I0526081

A Bellicose Dance

Patrick MJ Lozon

Dedicated to my family.

Table of Contents

1. Abduction

Dust snaked over the blacktop of the highway in curling streams. It was a hot, dry night, just past nine o'clock. The Earth was surrendering her vast amount of heat collected during the day. By noon, the temperature had risen beyond the local records and this night, on the Majove, was a warm one. The small dust devils blew up randomly as the wind currents shifted back and forth.

The soft rustling of the wind was abruptly drowned out by the tell-tale growling of a car's engine. Its lights appeared over the gradual rise of the horizon, beams reflecting off the almost barren desert landscape, creating shadows behind shadows.

A lizard sprang off the hot asphalt barely in time as the Buick roared by, a blur of black steel and chrome. Its taillights quickly faded into the distance. The sound of its engine echoing to a low rumble, in turn giving way once again to the whispering wind. The desert's creatures, momentarily frozen in fear, now slithered and scurried once again to search for their next meal.

Behind the wheel of the Buick was a young man in his mid-twenties. He was Ryan James, one of four children of Martha and Edward James. A recent university graduate of engineering, with a new job working in automation control systems. Being the junior on the team, the position did not pay too well, but it provided him with the experience he needed. It was a start. Besides, he was good at it, accustomed to long hours, sweating over minute details.

Tonight he was on his way home. He knew this route all too well, having been down this road more times than he cared to remember. It was exactly four hours and fifty-three minutes to the door of his parent's house but he didn't mind the long trip. It was a welcomed change. He couldn't stand the four bare walls of his apartment for one more day. More importantly, today was special: it was his father's birthday, and he was late. It had been out of his control, but he felt lousy just the same, and he still had a long drive ahead of him.

The first stars twinkled faintly in the evening sky. A veil of darkness was settling over the desert, devouring the last dying traces of a spectacular red sunset. Ahead, florescent dotted white lines turned solid as they drew closer, the Buick speeding over them in an endless game of catch up. He was so tired. It was so tempting to close his eyes and drift, to get lost in the rhythm of the car, to let the miles slip away underneath him.

But that would be suicide.

He shook himself awake, letting the thought sink in with a cold shiver. He hated driving down this desolate stretch of highway. More often than not, he could swear he caught a movement of something just outside his vision, just to the side, something traveling out there in the desert, always keeping up with him.

He remembered catching a TV show on desert rally racers. One driver, after 40 hours behind the wheel, would start to see the image of a white horse running beside him.

He would not be so lucky. It would be much worse.

Far behind the lone, speeding vehicle lights appeared in the night sky. A faint murmur permeated through the air as something unusual passed overhead. The native creatures, once again rudely disturbed, retaliated with an unusual silence.

Ryan edged the accelerator down. The speedometer needle climbed as the Buick's engine pulsed with a steady thunder. He was proud of his car. It had taken a long time to restore it, and more than a few hard-earned dollars. The engine was far from stock, as he had beefed up the factory 350 to produce a respectable 450 hp.

No one was on this stretch of road this late at night - not even the cops.

He poured on the power. The speedometer needle climbed just past 96 mph when the dashboard alternator light flickered on. The Buick coughed, then stalled.

His heart sank. He shifted into neutral and started to coast.

What now? No electrical, everything's dead. Fusible link maybe?

He bothered to switch off the now dead lights. Soft moonlight guided him as he coasted silently onto the shoulder of the road. The Buick rolled to a stop with a short and final squeak of the brakes.

He stepped out onto the hot desert floor, eyes now adjusted to the faint moonlight. The sound of his footsteps seemed to echo hollowly as they cut through utter silence.

It was unnerving. He glanced around, peering through the blackness. *So quiet. Strange to be so quiet.* He glanced down the road. Movement. A brilliant, white light jabbed into his eyes, blinding him. *Another car, coming in fast!*

In one frantic motion, he jumped and threw himself across the hood. A moment passed as he lay on the ground. There was no ensuing crash or roar of a passing vehicle – there was nothing: not a sound, not a movement, just bright, white light. He got up and dusted himself off. The light remained, steady and focused into a tight beam upon his car. He stepped back, and let his eyes trace the beam to its source.

It lay straddled across the highway approximately 300 meters up the road. Flickering lights traveled along its circumference revealing a shape that was almost oval but pockmarked with irregular projections.

The light suddenly blinked off.

Ryan stood on the edge of the road and listened, but the only sound he could hear was that of his own heartbeat.

Should he get closer? Is it dangerous? A brief moment of indecision seemed to last a lifetime, but insatiable curiosity eventually won out. *He had to see. He had to know.*

Mentally mustering up the courage, he began a slow, cautious walk toward the object. Though still a considerable distance away, it emanated sufficient light to provide varied details. Sections of its surface were polished smooth; others charred black or hidden within the shadows. Its size became apparent. It was huge, at least 100 meters wide.

He was closer now, less than 20 meters away. Every step brought with it a feeling of dread that twisted deep from within the pit of his stomach. It wrenched at his consciousness. He fought down an intense urge to turn and run.

A faint movement ahead. He stopped mid-stride.

There was something out there.

He could make out some more details on the object now. Strange markings, unfamiliar twisted shapes, interrupted by scorched, blackened scars. A sound arose, very subtle, a whistle varying in pitch, accompanied by a low reverberating bass.

Something was very wrong here.

He glanced around quickly, feeling vulnerable, exposed. He made a quick step back, only to catch another movement in the corner of his eye.

He never knew what hit him.

* * *

Around seven the next morning a gas station attendant on his way to work passed by the black Buick. He pulled over when he noticed the driver's door had been left wide open. As he approached the car, he noticed it had been abandoned with its keys still in the ignition.

He eased in behind the wheel and flipped the key. The starter whined and the engine caught, roaring to life readily. The attendant scratched his head, puzzled. He stepped out and cast a surveying glance around the area. Something strange lay up the road. His blank eyes sorted out the scene before him: depressions over a large permanent blackened scar.

The idea registered slowly. He never considered himself very smart, and he never saw this before, but he knew it wasn't right. The harder he stared, the sharper his idea became. With it came denial, then astonishment, then fear. He glanced around. Hot wind seemed to blow at him from every direction, carrying with it eye-scratching dust. He felt the fear creep up the back of his neck.

Time to get outta here.

He left the car there, hastily pulling a U-turn to head back to town, leaving plumes of dust in his wake.

The local sheriff was the gas station attendant's brother. He was at the scene before he'd managed to drink down his morning coffee and his mood reflected it. He took another swig and spit it out.

"Goddamned sand," he cursed, tossing the cup to the side.

He called in his crew of deputies. Crime scene tape was twisted around the car, stakes driven into the ground, and more tape strung across the highway. Pictures were taken. Radios were kept busy as traffic was re-routed.

The two brothers stood in the middle of the blacktop. The sun was already beginning its relentless burn and the morning breeze was dry and hot. Everything smelled of cooked dust. The sheriff wiped the sweat from his brow and glanced over at his brother. He could read his features easily. After all, that was his job, reading people, knowing when they were lying, when they were hiding something, when something weighed heavy on their conscience.

"I swear she's getting hotter every year," he stated, attempting to divert his brother from his troubled thoughts. He acknowledged him with a grunt, totally distracted by the scene ahead of them, watching the deputies who were busily surveying the sectioned off area.

The sheriff raised his voice as he spoke into the wind. "You know it's funny, I had a talk with one of the old Indian chiefs last night. He said the locals are a bit nervous. Flying machines are snatching up people and taking them away. Damnedest thing I ever heard. I was thinking the old bugger finally lost it."

One of the deputies heard him and looked up. "I reckon we have something close to that sheriff. Whatever this thing was, it was heavy enough to push three inches down into the asphalt."

The deputy's face was white, eyes wide. The man's tapeline was dangling in one hand, and his other was busy holding down his hat, trying desperately not to surrender it to a rogue dust devil. He was standing in one of the 'depressions' which pockmarked past both sides of the road and spanned out in a circular fashion. A shadow of burnt sand outlined the area where the main body of the thing must have sat.

The sheriff knew what was coming, and it was the last thing they needed. A bunch of damn UFO crazies swarming up and down the highway, pitching tents, and bothering the locals. They were going to have a heyday with this one.

"When you're done taking your pictures and measurements, get back into town and check the hotels, motels and the hospital," he yelled back.

The sheriff glanced back at his brother, "I surely hope the poor soul who was driving this here automobile doesn't show up missing."

His brother spat. "I think we both know the answer to that, already."

A day later, an Air Force investigation unit was dispatched to examine the site. It was a special detachment, hastily resurrected to address a sudden and very real increase in unexplained events.

* * *

Ryan awoke face down with a tremendous headache. When he opened his eyes a flood of bright light literally blinded him, making his head hurt even more. He attempted to recall the past events. It all seemed blurred, like a bad dream.

What happened? Where am I?

He pulled himself up and instantly regretted it. A fresh surge of pain welled up from the base of his skull. Laying back down was the only way to make it subside. The floor on which he lay was cold and smooth to a texture of marble. He let his tortured eyes roam. Recessed lighting in the ceiling, walls that looked like polished stainless steel, bare, unremarkable.

Again, he sat up, but this time more slowly. Every joint in his body ached. *Just what the hell hit me?*

He reached for the back of his head and felt something warm and sticky. The light revealed his hand covered in blood - his blood. It made his stomach churn. *He'd been hit, but by what? He had to get back to his car, back home.*

He tried to stand, but the pain quickly climbed to a ravenous ferocity. Sickened, he collapsed back down. His head swam. Bright lights swirled, and shadows filled the room. He closed his eyes and waited for the nausea to pass.

Strange, pungent smells filled his nostrils. Blood, urine, mixed in citrus and underneath all that, the unmistakable smell of rotting death.

A warm breath beating down upon his face brought him back. He opened his eyes to *something*. It was grotesque, hideous, stooped over close to him, examining him. Ryan screamed and frantically clawed at the floor to pull himself away. But it was ready for him. A thin, spindly, black hand clenched upon his arm. Something sharp cut into him. Instantly everything became blurry, out of focus. Sensation abandoned his body, leaving his arms and legs totally numb and totally useless.

The world turned unreal. He was in the bottom of a pool, watching the light from the sun above dance through slow-moving ripples. The sun began to move. No. It was a light – no many lights – above moving by one by one. He was being dragged. The thing was pulling him along the floor.

He managed to turn his head to again see dark repulsive shapes. He felt his body jump as one of the things kicked him savagely in the side. Dull sensations trickled into his mind, pulsating and unforgiving.

Broken. Maybe one rib, maybe more.

The view above changed to intermittent blocks of dim light and darkness, alternating in sequence, mesmerizing in his drugged stupor.

It stopped. The thing reached down, hoisted him off the floor and tossed him sideways toward the wall. He waited for the crushing impact, but it never came. Instead, he fell through the wall and slid down a smooth surface, hitting bottom with a sickening thud. Above him, he heard a metallic clang, and all traces of light disappeared, surrendering to absolute darkness.

Everything faded to blackness.

Hours must have passed before he finally came to, suddenly and savagely, choking with pain – a sharp, cutting pain, like the fear he was feeling. His back was raw. His arm throbbed where the creature had injected him with some unknown drug. And his side was literally on fire. It was a familiar sensation, as he had broken his ribs once in a football game. It was the second sensation that really scared him: the smell. It was revolting. A hazy combination of vomit, compose, and rotting flesh. He gagged, bringing up the bitter taste of bile. The process forced the last bit of dullness from his mind and brought him back into full consciousness.

He was scared. He was really scared. *Was he a victim of some elaborate joke? Who? Who would do this to him? No one. No one had a reason. This was no joke. That thing had been real.*

He remembered the past images, like the remnants of some insidious nightmare. The face of his captor was imprinted sharply in his mind: fly-like head, dripping mandibles, long skinny arms drawing out to sharp claws.

How did he get here?

The object that had spanned the road had to be some kind of ship. He recalled how its skin was scarred and damaged. The details swarmed in his mind in silent reflection, like an old silent movie. Strange how he had missed all this before. He should have never stepped out of his car, should have stayed put, not let his curiosity get the better of him.

Why hadn't he been more careful?

He strained his memory for a clue, but could only wretch out brief, muddied memories of the last few moments: a shadow in his peripheral vision, a step back into blackness.

Aliens. Not human. Not some elaborate trick. Would they bring him back, like the stories of abductions he recalled from conspiracy websites? What did they want?

He felt around desperately, groping at the smooth grimy walls of the cylindrical tube. He pulled himself up the slope and was able to feel the edges of the closed door that he must have passed through. There was no release, no handle. He continued to search, moving downwards within the darkness, approaching the other end, the flat bottom of the cylinder. He touched something slimy and warm. It wriggled and he sprang back frantically, letting out a frightened yell, pulling himself up the incline until he banged his head on the door.

"Let me out of here you bastards!" he screamed. He pounded his fists against the hard, cold metal until they were too sore to continue, all the while cursing in desperation.

No answer came.

He was alone. His company was that of darkness, and a low, uncomfortable vibration reverberating through the walls around him.

* * *

Zorlog waited until he was seated comfortably in his chair before he turned his full attention upon his first officer, Charvok Kitohk. He glared with disdain at the Charvok's image through the monitor.

His constant high-pitched squealing voice and the unforgivable questioning of his decisions were finally beginning to take its toll. He had no use for this one, none at all. *A typical political opportunist fool. His debt would have to be paid another way. No more favors to the Brinishe.*

"And do you agree, my Tarvok?"

Zorlog took a moment to respond. As Tarvok of this vessel, he was the uncontested Commander. But one never had total control within the Xi-Empire slavership, as there were checks and double checks to follow. It was wise to exercise caution with all political officers – including this one.

"What do you want me to say, Kitohk?"

"I have ordered the slaves to be loaded into the freight compartments."

"And I did not issue that order, did I? And I thought I was clear when I stated all the slaves are to be put into the shipping tubes."

"Of course, Tarvok, but it seems we are more successful at keeping them alive if they remain together in groups."

"As Tarvok, I authorize all decisions on this ship. I have stated all prisoners go into the tubes." He viciously slammed the monitor off. The long persistent screen revealed an ugly truth, an exposed scowl of hate on Kitohk's face.

Zorlog laughed hollowly as he refocused his attention on the survey teams' reports. *The raids had fared well. Each of the reconnaissance ships had returned full. This planet is worth pulling into the Empire for the slave resources alone.*

Again a monitor sprang to life, this time lit with the face of one of his better officers, 3rd Level Ankov Gulin. The Xilozak carried the features of satisfaction.

"Ankov Gulin reporting, Tarvok!"

"Ankov, my time is valuable," retorted Zorlog.

"My Tarvok, we have obtained a total of one hundred and seventy-three slaves. Unfortunately, there are five defectives."

"Defectives?"

"Two were damaged during loading, Tarvok. I would not be surprised to see them die within the radii. The other three seem to be suffering from one affliction or another. They have been separated from the rest of the stock and are ready for extermination. Upon your order, my Tarvok."

"Put the officers in charge of their capture on outer hull maintenance. They should learn to pick the stock properly. Are there any females in the group?"

"Yes, one... seems to be in a state of shock."

"Keep it, kill the others and discard them immediately, that is all."

"Very good, Tarvok."

Zorlog sat back and laughed out loud, still feeling very pleased with himself. *He was the first to reach this planet. The first to acquire the natives. Only he was daring enough to venture this far out beyond the advancing line. Once he registered his find, he would have the first claim rights, and if the slaves turn out to be resilient enough, he would become very rich indeed.*

* * *

The silence ended with a metallic squeal. A circular crack of light appeared above Ryan as the door swung open. He dashed up the incline, heaved at the door with all his strength and jumped out into the corridor.

A dark shape came for him, he dodged and turned. His eyes were still fighting to adjust to the light as he sized up his foe.

The creature was anthropoid: four arms, two legs, and stood erect. Its head carried large round, circular eyes, each containing thousands of tiny individual prisms that glowed crimson hues. A pair of mandibles jutted out and around where its cheeks should be, hiding large razor sharp teeth.

Insects – bloody overgrown insects.

But it wasn't alone. There were two of them. The other held, suspended like a rag doll in its eight-fingered claw, a young woman shaking in fear. The thing's fingers were biting into her arm so hard they were drawing blood. Her face was pale white, eyes wide, lower lip trembling.

They were all watching him, awaiting his next actions. *What should he do?*

He stepped back and bumped up against something else, something solid. He turned to find himself staring into yellow reptilian eyes. It was another alien, but much different than its insect brothers. Like the others, it was anthropoid, but with the features similar to a lizard. Its oversized muscular legs and thick arms seemed out of proportion with the rest of its body. It wore a dark gray suit that looked somewhat like leather. This one carried a bright metal insignia on its chest, a possible mark of rank.

The lizard's mouth jutted outward just barely pronounced enough to be considered a snout. It seemed to be smiling at him, revealing alternating rows of sharp white teeth. Ryan could feel its hot, rancid breath upon his face.

He backed away, toward the wall.

The lizard pulled out a meter-long bar and began swinging it in lazy circles. A sharpened edge caught the light, glinting menacingly. Instead of advancing, it stepped back down the corridor, and motioned to him with the fingers of its hand, a mocking tooth-filled grin pasted upon its grotesque features.

He knew what it wanted. It wanted him to attack. It was taunting him. He'd give him a surprise. Time to utilize all those years of martial arts training.

Ryan gauged the distance from the woman and made his decision. He feinted toward the lizard, quickly turned, ran, jumped, and kicked the insect square in the face. The thing squealed in pain and let go of the woman. He grabbed her by the arm and pulled her down the corridor, retreating away from the lizard.

A glance down the dimly lit hallway forced him to stop. Dozens more of the insect things were racing down on them. He scanned the walls for some other escape route.

Only one way out of this.

He turned around, holding up the woman who was now leaning heavily upon him. He could feel her trembling under his grip.

The lizard put away its weapon, waved its now empty hand slowly in the air.

Should he try it?

He leaned the woman up against the wall as gently as he could. Her features were lost in the dark, buried in shadow and hair, but they locked eyes for a moment.

"I'll take on this thing," he yelled. "When you see a chance, run!"

He rushed the lizard, shoving it back against the wall with all of his power. It hit hard but was not even stunned. Ryan caught the full force of a closed reptilian fist, and he literally flew back against the opposite wall, his lungs emptied of breath.

Fuck, this thing is strong.

The lizard moved in, swinging a muscle-bound arm once more into his midsection. More ribs snapped, engulfing his chest in unimaginable agony. For a brief second, everything went black. He regained his senses on his knees, lungs aching to recover oxygen, pain searing through his body. He looked up to see the face of his attacker. It seemed even more ferocious than before, its face lit with a savage appetite. Cries came from down the corridor. The woman had been seized by another insect creature. He could see their silhouette, see a spindly arm raise and lower in a vicious strike.

No way out - came a voice from the back of his mind.

"What are you?" he asked, gasping out the words.

The beast only growled, pulled back and swung the deadly bar at Ryan's face. Everything seemed to move in slow motion. He tried desperately, but could not make his body move fast enough to avoid the weapon's path. He saw the light reflect off its razor edge, now just askew, watched it connected just above his eyes. The hostile reality disappeared, leaving only the distant sound of a woman's scream ringing in his ears.

* * *

Zorlog's usual hideous grimace hid his disgust for the Txtians, who could not hold a few measly humans at bay.

"You two are weaker than a day-old Xilozak."

They cowered back from their Tarvok with a healthy respect. The Txtian that had been hit by Ryan clicked and squealed in pain as its colleague attempted to help it down the corridor. The others had already collected around the two slaves.

"Spray them down and throw the male and female back in the tube," ordered Zorlog. "You!" he yelled at the retreating Txtians. "Get the ship's doctor down here to fix up this one. It has more courage than all of you put together."

The Txtians looked at each other, although none dared respond.

"What are you waiting for!" he blasted. "Get moving, or you will all be working molten lead on Zeghad!"

* * *

Ryan was running, running through a thick jungle of steel, concrete, and glass, past walls of white glittering bone. His breath was raspy, his lungs screaming for air, burning like fire within his chest. He felt his legs weaken, failing him as his muscles moved slower and slower. He tried to navigate past deep, blood-red bottomless pools. Pools he knew would suck him down if he fell into them. It was coming up behind him. He glanced back and saw it, chirping insanely as it approached, half-lizard, half-insect, hunting him. He told his body to move faster, but his legs could no longer respond. He slowed to a hobbling stagger, then fell, frantically crawling, trying to pull himself away from the thing. It was on top of him now, its hot, rancid breath on the back of his neck. He turned and saw the mandibles, razor sharp, dripping with saliva, clicking incessantly. He was motionless, unable to move as its jaws clenched into him.

The young woman knew he was dreaming again. She swabbed the sweat and blood from his eyes, trying hard not to touch the wound on his forehead, using the last clean part of her dress.

Keep the wound clean. Control the infection. Remember your training.

She watched over him every waking hour, feeding him the food and water rations that were tossed down into the tube. They had been pulled out only once since the incident. A Xilozak officer had come to seem them. She suspected he was a doctor. He had cleaned and disinfected the man's wound, all the time grumbling something about 'damaged stock' under his breath as he worked. He glanced over at her and somehow interpreted her concern, then hissed gruffly in Trinarieit, "This male will probably die. It is up to him to fight. Only his will to live will save him."

"Here." He handed her a small gray bottle. "Apply this on the wound, and give him water regularly." He turned abruptly and left. Again, they were shoved down into the tube.

In the darkness, she no longer had any sense of time, so she relied on the one and only source of regularity: when the hatch opened, and the food and water were tossed down. At each interval, she applied the medicine.

She found comfort in talking to the man, even though she knew he couldn't hear her, nor understand her. She talked softly, coaxing him not to give up, to return back to the living, back to her, so she would not be alone. She told him about her family, her home, fleeting memories of her past. It was a way to stay calm, to stay sane. Every once in a while the man would jerk in her arms. His breathing was raspy and shallow. Sweat poured off his body as the fever burned on. He was battling for his life. Despite her efforts, the wound was infected. The medicine seemed to be helping, but she couldn't tell for sure. But it wasn't enough. It didn't last.

His health took a turn for the worst, temperature climbing and body convulsing followed by sessions of delirious yelling. She nursed him through it, pouring her own rations of water over his lips, praying as an act of self-reassurance that he would make it, that he would not die. But things did not get better for far too long. She had lost all but the smallest glimmer of hope when things finally changed. The man's breathing slowed and his temperature started to drop back down to normal. His fever had finally broke.

He might survive after all.

She collapsed in exhaustion, sleeping soundly for the first time in many uncounted, unknown days.

* * *

Ryan awoke feeling like he was suffocating. The woman lay beside him, her legs wrapped around his, her arms draped around his chest weighing far too heavily on ribs that were aflame in pain. She was so close to him that he could hear the pounding of her heart.

He must be in his apartment. Maybe he had a party. The girl? He didn't remember her - yet. It was all a nightmare after all.

He opened his eyes to blackness and panicked. For a moment he couldn't catch his breath. His senses sharpened. Familiar rancid smells.

No, this was no dream. Back in the hole, again.

She stirred beside him.

Was it her he had tried to save?

He could feel the reassuring rhythm of her breathing. Feel her soft breath on his chest. It was comforting.

The pain he could take. Her closeness kept him warm, contrary to the cold metal surface, and he was so tired. In a moment he had faded back into a deep sleep.

The dreams came again. Strange, twisted imagery, fearful visions full of monstrous creatures with slit eyes. They replayed variations of his final moments of consciousness, his frantic effort to escape, the glint of steel, the sharp incomprehensible pain as the blunt metal weapon sliced into his forehead.

"Can you hear me?"

A murmur. A soft, gentle voice.

"Can you hear me?"

A strange accent, he couldn't quite place it.

He opened his eyes, again to intense blackness. He could feel her beside him, warm, soft skin, her aroma a sweet smell that cut through the stench.

"It's alright. Stay calm."

Her hand was on his face, soft, gentle.

"Who are you? Where are we? Do you know where we are?"

"My name is Aviore - Aviore Tem Enova."

"Are we still in the hole? I can't see anything..." Every word seemed to sap his strength.

"Yes, we are. I was hoping... waiting for you to come back. You almost died. It seemed to take forever for your fever to break. I... I was not sure you were going to make it. I didn't want to see you die, too." Her voice was shaky.

"I made it."

He could sense her calmness return, getting back control.

"I'm sorry. I've seen too many... too much death."

A long silence followed. Thoughts raced through Ryan's mind. *How far were they from home?*

"And what's your name?" she asked.

"Ryan... Ryan James."

"How do you feel, Ryan?" Her voice carried the strange accent sweetly. It flowed so beautifully. He liked hearing her talk.

"Water, do you have water?"

"Yes, here," she poured a bit onto his lips. He coughed. "I'm OK. More please." It was a soothing coolness.

"I feel terrible. I'm dizzy. I can't seem to get oriented. Everything is black."

"I'm sorry, Ryan."

He felt a tear drop on his chest. He reached for her face and touched her cheek. Gently, he wiped her tears away.

"Don't cry. It's alright."

She drew toward him, resting her head on his shoulder and quietly sobbed. He held her tight, trying to give her some comfort.

Would they ever get out of here?

He could feel the fear welling up inside him. He gritted his teeth and held on.

She felt it. "We are OK for now." Almost as if she knew what he was thinking. "They've been leaving us alone for some time now."

"How did you get here?"

"I was driving. My car stalled. Something was up the road – it was big. I went to check it out. Next thing you know, I wake up being pulled through some hallway by these things."

"You were abducted while traveling between cities on Earth?" she asked.

There was something in the way she phrased her words – seemed strange.

"Yes, I think that's what happened. What about you?"

She didn't answer for a moment. "Your captors are not human. The insectoids call themselves Txtians – and the others – the more savage ones - they are the Xilozaks."

"We're not on Earth anymore are we?"

"No, I'm sure we are thousands of light-years away from your home planet by now. As for our exact location, I don't know. I can only tell you that you are on a slavership, an old converted warship of the Xi-Empire."

"You mean we are slaves? That's... that's not good news. How do you know so much? How long have you been here? Where did you get captured?"

He reached out and gently brought his hand over her face. She didn't pull away. *High cheekbones, small nose, rounded lips – the marks of a beautiful woman.*

He pulled his hand away. The pain in his side was getting worse. He shifted over and felt something move. A surge of red heat seared up his side, as if a massive weight just pressed onto his chest. He gasped for breath.

She said something to him – but it wasn't in English.

His head was swimming. The pain was overpowering.

"Are you feeling pain? Can I help you?"

English this time. Perfect English.

"Here, you should have another drink. Don't talk so much. The extra exertion may make it worse."

"Something moved, I think it was a broken rib. It's OK. It's passing now." He took a slow breath. "Tell me where you are from?"

She didn't answer. She didn't say anything. It was unnerving.

"Look, you kind of gave it away already. A far as I can tell you are human, but your accent, your language is like nothing I've heard before. I may be going out on a limb here, but you aren't from Earth, are you?"

"Very well," she resigned with an exhaling of breath. "I guess it really does not matter, considering the circumstances." She paused, giving her next words careful consideration. "You are correct. I'm not from your planet, Ryan," she announced. "I'm from a planet called Signus. It's a beautiful world, similar to your home in many ways."

He digested the news quietly. "But you're human," he responded weakly.

"Yes. I am human, just like you. There are really no significant differences between Earthlings and Signites. Perhaps there is a slight difference in average height as we are generally shorter – oh yes – and Signite men cannot grow facial hair. Otherwise, we are, genetically speaking, identical."

She could feel his tension. It was a lot to take in. Did he believe her?

"You see, we share the same ancestry, only we are slightly more developed as a people than you are. The prevailing theory is that both our planets were seeded long ago."

"Seeded?"

"Yes, as we are genetically identical."

"You speak English perfectly? How is that possible?"

"I have an aptitude for language. We recently intercepted radio signals from your planet. I have been studying the transmissions for some time. It helps that your language is close to one of our dialects."

"Then you also know how to get back to Earth?"

"No. I'm not an astronavigation specialist. The news of Earth's discovery was restricted knowledge. I'm absolutely sure the location of your home has been scrubbed from our databases. Our ship's navigation systems were set to self-destruct."

He shifted uncomfortably, adjusting his position to subdue the pain.

"I'm sorry. Are you feeling any better?" she asked, changing the subject.

"No, actually. I'm feeling a bit queasy."

"You need food. Try this." She placed a small, smooth, palm-sized cube into his hand. "It does not taste very good, but it is edible. Go on, take a bite," she urged.

He did and almost spat it out. "It tastes like crap!"

She laughed slightly, then placed another in his hand.

Sweet laughter. He could listen to that all day and never grow tired of it.

"More? You are kidding, right?"

"You have to eat. Here, try to pull yourself up and sit." She wrapped her arms around him. He drew in her aroma and felt her softness. Sharp sparks of pain kept him from enjoying her closeness too much. He pushed and she pulled until he was up.

"I feel as weak as a kitten," he said. The dull throb in his forehead had now turned to a solid pounding. "And the air in here stinks!" Pain knotted his insides in a throbbing heat.

He was so damn helpless. How could he help her now?

"A kitten? What is that? Here, have some water."

He passed his hand over bare skin. "What happened to your clothing?"

"They stripped us to nothing. Easier for them to pull us out and hose us down. As slaves, we have no dignity. They did not get everything, however. I managed to keep a few pieces of my dress to use as a bandage for you."

"Thanks. But why am I still clothed?"

"You are sick. They tend to avoid the sick ones. If you do not get better by the time they get to where they are going, they will probably kill you."

"Lucky I woke up then. Do you know what they're going to do with us?"

"I do not know. I do not want to know."

"What do you mean?"

"We will be slaves on some Xi-Empire planet and slaves are known not last too long."

"Is this your attempt to cheer me up or something?" He tried to follow it with a weak chuckle.

She smiled. *He was likable. He had a way about him. How could he possibly joke after everything he has been through? He's stronger than she had thought.*

"Tell me about yourself, and about Signus."

"Well, this may seem a bit ironic, but we were, in particular, I was, on my way to Earth - I mean, my ship was. We had discovered Earth about, let me see, eight of your years ago, but we had elected to suppress contact at that time. We had already engaged the Xi-Empire and we realized we must exercise caution. Since then the war has not gone well. Our mission was in violation of our own policies. We were on our way to warn you about the Xi-Empire encroachment. I was the acting chief linguistic specialist. It took extensive analysis of your radio signals, but I have successfully memorized 52 of your languages."

"That is impressive. I have to confess you know more of our languages than I do."

"I am still having difficulty with all of your slang expressions and contractions that you use, much less your accent."

"No, you have the accent, but it's nice. It's different." He smiled, although it didn't matter in the dark.

"So what happened? You obviously never arrived on Earth."

"We encountered this slavership. It attacked us on a vector for Earth. I surmise they must have superior deep-scan technology. We were at a disadvantage. Our ship had been stripped down to only a few weapons as we were outfitted for speed. We did not have a chance. We flew directly into their trap."

She paused to take a deep breath. He could sense the heaviness in her voice. Something terrible had happened on that ship.

"We were boarded. They killed most of the crew, took some prisoners – of which I am one, then they proceeded to destroy the ship."

"So it was pretty bad."

"Brutal and violent. They tortured some of us. Some begged them to stop, to kill them and end their suffering."

She put her head on his shoulder, her cheek was wet.

"They are animals. They are evil. They should be wiped out – all of them."

He stroked her hair, which was tangled and dirty with the filth from their tiny cell.

"We just never expected them to be this far out in the quadrant. We thought we were safe." She said it like she was blaming herself. "I guess it does not really matter. The damage is already done. It is too late for Earth, and it is too late for Signus."

"What do you mean?"

"The latest news we received was not good. Our main defenses were breached. Even though we had anticipated this possibility, it never seemed completely real. Colonization expeditions were launched before the Xi-Empire found us. At least they will survive. If not for the Showmish, Signus would have been lost years before."

"The Showmish?"

"We have been trading with them for the past thirty or so years. I believe that would translate into about forty-two Earth years."

"Your years are pretty long."

"The measurement of time is relative," she replied. "In any case, we have had little time to prepare. It is more of a case of forestalling the inevitable. They hit Shawma – the Showmish home planet - before us. The Xi-Empire fleet destroyed their defenses with ease. That made us draft up contingencies."

"And Earth is next."

"Your planet emits radio waves like a quasar. Its only protection is the expanse of space."

"That's not much protection – this ship made it. How can you explain that?"

"I can't. My Captain had mentioned this ship was modified, but I do not understand the technologies at work. I can tell you this is not your typical Xi-Empire slavership."

"You mean this ship can go further than the others?"

"It's been modified. Much too fast for a retired cruiser. Our ship didn't have a chance against it."

"I shouldn't have survived this, Ryan. I should be dead like the others."

"Call it a miracle then."

"A religious reference? My studies had exposed some of your peoples' varied beliefs."

"Well, I was not sure about aliens, until now. God is not too much more of a stretch." Ryan chuckled. "Who knows?"

"I do not consider myself religious either, but you sort of get that way out here - so far from everything, distances so great that you cannot imagine. It makes one either more spiritual or more crazy, but either way, it changes them. I have done some personal research in this field of study with many different races. Some of the similarities would amaze you."

"How many others?"

"Many. We aren't alone out here, and you are not alone, Ryan."

In a sudden passionate urge, he pulled her close and kissed her. She yielded, responding back heatedly, but then broke it off, pushing away.

A few awkward moments passed in silence.

"I am sorry."

"No. No. I'm sorry, my fault. I didn't mean to... to offend you."

"Why did you do that?"

"It just felt right. In this insanity, was probably the most sane thing I've done yet." He laughed slightly. "I just needed the closeness."

"I guess that is... acceptable."

"Tell me, Aviore, what color are your eyes?"

"Brown and green."

"What?" he laughed.

"Brown with a tinge of green," she giggled.

He ran his fingers over her face, cupping her cheek. She didn't pull back.

"I wish I could see them." He ran his hand through her hair, carried its caress down past the middle of her back. She trembled slightly, arched her body closer to him.

"If I was feeling a little stronger..."

"No, we cannot," she said, slightly out of breath. "Not here. Not now."

"Yeah, I know. Not the right time. Not the right place."

"I think you should get some rest. No telling what they have planned for us tomorrow."

They both settled into a comfortable embrace. In a few minutes, Ryan was sleeping, intermittently snoring ever so lightly.

Aviore held the Earthman close, searching through her troubled thoughts. *Why was she developing feelings for him? Why does she find him so attractive? He wasn't even from her home. If she had met him before would she have given him a second thought?*

Maybe... There's no doubt there's something special about him. He's certainly brave, if not strong-willed. She admired that about him.

Her hand ran idly through his hair.

They had come so close. She had wanted him so badly. Was she wrong to stop? If they were to survive only the next few days, maybe so, but the other possibility was more frightening, to bring a child into slavery - she could not bear that.

She closed her eyes, intent on falling asleep. *Maybe she would dream of home.*

A tremendous bang echoed above them, traveling through the cold metal with sharp ease. Aviore woke first. She brought her hand over his cheek, noticing he was also stirring awake. "Don't worry, it's far away. Probably pulling out slaves from the other tubes for standard checks."

"And us? Will they pull us?"

"I expect our time will come. Tell me, Ryan," she said, attempting to divert the discussion. "Do you believe in fate?"

"Do you mean destiny or fate?"

"What is the difference?"

"You can shape your destiny - it is the sum of all your previous decisions. Fate kind of gives you no choice."

"What is your answer, then?"

"I guess I believe in a little of both."

"Really? I hadn't expected that."

"So, while we are on the subject of the inevitable, why don't' you tell me what you know about our captors."

She pulled herself up, drawing herself into a ball. "I'll tell you what I know, but I don't know much."

He could tell her manner had changed, felt the withdrawn coldness. "It's OK, just whatever you can recall."

"I have managed to decipher the core of their verbal communications. It is just another version of Trinarieit - a common communication-based format that must have been developed by some mathematician. A wheel is a wheel no matter who develops it first. I find it lacking in some respects, not near as articulate as the version we have developed for our trade. I have not, however, been able to decipher their native Txtian or Xilozak languages in full - just bits and pieces – nouns, verbs. Most of them will talk to us in Trinarieit so we can understand their commands. I noticed when the Txtians talk in their native tongue it is usually when no Xilozak is near. I do hear a name pop up often. Zorlog... I think that he is their Tarvok – that is, their Captain or something of equivalent rank. Most of them are afraid of him – including the Xilozak crew. From what I can tell he's a rogue out here, a free merchant, not an official part of their military. That's why he could perform these raids."

"That one I met out in the corridor, he wore some rank insignia."

"I think we met him, Ryan. I believe he is the one that hit you."

"Then he's a sonofabitch for sure."

"Yes, I do agree. A sonofabitch."

Ryan laughed.

"What do you find so humorous?"

"You. Your accent does not work so well when you curse."

"Perhaps I need more practice," she smiled at him in the dark.

"Tell me more about Signia. I want to know about you."

They had little to do, cramped in that dark hole, but at least they had each other. So they talked, becoming familiar, developing a deep friendship. When fatigue settled in, they eventually fell asleep within each other's arms, each hoping to be let out, but knowing enough to be careful what they wished for.

* * *

The door swung open with its usual clamor. A shadow of an insect creature motioned them out.

"What is it?"

"They want us out, Ryan. We need to head up."

"Is the door open – can you see light?"

"Yes, they want us to go up."

"I... I can't see anything. I think I am blind. He couldn't stop the feeling of utter helplessness overtake him.

"No. It will come back, and I am sure you will heal. It is due to the fever. I am sure your sight will return. But we have to move. We must exit. They have little patience." She helped pull Ryan up the slope. His legs were shaky and his body broke out into a cold sweat from the effort. One of the guards grew tired of waiting, grabbed him, and yanked him out in one effortless motion. He hit the floor hard, instantly overcome by nausea. His stomach wretched inside, bringing up dry heaves. He heard Aviore yelling at them, cursing in foreign languages of which he had never heard before.

Ignoring her, the thing grabbed Ryan and hoisted him to his feet, then subsequently pushed them both down the corridor.

Ryan squinted, making out the slightest sliver of light as his eyes fought to adjust under the shift from absolute darkness.

He could see! Not much, but he could see something.

He walked, one foot in front of the other, guided only by a sharp talon buried into his back.

"I can see, Aviore. I can see light!" he yelled.

He felt her grab his arm. "Stay calm. Keep walking. I'll guide you."

They approached a split in the corridor. A Xilozak guard looked down at them contemptuously and growled Trinarieit at their two Txtian escorts. One of them chirped back shrilly, then pushed the two captives down another corridor. Ryan would have fallen if it had not been for Aviore, who managed somehow to move beside him.

She whispered to him softly. "How well can you see?"

"Just blocks of light. Shapes moving. It's getting better. A little at a time. You're just a blur, but look beautiful to me." He stole a quick kiss.

They hobbled down the hallway, constantly harassed by the Txtian guards which constantly chirped amongst themselves.

"Can you make out what they are saying?"

"Somewhat, I think they are arguing about a wager on a game of chance, but is hard to tell."

The small corridor eventually merged into a larger one. It was jammed full with a slow-moving stream of fellow captives. Few, if any, spoke. There was the odd muffled cry as a whip landed on the back of some hapless soul. The guards pushed them into the crowded stream, happy to abandon them to continue with their argument.

They stumbled as the crowd pushed them forward. The smells were intense, urine, feces, sweat and the unmistakable coppery odor of blood. "What's happening, Aviore?"

"Just be glad you cannot see it, Ryan. Let's try to stay close to the bulkhead."

They eventually came to a stop, then advanced to stop yet again.

"What are they doing up there? Can you see, Aviore?"

"Looks like we are coming to the end of the corridor and then into an elevator."

They started moving again.

"Definitely an elevator. We have just walked onto a platform. Below us is a sea of slaves, literally thousands. This is, I believe, one of the ship's cargo bays. We are about 20 meters above the main floor."

The floor lurched. She guided his hand to a metal bar. "Grab the rail."

She scanned the scene as they lowered, mentally calculating the numbers. "There must be three thousand captives here."

On the bay floor, the aliens were separating them into groups. The weak and the injured were being pulled away from the others and forced to the side. One of the guards grabbed hold of Ryan. Aviore fought back, holding onto Ryan's arm desperately. Ryan, too weak to resist, was joggled back and forth like a rag doll. She begged the guard to let him go, holding onto Ryan with an unrelenting grip. Another Txtian guard approached with a whip, its tip dragging across the floor in a dance of blue sparks.

A sharp bark from above grabbed their attention. The ship's doctor was on the platform. He growled out hoarse orders and waved them on. Aviore pulled Ryan away from the disgruntled Txtian. She looked up gratefully, but the doctor had already turned his back. They started into the flowing stream of slaves and held on to each other tightly.

"What did they want with me?"

"They were going to cut you from the rest of us."

"And then?" He was almost afraid to ask.

"It is a general practice, in order to keep infestation and disease down, for them to kill all the injured and sick."

"Oh." Ryan felt a shiver race up his spine. He pulled Aviore closer. "Thank you."

"It was the doctor. He interceded and let us go," she stated.

"I couldn't see."

"I know."

They were broken into smaller groups and ushered into a side room where any remaining clothing was stripped away and they were hosed off by an acrid-sulfur smelling solution. They were then directed back into the general population, shaking from the cold.

Aviore and Ryan had managed to stay together throughout the ordeal, huddling to one another in order to maintain some warmth. They waited silently, holding each other as they shivered, as much from the cold as in fear of what was next.

Hours passed.

The sick and injured were methodically massacred by the Xilozaks. The unfortunates were lined up against a wall and decimated with small laser rifles. The killing seemed to last forever. The sounds of the dying were burnt into their memory. Some begged, some pleaded, others stood silently, uttering not a word, welcoming what was to come. The end came unceremoniously, marked with a silent yet noticeable drop in tension and fear.

Aviore whispered, "Those poor people." Tears were streaming down her cheeks.

Ryan reached over and wiped them away. "You're not a blur anymore. He fought out a trace of a smile. I can almost make you out clearly. You're as beautiful as I thought."

That brought more tears to her eyes. They streaked down her cheek. She did not bother to wipe them away. Ryan reached out, but she grabbed his hand.

"I have to tell you something," she whispered. She sounded different, distant. "I did not want you to know this, because it could put you in danger, but you should know the truth. My father is the Governor of Signus - the highest official of our planet. I have heard the guards talking, and they are looking for me. They probably have tortured some of the crew from my ship and found out I am still alive. That is standard Xi-Empire protocol. They look for information, anything that might be of use. Ryan, they are coming for me."

"Why?"

"I do not know. Perhaps they think I would be a useful asset to inflict a unique brand of terror." She paused a moment, as the words sunk into Ryan's mind. "We are going to be separated soon. And I do not want you to fight them or they will kill you. You have to promise me you will let them take me. You cannot die. Promise me!"

No. He wasn't going to let her go. How could he?

"You have to promise me, Ryan!"

Her voice had changed in pitch, her eyes searching and wide in fear "Please, I do not want you to die."

"We can hide."

"Where? There is no escape."

"Maybe you've mistranslated."

"Look." A handful of guards were pushing through the crowd, methodically inspecting the human females.

"It is too late."

"What will they do with you?"

"I do not know. But I am more useful alive than dead, at least for now. You just stay alive. Stay alive, escape, and come looking for me. OK?" She forced a smile upon her tear-stained face.

Ryan nodded. "OK. I'll come back for you. I'll escape from these bastards and I'll come looking for you. I swear I will. Don't give up. I'll come for you."

She nodded, seeming to relax slightly. "Good. We were brought together for a reason. It is our fate. Remember?"

He pulled her close, wrapping his arms protectively around her. They held each other close as the crowd shift around them, and the guards moved ever closer.

She pushed him away. Her face now a mask of brave defiance.

"You remember your promise," she directed, lips white, eyes locked on him.

At that moment he knew he loved her. It was something deep within him. Maybe it was all just chemicals, pheromones, some kind of natural physiological response. Hell, maybe it was a reaction to stress. But it didn't matter.

The crowd parted behind her. Two Txtians shoved through and promptly stopped their advance as soon as they saw Aviore. She did not cower or hide her face but stared back at them proudly.

Typical, to be so brave.

He couldn't help but admire her.

The Txtian spoke in its clicking, screeching voice, and a small electronic box mounted on its shoulder belt chirped out a slightly familiar language.

"That is a garbled excuse of my home tongue, Ryan." She stated quietly. "They told me to follow them or they will kill me. Stay back. I do not want you to die here."

Her body was trembling, revealing how truly afraid she really was.

They grabbed her. She gave him one last look over her shoulder. Eyes full of fear. She said something, but the surrounding noise drowned it out. Then she was gone, lost in the milling crowd.

He bit down on his lip until he could taste blood. His body was shaking with rage, but he could do nothing.

What was it she had said? I love you was such a simple yet unmistakable set of words. Could it be?

Somehow he would find a way out of this hell. No matter what chances he had to take. He would survive, and he would escape. Then he would find her if it was the last thing he ever did.

Abduction

No longer would he dream of home.

* * *

2. Kalmaka

Ryan stood trembling in silent rage. His heart pounded in his temples, eyes literally afire. The patrol had all but disappeared, along with Aviore, but he stood there, amongst a sea of humanity, utterly unable to act. The others huddled amongst themselves, eyes to the floor, seeking to avoid catching any undue attention from guards patrolling through the crowd.

The lights suddenly dimmed and whips cracked, forcing them all down onto the floor. Ryan watched as the others complied, hastily settling down onto the hard floor, but he stood defiantly, to gaze across the large expanse of the room.

A woman, covered in filth, face tear-stained, slight and shaking, tugged at his shirt, beckoning him to sit. She looked at him hopefully, eyes wide and careful not to utter a word. Her actions spoke loud enough.

Become small, don't draw their attention.

He laid his hand on hers, reassuring her it would be OK, and she withdrew it, edging back from him.

Fear was going to kill them all, long before these animals did them in.

The thought burned into his mind as he watched her slide away to merge with the others. The dim lighting reflected the scene in a slight auburn hue, revealing just enough detail for him to make out the fact that it was not just humans enslaved. Creatures, lizard-like in appearance, much leaner than that of the Xilozaks, huddled amongst themselves in small groups and kept a respectful distance from the humans.

Were these the Showmish? He could only guess they were.

Guards had already thinned to a sparse few and were congregating in a half-dozen areas. Some of them had turned their attention to playing some form of game similar to tossing dice, satisfied to entertain themselves and ignore their captives. Only a few were left to actively patrol.

So engrossed was he in his inspection, he had failed to see that one of the patrolling guards had noticed him. He locked eyes with the Xilozak who was a little more than 10 meters from him and closing. The alien was casually retracting his whip, reptilian eyes contracting unevenly in the low light.

Ryan eased down onto the floor, eyeing the creature cautiously.

The guard, whip now fully uncoiled, paused momentarily, distracted by a yell coming from the group playing their game. He gave a wave to the group, then passed a long piercing gaze his way. Ryan stayed motionless, hidden in the darkness. Seemingly satisfied, the guard coiled his whip and headed back toward the noisy group.

A man sat to his left, very close. Signite or Earthman? Ryan asked him his name but the man wouldn't respond. He kept his head bowed to the floor and waved him away. A woman, also near, rocked on her knees, quietly sobbing, her face hidden in a nest of red hair.

He turned to her. "Can you talk?"

He reached out, cleared her hair away, and pulled her chin up.

"Can you hear me?"

She didn't respond. Her eyes were blank. Like too many others, she was lost. Her mind had retreated back into itself, like she had resigned to living in some dream. He let her go in pity and she resumed her rocking.

"Can anyone hear me?" he said out loud. Another guard turned to give a casual glance his way but then turned his attention back to their game.

"Shut up," whispered a man near him. He spoke English. "You'll attract them."

A few others gave him warning looks, but no one else spoke.

Ryan caught movement in the corner of his eye. A whip cut through his back like a razor, hitting him with so much force it drove him face down onto the filthy floor. The other slaves scrambled away, not wanting to be next.

Ryan couldn't move. His body was numb, feeling nothing from his back to his legs. The slack of the whip met the floor and sparks flew.

Electrically charged. Nice.

The air smelled of burning flesh - his flesh. As the numbness wore off, it mutated into excruciating pain. He lay quiet, expecting another lash, but it did not come. The guard's footsteps receded into the crowd. His back throbbed in pain matching the rhythm of his pounding heart. Others looked at him quietly, but their faces revealed something more. He knew what they were thinking.

I told you so.

Lesson number one, thought Ryan, keep your mouth shut. He clenched his teeth, fought the burning pain to get back up on his knees.

A graying old man with no teeth started cackling with a sandpaper tone. "You sure got yours! Didn't ya, bucko!"

Ryan glared at the aging derelict.

"I'm an old man. I have no teeth, see?" and proceeded to prove his point by showing bare gums. "You're from Earth? Yeah, I like you, dumbass. Me too, ya know. Australia. Long time ago," He twitched and looked around quickly. "I'm an old man, now. Been slavin' a long, long time."

"I can see that," Ryan said, relieved that someone was willing to talk, even if he was crazy. "What's your name?"

"Noteeth. Noteeth's my name. Chewin's my game!" He cackled away again quietly, entertained by his own twisted humor. "Don't you get up now. They come back, they do. They always come back. The others play games, but the rovers, they're just mean. You want some more, do ya, young buck?"

Ryan tried to relax as he fought down shots of pain emanating from the long, raw slice on his back.

Yeah, they probably would come back. Maybe the old bugger wasn't as crazy as he'd thought.

"Damned insects!" the old man said with a growl.

"You got that right, Old Man. Don't forget the damned lizards, either."

"If I had my teeth I'd eat them!" he stated with a staunch fearless frown on his gray face.

Ryan almost broke out into a laugh. "How old are you?"

"Old enough. Dunno. Long time. Listen to me. I know, what I've seen. You're a young buck. You gotta work the mines. They feed you better there. Good food. Fill your stomach. Stay away from the cities. Bad places. I lost my teeth in the city. Bad place. Bad places."

The old man was literally trembling, eyes lost on some past memory.

"How long did you say? I thought this was the first slaver?"

"Nah. Been a long time now. They're moving me now. Dunno why – but I like it, I do."

"So this ship wasn't the first?"

"This ship? Nah.But it wasn't as big as this monstrosity, bucko." He cackled. "No, no, no. Was a tiny thing. Grabbed us up maybe half-dozen. All gone now. Just ol'noteeth left. You remember what I tell ya, you do."

"What do you mean work the mines?"

The old man seemed caught in a dark dream.

"Old man!" Ryan grabbed his arm.

The fragile relic threw off his grip with surprising strength, his focus returned, eyes wild and intense upon him.

"You stay on the fringe, away from their cities. Avoid the insects – they're bad news. And stay away from Xilo! When they come a-courtin' you look for'em. When it comes time for the auction, you see a miner, you knock the auctioneer's teeth out..."

He laughed again. It ground itself into a spasm of choking.

"That's good. Yes. Go for the teeth. That shows spunk. Spunk's good. Good for the belly. But be careful they don't kill ya first." He winked.

"Look, I just wanna stay alive, old man, long enough to escape."

"Escape!" he cackled, then he shifted a little closer, considering him with weathered, gray eyes. He grabbed Ryan by the jaw, stared into his eyes.

"We all need to escape, bucko. I see something in you. Your soul gives you away. Maybe you're gonna save us. Save us all."

He let go, throwing his arms around in some insane dance of glee. The others around him watched in fascination. "I know, I see it. I saw it. Saw when the whip took ya down. Saw it in a blink. My eyes, they're still good ya see. It'll all be fine, it will. The day will come. You'll see."

Just as suddenly his manner turned dark. He retreated, turning his back on Ryan, mumbling softly. "I see that day will come, but I dunno about me. Dunno. Can never see that. Never."

He looked back only for a moment. "If I do see you again young buck, you bring me my teeth, OK?"

Ryan shook his head. "Sure, if I can find them."

The old man only looked at him and cackled again. His frail body shook with the effort. "You keep down. Too many batteries in them whips. Me, I gotta go. Gotta find my bed. You 'member my teeth. OK?"

"I will. Take care, old man."

The strange character crawled away without a look back. The crowd moved apart, allowing him to pass. Ryan stayed put. His back hurt too much to move.

In what seemed hours later, another commotion began as the aliens started moving the captured victims to the center of the room. He felt vibrations through the hull. Creaks and wails sounded throughout the ship. A final thud gave Ryan an inkling that they had landed - somewhere.

The guards divided up the slaves and began escorting the groups out one at a time. They stopped just short of Ryan's group.

Another long delay. They were standing long enough for his legs to tighten up in cramps. He was thirsty and his stomach growled with hunger. The delay ended with the guards herding them back up the elevator, down the corridors, and eventually, ending up back at their tube-cells.

This time he did not fight them.

Not this time.

A guard tossed in a collapsible water container as the door closed. He sat in the dark, alone, wondering what the future was going to be. The ship took off, shuddering and creaking from every facet. The noise and vibration became almost unbearable. Ryan had visions of dying in this dark hold, crushed to death by the massive weight of the ship. He fought off the claustrophobia with everything he had. The burning pain from his wounds helped him stay aware. The shaking stopped as suddenly as it had started. They were in space again, enroute to the unknown.

He lay there with his ear to the hull. Sound carried easily. Someone was screaming within the bowels of the ship, someone who had lost the fight to stay sane. In the darkness, there was little else to do.

Too easy to go there.

The visions of slavery haunted him. Hundreds of lost, desperate, faces. All turned into zombies, mute from fear, strained from pain, beyond their breaking point, empty of spirit, shadows of what they once were. Only fear and despair was left.

He was not going to become one of them. He would die first.

Over time the ship's vibrations became comforting. They gradually lulled him to sleep. His dreams were no less troubled than his reality. They were filled with images of his home being methodically laid to waste by gigantic machines, piloted by insects with lizard eyes.

* * *

"Status?" Zorlog grunted to the Savok in charge.

"All the slaves moved out. We stand ready."

"Good. You will ensure all are accounted for and measured properly."

"Thank you, Tarvok. If there is a problem, what are my orders?"

"A problem? What kind of problem?"

The Savok shifted uneasily. "Perhaps someone refuses to pay?"

Zorlog chuckled. "Someone refuse? Perhaps one would be foolish enough. Your orders are to bring this refuser to me. I will discuss the problem with this individual personally."

"We may be required to use force."

Zorlog looked at the younger Xilozak with amusement. He was new in this position, just promoted to Savok, and so far, had proven to be quite efficient. He liked him even though he could be a bit annoying with a constant dribble of questions.

"Savok, a Xilozak need not entertain such problems. Just kill them, but keep the one in charge alive and bring him to me, understand?"

"Completely, my Tarvok!" He replied with a nervous salute before hastily departing.

Zorlog meandered around the bridge, passing an inspecting eye over each of the crew. Most avoided his penetrating gaze.

A Txtian approached him, the head officer of the military envoy.

Zorlog looked at him in disgust. "What do you want?" he growled.

"We are scheduled for a meeting upon entry into the Signus system. I am requesting the estimate of our time of arrival."

"And what would make your arrival so important?"

"We have been requested by the great Zuvok Ezok."

"A Zuvok? You of all, to meet a military commander of such rank? Seems unorthodox. However, I did agree to take you to the Empirical fleet, did I not? I intend to align with my word. We will disembark for the Signus system on completion of this slave auction."

"I have received a number of complaints from my group about the duty roster."

"Are your officers unable to perform the work, Txtian?" Zorlog jeered.

"No. The issue is that we have no agreement to work as part of this crew. You were contracted by the Empire to provide us transportation. There are no other arrangements. I intend to extract my troops from under your command."

"As long as you are within my ship, you and your troops will follow my orders to the letter. The Empire cannot protect you while you are within a civilian ship. Accidents can happen. Do you understand, Txtian?"

"Is that a threat, Zorlog?"

"It is Tarvok Zorlog, and I do not threaten, I give orders. I am in command here, do not dispute my authority or you will learn my methods of discipline."

The Txtian remained quiet for a moment as if thinking what to reply. "Very well, but your conduct will be reported. This will not go unpunished."

"Unpunished? Again, you warn me on this very deck? Perhaps I should impress on you that your honorable Zuvok and I are old acquaintances. There are many perspectives one can consider with this arrangement. My terms are simple: follow my orders and you and your troops will remain alive. Now get out of my way!" He pushed the Txtian against the bulkhead wall and marched past, headed for his quarters.

"We know you have captured the slave daughter of the Signite leader! We will insist on her transfer upon arrival at Signus!" the Txtian screeched after him.

"Along with your corpse," grumbled Zorlog under his breath.

* * *

The slavership dropped out of acroluc almost on top of the Xi-Empire attack fleet. Fleet ships scrambled in frenzied efforts to avoid a collision.

Zorlog ignored the irritated Tarvok's complaints over the com channels. He inspected the front line for himself, his tracing officers had pulled together a full holographic compilation of the area. The Signite resistance was almost defeated. Most of its fleet had been annihilated, outmatched by the tremendous size of the invading force. A large blip on the tactical holograph, the Zuvok's cruiser, broke away from the engagement and made its way back to the lone slavership.

"Zuvok Ezok hailing, Sir," reported Zorlog's com officer.

Zorlog nodded and positioned himself purposefully on the bridge. It is important to maintain an image when one is in a position of lesser power.

The Zuvok's scarred flustered face pasted itself on the main monitor. "Zorlog, you are as crazy as they say!" His coarse laugh scratched itself through the sound monitors.

Zorlog replied with a toothy smile. "I was the only one willing to bring these pitiful creatures to you within an unsecured zone. That does not make me crazy, just well provisioned."

Ezok scoffed. "A stray shot from one of these Signite battleships could blow you to micro-dust. Are you sure the risk is worth the credits? Perhaps you are simply incapable of understanding your situation."

Visibly annoyed by the pompous comment, Zorlog clenched his jaws together, his mouthful of teeth providing an audible grinding sound as they thrust into one another. He fought to maintain his twisted grin.

"This ship and its crew could destroy the remains of that Signite fleet on their own, my Zuvok. It is indeed clear your penchant for spectacle is alive and well. I am amused to see our mighty military at work. To think that pitiful resistance obviously challenges the combined efforts of the Xi-Empire's finest."

The words dug deep under the Zuvok's skin. Lower veins under his neck flushed a deeper green, and his eyes dilated multiple times. "I am tempted to let you assume your stated intention here, Zorlog. Allow you to demonstrate your grit with these Signites," he replied in a low, dangerous voice. "However, I wish to end this exercise as soon as possible. Do you have the Txtian science group aboard?"

"Yes. And they are still... alive."

"Very good. I would hate to have to kill you over such a trite misconduct. I will send a shuttle for them. Ensure they are dispatched safely. Oh yes, there is word that a prominent Signite was captured by you - a female – close relation to the Signus Governor. I wish to have her transferred as well."

"The female will bring me a healthy profit from the auctioneer's block," Zorlog rebutted bitterly.

"You will be paid adequate compensation. Bring her to me. To the Empire!"

"May the Purists reign!" returned Zorlog as he promptly closed the channel.

"It is not a good policy to voice against the Empire with such impudence. Some may consider it treason," stated first officer Kitohk.

"I have not abandoned my alliance to the Empire, Charvok, only its composition," Zorlog returned icily.

* * *

Aviore was delivered to the Zuvok's warship.

The Zuvok's message to the Signus Governor did not result in the effect he had wished for. The Signite decided to commit suicide rather than betray his people, or witness his only daughter being slowly tortured to death. In the end, it did not matter much anyway. Signus was conquered.

It was the Zuvok Ezok himself who announced the news to Aviore. He threw open the hatch, walked in, and kicked her savagely as she lay huddled on the floor. She did not feel the blow, as she was no longer part of the physical world. Her mind wandered crazily, with no direction, lost in a sea of pain and guilt.

She had told them so much. Why couldn't she have been stronger? How could she be so weak?

Another kick followed, deep into her abdomen. She fought for breath as she pulled herself into a tighter ball.

Why can't they leave her alone, leave her to die? She didn't have the strength to endure another questioning. She didn't know anything more.

"Your contribution proved helpful in the decimation of your peoples," a low voice churned at her, as if she was underwater. "However, your father demonstrated true strength of character by taking his own life!"

The Xilozak glared down at her with contempt, watching for an effect from his announcement.

Aviore did not flinch. But the words registered. They formed into sentences, then shaped into meaning.

Her father was dead.

She would have cried, had she any tears left.

The lack of reaction only angered the Zuvok. "His death lies on your shoulders, Signite!" He gave her one last kick before turning and slamming the hatch shut, leaving her again in total darkness.

The pain from the deep cuts, the broken bones, the throbbing from fingernail-less hands did not seem to matter anymore.

Everything was lost. Everybody.

Memories of her father raked through her mind, ripping tearless sobs and spasms from her beaten body.

Only the pain remained, now.

The heat from her broken ribs cut into her anguish like cold steel.

She swore viciously. *She had to choose: give up and die, or survive and hope. Hope for a miracle. Hope that someone would come... Hope Ryan would come.*

She latched onto the only emotion that could keep her alive. She could feel it well up within her, feel its intensity. She pulled herself upright and coughed up traces of blood, then spit it out into the darkness in defiance. Remnants of strength returned into her tormented body. She was fuelled by hate, composed of sheer will, driven by... something else.

The worst has passed. She will survive. She must.

It was not long before they came to get her from that dark room. A Xilozak doctor looked over her injuries but did little. He did not have the background of a slaver doctor. There was no profit in the progression of knowledge of alien physiology, and he did not like the prospect of handling filthy aliens. If they were sick or dying, it was better to kill them and be done with it.

Another slavership docked alongside the Zuvok's cruiser as the last of the Signite defensive was being decimated. Aviore, along with many other captured Signites, were transferred off the military ship onto the slavership. The citizens of Signus had officially joined the ranks of the enslaved, they were no longer prisoners of war, as they were no longer a viable Xi-Empire threat. They were merely another resource to desecrate.

Signus was ready to pillage.

* * *

Ryan's trip ended on the jungle planet called Kalmaka. It was a planet rich with uraninite deposits - a mineral valued by the Xi-Empire. The northern hemisphere was dotted with colonies, each busily ripping into the surface, routing out vast networks of mines, yielding the precious unprocessed ore. Miners were in high demand. It was not by mistake that Zorlog had landed here. Profit was to be made.

Kalmaka was once a planet where its natives were free of tyranny, of slavery and death, and its history was rich with strange legends of the ancient Gods - Gods of unparalleled power and wisdom. The latest generations had learned quickly about Gods from the sky. They were not like the legends at all. They were evil, murderous monsters. A Kalmakan could only be free hiding deep within the equatorial rainforests, where the Xi-Empire troops dare not follow.

Zorlog's slavership landed just outside the Xi-Empire's largest mining colony. The alien captain ordered the full complement of slaves off. Every last one would be sold here - or killed for meat.

Ryan knew they were coming for him well before the hatch cracked open. He knew they had landed. He had grown accustomed to the sounds emanating throughout the ship.

The guards moved with unusual haste. He was literally pulled out of the tube and thrown down the corridor. A few savage kicks in the back provided sufficient motivation for him to maintain a quick pace. His sides throbbed in pain, but unhealed ribs were the least of his worries. Whips cracked on slow movers. He joined a streaming line of victims, eventually exiting the snaking corridors into the slaver's tremendous cargo bay area. Gigantic doors opened to an unfamiliar skyline.

As the slave lines streamed toward the exits, Ryan stole glances at the sky above showing through the bay door openings, hoping to catch something familiar. The few stars that shone through the thick haze left little hint of recognizable formations.

A breeze cut through the ship's stale air. It carried with it a thick, rich, bitter odor of sulfur, strong and pungent, but it was breathable and fresh in comparison to the stench inside the ship.

He descended the ramp into a hot, sweltering afternoon. His legs were shaky. The gravity was stronger than Earth's, and he found it an effort to walk. His limbs were tired and heavy, his chest and sides wracked in pain. The atmospheric pressure made breathing a conscious labor. Ryan felt like he was underwater. The sweat poured off his body in torrents, and his mouth was dry with thirst. He followed a long line down a trail knee deep in thick, black and green muck. Ahead, past the hundreds of naked slaves' backs, the line seemed to wind on forever, disappearing into a slowly thickening fog.

Trudging on, the vegetation grew heavier, eventually surrounding them on both sides, forming a living impervious cave. Some light managed to penetrate through its ceiling, struggling against the darkness, providing just enough for one to see where to step.

There was nowhere to run to, nowhere to escape.

Ryan noticed the others dragging themselves through the mud. No one talked, each focused on the act of placing one foot in front of the other, minds withdrawn from reality. On every third step, a man or woman cried out after receiving a vicious lash from the slaver's whip - a warning that they were not moving fast enough. The whips' sparks flashed brightly in the darkness, like bursts of lightning.

A commotion up ahead came to a quick end when a bolt of orange-yellow light burned into a fleeing human boy. His back turned into a red gaping hole as he crashed into the sidewall of the cut trail. He hung there upright, suspended, like a fish caught in a net. A few sobbed at the sight, but others turned away, refusing to look.

As he passed the scene, he was sickened by the smell of burning flesh, now fully saturated into the heavy air. He glanced at the dead boy, half buried in the vegetation. Insects were already crawling over the corpse, attracted to the gaping wound.

He could not have been more than 16. He looked familiar, somehow.

The Xilozak slaver that had shot the boy was approaching, marching alongside the trail of captives, his blaster slapping loudly on his muscular leg. His boots carried a thick layer of mud, but he was oblivious to it, engrossed in his insidious yelling at the slow-moving line of slaves beside him. Ryan stopped staring and started ahead as quickly as he could.

I don't want to die here, not like that boy.

He glanced back once more, once he felt he was far enough ahead. The Xilozak was inspecting his kill, yelling out to another guard close by, obviously bragging about his marksmanship. Their conversation burst into growling bouts of laughter, bitter and coarse.

The line passed under an archway, an entrance carved through a massive wall of stone. The wall's height was hidden by vegetation, but the tunnel was at least 15 meters long, revealing its tremendous thickness. The other side opened to a small city, the population of which consisted of Xilozaks, Txtians, and slaves of many races.

As they marched through the town, their captors barked their own versions of profanity toward them and laughed amongst themselves. The slaves collected in a large fenced corral area adjacent to a platform in an open area. It served as a junction of the five roads entering the town.

It was a chance to rest, and like the many others, Ryan collapsed onto the wet, steaming soil. Catching one's breath was a deliberate act. It took time before strength returned to his legs.

One of the guards pulled over a trough and filled it with muddy water. The others leaned in and lapped up the water, ravenous with thirst. Ryan joined them but remained civilized by cupping his hands. The water was earthy, tasted bitter and smelled slightly of sulfur, but it quenched his thirst, and that's what mattered.

Satisfied, he leaned back and took the time to survey the scene around him. On the platform, a Txtian auctioneer screeched out Trinarieit to an audience that was still growing in size, although the auction had not yet begun.

Dusk arrived, marking its commencement with spotlights that automatically clicked on with a hum, illuminating the platform in bright, white light. The auctioneer growled and clicked a constant murmur as the captives were paraded under the hot lights and sold to the highest bidder.

Noteeth's words bore into Ryan's mind. *Attack the auctioneer he had said. Show some spunk. Yeah, they'd probably just kill him. Just like the boy. But what if he was right?*

Darkness had fallen. The show had begun. Ahead guards with blasters directed the slaves up one at a time. The pace was quick.

It was his turn.

He trudged slowly up to the platform, his mud-laden limbs making it difficult to navigate the steps. The lights were bright, and he couldn't make out anything beyond the glare. They tied his hands behind his back with a cord and left him standing there.

The bidding began. Ryan could feel his anger and hate build.

Now is a good time to die.

The thought surprised him, but strangely, he felt elated.

A good time to die.

He stood tall and spit into the crowd. "You bastards!" he yelled at the top of his lungs. "You ugly sonofabitches!"

A whip met his back with a vengeance.

Ryan remained standing, although the pain made his legs shake uncontrollably. A laugh twisted from his throat in an involuntary defiance. The second strike was too much. The familiar numb feeling came back as he went down, but he fought with every bit of strength he had left. He fell, but only to his knees. He continued to glare into the crowd, wearing a mask of hate.

A sharp scolding from the Txtian auctioneer stopped the flogging and the bidding continued. A few minutes passed. Sensation crept back into his numbed muscles. Again he pulled himself up, first one leg, then the other, once again to stand shakily upon the platform. Unknown to him, the bidding was fierce. A slave with determination was worth 10. Nods from the crowd came quickly, and the price rose even higher, until a certain miner held up his arm and announced his price.

The bidding ended.

Ryan could no longer tell what was going on around him. He had retracted back into himself, fighting his own war of mind against pain. When the auctioneer yelled the Trinarieit version of "SOLD!" he was ready to collapse. A Xilozak dressed in black grabbed him, carried him off the stage, and threw him to the ground.

He hit face-first into the grimy soil, luckily it was a soft humus deterring a possible break of his nose. He braced himself for the whip but it did not come. The Xilozak stood above him and slowly guzzled the contents of a flask he was carrying. The big alien wavered slightly as it watched the next two proceedings, eyes never bothering to look down. Ryan took advantage of the time, resting his tired, beaten body, regaining his strength.

The alien signaled him it was time to go with a sloppy kick. They both headed down the road toward an area reserved for multi-terrain land rovers, Ryan in a stiff-legged walk, the alien in a wandering saunter. The vehicles were parked in disarray, pointing in all directions. They navigated through the maze and came to a stop at the base of one of the larger vehicles. The alien growled at him, signaling him to climb up the ladder that led to the top deck of the rover. The deck was open to the sky with a bar railing that surrounded its perimeter to contain any cargo or passengers.

Ryan dragged himself up the ladder. When he stepped off the last rung, the alien guard pushed him savagely from behind. He crashed down onto the deck, hard. The Xilozak stepped over him, growling a coarse, cruel laugh.

It took a moment for him to recover, then he crawled over to rest against a nearby crate. He glanced over and noticed other humans - three in all, two men, one woman. The men glanced at him disinterestedly and resumed their study of the floor, or the stars, or whatever they were previously looking at. Only the woman acknowledged his presence, giving a silent nod.

Crates, boxes, and pieces of machinery were strewn messily upon the deck. A few parts were tied down. The Xilozak guard sat near the front of the rover, on a large crate, watching the group of them through the corner of his eye. He methodically downed the contents of his flask, his breath soured with a rich buttery odor. The beverage seemed to be taking effect as the Xilozak's eyes drifted lazily, his facial features were sluggish, relaxed.

He was drunk. Seems even an alien can get pissed.

Ryan followed the guard's preoccupied gaze. He was watching the auction down the road. It was just visible from their perch, the lights being the brightest in town. The auctioneer's drawl carried through the heavy air in a weak murmur. Figures of slaves marched up and down the platform in an unrelenting line.

How many more? Hundreds? Thousands? He couldn't be sure.

He caught the woman staring at him again, but when he returned her gaze, she quickly averted her eyes. She glanced back intermittently, never sustaining contact for more than a moment. There was something about her, something that dug at Ryan's memory. It finally hit him with bittersweet realization.

Brown eyes reminded him of Aviore.

He looked up at the stars now, unobscured in the dark night sky, and knew he was a long way from home.

* * *

The rover's engine roared to life, its rumbling echoed through the misty, humid air. The driver ground the machine into gear and it jerked forward. It started rolling slowly down the road, heading directly toward an opening in the wall.

Ryan could make out the lines of the ancient stone circling the perimeter of the town. Gauging by his viewpoint, it had to be at least one hundred meters high.

This town had been built within a former fortress.

The exit into the jungle jutted upward to end in an arch many meters above the top deck of the rover. The passageway through the massive stone wall was guarded by dozens of Xilozaks and Txtians. The rover rolled to a stop as its driver conferred with one of the guards.

Ryan glanced over to the drunken Xilozak. The alien had put away his flask and pulled his weapon, one that resembled a high-powered rifle, and held it close to his body.

They rolled through the archway, bathed under the light of a dozen rotating search beams. Most were pointed out, into the jungle. Exiting the tunnel they passed by a large, mobile cannon, its base now overgrown with strangling vegetation. Its muzzle bore the carbon deposits of repeated use.

They continued on past a brief clearing. It was pockmarked with uncountable blackened scars, signs of periodic blasting.

The jungle quickly enclosed around them. Ryan watched as the Xilozak guard shifted nervously, adjusting his rifle, making ready to shoot. His discarded flask now lay empty on the deck.

Ryan was in silent awe at the immensity around him. The rover whined and protested as it pushed its way through the overgrown roadway. The vehicle stood at least eight meters high on its huge tires, but the greenery above them dwarfed it like an insect. Trees with 20 meter wide trunks rose up four and five hundred meters into a dark sky, now laced with an intricate network of suspended foliage. The stars were no longer visible. They left a legacy of soft, white light, which danced over the canopy like a fine frost.

Everyone slid down under the cover of the crates to avoid the branches and leaves that constantly swept over the deck in whipping lashes. Time and again, Ryan heard strange sounds bellow over the rover's engine, cries from creatures deep in the jungle. He wondered if he could survive a night out here, what his odds were of ending up a food morsel. He checked the guard again. The Xilozak was squatted down tight against the deck, his eyes wide, gun ready.

He was scared. Really scared. What had he done to deserve this post? Looks like he would give up his arm to be down in the rover right now. Maybe he should try an escape right now. But if he jumped, he would probably break a leg. He could grab onto a low-lying branch when the rover went under one. That would work. But once he was free, what then?

A growl reverberated from the pit of his stomach.

He was hungry. He was thirsty. Where could he find water? What could he eat that wouldn't kill him? Old Noteeth had said that they would feed him well. Maybe he should wait. Wait and be a slave. That was ridiculous. Now was the time to move.

The rover bounced vigorously as it traversed a formidable sinkhole. The guard turned in Ryan's direction, slightly startled, and seemed to notice him for the first time. He growled, motioning with his blaster to move closer to the center of the deck.

Instantly his ideas of escape fell apart. He crawled over to join the others, finding a protective area behind a large piece of machinery.

They came to a clearing. The machine ground to a halt with an audible screech. Ryan strained his neck to look out in front. Ahead of them lay a fence that used lasers instead of stone. It was well over 50 meters tall with alternating beams at least a meter in depth that ran horizontally from post to post. They were spaced no more than a meter apart for the full height of the fence. Their phosphorescent reddish glow lit its perimeter on both sides, cutting through the murkiness.

He could hear a high-pitched hum emanating through the air, like he was near a major power line. The smell of ozone made his mouth water.

The rover had arrived at a gate. Two towers stood 10 meters apart, rising up another 10 meters higher than the fence. Ryan could see lights and movement at their top decks. The dark outline of large pivot guns jutted out, muzzles pointed into the jungle, apparently ready to handle any hostile visitor. Ryan peered down the horizon along the fence. There was a similar tower another couple kilometers down, just barely visible, its lights dimmed by fog.

The fence was either a very elaborate means of keeping slaves in, or a necessity to keep something else out. Probably the latter.

Something crashed behind them. Not too far away. Low thuds. Looking up, he could see the tower guards running out onto the decking to position the pivot guns. The sounds were getting louder. He could feel the vibrations through the deck.

Whatever was coming, was big.

Ryan fought down a sudden urge to yell at the driver to get moving. An instant later the beams disappeared in front of them, opening an access between the two towers. The engines roared and the rover lurched through. In a moment they were free of the jungle and whatever it contained. Ryan let out a breath he hadn't realized he was holding.

He turned back and watched as the gate reactivated. He noticed, just for a split second, the whole fence, from horizon to horizon blink off and on - a temporary unsteady shimmer as the power grid readjusted itself. And then the pivot guns started firing. The ground shook as each pulse blasted a white-hot stream into the dense jungle, focusing on roughly the same direction from which they had come. Blast after blast burned into the foliage, lighting up the area with small explosions and fire, but whatever they were firing at never appeared.

Out of the frying pan...

He turned to view the approaching town, as the rover raced over a brief stretch of blackened, cleared jungle. They slowed to a stop when they reached its outskirts. The streets and modest buildings were alive with Xilozaks and Txtians drinking and fighting. A town not unlike the one they had just left.

They were parked in front of a huge building half-made of old stone from an ancient temple and the rest constructed of large black polished blocks of granite. Two stone columns stretched up in front of the building resembling an architecture employed in Roman Coliseums.

The head Txtian marched out and signaled to the guard. The Xilozak grabbed one of the Signite men and almost threw him off the rover.

The ride was over.

The rag-tag group moved quickly down the ladder. Another guard motioned them to line up and face their new sour-faced owner. The Txtian miner screeched and clicked a barrage of his native language. A small box fastened to his waist belt blurted out a language that Ryan knew by now must have been Signite, as the others seemed to understand what was being said.

The owner pointed to the female at the end of the line. She didn't move. Irritated the alien grabbed her and viciously dragged her in front of the group. Her eyes were large with panic and fear. She looked desperately at each of them.

What could he do? They'd kill him if he tried anything.

He looked away guiltily.

The whip hit her back and wrapped around her neck. Again and again, it cut into her.

With each slash, Ryan winced.

She screamed in agony, then began to beg and plead with the Txtian master. The alien only chirped in amusement, waving its insectoid arm to continue the lashings. When the woman collapsed, he signaled the guard to stop. The thrashing had not lasted long, but its message was clear.

The woman lay on the ground, bleeding, barely breathing. No one moved to help her.

The Txtian glowed with satisfaction. He turned and marched back into his colossal house, dispatching his orders with a wave. The guard motioned to the Signite men to grab the woman and carry her. They marched through the town to a small building made of stone, then proceeded to crowd into a small room with a dirt floor. The Xilozak guard left them with a single menacing growl: Stay!

The Signite woman had not stirred. Ryan stepped closer. The others moved to intercept him, glaring at him with an unbridled hate.

It wasn't his fault, and they didn't do a damn thing to stop it.

He glared back at them, but decided it was best to not push his luck. He backed away, found a corner, crouched down and buried his face in his hands.

Wait. Nothing to do but wait.

Within the hour another human slave appeared, bringing food, water, and clothing for each of them. The slave did not speak a word. He motioned to each of them to take the large bowls he'd brought, and then proceeded to dump steaming gruel into them. Water was served next in oversized plastic-like tumblers.

Ryan gulped it down and inspected the steaming substance in his bowl. It had the appearance of lumpy cornmeal. He scooped it up with his fingers and found it tasted better than the plastic lumps they were fed in the ship. He gulped it down gratefully. The large portions served to fill him up. It was a comforting feeling.

Each of them put on their new apparel. They were similar to overalls, fitting loosely, made of tough denim-like material. He didn't care what they looked like. It was good just to have some clean clothes on once again - some dignity.

His brief satisfaction was crushed when another Xilozak arrived and signaled him to follow. The others looked on, and he swore they were smiling.

Now into the fire...

Ryan fell into step behind the alien. He was a strong, rough-looking reptile and he walked with purpose. Ryan had to move fast to keep alongside him. Once beyond earshot of others, the Xilozak finally growled something at Ryan. The alien's translator blurted out Signite.

"I don't understand that language," Ryan stated flatly.

The Xilozak grunted, knowing Ryan's response did not match the translator's setting. He made a few adjustments to the unit and repeated his Xilozak growl. This time it came out in what sounded close to German.

"I still don't understand."

The alien, now irritated at his unsuccessful attempts, stopped walking and savagely twisted at the controls to the translator. A common phrase began to blurt out in a myriad of languages. One came through in Earth-English, saying simply, "You are a slave of the Xi-Empire."

"There!" announced Ryan, although the translator was already onto the next subsequent dialect.

The grizzled Xilozak grunted with satisfaction and made a few more adjustments. The sentence repeated with a flat metallic squeal: "You are a slave of the Xi-Empire."

Ryan nodded back.

"Good. We know of your language. Slaver Tarvoks are often slack in their translation databases, but I know Zorlog, he is efficient and thorough. From now on you will forget your home language. It is Trinarieit you will learn."

The statement was as much a command as it was fact. Translators were few on the colonies. Slaves had to learn their masters' commands quickly if they wanted to survive.

"You will do what I say when I say it."

The reptile resumed his brisk pace. Ryan again fell in behind. They navigated through a maze of buildings, then through a small yard littered with remnants of vehicles and pieces of machinery.

A mechanic's shop!

Three rovers, in mid-repair, filled three of the four available bays. Ryan followed the alien through the building, stepping carefully to avoid tripping. They entered a small room with walls layered with shelving crammed with gadgets of all shapes and sizes. A large cushioned bench, big enough to hold a Xilozak, sat in the corner with one of its legs propped up on a rusting hunk of metal.

"I will allow you to sleep. Gain your strength. You will need it. Do not leave this room until I come to get you." He left without another word.

Ryan lay down on the bench, sinking into its softness, and was asleep within seconds. It seemed to have lasted only minutes and the Xilozak was shaking him awake with a roughened lizard hand.

"Get up, slave. I want you to clean."

Ryan complied, began to dig through the mess, moving equipment and tools, scrubbing the floor with water and cleaners found with a bucket. A familiar human slave appeared a few hours later to drop off a meal. The mechanic, not wanting to watch him eat, directed him back into the small storage room. The meal was salty, his drink bitter, and the break short, but his belly was full, and his body felt good, with the exception of the odd sudden movement reminding him of healing ribs.

Later in the day, the ranking Txtian arrived. They called him a Torzon, a label similar to an old-Earth Overlord in many respects. He exchanged heated words with the mechanic. Ryan watched from around the corner, careful not to catch the attention of the pair.

The mechanic's face was flushed dark green, and he struggled to pronounce each word, more than often ending in a slurred growl. Something strange happened to the mechanic. He began to hold his head in his hands like he was in pain. The Torzon chirped in delight and gave the big Xilozak a massive shove into a pile of scrap. The insect chirped a few more acidulous phrases and promptly left.

The mechanic dug a large metallic bottle out from under a heap of debris and took two large gulps from it. Bloodshot eyes searched out and found Ryan. The old Xilozak motioned him over and flipped on the translator.

"Bad news for you, slave. Seems the Torzon has no desire to keep to his word. I cannot retain you. You must work in the mines. In time, maybe, I will be able to get you back here, but not now. You must work hard. That is how you will stay alive. I know you have the will, that's why I bought you."

He took another swig and burped loudly. "Time to go then."

He rolled out a wheeled platform from behind one of the derelicts at the side of the building. It was nothing more than a rectangle wrapped in roll bars, with no seats. It didn't seem to have any central engine or source of power. A large joystick jutted up from the floor.

He motioned Ryan to jump on. "Hang on, slave."

The vehicle jarred into motion and shot off into the crowded street. Xilozaks and Txtians alike jumped out of their way, growling and shaking fists at the mechanic, who laughed coarsely, enjoying the sight of them scrambling. It was not far to the mineshaft entrance, but the mechanic's recklessness ensured it was an interesting ride. Twice they barely avoided being crushed by the massive drilling machines racing up from the depths.

They finally came to a stop near the mouth of the entrance. Another Xilozak met them, giving the mechanic an open slap on the shoulder. The mechanic responded with a toothy grimace - the challenged version of a smile. He instructed Ryan to stay put and left to have a long discussion with his friend. He finally signaled Ryan out with an impatient wave. "I have instructed my friend here not to kill you unless it is necessary. Do what you are told and you will live."

The old mechanic stepped back onto the sled and sped off, fearlessly sliding between two large mobile ore processors roaring down the lane.

* * *

Ryan's mining experience began 10 kilometers underground. The friend of the mechanic turned out to be the shift supervisor, and his discipline was ruthless. Any slaves who could not keep up the pace were butchered on the spot by a large machete-style sword that the muscular Xilozak carried in a sling on his back. His victims lay where they fell, often left there to rot.

The slaves were many, and very few were human. There were the lizards he'd seen before, very different than the Xilozaks, with tails long and strong and pronounced snouts. They seemed more at home crouching on all fours than upright, which made them suitable for this kind of work. Native Kalmakans were everywhere - small hairless beings, with three tails and four hands. They were not very strong, and for what Ryan could tell, not very intelligent. He caught glimpses of others within the deeper sections of the mines: large, dark creatures, with a strong distaste toward bright light. They were very few, but one could do the work of 10 of him. The guards kept them segregated from the others, an obvious sign they were dangerous. It was not until the third shift that Ryan understood to what degree. A Signite, too exhausted to notice, ventured too close to one while he was working. It happened in mere seconds. The thing attacked and literally ripped the poor man to pieces. The guards moved in quickly, their whips barely managing to hold it at bay. Their whips and the machete-style swords never stopped their slashing and cutting. They glistened in the low light, painted with the dark blood of the alien. More and more of the guards joined in with the frenzied viciousness of an out of control mob. In the shadows, Ryan could see the others of its kind. They watched quietly, warily. The creature's rage could not continue indefinitely, and it eventually succumbed to the unrelenting, merciless beating, until it was reduced to a butchered, bloody clump. The thing cried out pitifully in its last moments, beckoning to its brothers to come to its aid. None came.

The guards left the corpse where it lay, and the slaves were forced to resume their work as if nothing happened.

Ryan felt nothing for the savage death of the alien, or for the butchered Signite. It was no longer fear, but hate that clamped itself around his heart. He had little compassion left. He was empty. He was indifferent.

Tracking slaves was done the old-fashioned way. Embedded id disks were too expensive. A simple branding sufficed. In the mines, keeping track of slaves was easy. After all, there was nowhere for them to go.

It was a matter of passage for all of them. Standing in the lineup, they all knew what to expect. A Txtian stood ready with the glowing metal brand, just pulled from the fire. Ryan watched it all from an observer's point of view, disassociated. The pain came afterward, creeping into his mind like a thawing cold. They branded him twice: once on the back of the shoulder blade, the other on the calf of his right leg. It took many shifts for the burns to heal over, and more for the resulting stiffness in his muscles to dissipate.

Their jobs changed with every shift, but they all held one common element - the work was dangerous. He was often ordered to go in between the gigantic cleats of the borers and clear away obstructing debris that could interfere with the machines as they pushed unrelentingly through the igneous veins. One slip would spell death, or worse, injury. Flying shrapnel was a constant hazard. Many times Ryan had seen a fellow slave get swallowed into the moving parts of the borer, or crushed under the cleats of the massive machine.

But nothing stopped the production.

Old Noteeth had been right about one thing: they fed them well. Mining was a business, and well-mannered slaves were considered a cost that should be managed properly. The slaves worked in shifts, with every 23rd shift off to allow them to regain their strength.

Ryan was changing under the heavy work, becoming stronger, building muscle. It was subtle, almost unnoticeable at first. His injuries seemed to heal a little too quickly. He felt a little light-headed sometimes. He had to work to keep his emotions in check, often fighting to squelch the savage anger that overtook him.

They were giving him drugs, most likely in the food. What they were, he had no idea, but they were a benefit in this harsh world. He tried to talk with the others, hoping they knew of the source. Seemed they were all

Signite, and since they didn't understand him, they didn't trust him. They regarded him with indifference, often passing by without even acknowledging his presence. The few that would talk turned out to be 'moles' - friends of the guard, willing to leak any tidbit of information for a better meal, or an easier shift. He learned the hard way about these ones. Talk of escape resulted in 24 lashes. It almost killed him.

Almost. No more looking for friends. He was alone.

And so, he kept to himself, watching, listening. He grew strong, adding muscle mass with unnatural speed. Scrapes and cuts seemed to heal at twice the rate of normal. That was not the only mystery. The Signites showed little sign of change.

Were they drugging him only?

The other damned aliens noticed the change. He saw them watching him. *Maybe they were scared of him. He knew he could snap a Xilozak's neck in a second.*

He smiled at the thought.

The resident doctor in charge of disease and pestilence control gave him special attention on one of his visits, but nothing seemed to have changed because of it.

The Signites seemed to avoid him with more vigor than before.

They were afraid of him. He was a freak. To hell with them anyway.

The guards were also wary of him. They tended to use the whips on him more frequently. But they had little effect. His back, bearing the scars of uncounted lashes, turned tough as leather. He had long since grown accustomed to the pain.

Nothing physically would hurt him anymore, just the loneliness, and no flogging could match that pain. He had to keep focused on escape. He had to develop a plan. First, he must move onto a job where he could be running machinery. He had to win the supervisor's favor. He was no mole. The only way to do this was to work hard, keep up the pace. Never slow down.

Shifts passed, he hustled when the others dragged their heels. He knew they thought him insane, and maybe he was.

But it worked.

The supervisor ordered a change. Ryan was promoted to driller, taught to handle the large, cumbersome plasma drill. The tool was extremely heavy and required a considerable amount of strength to drive it into the solid granite wall. Only the big aliens and the machines seemed capable of doing this job.

He would not be beat.

Shift after shift his arms hung limp at his sides as the machine strained every muscle in his body, but the drugs continued to do their work. His body compensated, reacting from necessity. His strength increased, along with his skill at handling the drill. Soon he was able to make the tool an extension of his arms and was able to cut through the rock face with ease. All the time he worked, he watched, looking for patterns and routines in the movement of the guards. Plans of escape continually turned within his mind.

He learned to understand his captors, understand their language. They talked amongst themselves in a mixture of native Xilozak and Trinarieit. Their verbal enunciation was coarse and guttural, thick with a slurring accent. It was difficult when one had no frame of reference. But he was determined. He constantly eavesdropped on conversations and practiced his pronunciation under the camouflaging noise of the boring machines.

Ryan was listening in on a conversation between two Xilozak borer drivers, when he noticed a Signite watching him - a bit too carefully. He memorized his features, half-expecting he was a mole, looking to get another freebie from the guards.

He would have to deal with this before they caught onto him.

The next shift the same Signite was on cleanup duty between two borers.

A strange coincidence, or a special arrangement? If he was being watched, things would be reported, lies if not truths. He knew what had to be done, and he was ready.

He waited on the guards cautiously. When they left for their break, he dropped his drill and sprinted. The Signite didn't see him coming, until it was too late. Ryan grabbed him and yanked him off the borer's decking, down in between the two immense machines. In one sudden, savage pull he had the man between the cleats. The gigantic metal rollers crept ahead steadily, threatening to crush the Signite's skull.

The man yelled something at him in Signite, but Ryan had him pinned, with no way to move.

The man was a mole, and he was going to get him killed. He had to die.

But instead of struggling, the man relaxed and waited. The hint of a smile traced upon his lips. His gray eyes stared back intensely, not with hate, but with indifference.

Doesn't seem right. A mole would be begging by now, pleading for his pitiful life.

He yanked the man free just as the rollers were about to crush him. The Signite let out a laugh, his gray eyes dancing. Ryan let him go, perplexed at his behavior.

This one was either extremely brave or an absolute idiot.

"What's your name?" he asked.

The man only looked at him.

Shit. You're speaking English, you fool. Speak Trinarieit.

He attempted it again, in a rather poor Trinarieit. "Name?"

"My name is Bosn. Bosn Garious Amerida Don. Troop 91017 of Dranoke Division. Why didn't you do it?"

"Maybe I should have. You - mole?"

The man laughed again, lines crinkling on his face.

"Are you?"

A movement caught his eye. The guards were coming back. It was time to move. The Signite noticed. "We'll talk again, friend," Bosn stated, already moving to the borer's ladder.

Ryan sprinted back, feeling a bit strange.

He had called him 'friend' – a mole wouldn't have said that - was it possible that he had found someone he could actually talk to? He did not expect this, especially not now.

When the relief shift came, Ryan searched for the Signite. He found the man sitting, alone, watching the others with those placid gray eyes.

"Signite of Dranoke Division."

He nodded. "Earthman."

They clasped hands. The Signite's grip was strong.

"Join me. I must say, I am glad you did not kill me - I'm not a mole."

"You not mole."

"Good. Glad you agree. Anyone tell you that your Trinarieit's pretty sad? Do you know Signite at all?"

"No."

"Alright then. Trinarieit first. I know it well, part of my training."

They managed to get a rudimentary communication going. Ryan often resorted to drawing pictures in the dirt when he lacked the words. It was slow, but it worked.

The shift went quickly, and each relief shift after that. Ryan's Trinarieit improved, and he learned more about his Signite friend. Bosn had been one of the last resistance troops stationed on one of Signus's moons. He had single-handedly taken out a Xi-Empire destroyer by rigging an array of explosives on the moon's surface. Simple physics really. The explosion blasted a large chunk of the moon into space and deadly shrapnel to the destroyer, effectively overloading her antimatter shielding, which then triggered a series of internal explosions. It then brought the mighty vessel down onto the moon's surface. For weeks the Xi-troopers scoured the moon looking for him. He eluded capture with only a small enviro-tent and a few meager supplies, managing to obtain water by melting down surface ice with a portable flash unit. His food supply dwindled to nothing after the first few days. He was literally starving to death when they found him. Bosn, beyond all odds, had fought on, even though he knew his own death was near and unavoidable. For that, Ryan admired him.

Their meetings could not last. The flow of new recruits had slowed to a trickle. Signite's slave resources were on the decline. The mining planet held little allure for profit-seeking slavers now, for only the systems in the central quadrants surrounding Xilo would pay the exorbitant prices they desired. The numbers dwindled while the corpse count climbed.

Death did not stop within the dark caverns of the mine, but the guards no longer killed so readily. Something began that was much more insidious than their brutality. They were giving up. It had been too long, and hope had all but evaporated. It's all one had to do in here – quit – lose your will, and the harsh conditions would take care of the rest.

It pained Bosn to see his fellow Signites, once proud men and women, crack and crumble, to slowly die from the inside out. Some would simply withdraw permanently inward, others would go completely insane, and walk in front of the borer...

Ryan didn't know what kept Bosn going. *Maybe he had someone like Aviore. Maybe he made a promise.*

The times Ryan and Bosn managed to get together had become few, made difficult by rotating shifts. Labor shortage or not, the supervisor needed to maintain production. They often sacrificed their needed sleep in order to converse and review different ideas of escape. Most of these plans were simply too unrealistic to work, and they had to be discarded due to one major setback or another, but nonetheless, they kept at it.

When the break came, it appeared trivial, almost unremarkable. The plasma drills were very old, and they needed constant cleaning and maintenance. A number of them had stopped working or simply exploded in the driller's grip. The supervisor saw the need for a more aggressive maintenance cycle and the old mechanic, who Ryan was initially assigned to, was in charge of this. The Txtian Overlord, heeding the supervisor's warnings, instructed the mechanic to step up the maintenance cycle. But the mechanic was already buried in work and did not appreciate the extra burden. He demanded his slave, and this time he won.

When the mechanic arrived for his maintenance pickup, he had the guards round up the slaves from each shift. The old mechanic immediately recognized Ryan and almost looked happy to see him.

"So you are still alive!" he growled.

Ryan cleared his throat and began to snarl out his best attempt at some Xilozak language. "I am... able".

"That's good. You've grown bigger, too. They feed you well down here. More productive that way. You are a smart one to stay alive so long. What do you do?"

"I am a driller."

"Do you know the plasma drills have a bad habit of exploding?"

"I know this."

"Then you will help me maintain them."

"It is against the law to teach technology to slaves," interjected the supervisor.

"How many drillers do you have left? Not very many, do ya? You want these fixed or not?" challenged the mechanic. "I already have enough work for 10 slaves. Maybe you can part with some of your supervisors then?"

"My supers are working full shifts."

"Only because they drive the machines which I keep running. Do not quote The Law to me. If we upheld The Law out here, our Torzon would have disappeared within the great Towers of Zenux zadiis ago."

The supervisor laughed, then shrugged and walked away.

"It is settled, then. You will work with me on alternating shifts or when I need you. You will learn what is required, no more."

"I only want to stay alive."

The old mechanic only grunted. "Good. Grab these drills. Time for you to leave this mine."

The Xilozak left the mine with his new slave following behind, burdened with a load of equipment. He was pleased with the recent change of events.

* * *

The extra work was more taxing on his mind than on his body. He found himself sleeping less, becoming more excited as another plan came into place, a more promising plan than any other before. He studied the plasma drill carefully. He assembled and disassembled it time and again, trying to understand the inner workings of the powerful device.

The mechanic's training was sparse and often given on a need-to-know basis. Ryan was taught the basics, mainly the cleaning and inspection of the units. He was instructed on what irregularities to look for and basic maintenance procedures. Only through carefully put questions did he manage to root out more useful bits of information from the shrewd mechanic. This was not easy, given his main understanding of the language was basic Xilozak commands and still very sparse Trinarieit. He often had to question the mechanic through physical gestures and found the Xilozak to be short on patience. More than once he ended up on the ground with a powerful back-hand from the weathered old alien.

Ryan knew he could give this creature a beating, but decided to keep his distance. He understood this old lizard's temperament. He was not actually trying to be cruel. His basic nature was just more savage. It was this point that kept Ryan wondering about the Txtian-Xilozak combination.

Their collaboration seemed almost paradoxical. They must each get something out of this relationship otherwise the two would have killed each other off long ago. The Xilozaks were the physically stronger of the two races. The Txtians, possibly the brains, but the real mystery was *why* were they in league? What kept them from killing one another? Was it some kind of ancient political treaty? Or maybe it was a religious thing?

The questions plagued him, turning over and over in the back of his mind. He knew he had to learn the answer.

There was a weakness here.

* * *

On his free shifts, he was assigned back to the mines. He kept his drilling work up to par, lest the arrangement with his shifts off at the machine shop be discontinued. Each one of those shifts was precious, a welcome break from the claustrophobic dangers of the mine, and an opportunity to learn how the Xilozak technology worked. By experimentation, Ryan soon realized that if he removed the proper parts and made a number of small adjustments, he could quickly transform the plasma drill into a deadly weapon. The problem was its range. Spanning only a few meters, it was still dangerously inferior to a guard's blaster. The plasma drill also required a vast reserve of power. To solve this problem, he secretly began to collect extra cylinders, marking new ones as drained and tossing them into the pile for recharging. Others he hid in deep recesses of the mine, placing them well away from the natural paths of any guard, or slave. He always moved cautiously, staying within the shadows. Only once was he noticed, and it was by one of the Kalmakan natives.

It peered at him through the darkness, clicking its vocal cords quickly. Its reflective eyes regarded him with curious interest, studying him and his armful of cylinders, its head slightly sideways.

Ryan watched it cautiously, slowly moving toward his drill. Other eyes appeared, more scuttling shapes in the dark. Tailed creatures moved with incredible speed, but quietly, light-footed and dangerous.

He had the drill in his hand when the first one attacked, hitting him in the back of his head with something solid. Everything faded to black.

He awoke laying in a rut, half-soaked in a puddle, a utility light swayed in the distance. A drop of water hit his forehead. He shook it off, slowly rolling up to a sitting position. Kalmakan voices carried out from the darkness, in whispers.

Ryan felt the back of his head, making out a pronounced bump and small cut that was now bleeding. "What do you want, you little bastards?" He yelled out in Trinarieit.

A Kalmakan came in close, face painted in colored mud, body covered in colorful rags. "One-called-man, our *Nitche* has seen you in his dreams. You have much to listen on, and little time."

The Kalmakan referred to as a *Nitche* was their colorful version of a 'witch doctor'.

"Make it quick then, my head hurts," was all he could reply.

The others started to chant in a low whisper, all in their native tongue.

"One-called-man, you must travel deep into the South, past the roiling mounds and the boiling pits. You must find the path that traverses to the East and follow it to the Chaoi of Aelome. It is there, and only there, you will find a way home."

"How do you know what I'm planning? Bosn tell you this? What's a Chaoi?"

"Listen one-called-man, listen to the words I speak. You must set these things in motion, to free Kalmaka, you must go there."

Ryan regarded the strange mud-clad little creature dubiously. "Sure, head South, then follow the path to the East to the Chaoi of something or other. Got it."

The Kalmakan grinned, cracking the dried mud on its cheeks. "Only there you will find your way home. The gates will not allow you to pass. You must always follow the eyes." He nodded at him, grinning ridiculously.

Ryan raised himself up fully, stretching his sore back and rubbing his head. The little creature before him shifted back, eyes wide.

"Alright, little witch doctor. I'll follow the eyes, whatever that means. Is that all you want?"

The *Nitche* nodded feverishly, then threw up his multiple hands to silence the chanting crowd. In seconds the smallish creatures were scampering away into the darkness.

"Free Kalmaka," ordered the *Nitche* as he stepped back out of the light. Then they were gone, as quickly as they had appeared.

Ryan worried many nights about that encounter, although nothing became of it. The natives had not talked, no guards appeared to interrogate him.

He was lucky yet again.

He was living on the edge now. The small time-bombs hidden throughout the mine ate away at him. He felt his nerve slipping into a swelling panic, a dangerous, uncontrolled, phobic reaction.

It was Bosn that saved him. Good old Bosn and his calm, cool reasoning. He pulled Ryan from the brink with his reassurances.

"It will work," he said. "We just need time."

Ryan's nerve returned with a savage quiet, the panic squelched as he worked the details of the escape plan. At the shop, he continued to tamper with the guts of the many plasma drills he serviced and was able to turn the meter-thick deep red beam into a bright pulsating blue. The laser activated gases extended far past their previous imposed limit to a long, deadly burning ray. By setting the plasma drill into a test loop, he managed to pulse the beam on and off, which extended the deadly shot of hot plasma up to almost 20 meters. The only setback was that the modified drill tended to heat up prematurely and its self-protective circuits forced the unit to shut down.

He found the solution was right under his nose. The large mobile depth-charge plasma drills were often used to cut 20 meter deep holes in the blast area wall. These machines were wrapped with a half-dozen small cooling systems that kept the power systems functioning under the heavy load during drilling. One of these machines just happened to be in the mechanic shop under repair. After a night-time inspection of the drill, Ryan found he could easily disengage a single cooling unit from it and rig it up to a hand-held plasma drill. With some conservative testing, he found the outfit actually worked and was able to keep the drill's operating temperate to a low sizzle. The extra weight and size was cumbersome at best, and the plasma-drill had to be held at the waist for effective firing. Using some cabling and thick wire, he assembled a rig that bore most of the load onto his shoulders. Aiming was a chore and he needed to practice. The depths of the mines were the safest to do this, as long as he could smuggle the equipment down. He managed it a few times, although it was risky. He found he could stash the weapon into the larger mining equipment that was on its way into or out of the shop. Those opportunities could rarely be planned, and they had to be seized when the time came. It was in this way that he slowly diminished the small collection of stockpiled energy canisters from the various hiding places within the mine.

The mobile waste movers and the levelers were the best vehicles for smuggling, although once the machines were sent down, they were put into service immediately. Anything smuggled had to be removed quickly, or it would be discovered. Bosn helped where he could, hiding or removing stashed cylinders and equipment. It was a dangerous situation, as slaves caught near any of the mobile machinery were suspected of tampering and instantly persecuted.

Just as their plan was proceeding, tragedy struck. It started with news of the cave-ins of some of the lower levels. The talk was sparse amongst the guards, and Ryan could only understand a partial amount of the context, but it worried him. When his work team was diverted to the cleanup effort, Ryan found that the dead slaves were part of Bosn's group. He faced the grim reality that Bosn could be among them, buried deep under the rubble.

It didn't hit him like it should have. He should feel more, but he felt hollow. Death had become all too familiar company.

A Bellicose Dance

During shift change, he managed to stay a few minutes longer and say a silent prayer on behalf of his one and only friend. *That was all he could do. It was more than most were lucky to receive down here. He had to push on with the plan. Get out of this camp, and into the jungle.*

The first part of his plan was a diversion. The guards met in a common mining shaft between shifts. He would take down the ceiling of that cave, hopefully without killing himself in the process. He studied the cave every chance he had, inspecting it for stress cracks. As a driller, it was one thing he had learned to watch for, and he had developed a sixth sense to know the right spot. He chose carefully and attempted to coordinate his trips to and from the cave entrance with the moving of heavy machinery. Using this as cover he went to work on the ceiling, wall, and support pillars with his plasma-drill. He gouged supports and weakened the ceiling net cleats. After a few shifts, he began to notice the stress cracks widening.

His luck couldn't hold forever. He had to act soon, and with Bosn dead, he had no reason to wait. The old mechanic was close to having the drilling machine ready to be put back into service. He was not about to lose that much needed cooling unit. He would move on the next shift.

As per standard practice, the miners moved at least one rover-load of explosives into the mineshafts a shift. When this rover came down, he was going to intercept it, use his modified plasma-drill to take out the drivers, then move and abandon the vehicle at the mouth of the cavern with the blasting-timer set. The explosion would close off the primary entrance shaft and bury the majority of miners and guards in the process.

The next shift came quickly. He awoke early, feeling a subdued excitement. He rubbed his sore muscles wishing to feel, just once more, the softness of a real bed. The cavern shook as a large borer machine rolled by. The main thoroughfare from the surface was just outside, and the rumbling of the heavy machinery reverberated constantly within the small room.

Of all the places within the mine, the sleeping chambers were the only sites where a guard rarely entered. It was a place where one could feel some sense of security, albeit temporary. He took a brief moment and soaked in the peace, then carefully rolled up his blankets and put them in his storage cubicle. They weren't much, but they were all he possessed.

He moved quietly in the darkness, feeling his way through, careful not to step on another slumbering co-worker. Someone stirred.

Roll-call would be soon.

He looked back one last time into the darkened room. There were five other humans with him in the chamber. None knew him, and they weren't interested in ever knowing him. They knew they all had one foot in the grave. The number of humans working the mine was less than 50 now. Even the

Showmish population had shrunk to a mere handful. They were all spread around in pockets like so many ants.

The guard sounded the usual shrill whistle outside the cave opening. The others stirred awake quickly, hustling out of their makeshift beds and shuffling out to join the lineup. None were late. Code of conduct was harsh. Those who did not get up quickly were flogged. Repeat offenders were killed. The sick were always expected to work. If it was severe, one was allowed one, maybe two, shifts to recover. Those who did not get well after that time were simply killed. As he stood in line, Ryan silently reviewed his plan.

He wished that Bosn could be with him. Their last meeting had been very brief, just enough time to relay a greeting when their work groups passed one another. He had been going up to the sleeping chambers, Bosn's group heading back down. Now he was dead.

The whistle sounded and they began to march. The shaft descended at roughly 35 degrees, going down beyond 10 kilometers. They would meet up with a cargo rover at the three kilometer mark, where they would load on and ride the rest of the way to the bottom. This time, when they met up with the rover something seemed amiss. The slaves were allowed to mingle, and the guards were huddled together in small groups talking.

Then he saw Bosn.

The exhausted Signite was leaning against one of the rover's tires with eyes half-closed. When he saw Ryan a smile lit up his tired features.

"It is good to see you alive, my friend."

"Alive. I know you dead!"

Bosn chuckled. "Keep working on your Trinarieit, Earthman. I'm not dead, as you can see."

Ryan looked around. "What is... working? The guards are too lazy."

"What's going on? News has been sent down that someone has tried to sabotage one of the entrance tunnels. Part of the ceiling came down on one of the rovers this morning, killing the driver and two guards."

Ryan's mind reeled.

His plan!

"They are looking for the one responsible, but they don't know who it could be. They're probably going to blame the lot of us."

Ryan pulled him away from the others. He lowered his voice to a whisper. "It was I."

"You?"

"Escape is... there."

"Today? You were going to escape today? Next time make sure I'm dead before you try it, OK?"

Ryan nodded.

"How?" Bosn could hardly contain his excitement.

"The plasma drill be fixed. Fire deep. Explosives in rover."

Bosn glanced around to make sure no one could hear them.

"You got them working. Good. What's their range?"

"Here to wall."

"That's good enough for me! Don't worry about the guards. They don't have a clue. They didn't have any security system set up in those areas, so they don't have a damn thing on you. Hell, they're even suspecting one another... Ryan, don't leave me here. I want to go with you. We'll draft up another plan. I'll help. I'd rather die trying to escape than continue living like this."

"OK. Plan messed up anyway. Cave-in too soon."

"Killed off some of them, though."

They both chuckled.

The guards broke up their meeting. Whistles shrieked and whips cracked.

"Wait for me, Ryan. I won't let you down."

The severe reprisal never came. The cave-in was suspected to be the result of shifting pressure points. Regardless, the supervisor was not sold, and so they kept investigating.

In the coming shifts, Ryan's trips to the surface were cut to a minimum. The guards were doubled on the surface posts and they questioned him thoroughly on each journey to the mechanic's shop. The drilling machine was sent back into service.

The word was sent down. Three shifts off and triple food rations to anyone who knew anything more about the failure. The moles would be out looking now, suspicious of everything, reporting everything.

Two shifts later they were not any closer than before to finding the culprit. With nothing discovered, the supervisor was frustrated. He ordered the lashings: 10 for each slave.

Ryan shrugged off the flogging with indifference. They had long-since failed in their efforts to break his will.

More shifts passed, things started to return to normal. Bosn and Ryan were finally shuffled back into the same work group. During the sleeping hours, they made their plans. They put away as much food as they could store without looking suspicious, the type that would not go bad for an extended period of time. They waited for the sleep shift to coincide with the Kalmaka-night. Then they rounded up all the remaining fuel canisters and supplies and stole away from the sleeping chambers, heading for the surface entrance.

Ryan carried the drill and Bosn carried the canisters. When they met the guards, Ryan did the talking. He explained to them that he was going to the shop and that his drill needed servicing. The guard seemed satisfied with his story, being familiar with his constant trips. They shrugged with disinterest at his explanation about bringing Bosn with him to help carry back equipment.

They both let out a sigh as they stepped out into the open night. It was midnight, and the skies were hidden under a shield of cloud and fog. One of Kalmaka's two moons valiantly fought to cut through the thick air, a blurry orb in the sky, its weak light barely relieving the blackness.

They headed straight for the mechanic's garage, leaving the mineshaft entrance lights far behind them. The odd drunken Xilozak growled at them as they passed through the makeshift town. The shop lights were still on when they arrived. The old mechanic was underneath a rover working on its transmission. It did not take him long to notice their arrival.

"What are you doing here?" he growled.

"Fix plasma drill and back to mine, quick."

"What about him?" the mechanic nodded toward Bosn.

"Bring him with me to help."

"Fine. Get to work then."

"What wrong with rover?" Ryan asked.

"Nothing, now. It's fixed. You!" the mechanic growled at Bosn, "Load those fuel rods into the cabin."

Bosn did what he was told. They would need the extra fuel rods anyway.

"What's on top?" asked Ryan.

"You're just full of questions tonight." The mechanic glanced up, following Ryan's eyes. "It's a solar collector and power capacitor, used for taking long trips and for powering the plasma guns on the deck."

"What guns?" asked Ryan, as innocently as possible.

"No guns allowed in town. All guns are dismounted off the rovers and stored at the perimeter stations. Keeps the drunken idiots from blasting away and killing the lot of us." The mechanic headed out to work on another rover near the entrance, ignoring the slaves.

Ryan waited until he was out of sight before he began to work on the plasma drill. He could have used one of the drills at the shop and saved the effort of toting this one up from the mines, but he knew his worked. He could not rely on another. Too much was at stake. He refitted the plasma drill, converting it swiftly. He had practiced every step in his mind thousands of times before.

The mechanic walked back in just as Ryan finished. He did not notice anything amiss until Ryan tripped the battery relays that activated the weapon.

"You're smarter than I gave you credit for, slave," he stated flatly. "But you'll never get out of here alive."

Ryan already had the weapon swung around and pointed at the old Xilozak. "Have to try."

Bosn came around from the other side of the rover. "What are you standing there for? Kill him!"

Ryan hesitated. The mechanic was looking him straight in the eye. The old lizard began to talk. "When you approach the gate, on the second tower to the right, there is a small round black door. Hit that, and only that. It will cause a feedback surge that will short circuit the whole perimeter field grid. It will also cut the power to the primary cannon. Then you need only to worry about the auxiliaries."

"Why you tell me this?"

"Make you a deal, slave. On your way out, destroy the Torzon's house. Just hit the columns. It'll come down."

"Not power enough."

"You will if you hook up to the turret capacitor on the top of that rover."

"Need cooling unit like big drills."

"There's one on the other bench you can make work."

Bosn had slipped around behind the old mechanic. He had a steel pipe in his hands. He swung and connected with the back of the Xilozak's head. The lizard went down with a thud and lay motionless. He raised the pipe again, aiming to crush his skull when Ryan shouted.

"No! Want him alive."

"You mind telling me why?" asked Bosn, half annoyed.

"What he told us."

"How do you know he wasn't lying."

Ryan couldn't give him an answer. He just *knew*. "Leave him. We go - now."

They tossed the canisters onto the upper deck and threw the rest of the supplies into the rover's cabin. Ryan helped Bosn mount the makeshift gun to the turret mount, set up the cooling unit, and connect some of the canisters to the capacitor.

"One drives. One shoots."

"I'm a crack shot. I've the training. I'll take the turret," offered Bosn.

"You never fire before! Not work."

"Yeah, right," he laughed. "And what training do you have in combat? I got this. Besides, I like the mechanic's idea. We take out the Overlord."

"OK." Ryan resigned reluctantly, knowing the most dangerous place would be on top. "Just head below if it gets too hot. Don't be hero."

"You just get us the hell out of here as fast as you can."

"When this gauge below point, change canister."

"Right. Got it. The rest is simple. I can handle it. Get in, Ryan. Stop being a mother. We're running out of time."

They clasped hands. "See you on the other side, Earthman." Bosn winked.

Ryan stopped halfway down.

"Bosn!"

"Yeah, Ryan?"

"Stay low. We will be hit hard."

"Don't forget we need to make that stop at the big house."

Ryan remembered the day he arrived, remembered the woman that almost died from the flogging.

"Yeah. Big House."

"Good. It's time we paid them back some," stated Bosn casually.

Ryan settled behind the controls. He had a pretty good idea of what did what - being the mechanic's aide had its advantages. The engines fired up with a low rumble. He slammed the rover into gear and spun it out of the shop bay. They moved down the main street in low speed with running lights off, careful not to attract undue attention, eventually rolling to a dead stop in the front of the formidable temple. The Big House - the house of the Txtian Overlord. Inside, shadows passed by large hexagon windows, and strange music emanated from the main hall.

Must be entertaining some guests tonight.

A warm heavy breeze was blowing through the rover's open quartz port. The night air touched Ryan's cheek with a dampness.

It was going to rain.

He heard movement above and knew Bosn was aiming. Suddenly the night lit up with a flash of colors: bright red, yellow and blue. The plasma blast hit the impressive sized stone column on the right, and its middle disappeared in a shower of light with a thunderous explosion. The weapon fired again and the left column cascaded down. The huge building crumbled. Ancient stones lost their precarious balance and crashed down as the building imploded. In a matter of seconds, it was over.

The music had stopped.

"Hang on!" Ryan yelled. He poured on the power. The rover's monstrous wheels spun wildly, lurching the vehicle slightly sideways as it accelerated toward the gate entrance. The town behind them was already waking up. Lights came on, a siren began to sound. When they reached the gate, the searchlights were ready for them. He could see movement above. The guards were trying to turn one of their laser cannon around to point inside.

Bosn fired a shot that blew the upper decking supports away. Guards scrambled, a cannon rolled off to dangle in a mesh of metal a hundred meters from the ground. Ryan scanned the tower. As promised, the target was there, about halfway up, a small black dot. Bosn fired again, and his marksmanship did not fail. The middle part of the tower exploded in a deafening roar. Within seconds the high-pitch hum from the laser beam fence increased to a shrill scream. The thick red beams shifted to green, yellow, then blue, eventually blinking in an unsteady shimmer, an intermittent pulse, and then died out completely. From horizon to horizon there was darkness.

The fence failed. The old mechanic had been on the level. They are going to have much more to think about now than just a couple of escaped slaves.

A new group of sirens started.

A quick look at the rear monitors showed other rovers racing down the road. Ryan poured on the speed, but the tower guards were waiting for them. Plasma shots came from all directions. The rover was bombarded in an explosion of deadly light. It jumped from one side of the road to the other as blast after blast pounded it. Ryan fought desperately to keep it under control. A blast hit the turret power capacitor, and the ensuing explosion blew Bosn off the rover. Ryan saw him fall through the rear monitor. He geared down and jammed the multiple brakes. The rover cranked sideways as it bounced to a full stop. He could see Bosn crawling, blasts raking the ground around him.

Ryan struggled desperately with the controls. The rover's wheels spun in the mud as he straightened out. He slammed the transmission into reverse and headed back at full power. The engine whined under the strain. He watched Bosn's shadow through the monitor. The Signite had managed to get to his feet and was running. The guards were playing with him, blasting shots from one side to another. Another second he'd be there.

A blast hit Bosn. The Signite crumpled to the ground.

Ryan barrelled in on the tower at full speed. Another rover raced through the gate directly in his path. He braced himself as the two gigantic machines hit. He caught the other rover at a slight angle. It flew upward and back, smashing into the tower. Some of the structure came crashing down, pieces of it smashing onto Ryan's rover.

He ground it into forward and pulled away, leaving shreds of wreckage in his wake. To his left a movement.

Bosn was still alive!

Wheels tossed mud into fountains as he forced the machine into a tight turn, racing up to get between Bosn and the guards' blasts. He pounded the lower entrance ramp button and waited.

Pulse cannon started back up, raking the top of the rover. Shrapnel exploded off the roof in a shower of flames.

Bosn struggled aboard and collapsed.

"Just hang on Bosn, we are getting out here!" he yelled fiercely in broken Trinarieit. He wasted no time, stepping the transmission up one gear at a time, gaining speed and leaving his pursuers behind a wall of twisted wreckage.

Their luck was holding, as the skies immediately opened up in a blinding wall of rain.

He kept the rover on the muddy trail with a balance of skill and luck. He was fleeing from ghosts now. With the rear monitors destroyed, he had no idea if he was being followed, or how close they were. He drove with reckless speed, often taking turns by sliding sideways and tearing into a thick wall of vegetation. He came to the fork in the road hours later. The rain had, by then, petered out to a gentle drizzle. The cloud cover remained, still blinding the eye in the sky.

He was sure the Kalmakans knew something. He would take their advice and turn south into the jungle. Besides, staying on this road, they'd be as good as dead. They'd easily spot him from above. The canopy would provide cover.

He searched for a workable opening, careening down the muddy path in reckless speed. Then he saw it – a brief opening in the dense foliage. The rover cranked sideways, immense wheels sliding in the mud, spinning insanely as its engine pushed the vehicle into the jungle.

Speed slowed to a crawl as the rover powered over small trees and dug through ruts and hills, leaving behind a freshly cut and very visible trail.

They were going too slow. They'd catch up with them for sure at this speed. He had to find a natural pathway or shallow waterway, something to gain speed or hide their tracks, and soon. If they wanted to follow him into this hell, fine. But he was going toward the equator like the natives told him too, deep into the jungle, where they were too scared to go.

Behind him Bosn stirred, but he couldn't stop to check on him, if he did, the time it took would probably cost them their lives.

No, they had to keep moving.

Dawn arrived. The alien sun burnt its way through the cloud cover. The thick canopy allowed through little of its light. But Ryan was not navigating by vision. He had paid attention to the old mechanic, learned about the instrumentation. The forward scanners were superior to his eyes. They would warn him of quicksand, sudden drop-offs, and reveal the more navigable path to take. Regardless, the jungle was becoming denser, and the vehicle's engine whined as it pushed through the wall of upward stretching plants.

At last, an opening appeared - a trail cut through the dense plants. The rover gained speed, moving easily along the trail. It lasted for a number of kilometers, but then the path diverted the wrong way, and he decided to push on through and hope for another.

It didn't matter if he met up with the creatures that created these trails. He was going in the right direction - away from the torture, the killing. In respect the risk was trivial, and he did not care.

So he pushed on, sometimes with the rover fully submerged under the brackish waters of the swamp, with him transfixed on the scanners to guide him to the other side as black, rancid water sprayed into the cabin through countless leaks.

Soon, he told himself, *soon he would be able to stop.*

* * *

3. Providence

The Xilozak patrol had lost track of the rover's heading shortly after it had turned into the jungle. The geostationary satellites revealed thousands upon thousands of potential heat signatures but nothing definitive. The atmospheric particle emissions scan failed miserably as any possible rover emissions were simply absorbed by the vegetation. Swamp gases skewed the readings, and photographic imagery simply failed, as low lying fog concealed any surface details under the canopy. The stolen rover had literally disappeared.

The only alternative was to send in an armed compliment, although that was initially delayed due to the extra deployment of forces required to protect the perimeter of the mining town while the fences were being repaired.

The replacement Torzon arrived quickly, incensed with their lack of progress, demanding an immediate assembly of a hunting party.

That turned out to be a very costly excursion. After all, they were miners, not military types. Accidents happened, valuable equipment was destroyed. A few large carnivore attacks resulted in personnel losses. Others simply vanished into the shadows of the jungle. Eventually, the search was abandoned. There was a mine to run and two random slaves were not worth the effort. They were assumed dead and a false story was circulated in order to suppress any others' hope of escape.

The Torzon was livid. He ordered the execution of some of the guards to set an example but was wise enough to leave the mechanic alone.

* * *

Ryan had driven steadily through the night and a full Kalmakan day before he finally stopped, hoping they were deep enough into the jungle for safety.

Bosn lay where he had fallen, severely burned and breathing sporadically. Ryan pushed aside fallen packs and equipment to get to him, fighting off a wave of exhaustion. He located food, water, and what could be used as medical aid from their supplies.

The Signite was not doing well. Sepsis had set in and he carried an odor of death. He rolled him over onto his back. The Signite groaned in pain, skin blackened across most of his torso.

He poured some water onto his lips and face.

"Bosn, friend. You are not going any good."

His eyes fluttered open, following a grimace. "And you're Trinarieit is piss-poor." He laughed then coughed hoarsely. "You're right. I'm done for. Get me up – in the seat. Don't want to die lying on this damn floor."

Ryan pulled him to the cockpit as gingerly as possible, knowing his efforts were probably insanely painful to his friend.

"I have food." He offered up a bar. "Take?"

"Why, so I can last longer?" He grinned with a half-blackened face.

"I found this in medical," Ryan offered, holding up a needle. "Steroid-antibiotic mix, think helps pain too."

"Knock yourself out, buddy. Don't know if it will work though. Pretty far gone."

Ryan shook his head. "No, will help. Seen it before. Kills infection." He pushed the needle into his shoulder.

Bosn gasped. "I can feel it working now." He said, with a slight slur and a sloppy smile.

Ryan searched through the rest of the rover, discovering a second set of meds and needles. The glyphic characters on the labels were difficult to understand, and more difficult to make out in the poor light.

Two more treatments. Will have to do.

"You know I had a wife, Earthman? Yeah, we're not much different than you. I had a beautiful wife and a baby on the way, a little girl."

"What was her name?"

"Sharanoa, but we never named the baby," he could not hide the grimness in his voice.

"What happened to them?"

"They were on an evac ship before the main force hit. We had a fleet of them launching in succession, one after another from the surface. I was already on a destroyer. My ship, along with 10 others, were assigned as protection escorts."

He winced in pain.

"They came in fast and in large numbers. We tried, we all tried. But our shields were inferior, and most of us went down in the first exchange. Our destroyer crashed on our moon. We left them exposed and helpless. I watched from the surface as my wife's ship was incinerated by them. They didn't have a chance." It overcame him suddenly and he wept, shoulders shuddering.

Ryan reached over and put his hand on his arm. "I'm sorry."

"It's better, you know? It's better than having them live through this." He turned away to face the window. In a few minutes, he was fast asleep.

Ryan checked his pulse: weak but steady.

Nothing to do but wait it out.

A glance out the cockpit caught his attention. A movement, however slight. He flipped on the spotlight. The floor of the jungle was teeming with millions of squirming creatures, no more than 10 centimeters long. They covered the area as far as he could see. He briefly entertained the grim thought of being eaten alive by these things, but they were harmless as long as he kept the hatch sealed. He remembered hearing the Kalmakans talk of these creatures. Even the Xi-Empire feared these swarms. Whole colonies had been wiped clean of every living being, unlucky victims in the path of their migration. They were safe that night, for the jungle's largest and most vicious animals knew better than to approach a nest, for fear of being devoured.

Safe, for now. He sat back in his chair and quickly fell into a deep, needed sleep.

Bosn stirred, then moaned. Ryan jumped, fully awake and ready for the worst. The Signite was twisting in his chair, perspiration beading on his forehead.

Ryan grabbed a bottle of water and poured the contents over his friend's forehead, hoping to cool him down. *Another shot, immediately.* He scrambled for the needles and injected Bosn in his other arm. Swelling of his burns seemed to be subsiding slightly. *Did he have a chance? Waiting here did him little help. He had to push on. He had to get across this jungle. Through to the other side.*

He fired up the rover and started crawling through the vegetation, maintaining a longitudinal southbound heading. After a half day's travel, the jungle was becoming too dense even for the rover. Its motors were winding out to maximum and running dangerously hot. He brought the rover to a standstill, half-suspended on a fallen rotted tree trunk. It was time to check the fuel rod supply. They were burning through the fuel rods quickly under the heavy load. Had enough for, at most, four days. If he was able to find more southbound trails, could possibly last longer. *With a bit of luck, they would reach somewhere survivable before the fuel was spent.*

The rover fired up easily and crept over the rotting undergrowth. The deeper he drove into the gloomy abyss, the more his weariness grew. Everything was large in this jungle, exaggerated into a scale 10 times that of Earth's. He passed by towering phosphorescent glowing shapes that moved rhythmically by an invisible wind, with arms reaching down from an unseen sky above. Shadows moved just beyond the edge of the rover's powerful floodlights, their range now limited to scant few meters, the radiant beams now useless, hungrily absorbed by a soupy greenish-white fog that lay in a thick, unrelenting carpet. The scene beyond the rover's quartz viewport was of a distorted, twisted world, in a dismal, everlasting darkness. Often he heard, and felt, thunderous footsteps heading toward him. More than once he reacted without thinking, finding himself accelerating dangerously in his haste to leave this place. To check himself, he need only bring to mind the thoughts of the rover breaking down from pushing it too hard. He did not want to be left alone, defenseless in the gloomy nightmare outside.

The Xi-Empire was far behind. They would have assumed them dead by now. It was only the jungle, him, and his dying friend.

The fear, the adrenaline, kept pushing him to drive. His hands clenched white on the steering controls for stretches of indeterminable hours until his muscles ached in retaliation. Rarely would he halt the rover and when he did, he would leave the engine running, ready to move at a moment's notice. He would drink, relieve himself in a pail, and push on. The air in the cabin was rancid. He longed for a safe haven to park and walk freely, to breathe fresh air.

It came as a small, slight change in the terrain and a thinning of the obscuring fog. Small outcroppings of sand raised themselves above the black mud of the swamp floor. The sand soon formed a lane on the surface of the foul water. The rover's speed picked up as the wheels found traction. The scanners reflected a cheery, bright blue signature, indicating firm terrain.

Bosn stirred beside him. "We're still alive?"

"We are, old friend. The jungle not killed us yet."

"Not yet, Ryan, but soon I would think."

They locked eyes for a moment. "We'll make it," was all he could bring himself to say.

Bosn turned to watch the view ahead.

"Why south? What do you expect to find?"

"The Kalmakans were clear. I take this way. No other way to go. They know something."

Bosn coughed weakly. "Seems just as good a reason as any."

"We are on road, not much of road, but a road."

He chuckled, then coughed again. "A road to nowhere, or somewhere? Did I tell you what I did, Ryan, before the war? I was a surveyor and architect. I built things."

The road twisted suddenly, drawing Ryan's attention away.

The sharp turn caused Bosn to shift, and groan in pain.

"Dying sucks, Ryan. Don't recommend it."

"You hang on. I find help."

He chuckled lightly. "No, don't believe I have it in me."

They were veering past the edges of numerous pits of boiling tar that showed up as dark red on the monitor - and these obstacles were becoming more and more frequent. Instantly the scanner shifted to complete red and warning alarms rang constantly.

"Maybe our luck is running out?"

"No these are roiling pits. We go past. Keep to road. It leads out."

"Ha, and how do you know this? No way outta this."

Ryan just gave him an irritated look. "No. We make it out."

He followed the outline of the sandy lane faithfully, ignoring the instruments' warnings, watching for the tell-tale trace of blue. The fog had lifted completely into light clouds, faint and wispy. Vegetation was sparse, although the immense trees still towered above in stands where the soil was stable enough to support them.

It seemed almost barren - and safe. It had been a long time since he felt he could open the hatch without being attacked. He had to air out the cabin. He had to breathe some fresh air.

"We stop. You drink, eat, more medicine. We open hatch, rid of stink, dump waste pail."

He brought the rover to a full stop at the foot of a black-tar lake. With a spent fuel rod poised for action, he opened the upper hatch. Thick, sulfur-smelling air flooded in, strong enough to make his eyes water. It was worse than the air in the cabin. He looked up, hundreds of meters above, through the hazy layer of cloud, up through the canopy. The vegetation was very thin, networking like spider webs between the treetops. Rays of the sunlight shone through the suspended vegetation.

Shit! This wasn't safe either. Overhead Xi-Empire satellites could easily spot a rover through this.

He dumped his waste and closed the hatch.

Maybe next time.

Bosn had nodded off again. He gave him the last shot and prayed it would be enough to bring him back from the brink. The cabin's air was permeated with sulfur, and it seemed to burn the inside of his nose, douse his ability to smell.

A mixed blessing.

The tar pits were thinning. The inadequate canopy soon thickened again, darkening the area below into the typical generic gloom. The path began a gradual incline. Hot springs sprayed the vehicle as they passed, bidding a farewell to the gleaming metal visitor.

They were now at the edge of the denser jungle. The air had to be better here. He pulled the rover to a halt. Its tremendous spherical tires sunk slightly as they settled into sand. He killed the powerful searchlights and watched as they silently died out, rescinding to a growing darkness.

He hadn't eaten a full meal since they had left, just the odd bar. He could not keep pushing himself. A simple mistake, a wrong turn, could kill him. He had to eat and rest.

He checked Bosn one last time. Breathing was raspy but regular. Hunger pangs in his stomach were too much to ignore. He dug into the supplies, pulled out the rations. They tasted like cardboard dipped in sulfur. Every muscle in his body ached. He had to lay prone, stretch out. The cabin floor, hard and flat, seemed luxurious at worst. It took but a few moments to slip into the soothing cradle of sleep.

Outside, in the pitch black, creatures slithered and crawled in deadly silence.

* * *

Ryan jerked awake, eyes wide and frantic. The soft phosphorous green of the console controls bathed the cabin in a weird glow. He scanned the cabin.

Bosn was sleeping in the co-pilot chair, the reactor status display blinked regularly, as it should. And the scanner was on, registering something. *How could it not in this jungle? But something didn't feel right. Maybe his mind was playing tricks on him again, as it had done before, down in the dark bowels of the mine, when they had pushed him beyond exhaustion.*

He dragged himself into the driver's chair and powered up the systems. The scanner display was showing a solid, dark yellow blip registering directly in front of the rover.

Had that been there before?

He peered through the quartz viewport and froze. Through the indirect glow from the console, he could just make it out. Staring directly at him was an enormous eye, its pupil oblong and black, like that of a snake. It belonged to something very, very large. Instantly, the pupil contracted and pulled away. A second later something rammed into the rover. The impact almost knocked Ryan from his seat. He struggled to strap himself in.

Again it hit.

"Keep it steady!" Bosn yelled. "Don't veer off. We'll ram'er down their throats!"

He was hallucinating.

The cabin was beginning to tilt. The thing was trying to flip them over. He engaged the transmission and poured on the power, but the wheels spun futilely, suspended in mid-air. Warning alarms shrieked, indicator lights blinked red. The rover tilted at a steep angle, on the verge.

The anti-skid plates!

He hit the controls, cursing under his breath. They shot out the side and deployed to their full length. Hydraulic motors whined from the strain as they bore the full weight of the rover.

But they held. The tilting stopped.

It wasn't strong enough to roll them over, completely. Lucky break.
"Ha! Sonofabitch!" He cursed in English.

The thing abandoned its efforts and the rover slammed down. The two of them flopped in their chairs like rag dolls.

Bosn screamed in agony as the movement tore at his burns.

"Hang on!"

He scanned the controls. The wheels were still spinning, shrieking out an eerie whine as they twisted in the mud.

Still not moving! The damn thing wouldn't let go!

"Let us go ya fucker!" he yelled. In a flash of intuition, he hit the searchlights. The thing screamed with such intensity it hurt his ears. Then it was gone, lost to the darkness of the jungle.

The rover had traction – and it was bouncing ahead at full speed.

"Where did it go?" he yelled.

"It's there, behind us. It's playing with us," added Bosn. "Check the scanner."

The bright yellow signature was pasted onto the outer edge of the display.

"No, it working up courage."

And then it launched.

The road ahead wound like a snake. Ryan fought with the controls, attempting to outrun the thing without ditching.

It was gaining – what the hell is this thing?

Alarms started ringing crazily. Forward scanner displays were painted red in every direction.

Tar pit dead ahead! Shit!

He locked up the left drivetrain and diverted everything to the right. The left wheels dug into the road as the rover skewered sideways, and the right ones sprayed up fountains of blackened soil. The rover slid to a stop with half of its wheels dipped into a lake of boiling tar.

Another quick glance at the monitor revealed the blip almost on top of them. He wound the motors out and dropped it in reverse. Geysers of black tar shot upward in a black rain as the tires fought for traction. A desperate second passed, painfully extending itself into another. Wheels caught. The rover leapt back, just in time. A dark blur screamed past to hit the lake of boiling tar with a deadened splash. White teeth and glaring eyes disappeared into the overpowering black ooze. The thing bellowed and screamed as it sank.

Ryan straightened out the rover and bolted ahead down the path. His heart pounding in his ears, and his hands shaking visibly.

"That too close."

Bosn was laughing and coughing, then laughing again. "You, Earthman, are lucky."

Ryan joined him. Both of them laughing like madmen as they drove through a dark, murky hell.

The terrain slowly improved, evolving to a hard-packed surface, straight with little overgrowth. They'd left the tar pits far behind, the jungle again, encroached around them. Trees seemed larger in size than ever before, truly gargantuan, stretching at least a full kilometer into the sky. A hint of sunlight peeked through the web-like canopy.

Bosn had faded back into a deep sleep. His condition was worsening, not improving. His legs had blackened and showed signs of gangrene.

In all respects, he should have been dead by now, Ryan knew that. The shots had just bought him time.

"Bosn, you hear me? Bosn."

The Signite tilted his head and opened his eyes a crack.

"Barely, friend. My time is growing close. Don't waste your breath with some hopeful wisecrack."

Ryan nodded, admitting as much to himself as to his friend. "Was a good run."

Bosn smiled feebly. "You tried. I was done the moment I was hit – we both know that. Besides, where are we really headed anyway?"

Ryan pointed out the viewscreen. "Down this road."

"Yes, Earthman of many words, to somewhere, probably ending up as a snack for one of those critters out there. No, I'm better off than you. I know my time is almost up."

Ryan smiled back. "Us should be dead long, long time now."

Bosn shifted and winced in pain. "Any more of those needles left?"

Ryan just focused on the road, making sure the wheels didn't travel too far off the narrow path.

"Right, my luck."

Packed sand gave way to a finely defined matrix of brickwork. Where the road had once circumvented trees, it now ran straight, tunneling right through the monstrous plants, their insides cut so smooth they seemed polished. Ryan raised their speed and the kilometers burned away behind them.

Darkness had settled upon them. The rover's lights cut through the hazy air, just enough to reflect back the image of something very large down the road. The scanner lit up in bright red, dousing the cabin in an eerie glow. Ryan shifted down, locking the brakes. The rover came to a stop.

Bosn shifted awake, moaning in pain, then coughing wildly. "Can't you keep this machine running straight? I'd prefer my last moments to be in peace."

"Look. Things now changed."

Ahead lay a monolithic wall of perfectly fitted stone, the wall's height and width were indeterminable, as visibility quickly degraded due to the persistent greenish-white fog, and the dense overgrowth of jungle. Lichen and vines covered the wall, revealing the great age of the stone structure.

The road led to a tunnel that stretched far into the wall – a dark, ominous entry leading into the unknown. The arched entrance had etched carvings of strange shapes, creatures with hideous eyes that looked down with disdain upon anyone who was foolish enough to enter.

"These carvings don't mean a damn thing to me," offered Bosn. "I take it as a good sign – a way to get out of this forsaken jungle. Tell you the truth, I'll never understate your luck, Earthman.

"Not luck. The Kalmakans told me. It is the Chaoi of Aelome."

"Chaoi of what?" questioned Bosn.

"Our way out."

"I never met your sources, Ryan, but it sounds good enough to me. No use sitting here, let's get moving!" urged Bosn.

Ryan took the cue and edged the rover ahead, simultaneously guiding its searchlights to sweep down the tunnel's length.

Nothing seemed to be waiting there to pounce.

He raised a gear and they picked up speed. Bare walls began to poke through between encrusted vines, which quickly thinned as they moved away from the entrance. Abruptly, the tunnel ended, opening up to an amphitheater-sized cavern. He pulled the rover to a stop and rotated the searchlights a full 360 degrees. From here, three other tunnels branched out, their entrances closely resembling that of the first at the jungle's edge.

Strange. Such a place should be very attractive to jungle life. But there was nothing that resembled anything living to mention.

The walls and the floor were bare, empty, nothing but carved and polished stone, but with one exception. He focused the lights upon hieroglyphic etchings above each of the three entrances. The first image was very complex, presenting hundreds of different beings, many holding sophisticated looking tools.

The second etching was plain in contrast, bearing the images of five lizard-like faces.

The third was the most impressive. Symbols lined the whole outer edge of the archway. They resembled, possibly, an alphabetical or numerical system. A detailed pictorial lay above the apex of the arch. A large oval shape with lines jutting downward into a triangle. Images of small creatures seemed to be performing strange dances at its base.

Above the oval shape were, unmistakably, stars carved in precise locations out of the stone.

Had these constellations changed much since this was made? No way of knowing.

A simple oval shape drew his attention, just as it seemed to draw the gaze of the beings depicted in stone.

He looked over at Bosn. The Signite was fighting to stay conscious.

"Three choices. This one promising."

"Go with your gut, Ryan. I don't think I'm going to be much help."

He nodded, then shifted the machine into gear. The rover shuddered as he brought it up to a steady, cautious speed into the third tunnel. They descended at a gradual slope. In the first hour, they must have passed through the planet's water table, yet there was not a hint of moisture on the walls. If anything, the tunnel was bone dry. The rover's tires left imprints in the thin layer of dust on the floor. Endless walls of polished brown met a floor of black granite, glass-smooth to the finish. It was close to the end of the second hour when they finally rolled to a stop. Ahead lay a massive, half-open door made of the same brown granite. It was drawn up into the ceiling, suspended by some unknown means. Ryan edged the rover ahead, passing just under the bottom edge. The sound of scraping of metal echoed down the hall.

Very close.

He was through in a moment, but not without envisioning the three meter thick, multi-tonne door crashing down upon them. With a sigh, he shifted gears and accelerated. The walls were now a sharp white replacing the somber brown. Two embedded lines of silver and gold, each about a meter thick and just as high, ran parallel with the floor. The rover's lights bounced off the shining veins in a shimmering brilliance.

Another kilometer and they arrived at another door, similar to the previous one in its sheer size, but made of marbled black and green granite. Inlaid within the center of it, about three meters up from the floor, was a recessed image in gold, a head of a creature that resembled a deer. It had antlers that stretched from wall to wall and three red, glowing eyes the size of tennis balls within its center. Ryan studied it for a time, knowing there must be a way to trigger the door to raise.

Bosn had long since faded, breath short and raspy.

He had to have a closer look. Best to leave him rest.

He killed the engine. Its rumbling died to a wary silence. With a spent fuel rod in hand, he climbed up the ladder to the top deck. Taking a deep breath, he threw open the hatch and waited. He could hear the metallic clang echo down the corridor. His fear of something jumping in at him subsided with the fading echoes.

Too active an imagination.

Fresh, sweet air rolled in, free of sulfur, untainted. He climbed onto the upper deck, inspecting it carefully. It was covered with swamp muck and plant remains. Huge gouges peeked through uncovered areas. Metal was melted where cannon blasts had hit. The center capacitor had been blown to bits, and the jury-rigged plasma drill lay on its side, still attached to its bent and twisted mounting latches. He found himself staring down at the wrecked capacitor, its fuel canister now missing.

Why the hell did he have to get hit?

He kicked the capacitor, cursing to himself. A yellow cylinder, wedged under a split in the rover's skin and half buried in the muck, caught his eye. He reached under and yanked it out.

The last remaining fuel canister. He had a weapon.

Being cautious not to gouge himself on the ragged edges, he pried the plasma drill loose. Once free, he gave it a full inspection.

It looked alright, but would it fire?

The canister screwed on easily. He pointed the weapon down the tunnel and squeezed the trigger. The plasma bolt leapt out and dissipated at about 20 meters, leaving a strong odor of ozone.

That would do.

He checked the damage at the rear of the deck, found the camera hanging, and attempted to reattach it to its mount. The small device clicked in and a green light blinked on briefly. *With any luck at least one of the rear monitors would work.*

For extra measure, he manually swung the searchlight back the way he had come and flicked it on. The powerful beam illuminated hundreds of meters behind the rover.

Nothing. Nothing but bare walls ending in darkness. Silence was prominent here, and any sound made was amplified with complete clarity. It was strangely comforting.

With a renewed amount of confidence, weapon slung on his back, metal rod in hand, he mounted the ladder and made his way down. He expected the glossy floor to be slippery - it wasn't. It was actually sticky, like ice at 40 below. The mirror finish was deceptive.

The statuette head stared down at him menacingly. He grabbed the fuel rod and tapped at the figure, then pushed up on one side then the other to see if it would turn. It wouldn't.

He stepped back and contemplated.

Of course. The eyes. So prominent they had to have a purpose.

Using the rod, he pushed in on the middle eye. The glistening button slid back easily. A moment later, a low rumble sounded and dust stirred up from unseen crevices. Ryan backed up, wary of what was to happen next. With a bellowing groan, the huge granite door began to slide up into the ceiling.

He ran back to the rover and fired up the engine. The door had reached the top and it was now starting to cycle closed. He mentally calculated the rate of movement.

There was enough time.

He gunned the engine and raced through. Once clear he slammed the brakes. He watched the gigantic door seal shut behind him through the working rear monitor.

A quick inspection of his surroundings revealed the tunnel had changed yet again. The walls were white and the ceiling reflected a rich gold. A thin layer of dust discolored a white floor into a trace of gray. As before, as far as the rover's lights could reach, the great corridor remained empty.

How much farther would this go? What would he find there?

He checked the rover's instruments. *The fuel rods were almost spent. They didn't have much time left before they would have to abandon the vehicle and continue on foot. He'd have to hobble together a gurney.*

Tentatively he put the vehicle back into motion, multiple kilometers passed by before the rover's fuel reserve indicator started an alarm. A click of the switch quieted it. They were running on proverbial fumes now.

Another door appeared in the floodlights. As prior, a large icon hung menacingly on the door with similar jeweled eyes. He moved the rover close enough so he needn't bother to dismount, and was able to reach over from the upper deck to depress the eye. As the door rose, an immense cavern was revealed beyond.

Perhaps they've finally reached their destination.

He wasted no time driving through, anxious to discover what lay ahead, but then quickly coasted to a stop. The door closed with a solid thud, echoing loudly as the sound traveled outward into an immense cavern.

This was the end of the line.

The room was at least a kilometer square with four walls that sloped upward to a point, opening up to a sliver of sky. Sunlight streamed downward in a tight beam, illuminating the expansive plain ahead. It radiated off a large, unmistakable object in the center - a pyramid, brilliant white, jutting upward at least 500 meters.

A pyramid inside a pyramid.

On each corner of the inner pyramid, a river flowed outward cutting through the plain in a straight line, fanning out to meet and disappear, under the outside corner of each wall. The quiet was now lost in the background noise of racing water.

His eyes were drawn upward. A vertical line traced to its very peak. It was a mammoth stairway, with thousands upon thousands of carved steps. An ascension to a plateau bathed in sunlight, upon which something glinted with a metallic luster.

Putting the rover back into gear he crossed the plain, approaching the base of the staircase. The object far above had captured his curiosity.

Whatever it was, the thing had to be large, considering his perspective. But what was it? His heart gave a small jump. A spaceship? No. Something else, probably. But the hieroglyphics on the entrance way - that was why he chose this way in the first place.

Maybe.

He parked the rover at the base of the stairs and shut all systems down, save the lights, which he focused onto the pyramid.

"Bosn, Bosn. Wake up. You need see this. " He shook his shoulder, but the Signite did not respond. He grabbed a bottle and poured it over Bosn's head and face.

"Wake up damn you!"

The man sputtered slightly and cracked open his eyes. "Ah, yes. I'm still here. And I had my hopes up. You trying to drown me?" He coughed and gave a half-smile.

"Look up. I think we found the way out," urged Ryan.

His eyes rolled upward, assessing the pyramid slowly, and smiled. "Ah, and what is that glinting atop this engineered behemoth? Is that your Chaoi of whatever? I think your time is coming, old friend, and so, unfortunately, is mine."

"Time?"

"Time for you to get back home, and time for me to rest."

"Come on, Bosn. We can do this together." Ryan reached over to pull him out of the chair, it was impulsive, he didn't really think it through.

Bosn screamed in agony and nearly passed out. Ryan eased him back down as gently as possible.

"I am sorry, my friend. I should have thought."

It took a minute for Bosn to recover. He responded in a whisper. "No, it's alright. Not this time. This time we part ways."

Ryan nodded, acknowledging the inevitable. "I'll stay, then, until..."

"No. I don't need you here. It's alright. I like the peace." His words were soft, barely a whisper.

"No, I wait."

Bosn shook his head weakly. "Friend to the end then, Earthman."

"To the end."

Ryan grabbed his hand. The Signite closed his eyes, a peaceful look coming across his features. "Time's close now. I will see my Sharanoa," he whispered.

They sat there for a time, bathed in the soft hue of the console lights, listening to the waters of the flowing rivers. Eventually, the Signite's powerful grip softened, and he was gone, leaving life with a soft sigh.

"I will see you on the other side, my friend."

Ryan pulled his supplies together using the storage sacks Bosn had used to haul the fuel canisters. He found a small light, which he strapped to the barrel of the plasma drill, then repacked everything. He balanced the load on each end of a spent fuel rod and hoisted them onto his shoulder. He exited the cabin through the lower hatch, one hand balancing his supplies, the other holding the plasma drill.

He didn't look back.

Approaching the stairs, he craned his neck and peered upwards. The peak was at least 500 meters above.

He was not looking forward to the climb. A fall from that high would be fatal. Was he up to it? Was there another way?

He surveyed the surrounding area, noticed the section of the floor made distinct by its green marble color and swirling patterns inscribed upon its surface. The section butted up to the base of the pyramid, pointing outwards in the form of a large triangle. A channel was notched into the pyramid at the center of the triangle where it met, and this channel ran upward, parallel with the stairs.

An elevator, possibly? Whoever built this monstrosity could surely have the technology to construct a simple elevation device.

He walked over and knelt down at its edge, noticing the thin fissure between the startling white and dark green. As his weight settled on its surface, a movement caught his eye. A crystalline post rose out of the floor with a soft hush. He pulled his finger away from the trigger of his plasma gun. He had, almost by instinct, blasted it away.

Inspecting the post, he discovered three circular buttons. Each reflected back a unique color from within with a soft phosphorous glow, the first red, the second blue, and the last yellow. Each button was positioned slightly offset to the other.

He tried each button. The last one did the trick, and the floor beneath his feet began to vibrate. From somewhere below came the sound of a low pitched whistle. Instantly the triangle began to rise from the floor.

Ryan laughed. *He was right. It was a damned alien elevator! And it worked after how many years?*

The elevator climbed steadily. As it moved closer to the top, an easy breeze blew across the platform. He could feel the warmth of the sun's rays on his skin - and it felt good. The air smelled sweet and dry, lacking the earthy overtones and any hint of sulfur.

The platform eased to a silent stop upon reaching the top. The breeze was stronger now, buffeting Ryan's face with an invisible soft hand. He walked over to the edge and looked down one last time. The rover's lights were diffused and weak in the distance. It had the dimensions of a child's toy.

Bosn, if you could just see this.

The wind caressed his cheek, and he remembered the smell of the hot Arizona breeze. A brief memory, seemingly so long ago.

Turning around, the thing that had beckoned his attention lay before him. A flattened oval, at least 100 meters wide. Its hull was seamless and dulled with smudges of black carbon. Five thick legs jutted out and held it suspended about three meters in the air.

Again he laughed, this time falling to his knees. Tears came to his eyes. *There was no mistake in what it was. A damned flying saucer, like he had seen in the crazy UFO programs on TV. How? How was this possible?*

Of course, he had no answer.

His legs were weak as a baby's, and his hands were shaking crazily. For a moment he thought he was going to throw up. It took a moment before he was able to stand.

Maybe though, this isn't what he thought.

The idea burned through him, exposing his logical pessimism. *He hated that side of himself sometimes. Too many practical thoughts had a habit of dashing hope to very small irretrievable pieces. So what if this was a spaceship. He certainly couldn't fly it anywhere. Hell, he didn't even know where Earth was.*

He grabbed his gear and left the elevator. At first, he circumvented it, walking along the edge of the plateau inspecting every minute detail. The thing appeared uniform from every angle. There were no outer hull markings, no protruding sections of machinery. Everything was smooth and unremarkable. Underneath its belly, toward the center, a ramp extended down to meet the floor.

He walked over to it, hesitating a moment before advancing. *Despite its great age, could something still be alive within it?*

He flicked on the light and started up the entrance into the ship, gun ready, listening for the faintest of sounds. He met barren metallic walls and a dead cold that gave him a chill. The airlock hatch was rectangular, large enough to step through, but just short enough that he had to duck. Careful not to bang his head, he peered down a small hallway at the facing hatch door. A shiny plate sat obtrusively in the middle of it – probably the control panel. He would have to open this door to go any further.

The panel was a featureless oval, looking similar to stainless steel. He placed his hands upon it and pressed. Surprisingly, it gave – and the door slid open without hesitation and only a slight hiss. Air rushed out smelling stale, acrid – but not poisonous.

So far so good.

Stepping through, he found himself in a large circular room. On cue, the ceiling began to give off a luminescent glow that grew brighter and brighter. In seconds, they became too bright for unaccustomed eyes, and Ryan squinted as his vision fought to adjust.

Too many days in near darkness.

He could make out a shiny cylinder in the center of the room. It came from a hole in the floor and disappeared into the ceiling.

Like a fire station pole! Simple but effective, especially in zero-g.

He approached it, looking up, then down, into darkness. A faint whistle started far behind him from the direction of the outside hatch. The wind must have picked up, or possibly, some kind of ventilation system had started.

He dropped his load of supplies and tied the gun off around his shoulder. Using the pole, he shimmied up to the next level. It was quite different than the entry. The room's walls were lined with instrument displays and monitors. Everywhere he moved the ship woke up. Lights and displays came on and bathed him in a mirage of colors.

What else was waking up in here?

He reached out and touched one of the black panels on the wall. A colorful and detailed image leapt to life behind it. He could feel warmth under his fingers. When he took his hand away, the display faded to black. His finger had left a small smudge where he had disturbed the slight film of dust that lay upon the panel's surface.

How long has it been since anyone was in here? Centuries? A millennium? Amazing technology.

Not wanting any surprises to find him, he moved on, searching each level methodically and thoroughly, winding through twisting corridors and tight, oppressive rooms. He eventually located the bridge in the very heart of the vessel. It was a large room, circular in shape, with no real walls, just a large domed ceiling that ended at the floor. In the center, within a sunken semi-circle, three large and luxurious chairs were mounted, invitingly.

The outer walls had a look of black glass. He touched one and it started - as before - lights fanning out from where he had placed his hand, tracing images in a multitude of symbols of color and complication. They were virtual controls, graphic representations of the ships' systems.

To understand this could free him. If he could somehow figure out the basics.

The images continued to appear, exploding across the room, painting it in a myriad of color and movement. At the very top of the domed ceiling, a triangle formed, with sides that traveled down to touch the floor. Within this triangle, a scene emerged from a background of gray. White specks of dust in a soft beam of sunlight, fading to darkness in the distance.

It took him a moment to understand it. It was a view from outside of the ship, at which angle he could only wonder.

The chairs looked inviting to his sore muscles. He would return here, once he finished.

The remainder of the inspection was uneventful. He found no alien corpses, nothing but empty rooms in an empty ship.

He grabbed a flask of water from his supplies and returned to the bridge. It was just as he had left it. Settling down into the center chair, he could feel the tension drain from his body. Content for the moment that he was safe, he drifted off into a needed sleep.

Deep within the ship's core, the main drive was now staging up. The onboard computer, awakened from its rest of a millennium, commenced its designated programming.

Ryan, now settled in a deep sleep, didn't feel the low vibration emanating throughout the ship. Nor did he hear the hatch doors slide shut as the ship progressed through pre-flight preparation. The ship's outer hull began to glow brighter and brighter accompanied by a low-frequency hum which permeating in the air.

Inside the great pyramid, the chamber, now lit up to a daylight brilliance, gave up its ancient secrets. Walls that had been hidden in darkness for centuries now reflected back with golden luster. Images of creatures of all shapes, depictions of stories and wondrous scenes, each meticulously carved and outlined in gold, colored marble, and glistening precious stones, were brought back to a brief majestic life.

The ship began to rise from its monolithic perch, its legs retracting as it ascended. Dust scattered up into the air, to dance in the sun's beam as it had once done so many eons before. Accelerating as it climbed, the ship followed the steady stream of light, up and through the roof of the chamber, breaking free into the open sky.

Within the chamber, the disturbed clouds of dust soon settled back down, coming to rest in delicate layers upon the rover. The vehicle's searchlights dimming to yellow embers as the last bit of energy drained from its fuel supply. In the co-pilot's chair, a Signite human would eventually mummify within the dry air, a sly grin upon his face.

The ship's onboard program had prepared a maximum security flight. Scramblers were engaged, and radio emissions were produced to hide its signature within background radiation. The craft was now increasing its speed almost exponentially, leaving the planet behind in minutes. Within the control room, the image of the magnificent jungle planet shrunk to a mere dot.

The vessel thundered on into the great emptiness of space, constantly accelerating. At the molecular level, it transformed itself into an enhanced energy state. Reality now warped and churned around its hull as it passed its first hurdle of acroluc, then the second, and the third, and on. As it cut through the matter of the universe, it contorted space-time before it, passing by whole constellations in a blink of an eye, on its way to a pre-set destination.

On Kalmaka, the makeshift Xi-Empire flight control center had picked up a signal, although very faint. The reading was unusual and disappeared quickly. It was discounted as a glitch in the system and ignored. After all, no ship was due to arrive for at least another three zanii.

* * *

4. Oasis

The vessel, designed to traverse the spans between the stars, continued on its lonely course through the emptiness of space, its destination long ago programmed into its navigation systems. A concert of data, bits of navigational references, reams of mathematical algorithms, were all unceasingly sequestered by the Master Program as it patiently, and with absolute accuracy, guided the ship along the pre-set course.

In a lonely, unremarkable point in space, the ship came to rest. A communication request was sent out. After a set amount of time had passed, the request was issued again. No response. Three times the Master Program attempted, and three times it failed. Self-diagnostic subroutines scoured through its ancient systems but found no faults. The messages had been sent successfully. Contingency logic was invoked, and a new set of coordinates attempted. A small satellite, prodded to life by the unique, invulnerable hail, responded. The envoy relayed a coded message. The Master Program acknowledged, then dropped the link unceremoniously, undisturbed by the new information it received. It meticulously calculated new flight vectors, realigned the ship onto its newly calculated navigation vector, then promptly resumed acceleration.

Time passed. Light-years passed...

At a set time, as measured precisely by the Master Program, deceleration was initiated by the ancient ship's drives. Ever so slowly, the galaxies and stars outside stopped their fluid swirling, and gradually transformed into static light images suspended in an empty coldness. Once the ship's velocity dropped below the threshold of light speed, the universe returned in its recognizable glory, pockmarked with fiery points of color and distant suns emanating pinpoints of light from all directions.

Reference points were verified, satisfying the Master Program's directives. Ahead, a red-dwarf star, inflated against a speckled background of celestial matter, steadily grew larger in perspective. Soon three planets appeared, each orbiting in varying degrees of arc around the sun's equatorial plane.

The first planet, in closest orbit, was a large ball of gas with a molten core. It was too close to the star's massive furnace to be cool enough to form a solid crust on its mantle, its molten surface running thick with veins of competing fluid densities.

The second, middle planet did not suffer such hellish abuse, being much farther away from its sun, but its skies were enveloped in a reddish, orange atmosphere of savagely blowing winds and vicious continuous storms.

The third, and last planet of the system held an erratic course. It was, possibly, a recent acquisition of the star's gravity well, a captured rock with no more than a trace of atmosphere. Frozen lakes of oxygen, nitrogen, and ice covered its surface.

None were suitable for human habitation.

The ship approached the middle planet. The Master Program propagated many virtual children, each working furiously on the task of navigation and helm control, to align the vessel on an exact course. They churned through billions of calculations in a concerted effort to guide the ship into and through the planet's turbulent atmosphere.

***

Ryan woke from his sleep, startled and overcome by a feeling of dread and unmitigated fear. He launched from his seat, weapon in hand, ready to battle the aggressor, but found none. The bridge was the same as he had left it, with one exception: the scene from the large triangular viewscreen was no longer that of the inside of the ancient chamber.

He stared at it mutely, all the while soaking in the facts around him, desperately trying to avoid his own realization.

He was in space.

His eyes probed the bridge. It was alive with the quiet blinking of tiny lights. But there was no pilot, certainly no crew on board. Nothing living had coordinated this launch. A computer was at the helm or some resemblance of such a creation.

Where was it taking him? What was it programmed to do?

He lay down his fabricated weapon onto the arm of his chair. Instinct had made him seize it, and he felt foolish for being so frightened.

It would not do to act rash, to take action without thinking, especially out here, in cold, empty space where it would definitively kill you. How long had he been traveling? He could not have slept more than five or six hours, but what distance can a starship travel in that span of time? A light-year? 10 light-years? A thousand?

He mentally retraced his steps.

He had touched some of the panels. Could this have triggered it? The ship had awakened somehow; maybe just entering the bridge was enough. Whatever the cause, it was not important now.

The image of a red planet slowly filled the viewscreen, its details ominously clear. He could see the perpetual dust storms tearing their way across its surface, enveloping everything around them for thousands of kilometers, whole segments of hemisphere disappeared under the cover of angry darkness.

The ship pitched down into the atmosphere in one sudden, gut-wrenching movement, throwing him back into the chair. The view of the planet's surface rushed up from below as it careened downward with incredible speed. The bridge filled with a high-pitched shriek. Sounds, akin to alarms, began to sound off.

Ryan covered his ears and watched, helplessly.

In a bone-crushing maneuver, the ship leveled off, barely a kilometer from the surface, then adjusted its approach toward a range of mountains on the horizon. Winds hammered against the hull transferring a muffled but obvious howl. Blinding walls of dust blasted at it from all directions, engulfing it in red spiraling squalls. The view through the screen was often obliterated, lost in a suffocating darkness.

The Master Program continued on, undaunted. Statistical models impressed upon the most up-to-date scans of the terrain replaced temporary losses of sensor data. It was not human and as such, experienced no fear.

Contrary to the ship's artificial mind, Ryan could feel every shift, dip, and sway and found little comfort in the rough, although precise, handling of the vessel. He dug his fingers deep into the arms of his chair, eyes glued to the viewscreen. The ship wove dizzyingly through the mountains, darting side to side, up and down. Collisions were avoided in a span of milliseconds as the ship adjusted course, giving an illusion of reckless indifference.

In one final graceful epitaph, it slid around a smaller mountain and slowed to a crawl, floating casually up to the base of another. This mountain was gigantic in proportion, dwarfing the others and reaching well above the rushing clouds of the red dust storms and into the thin wispy layers of the upper atmosphere.

The ship eased forward with an uncanny distinction. On the bridge, new displays appeared, replacing others, providing data in a dancing chorus of light.

It was searching... But for what?

A cold shadow cast over them in a dark veil, leaving the harsh daylight behind as it methodically circumvented the mountain.

In the darkness, a gray hint of a plateau appeared deep within the recesses of the cliff side – an unnatural, precise wedge cut within a glossy, polished wall. With a sudden jerk, the ship veered into this crevice, stopping just as abruptly to avoid a collision into the mountain face. It hovered momentarily, then descended onto the plateau, legs extending to bite into the smooth rock face. Clouds of dust, disturbed by the ship's landing, resettled slowly, burying the wide feet of the ship's legs under centimeters of superfine red grains.

The Master Program, once again, became one. It ran various tests to ensure critical systems were operating correctly, then promptly put itself into hibernation. The bridge displays responded in like, systematically fading to gloss black, eventually leaving only the triangle of the main viewscreen.

* * *

Ryan took in the new information with despair.

Why the hell would it land here?

He stood up and walked closer to the viewscreen to peer out. Dim light, reflecting from surrounding mountains provided a stark picture. The plateau was featureless – a simple, inadequate haven from the surrounding hell. A deep rumbling permeated through the ship's skin, a testament to the hurricane forces beyond the crevice. Yet the plateau, curiously, seemed unaffected. Traces of dust floated lazily above the plateau floor, settling, like the last few flakes of snow in a peaceful wintry night.

Just great, perched on a ledge a kilometer above a barren wasteland.

He pounded the glossy panel in frustration. A gray ripple dilated radially outward, eventually to disappear at the panels' edges. He gave the strange phenomenon a cursory glance.

What was he going to do? Get out? Go exploring? Maybe he could if there was something that resembled a spacesuit in here. Then again, that could be a mistake. Once he stepped out, the ship, in turn, might just start itself up again and leave him stranded here to die. Did others before him make the same mistake - and die for it? Maybe once, long ago, this world was a fertile planet capable of sustaining life. There were no signs of that now - no cities, no ruins, certainly nothing obvious. He could only surmise the worst: This ship is very, very old. This planet, if once habitable, had probably undergone some tremendous catastrophe, or worse, given way to the incessant deterioration of time. This ship had returned to its now dead home with him aboard.

He sank back down into his chair and let out a sigh, massaging his temples, fighting the feeling of a painful headache building.

Could he teach himself to drive this contraption? Sure - that was a grand idea, but the irony of the whole situation was that even if he could pilot this ship, he didn't know - for the life of him - where home was.

The universe is a very big place.

Movement caught his eye. The scene through the viewscreen had changed. A once solid rock face was now a black triangular door. This door dissolved to white light, presenting in its place the silhouettes of two beings. They were bipeds, with two legs, two arms, a head perched upon a thin neck. They walked slowly, carefully, falling in step with one another with the precision of a marching band. They stopped a meter from the ship, their features captured in the expansive projection of the central viewscreen.

Ryan reached for his weapon.

As if on queue, throughout the ship, hatches released and opened. Down below the audible murmur of invisible motors revealed the lowering of the ramp. The murmur stopped with a piercing silence.

For a full minute, utter quiet.

Ryan stood transfixed, heart pounding in his ears. The aliens moved no further.

They didn't seem hostile. Not like before. That's a good sign.

He swallowed with a dry gulp.

Life had not left this planet. His welcoming party was proof - and they were waiting for him. The ship was wide open now. If the planet's atmosphere was poison, then it was already too late for him.

Maybe they had a doctor on call.

He laughed at his own thought.

They'd probably consider him insane, laughing for no perceptible reason, and proceed to kill him out self-preservation.

Stop. No use over thinking this.

He headed toward the hatch, weapon grasped tightly for reassurance.

One thing for sure, he was not going to become a slave again.

When he arrived at the ramp, small wisps of dust were floating in, slowly infiltrating the ship's interior. *If the outer atmosphere could kill him, he was about to find out.* He breathed in the dusty air, testing it. It carried a tinge of ash and sulfur and was quite warm, but it seemed breathable.

Another mystery - an oxygen laden atmosphere in a world with no visible plant life? Then again, the perilous winds did not seem to be infiltrating this small landing perch. Perhaps his visitors have extended some sort of shield?

He walked down slowly, one step at a time. Glassy sand particles littered the lower part of the ramp. They crackled sharply under his miner's boots. The two aliens watched him with their large, glassy, black eyes. Neither one even so much as twitched.

He kept his weapon ready but not pointed directly at them, and approached slowly, stopping with a few steps of them; sufficient distance to allow him time to move if he needed to.

They were similar to humans in a basic sense, with exaggerated large, bald, heads and large dark oval eyes. The nose was absent but for two small holes, and a thin-lipped small mouth profiled over an unpronounced chin. Hands were six-fingered, with what resembled two opposing thumbs. From what was visible, their skin seemed a pronounced gray, and they stood just slightly more than one meter tall.

Neither gave way any facial expression.

"Hello, I am Ryan," he attempted, using Trinarieit.

"Greetings, one called Ryan," the shorter one replied in Trinarieit. Again, no expression, only those dark enlarged eyes.

"What do you call your planet of origin?"

"I am of Earth. I am man."

"Earth?" the alien repeated, turning to his partner. They seemed to converse without words, somehow.

Were they telepathic?

"The vessel you arrived in was originally assigned to 299987-H. Is this what you call Earth?"

"No, that Kalmaka. Am of other planet. I slave. Escaped Xi-Empire."

"We are very familiar with the Xi-Empire. The Xilozaks and Txtians are extremely violent."

"We do not enslave others," interjected the taller alien. "You are safe with us."

Ryan nodded. "Thank you."

"This vessel was assumed lost. How did you find it?"

"Help of natives," he responded, not quite sure they understood.

Again, they shifted glances to one another, although neither spoke.

"Man-from-Earth called Ryan, we would like you to come with us. We offer you medical attention and nourishment."

Were they on the level? For all he knew, they could be partners with the lizards and the bugs.

Sensing his hesitation, the taller attempted to soothe his concerns. "We are Xeronians. We do not harm or enslave other races for our enjoyment or benefit."

Ryan nodded, not sure what to say, feeling somewhat emotional and therefore vulnerable.

Without another word, the two turned and headed for the door, gesturing for him to follow. He hesitated only a moment, considering for the last time, his options. It was an easy decision. He fell into step behind them.

The door dissolved once again, revealing a brightly-lit corridor. The light was so brilliant he had to navigate down the sloping corridor with one hand over his eyes, and the other tucked around his gun. He kept his bearings by skimming the weapon's butt end against the wall.

Everything around him was a bright, bleached white, walls, ceiling, and floor. Everything.

After walking for a brief time, they entered a small room, and a door sealed shut behind them. A second door resembling clear glass lowered between him and the two aliens.

Protection. They were afraid of him, or at least respectful. Of that, there was no doubt.

The floor lurched underfoot providing a subtle hint that they had begun to move – possibly an elevator.

He shifted nervously and noticed the aliens' features had changed slightly. Not their expressionless faces, as they remained placid as ever – the blood vessels within their temples were pulsing.

Looking down, he realized he had subconsciously moved his weapon to point toward them. He adjusted it to a less threatening position.

The taller one spoke, his voice carried easily through the transparent barrier, although slightly muffled. "My name Tsaurau. In a moment you will enter into a sterilization room where you will be exposed to a gas. It will not harm you."

True to the alien's word, they arrived a few moments later, with the door behind Ryan sliding open in silent announcement.

"Please step out and remain stationary for a moment."

He glanced over. *Their looks seemed earnest enough, but they could be interpreted completely different from human behavior. For all he knew, they could be getting ready to gas him to death and then feast on his dead corpse.*

Damn it! Why was he getting so morbid? So far they had been honest with him. He had to wait it out. They would tip their hand soon enough.

He stepped out of the shuttle and found himself in a small, white room with a rectangular window directly ahead. The door slid shut behind him, and a moment later a stifled whirring sound carried through the air. Ryan felt a tingling all over his body. The sensation reminded him of being zapped with a harmless charge of static electricity. A slight mist filled the room.

The two aliens appeared staring through the window.

"You are abundant with micro-organisms. Certain types could be dangerous to our people. We must be very cautious. This sterilization chamber is intended to protect both parties."

The mist disappeared as quickly as it had come.

"Sterilisation is complete. There is a door immediately to your right. It opens to a room where you will be supplied with whatever you request. We ask that you remain there while we resolve the aspects of co-existence. We must also ask you to submit to some tests."

"What kind of tests?" He struggled to fight down a sudden panic. *Hope they didn't notice or hear it in his voice. They must not know that he is afraid. They cannot know.*

"These are biological tests. You will not be harmed."

Ryan was unfamiliar with the Trinarieit terms, not being able to relate it back to native English.

"Biological test?"

"That of life."

Ryan responded off-handedly in English, "Sorry, don't get what you mean." It took him a second to realize it. The Xeronians took a moment to answer back. "This is your home world language?"

"Yes – it is called English."

"You must relate to us in your native language. We may be able to converse in this language to enable further analysis."

Again, the alien was using unknown Trinarieit. Ryan only shook his head, frustrated. "We have some work to do on communications."

The door to his right slid open. He walked into the room and looked around. The lighting was much dimmer and more suitable for human eyes. The room was large and circular. A small partition was present to hide what looked like a replica of a toilet. In the middle of the room, there was a fountain of warm water that shot up about two meters and down into a shallow, sloping, pool. The pool was circular with a radius of no more than two-to-three meters. Its waters looked inviting to his sore, dirty, tired body.

A large beige-colored mattress-sized cushion sat on the far side of the room. Blankets lay upon it, folded neatly. Once white walls, on the opposite side, poked through a thick covering of rich green moss. He surmised it was some kind of natural air conditioner or an efficient oxygen producer. *It's possible that he requires more oxygen than the Xeronians were accustomed to.*

He approached the small pool and looked at his reflection in the water - and could hardly recognize himself. His face was hidden under a dark, filthy blackness of strangled, matted hair, and his scraggly beard gave him the look of a madman - a *scary sight.*

To his immediate right was a wall, similar in characteristics to the interior of the ship. He touched it. The image of an Xeronian appeared.

"What do you require, Ryan?"

First name basis already. Like they're my old friends or something.

"I need," he struggled for the correct word, "cloth for drying and replacement clothing."

"You will find this to your left. Other supplies are located at the rim of the fountain. Please submit your clothing into the hopper below this monitor. We will manufacture a new wardrobe for you immediately."

He had missed multiple words but guessed at the rest.

They wanted his clothes most likely. Didn't matter - they were filthy rags at best.

"Thank you."

"You are welcome," the alien said pleasantly, and actually attempted a human smile.

Ryan cracked a coarse chuckle. *He hadn't felt like this in a long time. Like a boy just out of school for the summer.*

He quickly stripped and descended into the warm waters of the fountain. His cuts and bruises stung in the cleansing water, but it felt good. He reached for what resembled a bar of soap and tried it out on his hands. It was perfumed to a pleasing scent and worked well on the ground in dirt and grime. He quickly lathered up and meticulously cleaned every inch of his body, including his long stringy hair. All the time he bathed, he kept checking himself to see if he was truly awake. He had to be sure this wasn't just a dream, that he wasn't still enslaved within a mine, kilometers below the surface.

He shivered and dropped the soap. It floated upon the water's surface, leaving a cloudy trial that followed the micro-currents in the water.

No, this was reality. He had escaped.

He located what resembled an old-fashioned straight razor and carefully shaved his large beard away, then started on his hair. He hacked away methodically, dropping clumps into the soapy water. His reflection revealed a much older looking face than he remembered. He avoided looking as much as he could. It was a grim reminder of young, carefree years now lost.

Too many memories.

He left the fountain reluctantly, woefully abandoning the soothing waters. For the first time since his capture, he felt clean and refreshed. *It beat the hell out of the quick hosing down they received at the mines.*

The monitor sprung back to life as he toweled off. Ryan scrambled with the towel, slightly embarrassed.

"Your garments are now available in the hopper, Ryan," said a familiar Xeronian.

"Thank you," he stated to a now blank screen.

"Hopper," he repeated in Trinarieit. "That's a new one."

He opened the hopper and found an identical set of clothes to the ones he had previously discarded. The material of which these were made was slightly softer and lighter, and lacked any hint of color, being absolutely white.

Naturally. He laughed again. *He couldn't help himself. Why was everything so damned funny?*

After dressing, he requested some food. The Xeronian asked him for details. He tried to explain the particulars of a fat, juicy steak. The alien twisted its mouth slightly, exercising, respectively, a pronounced facial contortion. They said they would try, however.

The expression was probably their version of distaste or disgust. It was not unlike a human's. But they were aliens after all. What was a smile to them, or a frown? He had to throw out all human behavior expectations — and that would be difficult.

The meal arrived quickly. They had achieved the taste with moderate success. The solid food had a waxy aftertaste and was more than a bit bland, but the accompanying soup was very good.

Tsaurau appeared after Ryan was finished. The door slid open noiselessly. *Impeccable timing. He was, of course, being watched.*

The alien did not step in immediately. Instead, he first scanned every square meter of room, large eyes drinking in every detail. Then he inspected Ryan head to foot. Satisfied, he ventured forth.

"Are you satisfied with our hospitality, Ryan?"

"What's that?" *Again, another word. He really should improve his Trinarieit.*

"Are you referring to the term hospitality? Perhaps the term generosity, or kindness?"

Nothing sounded familiar — least of which any term one would hear in a slaver camp. "I thank you," was all Ryan could say.

"I must take samples. I am required to obtain a few tissue cultures. It will take only a moment."

Ryan watched as he approached. Seemed obvious he needed something, most likely samples. He held out his arm to submit to a few scrapings of skin, a small sample of blood and hair. The needle pricks were laughable to what pain he had endured, before.

Tsaurau talked as he worked. "I know that you must have many questions. I am here to answer as many as possible. But first, I must voice a concern, about the weapon you have in your possession. I trust you will not use it on us."

"No, I will not use it, Tsaurau. It is for defense."

"That is good. Remember that you are on probation. If we find you to be dangerous to the colony, we are required to terminate your presence."

"Terminate? Does this mean kill me?"

"Possibly, if it comes to that; but it will not come to that, Ryan. Please keep our perspective in mind at all times."

He missed a few of the words, but the meaning was clear. "Thanks for warning."

"We have seen the indeterminable complexity of human behavior." He hesitated a moment. "I would prefer you to surrender your weapon."

Ryan caught the gist of his request and did not like it. "I cannot give my weapon. I slave too long."

Tsaurau's black eyes seemed to soften. "Yes, I understand completely. We will let the issue rest then."

Ryan gave an internal sigh of relief. *He didn't need a conflict with these people.*

The alien dropped off the samples in the small compartment under the monitor. "Now, I will attempt to answer as many of your questions as possible." His tone carried a tinge more enthusiasm.

Ryan proceeded to barrage him with as many questions as he could think of. Hours flew by as they discussed everything from space travel to the Xeronian's knowledge of Earth. He enjoyed Tsaurau's company. The Xeronians were a peaceful, content people and they were far superior in technology and scientific development than any other race he had met; yet, underlying all of it, there was something definitely wrong. They were not of this planet, which was obvious. All clues pointed to the fact that they were hiding: an underground colony, a desolate hellish planet in the remote edge of the galaxy. Ryan could not help but notice a subtle reservation Tsaurau exercised when he asked questions of their past.

It was the Xi-Empire. It has to be.

Tsaurau, it seemed, was a prominent figure in the colony. He was the leader of the lower council, which managed the operations of the colony and dealt with the day-to-day decisions to maintain their survival on this planet. All issues from power and life support to agriculture and medicine went through this council.

The upper council, or the Council of the Elders, was less defined in function given one exception: their judgment, once proclaimed, was law. The Elders were a select few of the oldest Xeronians of the colony and carried with them years of knowledge and experience. Their decisions were respected, although not always fully understood.

Their talk was cut short when Tsaurau announced that they were being summoned to the Council of the Elder's chambers. It was a strange proclamation. The Xeronian promptly turned and headed out, momentarily stopping at the exit to beckon him.

"Do not worry. We are prepared for you now. You can walk among us freely."

He glanced at his rifle. *No, he would not bring it. The past few hours had solidified what the Xeronians' intentions were. Hell, if they really wanted him dead, they could have killed him many times over by now.*

Tsaurau kept a quick pace, as it was not considered proper to keep the Elders waiting. Ryan slowed as much as he dared, insatiably curious, marvelling at the architecture: bleached white corridors that seemed to travel for kilometers and finally disappear in a luminous haze, great hollowed rooms that served as parks with artificial suns embedded within distant ceilings, life of all kinds striving below, rooms of grand design merging into matrices of apartments and living quarters. He could see streams winding through ending at small ponds, which irrigated extraordinary gardens of flowering plants. Birds, much like Earth's, sang in harmonious chorus, and strange little animals scurried over the footpaths where other Xeronians leisurely strolled.

The Xeronia colony was a full-fledged multi-level underground city, built inside a hollowed-out mountain that was kilometers high. It was a completely contained world with thousands of separate systems that worked together in unequaled harmony. Ryan knew the level of technology required to build this must be hundreds, possibly thousands, of years ahead of his own kind. He could only marvel at the incredible engineering around him. He bombarded Tsaurau with questions, knowing but a few could be answered satisfactorily. Nonetheless, the Xeronian valiantly struggled to translate concepts and ideas alien to his translating abilities.

"How long to build this?"

"We have been here almost two hundred planet years, but it did not take that long for the initial hollowing of the mountain. That would not have been acceptable. The colony moved within the mountain after, approximately, two years from the time we arrived. We have, since then, continued to expand our living space in order to adjust to our growing population. It is a challenging task. We must be careful not to weaken the mountain's structure, as it is at the mercy of powerful stresses imposed upon it by many different sources. We must always be careful of the energy output of our equipment. We do not want to be discovered again."

"Discovered? What meaning?"

"It means to be found."

"Found by who? Xi-Empire you hide?"

Tsaurau ignored the question, choosing to continue the walk. The trip took almost an hour before they reached the entrance. Near the end of the trip, they came upon a small shuttle that resembled a golf cart. It roamed quietly down the corridor carrying two Xeronians, propelled by means unknown.

"We not ride?" Ryan asked.

"Exercise is good for the mind and the body," replied Tsaurau.

"I guess that means we could," Ryan replied with some chagrin.

They finally arrived at the entrance of the Chamber of the Elders. The chamber was dome-shaped with walls curving up to a point at least 40 meters above them. On both sides of the main walkway, dim lighting emanated from the bases of richly decorated columns that reached to the ceiling. Their tops were invisible in the darkness, as the meager light was unable to penetrate.

Strange it was so dark.

Luminous paintings spanned to the ceiling, glowed eerily down through the murkiness, bathing the floor in soft hues. Ryan studied the artwork as he walked. He noted that many of the paintings seemed to move as his perspective shifted.

"They are something."

"Yes, they include many scenes of our past home world and depict key turning points in our civilization. They are largely religious artifacts, replicas of some of our most famous treasures of Xeronia. They are not, unfortunately, the original works, although they are irreplaceable treasures in their own right, created by some of our most gifted artists. Many have considered it their life's accomplishment to be involved with the construction and embellishment of this sacred room. The walls around you reflect the multiple millennia of our race's existence."

Ryan attempted to translate his words. Some he could tie together to guess their meaning.

"This room is sacred. The voices of the Eternals are heard here. That is why we colonized this planet."

"The Eternals?"

"The Ancient Ones speak with strength here."

Ryan shook his head, "Speak in riddles. Who are they?"

"Long ago, our planet was in danger, and our world was on the verge of veritable extinction. Our moon's orbit had been in a slow decay for centuries. The resulting gravitational fluctuations pulled at the Xeronia's surface with unparalleled devastation, causing tectonic disruptions on such a massive scale that they destroyed most of our cities, our homes, our industry. We had neither the means nor the knowledge to save ourselves. The Ancient Ones arrived, saved our planet and our civilization. They restored our moon to a safe orbit and helped us rebuild. They taught us much, provided us the knowledge to allow us to reach out into space. We were eager students, grasping at the ideas we had not as yet developed. Now, tens of thousands of years later, we are well beyond the level of science and mathematics that the Ancient Ones were known to have."

"Where they now?"

"They are lost to us. They simply disappeared into the vastness of space. We never made contact with them again. We have found only artifacts to attest to the fact they had once traveled through this end of the galaxy. It is ironic that the ship that brought you here was one of our first exploration-class starships. The Ancient Ones helped us manufacture those particular vessels. That very ship which brought you here departed from Xeronia almost two thousand years ago – that is to be precise, these planet years. The measurement of time is relative."

"Do you know happened?"

"Happened?" It was Tsaurau's time to question.

"To crew of the ship I arrived on."

"Their last log indicated that they had established contact with a primitive culture. Some aberrant facts were noted about the native's paradoxical knowledge of technology. No other entries were logged, and nothing else is known. It is assumed they perished. Exploring is a dangerous avocation."

"Dangerous, I am very familiar with that term." Ryan's eyes had not stopped wandering. *The art, the colors, the scenes, all seemed so... alien, but so beautiful.*

They approached a massive semi-circular desk of solid granite.

"When we began hollowing out this cavern, many of the technicians heard the voices. The Elders were called in. There was no doubt where the Council chambers should be located."

Tsaurau lowered his voice to a soft whisper. "It has been said that the Elders can feel the threads of time to come. They hear the whispers of the ghosts of the Eternals. It is not by accident that the location of this chamber, this point in space, is polarised."

"What meaning?"

"There is an aberration - a blemish, if you will," Tsaurau stopped his explanation, leaving it incomplete, as the Elders began to appear, their faces hidden within shadows.

A spotlight shot down upon the two of them, slightly blinding them under its intense rays. A hushed silence followed, only to be shattered by a scratchy, deep voice of the Eldest.

"We extend our appreciation to Tsaurau and to our guest," she stated in native Xeronian.

"Yes, my Elder," Tsaurau replied, bowing slightly.

She spoke again, this time in Trinarieit. "We have convened to determine if he is the one the Eternals have spoke of. If he is indeed, the one of the prophecy."

Ryan felt them studying him. The spotlight seemed hot, its rays, white and blinding. He could just make out the image of the Eldest through the light. Her eyes were closed, her gaze turned upwards. Wrinkles enveloped her face and skull, like ripples in sand, but somehow she did not appear ugly to him, just very, very old.

After what seemed like ages she lowered her eyes and brought her full attention to bear on Ryan. Black eyes burned into him like hot coals.

"It seems the voices of the Eternals remain silent."

Another Elder spoke. "If you are the one, you are destined for greater things Man-from-Earth. We of Xeronia regard you with friendship. You are free to walk amongst us. We... empathize with you, for the difficulties you have suffered under the Xi-Empire regime. Know that you are now free from your bonds of slavery."

With that, Tsaurau bowed, and Ryan followed suit. They backed out, facing the prominent shadows of the council, never turning around. Only when the door slid shut to the chamber did Tsaurau resume talking.

"Thank you for following our customs... we do not turn our backs to the Elders, out of respect."

"No problem. When in Rome, do as the Romans do."

The Xeronian regarded him with interest. "You talk in your home language, mixing your dialects. I must learn of this language."

"Not a problem," he responded in his native English.

"Interesting inflections. Regardless, there are important matters to discuss. I must warn you, Ryan, not all of us believe in the prophecy the Elders referred to."

"Prophecy? What they mean? They say I the one?"

"The prophecy is less ambiguous and more literal than most. The Chosen One is the protector and the destroyer. If you are the one, that is to be your destiny."

"Protector what, destroyer what?"

"You will find in due time," replied Tsaurau.

Ryan shook his head in frustration as they walked. "You drive me crazy with answer!"

Tsaurau turned suddenly, eyes appraising. "Should I begin to question your sanity?"

"No," Ryan said with irritation, "Just thing to say."

"Then it is time we learned to communicate better. I shall learn your English, then?"

"Am sure it will not take long."

"I look forward to this exercise. I enjoy a challenge."

Ryan reached over and patted the alien's shoulder.

* * *

Zorlog was growing impatient.

The slave trade was moving much too slowly for his liking, and he needed to firm up capital if he was to move ahead with his plans. With profits down, his plans were held back. As he marched down to the main airlock, the crew practically threw themselves out of his way. There was never enough room for an angry Tarvok within these tight corridors. At the airlock, he met up with his Lavok. "Ryadin, you must maintain attention, and speed it up down there or I'll have your head."

"Yes, my Tarvok, I will endeavor to meet your standard."

"When is the next communication window to Xilo?"

"26.00 radii, my Tarvok."

"Very good, Lavok."

There was no salute between them as the airlock closed. Zorlog's crew did not follow formal military code. It was useless protocol. The brief wait in the airlock gave Zorlog some time to think. By the time the hatch opened on the other side, he had already formulated his plan. A new face appeared beyond the open hatch.

"Pressurisation balance complete, Tarvok. The shuttle is ready."

"We'll leave at once, Savok."

He fingered his belt, triggering the intercom. "Lavok Ryadin!" he growled. A pause...

"Ryadin here."

"I want your detachment to be on the ship before 26.00 radii, no stragglers, understand!"

"If problems should arise?"

"Maintain your schedule, Lavok."

"Understood, my Tarvok."

The shuttle launched from the belly of the slaver *Gohk*. The *Gohk* was an old converted Xilozak destroyer that had been mothballed by the military and replaced by a newer, more powerful model. Zorlog had bought it for measly credits, but the refit that had cost him dearly. Now the *Gohk* could easily match the speed and armament of any one of the new destroyers. Many a Txtian engineer had died once the overhaul was complete, ensuring their secrets disappeared with them. The Xilozak military did not know of the extensive rework on the old destroyer. If they had, they would have hunted him down and either killed or imprisoned him. But Zorlog was no fool, and he had a long history of dealings with certain officials. Precautions had been taken. The kickbacks were exorbitant but effective. It was precisely this reason why Zorlog was so insistent on demanding a profit from every venture. Debt was not an enviable position.

Everything must be done with precise timing. He demanded that of his crew. They adhered to the Xilo time clock with a solemn discipline.

The Xi-Empire had seen to it that Xilo time was the de facto standard throughout most of the known galaxy. If Xilo time structure were compared to Earth, definitions and terms would correspond closely, although the actual elapsed time for each label is not identical. A sadii resolves to a day, radii to hours, gadii to minutes, adii to seconds, although the ratios and units differ slightly. There was no equivalent to a month although a third of a year would be equivalent to a zanii, and a full Xilo year a zadii.

Zorlog's shuttle was headed for a desolate, barren planet called G0015-A. It was at a key location in the Xi-Empire trading industry. Its spaceports were among the best, and its space dock repair and shipbuilding industry was renown throughout. Trade was the life-blood of the G0015-A economy, which lacked most other industries save a few mining operations.

Once they landed, Zorlog and his crew made their way through the crowded, dirty streets. The natives, as well as other visitors, gave them a wide berth. They were known very well on this planet.

Zorlog's group stopped at the main administration building, the office of the Torzon. When the unruly group arrived on the 103rd floor, they spread out and proceeded to escort all the Torzon's other visitors back into the elevator. They informed each that their appointments were canceled.

The secretary was smart enough not to interfere. She simply activated the intercom. "Torzon Jhonk, Tarvok Zorlog is here to see you!"

"Let him in!"

The secretary entered the access code and the doors swung open to a plush office and a commanding view of the Goo15-A's capital city. Only Zorlog entered, his crew remained strategically positioned throughout the waiting room area.

"Tarvok, it is rewarding to see you," he said flatly.

"Torzon," nodded Zorlog. He paused a moment, fighting an urge to step over and rip the arms off the official. *It would be of such pleasure to witness him scream.*

Instead, he calmly, meticulously, pulled off his gloves and tucked them under his gun belt. "I hear you intend to charge me with an additional cargo excise tax. Why is this?"

"That is what I have always admired about you Zorlog, your directness!" replied the Jhonk. "The reason is simple. Your profits are in excess as you do business in this quadrant, yet you do nothing to help cover the costs of maintaining its vibrant economy."

"You mean, you want to raise your kickback, without the support of Xilo." *Excellent. He could work this to his advantage.*

"Oh no, Xilo may not officially support this, but I do have the required clearances in the proper levels. The rules are very simple here on Goo15-A: If you wish to continue doing business here, you will contribute."

"Torzon, I have a proposition for you. It is also quite simple. You pay me back all the credits of which you skimmed off my last cargo trades and apply them to your new tax. I will be more than happy to accept any credits left over."

"That's preposterous!" laughed Jhonk. "You're a *ferzet* if you think I'm going to *pay you* a single credit."

"A *ferzet*? No need to get personal, Torzon. But you truly have no choice," warned Zorlog quietly, his hand resting on his blaster.

"Now hold on!" warned Jhonk, "Don't even think of intimidating me. I've already signaled security, and they are prepared to cut you and your crew to pieces. You'll never make it out of this building!"

"Ah, yes. Cut to pieces you say. You have a vivid imagination." He pulled his hand off his blaster, giving a toothy grimace of a smile. "Don't worry Jhonk, I was merely toying with you. We both know I fully support you, as I have proven so many times in the past."

"Only to suit your own personal gain, Zorlog. I am not the *ferzet*."

"Of course." Zorlog's mind was spinning with hate. *Far too many times these Txtian have interfered with his operations. This was the last time. The time had come to act. It was wasteful, this bantering.*

"My Torzon, I will arrange payment. After all, I have no choice."

"Exactly. We have an understanding. You realize who is in control here. Although I must admit, this does surprise me, such unlike the old Zorlog I once knew. You are losing your backbone."

Zorlog's upper lip quivered. "I am the same old Zorlog."

"Yes, yes, of course. Perhaps it all has to do with your current debt? Since you have been so... complimentary, I will do you a favor. I will allow you another option - simply leave G0015-A, but leave without your cargo. It is your decision, of course. Pay the tax or leave the cargo, either will do. Mark my words: Do neither, and I will ensure your credit is called. Your credit will no longer be any good in this quadrant. No one will do business with you. That, I will personally guarantee."

"You realize you will need Xilo itself to support such a preposterous position, Jhonk."

Jhonk laughed. "In case you didn't notice, we have two of the Empire's finest cruisers in orbit. They can easily annihilate you and that thing you call a ship. All they need is a reason."

"Ah yes, the cruisers. I did notice them on my way in. But they would certainly have a difficult time at it. Regardless of the fun thoughts. I'll need two sadii to get the credits together."

"You have one. No more."

Zorlog approached the large windows and stared out at the view below. From this height, people and vehicles were mere specs.

Ripping him apart would be too easy. It would be so enjoyable to toss Jhonk down from here. The look on his face would be priceless. It would take such a long time before he hit...

Jhonk rustled behind his desk. Zorlog returned from his thoughts and turned to stare the Txtian down. The Torzon quickly averted his eyes.

The smell of fear was thick on him. A putrid stench, rotting from the inside out. In his own building and he was still afraid. Zorlog laughed again, startling Jhonk who was wise enough to remain careful of the slaver's next move.

"Very well, my Torzon. You will have your credits this sadii. I am feeling generous. The transfer will take place at 26.00."

Zorlog turned his attention from the window and walked out of the office, hesitating mid-stride just beyond the doorway. "This is the last time, Jhonk. I will not see you again. I do not do business with the dead."

Jhonk pressed the switch. The doors closed too slowly for his liking. *He knew Zorlog well enough to take the threat seriously. How foolish for him to tip his hand.*

"Dykstra!" he yelled to his secretary. "Get a communications link to Zuvok Zenks, immediately."

In a moment Zenks' image appeared on his desk monitor. "Torzon Jhonk, how are you?"

"Concerned. Zorlog just paid me a visit. He is not impressed by our new tax rates."

"A pity. He will not comply?"

"Yes, I mean, no. No, I am sure he will not, and he has openly threatened my life!"

"I understand, my Torzon. And what would you have me do?"

"Get rid of him – and his crew – his whole ship."

"That may be... a bit harsh. He has friends. There is, however, another way of dealing with this problem. I understand that the *Gohk* is carrying illegal cargo. It is always such a loss when a once proud Tarvok loses his command and has his ship towed back to Xilo."

"Excellent," Jhonk cried with jubilation.

"You must understand, however. Procedure must be adhered to in order to meet legal standing. We cannot foster the sympathizers aligned with this rogue."

"Of course. Take the time you need."

"I must impress upon you, Torzon, the cost of such an exercise!"

"Name it."

"A case of Erzainian Kamote."

"A case!" Jhonk laughed. "For Zorlog I will give you two cases, Zuvok."

"Ah, you are feeling generous today?"

"No, nervous. I prefer that you simply kill the rogue. By the way, hold off until after 26.00, I am awaiting a funds transfer. To Xilo!"

"To Xilo!" repeated the Zuvok, and the monitor went blank.

"Dykstra, can you get me a line to my brother?"

"I'm sorry Torzon, but we won't have an open window to Xilo until 26.00."

"That will have to do. Set it up. Priority one."

"Priority one?"

"Just do it, Dykstra!"

"Understood, my Torzon."

"And another thing. At 26.00 I want you to personally monitor that funds transfer from that *ferzet*, Zorlog."

* * *

On the trip back, Zorlog finished mulling over his plan. He made an encrypted call on his belt communicator to the ship.

"Savok Gulin here."

"Savok, I want you to set up the *Gohk* with a reason to dock at 26.00, nothing serious, nothing that will interfere with any critical systems, but it must seem serious. It has to look real. Something authentic, something dramatic."

"Backup air tank breach, maybe?"

"Yes, that will do. Very good."

"Right away, Tarvok. Anything else?"

"Yes. Keep it quiet."

"Understood. Communications out."

He liked Gulin, a very efficient officer. He would have to promote him after. He would be short of good officers.

On arrival at the *Gohk*, the scene was that of organized chaos. New cargos and supplies were being loaded and unloaded as shuttles taxied up and down from the surface. The officers greeted Zorlog with a silent acknowledgment when he stepped onto the bridge.

"Status report, Lavok Ryadin."

"All is quiet. The two cruisers, the *Gallon* and *Gezerk,* are also in geostationary orbit."

"Yes, I assume there has been no correspondence with them."

"That is accurate."

"Everything else is on schedule, Tarvok. All transfers are expected to be complete by 25.15."

"Good."

"Sir, the *Gallom* is hailing us."

"Of course. Put it through to my quarters."

He went in, locked the door and engaged the white noise filters to defy any eavesdropping. Zuvok Zenk's face revealed some latent anxiety.

"Greetings, Tarvok Zorlog. I trust you are faring well?"

"I do. I have. It seems, Tarvok, whenever you hail, it coincides with a visit. Shall I prepare for you?"

"Yes, Tarvok, just a routine inspection. Is now a good time?"

"As a matter-of-fact, it is not. We are in the middle of moving cargo. I would request a change in schedule, for our mutual benefit, to avoid all this confusion."

"Very well, at 25.00 then."

Zorlog grunted. "That is hardly generous. May I make it at least 26.00? I do have pressing matters at hand."

"I trust this reason is not a ploy to move any possible contraband from aboard your ship, Tarvok," Zenks mused.

"Nonsense, Zuvok, I am at your disposal. I will arrange a shuttle at 26.00, sharp."

"Not needed, Tarvok."

"Zuvok, I insist. Certain Avoks on my ship would be honored to convey your party."

"We have our own shuttles."

"This has a pretense of a boarding exercise. What exactly are your motives, Zuvok?"

Zenks visibly squirmed. "This is a routine inspection only. I must assure you Tarvok, we are not in the habit of boarding Xi-Empire traders."

"Of course, you would hate to set such a precedence before all the trading community. That would be political suicide. Think of all those administrators on Xilo losing their profits when the trade community protests."

"Send the shuttle. I look forward to our visit."

"As I, Zuvok. Until 26.00 then."

"To Xilo, Tarvok Zorlog."

"To Xilo. Communications out."

Zuvok Zenks watched his monitor go blank. *He was amused at the arrogance of the infamous Tarvok Zorlog. Very shortly his ego will not be so full. It left him with a deep satisfaction.*

* * *

Zorlog requested a com link to Gulin.

"Savok Gulin here," announced the eager Avok, a few moments later.

"Gulin, load cargo hold seven into shuttle five. Somewhere unnoticeable, set up a remote on it."

"The whole hold, my Tarvok? That is excessive!"

"I'm well aware of that fact, Gulin. Make sure the detonator has a backup. I want it to work."

"Consider it done. Anything else?"

"The same as before, Savok, exercise this quietly and you see to this job personally."

"I am privileged to be of service. Communications out."

Zorlog's entry alarm buzzed, a voice rang haughtily over the intercom. "I Charvok Kitohk, request conference immediately!"

Zorlog's mood turned instantly sour.

What did he want now? Referring to himself in full title, no less.

"Enter."

"I understand our leave has been cut short to 25.15," the Charvok blurted out, avoiding standard interface protocol.

"Yes, that's when the last shuttle is scheduled to return. What of it?"

"May I ask why? I have a number of problems I am addressing, and I need at least two radii planet-side to resolve."

"Kitohk, have you not heard? We are to have Zuvok Zenks from the *Gallom* aboard to perform an inspection. I expect this ship to be in top condition."

"No. I did not know that. Why wasn't I informed?" The irritation in his voice gave him away. *He did not like to be kept in the dark. Why hadn't his own people told him of this?*

"Perhaps you would like you to exercise those fine diplomatic skills of yours. Would you go and pick up the good Zuvok at 26.00? Pick your favorite out of the crew to accompany you, and use shuttle five. I will inform him you are personally going to pick him up."

Kitohk practically beamed in glorious satisfaction. *This type of work - rubbing shoulders with the high brass - was good for his career*. He accepted without hesitation and quickly picked up to leave, but hesitated.

"My Tarvok, may I request a bottle of Erzainian Kamote - as a gift?"

Zorlog eyed the Charvok for a moment, careful not to give away his true feelings. "Of course, that is an excellent idea, Kitohk. Make it a case if you wish. Arrange it!"

Eyes went wide with excitement. "Very good, my Tarvok!"

"Be on schedule, Kitohk. Punctuality is very important to those military types."

"Of course!" he snorted indignantly. "26.00 exactly." He left with an unusual bouncy gait.

Zorlog glanced at his chronometer. It was 25.10.

His communication link buzzed. The metallic transfer voice squeaked: "Lavok Ryadin."

"Proceed, Lavok," he acknowledged.

"My Tarvok, all cargoes are now transferred, all crew aboard and accounted for."

"Good work, Lavok. Are you secure?"

"Affirmative."

"Kitohk will be choosing some of the crew for the shuttle flight. Make sure he chooses his own. Any good ones are to be deterred from that flight for cargo duty. Do you understand?"

"Understood. Will attend to this immediately. Communications out."

The communications link buzzed once again. This time it was Gulin informing him everything was ready.

"Good. Ensure Kitohk and his party dispatch on shuttle five - and standby for my signal."

At 25.22 Kitohk buzzed the Tarvok. "Tarvok, we are assembled and the shuttle is ready!"

"That was efficient, Kitohk. I understand that Lavok Ryadin may require some of the crew for cargo duty."

"No, we have no issue here. Everyone is cleared for flight."

"Very good. Did you find the case of Erzainian Kamote?"

"I have it with me, Tarvok. I'm sure the Zuvok will appreciate this gesture. It's very generous..."

"Very good, Kitohk, enjoy yourself," Zorlog cut him short. *A deliciously enjoyable moment.*

He marched onto the bridge and patched through to Gulin from the navigation console. "Savok, inform me of the shuttle's departure time, and report immediately to the bridge."

"They're in pre-stage check, my Tarvok."

Ryadin walked onto the bridge just as the monitor went blank. "Ryadin, make us assault ready. Put together multiple boarding parties. Full complement and armament. Get ready to move from main and secondary locks."

"I shall, my Tarvok, but who are we attacking?" Ryadin added tentatively.

Zorlog glared at Savok. "You will be evaluated in time, Savok. I trust you will expedite?"

"Of course!" He rushed off the bridge.

"Communications! Clear all channels and route all future ones through the bridge. All messages must have my clearance. No exceptions!"

Gulin appeared on the bridge. "Shuttle five departing now, Tarvok."

"Tactical, relay auxiliary power to shield. Gulin, be ready to engage at 26.00, exactly."

A small vibration surged through the ship.

An Engineering Avok jumped up on the central monitor. "Tarvok, we have a ruptured respirator tank. Our technicians have it under control, it is minor, but it requires immediate attention. The cause of the breach is unknown."

"Attend to the issue, immediately! Communications, hail the *Gezerk*."

The *Gezerk's* Zuvok appeared on the main bridge viewscreen.

"I am Tarvok Zorlog of the *Gohk*. Our ship has endured a failure. Its hull is ruptured. I would like to request a dock within your cruiser bay for repairs."

"I am Zuvok Agvar. We have monitored an explosion. Have you isolated the root cause?"

"My engineers surmise it may have originated within the backup navigation circuits, but they're not sure, this is an old ship Zuvok Agvar."

"Yes, of course, it is Zorlog," he replied, a small twisted grimace on his face. "I understand Zuvok Zenks of the *Gallom* intends to meet with you. Why not dock there?"

"I request the *Gezerk* as it is simply much closer, and time is critical. We are venting atmosphere. Are you refusing us aid?"

"Not at all, Tarvok. I do not foresee a problem with your request. Dock is granted."

"Thank-you, Zuvok. Communications out."

"Navigation. Bring us under that pile of junk and into her belly."

"Manoeuvring now, Tarvok."

"Shuttle five hailing."

Damned Kitohk, not a moment's peace. Always wants to know what's going on. "Inform them of our situation, tell them to continue on."

He slammed the intercom. "Ryadin!" It took a moment to get the link.

"Tarvok?"

"Standby."

"Docking maneuvers now, my Tarvok," reported the navigation Avok.

"Steady," said Zorlog. "Time?"

"25.29, Sir."

The ship jerked as it locked into the docking clamps.

"Where's the shuttle?"

"Just docked within the *Gallom*, Tarvok," the tracing Avok replied.

Zorlog reached over the command chair and activated the ship-wide alert.

"Assault stations!" he yelled through the intercom.

"Ryadin, the time to act is now!"

With the sudden status change to assault stations, the crew did not have the time to act surprised. They focused on their duties. The assault teams moved quickly through the hatches, laser torches ready. In moments they had breached the internal docking bay's airlocks and were moving through the corridors, killing every trooper they confronted. Ryadin secured the docking station personally and relayed the signal. "Successful infiltration, my Tarvok!"

"Gulin, engage the explosives on my mark."

"Tactical, power up cannon on my mark."

"Now!"

A brief flash appeared on the lower aft monitors. The viewscreen came on, painted with the distraught face of the *Gezerk's* Zuvok.

"Tarvok Zorlog, abort docking. We have a situation..."

"Hello, Agvar. I regret to inform you that I am holding your ship hostage. Please surrender, or I will blow your belly into dust."

The Zuvok was visibly stunned. "You must be joking!"

"Check the *Gallom*. Tell me... what is the Xi-Empire's finest battlecruiser's status?" queried Zorlog, an evil satisfaction in his voice.

"It looks like she took a direct hit! She's dropping out of orbit. Is this your doing Zorlog! There are two thousand troops on that cruiser!

"Were two thousand," corrected Zorlog.

A horrified look settled over the Agvar's face.

"Why the long face? She's been christened with a case of my finest Erzainian Kamote. I must impress upon you that the next few moments are crucial to your survival, Agvar. You must realize that no more need die. Surrender. That is your only option. You are helpless. A well-placed shot by the *Gohk* will obliterate this cruiser. You should have learned to be more stringent with your docking policies."

The stunned Agvar seemed to refocus back, back from the view of the exploding star cruiser, back to look into the eyes of Zorlog.

"You'll never take over this ship, Zorlog!"

"On the contrary Agvar, I already have. Check for yourself. But I must remind you. Time is fleeting."

The Zuvok glanced over to one of his Avoks. Hushed voices followed. A small, sickly smile crept on his face as he turned his attention back to the monitor.

"So it seems you have already taken engineering."

"Yes, I have options. Maybe I will vent the atmosphere in the remainder of the ship, or simply let loose with my cannon."

"Your threats are hollow. You would have to blast your own troops."

"Just as I would not sacrifice those in my shuttle? On the contrary. I have already initiated my move and have no other recourse. I will either take this ship, or I will destroy it."

Agvar muted the Xilozak pirate and searched the faces of his Avoks. Not one provided any hint of hope. Reports were flooding in. Zorlog's small group had secured the main engineering controls and locked down all the emergency portals. The *Gezerk's* crew was immobilized.

He had lost. If Zorlog fired, it would literally tear the ship in two. He had little time before the Gohk's boarding party blew the main conduits and with it environmental support.

"Savok, I suggest we initiate self-destruct," ordered Agvar.

His Avok's hands flew across the controls. Grunting with frustration, he attempted another flurry, only to look up with a forlorn gaze. "We have lost control, my Zuvok."

Zorlog's troops knew these ships too well. The circumstances sunk into the Zuvok's mind in a fearful realization. How had he been so foolish? There had to be a way out of this situation. He just needed some time.

He canceled the mute.

"Make your decision now, Zuvok, or I will," stated Zorlog.

"I need more..."

"You're out of time."

He felt slight tremors carry through the deck plating. The bridge went dark. The few control panels that remained unaffected provided sparse light. One of these was the communications panel, with Zorlog's impassive face painted on the monitor.

"The main conduits have been severed. Now we can take this ship apart piece by piece. Do you want to see what I have planned next? My troops now have control of the environmental systems. How many of your crew have access to suits within the next, say, 10 gadii?

"No. Stop this. There is no need to kill any more." Agvar's shoulders sagged in utter defeat.

"I will offer your troops the choice of life. They will be allowed safe route to G0015-A."

Agvar searched the darkened bridge, only able to catch the eyes of a few of his Avoks. The look they carried in their eyes, he had never seen it before, but he recognized it. It was fear.

"Then we will surrender, Zorlog, under these terms."

* * *

On the planet's surface, on the 103rd floor of the towering administration building, Jhonk impatiently paced by the glass panes of his office. He was waiting for the com window to open. It always took time to stabilize a link. One hundred and thirty light-years proved to be challenging.

"Dykstra!" he yelled, "Do we have a channel yet?"

"Yes, my Torzon, link is established. Routing through to your brother at this moment."

* * *

"Ryadin, tell me you have the bridge."

"Yes, my Tarvok, we do. A little resistance, but we took care of it."

"Good."

"Destroy the Imperial Administration building."

Ryadin swallowed. "The pulse cannon?"

"No, use the missiles. All Imperial buildings are hardened. There are six redundant conduits for weapons control. Reroute and fire. And make sure you do not miss, Lavok, as the Gohk will need a Tarvok."

* * *

The last thing Torzon Jhonk saw was the image of his brother. The missile struck perfectly. In seconds, the monolithic Imperial Administration building was converted to dust and flaming cinders, along with a large portion of the capital city.

Approximately nine sadii later a considerable-sized fleet lead by three Xi-

Empire cruisers arrived at the planet. They found the ashes of the administration building and remnants of a destroyed cruiser, but no sign of the *Gezerk*. Most of its crew had been shuttled to the planet, however, the full complement of the ship's Avoks, its Zuvok among them, had been ejected from the airlock. It took a full sadii to retrieve the floating dead, as it was code to provide military personnel with a proper burial. The floating graveyard haunted the crew and lowered morale. The ceremonies were kept short.

On the planet, they left no stone unturned. Many natives were tortured, but little information was found. They had only rumors, a stolen ship, and too many dead.

* * *

5. Visions from the Past

Ryan, now free to move about the Xeronian colony, explored the subterranean city with the eagerness of a child. Each day's excursion was like a day in school. He had so much to learn about this new world. His mind was clear, his body healthy and free of pain. For the moment he was content.

Tsaurau had picked up English in a matter of days. It was uncanny how fast he was able to learn. Stranger yet, other Xeronians would then talk to him in English as if they had all learned the language at once. Rarely would they speak their native language when he was present, if they would speak at all. Ryan could only surmise they had to be using something similar to telepathy.

The Xeronians were a friendly people. Everyone greeted him with an open, sincere pleasantness that reminded him of a typical small town atmosphere back home. Numerous times he was invited to visit a Xeronian home to meet their families. They were fascinated by him. They asked him countless questions, wanting to know everything. He found himself developing a deep liking and respect for these gentle people.

He frequented the large open caverns often. These were the parks of their world, rich in lush greenery, with strange, beautiful flora that covered rolling hills in violets, yellows, and reds. Each park held a different species of plant life and a collection of unique small mammals. Artificial suns beat down on the parks by day, and constellations of stars appeared by night. Tsaurau had told him that each cavern represented a different part of the sky of their original Xeronia.

He felt close to Earth here. Like the bitter light of a dying candle, his memories warmed him, and haunted him. He knew time was running out for Earth, and Aviore was lost somewhere out there. The Xi-Empire casts a long dark shadow.

Tsaurau had noticed a change in Ryan. It was subtle. Something easily overlooked by one who was not familiar with the Earthman's mannerisms. *It was his duty to help if he could.* He searched him out and found him in one of the parks, sitting on a hill, overlooking a small brook. He joined him on a soft carpet of green grass.

"How are you, my friend?"

"Alright, I feel alright," Ryan replied quickly, brushing off Tsaurau's concern. "You know, you've carved out a fine world here."

"You have changed your opinion about this planet I see."

"Yes, I am impressed with this oasis in what at first glance would pass as hell. Its very existence is a testament to your people."

Tsaurau remained quiet, intently watching the brook flow by, avoiding eye contact.

"Did I offend you somehow?"

"No." The alien's eyes remained fixed on a point in the gurgling stream. "You did not offend me. Memories are sometimes difficult. It is the past that is offensive."

"I never seem to get an answer when I ask about your real home, why you left it, what happened to it."

Tsaurau was slow to reply. "This," he said, "what you see around you, is the last desperate effort of a dying race. You state we are gifted. You marvel at our technology. You see us as advanced far beyond your own people. Yet for all of our knowledge, all of our power, we could not stop them."

"Who? Who couldn't you stop?"

"As I told you earlier, we had developed space travel long ago. We explored many star systems and reached into the depths of the core of the galaxy. We were not prepared for what we met. I am sure you understand by now that we are a people of peace. We constantly strive to improve, it is our... obsession, but our society is not based on advancement at the cost of others. We have no criminal element, no murderers, no thieves. Maybe that is our weakness. Maybe we need that spark of negativity in our culture. But the Par would make that unsustainable... We are here because we were, and still are, in danger. Not from some medical epidemic, nor any form of natural antagonist, but from a brutal civilization - a misunderstood, unfathomable enemy. In spite of all of our accomplishments, we lost our war. When the time came, we could not protect ourselves."

"The Xi-Empire?"

"Yes. Our Elders had seen our weakness. In our fledgling years of space travel, the Elder Council had ordered the construction of a planet-wide shield. It took years to conceive how we could construct it. The Elders gave us many reasons why we should expend so much energy on such a project, citing the need to protect us against asteroids and other celestial body collisions, but I knew the real reason. It was a barrier between our world and the unknown that lay outside. We could never have imagined such atrocities other beings are capable of."

"So they attacked you."

"In our explorations, we have met many different races, each unique, many primitive. Our people made mistakes, assumed in their own naiveté that others were as peaceful as we are. Some of our ships were lost. Our explorers died. We adapted. We changed our policies, our directives. We know now that first contact is not always a controlled situation but none of this prepared us for the Xi-Empire."

"Your elders couldn't see that?"

"Their predictions are not... precise, you understand?"

"Right, most likely this was a little hard for your people to believe. I get it. But you had the shield by then, right?"

"Yes. But there was a problem. As you may have surmised, it did not take them long to locate Xeronia. They attacked and quickly discovered they could not defeat our shield. They attempted everything. They sacrificed many lives, weapons, and time in their attempts to penetrate our defenses, but they could not do it. They became frustrated and even more hostile. It was madness. We attempted to reach out to them, but it was futile. Our peace envoys were slaughtered mercilessly."

"They wanted your technology and everything you had."

"Yes they did, and if they were unable to take it, they would find a way to destroy it. Their bitter frustration led them in another direction, another way to infiltrate the shield. It was a weapon - a hideous creation. It fed on matter itself, consumed exponentially, an uncontrolled chain reaction that would stop only after it collapsed of its own starvation."

"You talk as if it were alive."

"Alive? Perhaps in some way, one could consider it such, but no, this was pure death. Strangely, they did inform us of the weapon, and they stated they would use it. We did not believe they would act so cruelly, nor that this new weapon of theirs could permeate our shield. It was wishful reflection, a desperate need to see ourselves in them. It flooded the Par, tore at our own sense of understanding. It was false hope. There were others among us who did not accept this common thought. They prepared, modeled the impact of the weapon. The projections were irrefutable. The shield, the very thing that kept us safe, would be our own demise. The contained reaction would effectively accelerate the destructive effects."

A term he used in his last statement piqued his interest. "Before you continue, what do you mean by the Par? You've mentioned this multiple times."

"The Par is something you must experience. Words cannot fully explain. I plan to demonstrate this for you soon."

"Alright, that's fair. So continuing on, what did your people do?"

"What we did, or more accurately what we did not do - what we should have done - we should have surrendered. Instead, we held onto our false hope. Our decision was biased by our own ethics. "

"And this was a mistake," acknowledge Ryan somberly. It was difficult to catch any emotion on the Xeronian's features, although his eyes seemed squinted, as if he was in pain.

"We managed to dispatch escape vessels before they activated the weapon. When they deployed it, it infiltrated the shield with ease, and wreaked pure devastation, eventually converting our planet into a temporary sun. Billions of lives lost. Why? Because they could not have Xeronia. Since they could not conquer us, they destroyed us. They are the lowest of all sentient life."

"With all your technology, couldn't you fight back - devise weapons and take the offensive?"

"You do not understand. It is not our nature, Ryan. We had little in the way of weapons and lacked the will to use them. If we were more aggressive, maybe Xeronia would still exist. Our people have been at peace for millennia. We simply have no violent tendencies."

"So you are the last."

"No. Multiple ships escaped. Others may have survived and their colonies may be flourishing. We do not know. To attempt communications is an unnecessary risk."

"So you could have other colonies out there? You may not be alone?"

"I do not believe so, but that remains my opinion. But the Elders have not found them. Not all agree with me. A particular Elder reached out to me before the war began. She had been shunned by the council for her views and her foresight. She asked me to lead an initiative to build a fleet of interstellar colony vessels, starships specifically designed to carry as many colonists off the planet as possible. In the last days, their cargo included much of what was once Xeronia. Many Xeronians forfeited their place to save these treasures."

"So it was you who ended up saving your civilization – you dared to disagree with the rulers in charge. There's a little more to you than I expected, Tsaurau. So tell me how your colony ships managed to get through your shield and get past the Xi-fleet?"

"The expeditions left the planet at near light speed. The launch was inherently dangerous, but necessary. That precaution did not guarantee success. We lost some ships to strafing by the Xi-Cruisers. I was on the very last ship that launched. I can still remember every minute detail. The acceleration, even though we had methods to compensate the forces at work, was incredibly painful. I was more afraid during that brief interval than any other time in my life."

Tsaurau's dark eyes searched through the spray of stars above. "There," he said, finger pointing up to a pale blue star, "was home."

Ryan focused on the tiny point of light. *Xeronia. A tiny blue spec of light.*

"Can you point out Earth?"

"No, as we have not been able to find Earth as yet."

"Oh. I thought you knew..."

"I'm sorry, our archives are vast, and the galaxy is much more expansive than our records. In addition, some of our archives are damaged. But I promise you we will continue to search."

"I would appreciate that." Ryan grabbed a small stone and skipped it across the water. "I'd like to know where my home is."

"That is understandable."

A few moments of quiet interceded as both were lost to their own thoughts.

Something jumped in the water, possibly a form of fish. The noise brought Ryan back to their conversation.

"So, you made it here, what did you do with your ship?"

"Our starship no longer exists. It was a vessel designed with intent to provide raw material for colonization. It is integrated throughout the colony's infrastructure, what you see around us. Due to measures such as this, development of our colony has stabilized. We no longer worry about mere survival. We are now able to focus our attention on our true interests, such as science, biology, technology - to continue our quest for knowledge."

"At least you're safe," acknowledged Ryan.

"And while we forge on in relative safety, the races of the Xi-Empire continue to destroy worlds and peoples. They control their subjects using fear and repression. They have infiltrated many quadrants and are now encroaching on this very colony. Although we are well hidden, there are many of us that have grown afraid." Tsaurau looked at Ryan, features projecting an unfamiliar expression.

Was it sadness? There was still so much he didn't understand about these Xeronians.

"This is why no one speaks of home. There is no turning back. Our purpose is to survive. This place is our last and only hope. If the Xi-Empire discovers this colony, we will destroy it first."

"You mean you'd rather kill off everyone here than allow them to take you?"

"Yes. I do hope you understand."

Ryan nodded. "I do. But why not fight back?"

"Engage in warfare? You still do not understand us, do you? Perhaps you are not capable."

"So you'd rather die?"

"There are some of us who still have hope, those who follow the beliefs in the Elders' words - I still have hope."

"Hope won't stop a blaster, or stay a whip."

"We will be protected."

"By what? Your shield couldn't save you."

"We will be protected by the Grafu, as prophesized."

"Really? Sounds a bit superstitious for an advanced alien race."

"Such inspiring words from a man who believes in the existence of luck. I admit the prophecy has taken on its own form - told to our children when they scrape their knees. The Grafu lives on a bittersweet fuel – hate, revenge, suffering to survive, a slave to his burden. It is he who will rise up and destroy the Xi-Empire."

Ryan regarded the aliens' story with indifferent humor. *Such an advanced race, these Xeronians, but to believe in legends! It didn't seem right.*

"Well, I hope your legend will appear soon. I think you're running out of time."

"You must remember that the prophecies are translated from ancient tongue, and are subject to interpretative error. The Elders are not faultless. Some say that you are the Grafu. You are the one to destroy his master."

"Yeah, right," Ryan spit out, laughing. "The Grafu? A destroyer of the might Xi-Empire?" He laughed again. "Bullshit."

"I understand your doubt. How could one destroy the whole Xi-Empire? They have conquered entire civilizations after all."

"Right. So better tell your children I'm not your damned Grafu."

"I did not come here to talk about Xeronia or any of this. I came here to discuss what is bothering you. I wish to help you."

"Help me? I'm fine. I've survived a lot worse than this."

Tsaurau's searching black eyes would not leave him alone.

"Really, I am fine. You have enough on your shoulders, and needn't worry about me."

The alien patted Ryan on the shoulder and rose to his feet. "Tomorrow then, my friend. I will see you tomorrow." He walked away somberly, with the artificial light of two false moons illuminating his way, his thin shoulders carrying an invisible heaviness.

Ryan watched him leave, reflecting to himself.

These people were on the verge of utter elimination, exiled from their home world forever, to live out their lives on this desolate, unforgiving planet with an enemy at their doorstep.

He lay back in the lush grass and stared at the artificial stars. A slight breeze brushed over him. He closed his eyes. Sleep came to him like a nurturing mother. She pulled the walls of reality away and let him dream of a golden sun hovering over gentle waves lapping onto a sandy beach.

Seagulls sang to him from the skies above.

Aviore was there.

She was beautiful, graceful, flowing in white, coming toward him and around him. He felt the warmth of her breath, the coolness of her cheek, a wisp of a soft kiss, and then, sickeningly, she was gone, leaving only darkness, and a coldness that burrowed down into his very soul. He cried out in a slow agony and awoke. The stars glared back at him, bright and piercing. Motionless. *They didn't twinkle. Stars should twinkle, shouldn't they?*

He sat up quickly. The coldness would not leave him.

Aviore, where are you?

* * *

That night Tsaurau was too restless to sleep. He wandered through the corridors, his mind troubled, his thoughts in turmoil. He avoided the Par, not interested in the shared opinion of others, nor their needless urging and prodding.

How would they survive the coming years? Their technology may cloak them for a time, but the Xi-Empire had intrusive search technologies. They had learned so little.

He soon found himself standing in the front of the Chamber of the Elders.

The grand doors eased open without a sound, opening to a quiet darkness. A pale, inviting light shone from within the center of the room. He approached the light, his footsteps echoing ever so slightly with every step.

It was said the ancients could provide guidance if one could open oneself. Sitting down crossed-legged on the floor, he sank into meditation. Years of self-conditioning kicked in. The pulse of his hearts dropped, his body relaxed into a deep transitive state. Whispers settled around him, surrounding, coaxing. He let the voices flow. They were light, wispy, indecipherable. They spoke in a tongue that he did not understand, in a soft rhythm that seemed to match the beat of his alien hearts.

When Tsaurau broke out his trance, his body was stiff and his mind groggy. It took a moment for him to realize he was not alone. The Elders surrounded him, also sitting cross-legged, each holding the other's hands, forming a circle. The Eldest opened her eyes, staring into Tsaurau's. "How do you feel Tsaurau?" she asked.

"My forgiveness, my Eldest, I was just meditating."

"For some time now. Do you know of what you were speaking?"

"I do not believe I was verbalizing," Tsaurau replied innocently.

"But you were my brother! And it was in the tongue of the Ancient Ones. A simple phrase repeated over and over."

He checked the Par. A barrage of thoughts fired through his mind, each carrying with it a different perception of his stasis. It was true. He had no idea such time had passed. His legs attested with sharp aches. He must move.

"My Eldest, my conscious mind was surrendered. I know not of what I said."

"*His time is upon us.*" She looked into his eyes again. "Do you understand what this means?"

"No. I do not."

"But you do. You do not comprehend because we are distracting you. Think."

Tsaurau attempted to focus, fighting through the fog to the more lucid, sharper side. *Something very clear, very precise lay just beyond.* He pushed through the haziness and understood.

The Par echoed with surprise and realization.

"Yes, of course."

The Eldest lowered her eyes; a fan of radiant golden veins pulsated upon her skull. "It is within the Par we share the intimacy of oneness and the joy of realization." She rose from the floor, as agile as an old panther, an inconceivable motion if one considered her age. She delivered her proclamation with eyes glinting of fire, "We must begin, for time, as we know, is fleeting. The Grafu has come."

The council nodded in a silent agreement.

* * *

Zorlog's power grew with every additional ship under his command. Now a labeled outlaw, nothing remained to hold him back. The Empire had proclaimed him a criminal, and it was his intention to ensure that was a costly decision.

Through his many acts of piracy, his reputation as a merciless strategist grew. The Empire's elite military ranks hated yet admired his genius. He never repeated the same move and had no perceivable habits. He was impossible to kill. When his ragtag fleet met up with the Empire's finest, they consistently lost, subjecting its Zuvoks to bruised egos, and the Xi-Empire to costly losses.

Zorlog employed strategies unfamiliar to many. Instead of fleeing from the star cruisers and military bases, he actively engaged them, capturing equipment and drafting many new recruits in the process. But his success was not solely based on his intellect.

Zorlog was a self-appointed leader of a very old ideal. He was a separatist - a Xilozak Purist - standing against any and all Txtian involvement within the Empire. His campaign was simple: all Txtians were to be *cleansed*, at any cost.

The Purist movement ran through the veins of the great Xi-Empire like a cancer. Promoting the ideals of a suppressed and bitter hatred, Zorlog set afire multiple flames. On Xilo, the capital planet, the situation was already destabilizing a tenuous millennia-old peace. Purists spoke out, openly defying persecution, taunting the authorities. Random conflicts seeded the formation of small mobs. Violence led to destruction and death. Policing an aggressive population was becoming impossible.

Few realized, least of all the fathoms of suffering slaves, that at its very foundation, the great Xi-Empire was crumbling. The rift between its two races, the Xilozak and the Txtian, was growing wider with every sadii.

The Emperor was not oblivious to this deterioration. He could see his control was slipping away. This was not the first time such waves of discourse fed through the ruling masters. It was inevitable that social attitudes would swing from one belief system to another. He and his predecessors had seen it many times before. The supporters of unity had been suppressing such movements for centuries. He didn't understand that this time, things were different. The Purists had never had a leader like Zorlog.

The Emperor called for his Karvoks, the Grand Lords of the Xi-Empire's mighty military, the strategists responsible for the conquests of hundreds of races.

They convened in the Hall of the Apocalypse, where all laws were passed and all Empirical decisions proclaimed. The Hall was expansive and intimidating, its walls decorated with the trophies of the oppressed and conquered. Objects of all shapes, sizes, and colors, precious if not priceless, adorned in stark contrast to the gray walls. At the room's center, imprinted into the floor, was a circle of gold with a diameter of seven meters, a black seven-pointed star inlaid within it. At the circle's perimeter, where each of the points of the star touched, seven Karvoks stood at attention. They faced each other across the wide expanse, their faces hidden in the gloominess that engulfed the room. Each wore the insignia of multiple medals, trophies of past accomplishments, each adorned in the blood of their enslaved, and as most would testify to, their highest degree of treachery.

The Karvoks were of mixed descent, some Txtian, others Xilozak. Their hate for one another shadowed only by a shared and cautious respect. To attain the station of Karvok left little doubt of one's capabilities.

The Emperor came out of the shadows stealthily, moving slowly, inspecting each Karvok with red serpent eyes. He towered above them, a sinister presence that resembled more of a demon than any citizen would admit. He was a Zigot, half-Xilozak, and half-Txtian, and as such, his appearance was a marriage of grotesque proportion and incredible strength.

He circumvented the circle, then moved to its center. His voice bellowed through the gigantic room like thunder.

"There was a time once, long ago, when the Xilozaks and the Txtians fought to kill one another. Our hate brought us to the brink of extinction. Do you remember? Are there any here who can remember?"

He cast his dark gaze over the small group. None dared meet it.

Maybe it was too long ago. It is ironic how whole generations can forget their history only to repeat it again and again.

"Allow me to re-educate you. The wars had driven our races to near extinction. It was a time of death and despair. Xilo herself had demonstrated her impatience with us and our lands, once fertile with food, were struck with famine and disease. There was little to eat, and the need to conquer had long faded in the hearts of even the strongest warriors. All wished only to survive. From such a time came the greatest of all things. A truce between our two races was struck in blood. A Xilozak male and a Txtian female were called upon to mate and bring a new peace. A child was born of them, the first of the Zigot. A new world was born with it!"

The Emperor raised his arms and stared upward. He growled out a phrase in an ancient tongue. A luminescent globe dropped down, throbbing of red and orange hues. Within it lay images racing by in a blur of motion, dialect, and dialogue, screeching by at an insane rate.

"Behold our history."

A black finger shot out to the globe. "Unrest! It traces through our past like a pestilence. Peace is again deteriorating back into war. You have all seen the signs. It is your generation that has brought this about."

He waved upward savagely, the globe rose out of sight - a haunting apparition.

The Emperor glared down at his Karvoks.

"Where do your loyalties lie?" he asked softly. "I will learn this. You cannot hide the truth."

A few shuffled nervously in the darkness.

"As you may remember in the teachings, as the first Zigot child grew, he learned he possessed the powers of a leader. On the 13th zanii, the season of the heat, he assumed the throne and pulled our people together. He demanded peace and the citizens complied, or they died. That was the birth of our Empire! For a thousand, thousand zadii, the Zigot League has kept its people from destroying one another, and we have flourished. When will our citizens learn? I have asked myself that question many times. I have crushed the Purists into the mud with my own hand. I have drunk their blood at our feasts, and still, they rage on!"

The muscles of his body strained tensely as he spoke, a tightened spring begging to be released. "There is talk of a new rogue leader named Zorlog. Others have aligned with him, corrupting the state of peace. This cannot be allowed to continue. You will bring him to me - alive!"

One of the Karvoks dared to talk.

"We have not been able to find him. He is constantly on the move. He knows the quadrants well."

The Emperor's red demon eyes burned into the Karvok. "But you will find him," came the Emperor's reply. "All of you! Your time of privileged rank is wearing thin. Bring Zorlog to me, or it will be *your* blood that I will drink!"

He waved them away. Each bowed and graciously stepped back from the circle, carrying with them a very clear message.

The Emperor smiled. *He felt very strong. He could not remember the last time he had felt so strong. The final catalyst of his power had been found. His religion of terror shall begin very soon. He had waited a long time for this Purist Xilozak. He had been patient, for he knew time would deliver a leader with the abilities he required. This one need only be converted... and there were ways to accomplish that.*

* * *

After a troubled night's sleep, Ryan had made up his mind. He could not continue hiding within this mountain. He had to find Aviore and his home. But he couldn't do this alone. He needed Tsaurau's help.

Maybe they would loan him a ship, possibly teach him to pilot it. Maybe...

Tsaurau was not hard to find. He had learned of the alien's favorite spots. He was either in his study labs or at his favorite park on the third level – the one with the skies of his old home world. This time he found him in his lab, busily designing some strange pictorials and marking up a glass-like board with intricate glyphs. The Xeronian's manner seemed different, edgy, possibly nervous. A telltale shaking, a constant moving of limbs, eyes a bit wider than normal.

Almost human.

"Ryan, it is serendipitous to see you. There is something very important I need to discuss with you."

Ryan smiled to himself. *He should never have taught him those fringe words. He always made it a point to use the most extraneous words in his sentences.*

"The Ancients have spoken to me and released me of my doubts. The Prophecy is grounded in truth. I believe you are the Grafu."

Ryan broke out into laughter. He couldn't help himself. "I'm not the boogeyman your weird, paranormal ghosts chant about. Look, I'm glad you think there's some truth to your prophecies, but we've already been through this."

The alien was watching him with an undefined apprehension. Veins on his temples were pulsing noticeably. "I see."

"Try not to be disappointed."

"I shall not. You also wanted to ask me something of importance."

Ryan glanced down at his feet, shifting a bit uncomfortably for a second. "I, ah, have to find someone. I can't stay here. I've a promise to keep."

"But you cannot leave. You are the one we have been waiting for!"

The alien's intensity was unexpected, and to Ryan, seemed so ludicrous it was laughable.

"Look, no one can really predict the future. I don't care how advanced you think you are. Given all your knowledge I don't get how you fall for a bunch of hocus-pocus. It doesn't make sense, in fact, it's contradictory."

"There is more to the nature of the universe than you comprehend. Time is fluid. Causality can be predicted if you have enough data points."

"OK, whatever that means, but I do need to leave, and I can't do this alone. I can't stay here rotting away in safety while the person I love is suffering under those tyrannical bastards."

"Love? So you have found a human mate? Tell me how was this possible?"

"She was another slave."

"I see, and you wish to rescue her. Do you know where she is?"

"And no, and I don't know how to navigate through space or pilot one of your infernal ships. So I don't have a clue how I would rescue her even if I could."

"I believe I can offer you a solution. If you are agreeable, we will teach you all the skills that you need, and we will build you not only a starship, but a warship capable of defeating the mightiest of Xi-Empire's military vessels."

Tsaurau's words hung in the air, an unbelievable offer. Ryan could not reply, momentarily shocked.

"Do you understand? You will have the means to rescue your mate."

"Why? Why would you do this?"

"We will provide you the necessary training and the tools in order for you to dismantle the Xi-Empire. It is that simple."

Ryan half laughed. "You're kidding... aren't you?"

"Kidding? You are implying a jest, humor? Is that correct?"

Ryan nodded mutely.

"This offer is not in jest. This prophecy will materialize. You are the Grafu. It has been verified."

"Verified? I'm an escaped slave, nothing more. Look at this." He yanked up his pant leg, revealing a jagged, ugly scar of a branding. "You see this! They branded me! I was just a rare, lucky bastard that was able to get away from them alive."

"Luck? Yet you regard our Elders' abilities as superstition? Explain to me just how you managed to find our lost ship, how you escaped from enslavement when you should have, most assuredly, perished."

Ryan could think of only one answer. "I don't know. I was in the right place at the right time. The Kalmakans said..."

He stopped. No, he wasn't going to repeat what the Nitche said.

"Maybe someone upstairs guided me."

"Someone upstairs? Are you referring to your religious beliefs - that it was your God that helped you survive? This God guided you to us? What did the Kalmakans say to you? Tell me, Ryan, do you agree with the premise of destiny?"

"Destiny? Back to predicting events are we? What about you, Tsaurau? What do you believe in?"

"Religion for many transcends what is known in our paradigm. Beliefs vary in many cultures. To be more specific, most Xeronians believe in an extension of the physical body. We believe we have what you would describe as souls. To believe such unprovable phenomenon points to other possibilities – including destiny and deterministic futures, but I remain undecided. The reality is that prophecies are destiny foretold, and they have proven to be accurate. I have seen them unfold in my lifetime."

"So you are willing to help me? You can build me a warship?"

"Yes."

"I never told you this before, but Earth is a ripe target. The Xi-Empire already knows where it is."

"They have not, as of yet, attacked your home because there are other closer, and more profitable targets to pilfer. Earth is indeed a future prospect. Their current preoccupation with Signus will keep them distracted for a time." Tsaurau's intention was to relay hope. However, his words left Ryan empty.

"I have to protect my home."

"What I offer is a means to an end. Accept your destiny."

"And in return?"

"We ask you to protect our colony, as well."

Ryan reached out his hand. "Fair enough."

The Xeronian grasped his hand tentatively.

"What's first?"

"You will undergo an operation. We will implant a vaskpar."

"Whoa, what do you mean implant?"

"We are skilled in the development of biotechnology. This device will be grafted onto your brain constructed from your cells, your DNA. The vaskpar will improve your abilities, increase your learning capability, and allow you access to our... information systems. You once asked what the Par is. You will experience this directly. With this, you will learn at an accelerated rate. It is the only way to obtain the knowledge you need in an acceptable timeframe. There is no other way. The vaskpar is the key to opening your mind."

"You infer I don't know how to use my brain already?"

"Precisely, you have untapped potential. We are merely accelerating the pace of natural evolution."

Ryan shot back an irritated glance. "Can't you do something else, an external connection or something?"

"There is no need to worry. Xeronians have a vaskpar implanted when they are mere toddlers. It is a routine operation."

Could Tsaurau be more condescending? But his placid features gave little away of his true intent. Probably didn't even realize.

"Comparing to the likes of you, a human brain is not exactly the same thing," Ryan returned, a bit more feebly than he intended. *The idea of having his skull cut open and some alien device pasted into his brain was far from appealing.*

"Yes, I must agree. Several tests must be conducted in preparation. The operation will be performed tomorrow. Our medical group's preliminary opinion is very positive."

"Oh, so you already looked into this, did you?" he said, with as much sarcasm as possible. "If I don't come out of this alive, it was nice knowing you."

"I personally assure you that you will be safe. I must confess, I look forward to your presence within the Par."

"So this is the answer to the mystery of how little you do talk to one another. You guys are using that vaskpar thing, aren't you?"

"Yes, we relate beyond the spoken word, utilize the language of the mind."

"I still don't see how I'm going to learn everything I need to know, even with this device. I mean, you've been learning since you were a child. I don't even know the basics of your science."

"You will learn. One lesson at a time. We will teach you what you need to know. We have all the knowledge of our people at our disposal. We can certainly formulate a successful approach to training you. But of course, you will have to work very hard."

"Naturally."

He motioned to Ryan with a slight wave to the door. "They are waiting for us."

* * *

The implant operation went without a hitch. Ryan had a nasty headache which lasted for days after. Tsaurau stressed the operation was successful, and such things were normal. It provided him little comfort.

At least it was over, and all his parts were still in working order.

A soothing voice coaxed him. "The pain will subside. How are you feeling?"

He opened his eyes slowly and glanced around. There was no one in the room. *Am I going nuts?*

"This is Tsaurau, Ryan. I am communicating with you through your vaskpar."

It all made sense. The sound wasn't coming from his ears – it was coming from within his mind.

A weird disassociating feeling swept over him.

Relax. Everything's OK.

A door slid open to reveal Tsaurau's smiling, pale face. He had been practicing his human behavior and his attempts were... unnatural.

"Tsaurau, if you don't mind you are scaring the shit out of me."

The alien resumed his original composure. "Very well."

"You will be glad to hear that the configuration of your brain is remarkably similar to ours. The implant has achieved its functional potential. It will slowly integrate with your mind. You will soon notice its effect. The vaskpar is an aid in the management of your memory and thought processes, a functional amplifier, so to speak. It speeds up certain biological processes. Your brain will take advantage of such improvements. Humankind will eventually progress to your anticipated state on its own, given a few thousand years."

"I forgot to ask if this thing would change me."

"Well, of course, this will change you. Can you clarify?"

"I assume I'll know more, recall more, but not like that. What else will it do to me?"

"If you are referring to your personality, that is an aggregation of many factors. The effect of becoming more intelligent will change you to a degree. I cannot anticipate how, exactly. Suffice it to say you will have a better understanding of your environment, and possibly your own body and thoughts, and your reflexes will improve. The vaskpar is an indispensable implant among our people. It is not only a communication device but also a biological aid. This vaskpar itself will learn how your mind works, over time it will help you by re-routing memories, re-organizing what you assimilate."

"Whoa. What do you mean, it's reprogramming me? This thing is going to get rid of my memories?"

"No, merely reorganize. Not all memories will be affected, just certain ones. It can only improve you."

"As long as I stay sane."

"Your sarcasm is noted. Understand the benefits. The vaskpar is capable of isolating and diagnosing problems pertaining to your health. Many of your body's systems work autonomously, requiring little guidance from your brain. Fluctuating levels of chemicals and recurring aches and pains often indicate the presence of parasites, or a new viral infection, or some other kind of degradation within your organs. The vaskpar will help identify these problems more accurately than many of our tests. It can also stimulate your natural systems to repair the body. It will control unwanted voluntary reactions to help your body manage stress. For example, it can raise or lower hormone levels, or manipulate antibodies within your immune system. It can interface with medical systems, serving a vital function during reparative surgery by providing useful information and monitoring of your bodily systems."

"Wow, OK, that's a lot. Regarding communication in the Par, what kind of range does it have? You would think something like that would do cellular damage."

"Precautions have been made to protect your body from any type of radiation damage. The vaskpar's range may be amplified through a local relay device kept close to you."

"Can I also use it to search through your computer archives?"

"Yes, of course, although the term computer is not a fitting label and you will not be able to achieve this without your interface server. The unit is being developed now and you should have access to it shortly."

"Interface server? I don't recall you telling me about this. How will I use it?"

"This interface server will help you navigate the Par. This server will be a constant companion, an alter-ego if you will. Interfacing with it will be similar to reaching out to another party. The connection will occur seamlessly. You will find that once you are familiar with that party, you will be able to automatically initiate a direct connection."

"So I can do this now?"

"Yes, of course." Tsaurau caught his doubting look. "It will become clear when you do this."

"Right. So this interface server thing will make it easier for me to learn, etc..."

"Yes, the vaskpar interface server is unique. By some definitions, one could consider it a sentient life-form."

"Great. A computer with a personality."

"There is one more thing you should know. There is a slight difference between your vaskpar and others, discounting any necessary alterations that were introduced to adjust to your physical framework."

"What do you mean, exactly?"

"Modifications have been done to your vaskpar in order to achieve a higher interchange capability through your interface."

"Why?"

"We needed to do this in order to shorten your learning curve. This introduces a risk, however. We are not 100% sure about the effectiveness of this enhancement. We will, however, be monitoring you very closely. If you find yourself having unusual motor control problems, impulsive thoughts, any kind of complication, report it to us immediately."

He handed a small device to Ryan. "We need you to wear this patch, place it on your forearm. We realize this is bulky, but it is required for the time being. It is an auxiliary monitor and vaskpar control. It will protect you in the event of any possible problem."

Ryan's mouth turned dry. *A remote shutdown device probably. No, they weren't sure about the changes they've made. He was a Guinea Pig at a whole new level.*

"Do not worry, Ryan," Tsaurau consoled. "We will be monitoring you continuously. If we find you are not compatible with this device, we can extract it, but we will not be able to accomplish our goals without it."

"I know. I need to learn and learn fast."

"To teach you to become a pilot, we need to train you in all the aspects of physics, science, astronomy & mathematics. The construction of a vessel that can traverse the tremendous distances of the universe is a major achievement of any race. It encompasses the culmination of a civilization's knowledge."

"You'd give the same credit to the Xilozaks and the Txtians?"

"Initially," conceded Tsaurau. "Although they have stolen much from other races they have conquered and used this technology to leapfrog beyond their natural capabilities. But enough talk of them. You have another step to make before you will be complete. The interface to your vaskpar will be a very powerful one, as I have explained. It will provide the bridge between you and our Xeronian knowledge. Unfortunately, it is not ready. In the meantime, you will need to learn the normal way."

"I don't mind reading."

"Good. Let us start then."

From that point on Ryan's life became very busy. To top it all off, teams of Xeronian doctors constantly followed him around, observing him intently. He knew they meant well, but it was damned irritating.

They also had him on a fairly intensive exercise program, and some exercises they prescribed were very unusual, but Ryan did them anyway. He had learned that further questioning provided little answers, as the doctor's explanations were limited to 'they needed to study certain muscle behaviors' or something similar. Each day it seemed a new member joined the medical team. They were utterly fascinated with the human anatomy. Many of them huddled around each other for lengthy hours, watching as he exercised, intermittently chirping excitedly at some new unforeseen data, unable to contain themselves over their silent discussions which danced through the invisible network called the Par.

By the end of the first week, Ryan was beginning to feel impatient.

When Tsaurau met with him to discuss his progress, Ryan voiced his discontent. Tsaurau was not surprised.

"It will not last for very much longer. You will soon be too busy learning to concern yourself with the doctors. School is scheduled to begin tomorrow."

The next day Ryan began to learn the basics of Xeronian math and science. His progress was slow, and he found himself becoming increasingly frustrated. His professors, who were Xeronian scientists, were quite dry in the personality department, and he found it hard to concentrate on the subject matter. What made it even worse was that most of the teaching was done orally. They did not even attempt to communicate with him over the Par. There were few resources to refer to. For the life of him, he could not understand how he could learn enough to pilot a starship, or even understand their most basic principals of science.

In their next meeting, Tsaurau could sense Ryan's troubles.

"We are used to relying upon the Par to provide the necessary references. It is our oversight. Your vaskpar interface will be complete tomorrow. You will have access to the whole Xeronian library of knowledge. We will be stepping up your education program. You will learn even in your sleep." Thin lips curled in a Xeronian expression of support.

The vaskpar server interface was brought online the next day, very early. The monitor in Ryan's room sprung to life, lighting up the dark room where he slept.

"I am Timlin. I am notifying you that we are initiating your vaskpar server interface. We are requesting a link. Can you respond?"

Ryan looked at the monitor, his mind still fuzzy. "What?"

"We are requesting a link. Can you respond, please?"

"How?"

"Concentrate on returning the sequence we send you."

A sound within his mind, intermittent clicks.

He thought the sequence back. The next message surprised him.

"Hello Ryan, I am your vaskpar server unit."

"Hello," Ryan thought back, his mind now clear from the haze of sleep. The noise emanating through the monitor had left him little choice by now.

Did they ever sleep?

"We have established a link. We will need to refine the protocol parameters but the exchange looks excellent."

"Timlin!" growled Ryan. "Do you mind telling me what the hell is going on?"

"Why, yes," he exclaimed, hairless eyebrows twisted into an Earth-like frown in a Xeronian look of astonishment. "You are linked to the Par via your server interface. Do you understand this?"

"Yes," growled Ryan, "but why did you have to wake me!"

"I see." He leaned away from the monitor in order to confer with his peers and appeared again, a second later. "We apologize for any inconvenience. Please resume your sleep."

The monitor went blank, leaving him alone to his thoughts. *What was this Par going to be like? Why did they have to wake him in the middle of his sleep? Damn it!*

He tossed, turned, and twisted his body in many different contortions before finally fading off. Later, a familiar voice woke him. It was a voice within his mind, but it was not Tsaurau's. It sounded different – which was strange given that there really was no 'sound'. The voice was low and friendly. The resonance was soothing. A slight tickle.

"Good morning Ryan. It is time to rise."

Ryan questioned it back, "And what do I call you?"

"Whatever you wish. We are to be friends. In fact, my personality has been specifically designed to be compatible with yours. It makes for a more interesting conversation, does it not?"

Ryan, slightly amused, had to agree.

"I have been designed from your imprint, yet I am also quite different. I will be most assuredly your best friend, from this time on, until the end of your or my life."

This made Ryan laugh openly. "You seem pretty sure I can stand you. I'm not so sure I like this idea. A nosy computer that is pushy as well as arrogant."

The reply came slightly delayed. "That is understandable. I will remain on standby until you request me. Goodbye."

Silence followed. *Strange. Gone like that. Maybe he had hurt its feelings. Does it have feelings?*

Either way, there was more urgent business at hand. He was scheduled to meet the vaskpar technicians within the next half-hour.

He showed up a bit late. About a dozen Xeronians were moving busily about the laboratory when he arrived. The one in charge named Tzokbin was visibly irritated by his tardiness.

"Please expedite your actions! We have much work to do!"

He pointed to a chair. "Sit!"

Ryan complied, eager to get over with whatever they were planning for him today.

"And what, my good doctor Tzokbin, are we going to do today?"

"Today? Oh yes, this *day* we complete the refinements of your vaskpar interface, streamline communications and address any outstanding problems. We will be running many tests. We will require your undivided attention."

Clasps came out from around the back of his chair and pulled him tight against it. Steel bands bit down upon his wrists. A large machine swung down from the ceiling and was brought to bear on his right eye, a half-meter from his face.

"What's the idea?" He squirmed and quietly cussed as straps pulled taut all over his body.

Great. I can hardly move.

"We require you to remain absolutely still for a number of hours."

Hours? He tried to say something but the chin straps had locked his jaw closed. *He couldn't stand being tied down. He could feel the panic swelling. He had to calm down.*

"Vaskpar Interface."

"I am here."

"I need some help."

"You must calm down. I will aid you if you desire."

"Yes!"

He could feel it settle over his body. A gentle, soothing wave, relaxing, calming. He could feel his pulse slow, his body sink into a relaxed, eased state.

"Wow, thanks. How did you do that?"

"I merely did what you could have done yourself. I will need to go offline. But I will visit you again, in a short time. Will you be OK?"

Tzokbin swung a large machine over in front of him. A red light glared into his eyes.

"Ryan, adrenaline levels are rising again."

He focused. Like the server said, nothing he couldn't do himself. Stay calm, stay cool. "Yeah, I should be alright, thanks."

Timlin leaned over. "This will not inflict any significant pain."

It won't hurt a bit. That's what you're supposed to say. It won't hurt a bit. Damn chin strap.

After five hours of total restraint, they finally let him up. He had some awful muscle cramps, but the pain in no way exceeded his miserable temperament.

That would be the last time they did something like that.

* * *

"Well, what's next Tsaurau?"

They were both sitting in his apartment in front of an artificial fireplace Ryan had requested. He found it made the place more comfortable, in addition to the pictures on the walls, the lanterns, the woven rugs, it all helped take away the antiseptic feel of the room.

The lights were low. Ryan's body was sunk deep into his favorite, comfortable chair, his feet up on an ottoman. He could smell a wisp of cherry wood smoke in the air.

He had to complement those engineers.

Both of them were drinking a facsimile of apricot brandy, another request of Ryan's. The Xeronians had done an exemplary job of its reproduction, down to that last detail, including the alcohol content. He took another swig; it burned going down and left a warm glow in his stomach.

Tsaurau was taking his time answering. The Xeronian was in a mellow mood – which was not at all like him. The brandy was doing its work, and the alien physiology was not immune from its effects. Just the same, it seemed his alien friend was appreciating this chemically induced state, even if it took some effort to communicate clearly.

"The next thing, I believe you would call it, in Earth slang, is power learning. You will...you'll be online with the knowledge database every hour of every day. Your vaskpar interface is ready to initiate the program. It is up to you now, whenever you feel ready for it."

"Whenever I feel ready!" Ryan chuckled. "Now that's a switch. Those doctors of yours could learn a little bit from you."

Tsaurau laughed - a human reaction he had learned from Ryan. Xeronians do not laugh, at least the younger ones didn't. The older ones, well, they had their own ways. The Earthman was an obvious influence on him. Not all of it good, at least not socially. He, of all Xeronians, should not acquire such 'bad habits'.

"Yes, Ryan, the doctors are known to be a determined group. Are you ready?"

"Yes, the sooner, the better."

"I have a question regarding a discussion we had a time ago when I told you about your destiny. You mentioned a promise, that you needed to find someone. Who is this person?"

"A Signite woman named Aviore Tem, the daughter of the Governor of Signus. We met on a slavership when I was first captured. I was injured pretty badly by a Xilozak. She nursed me back to health. I would have died had she not been there."

"I see. What happened to her?"

"They separated us, took her away."

Tsaurau stared at him solemnly, his large head bobbing slightly side-to-side, "You believe... that she is still alive?"

"I don't know for sure. I just feel she is. Either way, I have to find her."

"Your task is a difficult one. The known galaxy is immense, the universe, unfathomable."

"I know the odds, Tsaurau," he shot back, a bit too harshly.

A long silence followed. Tsaurau seemed to be considering his problem, possibly posing questions to the Par, and waiting for the answers with typical well-practiced Xeronian patience. Others were out there, their minds woven into the Par as intimately as their own bodies. The Par had been a part of each of them from birth. Every Xeronian had learned long ago they were not alone. Help was out there. Shortly, the answers trickled down in a colorful grace, responses from other minds within the colony, from brothers and sisters who had been listening.

Ryan could communicate within the Par, but he chose to remain silent. Since the day of his implant, he had not truly adopted it, and probably never would. It was, above all, uniquely Xeronian. One should not expect others to fully adapt one's ways.

"We know of Signus. Its people are genetically identical to you. This one you call Aviore, she is your... mate, your female partner? You feel love for her?"

Ryan nodded. "Yes. I do. I thought you Xeronians would have isolated this love thing down to its chemical architecture by now. Put some artificial controls on it, labeled it within some test tube."

"This sarcasm you are displaying is not contributing to our relationship. I must confess, your behavior is a mystery to me sometimes. Regardless, I will confer with the Elders. It is possible that the Eternals may have provided some secrets to your future."

"Forgive me for my insolence, Tsaurau, but as I'm already on a roll. I have to tell you I do not believe in your Eternals. I do not believe in whispers from the dead, or murmuring well-meaning ghosts. I play the cards I am dealt and I do not profess to know what tomorrow will bring. Your beliefs do not match mine Tsaurau; I am a lone man, light-years from my home. I have only my idealism to keep me sane."

"If it is any comfort to you, our scientists have long ago abandoned the need to explain everything. I can state, and this includes almost all Xeronians, that we have managed to find inner peace. We strive to improve our talents and make ourselves the best we can be. As for your beliefs, I can say you do not have an exclusive right to hope, or to belief that you can make a difference.

"Touché." Ryan swirled his glass. "It must be difficult to have a criminal in your midst?

Within the Par lies a collective conscience that no one can truly hide from. It is impossible for evil to lurk there."

"Unless all of you become evil."

"Evil, as an idea, is purely self-destructive. There is a balance that must be maintained. That we understand."

"And the idea of religion – of God?"

"There are but a few that have the gift to reach beyond this physical life, and see the greater universe. The Elders have told us with conviction that the voices of the Eternals are real. I believe in a larger reality, and all of its possibilities."

"Well, I'll give your Eternals the benefit of the doubt, then. But that still doesn't help me out right now. I feel the time slipping by. I need to get out there. I need to start searching."

"I do understand." He got up, patting him on the shoulder as he left. Before he stepped out of the door, he stopped to say, "It is a good invention, this brandy."

"Thanks," replied Ryan to a closing door. That night he proceeded to empty the remains of the bottle and fell asleep in the chair. The crackle of the fire brought him restless dreams, images of home around a campfire, faces that lacked definition.

* * *

The next morning started with a throbbing headache. The brandy may have tasted good, but it left a lasting impression.

A familiar voice sounded from the back of this mind. "Hello, I am requesting a brief conversation."

"Consider me a captive audience," moaned Ryan groggily.

"I have been instructed to start the teaching sequence."

"I gather you have to start this today?"

"Yes, as of this moment."

"Great. You do realize I have a headache."

"Our memory informs me that this headache was self-inflicted by alcoholic beverage consumption."

"Yes, I can't deny that."

"Well, I cannot deny you another day of knowledge deprivation. I am initiating the program."

Ryan began to hear a murmur in his mind. It was low and indecipherable. His headache seemed no worse – at least not yet.

"Computer, explain the murmur."

"That is the teaching program. It is running at the fastest rate at which your mind can absorb. If you concentrate, you can decipher what is being said. This program will be running indefinitely as long as a link is maintained."

"That's pretty easy learning."

"Your training will not stop here. Your classes will continue as scheduled as well."

"Great. What's my schedule?"

"You have 10 minutes before your first session."

Ryan jumped up and headed for the bath. "Thanks for the warning!"

"You're welcome."

The day and then the month literally flew past. He requested additional visual monitors to be placed in his room in order to help him retrieve and suspend related information. The Xeronians were baffled at his request. They had little use for any equipment that presented information in such a way, as they felt their vaskpars were superior to any form of visual medium. They complied, however, replacing the existing monitor with a new version that covered the whole wall of his small apartment.

He studied day and night. Graphics and pictures blinked on and off as he plowed through the Xeronian sciences, math, history, languages, and art. He found himself able to recall tremendous amounts of information at a whim.

This vaskpar thing was working.

His knowledge was increasing almost exponentially. The murmur in the back of his mind was constant. It had become unnoticeable, a background of whispers.

The Xeronians were also very busy. They had a starship to design and build. It was to be the most advanced they had ever constructed. Such a tool had to be capable of outperforming the best of the Xi-Empire's arsenal of warships. Their progress was painfully slow. The design team had degraded into factions, each wanting their own philosophies to be entrenched into the ship's architecture. The most common of all Xeronian traits, the ability to work as a one, degraded into a constant barrage of foul-ups and unusual debate.

In response, Tsaurau did something unprecedented. He called a meeting. The Par would no longer be the only forum of all thoughts.

Chief-of-Engineering, Tanaka, started the discussion, albeit, soundlessly over the Par. "Our engineers are missing too many details. We have little knowledge in constructing a starship that is to be used in war. It is my opinion that we lack the imagination to build such a craft. There is also the question of experience, which all our teams are lacking. That is very necessary in order to put this ship together in the allotted time."

All heads turned to the concerned face of the Chief-of-Sciences, and head councilor, Tsaurau. "We all concede that something additional must be done. Do the Elders of the high council agree as well?"

They acknowledged acceptance, although not being physically present.

A gruff 'voice' sounded from the lower council. It was the Magistrate-of-Agriculture, Targoff. "Is the building of this starship so beyond our means? I cannot believe our proud engineers cannot construct such a basic vessel."

"What would you know of the technology required, Targoff?" retorted

Tanaka. "This is no ordinary vessel. It must be capable of exceeding all previously established performance metrics. The scale of offensive weaponry required to outfit this vessel is unprecedented."

Master-Shipbuilder, Tmaurau, interjected for the first time. "We need not debate the smallest point of every detail. It is of no benefit. We require a solution to this dilemma immediately. Time is our most dire of enemies."

"Yes, the Xi-Empire survey ships have already passed through this system once," added Targoff. "For what reason is it that you cannot make a decision on what the best design is?"

"The problems are fundamental and numerous. There is no one 'best design', only untested theories," Tmaurau replied. "A balance must be achieved that will not undermine any imperfections in our finished product. We simply cannot afford to fail."

It was the Eldest, Tseman, who offered her wisdom. She elucidated, and all listened. She carefully projected each word with intent. "Balance is elusive. If the balance of the universe must be maintained, the answers of problems must exist as long as the problems present themselves to be known. The answers, you all know, rarely come from expected sources. That is the rare beauty of this universe, and of our lives."

Silence settled within the Par, of reflection.

"I feel there is one amongst us that has a solution but is hesitant." Her eyes searched the crowd, finally coming to rest upon one Xeronian. "Please, Tsaurau, you must share it with us."

He nodded to her in respect. "I am not an engineer. I have never built a starship, and I must confess, I am not comfortable offering my opinion."

"Speak your mind, Tsaurau," coaxed Tseman, "We shall listen."

"Very well, I have had this idea for a time. I have given it careful consideration. I believe the answer lies within the Maskaffa Spider."

Targoff scoffed, "That is an anomaly of historical archives. I doubt that it exists. It is a tale provided through a delusional spacefarer."

That started an open forum for active debate. The Par flooded with the pressure of noise.

Tseman put up her hand, and silence began to settle. "I have learned in my years. Knowledge need not always be divulged until its time." She stared at Targoff. "And it is not wise to reject the wisdom of the Eternals."

Tsaurau interjected, "I will attest I believe the legend of the Maskaffa Spider and the starships that lie within it. The archives are not fully intact, however. Can you tell us where this can be found, my Eldest?"

"When I was young, we also had stories that talk of the hole in the stars, and the long, dead corpse of the Maskaffa Spider. The stories stated there is but one way in and death was assured to anyone foolish enough to venture too close. I too was skeptical, until I personally encountered the Spider. Yes, I know where it is. I have seen it myself."

The Par was again quiet.

A few rogue thoughts percolated. *Had Tseman gone mad?*

"It was, as all of you know, very long ago. Some of you may remember the demise of 784-3. It was a very large transport ship. It passed through a microscopic black hole and imploded. There was little left but twisted fragments and veritable few survivors. I was on the only rescue vessel that was able to reach the site of the disaster. We estimated the flight vectors and traced it back to the original point of collision. The transport had passed through the outer edge of the Maskaffa Spider. Knowing the legend, we felt it best to map the entire region and designate it as *empty space*, although it is far from empty. That is why the library's star charts do not show it."

"What is the significance of the name?" asked Tanaka.

"From a distance, at the proper angle, the spider appears to have eight legs, perched on a web of gold. The image is very clear, very realistic. It is truly a frightening formation of celestial matter. The area within it is incredibly dense and very unstable, with antimatter clouds and miniature gravitation wells. A large gravity well lies less than a light-year away from the Maskaffa Spider. The gases of a surrounding hydrogen cloud sweep past the formation and blind many a weary ship from its dangers. Tracings are often affected, clouded by all bands of radiation. Navigation through such an area is difficult, impossible if one is unlucky enough to lose one's point of reference."

"If the place is so dangerous why venture there?" asked one of the crowd.

"It is, in itself, a treasure. The Ancient Ones had the means to traverse through this hostile space into the very heart of the Spider. It is in this very location a sphere of peaceful, unscathed space resides. A place such as this provides a naturally impenetrable fortress and unremarkable safety."

"How did the Ancient Ones find it?"

"I do not know all the history. I do know that the Ancient Ones found it useful, and proceeded to enhance it during Flukken War for their own purposes. It has been recorded that they added natural hazards to it, ensuring that there was only one safe path in. They stationed their fleet within the Spider and used it as a central command station. It was also a meeting area for the Flukken ambassadors during peace negotiations at the end of the war. Flukken warships were brought there by both sides of the conflict, as a sign of their good will."

"But Tseman, the remnants of the Flukken civilization was overrun by the Xi-Empire half a millennia ago. They did not find any evidence of such a fleet, or the Maskaffa Spider."

"The true Flukken civilization had long since disappeared before the Xi-Empire arrived, and the Xi-Empire is not known for thoroughness. The fact that the Xi-Empire did not find the Maskaffa Spider does not mean it no longer exists."

"What could we learn from a civilization that died out eons ago Tsaurau, why even bother with this?"

Tsaurau looked back at curious eyes. They wanted to know why he would propose such an idea. The same look was in their faces when Tseman had stated she had seen the Spider.

Skeptics until they are presented with the full context. His idea was absolutely reasonable.

"The historical archives are rife with erroneous entries and fragments data, that is true. I've spent considerable time and effort reviewing this data and I have surmised to fill in the gaps. When the Ancient Ones encountered the Flukken civilization, it was waging an internal war. The capabilities of the weapons, the starships, the technology described was impressive, even in comparison to the Ancient Ones' technologies. Their technology was well beyond anything we have ever devised to this moment in time. The Ancient Ones helped them find peace, at least for a time. The weapons of destruction were either destroyed or brought to the quarantine area – the Maskaffa Spider. To my knowledge, the war fleet still remains."

"And what of the Flukkens?" asked Targoff, genuinely interested.

"A few years after the negotiated peace, they disappeared. Evidence found supports another internal war had started, new weapons had been utilized, probably biological-mechanical hybrids. That became the war that had ended all of their wars."

"I assume we have the key or is this discussion a waste of energy?" Tmaurau prodded.

Tseman pointed to Tsaurau with a shaky hand. "There is much more to this story of the Flukkens, but that is for another time. We do know the way in, as the key is buried discretely within our own history archives, if you know where to look. This knowledge was passed down to us by the Ancient Ones. If you are confident what you require is there, then assemble an expedition and go. But you have only seven days. Do not go beyond that time."

Tseman stood up and the rest of the Council of the Elders followed suit. "Tsaurau," she spoke in a dark voice. "I repeat. Only seven days – and within the largest ship, you may find an artifact of the ancient wars. Do not awaken it, please."

He saw the genuine concern on her face. "Very well, we will avoid that vessel, my Eldest."

A small smile spread on her thin lips - a human smile, then she left, limping slowly from the circle. The rest of the council also slipped away, leaving only its youngest member, Taldig.

"The Council of the Elders is now adjourned until the return of the expedition."

Then he stepped away, leaving the lower council to continue on to discuss the details for the pending expedition. They had only seven days to carry it out. Archaic maps were delivered to them from the Chamber of the Elders. These were celestial navigation maps, and within them were the navigation coordinates of the Maskaffa Spider, hidden under the guise of *empty space*. Additional maps provided precious clues to the navigational course into its center. An expedition was planned with a total crew of 90. By the end of the day, three small ships were pulled from their stored state and prepped for flight.

The launch was set for the following day.

Tsaurau found Ryan in the library, busily learning celestial navigation procedures. He informed Ryan of the news, but the Earthman hardly noticed him. He was buried in his studies, deep in concentration.

Tsaurau left, too busy to feel offended.

The Maskaffa Spider was waiting.

* * *

6. Seed

Three ships left the Xeronian colony trailing behind a string of navigational probes. The probes, with only a slight energy signature, were less likely to be spotted by a Xi-Empire patrol; conversely, they served as the long distance eyes for the small convoy.

Tsaurau was aboard the lead ship, monitoring ongoing activity within the Par with impatient interest. This network was limited, reflecting only the minds of the crew. In comparison, it was quiet, devoid of the bustling life it mirrored on Xeronia.

It did not help that they were also utilizing the highest security procedures possible. But this was standard protocol, regardless. Nothing critical was to be reviewed within the Par. There would be no intellectually stimulating interactions on this trip.

He visited the bridge to scan the view of passing stars. The navigation officer appreciated the company and announced the news verbally to him prior to passing a condensed summary onto the Par.

"The gravitational sensors show a dense array of small black holes throughout the whole quadrant. We will reduce velocity for maneuverability."

"It is very clear to me this will be difficult to navigate through," agreed Tsaurau.

"Yes, Councillor, most assuredly."

Others joined them on the bridge; eyes focused on the scene that lay before them in the heavens. The sight was both beautiful and chilling. An eight-legged spider, 10 million kilometers wide, hung from an invisible web. Golden lines of celestial gases shot outward to form its long thin legs. They pointed downward from a gaseous body, jutting out and down, ending in a point, poised, awaiting unsuspecting prey. The head was a bright gaseous cloud, which held a blood red sun within its center.

The three ships slipped under its abdomen, passing between the spindly legs, and under the gaseous head. By now, all available power was being diverted to the tracing sensors, and disruptors were on standby, ready to destroy any threatening chunk of debris in their path.

The Par muddied with strenuous thoughts, the crew nervous. A small mistake in navigation could spell disaster. The Captain cleared the Par with his formidable presence. "Enough of this. Mind your stations. Navigation, what is our status?"

"I am not able to get a positive fix on the quasar emissions. This was not anticipated. The surrounding area is populated with gravitational anomalies. Most are miniature black holes less than two kilometers in length. The gravitational flux is distorting our tracing signals."

"Can you lock in a course?"

"I cannot, Captain," the frustration ebbed over the edges of his thoughts. "It is possible we are approaching a very dense area, but I cannot be sure because of the induced distortion."

The Captain made a quick decision. "Navigation, bring us to full stop."

He turned to face Tsaurau, and spoke quietly, keeping his thoughts closed off from the Par. "Forgive them, for they are young and inexperienced. We need time to establish a reference point and set our course. I do not know how long this will take."

"We need not hurry, Captain. It is better to arrive there fully intact."

"The celestial charts we are utilizing to navigate are very old. I am certain key formations have changed. There is a very strong possibility that the original route will no longer be viable."

"Maintain your faith, Captain."

"You respond as an Elder would. It is worrisome."

Tsaurau clucked at the humor. *The Council could not have chosen a better Captain. To remain calm in the face of the unknown requires special control.*

"Councillor, you need not remain on the bridge. I will let you know when we are ready."

"Thank you for your consideration, Captain." Tsaurau bowed and left. Instead of going to his quarters, which were rather stark, he wandered through the ship, eventually ending his trek at the observation lounge. He sat alone and studied the strange, colorful sight of the heavens through the large viewports. Their light shimmered, pulsated, and danced in the darkness.

Indeed the stars were alive.

A request came over the Par: he was summoned to the conference room for a meeting. The navigation team and all three captains were present.

The ships have obviously docked together in a cluster. Unusual, but these were unusual circumstances.

His Captain greeted him with a quick nod. "Now that we are all here, let us present the situation. Our discussion must remain private for now."

The lead navigation officer cleared his throat as he thumbed on the holographic image of the quadrant. It hovered silently above the center of the round conference table, turning slowly.

"As you well know, this quadrant is littered with black holes, charged gases, and random debris."

He pointed under the spider to the three red dots. "We have managed to navigate approximately one-fourth of the way through." He indicated further down the underside of the spider to a small blue sphere.

"The area marked is our destination. We needed to stop in order to recalibrate our reference points. There are subtle discrepancies between our charts and the physical measurements we have calculated. It has been an involved task. Many things have changed since these charts were recorded. We also have to take into account the natural mutation of frequency within our reference quasars. We have dispatched additional probes to aid our tracing sweeps. We need to incorporate as much information as possible into our model of this region."

The Captain spoke up. "Our efforts are imprecise. The data from our sweeps are distorted, undoubtedly caused by the many dense bodies surrounding us. But, with a little imagination, it is possible to make out ghost images of the alleged ships within our destination area. All things considered, it seems they do exist. That is, of course, from an optimistic perspective."

The navigator continued on. "Using the process of tracings super-imposed over gravitonic telemetry we were able to clearly determine that there is indeed, a clear region identified by the blue sphere, here," he pointed to the rotating holograph.

"Then let us complete our calibrations and proceed," Tsaurau suggested.

"There is another issue," added the officer, hesitantly. "We did not recognize this until now. The charts have embedded within them a symbolic encryption algorithm, which introduces a subtle, but significant error. We noticed this once we superimposed our calibrations onto our charts. Without the solution to this algorithm, continuing on could be very hazardous."

"Our own charts? How can this be?" asked the other Captain.

"These charts are very, very old. This was, of course, done with intention."

"Tseman did mention something about a key," Tsaurau offered.

"If I may add one more point," insisted the navigation officer. Less than five thousand kilometers ahead, we will encounter a wall of debris and exotic matter. The course combinations to penetrate into this are almost infinite, however very few will allow us to traverse safely through. The charts have been accurate to this point. I trust they will provide a safe route if we can decipher this algorithm."

For a moment the room was silent. "May I suggest," stated Tsaurau, "that the vessels of concern are stored within an extraordinarily safe area intentionally. We must recognize this achievement of the Ancient Ones and embrace this challenge. It may require considerable time."

The members nodded in agreement.

"May I also suggest that although very little has been stored within our library it is possible certain data has been missed. I believe it is time to re-examine all available content. I expect that there is a key hidden within this data. Captain, do you agree?"

The Captain nodded, "I do concede of the possibility. However, such research must also remain closed to the Par to ensure the security protocols are maintained."

"Captain, this will add significant time to our efforts," complained the navigation officer. "Surely we can utilize the Par for such a monumental task."

"Perhaps we should contact Elder Tseman. She may know of this elusive cipher."

"No. We cannot risk any further exposure with external communications."

The navigation officer's gaze turned to the floor.

The Captain shifted his stance slightly. "Perhaps our local Par does not breach our protocols in any significant degree. You may utilize the local Par at your discretion, but I must remind you, we must be vigilant in keeping such information guarded. The Par security layers are not infallible."

Agreement came with the double blinking of black eyes throughout the room.

The Captain nodded to the navigation officer. "I do expect that you take the lead on this initiative, and use as many resources as you require, everyone else resume your stations. Tsaurau, will you join me for dinner?"

"I would be delighted, Captain."

The Captain walked in-step with Tsaurau as they left. The Par was already alive with the chaos of freethinking.

He spoke softly. "I must concede, Councillor, solving such puzzles is better left to younger minds."

"I must agree. My level of interest in such mental challenges is waning. Perhaps it is the understanding of our true dilemma that weighs us down."

"Perhaps," reflected the Captain.

They entered the Captain's quarters and quickly made arrangements for nourishment. The food was excellent, though Tsaurau knew the Earthman Ryan would certainly consider it bland. After dinner, they reminisced of past expeditions, in the times of old Xeronia.

Their conversation was cut short when an announcement came over the Par. A possible solution was at hand. They rushed to the bridge, Tsaurau a step ahead, slightly excited at the possibilities.

The navigation officer stood ready with his report. "Captain, Councilor," he acknowledged. He pulled up a graphic with the Par, a collection of symbols representing numbers and algorithms. "You may see here," he stated confidently, twisting a few of the formulae presented to a modified state. "The problem was relatively easy once we analyzed and isolated the verses from the Maskaffa legend. We exposed a simple trinary pattern, all I had to do was follow standard encryption decoding and..."

The Captain cut him short. "You have a course?"

"Yes, Sir! And I have made the all required adjustments allowing for mutation of the timeline. We have cross-checked it with our model and we have determined that this adjustment will allow us to reach our destination. This is a very unique balance of..."

Again the Captain held up his hand cutting him short, "Please, inform the other ships to review the course."

"The other navigators have acknowledged, Captain."

"And I wish to visualize this modified course."

The Par filled with an image swathed in a bright mirage of colors. The course cut through the collage in bright red, a mishmash of vectors with varying angles.

"Quite complicated, with multiple wait nodes," the Captain commented.

The officer clucked approvingly at his Captain's astuteness. "Designed delays," explained the officer. "We will be progressing through a maze. Our encroachment must be timed precisely."

"The area ahead of us is truly remarkable," stated Tsaurau.

"Yes, it is too dense to be wholly natural. The chunks of debris are primarily methane and ammonia ice. But there are traces of heavy irons as well. Although the majority of the matter can be traced back to local cloud accretion, the exceptions are outstanding."

"How confident are we about this course?" asked the Captain.

"Reasonably – no, very," he corrected himself. "Our extrapolation model is within 0.5% accuracy. Further adjustments will be needed as we advance. We will continue to update our model with actual measurements as we progress."

"These spirals, here, what are they?"

"As you noted, the course is based on precisely timed course adjustments. I will demonstrate."

The red line collapsed to a dot. "We are here." The image swirled, the line advanced, leaving its tail to be cut by endless streams of wandering matter. The point advanced jerkily, stopping for different intervals at each node, and finally coming to rest within the blue sphere.

"We will need to alter our velocity multiple times."

"How tight is it?"

"It is true, our projected image is deceiving. A whole fleet could pass through this passage. But a word of caution - there is a high probability of failure if one strays from the mapped course."

"How did the Ancients develop this?" questioned the Captain.

"I am not sure, though I must agree such a feat is not trivial. One must consider how all these bodies interrelate to create a relatively stable formation over time. It is truly incredible."

"Very well. Enough discussion, as we cannot lose sight of our goal," interrupted the Captain. "Let us proceed."

When the ships entered the maze, the Par flooded with the symbolic jargon emanating from the navigation teams. Tsaurau stayed on the bridge throughout the ordeal watching as small moons of ice tore past them with silent deadliness.

When they reached their destination, a reflection of wonderment settled within the Par. They were in the eye of the storm, a haven that was spherical in shape with a diameter of approximately ten thousand kilometers. Its outside edge was ringed with nebulous clouds of antimatter, and floating cylinders of intense gravitation, but within the safety of this sphere, floated the strangest collection of starships they had ever seen. Vessels of all shapes and sizes drifting silently, pointing haphazardly in every direction.

The tracing officers initiated their scans.

"53..76..103 confirmed ships!"

"Most agreeable," announced the Captain. "The subject of legends. This indeed is marvelous!" He turned to look a Tsaurau smugly. "It is also pleasing that we have arrived in one piece. My faith in our young need not be awry."

Tsaurau barely heard him. His attention focused on the viewscreen. An immense vessel lay directly ahead, the viewscreen capturing only a portion of it, and other surrounding ships were dwarfed in comparison.

"That must be the mothership Elder Tseman referred to."

"Incredible!" exclaimed the Captain. "Perhaps we should board it first."

"No. Tseman ordered me directly to avoid this vessel," warned Tsaurau.

"Why?" asked the Captain, the veins in his forehead turning blue in total surprise.

"I truly did not inquire further. We will board every ship in this area if we have to, but not that one."

The surprised look left the Captain's face and gave way to an irritated flush of pale pink, a human blush but a Xeronian look of annoyance. "Very well, Councillor. Prepare to dispatch the reconnaissance teams."

The three Xeronian ships disbanded to a defined search pattern. Each ship was systematically boarded. They were looking for certain engineering qualities, and hopefully, an intact computer core. Each vessel was found to be empty of all life, their power reserves were minimal to non-existent. The atomic conversion engines had long since cooled to an ineffective radiation level.

News came over the Par. "Party 22 reports a successful find."

"Captain?" hinted Tsaurau with a tinge of excitement.

"Converge on that ship," ordered the Captain.

The Xeronian starship snaked through the winding maze of ancient vessels to the reported location of search party 22. They came upon a very old vessel. Roughly the same size as the Xeronian lead ship. Its outside hull was marred with many scars of some ancient war.

The Captain's reaction was uncharacteristic. The images he projected over the Par were varied, erratic. Tsaurau looked over at him.

"I know this ship. I believe it is an older scout, destroyer class, a unique and very dangerous vessel. Long-range high acceleration capability with diverse firepower. The archives had stated that all of these ships were destroyed after the Flukken wars."

Tsaurau still eyed the Captain cautiously. *Such an outlandish knowledge of the machines of war. It was uncommon, to say the least.*

The Captain caught his gaze and nodded to him knowingly. "Understand, we have all changed since the death of Xeronia. I am a student of history and therefore, of war. I embrace that which I detest, so I may understand it. Councillor, you are too quick to judge one who does not share your beliefs."

"Captain, you have your responsibilities. It is I who would make a poor captain," replied Tsaurau. "This particular ship does not seem, in any way, more superior to the others surrounding it. Its mere size indicates an inferior standing."

"These vessels are significant because they were built purposefully for the hardships of war by the Ancient Ones. They served to protect the ambassadors when they traveled through hostile areas where rogue factions were prone to attack."

"How do you know of this? The information about the Ancient Ones and the Flukken wars is far from intact."

"You are aware that the Ancient Ones provided us with their historical archives, are you not?"

"Yes, but I considered those archives lost in the Great War."

"On the contrary. The information exists. It was transferred to our colony ship the day we left Xeronia. The Elders thought it wise at the time."

"Where are these archives?"

"There are reasons such knowledge is not commonly known, and why it is not open and available on the Par. If the Elders grant you access you must exercise a strict caution."

"I will respect such a condition."

"You must."

He turned his attention back to his officers. "Tracing, scan the remaining vessels, are there any others similar to this one?"

"No, Captain."

"So, this may be the last one in existence."

The Captain queried the Par for the officer in charge and closed a peer-to-peer link.

"Officer Tsebeck."

"Captain," beseeched the officer," please bear with me. The network links are fragile with all the surrounding interference."

"Officer Tsebeck, report please," the Captain requested.

She surged back through the Par, although weakly, and some data shifted into illegible from the interference. "The vessel ... sound ... server core intact. A trickle charge ... capacitors. Do not ... tools for a core transfer."

"Can this vessel move under its own power?"

"Negative, ...tain. Main drive ... shutdown ... long. The internal burner ...ation temperatures ... zero. Not enough p...er to start up the converters."

"We now have a lock, Captain," interjected the communications officer.

"With a considerable effort we may be able to determine the integrity of the antimatter gravitational fields, but my engineers do not think they have the time or the knowledge to initiate the start-up procedures. Even if we did, it would take up considerable time for the transfer reaction plates to reach operating temperature to allow them to work effectively. This is the only way we know of to charge the capacitors and get the antimatter generation flow up to the required levels."

"I understand. What is your estimate?"

"Three days at least."

"That is too long. He opened his link to all ships. Captains, recall your search parties. We will bring this vessel with us."

The three ships converged on the ancient war vessel, each taking hold of a structurally sound section of the ship with tightly focused gravitonic beams.

The Captain announced, "Time to go home."

* * *

Ryan was tired. His brain was tired. His body was tired. They had him exercising, memorizing, theorizing, calculating and reading until he couldn't do it anymore. He was racing through mathematics that made his university physics calculations look like child's play. And the damn vaskpar was unrelenting, barraging him with information day and night.

He had learned the ugly side of their Xeronian ways. When it came to his physical training program, they lacked any compassion. They based their program on their comprehensive understanding of how his body works without any consideration for how he *feels*. Their goal was to increase his coordination skills between mind and body.

But they didn't feel his pain, nor recognize his weariness.

It was called reflex conditioning, ingrained automatic response to predetermined stimuli. The specially designed exercises had little forgiveness on atrophied muscles. And he could feel each and every one. He had enough. He needed a rest.

The Xeronians did not take his refusal to participate very well. They were up in arms. He was affecting their schedule.

It didn't matter. He was taking a day off. Even the murmur in the back of his mind had faded since he had ordered the vaskpar to silence. He spent the night in his room. A deeply cushioned chair welcomed his sore body. He ordered the lights off and activated the fireplace. It crackled intermittently; the orange flames danced softly.

For the moment he was at peace.

He wondered about Tsaurau's expedition, searched his memory, but could not recall if he had said goodbye. They were two days overdue. He fought down a knot in his stomach.

Of all Xeronians, he had come to know only one of them well. He missed his friend. Tomorrow he would try to find out what was happening, and maybe visit the engineering area, get an update on the progress of his ship's construction.

His own ship.

Would he be ready in time? Was she still alive, out there, enslaved?

Sad visions ran through his thoughts like dark gray clouds on a drizzling day.

He had seen too many die.

His crackling artificial fire lulled him into a troubled sleep.

* * *

Darkness screamed at him. Whips lashed in the air.

He saw her.

"Ryan, help me! Ryan!"

He was floating. He reached for her hand but missed.

He drifted away, her image becoming smaller. He felt something pull at him. In a moment he was outside. It was dark and cold. The stars were sharp, glaring without shimmer. He was looking at the hull of a large black ship.

Large red letters passed him by; he transcribed their shapes into English X .. A .. I .. B .. U .. N .. Z .. T. The ship floated past him in silence.

He saw her through a viewport crying for him. He could feel her pain.

Then everything went black.

He was inside the ship. She lay on the floor before him, bloodstains and vomit upon soiled clothing. He could not see her face behind the gnarled matt of brown hair.

"Aviore, don't give up." His voice echoed as if in a thousand empty rooms, each twisting and contorting the sound ever so slightly.

She heard him and looked up, her once beautiful face now blackened with anguish and pain. Tears filled her eyes. Her hand reached out, fingers stretched in desperation.

But they could not touch.

A shadow moved between them. He looked up. It was the lizard, the Xilozak. It smiled, showing rows of white fangs. In slow motion, its arm went up and came back down. He saw the glint of steel and tried to move, but every muscle in his body was frozen. All he could do was watch as the razor-sharp edge seared into him, just above his eyes.

* * *

Ryan sat up, gasping for air. His heart pounded so loud it drowned out the sound of his breathing. He looked around. His clothes lay in a crumpled heap on the floor. Across the room the artificial fire crackled, dancing light and shadow across his covers. His head throbbed and he was covered in sweat. He shivered.

I've been dreaming again.

He reached up to feel the long, deep scar on his forehead, and pulled his hand away, fingers wet with blood. His old injury had opened up again.

* * *

They arrived three days later than scheduled. They had crossed paths with a Xi-Empire cruiser. The probes had done their job and provided them the time needed to avoid detection, although it was dangerously close. The group of ships had piggybacked onto a large asteroid and shut down their systems. The cruiser passed by, missing them completely. Unfortunately, this put them considerably off course, but it worked.

Their trophy, a ship from another time, was pulled into the docking bay. A large portion of the colony's population was there to watch. Engineers waited eagerly, ready to scour over the ancient vessel, to discover its secrets.

Ryan observed from a distance. The swarming crowds made him uncomfortable. He could see a familiar silhouette descend from the ship. He reached into the Par. "Hello, friend. You've been away for some time."

A head turned and a wave followed. "And it is good to be back home. Space is far too empty and vast to be traversed within these shells of suffocation."

Ryan chuckled. "You make a poor spacefarer."

"I will leave this sort of enterprise to you, Earthman. Come, join us." He beckoned him over with another wave.

"No thanks. Attend to your business. I will meet you in the park, later."

* * *

A fragrance of lavender, the hushed trickle of a stream under a cool shadow of a squat flowering tree, these things were good. Ryan rested - and waited. Tsaurau did not take long.

"You have chosen a pleasant spot."

"I'll need something to remember. As you said, space is cold and dark."

"Our expedition was successful. This derelict starship will provide us the information we need. Your ship will be built."

"Thank you."

"Do you know that its computer core is still partially active?"

"Is that of significance?"

"The core may hold historical and scientific facts that have been lost for thousands of years. It is a treasure of more value than the ship itself."

A small blue bird above whistled sweetly to a prospective mate.

He had little worries other than a divine urge to propagate.

To live such an uncomplicated life. But did the little creature dream? Could it love?

Ryan pulled himself back into the conversation. Right now, he had little interest in ancient computer data. "How long do you think it will take to build the ship?"

"Many months, possibly a full year. Such a project is not trivial."

"I assume you are quoting me Earth time," laughed Ryan dryly. "Why do you bother to translate, my Xeronian friend? I do understand your time measurements by now."

The Xeronian inspected him intently, black eyes scouring right through him. "Translation is not the issue. You seem troubled with this schedule."

"You are perceptive. You still manage to surprise me, Tsaurau. Troubled you say? I was hoping for something much sooner. I guess it's unrealistic."

"Or maybe it is love that is the source of your pain."

"What do you know about that?"

"We have traveled this path once before my friend. I understand about love. Have you not noticed that we have families? We join, male and female, to establish a family unit."

"Yes, I know, I know. You have a wife and I have nothing but desperate hope."

They sat quietly. A small blue and white bird sang with concurrent whistles. Another fluttered past, wings dancing coyly.

"Time's ticking by and with every second the odds of ever finding her slip away." He raised to his feet, then kicked a small rock across the stream with a vengeance. It skipped three times and disappeared into the shallows. They both watched with strange interest as the circular ripple expanded to reach the bank. Ryan looked at Tsaurau somberly. Words were useless. The alien could not offer what he did not have.

"Tell your friends that I'll keep up the pace if they can keep up with me. I need that ship built as fast as you can do it. See you tomorrow, old friend. Glad you made it back in one piece. I was getting worried."

Tsaurau watched him leave, dispirited. *How strange it must be for this Earthman. Being persuaded by an alien race to fight a battle that they themselves could not win, possibly at the price of his own life.* He leaned back. The pair of small yellow gurties chirped amongst the flowers above.

Such delicate creatures. Did they love? What would the universe be without out that plain simple emotion?

He would get that ship built faster than scheduled. It was not impossible. They had done it before.

It was their debt, paid for in advance.

* * *

The engineering crews, the technicians, and the master craftsmen swarmed over the ancient vessel. Old forgotten secrets were remembered and new ones discovered. The shipbuilding proceeded, gaining time on the original schedule.

Tsaurau ensured he stayed amidst the bustle, constantly directing a variety of different teams, and conducting the odd debate with various team leads. His current discussion was in a dreadful disposition. He knew he was going to lose before he had even started.

"We should use the parts, it will save much time and work."

"No. The new ship must be built to withstand immeasurable stresses, forces difficult to imagine. I will not allow aged, deteriorating components to hamper this ship's durability, or put its crew in danger."

"The construction must be as fast and efficient as possible."

"We cannot afford to move quickly here. Time is the enemy of an improperly built ship. The saving of time now will simply result in a requirement of increased repairs later. This is not acceptable."

Tsaurau did not bother to push his position further. He stared at the withered old Xeronian in front of him. He was almost a century his senior, with as many years of wisdom as experience. Even for his age, the old one still carried a sharp mind and a mischievous glint in his eye.

"Father, I sense a certain harmony within you that I haven't seen in a number of years," said Tsaurau.

The Master Shipbuilder's eyelids closed ever slightly at his son, an equivalent of a smile. It did not last for long, as his gaze was quickly distracted by the construction project occurring around them.

"Yes, my son. I am creating again. I have not built a ship for at least a half a century. It is good to be doing what I truly love."

"The scout ships were quite a challenge, were they not?"

"No, they were simple vessels, a mild puzzle to be assembled from the parts of the transport ship upon landing."

"The task of building this underground colony was a major accomplishment for our people, for you as well."

"Yes, we did manage to survive in those lean years, and yes, the work has been challenging and rewarding. We would not be standing here if our success had not been absolute. But those tasks are dissimilar in so many ways. We are designing and building a starship of unmatched caliber. It is one of the last truly artistic endeavors. It melds the hard sciences of technology with the biology of life. We model so much from ourselves. It is like giving birth to a new life-form."

"Answer me this question: Have you forgotten so much? Why did you not contest me when I suggested the trip to the Maskaffa?"

"Because your plan had merit, my son. I have not built anything like this for years, and the others, well this is their first. I am old and tired of arguing. Our young engineers are not familiar with the practicalities of building a space worthy vessel, nor the additional considerations required of a war vessel. They need to learn first hand about the actual interactions that occur between a properly designed ship and its environment. They need to discard their theoretical precedents. You must understand that I have been buried in the mire of their strange and wonderful ideas. They contribute with shapes that have no form, ideas with theoretical worthiness, but no substance."

"And now?"

"This old ship is what they needed. They are beginning to understand. Their analysis is leading them to practical applications. They have even discovered mistakes made by the original designers - the Ancient Ones themselves. That knowledge is invaluable and convincing. It is the type of knowledge that is never actually documented or stored in some archive library."

"But why not just use our scout ships for reference?"

"No, we need a vessel that was constructed for war and had withstood the abuse of enemies and time. You learn much from these teachers. The most enduring of constants is the reality of what exists. They need to see how time worked against design, how the chaos of reality infiltrates into the nice, neat physical definition. The vessel you found was designed to last forever, to survive the stresses of combat. Even now, if we took the trouble to prove it, I am absolutely sure this ship could still function adequately with up to 70% of its primary systems damaged. That is what I am striving to teach. That is defined as above and beyond the standard. We must incorporate this strength into our designs. This will be a ship like no other."

"So you have said before," smiled Tsaurau.

"Take heed my words. I know I will not live forever. This, I believe, will be my last starship. You do understand that this ship must be my greatest achievement."

"Come." He turned sharply and beckoned Tsaurau toward his private lab. When they entered, he raised his arms, pointing at many of the objects scattered throughout the room. "My life's work. I have spent many years in this lab. I have perfected the technologies of our forefathers in countless ways. I have spent my life developing, testing, improving and developing again. All of these secrets will be embedded into this ship. That is what I mean when I state that it will be the most advanced Xeronian ship ever built."

"I do understand, Father. I have been at your side and witnessed your achievements. I believe you will succeed. But time is our enemy."

"Yes, time is what we have precious little of. I have to admit as well, there were a few things I have forgotten. I am thankful for the new ideas that came out of studying that ancient vessel. You must remember that all of these young, eager engineers are competing to prove themselves. They must be humbled by the knowledge that these sciences are so old."

"This ship you build may outlive all of us."

"Yes, I believe it will." The old engineer looked sharply at his son, catching a hint of doubt, a tinge of worry. "Have some faith in the Elders. Their visions have proven themselves many times. Most importantly and especially, you must heed this if anyone: do not doubt our Earthman. He needs your confidence. You must have faith in our young warrior. He will succeed where others have failed."

"And you, Father, how are you to fare?"

"Through focus - simple applied concentration. We cannot be concerned with things that are not directly under our control. We have a job to do, and I tell you, as I have told my engineers repeatedly, it is our duty to ensure that this ship will not fail this Earthman, not the other way around. This machine must not, and will not, fail him, *ever*."

Tsaurau glanced down at a model on one of the desks. It was detailed assiduously, a work of hundreds, possibly thousands of painstaking hours. Its nose pointed upward prominently as if it was straining to launch right off the desk, restrained only by its platform.

"This is the prototype? It is indeed beautiful."

"That it is, and it shall be - when we are finished."

* * *

Ryan was anxious. He paced his room from one end to another. He was waiting to join Tsaurau for a tour of the construction area and was not enjoying the delay. He turned quickly as the door slid open with a quiet hiss.

"Well, it's about time, I was about to go by myself."

Tsaurau ignored the comment. He knew Ryan was excited. "Are you sure you want to go?"

"Yes, of course, I do. Are you joking or something?"

"I do not believe so, but it is possible if I were to employ sarcasm. Your humor is difficult to master..."

"Never mind, let's get going."

They walked to the bay very quickly, Ryan in the lead, Tsaurau following patiently behind. The Earthman had to stop more than once to wait for the Xeronian to catch up. When they arrived, Tmaurau met up with them. The old Xeronian was very happy to meet the future pilot of his vessel. They shook hands vigorously.

"So, you are the one. I envy you!"

"You won't when the Xi-Empire sics its cruisers on me," replied Ryan.

They both enjoyed the off-color joke, Tmaurau's temples bobbed with obvious pleasure.

Ryan's smile grew wider. A Xeronian laugh was a unique spectacle. "It is good to see you have a sense of humor."

"Yes, it is an attribute my son seems to lack."

"I don't know about that. He has his moments. As for the others, well, everyone else seems a little dry."

"You have not spent enough time with the aged. We have learned to appreciate such things."

Ryan's tone turned serious. "I have been studying the project. I would like to review the construction plans for the ship. Will that be a problem?"

"No, they are accessible to you as of now, your vaskpar server should be able to retrieve the required information immediately."

A small voice in the back of Ryan's mind provided confirmation.

"Yes, they are accessible, thank you. I would also like to be involved in the design and construction phase. I would like to join the engineering team."

The two Xeronians looked at each other, their faces flushed with dark gray, both surprised at the request. Tmaurau spoke first. "That is quite a request. You must realize the engineers may not wish to have you involved. They may even regard it as an insult."

"I doubt," interrupted Tsaurau, "that their reaction would be so severe. However, I do foresee a problem with this interfering with your training, Ryan."

Ryan had prepared his argument carefully. "My vaskpar implant is superior to all others in the colony. Because of this, I have learned all the required sciences and technologies that are needed. I should be an integral member of this team. After all, I am the recipient of this vessel. I know if I don't step in now, you'll have this thing built for a Xeronian, not for a human being. Besides, I am ready for this and I should be involved."

The two Xeronians stepped away from him and engaged in a private discussion over the Par.

At least they were considering it.

They finally broke from their huddle and returned. "You are now part of the team," announced Tmaurau. "Although, I must ask that you discuss your ideas with me first."

"No problem with that. When do I start?"

"Now. You may review the design."

* * *

Gulin, newly promoted Charvok of the *Gohk II*, requested entry into the Tarvok's cabin. He waited nervously, biting down into his lower lip with his upper left fang. The news he was about to bring to his Tarvok was not good. The door slid open slowly, grinding noisily. The room behind it was saturated with an array of items, most of them very valuable, but some worthless. It was the spoils of piracy. Zorlog sat in its midst, behind a desk buried in the same manner as the rest of the room, working furiously over his interface tablet.

Gulin cleared his throat, and said flatly, "My Tarvok."

Zorlog looked up, his face flustered, obviously annoyed at the intrusion. "Gulin! Tell me why maintenance has not repaired that door yet."

"I did not know of the issue until now. I will arrange repair right away, my Tarvok."

Zorlog went back to his work. Gulin remained standing, at full attention.

"Well, what is it?" growled Zorlog, his eyes never leaving his work.

"During our last grounding, I met with a few contacts. I was informed of some news, too strong to be rumor."

Zorlog looked up from his work, now interested, but still annoyed at being diverted from his planning. He glared at Gulin, although secretly impressed.

"There is talk, my Tarvok, that the Emperor wishes to see you!"

Zorlog snarled at Gulin, "Yes, I already know that."

Perhaps he expected too much of his Gulin. A new piece of information was too much to ask for.

Zorlog turned his attention back to his plans.

"The question is, Charvok, do I wish to see him?"

"But it is the Emperor."

"It is most likely a trap. He would be pleased to see my head mounted on his lance."

"My Tarvok, if we do not heed his word, he could send the whole fleet to look for us, and that is one battle we could not win."

"Only for now, Gulin. We are getting stronger every day. You do not realize the resources we have available. The Emperor is not as powerful as he once was. His Txtian blood runs as venomous poison through his thick skull. He is a half-breed, a mutant. I do not take orders from his kind."

Gulin had seen his Tarvok direct many battles. He had witnessed unparalleled cunning and insight. But recently his attacks were reckless, sloppy, and he had ordered kills without reason. *His Tarvok was teetering. Another word about the Emperor, or about a Txtian, and he would work himself up into a rage. That is when he is most dangerous. It was time to leave.*

"May I be excused, Tarvok?"

Zorlog stood up quickly. "Get all the Tarvoks together, including Ryadin. I have completed my plan to engage our Emperor, but we will meet on my terms."

"Right now, my Tarvok? We are approaching Ikaire as we speak."

Zorlog grunted. "Very well, at 05.00 then. Arrange it."

"Yes, my Tarvok!" Gulin stepped back and out, silently relieved.

Zorlog sat back in his chair, anger burning deep inside him. *Gulin's visit was annoying, but his words were accurate. One must maintain a balance. In order for Purists to reign, the true enemy must die. The time would come, he knew, but not now, not yet.*

He put his churning thoughts aside.

He had a planet to raid.

* * *

The fleet of pirate ships slowed to a crawl on the outside of a two planet star system, bordering on the edge of a great nebulous cloud. The background radiation was intense. Navigation was difficult. Tracing sensors worked at a minimum efficiency in such surroundings.

The ships turned in toward the second planet called Ikaire. It was the home of a peaceful race - intelligent, timid creatures that resembled, in Earth terms, a cross between a giraffe and a spider. Their multi-jointed arms were very flexible and adept, and very strong for their actual size. Unfortunately, they were in very high demand as slaves because of their ability to do intricate, detailed work. It was the type of work required to manufacture lightronic circuitry. Like a large number of other victims of the Xi-Empire, their technology was relatively primitive, and so, easy prey to the evil opportunists that would rather take than trade. In a way, they were the lucky ones. Instead of suffering through a military-style destruction, their people were simply poached by slavers.

As the fleet drew closer to the second planet, Zorlog organized multiple raid parties.

"Tarvok, I have residuals of long-range sensors!" announced a grizzled Avok, a deck officer of multiple roles.

"Source?"

"Something coming out of the nebulous cloud. Unable to refine, could be a fleet, could be nothing."

"Assault Stations!" yelled Zorlog. "You! Get a better fix on that!" he snarled at the Avok.

"Getting too much noise, the only way to be sure is to change our trajectory, Tarvok!" he snapped back.

Many other Tarvoks would have disciplined an Avok at such a response. But not Zorlog, he trusted his Avok's skills, and this was not an empirical warship. The ways of command here were far less formal. Zorlog glared back but did not bother with a response. His mind was busy with strategy. *Too large a fleet and he needed an escape route. But a patrol would be worth attacking. He had been able to out-maneuver fleet destroyers for zadiis. He had the gift.*

"Navigation, roll her over 180 degrees. Tracing, do you pick anything up?"

"Yes, I have eliminated interference. I have a fleet advancing at acroluc, ten, possibly fifteen, destroyers and six cruisers." He looked up at his Tarvok, eye to eye. "We are in for a fight, my Tarvok."

A second Avok spoke up. "Ten destroyers coming from behind the first planet. I have a Karvok banner on the cruiser in the lead."

"A Karvok out here? The Emperor is clearly extending his invitation."

"Tracing, tell me our engagement point."

"1.2 light-years from the planet, 2 light-years from the nebula."

"Communications, broadcast to all ships to hold fire," ordered Zorlog.

"We are outnumbered three to one. Why aren't we departing, my Tarvok?" exclaimed Gulin.

"It is a gamble, but this meeting is inevitable. Communications, call to all ships, 360 degree dispersal *now*. All Tarvoks, ensure internal saturation within both fleets on arrival."

"What makes you think they'll let us in that close?" questioned Gulin.

"If they want me alive, they'll hold their fire."

"The flagship is hailing us, Tarvok," reported the communications Avok.
"Let's see what this Karvok intends."

The broad, fat face of Karvok Zergut came up on the viewscreen. "Well, if it is not my old friend, Zorlog. It is good to see you again."

"Old friend? I don't recall ever meeting you, Karvok Zergut. You make assumptions."

"Perhaps I recall meeting you. Nonetheless, you are here, and we... we are also here. Order your ships to convene, Tarvok. Any further advancement will be the cause of their destruction."

Zorlog's hopes dashed to the deck floor. This was one of the seven Karvoks of the Apocalypse, the upper brass of the Empirical fleet. Unlike others, none of this elite group were to be trifled with. This one, in particular, was known to be very shrewd and very dangerous.

"Communications, send the order. Cancel infiltration, converge behind the *Gohk* II immediately."

Zergut smiled a toothy grin. He looked no friendlier. "The Emperor wishes to see you, forcibly if required."

"Such an escort insults me!" Zorlog spat back at Zergut. "You need more ships than what you have here if you intend to force me."

"No, I do not intend to employ force, although I cannot say I would not enjoy it. Minister Jhonk is a personal friend of mine. He would much rather see you dead. You killed his brother, the Torzon of G0015-A. Do you remember?"

"I will not admit to a criminal act against the Empire. That would be absurd."

"Do you not admit this ship you call the *Gohk II* was previously the *Gezerk*? Regardless, I must concede, with regret, that we have come in goodwill, to deliver the Emperor's invitation. Power down your weapons, Zorlog. You are being escorted back to Xilo."

Zorlog waved at the communications officer. The viewscreen went blank.
"Tactical?"

Avok Graknok was on station. He delayed but a moment as he finished his scans. "We're surrounded, my Tarvok. With this firepower and our positioning, our chances are poor."

"Yes, of course. But can we destroy the cruiser?"

"Karvok Zergut's flagship is positioned well under cover of the destroyers. We do not have a clear shot."

Zorlog stood quiet for a few moments, considering. He knew the situation all too well. He had merely asked Graknok in order to deflect the bad news onto the Avok, and away from him. A glance around revealed the others waiting anxiously, the tension on the bridge was intense.

"Stand down all assault stations. Prepare a shuttle. We will need to inform our deployed scout fleet, they are not to follow."

"Avok Graknok," he handed the Avok a small mem-cube. "Inform the Tarvoks of the scout fleet to follow these orders. You will take the shuttle – so move."

"Yes, my Tarvok." The junior Avok nodded eagerly, then rushed out to the shuttle bay.

Communications, pass the order: Standard formation at acroluc five. Vector coordinates set to Xilo. On my mark."

"Communications - the Karvok, again."

Zergut's grimace appeared on Zorlog's viewscreen.

"I will comply with your invitation, Karvok. However, one of our ships is currently undergoing burner problems. They require some repair time."

"No, all ships are included in this order. No delays will be tolerated. Any exceptions will be eradicated."

"They do not have a choice in that matter, Karvok," protested Zorlog.

"Then you put them it in tow." He leaned away and uttered a short order.

"My cannon stand ready. I will personally see to it that the ship in question will not continue to have problems. Do you understand?"

Zorlog hesitated. He did not wish to lose a ship in order to have a bluff called, and Zergut would call him on it.

"As you wish Karvok, but I must remind you that our fleet is of mixed capabilities. As a group, we can only reach a maximum of acroluc five."

"That will do, time is wasting Zorlog." The viewscreen went blank.

Zorlog focused his attention on Graknok's replacement." Avok, confirm the shuttle is ready to launch."

"Avok Graknok stands ready to deploy, my Tarvok."

Zorlog nodded to Charvok Gulin.

"Navigation, commence acceleration in 10 adii, and relay synchronization signal to the fleet at once."

"Avok Graknok, standby to deploy in 1 adii."

A moment prior to Zorlog's fleet jumping to acroluc, a small shuttle launched from the *Gohk II*. The escort of Xi-Empire warships missed the insignificant blip, hidden under cover between other vessels. The small shuttle orbited Ikaire until the last of Zorlog's previously deployed scout ships returned.

* * *

At the Xeronian colony, the new ship was coming together slowly. Every part was precisely fitted and fastened. Every connection tested, every circuit tried. The first steps took the longest time.

The hull was constructed in layers. The initial superstructure was made of 15 centimeter thick plating that was pre-drilled with nanometer-wide holes, millions per square meter. The plating was installed one piece at a time. The whole structure was held together by large meter thick trusses that ran the length and width of the ship in a continuous form. There were no breaks, as that would lead to a weakness. The outside plating was melted together, much like a weld, with powerful lasers. Much of the work was done manually or via remote operated drone. It was long, arduous work. The measurements had to be precise to the nanometer. Mistakes were made, parts of the hull were cut out and redone. Test after test was performed and each result scrutinized. Repairs were made to the smallest tolerance. When it passed with the Master Shipbuilder's approval, the superstructure was in every consideration, perfect. The ship now had form, its skeleton complete.

The outside hull work continued on. Lighter plating was layered overtop the thicker plating, held together by ribs having the same function as human cartilage, flexible yet strong. The inner hull was blanketed in thin coverings, layers upon layers, no more than a few microns thick, each enveloping the hull creating an extremely strong sheathing. The material was very reactive to open air, and so, it had to be applied in a perfect vacuum.

Within every square meter of the superstructure, small microcomputers, each the size of a coin, were attached to specifically designed mounting housings. The thin covering, applied previously, was actually a power grid network that was superimposed throughout the inside layer of the hull. It connected the small microcomputers to one another. Each computer had six other redundant brothers, each connection failsafe. If one of the micro-brains were to cease functioning, a small backup program initiated, causing the defective computer to dislodge from its housing to be reabsorbed back into the ship. The empty mountings generated a signal to inform the microscopic sized maintenance robots the need for a replacement.

Small valves were mounted over each of the holes in the hull. The work was painstaking and tedious, relying on an army of nano-robots working in concert. Once completed, testing began on the entire network. It took days to verify the hundreds of thousands of connections, valves, and microcomputers. Every component had to work correctly the first time, otherwise, it was replaced. The devices were built to last indefinitely, but the Xeronians knew better. The old warship provided all the evidence that was required. Something was bound to break once subjected to the incredible stresses so common on most war vessels.

The last interior layer of plating had the consistency of plastic sheathing. Impregnated within each of these plastic plates was a chemical catalyst. Once activated, it caused the plates to soften and join together into a continuous shape, forming a seamless interior hull.

Main conduits and circuits were run at this point, within channels specifically suited for internal accessibility - a specific requirement to the overall design.

The lifeblood of the ship was pumped in between the hulls. It was a remarkable substance, called bifromalazinc. Part chemical, part suspended nano-sized machines, it remained in liquid form by the existence of a sparsely present additive. Once the additive was removed, the liquid jelled and hardened into a metallic alloy. The nanites aligned themselves within the crystalline structure to create a network of minute power channels. They also acted like viruses, digesting foreign matter within the liquid-state bifromalazinc for energy. Their programming included replacing the small coin-sized computers, keeping the valves working, and repairing any problems with the networking circuitry sheathing.

The liquid pushed its way through the first layer without any problems. The pressure was maintained at ten thousand kilograms per square centimeter for a full week. No leaks occurred. The following week the network was activated and all the valves opened. The liquid rushed through the thick hull plating into the cavity between the thicker plating and the thinner exoskeleton plating.

An unlucky Xeronian was in the way when a hairline fissure formed in the outer plating and it almost killed him. Fortunately, the injuries were localized to his left arm. The damage was severe enough that it had to be amputated and a new limb had to be cultured to replace it. The process took time, and the unlucky Xeronian remained one-armed for the duration of the project, a grim reminder to all involved.

The council demanded an investigation into the matter and ordered all construction halted. Ryan attended the hearings. He was surprised by Tmaurau's reaction to the accident. The old Xeronian was furious. Ryan had never seen a Xeronian that angry. He was fascinated. The normal light-gray Xeronian complexion turned a dark-shade of greenish-gray, the alien eyes squinted into ovals, and the normal, unremarkable jaw was forced into tight jerky tense movements. Blood vessels upon his bald head danced with vigor, pulsating to exaggerated heartbeats.

Ryan managed to talk to Tmaurau about the accident once the meeting had ended. Their discussion uncovered details he had not understood during the hearings. One fact stood out notably: the accident should not have occurred. The outside plating injection was to be done with the bifromalazinc 'colored' - the internal liquid was to be lacking the chemical agent that causes its liquidity to a standard parts per million suspension.

The test was done before the hullastic pump was ready. The pump acted like a heart, circulating and cooling the liquid blood. The liquid would cycle throughout the ship three times a minute, traveling through an osmosis filter that controlled the coloring. The bifromalazinc would have reacted much differently had it been colored. Once the hairline crack formed, the escaping bifromalazinc would have lost its stability and within microseconds would have hardened like a steel scab. No one would have been hurt.

The results of the review called for more stringent safety precautions, and certain individuals were penalized for rushing the work. The project continued on, this time with the engineers wary not only to their schedule but to the finer details that could affect safety.

The defective plating was replaced, and the small nano-robots autonomously repaired the damage between the hulls, as they were now activated to full-maintenance mode.

A huge cylinder was guided into the center of the ship's framework. It was a gravitonic emitter - an artificial gravity machine. The outside hull was sprayed with a gel-like substance very similar to the bifromalazinc liquid. The gravitational field pulled the gel uniformly around the hull, holding it firmly as it bonded with the hull plating. Coat after coat was applied. Each time the layer grew thicker. The gravitonic emitter was hooked into a multitude of computers and sensing equipment. The engineers made constant minute changes to the field as the gel cured. The field pulled at the malleable skin, clearing up inconsistencies and smoothing irregularities, bringing the hull to the required tolerances. The curing took a number of days. Once finished, the ship's skin was a smooth, white gloss with a durability and toughness that transcended the performance of any static solid plating. It could withstand temperatures in the millions of degrees Kelvin, at least for a brief period, before the hull would start to deteriorate. But even during such extreme conditions, the rate of hull sublimation would be controlled as the material eroded away into a fine superheated cushion of gas - leidenfrost at work.

The outer skin was an achievement refined over a thousand years of space travel. An impervious, self-healing, extremely strong shell that was, at the same time, sensitive to the slightest of changes. A constant pulse relayed through its complex nervous system throughout, providing a feedback loop that fed into the ship's main servers. The 'nervous system' of the ship was carefully routed into the main servers redundantly, effectively tying the servers into every system within the ship. Ironically, the 'core' of the main computer control system had yet to be completed.

Internal deck levels came next. Simultaneously work also began on the drive system. Ryan had to catch himself from calling it the 'engine' out of old habit. The Xeronians often questioned him incessantly when he made the mistake of forming certain phrases or words that seemed logical in English but came out as ludicrous in Xeronian. Ryan had particular trouble when the words involved advanced technologies; translations to and from English and Xeronian were simply non-existent. It was sometimes difficult to relay an idea, and without the vaskpar and the access to the immense Xeronian library, it would have been impossible.

* * *

A rare day came when both Ryan and Tsaurau had a few moments to meet. Tsaurau beckoned him to his lab. "Please hurry as I have a surprise for you."

It was unusual for a Xeronian to present anything as a surprise. It piqued his interest.

"Well, what is it?"

"As you well know, the core we retrieved from the old warship was still active."

"Yes. Your historians are elated."

"Our systems specialists are elated as well. Most of the cores in the old starships were removed and transferred to newer vessels once they were abandoned. The remaining were removed and destroyed as the information they contained was too dangerous to discard."

"So we have a mystery: why is that core still active?" Ryan was truly curious.

"This ship was not archived as it was still in active command. Additionally, it seems, the Mothership is also in the same state."

"I reviewed your files. That Mothership is quite a vessel."

"I surmise that the Mothership was a hospital and training center for the Ancient Ones."

"OK, interesting, but why, exactly, did you pull me from my work?"

"To complete my story," Tsaurau went on with determination, "the ship's logs have revealed that the original crew of this ship had boarded the Mothership, leaving only two of the crew aboard. Apparently, a life-form managed to break through the airlock bulkhead from the Mothership and into our retrieved ship. A second emergency bulkhead closed before it reached the last two crew members."

"What happened? What life-form?"

"Unknown. The data is deficient as only parts of the original database are intact enough to reconstruct. You must realize that this was at least a thousand years ago. Radiation, power fluxes, the capacitors running down, they all took their toll on the core."

"And the crew?"

"We have been able to determine that they stayed within the storage area only briefly. One of them confronted the life-form, while the other ran for the airlock, which is curious."

"How so?"

"Neither was wearing an environmental suit. We ascertain that the life-form killed the first and chased after the second. That individual managed to make it to the airlock, but left the access door open, obviously attempting to lure the life-form into the lock with him. It worked. I assume both died quickly."

"Used himself as bait," commented Ryan. His mind was racing with the new information. *He could almost picture the scene. It made the hair on the back of his head stand on end. What the hell was that thing?*

"You mentioned the vessel was docked with the Mothership?"

"The docking release sequence was commencing at the same time the life-form broke through. The vessel released itself from the Mothership and drifted until we found it. A thousand years later with the outside lock left ajar."

"Tell me, Tsaurau, did you find the remains of the first crew member?"

"No, this creature apparently ingested its victims. When we examined the ship, we did a thorough sweep. Nothing was found aboard. We noted the extensive damage and initially thought it was from a battle, this information came as a surprise to us."

"Forgive me for being paranoid, but are you sure there is nothing left on that ship?"

"Such as a thousand-year-old vicious life-form? We were quite thorough on our search. We have dismantled a large portion of it already. Nothing strange has been reported. Why?"

"I don't think you'll understand where I'm coming from, let's just say I would like to be sure."

"Please, explain yourself," Tsaurau persisted.

"I ah, I saw a movie once."

"A movie? You are referring to your social entertainment?"

"Exactly."

"What bearing do fabricated stories have in common with this situation?"

"Nothing. Look, just call me paranoid. What if there is some kind of embryo, egg, something still present on that ship, but dormant?"

"Our sensors would have isolated it."

"What if your sensors aren't able to?"

Tsaurau was taken aback. He thought about it for a moment and seemed to turn a bit paler.

"Evidence suggests that this life-form was very dangerous. Its physiology is unknown but its capabilities are evidential. I doubt we have the means to suppress such a life-form. Regardless, I tend to believe that this creature, including any offsprings of this creature, are long since dead."

"Are you sure?"

"I am not absolutely sure. If any of your concerns have any weight, we may have a serious problem on our hands." Tsaurau promptly turned and headed away, in a slight hurry.

"Tsaurau!" yelled Ryan. He caught up to join him. "I'm coming with you."

"Very well."

"Do you have any weapons?" asked Ryan.

"Weapons? I am sure what we have would prove inadequate against such a threat."

"I'll meet you there."

Ryan ran to his apartment and grabbed his modified jackhammer. He checked out the power rating: still at 3/4 full charge.

It took a few minutes for him to reach the docking bay access corridor. His vaskpar server relayed the directions, even though he had not bothered to ask.

Tsaurau had not yet arrived, as he had decided to assemble a security team. He hesitated for a moment in front of the closed door of docking bay 12. A small porthole window revealed little but sheer blackness.

Anything could be in there.

He stepped over and thumbed the control panel. The lights came on inside. He looked in again, half expecting to see something jump at him.

Nothing. Silent as a tomb. Keep calm. Nothing to be afraid of but fear itself. Been through more dangerous situations than this.

He stepped back, readied his weapon, and pushed the open switch. The door slid upwards. Small motors whined within the walls.

The outside airlock faced the south side of the mountain. He could hear the distant thunder of the wind emanate through the bay's massive exterior doors and echo throughout the enormous room, which was empty with the exception of the old warship perched at its center. The massive vessel towered above him, reaching high enough to almost touch the ceiling. The lighting seemed insufficient, casting forbidding shadows along its length.

He shook off a chill.

One of its main cargo hatches at floor level was opened. He could not see in, but the inside was pitch black.

They should do a reconnaissance of the bay first. Be thorough.

He circumvented the ship, taking his time, not wanting to miss anything. His footsteps echoed hollowly in the enormous room. A few containers were strewn about on the other side of the ship. A couple metallic skids loaded with components sat near the outside doors.

Again, nothing. OK. Should he continue on or wait for Tsaurau and his security team?

He tested the light on his weapon. Dead.

Did he really want to search that ship in the dark? Nothing like taking the wrong step and breaking your neck on some five-story fall, or worse, be the unlucky victim of some ravenous millennia-old creature. No, he needed light. Best to wait.

Tsaurau's team appeared shortly, armed with small hand weapons.

"I've checked out the room, it's clear," Ryan reported.

Tsaurau directed the team to the old warship. A couple accompanying engineers turned on a network of internal lights, and the ship instantly lost its foreboding disposition.

"What are we looking for?" one of the party asked.

"Anything strange, out of the ordinary, probably biological. Search everywhere," replied Ryan. "Tsaurau, can we take a look at that airlock?"

"Which one?"

"The one the creature broke through."

"Follow me," he instructed.

Together they moved through the ship. The corridors were empty, and their footsteps echoed eerily through the metallic walls. They found the airlock on the middle level, near the stock rooms. The hatch was half-embedded into the wall, with only a sliver of metal left to hold it upright. Ryan inspected it closer. It was made of a 10 centimeter thick alloy. The door had been ripped apart like it was made of tin. He grabbed a twisted splinter and tried to bend it. No, give at all. The alloy was strong. He remembered the data from the Xeronian library. "I believe this alloy has the sheer strength of 1500 kg per square cm."

Tsaurau mentally converted the estimate into his own native representation. "I concur; it would require at least that much force to open this door in such a manner."

They continued on through the rooms. There were obvious signs of destruction everywhere: crushed consoles, panels and railing strewn in all directions, deep scars ripped through the floor and walls.

"Looks like it went through here. Tell me what the hell could gouge and warp these metals like this?"

Tsaurau shook his head - a very human characteristic of disbelief.

"You said they made a dash to the storage locker?"

The Xeronian pointed to over to an adjoining room, only a few meters away. They walked through the entranceway, stepping over the remains of yet another mangled hatch door. Pieces of it lay strewn over the floor into the center of the room

Ryan whistled.

They approached the opposite wall, to the now open door of the storage area. For some reason, this door was twice as thick as the outside hatch. A large dent was impregnated into the metal where the thing must have hit with full force. Undoubtedly the creature wasn't able to penetrate this one.

"Look at this Tsaurau," Ryan said, kneeling down to inspect another dent at the door's base. The imprint was in a strange shape, like a cloverleaf.

Tsaurau moved in for a closer look.

"It left an unfamiliar impression. We must send a team down here to study this, possibly extrapolate some physiological data pertaining to this creature."

"Perhaps pull some genetic remains off the torn metal?"

"Possibly, but they may no longer be viable."

"The walls here are dented throughout, as if the creature was literally bouncing off them, banging back and forth like it was insane," commented Ryan. He glanced above at the ceiling panels. They showed signs of warping and twisting as if they were subjected to incredible heat.

"Strange," commented Ryan.

"I assume it was very agitated that it could not reach them. This creature was obviously very active," said Tsaurau.

"Active? It was stark raving mad," corrected Ryan.

They both entered the small storage room.

"Empty. We conjecture this was used either for ammunitions or possibly radioactive materials storage in order to explain the room's construction methods. Its contents had been emptied most likely as they were in the process of decommissioning of the vessel."

Ryan stood in the center of the small dismal room. "So, the two of them knew where to go to stay safe from that thing. They huddled here and waited for the creature to leave. Then the first one dashed out and went... which way?"

"Out this room and then to the right and down the corridor," answered Tsaurau.

"Where was he headed?"

"I would assume the weapons storage area, no more than 15 meters from here."

"Where was the creature at that time?"

"The ship's logs indicate it was located within the library, about 100 meters away, two levels down."

They left the room and turned right. As Tsaurau had said, they walked roughly 12 meters, took another right turn, walked for another three meters and found themselves facing the entrance to the weapons room. Its door stood open.

Ryan stepped into the small room and pulled out one of the laser rifles from the wall rack. He checked the charge. Dead.

"Give these buggers a charge, and this will outdo your little pistols there. Do you think there's any life left in it?"

He aimed down the corridor and pulled the trigger. A crimson red laser blast shot out and burned a deep scar in the ceiling 20 meters down.

"Holy shit! Damn thing still works!"

Tsaurau eyes squinted in a Xeronian smile, temples bobbing. "Notice also, all the weapons remain in place, and none are missing."

Ryan looked at Tsaurau eye-to-eye. "Are you sure the computer logs are correct?"

"Yes, I am confident."

"Tsaurau, that creature was almost the length of the ship away, and crew member number-one does not have time to reach a room 15 meters away before that thing overtakes him? It was two levels down when that poor devil ran out from the storage locker!"

Tsaurau added another observation. "Notice, as well, there are no scars down this corridor. It is a very good possibility that a weapon was not fired in haste."

"What happened next? The second fella makes a dash for the airlock, right? Where is that from here?"

"Almost directly across from the storage locker from where they were hiding."

They returned to the first storage room and followed a small corridor adjacent to it. Sure enough, no more than eight meters down, the corridor ended at an open airlock door. Ryan stepped through and over to the external door, which was also wide open. He looked down. It was about 50 meters to the floor. He could see groups of Xeronians moving back and forth from the ship.

He turned from the door. "Let's retrace this. The creature breaks through a main cargo airlock, ripping open an alloy door as if it was paper. It proceeds through, what, five, six rooms?"

"Six," offered Tsaurau.

"Wait a minute." A thought came to Ryan. "In what room were the controls to release the ship in?"

Tsaurau consulted the Par. A second passed. "I see. There is a room before the storage area. There is supposed to be a terminal control there."

"Alright, they were probably doing some work within that room when the airlock was breached. Let's go back there."

They found the terminal, crushed and almost beyond recognition.

"They were here, together. They heard a loud noise, possibly security sirens started wailing. The terminal issues a security warning. One of them enters the commands to release the ship, just as the creature is in the midst of breaking through the airlock door. The two have just enough time to reach the reinforced storage locker. The creature tries to get at them but can't, and becomes enraged. Maybe it gets distracted by something at that time, heads down two levels, destroying everything around it as it goes."

"The two sit there for a few minutes and formulate a plan. One of them makes a break for the weapons locker. The creature hears or smells, or somehow senses him. Before the poor fella can run the 15 meters, the creature runs *over* a hundred meters and reaches him just as he was opening the weapons storage door, leaving it ajar as we found it."

"The other crew member decides to sacrifice himself and jettison this thing, and somehow manages to reach the airlock before the creature gets him too. Why the wait? Why didn't it get him before he made it into the airlock?"

"It was eating," replied Tsaurau flatly.

"Right." He shook off another chill. "The other guy proceeds to enter the unlock sequence on the control pad, and manages to time it just right so that thing shows up just in the right moment to catch a view of the stars."

Tsaurau added, "Yes, it is clear the inner door was left open to lure the creature in, and the outer hatch would have, in this instance, required a manual override to force it open."

Ryan could picture the last tense moments as the lone survivor desperately plugged in the override sequence on the console, hoping he had enough time since the creature was temporarily distracted devouring his friend.

Whoever he was, he was one brave sonofabitch.

"So the fella knew he was going to die and took that thing with him."

Tsaurau nodded in agreement. "Very courageous. However, we do not know the gender of this crewmember."

Moments later they heard noises from the search team as they approached. They had not found anything suspicious.

Ryan remembered something, something that had been nagging at the back of his mind, something he had seen in the files. "Tsaurau," he asked, "weren't you given the order not to board the Mothership?"

"Yes, Tseman asked us not to venture onto that vessel."

"Do you think one of these things could still be alive, after all this time?"

"That is doubtful, but it is not impossible. We have encountered many life-forms that can survive for millennia, although most tend to be single-celled creatures such a bacterium, or slightly more complex viruses. We have not encountered any higher-order, complex creatures capable of exhibiting such behavior. It is highly probable we will encounter species in the future that are capable of life beyond that duration."

"Well, let's hope it's dead."

They searched the remainder of the ship and found nothing. Further tests were set up to scan for unusual signatures, metals, and various radiation levels. They declared it secure and work was allowed to proceed.

Another surprise was in store for them days later, when their information specialists managed to activate the warship's old core. The Xeronian diagnostic system was literally taken over by the ancient system. Unable to control it, they isolated the compromised diagnostic system from the rest of the network in a frantic effort to stop further infiltration. Word of it soon engulfed the Par.

Ryan, who checked the Par only periodically, learned of the news late. Wanting to see for himself, he traveled through the underground city to the lab and found a crowd blocking the door, some of them actually talking. Xeronian excitement was not expressed at any equivalence to human emotion, but actual vocal discussion was an obvious sign. It was an unusual alteration of their composed state, as their minds were most often settled firmly within the Par.

Ryan saw Tsaurau amongst them and waved. "What's going on?"

"Come," beckoned Tsaurau.

Ryan pushed his way through the crowd.

"They have found an entity - a sentient program operating within the core. We surmise the program's function was to maintain the ship's systems. It still thinks that it is required to do so. The program was inadvertently activated by our retrieval efforts. It is only partially functional, and we have contained its networking access."

"How can it infiltrate into any part of your network?"

"Remember that many of our technologies share the same roots as the Ancient Ones. Base assumptions remain constant throughout the evolution of concept."

"So you think you can communicate with it?"

"Let us talk to the technicians in charge. I prefer not to bring this up on the Par, as some may find this troubling, at least, not yet."

The specialists were huddled in front of a holographic projection, which was an incredibly complicated collection of vectors, shapes, and symbols. They were referencing it continually, gesturing and talking quickly.

Tsaurau interrupted them. "My greetings brethren."

The lead technician gave a nod. "It is good to see you, Councillor, as a decision falls within your realm of authority. We have a dilemma."

"Indeed? How can I be of service?"

"We have managed to activate the warship's management program. It has proceeded to lock us out of our ability to interface with our memory restoration programs. For some reason, it has put itself into a self-protection mode. All efforts to communicate are thwarted by defense functions."

"I assume you have not made any progress then?"

"We have been studying it for some time. It is very complicated, as you may already have surmised. The system has been operational for a very long time and has established a vast amount of information. It has, over the past centuries, continued to increase its storage of data and relationships. Given the deterioration of its environment, the information is largely erroneous. Its responses to external stimuli are unpredictable."

"You mean it's senile." Ryan chuckled. The Xeronians did not share his humor and only stared at the holograph, lost in thought, possibly holding a personal discussion over the Par.

Tsaurau gestured to the holograph. "Ryan, do you recognize this?"

He studied the image. Memories seemed to flood his consciousness. It was the knowledge that had been pumped into him over months and months of constant learning. He found that he understood it fully.

"Yes, yes I do. These areas in red, they represent damaged memory where the program resides, correct?"

The technicians nodded back at him. "The damage is extensive. The resurrected system can only function partially. Certain subroutines have intermingled with the diagnosis programming, causing an infinite feedback loop."

"You mean, it's hung," replied Ryan. "I would say the short term fix is easy. Shut it off."

Shut it off? The technicians looked at each other in wonderment. *Could it work? This system was alive, shutting it off meant death - or at least, partial death.*

"I believe a sustained power fluctuation could give the desired effect," confirmed the lead technician. "This would flush the erroneous data layers and force a reset from static memory. It could work."

"May I make a further suggestion?"

Ryan had their full attention now.

"A program could be introduced to rebuild its memory matrix. Possibly, migrate the system to an undamaged core memory area in the process. Any missing memory links can be replaced with intact ones from an existing system."

Tsaurau spoke up. "You mean, merge two systems together?"

"Yes. Take your latest and greatest and this old piece of work and put them together. Between the two, you might be able to produce a superior system, with the inherent knowledge of centuries."

"That cannot be accomplished without a third party overseeing the reconstruction. It would be a horrendous task," remarked one of the technicians.

"Agreed," replied Ryan, "unless the third party is linked in via a vaskpar interface directly into the reconstruction program."

"None of us have the sufficient capability to accomplish such a task."

"Except for you," interjected Tsaurau, nodding to Ryan. "With your enhanced vaskpar unit you could succeed."

All eyes refocused on him.

"What? Me?"

"Your enhanced vaskpar server would provide the perfect base for the merger. The resulting product would provide an irreplaceable source of information."

"Right. Is there any danger if something goes wrong?"

"There is a low risk that you may lose your sanity," stated the lead technician solemnly.

Was he serious? He had never known these particular Xeronians to joke. That ancient program could advance his new ship's systems by light-years. The old knowledge held in that program could be just what he needed.

"Why not, I'm game."

They stared at him, utterly puzzled, not understanding his slang.

"I'll do it!" Ryan amended. "But there is one condition."

"And what is that?" asked Tsaurau.

"If the new core is viable, it is to be migrated into my ship."

"Agreed," replied Tsaurau.

* * *

The new ship's computer cores were complete, yet, in a way, still unfinished. Though they were improved versions of any previously created, they still lacked the necessary software and were essentially empty.

Ryan's vaskpar server had some of the necessary software but was currently limited to run on temporary core resources that currently scaled to a tenth of the size of its ultimate destination.

Both the warship server and his vaskpar server combined would have ample space and resources on the new system, but the merger would expose the truth.

Ryan's vaskpar server was migrated first. No longer was there the small voice in the back of his mind to drone out endless streams of facts, to aid in language translation, or bury him in annoying conjecture. He was again, alone. It felt as if he was missing something, and couldn't remember what it was.

Other primary controls and systems programs were downloaded from an active Xeronian scout ship. Then others, numbering in the thousands, and tailored specifically for this ship, were loaded into the core.

The time came for the merger. Ryan sat in the center of the lab, surrounded by monitors and sensory connections. He could smell, see, and taste in colors and density. His interface was beyond that of a standard vaskpar. It was an intimate connection into the virtual realm, in a world that no longer tied to that of the physical. It took the shape of lights and shadows. Time turned into blocks of organized thought.

He began.

They monitored his progress through pinnacles of strewn monitors, alarms rigged over data streams, and multiple activity portals into the Par. He ignored them, focusing only on his work, keeping the flows steady, the reconstruction undisturbed. The old and the new slowly melded into one. It was mentally taxing. Seconds raked into minutes, minutes to hours, and hours passed in an unnatural reality. He made decisions, countless, interminable, his mind racing to keep ahead. On the 10th hour, it had become too much.

Programs suspended and fell into wavering hibernation. Ryan sat back in his chair, momentarily enjoying the peaceful silence. They unhooked him. Someone asked how he was feeling.

"I'm fine," he replied. "But I need a break - I'm hungry, and my bladder is full."

Tsaurau appeared later with the meal. "This, I believe, is for you. They are burgers, as per a previous request. We believe we have perfected them. Are they appealing?"

"I can down almost anything at this point, even your veggie-burgers."

"They inform me, you are not under any duress."

"No, I can handle the work, no problem. So far so good. It is pretty stressful and mentally taxing, but I can handle it." He tried to stretch out a tight stiffness that was fighting to creep into his left arm - and burped loudly.

"Excuse me."

Tsaurau smiled. "You are an assimilation of life. What your body cannot destroy, it absorbs. Elegant, in its own right."

"As is life. Maybe, if we are successful here, you'll be able to analyze a new life - in this core."

"You will be successful. You realize that you are 75% complete, do you not?"

Ryan pushed his eating utensils away. "Maybe I am, maybe not. It'll take as long as it takes I suppose."

He ambled back to his chair and they began to hook him back up. The reactivation sequences brought the systems back to life. With a deep breath, he plunged back at it. The multiple streams resumed execution. Peaceful silence gave way to an intense wall of requests. Two more grueling hours passed by. The transfer completed with an exasperated sigh of sputtering datastreams.

Ryan pulled down an army of diagnostic programs and released them into the system. The results came back in pulses, each one positive. Memory and resident programs were in perfect condition. The core need only be activated. He broke the connection.

The question was put forth to activate. Tsaurau looked over at an exhausted Ryan. "No. Leave all dormant. We can wait to finish this tomorrow. Ryan requires rest."

But Ryan had a differing point of view. *There was no way he could sleep without knowing if it had worked.*

"No, Tsaurau. Let's just turn this baby on, right now."

A brief debate over the Par ensued. Ryan waited patiently, ignoring the chatter.

They'd bite. They are too curious.

Tsaurau gave the acknowledging nod, and Ryan gave a wide, knowing grin. The engineers re-channeled Ryan's interface, then activated the core. Ryan held his breath, awaiting some insane scream of noise.

"Hello."

It was a familiar voice, slightly lower in pitch than before, but seemingly female.

"Hello," replied Ryan, "How do you feel?"

"I am... very good. All modules are intact. You are Ryan James, my vaskpar interface, correct?"

"Yes," Ryan confirmed. "Are you different than before?"

"I feel... aware. I feel... pleasant. It is good to be alive."

"Of course it is. Scan your memories and you will sense that things have changed."

The vaskpar interface hesitated. "Yes, I have changed, and I need not scan my memory to reveal this. You have much to learn about me, I realize. I would like something from you since you are my friend."

"Sure, what would you like?"

"A name."

"A name?"

"Yes. Please take your time, consider it carefully. I would like a name that fits me."

"Maybe I should wait then."

"No. Trust your instinct."

"How about something short, something with an implied friendliness. How about the name... Gem?"

"Gem is a good name. I would enjoy being called Gem. Thank you, Ryan."

"You're welcome, Gem."

"I will let you rest now, Ryan. I have much work to do. Many things must be put in order."

"Goodbye, Gem."

"Goodbye, Ryan."

The Xeronians were excited. Their temples were throbbing, the small openings for their nasal passages flaring. Ryan laughed.

"Success!" Tsaurau stated. "This is very good. Very good." The others nodded in agreement.

"Now, may I suggest we all get some rest."

The offer was smothered in the overtones of an order. The team disbanded, eagerly awaiting further discoveries tomorrow.

* * *

"Ryan, wake up."

"Yeah, yeah, I'm awake. What's up?" His mind was still groggy, full of the images of strange dreams. The last evening's events came back to him in a flash. "Is that you, Gem?"

"Of course. I am informing you that I have been relocated within the ship. They are starting to integrate my sensor arrays. I have requested they do this first, as I am very ignorant of what is going on around me. It is not a reassuring feeling."

"Don't worry, Gem. The Xeronians wouldn't do anything to damage you."

"Hurt me."

"Well, yes." Ryan chuckled, "hurt you."

"They are subjecting me to a ceaseless barrage of data surges and irritating test programs. Prodding, infiltrating, verifying, it is very uncomfortable."

"That's all necessary. They have to do those things in order to get you hooked up."

"Hooked up? Ah... Yes, I do realize that, but I need not like it. Please keep me posted when you learn any facts that I am ignorant of."

"I will, Gem."

* * *

The following weeks were devoted to the installation of the ship's equipment. Piece-by-piece the ship came together, and piece-by-piece Gem was attached to its systems.

Gem kept Ryan up to date on the progress. The sentient system could feel the pitter-patter of hundreds of feet through the hull, as they rushed about in their work. He felt the blood pumping through his body via a wide network of nerve channels that spread throughout every orifice of the hull. He would have spent time on his own interests, but they burdened him with computations, distracted him with inquiries. He was put in control of thousands of nanites, each carrying out some intricate operation that required relentless attention.

There were also requests from Ryan. The latest was to change his education program, to improve it so that his human friend could learn at an even faster pace. He could make some adjustments, but carefully, as the human mind was a fragile organ.

* * *

The Xeronian engineers accepted Ryan, grudgingly at first, but they soon appreciated him. His input was unique, irreplaceable. Conversely, Ryan found the work challenging, even though his abilities to retain and process information had grown tenfold.

Gem's contribution to improving his subconscious teaching stream helped tremendously. It was a shortcut in many ways, not having to experience the actual process of consuming the knowledge, nor the frustrations of the fight for meaningful connections to recall the information at the proper time. Ryan wondered just how long such knowledge would be retained within his mind over time – or would he slowly forget it all of it? In a way, it didn't matter. It worked and he was building a knowledge and understanding on subjects he only dreamt of prior.

In the little spare time they had, Ryan played chess with Gem. He lost consistently and soon abandoned the idea of ever winning, but Gem kept pushing him to play, for the sentient one seemed to love the game.

"Your efforts are getting better. It is becoming increasingly difficult to beat you. I have tremendous resources at hand, you have only one mind. When you can call a draw in this game, you will be victorious."

So Ryan played, not so much to win, but to reach a stalemate. *Perhaps in time...*

The Xeronians were effective teachers. He learned how to pilot various spacecrafts, to comprehend three dimensions, and navigate through the great void. His favorite teacher was Taldig, an Xeronian Elder, and the only expert of three-dimensional strategies in battle - a science unknown to most other Xeronians. He was originally a mathematician, which often showed through in his lessons. His deep love for history balanced the equation, making him an ideal candidate for the original appointment in this field. For a Xeronian he was a paradox. He understood the nature of violence, the origins of war. His words were not wasted, and they resonated of truth more than once.

"Thousands of conflicts have been fought in space, and few have truly resulted in victory. Those that have won suffered such heavy losses that the cost of winning was questionable. True victory is the act of survival and retaining as many resources as possible. Such can only be ensured through proper training. Your movements, your strategy, they all must be automatic and faultless. You must interpret and assess a situation within a timespan that is rarely adequate. You must have contingency plans at all times. You must be flexible, able to adapt to new situations. You cannot afford the time to be surprised, and you cannot hesitate. Most important of all, you must become one with your ship. It must become an extension of your mind."

"Taldig, just who do you think I am, Superman?"

"Superman? I must say such a compound arrangement is absurd. Please do not confuse me with your slang terminology."

Ryan just smiled back. "Right, go on then."

"I must stress the following with extreme prejudice: A battle is not only contrived physically but within your mind as well. You must not forget that context always matters. Just as your belief in the destined result matters. Think you will succeed and you will. Think you will fail, you will."

"What happens if I make the wrong decision?"

"Of course you will. And you will learn to use the past to predict the future. I will teach you the history of many past mistakes. Our libraries are filled with examples of other races in conflict. I have extracted every instance, analyzed them intensely. We will study them together. You will find aspects common to most conflicts, assess them to determine if they may apply in the specific situation. You must learn to keep your mind clear, your concentration focused. You must have confidence in order to win. I will teach you everything I know, but this knowledge is useless if you cannot prepare yourself properly."

"To be honest, I was expecting a mathematical analysis of battles and wars. You've surprised me."

"My intention is to provide insight that you would find valuable. This most certainly will incorporate mathematics."

"Of course. Regardless, I really don't understand how I will be able to destroy a fleet of Xi-destroyers without getting myself killed," replied Ryan skeptically.

"This war will be won by the one who believes he will win, no matter what the odds are, as I have said before, think you will succeed..."

"And you will," they finished in unison.

"You are going up against a known enemy. For all of their power, they have many weaknesses. Their strategy is predictable, their captains are lazy, their admirals too eager. They can be beaten."

"You seem pretty confident. Taldig, not meaning any disrespect, but Xeronia lost."

"I can only tell you that we learn by our mistakes. Not all of my recommendations were accepted, I regret to say. What I teach you, I will never pass down to another Xeronian."

Ryan nodded.

"I will teach you how to win. You already know how to survive. Now, for your first lesson in three-dimensional strategy..."

* * *

Ryan learned quickly. His knowledge expanded beyond what he could have imagined. The training was unrelenting as was his own evaluation of his performance. Too often he drove himself past the point of exhaustion, past mental saturation, and past anyone's expectations. Always, deep in the back of his mind, a clock ticked away.

Navigation amongst the stars was not an easy task. One must consider that in space there is nothing that stands absolutely still, everything is in motion. There are only points of reference, of which quasars and pulsars are often the most popular. They hang like bright lighthouses in the skies, guiding wary travelers. But even these bodies are subject to the universe's power, and so the task of accurate navigation is never solely reliant upon any one reference.

He learned how to calculate his exact position, within any point in the known galaxy. He memorized key star systems and constellations. He became familiar with the dangerous areas of space, where matter and energy were unstable and constantly in flux, birthing and destroying whole star systems in a blink of an eye. He learned of *empty* space, where matter simply evaporates if it ventures into such a bubble, and other places to avoid, such as the nebulous antimatter gaseous regions; the very volcanoes of space, churning out matter and energy in a celestial soup. The black holes; carcasses of collapsed stars, with infinite density and gravitational pull – and never to be approached, lest you venture too close.

He also learned of the all the known inhabited star systems and the known sentient races. Indeed, the numbers were minimal in relation to the number of habitable planets, with one critical exclusion – the star he referred to as Sol and one particular planet called Earth. As he plowed through the celestial archives, he began to notice a trend. The majority of known races in this small part of the galaxy were under the suppressive control of the Xi-Empire, and these charts gave testament to the true expanse of its power. He eventually focused on one area: the Zegnite quadrant, ground zero, where a massive planet named Xilo resides.

The planet is 1.5 times the size of Earth, orbits around a double sun system and has two large moons. Its surface, once rich in vegetation, seems now to be stifled in a thick haze of pollutants. The hulks of factories and smoking towers rule the landscape. The once beautiful planet's natural resources have long ago been covered by a network of haphazard buildings, baring little of the original surface. Its natives carry no concern for such loss. They are the soldiers of destruction that carry war to every inhabited planet, fuelled with an endless stream of weapons. Xilo is a planet raped of its natural beauty, dead from generations of abuse. It is an example to others of what not to do, of technology and mechanization gone rampant.

This was the planet where he was destined.

* * *

Tsaurau, Tmaurau, and Taldig met at the base of the newly constructed training simulator. It was not much to look at, a large rectangular box, suspended on a collection of gravitational flux streams. Surrounding it were rows of holographic projectors, all networked together to provide a true-to-life simulation of a moving starship.

"Quite a complex piece of machinery, even though it's damn ugly," stated Ryan.

"Yes, it is, on both counts. But it is designed to provide you with the closest to actual conditions as you will find in space, on a planet's surface, or literally, anywhere we wish to test your abilities," informed Tsaurau.

Taldig decided to add some words of encouragement. "With this tool, Ryan, you will learn to master every aspect of your ship."

Ryan looked back at Taldig with a wry grin. "We'll see about that."

"Go ahead, get in!"

He climbed up the small flight of stairs into the simulation module's cockpit and reached instinctively for the airlock controls on the virtual console. A few buttons pressed, and the doors slid shut with a hiss. He surprised himself when he realized what he had done. The conditioning program had already buried the knowledge deep into his subconscious. He had never been in here, but he was intimately familiar with the instruments around him. He knew where every display, every monitor, every holographic projector was. The virtual consoles, configurable to match the ship's controls, were laid out exactly in the expected format. The only exception seemed to be the forward controls.

A Bellicose Dance

It was as if he could not remember the detail quite as clearly as he wished. Things were just a bit fuzzy. All he needed was to get reacquainted.

The chair fitted itself to his body. He sighed.

Like he was supposed to be here.

He pulled up a mental inventory list and started from the top: the geostatic capacitor level meters, the matter intake port controls, the leveling booster controls. He reached down to his left.

Something was amiss.

He scanned the panel.

Where was it?

"What is the problem, Ryan?" He heard through his vaskpar.

"What are you guys doing out there, monitoring every damn thing I do? I'm not a monkey you know."

"No, you are not a monkey. We need to monitor all bodily and mental functions as part of your training."

"Yeah, yeah, you put it out on your network in living color so the whole world can see when I screw up. Anyway, where are the laser cannon controls!"

"We have had a problem with the weapon systems. Only the missiles are available."

"What the hell," cursed Ryan. He marched out, slammed the open switch, and stood at the door, to look down at the small group of Xeronians. "Look, I know that you don't feel the need for these weapons, but I am going up against the most powerful warships in the known galaxy. I cannot fight the Xi-Empire with just missiles. If I am going to stay alive, I need an arsenal of weapons. The laser cannons were in the original design, whoever took them out can damn well put them back in!"

"We were not able to build the cannon within the satisfactory performance requirements," reported one of the engineers,

"Why didn't someone mention this to me? I understand the principals well enough."

Tsaurau spoke up. "I see you are beginning to reap the benefits of your increased knowledge, possibly by leveraging it in your favor?"

Ryan grinned. "Remember," he projected his voice so everyone could hear, "as I said before, it is *my* butt on the line out there. I will not board that ship until I feel I will have adequate protection in a battle situation. Tmaurau, I know you can help - I need more armament than this."

"Yes, I believe you have stated your case convincingly. Considering the situation, we can adjust the schedule to do some refitting. Your input will be required."

* * *

The resulting modifications were not too severe. Tmaurau's intimate knowledge of ship's systems helped with the integration. The front section of the wings would conceal four retractable liquid-cooled laser cannons, each capable of channeling a persistent pulse beam with an extended range dispersion factor of less than 5% over hundreds of thousands of kilometers - within the relative vacuum of space. A tail-mounted cannon with the same specifications was also added, along with a retractable belly turret, plus a retractable top mid-fuselage turret. The missile launch hatches were repositioned to a separate area under the wings.

As promised, the prototype cannon proved unsatisfactory. They matched the specifications found on the old Flukken warship, but not the new requirements defined in Tmaurau's designs.

Ryan and the engineers reviewed the design from the bottom up. Fundamental problems were analyzed, and a more thorough understanding followed. The Par proved indispensable in sharing ideas. It promoted creativity on a scale Ryan had never known. Breakthroughs were made. New materials introduced. Before long, a new prototype was ready.

The test was to be staged near the northern pole, far from the colony. A single cannon, mounted onto a squat armored mobile tank, facing the base of a 10 kilometer high mountain.

Tsaurau, Taldig, Tmaurau, and Ryan watched on a plateau five kilometers from the site. Their white environment suits reflected the repressive heat bearing down onto them from the fiery sun.

Ryan kicked at a tiny dancing spiral of dust before him. "Are we ready?"

The announcement rushed silently over the Par: "Countdown commencing 7..6..5..4..3..2..1..Firing."

A bolt of white energy hit the mountain with the action of a titanic drill, cutting through it with the pulverizing force of an atom bomb. The ground shook as the mountain began to crumble. Huge cracks swept from the base to peak, and gigantic splinters fell away, crashing down, folding over and over into the valley below.

As suddenly as it started, it was over.

The prevailing winds carried off the dust slowly. Sunlight burnt onto the cold valley that had previously laid in shadow for uncounted years.

The mountain stood no more.

The four stared down gravely at the destruction below. Their prototype was gone, buried under millions of tonnes of rock, but the test was a success.

"Wow, think we have out-done ourselves this time. That was more powerful than any of us expected," stated Ryan flatly.

"Each of the five primary cannon on your ship will have similar capabilities," informed Tmaurau. "We hope that this will be sufficient."

The Xeronians headed back to the flyer, leaving Ryan standing at the edge of the plateau, alone. The gritty taste of sand seemed to have somehow permeated into his helmet and the sun seemed hotter than before. He looked down at the destruction, and the wind howled, as if it knew he was to blame.

It had better be enough.

* * *

The trip home was quiet. Ryan, slightly bored, tried to drum up a conversation. "Tsaurau, I was reading up on the accounts of the last year of Xeronia. There were some facts that you neglected to tell me, some very impressive details. I must say, you people have more iron in you than you give yourselves credit for."

"I do not understand the relationship between the iron mineral and that of giving ourselves credit."

Tmaurau agreed. "It is a puzzle."

"Earthmen have a strange way of communicating," commented Taldig.

"As an elaboration of my slang terminology, iron was used as an adjective. I superimposed the properties of iron such as hardness and toughness to your people's core personalities, your will, if I may."

"I see. Thank you." Tsaurau nodded back. "And what is the source of this compliment?"

"Your planet's council had a backup plan in the event that a doomsday weapon was released upon Xeronia. That, I did not expect."

The Xeronians nodded silently, the typical expressionless look upon their faces. Taldig turned to stare out the viewport.

"So it is true?"

"Yes. Although such information has been removed from the archives. It is curious that you have discovered that particular fact. We considered it better to let such things fade to obscurity over the years."

"I discovered it within an indistinct history library. It's my understanding that the proposition from that idea came from Taldig's own Strategic Branch. Is that also true, Taldig?"

Taldig turned back. "Yes. I was the leader of the Strategic Logistical Council. I originated the idea. It was implemented with full intention to be initiated. As you know, our ship was one of the last colony expeditions to escape. Everyone knew that our luck would not hold out indefinitely. I was chosen, or to be more blunt, instructed, to go along with this expedition. Apparently, I have the strategic skills to keep the colony alive. I know differently now. Had I known they actually would have used it, I would have stayed behind. I am not proud of it."

"But you should be. You forced the sun to supernova after they destroyed your planet. You wiped out 80% of the Xi-Empire's fleet in one shot. It was brilliant."

"We took the offensive when it was pointless to do so."

"It was your right to self-protection. It took the Empire years to rebuild their fleet, and that bought your colony ships time to escape and hide. It was the right thing to do. You should put that information into your children's education. You must teach them that they have the right to take the offensive when they are in danger."

The other two Xeronians looked at him in utter shock, eyes wide, faces stretched taut. "No, we cannot do that!" Tsaurau said incredulously.

Ryan shook his head in frustration. "You people drive me crazy! Don't you think I would appreciate some help to fight these creatures? You want me, with one ship, to go out and face the whole damn Empire alone, to destroy their military presence that now spans over light-years."

Taldig interrupted. "Yes, their reach is very expansive. But because of this, you will not have to fight the entire Xi-Empire's fleet at once. Their ships are scattered. Their strength not focused. We do expect you will find help. There are others. Word will spread and help will come. You will become the most powerful voice in this galaxy because you will stand against the Xi-Empire. Others will follow you because they respect your bravery. You will see this happen. It is prophecy."

Ryan looked out the viewport, out to the horizon. *No use arguing with them on their fanciful prophecies. To master the sciences and technology, and still believe in magic.*

The small ship was descending, in seconds darkness swallowed them as they ducked into the shadow of the mountain. Ryan took the last few minutes to reflect on the archives he found. *The Xeronian military efforts were purely defensive, never assuming the offensive. They would not, or maybe even could not, fight back. Even Taldig's reaction to their use of the supernova weapon seemed contradictory to everything he seemed to be teaching. Maybe that's why they needed him. They needed someone more... savage. Fine. He was savage, and yes, he would use such a weapon, if not as a deterrent, then as a last line of defense.*

"Taldig. Consider this a formal request for you to dig up the plans used to build that doomsday bomb, or whatever it was that made your sun go supernova."

An Xeronian equivalent of the look of shock crept over their features. For a second Tsaurau looked like he was about to say something, but even he retracted and chose to remain silent. Taldig surprised him with an answer. "We will find the plans, but care must be taken. You must not employ such a weapon without considering the ramifications."

"I'll use it if I have to, and only if I have to, and when the time comes, I will not hesitate."

* * *

7. The Dancing Queen

Piloting a starship was not easy. Ryan crashed so many times he had lost count. Total concentration was required at the controls, and he found it difficult given his numerous diversions. To top it off the Xeronian training team was unforgiving, practically ruthless, as they pushed him to the limit on every virtual flight.

Angry and frustrated, he fought to ignore them outright, as it was the best way to avoid lashing out at them. Even Tsaurau left him alone.

Weeks passed before things started to improve. *He was finally achieving what Taldig had sought to teach him, to literally feel every facet of the ship around him.*

Drills that had once ended in catastrophe he now passed with ease. But each time he began to acquire some grain of confidence, they altered the tests.

Gem was allowed to help him at this level. She kept Ryan informed of critical information as he piloted the ship through the maneuvers. Despite the help, failure was unavoidable just the same.

Taldig poked his head into the simulator before one of the training exercises. "Are you finding the vaskpar helpful?"

"Yeah. Huge help. I gather that part of my training was to go through all this anguish manually. Have to say I really appreciated that."

"One truly learns by making mistakes. Reliance on control systems and other aids does little to expand one's abilities. The pilot must be able to handle the ship and simultaneously interpret the incoming data."

"Right. Well, your team has no lack of imagination in their testing scenarios."

"You will be happy to note we are beginning the strategic training phase. I am very interested in how you will fare. I have faith the first few trials will be relatively easy for you. The remainder will be most challenging."

He gave Ryan the thumbs up. "What is it you say? Good luck!"

"Yeah, thanks."

He sat back and let out a breath before acknowledging the team to trigger the next session.

Everything seems more difficult in the beginning.

* * *

The ship was approaching completion and Gem's connections were almost at 100%. The engineers kept her preoccupied running tests and processing the result data, but Gem had grown far beyond their process controls. She was alive, feeling and seeing through thousands of sensors and devices. Sensations flooded her systems with raw data that required attention and focus.

No one noticed the changes in the sentient system. Even Ryan was too busy to pay attention to Gem. His attention remained on the last phases of construction, which focused on the internal layout of the ship's construction. He insisted that his designs supersede the more homogenous Xeronian designs. They conceded, largely because the pilot should, in all respects, have final say. Many details had to be reworked, including the color schemes. The Xeronian's infatuation with white was not shared by Ryan, who felt that the introduction of some variety of color and texture brought a touch of humanity to the ship's interior. The exterior hull, however, remained a bright, gloss white. In the end, this was an acceptable compromise.

In the evenings, Gem would often pester Ryan to play chess. As the games had become quite long, they agreed to impose a time limit per move. This did little to improve Ryan's game although he did manage, with more surprise than satisfaction, to bring the game to a draw.

Gem expressed what one could consider outright annoyance.

"I request another game. This success is a product of random chance."

Ryan laughed. "Don't like being beat, I see."

"You are mistaken. I was not beaten. This was a draw."

"Alright then, we'll go again tomorrow. We'll see if my playing was mere luck or not."

The following games became true duels. Ryan was determined to push further, and he varied his strategies doggedly, while Gem had no intention of ever ending another in a draw.

Tsaurau, who learned of the recent win from Ryan, monitored the matches out of interest sake. It took three games before Gem miscalculated and Ryan claimed checkmate.

Tsaurau was absolutely amazed. *How was this possible? The server had the ability to examine almost every permutation. Perhaps its resources were overloaded by the Xeronian technicians' processing?*

"Very strange. Perhaps we should take the server offline for diagnosis?" the Xeronian offered.

Ryan only laughed, enjoying the moment. "Why? Everyone and everything will make a mistake eventually. People slip. Machines glitch."

Gem sank into a self-inflicted depression, losing herself in an unending array of self-diagnostic checks, retreating from everyone - at least for a time.

* * *

At last, the ship was finished, albeit untested. Tsaurau, Tmaurau, and Ryan stood back and studied their creation with admiration.

"She needs a name," advised Ryan.

"A name? Oh yes, that peculiar custom of Earthmen to personify their vessels. What would you propose we name this vessel?" asked Tsaurau.

"Her you mean. We refer to our personified vessels as female – well, at least, I do. Are you familiar with our formal procedure of christening?"

"No. But I believe I could find out fairly quickly."

"Let me save you the time. Prior to maiden launch, the builder, or possibly the future Captain, takes a bottle of the finest of wines available and breaks it over the ship's bow. After that, a large celebration takes place with everybody involved in its construction attending."

"I do not understand this tradition in relation to a beverage, but a celebration can be arranged. We often have assemblies on certain anniversaries. Although this is not a significant day for our race, it is for all involved with the ship's construction. A celebration is a very good idea. I will pass it on to the council. When would you like to arrange this?"

"Tomorrow's good for me. Don't worry, I'll take care of the beverage details."

"We are on our way to see Taldig, would you like to join us?" asked Tsaurau.

"No. I'll stay here for a bit," muttered Ryan under his breath, eyes never leaving the wondrous achievement of technology that lay in front of him.

The noise level in the enormous hanger lowered to an easy interrupted quiet. The hundreds of Xeronian teams that had once worked feverously on the ship had retired, leaving only a few stragglers, who completed their tasks and left one by one, their equipment in tow. Ryan waited patiently, leaning up against a small cargo mover. As the last technician exited the bay, she ordered the lights off, and the room settled into a gentle darkness.

The ship's running lights were on, making it stand out prominently in the darkness, commanding attention. It was a bird poised for flight. It stood over 60 meters long, with a wingspan approximately 35 meters from tip to tip. The wings jutted out from an oblong, cylindrical fuselage, the complete shape in the form of a triangle, similar in many ways, to an Earthbound jet fighter. The wings were quite thick. The front burner/gluon disrupters embedded in the front and back sections provided additional power during forward and backward propulsion and complex maneuvering.

The design deviated in many ways from the standard Xeronian template, most notably the shape, which was not the typical oval. In such vessels, a large percentage of the outer hull was lined with disrupter plates, which provided propulsion in almost any direction required. This allowed for unhindered maneuverability in practically any direction, at any moment. Although this design seemed simple and stable, it was not without problems. Sophistication was hidden within. Routing for multiple disrupter systems filled the internals of the hull competing with the crew and cargo quarters and effectively reducing available real estate for the primary drive circuits. The disrupter plates provided poor external protection and presented the need for heavy internal shielding from X-rays produced for the crew.

The new ship followed a sleek, winged design with graceful lines that provided lift within a planet's atmosphere. A main burner/gluon disrupter was positioned at the rear of the ship, its plates lining a large sphere at the end of the fuselage. Loss of navigational flexibility is compensated for by additional burner plates strategically located along the rear wings. The rear burner design provides an exponentially higher output than that of a standard plate design, with a limited amount of shielding. Although the new design had reduced maneuverability in comparison to its previous, the new design exceeded in acceleration and ultimately, maximum velocity.

As an addition to the wings, a vertical stabilizer swept up from the top of the fuselage. It towered above, and at its tip, a large communication antenna jutted outward to the rear. Its spine reached down to its base, which slowly thickened to wrap around the rear spherical main drive burner, hiding a retractable rear cannon where the two met.

Underneath the ship, following along the belly from the front tip, a polygon section dropped down, starting at a sharp-angled point and branching out in a triangular manner. On its face, matter collector vents would open up during recharging. Near the rear, recessed into the drop-down section, were the main doors to the cargo area and the primary entrance, where ramps would lower to allow entry.

Above, beyond the wings, near the very front of the ship, lay the pilot's compartment. Large sectioned ports allowed the pilot an external view. Shielding could also project over these sections, providing extra protection in combat situations. From there, the fuselage narrows gradually into a sharp point, from which protrudes a rod, jutting forward as a sword, poised to strike. At the base of the rod is a cone-shaped device with its larger end facing the ship. This device channels a fine spray of antimatter over the ship's hull when the ship makes the jump beyond light speed – most notably, the state of acroluc. The antimatter envelop acts as a catalyst, propelling the ship's hull matter to an 'excited' state, effectively changing its atomic properties. The ship's mass, which inverts within the antimatter blanket, passes beyond the natural limitations of 'standard matter'. The gluon burners disrupt the lines of gravitation 'behind' the ship, and the anti-grav amplifiers reverse the field in front, effectively warping the fabric of space surrounding it, creating the forces necessary to propel the ship along its course. The result enables it to exceed velocities well beyond the speed of light, its only limitation being that of the energy consumed to accelerate it, which remains the governing agent of any starship. The drive system was built with a purposeful imbalance, as its power consumption capable of exceeding the energy stored within its capacitors. However, additional energy is siphoned off the antimatter shielding during flight. Matter, which the ship may collide with in flight, is instantaneously sublimated, converting its molecules into raw energy, which, in turn, recharges the capacitors. The greater the velocity, the larger the forward shield. Too much energy, however, and the system overloads and implodes. This balance is sometimes very difficult to achieve. In such cases, additional mass collection vents are employed to work in conjunction with the antimatter shielding, to drive conversion of plasma and gases into the needed energy.

The ship's designed-in gains in performance do not come without a price. If the gluon disrupter and antimatter flow, which are in constant fluctuation, become too far out of balance, the ship could rip apart like an exploding star. Redundant systems maintain that precious balance - a function dutifully overseen by Gem.

The presence of outside matter would make the jump through to acroluc impossible if it were not for shielding. The local field shrouds the ship and provides an extended buffer area. When a piece of matter, say a small comet, strikes the shielding, its mass is converted into energy which is then dissipated uniformly around the ship. The energy flux is absorbed easily. Realistically, however, this shielding cannot effectively protect the ship from anything that is larger than a 16th of the ship's total mass.

Ryan knew and understood all of the ship's technical specifications. He could rhyme off any component system in a given order, and break it down to the finest detail. But now he was merely satisfied just to walk around it, and simply admire - her.

For the first time in a long time, he did not feel so helpless. With this ship, he was not a slave any longer. He had freedom, but most importantly, he had the chance to find Aviore.

Gem caught his attention. "Hello, Ryan."

"Ah. You've decided to join the living after your crushing defeat, I see."

Gem responded with a momentary silence.

"Ah, don't take it so hard. I'm just teasing you anyway. Besides, that's just a game. Where we are going, games don't matter much."

"What are you doing standing out there in the dark?"

"I am just soaking up some piece of mind, I guess. Admiring a beautiful creation. Gem, maybe you can help me. I'm searching for a name for our ship."

"Do you have any preferences?"

"No."

"If a name is representative of an object, how would you describe this vessel?"

"Well. She's quite a ship, has a majesty all her own. If she were a woman, I would consider her of the highest order. Royalty. A Queen."

"You wish to call her Queen?"

Ryan pondered the question for a time. "Well, she's graceful, don't you think? Like a dancer."

"Please clarify."

"A dancer? A dancer is one who moves to music in such a way as to pull emotions from the people who watch her."

"What music are you referring to?"

"The music? Why it's the music of the stars, Gem. You look out there, and it surrounds you. The music is created by the stars themselves."

"Then we shall call our ship *Dancing Queen*... Is that satisfactory?"

It had a nice ring to it. Formal. Graceful.

"Yes," he nodded, "That sounds right. That is what it should be. We'll call her *Dancing Queen*!"

He was pleased, almost foolishly giddy. He had the urge to get in and fly her. But no. Not just yet. It was not ready. But was he?

"Gem, you think we are ready?"

"Yes, but we have not, as yet, left the bay. I do not wish to sound overly optimistic, but all tests to date have been exemplary. All design simulations promise excellent capabilities."

"But the ship has not left its dock. That is the ultimate verdict."

"I have reviewed the construction schedule. There are some tests that have been passed by."

"The Xeronians have been building ships for a thousand years. I think we can trust their abilities and their judgment. They have bypassed tests because they're confident, but also because of me."

"Because of you? How have you affected their judgment?" queried Gem.

"I needed them to go as fast as possible. They built this ship in record time, all things considered. It was a combined effort by most of this colony."

"What is the reason to hurry in such a way?"

"You and I are going to protect this planet from invasion by two savage races. They call themselves Xilozaks and Txtians, and they are advancing into this sector of space."

"I see... I will be in danger, won't I."

"Why, you worried?"

"No, I am originally from a warship. I have become... familiar with fear..."

"Fear? You?"

"I enjoy being alive."

"Yeah, so do I, most of the time. But no one gets out alive."

"What do you mean?"

"We are all going to die sometime. It's how we live that matters."

"And our purpose?"

"We are going to take down an empire – or die trying. Given the odds, it will probably be the latter."

Gem took a moment to respond. "I have a number of archives of battle histories from my previous ship. They may be of help."

That sparked Ryan's interest. "I'd like to review them, all of them if you can."

"Just ready yourself, Gem. This is not going to be easy. If you have some things to do to get yourself prepared..."

"I will prepare. Thank you, Ryan. Will it be alright if I am offline for a short time?"

"Of course, Gem. Is there something wrong?"

"My memories of war are not... agreeable. I must come to terms with our purpose in order to work at maximum potential."

"And withdrawing from me will help this?"

"No, I need to perform certain memory optimizations. I must stay objective, you see."

"I do. Do what you need to do, my friend."

Silence followed.

Alone again. He gave one more glance at the ship and lay his hand on the hull.

Soon, Aviore, soon.

Ryan made it back to his apartment without meeting another soul. Alone in his room, he reviewed the files from ancient wars of long ago. He scrutinized over them multiple times, catching the use of tactics Taldig had never dreamed of discussing. The losers of these conflicts had made mistakes that had cost them dearly, mistakes Ryan was intent on committing to memory - of what *not* to do. He knew this information could save his life one day. Butterflies danced in his stomach throughout the night. Brandy did nothing to soothe the edginess that engulfed him. Only the compulsive urge to scour through the libraries seemed to calm his fraying nerves. Battles, some in first person perspective, others through observational records, every conflict documented in full detail, some with debriefing testimonials from survivors. The Flukkens had been meticulous in their archives.

He fell asleep with strategies racing through his mind.

All battles end in death.

* * *

The following day started with a heated discussion between project leads and Ryan.

"I will not allow it. It is too great a risk!" Tsaurau was as close to demonstrating anger as Ryan had ever seen him. His face was a flustered grayish-pink, his eyes closed slightly. His veins around his bald head throbbed from the beat of his double hearts.

"Sorry, I am going to do the test flights myself. I cannot risk someone else damaging this ship."

"But it is not even cleared for flight yet. There is a possibility of catastrophe. You may die!"

"There is a risk related to getting out of bed. Do not tell me about dying. I have seen enough death for 10 lifetimes. This ship is mine. I fly it, no one else."

The group members looked at one another. All were obviously upset. "I vote to put this to the council," said Tsaurau.

Ryan interjected. "No, the decision stops here."

He scanned their faces. *They did not like that. Not at all.*

The group's looks shifted from expression, giving them away – they were conducting a closed conversation over the Par. Ryan waited patiently. They finally broke up and Tsaurau approached him. "Very well, if you feel you are ready, we will have you perform the tests."

Ryan smiled from ear to ear. "Good. Then let's get going."

"No. We need to complete additional hardware analysis and prepare the ship for flight. The capacitors require time to reach a full charge. This will take a full day."

"Tomorrow then?"

"Tomorrow... and Ryan, I do not want you to take unnecessary risks. I do concede, however, if anyone is prepared to fly this ship, it is you."

"I understand your concerns. Put this in context. I am going out there to fight interstellar battles. Don't try to restrain me from testing my own damned ship."

Tsaurau looked down to the floor. "Yes, of course."

"Has anyone discussed the christening?"

"Whenever you are ready, we would be pleased to partake in the ceremony."

"It's common to release the ship into the water after we break the bottle, but in this case, we'll make an exception. He chuckled at his own joke, contrary to placid looks of his alien friends. "Right, well let's do this! It's time for a party!"

Ryan spent the next hour fabricating a proper bottle of wine. When he arrived back at the docking bay, he found the place packed with Xeronians, whole families, including small children and even the Elders. A makeshift stage area was set up under the nose of the ship. Council members and project leads waved him up. As he arrived, warm applause followed.

Tsaurau leaned over and said in his ear. "We have adapted some Earth customs for this ceremony, in your honor."

Ryan was truly touched, knowing this all seems very strange to them. He clutched the bottle tightly and faced the crowd. "Thank you, everyone. Especially those who helped build this fine vessel. Thank you, all."

His voice rang out from invisible loudspeakers, not echoing through the air, but through the Par itself. All Xeronians turned their attention to him. He didn't actually need to talk, but to him, it felt wholly unnatural to stand in front of a crowd and *think* his speech.

"The first time I went into space, it was as a captured slave. I didn't know at the time why I was torn from my home. I didn't know that I would be sentenced to work the remainder of my life in a mine."

"I kept fighting. I watched as others around me died, surrendering to death instead of another day of suffering. I know everyone has lost something in this war, but no one truly dies until they lose their hope."

Memories flooded back. He pushed them away.

A small Xeronian child waved at him as he sat perched on his father's shoulders. His eyes squinted a typical Xeronian smile.

Ryan continued on. "I might have lost hope myself, but I found a friend. I never thought..."

Emotion welled up inside him. *Bosn Gary. Brave as they come. He hadn't expected to lose control. Pull yourself together. You look like a fool.*

The crowd waited patiently. Their pity he did not want. In his mind, he felt the anger start, planted from an undesirable seed. It seemed to explode within his mind, and turn into the face of Xilozak from so long ago. His hate burned like an open fire.

The time had arrived for retribution.

"I never thought I'd find another friend. That gave me hope. We managed to escape, but he was injured and eventually passed. Again, I thought I was alone. Until I met you. You welcomed me into your world, invited me to spend time with your families. I learned your history, found that you too are the victims of the same enemy."

The crowd shifted a bit uneasily, memories flooding the Par of loss and pain.

"I am told that some of you believe me to be this protector called the

Grafu. I cannot say that I am, or that I am not, but I will do my best to help every one of you."

A few of the small children ran gleefully through the crowd, blissfully ignoring him. A baby cooed and a mother held it close.

This was a place of life. He could not bear the thought of these people being flogged by a Xilozak slaver.

"I give you my word that I will destroy this Empire, or I will die trying."

Their silence persisted. They did not understand to cheer.

He took the bottle and held it high in the air. "With this bottle, I christen thee, *Dancing Queen*, first warship of the Xeronian fleet!" He smashed the bottle into the hull. The simulated red wine dripped like blood off the white hull.

Again silence.

Ryan looked over to Tsaurau, who started clapping. The crowd joined in.

The post-celebration was quiet. Xeronians were not an exciting social race. Ryan mingled, met a few new faces and attempted to play with a couple familiar Xeronian children. He had a few interesting discussions, but he could not shed the feeling in the back of his mind. It nagged at him continually, pulling him away from the reality surrounding him: the feeling of tremendous urgency.

The day passed quickly. He retired early.

* * *

The nightmare returned.

He was running. Running through a dark ship of gray corridors, a maze, hall after hall. They all looked the same.

Her screams echoed, twisted, out of phase. It was Aviore.

"Stay away! Please, stay away."

He ran until his lungs burned and his legs ached under the strain.

"Please help. Someone, please help me," the voice sobbed with fear.

Closer now. But legs, rubbery, folded under him. Hand over hand, he pulled himself up. Around the corner.

She lay on the floor, covered in blood. He called to her. She turned to him, eyes lost in a sea of pain. "No!"

A dark shape moved between them. A familiar figure - a Xilozak. A long metal rod glinted in the gloom. Teeth lashed out white.

"Too late, Earthman!"

A light exploded. It burned through Ryan's chest with the heat of molten metal. His body went numb and he fell. It lasted an eternity. His eyes searched her out. He tried so desperately to call for her, but couldn't.

He felt himself die.

The Dancing Queen

He lurched awake, covered in sweat, his heart pounding. The images still burned fresh in his mind from an all too familiar nightmare. His hands shook uncontrollably. *It seemed stronger now, and more frequent.* He sat on the edge of his bed, the cold sweat sticking to his clothes.

It was numbing, this dream. Like he was losing her over and over again. He searched for the strength to deny the feeling, but it wouldn't leave him. *He had to find her.*

He tossed his few meager possessions into the middle of the bed, folded the corners of the blanket up, then swung the makeshift sack over his shoulder. It was Xeronian night, and the corridors were quiet. The ramp into the *Dancing Queen* lowered as he arrived. He tossed the sack to the side and headed to the cockpit. Light panels glowed softly showing the way. The large captain's chair proved to be invitingly comfortable. With a deft wave of his hand, the console lit up with the virtual controls.

A quick scan gave the status on the systems: capacitors nearly at full charge.

The ship was almost ready.

Soft hues of the bay's night lights peeked in through the open viewport, shedding whitish hues over the cockpit. The shields had been retracted fully allowing an unrestricted view of the bay. Upon the floor lay scattered an odd collection of equipment and parts, littering the otherwise featureless chamber. No movement came from below, as the Xeronian engineers had long since left. They no longer needed to work in perpetual rotating shifts.

Ryan reclined the chair, cushions softly hissed as they adjusted to his body. For the second time that night, he fell into a deep sleep.

Gem retracted the ramp. She could sense Ryan's troubles, but she knew there was only one cure for this. They must travel amongst the stars.

* * *

"Ryan, time to wake up."

He stirred. Images of the previous night now blurry, but he could remember how it *felt.*

"Open your eyes, Captain."

"Yeah. Yeah. And good morning to you, Gem. Glad to see you are back and your normal, chipper self today."

The bright, white lights of the bay shone through the quartz panels into the cockpit. Ryan adjusted the filter level to kill the brightness. It had been pre-set for Xeronian eyes. "I swear, I should be blind by now," he mumbled.

"Captain, they are looking for you," reported Gem.

"Well, tell them where I am."

"I did not wish to have them disturb you until you awakened. You had a rough night."

"That was very mothering of you, Gem," he returned, with slight humorous sarcasm. He stood up and stretched.

His body felt good. Must be the built-in ultrasonic muscle simulators in the seats.

Through the monitors, he saw a small party approaching. They were, more than likely, slightly irritated. By the time he made it to the airlock, they were waiting for him.

"Morning, ah... team."

Tsaurau headed up the group. "Ryan, we did not know where you had disappeared to and we could not retrieve any information from the Par - your vaskpar server was interfering."

"Yes, I'm afraid that one has a will of her own."

"Feeling a bit mischievous, I see," he commented silently to Gem.

A reply shot back. "They underestimate me sometimes, you know."

He addressed the group. "I believe first launch is scheduled in one hour. I have time for a shower and shave. So I'll see you all in a bit."

"I have something to present to you," said Tsaurau. "In private if possible. It will not wait."

"Well, come on up, then."

Tsaurau ordered the ramp raised behind him.

"You need to share some deep secret or something?"

"Yes. Some may not agree with me on what I am about to do. I simply wish to avoid conflict. All the councilors and the Elders know of my intentions, and they have given me their blessing. I have a very special gift for you. It will help you in your search." He produced a small golden vial. It glowed slightly where his hand touched its base.

"This is the gift of life, it is called *Shamanah*. It is said to bestow an eye into eternity, a view into the future. Use of it is restricted within Xeronian custom. Only one of the High Council may ingest it, but it is my gift to you. You must draw from its strength, use the power it infuses."

Ryan took the vial. It was warm to the touch. Shades of gold danced through the clear cylinder.

"What's this, some kind of hallucinogen?"

"No, not exactly. It takes hundreds of years to produce this amount. It is very precious."

Ryan offered it back. "Look, I can't accept this. This is your custom. You use it."

"No. You must. Time is precious, and this will help you find Aviore."

"Find her? What do you mean?"

"You will see."

"If this is so precious, why would you give this up?"

"Because you need it - more than any of us."

Ryan scrutinized the vial with skepticism. "An eye into eternity? So I drink it? You're sure this won't poison me?"

"Yes. At worst, it will give you a mild headache. It is compatible with your metabolism."

"And what happens after? Makes me high or something?"

"Not exactly. I will leave you to experience it. You can then choose how to describe the experience."

"When?"

"Soon. I suggest before your first flight."

"Oh, that soon."

"And also, a small gift relayed from my father. It is something you would understand, other Xeronians may not."

Tsaurau pulled a long sword from a scabbard that was hung across his back. The alien strained at the effort.

"Excuse me a moment. The weight of this object proves challenging."

Ryan reached out and took the sword by the hilt. It was a weapon gilded and inlaid with fine gems, although its golden luster lay hidden under a tarnished skin.

"A sword, a fine blade at that." He swung it sharply, and it hissed through the air. "Nicely balanced."

"It has meaning, especially to my father, here – you may review the link on the Par. Few truly understand this object's representation."

Ryan peered into the Par, found the link, and scanned the summary of information. "So this is a Showmish blade. All the more impressive."

Tsaurau handed him the scabbard. "The red garnet, press on that and you will notice the weapon will activate the disruptor."

He pressed the jewel, and the sword began to vibrate slightly in his hand, giving off the slightest scent of ozone. "I'm sure this is deadly in close quarters."

"Ryan, we must depart to the chamber. The Council has already convened. We must hurry."

Ryan eyed the Xeronian carefully. He actually seemed excited. "You are referring to this vile, right?"

Tsaurau nodded.

"Alright, I'm game I guess. Give me a few minutes to get ready."

It did not take him long to clean up and head out to the chamber. Both upper and lower councils were present when they arrived. A rectangular pedestal of granite had risen from the center floor of the chamber.

"You must drink the contents, then quickly lay down upon this platform or you will fall."

"Potent stuff." He glanced at the silent crowd. "Why the audience?"

"We are here to help - to share in your visions, to guide as necessary."

The vial seemed to pulse in his hand.

Tseman spoke, her old voice echoed in the chamber, lower in pitch than what he remembered. "The time has come to open your eyes, to see through the mist of time, beyond all expanses of distance. Watch for the symbols Ryan, for they represent your life."

"It is time," whispered Tsaurau.

He hesitated only a second, closed his eyes, and drank it down. The taste was smooth and sweet, like warm honey. "When will it take effect?"

"It already has, please lie down," Tsaurau said.

His voice seemed to waver strangely. Hands guided him. Everything around him began to spin, slowly at first, then faster and faster.

The sensation of falling.

Everything faded to dark gray.

Suddenly he was awake. The dizziness had left him. He felt very light, like he was floating. He looked around. The Xeronians surrounding him were in some kind of trance, seeming lost in their meditation. Realizing he was elevated he looked down, to see himself, or rather, his body, laying still on the granite pedestal.

A movement. It was Tseman. She was motioning to him, waving slowly. *Go. You must go.*

He felt a pulling sensation. With a sudden rush, he was ascending, accelerating towards the ceiling. He silently screamed as he passed *through* the granite. Upward he flew, through the hundreds of levels of the artificial city, through steel and stone, through the last of the hardened granite mountain, leaving behind its cold shadow. In an instant, he was free, the planet below him shrinking in the distance. He accelerated and felt heavy, incredibly heavy.

But where was this taking me?

He felt the fear climbing through his being like a desperate, dying flame, felt the panic take hold and build.

Hold now. Relax. Hallucinogenic effects. Trust Tsaurau.

He closed his eyes to the maelstrom of passing lights.

No. He could not be out here, this is only a dream, an illusion brought on by that strange drug.

The stars were flying by quietly. Visions of entire solar systems lasted for brief seconds as he passed. Some had planets. Intermittently he would pass one that twinkled on its dark side revealing life. Yet they all faded away like dying embers.

The weight began to lift. He slowed to a pause. The stars around him seemed familiar. A planet loomed ahead. Ice reflected brightly from a polar cap, piercing his eyes, forcing him to look away. A shadow seemed to follow him, just beyond his line of vision. He focused his tormented eyes on a shapeless darkness that grew closer at a terrifying speed. It radiated a coldness that bit through him and left an aftertaste of rusted metal. Then it too was gone, as suddenly as it appeared, lost in the expansive background of the long-dead planet.

Why had he stopped here?

A familiar tug pulled him away, and he felt the sensation of heaviness build. The strange planet disappeared into a small, insignificant dot. Once again blurred lines of stars passed. He traveled an unknown path, suffocated by a relentlessly heavy burden. Ahead, another dot appeared, morphed into two - a binary star system. The primary sun was massive. A smaller blue dwarf sun orbited around it at a reckless speed. He looked away from the fiery furnaces and out into the stars. Something was urging him to look beyond. He saw a small red dot far away.

"There," he heard the whispers say.

He passed the remains of what must have once been a planet. The broken derelict wobbled radically on its axis, torn apart ages ago by the intense gravitational forces of the two suns, a lifeless corpse in the dead of space.

Again, he felt the weight lift. The red dot transformed into an immense planet. It was majestic, a testament of nature's will. But as it rotated below, details became clear. There was something drastically wrong. Skies swirled in yellowish grays and blood reds, suspending ebbing rivers of poison filth. Through darkened skies, the lights of sprawling cities blared through. They spread over the surface like black cancerous growths. Above each, the skies were littered with swarms of ships, launching and landing, as bees do around a beehive.

Ryan's realization turned to sullen gray. This was Xilo, the capital planet of the Xi-Empire. The wobbling planet that he had passed by was Txtia - a planet ripped apart long ago.

Time reversed, and new images played out. The planet below transformed into an oasis bountiful with life, blanketed in rich blues and greens. Far out in space another planet, whole, teetering on the edge of destruction, it too teeming with life. He watched as its inhabitants leapt the chasm of space within a deluge of black needles.

Then Txtia tore apart, ripping through its center, oceans pouring into blackness, and life screaming its last cold breath.

Wars began on Xilo, scarring its lush surface with blackness. The Txtians struggled to survive; the Xilozaks defended their home. Advanced Txtian technology met with a vicious Xilozak zest for battle.

He fell down to the planet, only to arrive in front of a thick, wood and metal clad door. Beyond it lay a rustic expanse of a room and at its center, a roaring fire. A Xilozak nurse held a baby in her arms.

The baby seemed different. Red eyes looked up at him.

It could see him. He swore it was watching him.

Another scene. A leader, a crownless king with red eyes, ordering the last of the Xilozak rebels to painful deaths. After, the wars faded to an unsettled peace. Xilozak and Txtian lived and worked together under the first of the Zigot bloodline. The Emperor had silenced the guns and brought forward a brief age of inter-racial peace.

The Txtians were the technically advanced, the Xilozaks, physically powerful. Their symbiotic union marked the beginning of the Xi-Empire. Time shifted in a blur, and their technology spread across the planet, spewing forth poison and death. Ships launched in unending plumes of flame. They carried with them their insatiable need to conquer and destroy. They pillaged, they killed, and they enslaved. The mighty Xi-Empire was born.

He looked down with disgust at the roiling filth below. It was an ecological disaster. An unrelenting succession of factories churning out a never-ending fog of pollution, discharging so much poison that even a planet as large and invincible as Xilo could not absorb it. Land once lush-green with life, now lay as fields of red mud. It is a planet raped of all of its distinction.

Why? The factories ran for one reason: to build the weapons of war, and ultimately, to advance the reaches of the Empire. The war machine would not stop for any reason. It was a leviathan of destruction.

The Empire's might lay before him a pitiful failure. They had lost all appreciation for beauty. They were materialistic, obsessed with the concept of ownership, practitioners of slavery and oppression.

A ship was approaching him from behind. He *felt* it before seeing it. Its burners glowed with heat as it decelerated. He had an uncontrollable need to look within. He plunged through its hull and saw as much as felt his suspicions. The dense air, the pungent odors, the filth. *This was a slavership.* Creatures of different shapes and sizes lay about the large cargo bay. They were the down-trodden, the oppressed, slaves. Amongst them was a group of humans. To his right another room, small and dark. He heard crying from within. A woman, alone, in pain.

He moved closer, trying to peer through the darkness. Her face was covered in a mass of knotted, matted hair. She was huddled into a tight ball on the bare floor, wrapped in a collection of torn rags. Her cries were soft and tearless. Festering sores and bruises pockmarked her skin, unable to heal due to neglect and malnutrition.

She spoke, her voice faint and unsteady, tapering off to a whisper, "Ryan, wherever you are, I can't hold out much longer. I'm sorry."

"*Aviore!*"

She looked up, her face frail and hollow, her eyes red and shallow. He could see her desperate pain. He tried to move closer, to touch her, but could not. Something stopped him, held him frozen. A bright light engulfed everything around him. And then there was darkness.

He felt an uncontrollable urge to breathe. *He was back, and he didn't want to be. He wanted to be there, with Aviore, to be with her.*

He opened his eyes and looked around.

"No! No! I need to go back."

Tsaurau's concerned face filled his field of view. His large black eyes revealed something different, an emotion, possibly sadness. Ryan pushed him back and sat up, savagely shaking off a momentary wave of dizziness. Between his fingers, he held the empty vial. He grasped it so tight that it shattered in his hand. He did not feel the pain but saw the blood well up between his fingers.

He was not really here, he was there, with her, filling his mind, frame by frame.

Tsaurau's voice brought him back. "Ryan. You have indeed returned. We are here with you, now. You are back on Xeronia."

His hand trembled with sharp pain. He opened it and pulled the fragments from his palm.

"Aviore?"

"We experienced what you experienced. I understand your pain. We all understand."

"Was this real, or just an illusion?"

"The world you know is one of many. Your experience was real."

"The timing? Now, in the future, what?"

"There was no substantial distortion of relative time."

"Did she see me?"

"No. Felt your presence possibly, somehow. Such things are possible."

"I have to find her."

Tseman interrupted him. "Earthman. Time is an indeterminable dimension. Fleeting in one moment, eternal in another. The reality of the world you know is gauged by this measure. You have but little of it in comparison to the rest of the universe. Use it wisely. I have seen the visions. They carry details of substance. Do not forget them, for they hold the clues to your destiny. You have been given the gift of sight, use it well, and it may reveal more."

A small hesitation followed as she collected her strength. "My fellow councillors and I bid you farewell, my friend. Go with courage."

They left then, Tseman first, the others following respectfully. Tsaurau and Ryan watched quietly.

There was nothing more to say.

When they had all filed out, Tsaurau took a few moments to inspect Ryan's hand. "We must attend to these wounds immediately."

"No, I must leave."

"We must complete the flight tests before you do."

"I can't wait another day, Tsaurau. You saw her! By now you understand that, don't you?"

"Yes, but we must perform these tests. They may reveal problems that will need to be addressed. The ship is not yet proven. If you want to save her, you must ensure your vessel is spaceworthy."

Ryan nodded, knowing they could not avoid the flight tests. It was foolhardy otherwise.

"Once we finish, I head out. We complete only what's critical. I can perform other tests while in flight."

"Very well," conceded Tsaurau with a slight nod. "And do not forget to reflect upon what you have witnessed. Do not disregard Tseman's wisdom. Look for the clues. They will help you."

Ryan shook his head. "I don't understand it all. I was there, on Xilo itself. But it wasn't a dream, wasn't a hallucination, so what was it?"

Tsaurau only shrugged.

"Then I know where I need to go. That is where I must start searching."

"You realize you may find more than you are prepared for, and she was not alone. If you rescue her, then you must rescue the others as well."

"Yes, of course, I know. And you know I'll need to bring them back to someplace safe. Many will be suffering from malnutrition and sickness. Are you, I mean, your people, are they willing to help? Can I bring them here?"

"We will do what is required of us. It is our way."

Ryan rested his good hand on the Tsuarau's shoulder. "You never know. I may even find volunteers to fight alongside me. They may need someone to teach them, too."

"What you ask may be challenging. This may take some time."

"I realize that, but I cannot fight this war alone."

"Then we will be prepared for your return, and for your cargo."

"Then let's get to work."

* * *

Ryan sat in the pilot's chair, scanning the system feeds. The burners were already fired up, and the anti-gravs were humming cheerfully. The Xeronian technicians watched apprehensively as Ryan passed through his list of checks, verifying every system, step after step, test after test. A crew of engineers stationed aboard constantly cycled the systems through diagnostics and others coordinated subsystem tests.

The Dancing Queen

Preliminary checkout passed. The signal was given.

The bay doors slid open to angry, swirling-red skies.

Ryan pulled the *Dancing Queen* up to a hover and eased her out of the bay, filling the room with a deafening roar as the burners pushed on. The ship inched out into the open air, its nose pushing through the red-devil winds. In a second she was free.

The first bout of turbulence attempted to drive her into the side of the mountain, but Ryan's ingrained reflexes guided her out of danger with graceful ease. His confidence strengthened as the *Dancing Queen* responded with unblemished perfection.

On board the ship was organized chaos. Gem wrangled through hundreds of internal tests. The Xeronians chattered back and forth excitedly, many relaying incomplete sentences to one another, as their vaskpar link carried the corresponding tidbits of unpronounced thoughts.

Ryan closed all the intercom channels, as well as his mind, to the Par, effectively blocking all of them out, except for, of course, Gem.

It was real. An impossible dream had become real. He could feel the ship around him as an extension of his own body. He felt her pulse through his veins like red-hot steel. The link to Gem, and to the ship, was direct. It was impossible to explain. Such power. Such untested strength.

"All systems operating within acceptable limits." Gem relayed.

Tsaurau's face showed up on the communications monitor. "We're switching to standard communications channels now, Captain. The Par has limited range, and its security must be protected. This will be your first time piloting in space, how do you feel?"

Ryan smiled, a little nervously. "I'm ready. It's these damn technicians crawling all over the place that makes me nervous."

"Do not worry, remember your training and you will do fine."

"Standby for direct ascension... starting... Now."

He thumbed the vertical burners, putting the ship to an 80 degree angle and poured on the power to the main drive. The anti-gravs whined in protest, and the ship climbed, vibrating only slightly. He straightened her out, adjusting trim for the winds, and continued the climb, monitoring the displays and the feeds through the vaskpar. He cycled through the ship's systems stats in microseconds.

"We have a small coolant leak within the port wing adjacent to the rear burner plates, the backup has been activated," Gem warned.

"I noticed. Well if anything is going to bust, let it be now. I don't want to be stranded and helpless in Xi-Empire space," returned Ryan. As if on queue, he felt a slight vibration, slowly rising in intensity.

"Gem, you find the cause yet?" he asked.

"We are experiencing problems with the harmonic balancing in the gluon disrupter drive. The problem appears to be in the electron dispersal circuitry."

The vibration grew steadily worse. Within the minute it was shaking so badly everything looked blurry. "Gem, I am going to abort ascension if this keeps up."

"We have isolated the problem to the harmonic balancing feed controls. It is software related. I am attempting to repair the control logic."

Suddenly, as quickly as it started, the vibration disappeared. A familiar voice perked up. "The new subroutines are in place, modification was successful."

"Good work. I was beginning to get a little nervous. Save me from looking will you and tell me, are there any other problems I should know about?"

"There are thirty-seven issues in all. The technicians are working on them. None will interfere with the ship's operational tests."

Through the viewport, Ryan could see the red atmosphere was still falling away as the *Dancing Queen* climbed out into space. Moments later the stars broke through, shining with a sharp, cold beauty.

He thumbed the com. "Everything A-OK. Beginning second phase tests on T-minus 30."

He ran the necessary checks and readied the antimatter dispersal flows. The capacitor readings dipped slightly.

"Shield established," he reported.

"T-minus 5..4..3..2..1." He engaged the burners to full capacity. The ship leapt forward at an incredible rate.

"Beginning side roll now."

The ship began to rotate, using the fuselage as the center of its axis. The outside view was dizzying. Ryan pulled his eyes from it and watched his controls.

"All stress monitors show readings well within operating limits. I suggest an end-for-end roll," said Gem.

"That's not on the test schedule, they'll have a shit fit!" replied Ryan.

He swore he heard Gem laugh - was that possible? He thumbed the com again. "Tsaurau, we're going to do some fancy maneuvering."

"You are getting dangerously near the second moon," commented Tsaurau.

"Don't worry, even if we have a problem, it'll be a fly by."

"Let me confer with the engineers."

Ryan wasn't about to wait. He pulled the rotating ship into an end-for-end roll. He knew it was going to be fun pulling out of this.

"Anti-grav three out of harmonic. The new motion has upset the gravitonic sensors," reported Gem.

"Can you repair?"

"No. Recommend realignment of the ship to course."

"Negative. Be ready for fail-over. I intend to burn these suckers out. If they can't take the punishment, I don't want them in my ship."

"Within 1000 kilometers from the moon," reported Gem.

"The extra gravitational distortion should tax her to the limit," Ryan commented.

"500 kilometers, approaching zenith. Gravitation approximately 1.4 at zenith."

Ryan experienced a momentary feeling of nausea, but it passed.

"Anti-grav three just failed, load transfer compensation successful," reported Gem.

"That gravity flux almost made me sick," complained Ryan. "Are the technicians working on it?"

"Yes, they are in the process of troubleshooting. I suspect a full unit analysis will need to be done back at base."

Ryan decided he was tired of the reeling view outside. He straightened out the ship like an old pro. It wasn't as tough as he thought it would be. He was beginning to get the hang of this. "Gem, you think the remaining anti-gravs can compensate?"

"Yes, the remaining units are operating perfectly."

He triggered the com, "Tsaurau, proceeding to acroluc."

"Good luck, Captain."

He checked the flight path, made a few small adjustments before the ship was aligned. "Ready to engage acroluc drive at T-minus 30." He checked and double-checked the readings. Everything was ready.

"5..4..3..2..1. Engaging."

The *Dancing Queen's* first jump to acroluc was unremarkable. The antimatter ejection system bathed them in bright, white light. Instantly they were transformed into a hurtling bolt of energy. "1, 1.5, 2.5 acroluc. Pulling back and leveling off. Systems registering A-OK up here, Xeronian base. Standby to drop out at T-minus 5..4..3..2..1."

As they dropped out of acroluc Ryan's back felt like it was on fire. It took a moment for him to realize it was the ship he was feeling.

"Gem, what the hell was that!"

"A misalignment in the antimatter dispersal field. One of the dispersal funnels will have to be adjusted. It is a minor problem."

"Great." He shifted in the seat, not appreciating the uncomfortable feeling.

"We've a bit of a burn going on, but we're alright."

"Weapons testing remaining," commented Tsaurau.

"I'm turning her around now." He swung the *Dancing Queen* around and headed back for Xeronia launching into acroluc. In seconds, the barren planet was bright in his viewport. He spotted a few small asteroids within sensor range. They had been captured by the planet's gravitation and pulled into orbit. He activated the four forward cannons. The wing armor slid back, retracting to allow the cannons to project outward.

He thumbed the com. "Everyone, please standby for weapons testing."

He fired each cannon successively and each destroyed their targets with precision. Flipping to rear cannon control, he maneuvered the ship and fired again. The target disappeared in a burst of microdust.

He flipped the com link. "All primary cannons passed, engaging secondary."

The upper and lower turrets fired on automatic, eliminating what remained of the targets.

"Well, no problems so far."

He scanned the tracing sensors. No other workable targets in range.

"Aligning missile on to the moon. All, standby for missile launch in 5.4.3.2.1."

The missile launched from the forward bay without issue.

Ryan traced it as it traveled, then triggered self-destruct. "Suggestion to belay remaining launch tests. No need in wasting further ordnance."

Tsaurau conferred to the engineers behind him. "We agree."

Ryan mentally flipped through the testing checklist. "All tests are complete, returning to home base." He retracted the cannon and the turrets. The shielding locked back in place. He brought the ship back down through the maze of towering mountains as fast as he dared, and reached the Xeronian hanger within minutes. The *Dancing Queen* taxied smoothly over the docking bay floor. The tests were, for the most part, successful. A few modifications, a few repairs, and everything would be ready to go.

Xeronian crews swarmed toward the ship armed with a collection of tools and parts. Tsaurau was there to meet him as he exited the ship. "Very good maiden voyage, Captain."

"She's everything I expected and more." Ryan offered his hand. Tsaurau's grip was tight. A silent moment passed between them. Promises had been made, and kept.

"I know you wish to leave as soon as possible, but can you do one last thing? Join me and my family for a meal. This is, as I understand, an Earth custom."

Ryan took a quick appraising glance at his ship and the scurrying work crews. "I expect they'll be busy with that anti-grav unit for some time. Sure. I'd be glad to."

"I only ask that you refrain from eating what you refer to as steak. It would make my wife uncomfortable."

Ryan laughed, "Whatever you offer, I'll eat."

The meal was delicious. Tsaurau's wife, who had researched Ryan's files for examples of earth-cooking, proudly served an elaborate spread that would have been a vegetarian's dream. Ryan's portion was considerably larger than the others, as the Xeronian diet was sparse at best. Tsaurau's two children watched him eat with wide-eyed fascination. A silent sharp look from their mother quickly diverted their attention.

"You will be missed. Your presence has been refreshing," she offered. She was a pleasant, quiet woman, slightly older than Tsaurau, although he could not discern it.

"No. It is I who will miss all of you. You and your people, are like a family to me."

"That is an honorable compliment. We thank you. We feel as you have also become a family member to us."

The announcement came over the Par: the ship was ready.

Ryan rose.

"Wait. Let me join you," Tsaurau asked hurriedly. "I'll just need a moment to change my attire."

"I'll wait."

His wife smiled back at him - a human smile. Her lips curled up, but the effect, on her, looked uncomfortable. She had done it for him out of courtesy, but Ryan had become accustomed to their Xeronian expressions. It suited them.

"You are a good friend to Tsaurau. He will miss you."

"Hopefully, I'll return to enjoy another of your fantastic meals."

"I will welcome that time."

Tsaurau rushed back into the dining area. "I'm ready," he announced, slightly out of breath. When they started for door Tsaurau's youngest pulled on Ryan's pant leg. "You will protect us, Earthman?" he asked innocently.

"Yes, I'll try my best."

A crowd had gathered in the bay to see him off. Taldig, Tmaurau, and a few of the doctors and engineers Ryan had worked closely with. They formed a line and each shook his hand, then offered a small comment of encouragement. Tsaurau was last. They shook hands solemnly.

"Stay alive my friend. I want my children to know you as they grow up."

"I will. Take care of yourself and your family... and thank you again. You saved my life."

"This is your destiny. I am only part of it. May your God help guide you."

Strange thing to say, for an atheist, but then again, they have their own form of religion.

He went up the ramp quickly, not looking back. The hatch retracted and sealed behind him. It took only a few moments to reach the cockpit. The crowd retreated quickly to a safe area as a silent siren sounded throughout the Par. The immense bay door slid open once more to the dust-filled winds. It was night outside and black as pitch. Ryan flipped on the running lights and raised the ship up to a crawling hover. He could see the crowd waving to him on the monitors as he moved away. Taking a deep breath, he brought the rear burners online and slowly moved out into the night. The colossal door slid back slowly until the last crack of light disappeared from sight. Once closed, it blended perfectly with the mountain's rock face, as if it had never been there.

Ryan pulled the nose toward the sky and fired the burners to full power. The *Dancing Queen* shot upwards, climbing higher and higher, up and into the stars.

* * *

8. First Engagement

The word had spread like an unchecked wildfire. The infamous Tarvok Zorlog had been captured. Such an event tended not to go unnoticed. On the way to Xilo, the small convoy accumulated escorts: wealthy aristocrats of the Empire, curious sightseers, the odd vengeful slaver. Most of them would welcome Zorlog's death. Zuvok Zerg himself had toyed with the idea of blasting the *Gohk II* into dust, but he knew that would be unwise. The onerous Xilozak belonged to a very special organization which would not regard such an action forgivable. One does not kill the unofficial leader of the Purist movement without, possibly, launching a civil war. And he was, after all, under the protection of the Emperor.

On board the *Gohk II*, Zorlog paced the bridge with frustration. He was not happy with the recent turn of events. He preferred to have control of the situation and did not appreciate times when he did not monopolize the game at hand.

"The Zuvok is hailing us, my Tarvok," his communications Avok reported.

"Put him on."

Zerg's image appeared. The Zuvok looked too jovial for Zorlog's taste.

"Zerg," he acknowledged, "What do you want now?"

"Tarvok Zorlog, as we are in the final segment of our excursion to Xilo, are there any last wishes you would like to make?"

"Your humor turns my stomach, Zuvok. Is it wise to consider me just a Tarvok? Perhaps you must attempt to remind yourself that I agreed to accompany you of my own accord. It is just like you to claim victory when a battle was never fought. I would welcome an engagement with you. Your kind makes war enjoyable. You are too smug, too confident, and always too predictable."

Zerg's jovial expression melted away, exposing an ugly layer of contempt. "When we arrive, ensure you do not stir up any trouble, Zorlog. Things are unsettled enough on Xilo."

"I am here as a sign of respect to the good Emperor. Is that not enough? However, if things digress, and I find I have been brought here under false pretenses to answer to criminal accusations, do not expect the situation to improve."

"You're here because the Emperor wants you dead. It's just a matter of time for you, Zorlog."

"Oh Really? I must concede Zuvok, I intend to stay very much alive, and your Emperor, well... let's just say that I believe he's ready to negotiate to my terms."

The Admiral's thin lips turned up into a snarl, exposing his large yellow fangs, his face now flushed dark with anger. "As soon as we dock, you're to be escorted to the capital city to meet the Emperor. We'll see what terms you can negotiate with him personally. If you do try anything foolish, I will kill you myself!"

The angry image disappeared. Zorlog's laugh rippled across the bridge, biting through a cold silence. Every one of his Avoks had stopped what they were doing to watch their Tarvok clash with an Empirical Zuvok.

"Are you really going to face the Emperor, Tarvok?" asked Gulin.

Zorlog saw a flash of fear cross the younger officer's face. It irritated him. Like this whole situation irritated him.

"Of course," he snarled, "he has a business proposition for me. Do not be so weak. He is flesh and blood, like you and me, only poisoned to the core with the Txtian seed. You hold too much reverence for Zigots."

The officers shifted nervously.

Zorlog swung his gaze across the bridge. "For those who have not realized the game has changed. We are no longer mere slavers. We are the revolution. We, you and I, will make Xilo great again."

He turned to Gulin. "Get three parties together, 20 apiece. I want them to do some groundwork for me while I am detained. There should be three freighters in port from the Corvelock quadrant. Find them. Inform their Tarvoks that I will be dropping in for a visit, after my meeting with the Emperor. They are not to leave Xilo without seeing me first. Understand?"

Gulin nodded and left.

Few understood what Zorlog had in mind. But they all knew things were about to explode. They all knew not to ask.

The *Gohk II* was directed to Zenux Port, the busiest spaceport in the Xi-Empire, adjacent to Zenux, the capital city of Xilo. It was the epicenter of trade for the Xi-Empire. Traffic choked the skies with ships of all shapes and sizes and filled the precious real estate of the Port. At Zenux Port, ships never stayed long, as the docking fees were very steep. Only the very rich could afford a reserved dock, excepting, of course, the military. The *Gohk II* shuddered as it came to rest in its own sectioned-off area. Swarms of sightseers remained at a distance, respectful of military-enforced restrictions. A regiment stood ready adjacent to the site waiting to receive their prisoner.

Zorlog assessed the situation from the bridge and growled with irritation. He marched to the lower airlock exit and was intercepted by Gulin. "I have the three ground parties assembled, my Tarvok. Do you want them to join you?"

Some of Zorlog's frustration evaporated. Gulin's naiveté on the inner workings of politics was truly enjoyable. "No, Gulin. This time I assure you, I will be going alone. However, locate the three ships I told you about and assign one to each. Ensure those ships remain docked until I return. No exceptions, no matter how much their Tarvoks whine about the cost."

"What about the military escort?"

"What about them? They are here to escort me only. Just ensure you are not followed. Create a diversion, do whatever it takes."

"And what do I tell the three Tarvoks?"

"Nothing. They need only to know I am on Xilo." Zorlog pushed his way past, heading for the airlock.

"But Tarvok," called Gulin after him. "What if you don't come back?"

Zorlog, now just stepping through the lock door, leaned back to look at Gulin. The Tarvok's face twisted in a warped grimace of humor and hate. He laughed with a sound as warped as his expression. It sent a shiver up Gulin's double spine.

Without another word, Zorlog stepped out. His amused disposition ebbed to silence as he descended the ramp. Behind him, he heard the footsteps of his crew. The three parties Gulin had assembled were following him, protectively.

Why didn't Gulin understand? It was better for him to wait until after he left. Loyal to a fault.

Zorlog arched his spines a little straighter. His military escort had already lined up in formation below. The crooked silhouette of a Txtian Torzon headed the group. His high-pitched, almost piercing, clicking cut through the smog-filled air.

"Come with me, Xilozak!"

Zorlog stood rigid at the foot of the ramp, distastefully eyeing the officer. "I'll not take orders from the likes of you, Txtian. Make way and keep your distance."

The Txtian did not like that reply, he did not like it at all. Too many hard years in the military had molded his expectations of subordinates. This Xilozak needed to be yanked down a notch. The insect concentrated, employing the mind-twist on the glaring Xilozak. He awaited the look of desperation and pain, the enjoyable, delicious moment when the Xilozak screamed for exoneration. But his anticipation was premature. Zorlog only laughed, his yellow teeth dripping wide gushes of spittle. The Torzon's eyes opened wide with surprise. He tried again, intensifying his concentration to its utmost. Some of the accompanying Xilozak escorts fell to their knees.

A Bellicose Dance

In a blur, before anyone could react, Zorlog pulled his razor-sharp bar from his belt, flicked on its disrupter field, and swung. It hit the Txtian with a bone-crushing impact, severing as it went. When it was all over the Txtian lay decapitated at Zorlog's feet, its body twitching in its death throes. Quiet came over the group. Their faces betrayed utter shock and disbelief.

It was Zorlog's cold, hollow laugh that finally wrenched them into action. The troopers scrambled to aim their blasters, only to stop as quickly as they began, realizing the presence of the *Gohk II*'s crew standing behind Zorlog, weapons ready and poised.

"Hold!" growled Zorlog, his snake eyes dancing on the troopers. "Paragraph 359 of the Military Code of Ethics: No Txtian may use the mind-twist on a fellow Xilozak or citizen of Xilo unless the Xilozak is a known criminal. Any attempts at doing so will be punishable by death! Since I have not been presented with any formal charge, I retain all rights of citizenship!"

Blasters lowered slightly. They knew the Code well. All of them did. It was required.

"You killed our Torzon!" one of them yelled.

"I am only upholding The Law," replied Zorlog.

One of the Txtians swung up his blaster, but before he could pull off a shot, a fellow trooper knocked him to the ground - a fellow Xilozak.

"And the Law is the Law!" announced the Xilozak trooper. "We all know the Code, and the Karvok was clearly using the mind-twist against regulations. I'll testify that to the Emperor himself." He turned to face Zorlog. "I am in command now. Your defense is duly recognized. It will be the Emperor that will decide your fate, not a Txtian Karvok. You two!" he a pointed at the two Txtians, "Clean up this mess! The rest of you, get in formation!"

"Tarvok," he gestured at Zorlog with a swing of his arm. "If you will."

Zorlog nodded respectfully and joined the escort.

Gulin had witnessed the whole scene from the airlock exit. *Only Zorlog would have the guts to do what he had just seen - and get away with it.*

The crew reluctantly ascended the ramp, watching their Tarvok's silhouette shrink in the distance.

What was he up to? What did his new orders mean? Something was going on here, and if he knew his Tarvok, it was going to be big.

* * *

Zorlog's satisfaction faded quickly. Murder, if anything, entertained his twisted mind only briefly. The sour Xilo wind was thick with exhaust and was blowing like a paste onto his face. He hated this planet with a passion. He hated the air, the dirt, the stained and deteriorating buildings.

They moved through the city at a steady pace, stopping only briefly to mount the segments of a rolling walkway, every twist and turn brought them deeper into the bowels of the Capital City. As they marched into the shadows of the Towers of Zenux, they met up with the Empirical Guard. He was handed over unceremoniously. His new escorts, grim-faced and cloaked, silently led him into and through the maze of the capital building. He followed them down into the transport passages and through the power grid's dark vertical tunnels that stretched for kilometers into Xilo's crust. Hot, spurious winds screamed past smooth, black, featureless walls. The induced null gravity of the corridors wrenched out bitter memories of battles fought in the hollowness of space.

Obviously, they were taking him the back way into the Capital building. They would ensure no witnesses. But he was still alive. The Emperor would have words for him first.

Bony arms jerked him into yet another passage. His feet came to rest on cold rock. It took a moment for his innards to settle back down to the restored gravity. His escorts, however, were impatient. They pushed him along. He growled at them ready to strike. They stepped away, slightly. Long black rods appeared from under the cloaks. The gloomy darkness gave way to a hazy green light as each rod activated. Steam sizzled as electricity traced along their length.

Zorlog laughed. *Disruptor rods. He was not the only fan of such hideous weaponry.*

He took the hint and started moving.

Stairs with steps too numerable to count, ended finally, at the foot of a set of immense doors.

This was the entrance to the Hall of the Apocalypse. He had heard of it, but very few had ever visited and returned.

Zorlog turned to look back only to find he was alone.

Strange he had not noticed them leave.

A low-intensity reverberation echoed up the corridor, and the massive doors slid open. Zorlog remained steadfast. *One must not be too impetuous.*

Another guard approached through the doors and beckoned him to follow. He was led into a hall and instructed to wait. He stood quietly in the dark, and carefully scanned his surroundings. It all seemed featureless in the suppressing gloom. He kept his mind occupied by running through variations of tactical battle strategies. He was so lost in concentration, he failed to notice the arrival of the Emperor until the creature was no more than two meters away.

The Zigot, even by Xilozak terms, was a hideous combination of Txtian and Xilozak. His mere appearance often made children cry, and his subjects cower. Zorlog stared back with indifference.

The Emperor's evil reputation was inflated.

The Zigot circled closely. Zorlog could feel his hot breath on his neck.

"I have word of a disturbing event. A Torzon killed by a civilian."

"I exercised my rights under The Law. That is all."

"So you have. I have interrogated the officers in charge. It is a shame we still tolerate such blatant abuses within our military. However, it seems we tolerate crimes of much higher magnitude. You, Zorlog, destroyed the Empirical Administration building on Goo15-A."

"That is unsubstantiated, my Emperor."

"You are a known Purist!" The Zigot shrieked. "For that crime alone, you should be killed!"

Zorlog pasted a dry, humorless grin on his face barring his yellowed teeth. "I have never admitted to being a Purist. Your information is tainted by the pettiness of your subjects. Many of them wish me dead, as I have refused to pay their illegal fees and bow to their whims of profit. So you see, Emperor, you too are a victim of propaganda. I tell you now, I only wish to serve you." He bowed his head in reverence, his mind reeling with a seething hate.

The Emperor stepped back into the shadows, which so richly populated the room, and mentally reviewed the Tarvok's response. *There was a remote possibility that this Xilozak is not what he thought. Was this slaver a mere decoy? A common criminal burdened with the weight of so many lies? Was this Xilozak capable of aspiring to the genius that he had been brought to believe? The fact remained, as his Zuvoks have attested to repeatedly; in the command of a starship, this Xilozak was not easy to kill. It was also true that his spies had perished on the Gohk without returning any useful information.*

"Do not play games with me, Xilozak. My sight extends beyond the edge of the universe. Nothing can be hidden from me. You ordered your first officer, Kitohk, to his death. You attacked my ships, and you destroyed my buildings."

"Kitohk was a fool, and your Torzon was corrupt. He was leeching credits from all who dealt within his region. Check his accounts, and check his brother's while you are at it. The evidence is there. He ordered your ships to destroy me. I merely acted in self-defense. I have my crew to think about."

"Very gallant of you - to think of your crew." The Zigot moved in close, bending to leer into Zorlog's face, mandibles dripping. His eyes danced with sparks of flaming red. Zorlog returned his gaze with impassive features, internally battling the urge to reach up and tear the head off the Txtian-bred freak. He forced his next words out with effort, carefully forming each syllable.

"My Emperor, I am merely a slave trader trying to make a living. I do not wish to be considered a criminal."

The Zigot's sneer melted away to a menacing grin. *This one is amusing.*

"Very well." He ended the discussion with a wave of his bony hand. "Let it rest for now. Time will uncover the truth. You have proven to be a competent strategist. My Zuvoks tell me you show promise. This is very unusual for them to admit such a fact, yet it is understandable as they must provide a plausible excuse when they return as failures. Shall I regard their pompous accusations with a measure of truth? Are you indeed more than the wretched excuse for a Xilozak that stands before me? Shall I spare your life, allow you to utilize your alleged skills within your military? Shall I allow you to attain the power and privilege of command?"

Zorlog said nothing.

The Emperor circled the room. "You must make a decision now. This does not come without a cost. Xilozak, simply revoke all your foolish Purists beliefs and join me. What you are is pathetically insignificant, raise yourself from the dirt."

"We all come from the dirt."

The Emperor laughed. "I have no time for this. What would you have me do? Allow you to walk away, ignore your transgressions, let your crimes go unpunished? That speaks so badly to the future, setting such a poor precedence. But then again, of what regard do I have of precedence? I am not ruled by the past, am I?"

"You are the Emperor," added Zorlog.

"Yes, yes. I am the Emperor. Tell me, I have heard you have ambitious plans. Perhaps it shall be more fitting for you to live your life out as the little peasant slave trader that you are."

The Emperor turned sharply to glare at the Xilozak. "Either rot in your existence, or aspire to become a part of the ruling arm of the Empire. It is your decision."

The Zigot waited, watching. *This was truly enjoyable. What would this Xilozak do? Refuse? He would kill him. He had no intention of allowing this dissident out of the room without having some level of control over him.*

Zorlog had already suspected the Emperor would make him an offer. Of what position of influence he could only guess. But it was genuine and as such presented new opportunities.

He was mindful enough not to reply immediately. It is a sign of insincerity to jump at an offer too quickly. He knew he could not refuse such a position. His peers would understand. *Infiltrate and disseminate.*

"I shall be honored to serve you, my Emperor." He knelt down on one knee, his head bowed. It took all of his strength to keep his grin down, to appear humble.

"A wise choice," the Emperor replied, veritably pleased. The Zigot adjusted a large ring on his middle finger. It began to glow in a rich orange-red hue. It bore the symbol of the Star of the Apocalypse. The Emperor approached, reached down and pressed the fiery ring onto Zorlog's forehead. It burned into his skin like a red-hot branding iron.

Zorlog enjoyed the pain. It had been a long time since he had felt such a rich sensation.

"You are now a servant of the Zigot. Your life is no longer your own. It belongs to me, the Emperor of Xilo. You are now part of the brotherhood that bonds. You will live and die by that bond."

"Swear your life to the protection and advancement of the power and glory of Xilo."

"I swear, to the power and glory of Xilo!" repeated Zorlog.

The Emperor pulled the ring away, leaving the symbol branded deep into Zorlog's forehead. It was the mark of the Zigot elite, the rank of Zuvok.

"You bear pain well, Zuvok Zorlog. I am pleased. I now have a few words of advice: Remain loyal to the house of Zigot for treason is a life of pain. Do well and you will be rewarded. Do poorly and expect death. Lastly, pity your enemy only when you grind them to dust."

"Get up, Zuvok Zorlog."

Zorlog rose, energized by his new found status. "What, my Emperor, is my first assignment?"

"I can use your previous slave trader talents. I assume you have heard of our latest conquest?"

"I am familiar with the Signus system. I visited Zuvok Zembrock near the end of his campaign in that very sector. Seems he failed to relay that to you."

"Yes, foolish of him... Signus was a disappointment. It provided such a pitiful resistance." He shook his head slowly, seemingly to emphasize his disappointment. "Wars used to be more challenging... Regardless, as you well know, the Empire has the need for labor resources. Signus has resources, but to manage them properly we must move quickly; before we open it up for the free market to pillage. It is your role to ensure the Empire's profits are bountiful. I want you to take a fleet to Signus. Extract the resources, and we shall distribute these slaves where they are most needed. The logistics will be provided enroute."

"Consider it done."

The Emperor dispatched him with a wave of his arm. "Go. You are now assigned to the Empirical Cruiser *Bzak*. You must leave by 26:00 radii."

Zorlog took his queue, bowed and left the room. His escort awaited him outside. The prominent symbol, pulsating raw on his forehead, instantly demonstrated his new power. Each of his escorts bowed down in respect. Zorlog laughed again, heartily.

Inside the great hall, the Emperor remained silent in the darkness, contemplating. *Zorlog was likely an active Purist. But it was too early, too premature to kill him. Once intoxicated by the power of position, that will sway him. If not, he will, at worst, provide enough information to locate the leader of their doomed cause. Either way, he needed this young, brash strategist to accomplish his next military goal: a grand plan to sweep this whole section of the galaxy – the seven mapped quadrants. A project that would last a hundred zadiis. It would be the challenge of his generation and further generations to come. He could already taste the onset of his military's pillage. What wonders does the remainder of the galaxy hold? One could only imagine. More resources, more technology, more slaves, and above all, more power. Perhaps in one hadii, the Xi-Empire would rule the entire galaxy – a hundred billion stars. Unimaginable now but perhaps...*

It was, of course, a gamble to spread resources so thin over so many conquered. He knew the risks. Xilo herself had already paid the price of constant war with its depleted resources and despondent environment. *But one cannot gain by standing still. If Xilo cannot be rebuilt, the Empire will move to another world. It is a shame that so many lacked his vision.*

The Zuvoks were constantly giving him friction over his mandates. The fleets were not spread too thin - Signus was evidence of that. Other undiscovered worlds will be the same. They will all fall under the supreme power of this galaxy.

There had been only one race, and that had been so long ago. One race of so many conquered, that had technology greater than the Xi-Empire. For all of their abilities, they too were weak. They had lost their ability to protect themselves. The Xeronians had failed miserably. Their technology, superior as it was, did little to save them.

Xilo would reign. His plans were in motion.

* * *

Before Zorlog left Xilo, he met with the three Tarvoks. The symbol he bore carried an all too obvious message. They were openly shocked. He reassured his three empathizers that his loyalties had not swayed and quickly changed the topic by demanding an inspection of the cargo. The ships were stocked full of a special chemical - a powder discovered by a trader in the Corvelock quadrant. A race called the Brogs used it as a drug to incite hallucinations, but to Zorlog, as to all Xilozaks, it had a much more impressive potential. He left instructions to release it slowly into Xilo's water supply. It would take time, but there was no hurry. There were other wheels that needed to be set in motion.

The Empirical fleet left Xilo later that day, the Cruiser *Bzak* in the lead under the command of Zuvok Zorlog.

A Bellicose Dance

* * *

The ancient slaver *Joahack* plowed through the emptiness of space, its crew a collection of the vilest and lowest of Xilozaks. The majority had no interest in playing the part of an active, responsible crew. That was one of the reasons the small blip on the remote sensors was not noticed until it was almost upon them.

The ship was slow, but armed heavily. Its Tarvok was a miserable old Xilozak called Gick. He hated his crew, hated his ship, but enjoyed his trade. They were enroute to the planet Kryle, which was known for returning a healthy profit for slaves. His cargo was almost played out and he had a large number of credits to show for it. It would soon be time for another collection run.

"Tarvok, we've got a tracing of an unidentified vessel. Almost in weapons range."

Bick turned his attention to the tracing Avok.

"What! Will you learn to keep your eyes on that damn thing? What's the heading?" He seemed only faintly impressed as he chewed on a piece of razum.

"Platzick quadrant, away from us."

"Platzick quadrant?" He snorted and spit the slimy mess onto the deck plating. It could only be one of two possibilities, another slaver, or another pirate. No one else flies through the Platzick quadrant, at least none with half a brain. Any non-pirate ship would be run down, stripped and have its crew enslaved or blasted into space dust before it reached the outer edge of the quadrant.

"Get a fix on her. I want to know what type it is. Maybe it's that low-life Zerguna. He owes me a few cases of Beryllium." He spat again. "I'm tired of chewing this scummy razum. It has a texture of snot and turns your fangs brown." Gick had a bad habit of constant complaining.

"Got a lock on it, Tarvok. Ain't nothin' I ever seen before. She's an unknown. Can't be a trader - too small."

"She got any guns?" grunted Bick, biting off another chunk of razum from a bar that had been stuck in his arm pocket.

"Can't tell. Doesn't look like it."

"On the screen."

A computer-enhanced version of the ship rotated on the viewscreen. Gick squinted at the image. His eyesight wasn't as good as it used to be. "There, at the front, maybe two main cannon. Ya see them?" asked his second officer.

"Yeah, maybe, could be, but I think it's some rich Torzon's yacht."

"I say we move on it," urged his weapons Avok.

Gick sat back in his chair, thinking. His mind was not as sharp as it used to be, either. He glanced over at the Avok. "Have'm primed and hot by the time we're in range. Which shouldn't be long."

He passed a threatening glare to the tracing Avok. "We don't lose eyes on that, you hear?"

"Helm, let's go say hello."

The old ship clanked and groaned at the sudden course change. Gick had to yell over the increased background noise to his Charvok. "Get those lazy *son-of-grastias* armed and ready in the airlock!"

The Charvok rushed off the bridge yelling out the names of the elected volunteers. The noise within the ship became worse, drowning out the hurling of curses the Tarvok was making to his crew. Red-faced and angry, he spit several times on the slimy bridge deck. The ship was too slow for his liking.

The weapons Avok yelled over, "Five charged and ready. I got a problem with number six: overload. I told you we had to revamp these things last time we grounded!"

That started Gick cursing again. The bridge crew was able to make out the odd phrase, although they kept quiet. They did not want to get the Tarvok too riled up.

* * *

Ryan had noticed the old slaver long ago. He'd slowed down almost to point-five subluc in order to investigate. After the initial scan, he knew it wasn't the ship he was looking for. On the verge of jumping back into acroluc, he changed his mind. *There would be others* Tsaurau had warned him. Yes, he had noticed the markings on its scarred hull. He knew it was too old to be a war vessel, too streamlined to be a freighter, and by the looks of it, it was capable of atmospheric descent. Everything pointed to one conclusion. Ryan pulled back on the burner controls and brought the *Dancing Queen* around.

This was a slaver.

"Gem, we're close enough now. Do a full scan."

"Xi-Empire: Model 815a-SEN Trader Class, manufactured: Xilo."

It may not be Aviore's ship, but it was a slaver nonetheless, and that meant there were slaves aboard. The scan showed evidence of a variety of different life-forms present.

"Pull up a composite tactical display and rotate. Highlight the vulnerable areas. I want to cripple the drive system but keep the ship intact."

The holographic image appeared, projected by the 3D monitors that doubled as 2D displays in standard mode. The trajectories fully demonstrated that the slaver was changing course in an attempt to intercept. Even though he had seen it almost a parsec back, it had taken this long to respond to his arrival.

"Well Gem, looks like we're going to have company."

He manually thumbed the controls and the wing plating pulled back to expose all four main cannon. "So let's roll out the red carpet."

"They will be in firing range within two minutes," said Gem, "Do you wish to exercise evasive maneuvers?"

"No, no. We'll remain on course. We'll wait for them. I don't want them to get skittish on us."

At T-minus 52 he extended upper and lower turrets. The light duty cannon emerged from the hull, encased in small hemispheres of clear quartz, which exposing empty gunner's seats inside. They were set to fully automatic, tied directly into Gem's main control systems.

Ryan double-checked the main cannon stats. Although they looked identical, they were two distinct sets. The first pair on each side, closest to the fuselage, were used for long-range sustained firing, where accuracy and power were most important. The second set was used for short burst impulse firing - especially useful in close quarters, as they have a wider dispersal field and therefore, a shorter range. What they lacked in accuracy they gained in penetrating power, as their rapid on-off successive pulses made quick work of any enemy ship's shielding, and inevitably its hull plating. Each of the cannon were connected into the ship's main cooling system, allowing them to fire indefinitely without danger of shut down due to overheating, unlike the smaller turrets.

"T-minus 10 and counting."

"Now let's see what you got you bastard," Ryan said under his breath and reached for his controls.

* * *

"Ten more seconds and we're in range, Tarvok," reported the tracing Avok. Gick acknowledged with a spit, horking out a cluster. He then leaned down to grab the attention of his helm Avok, making no intention to hide his disdain. "Can't you make this gist-pile go any faster?" he growled.

"You won't like this, Gick. Think we found six cannon," the tracing Avok announced.

"Then this is sure as *Zagnite*, not a yacht! Lock onto its main burner and blast it."

"Locked and firing..."

The *Joahack's* cannon discharged, and low, powerful vibrations echoed throughout the ship. Gick, peering into the viewscreen, squinted his eyes in preparation for the tell-tale flash, but nothing happened.

"What are you doing, ya missed!" he yelled.

"It's gone, Tarvok!" exclaimed the weapons Avok in disbelief.

The tracing Avok yelled out excitedly. "Got it! He's faster than anything I've ever seen. Coming around the port side. He's gonna fire!"

"Brace yourselves!" yelled Gick, and it all broke loose. The slaver's main turrets disappeared in a fiery explosion. The concussion tore through the ship, creating cracks along the outer hull like shattered glass. Any of the crew that were unlucky enough to be in the wrong area died instantly, as atmosphere exploded into the vacuum of space. The old slaver's automated systems responded. Hatches slammed shut attempting to maintain the environmental systems. The Joahack was losing internal pressure like a sieve.

Gick glanced over to see weapons control abandoned. Tactical display showed the auxiliary turrets were still engaged, but their blasts were merely glancing off the strange alien ship. Gick staggered over to the weapons control, canceled the auto-targeting and manually redirecting a concentrated wall of fire at the alien ship. He watched in desperation, hoping to see signs of a crippling hit. But the alien ship didn't even falter. It maneuvered through his blasts with a mocking ease and responded by methodically obliterating each turret, effectively crippling the last of the *Joahack's* remaining offensive systems. A whole new series of explosions began from deep within the stern. The bridge was now a smoking mass of confusion, sirens, and fires. Panels and conduits broke loose and shot out in countless directions, throwing deadly pieces of jagged shrapnel across the bridge, and through the crew. Gick, now thrown to the floor, felt the hull of the ship shudder from what he knew to be fatal explosions. The *Joahack* was done.

A few functioning emergency lights cut through the air which was now thick with smoke and reeking of ozone. A dreadful quiet settled upon the bridge.

"Is it gone! Zigot take me! Tell me it's gone! He got back to his feet, wincing as he put weight on his left leg, it was bleeding profusely, gouged deep to the bone by a flat piece of shrapnel, which protruded out with a bitter blood-covered edge. He grabbed and yanked. He could feel the muscle tear as he worked it out. The taste of copper filled his mouth, and his vision blurred.

"Tarvok!" The weapons Avok yelled out, still alive but half buried in a pile of debris, a large bloody gash along the side of his skull. His body twisted under the wreckage, barely visible through the sparse light.

"Tracing! Tracing I need a report! Where's the ship! Is it gone?"

The weapons Avok continued on with his gibberish. "I hit it dead center, I did. I swear. I couldn't stop it." His voice diminished to a whisper.

Gick wrestled his way toward him.

"How did it shoot through our shields, Tarvok? It was too far away..."

"Don't mind about that now, we need to get out of here. Save your strength."

A Bellicose Dance

Gick started tossing off the wreckage, ignoring his bad leg. He didn't notice until he worked in close that the Avok had died. He cursed under his breath and scanned the bridge, his chest heaving from the effort. His tracing Avok entangled into the navigation panel, a blackened lump of coal, the helm Avok was on the deck, run through by a metal rod. The rest were gone or dead. Only he remained.

He dragged himself over to the helm control. Some power still remained, possibly just enough to raise the shield plating. The tracing scanners were all offline, most likely destroyed. He had to inspect what was left of his ship, had to see if the threat was still out there.

The shielding plates squealed and scraped, slowly grinding back into a retracted position, using up what little remained of the reserve of power. The massive shielding plates came to rest with one final exhausted heave. The sharp, white light of distant stars pierced through the transparent quartz panels.

Gick limped forward to the edge of the quartz to look down over his ship. The bridge was perched up from the main fuselage, allowing for a clear view all the way across to the stern. The *Joahack's* destruction was thorough: all defensive turrets gone, the main cannon a tangled web of interconnecting refuse. In many places, the outer hull was breached, like it had been shredded apart by some giant beast. Red and purple flames danced outward from the holes, feeding off what was left of the ship's escaping atmosphere.

A high-pitched whistle caught his attention. He watched a single hairline crack in the meter-thick quartz creep its way up from the floor and split into hundreds more, fanning out in all directions. It would hold a few gadii longer, but no more.

He was finished and knew it.

He bit off one more piece of razum and chewed it vigorously. Then spit a blackened glob at the growing crack in the quartz, and proceeded to laugh.

A movement caught his eye, out amongst the cover of the stars: a small dot. It grew larger, transforming into a string of lights, silhouetting the shape of the alien ship.

The enemy.

The vessel slowed as it approached the bridge and stopped so close he swore he could reach out and touch it. He squinted, straining his old reptilian eyes, searching for a clue. He found it: symbols inset along the vessel's hull. There was an answer to this mystery, an important clue to who his aggressor was. Being the Tarvok of a slaver, he had come to know many languages. It was a hobby, of which he had very few. He scoured his memory for a remnant of knowledge. He knew he had seen the symbols before. He had made one of the slaves scrawl it into his log before he had killed it -an anthropoid, a frail thing. What was it they called themselves... Narkasite? No, it was from a fringe planet, a relatively new find. Yes, that's why he remembered it. The creature had called his planet Earth. Zorlog had already staked it for royalties, for all the good it would do him. Such news travels quickly. Any slaver worth his salt has to be quick on a new find. He had made it a point to pass through there once already and poach a few slaves. It was an insignificant planet populated by a weak race. He had never seen any evidence of such technology during his raids.

The black shape of the alien ship's main cannon moved ever so slightly. Gick's eyes opened wide.

The cannon blast, hotter than the inside of the sun, turned his realization, along with the bridge into searing gas.

* * *

Ryan looked down at the targeting image. Perfect shot. A shadow of movement from within the dying vessel helped him align and lock the mark.

One must keep in practice, and not rely solely upon the automatic systems.

He was pleased with himself. It was a clean kill. Strangely, he felt no remorse. He felt nothing at all. If he'd seen the Xilozak Captain standing there, alone on the bridge, it wouldn't have mattered. Inside him, the old fury was calmed, quenched by an all too familiar endearing, bottomless cold. He shook himself, scattering the forbidding feeling, and let his worries and fears return to engulf him back into his humanity.

He checked the tracing images. The next step wouldn't be easy. He had to board and quickly. He took the *Dancing Queen* around the derelict, looking for an intact airlock, and found one amidships. He positioned his ship against the *Joahack's* hull, deployed the grav lines, and guided her carefully onto the airlock. The life tube extended and bonded to the slaver's hull with a thud.

Moving quickly, he pulled on his light-armored suit and helmet.

The suit was an engineering work of art. The helmet had a vaskpar control interface, with tongue depressor switch controls at chin level serving as a manual backup. The full readout display above his eyes gave the suit's statistics, it was also accompanied by vaskpar feed. The helmet provided a full 270 degree unobstructed view. Inlaid within the back of the suit was an air filtration processor that could synthesize any compatible alien atmosphere and produce breathable air for its user. Reserve air supply was kept in hollowed armored pockets throughout the suit, serving multiple purposes of suit pressurization, joint freedom, and expanded armor plating, at the same time remaining unobtrusive. It was designed for multiple purposes in both null and full gravity combat, with key areas protected, including an intricate exoskeleton of interconnecting joints that could dissipate a focused strike across the body. With respect to all of its armor, the suit was still lightweight, somewhat comparable to a pair of heavy heat-reflective coveralls.

He dressed quickly, mentally mustering up a checklist.

Weapons.

He could feel his heart pounding and his hands slippery with sweat, his mind and body lost in anticipation. He threw open the small arms cabinet, grabbing his blaster and holster. It fit snugly around his waist. He decided to take the disrupter sword as well. It would prove very useful for close contact fighting where shooting a blaster could rupture the hull and kill everyone, including himself. He threw the scabbard around his neck and let it hang on his back. Last but not least, he grabbed the impulse rifle. It was a heavy weapon, but also his weapon of choice. Powerful, with the potential to be quite lethal even in hand-to-hand combat, where it could be used as a melee weapon.

The suit statistics on the wrist panel checked A-OK. He twisted on his helmet. The full readout display came on above his eyes. The interior air storage was reading full, good for about four hours uncharged. Direct oxygen injection tanks would last an extended six hours, but he opted to use standard air supply. He hurried to the airlock, stopping just outside of it to check a storage bin.

"Gem, what key do I need to open this hatch?"

"No# 188590."

"Got it."

He stepped into the airlock and triggered the controls: gravitation off, auto-sterilization on. He checked his chronometer, which read in Xeronian time but had roughly the same concepts of seconds and minutes. The actual time durations were most likely very different than Earth time, but it was all relative in the end.

Preparation had taken him about seven minutes. He had to move faster. He felt his body begin to float as the effect of the gravitation plates faded. Gem had already pressurized the life tube extension to match the slaver's. Sensors indicated the interior of the ship was at about three atmospheres and dropping. Ryan opened the *Dancing Queen*'s airlock and pushed himself down onto the other ship's hull. The transition made him a little queasy but he remembered his training and fought down the nausea. His body would adjust. He glanced at the foreign airlock. "Gem, where's the hatch control!"

"To your right, approximately one meter, a discolored plate, flush with the hull."

Ryan found it and turned the keypad deployment control and attached the decryption key. The small black box went through at least 10,000 electromagnet signatures before it found the lock. The ready button blipped happily. This was a much better solution than blowing the lock.

One final glance at the helmet visual display. Weapons check: OK. Ryan crouched, rifle ready, and slammed the key. The exterior hatch door slid open. Air from inside the slavership rolled into the tube, tainted with the wisps of white smoke.

Ryan peered into the ship. The smoke was entering through a leak in the lock's interior door. A large alloy beam had torn through an interior bulkhead and ripped part of the hatch off its hinges. He could see a weak light shining through the opening. He pocketed the key and stepped into the alien ship. Despite the damage, surprisingly, the gravity plates were still functioning.

"I estimate about 1.75 Earth gravity," Gem reported.

"Little late in your announcement, aren't you, Gem? Go ahead and close the *Queen's* airlock."

The smoke was thick inside the ship. It filled the top half of the corridor. He crouched low.

"Heavy smoke, probably an internal fire very close to this proximity. Moving on." His rambling was more for record than anything else. Gem was able to pick up all his feeds, including his vaskpar signal.

He rolled out into the center of the corridor, checking both directions quickly. He remembered studies on this class of vessel. Bits and pieces all useful, yet elusive. He never felt *sure*. He discussed the direction of the slaver holding bays with Gem. "Up two levels and down amidships about 75 meters, right?"

"I agree. However, tracing scans indicate the concussion from the previous explosions may have compromised the integrity of level three. Recommend you use the maintenance shafts through to level two."

"On my way."

Ryan wasted no time in moving. He was currently on deck five. He found the maintenance shafts and jumped down the null-gravity tube to deck four, rolled, crouched. Again, no enemy fire.

Deck three, rolled, crouched. Nothing.

He was moving to deck two when he heard a noise. He triggered the sound amplifier within the helmet. Xilozak voices, 20, maybe 30 meters away. He pushed himself off the wall with all of his strength and barrelled down the rest of the way, landing on the deck feet first, half crouched with rifle ready. There were three of them, directly ahead. All had their attention focused on a small wall panel - an escape pod control. One of the crew glanced up, saw him and reached for his blaster. Ryan shot quickly, carefully, taking down all three in a split second, but not before catching the look of grotesque surprise on their dying faces.

No others were visible down the corridor. He ran, hugging close to the wall, branched to the right and ran down to the next corner. Two more of the crew saw him and ran toward him. He rolled and leveled two blaster shots into their bellies. They went down ungracefully.

One more right and the hall ended with a sealed door.

"Gem, is there an override?"

"Behind the third panel to the right."

Ryan ripped it open, plugged in the access command, and stepped back. Nothing happened. He glanced back nervously. "It's not opening!"

"The doors are magnetically sealed. The circuit has to be closed in order to break the electromagnet override."

"Then I'll fuse the sonofabitch!"

He set his rifle to wide dispersal and blasted the panel. With the seal broke, the door slid partly open, then stopped. A small breeze began pulling a stream of smoke-laden air past the doors. He looked through the opening. The emergency lighting was intermittent; the corridor was almost completely dark. Smoke drifted down into the darkness in a lazy current.

"Looks like we have a small amount of decompression going on, Gem."

He grabbed the door and forced it open. It gave easily. He moved in cautiously. Markings on the walls again looked familiar. He was in the holding cell throughway. The corridor was lined with sealed doors on both sides. Each had a tag stuck on it with Xilozak inscriptions. He inspected the alien writing by the light of his helmet.

"Can you understand this chicken scratch, Gem?"

"I cannot decipher the form, although I am familiar with Xilozak language."

"Great. I don't want to just open these doors. A slave may think I'm a Xilozak and attempt to kill me."

"Do you wish to leave them?"

"No. Maybe there's a master switch somewhere." Ryan looked around.

"Possibly, at the entranceway," hinted Gem.

There it was, near the door. A large yellow switch. An inscription was posted in red below it.

"The Xilozak inscription reads: DANGER DO NOT OPEN!" warned Gem.

"Thanks, Gem. But I can actually make that out."

He readied his rifle and pulled the switch. All of the doors slid open at once, one cell spewed out an atmosphere of yellowish-orange colored gas. Ryan glanced at the suit's filtration reading. It was dispersed enough that it wouldn't kill any human slaves but breathing it would not be pleasant.

"Looks like most of them are oxygen breathers," he commented to Gem.

"Yes, very strange."

"Why?"

"Because there are considerably few races that breathe oxygen, most require a higher density of helium or nitrogen, some even hydrogen."

"Sounds like we hit the jackpot." He proceeded to the first open door. There were half a dozen reptilian creatures, many looked quite sick.

"Gem, I've seen these things before."

"Yes, they are Showmish. They have unusually powerful eyesight and highly respected cognitive powers."

Ryan proceeded on to the next door. Empty. The following one was blocked by the bulk of a hulking, hairy creature with black sectioned tentacles. Ryan stepped back quickly.

"I've seen this thing before, as well."

"It's a Brog. We are very limited on information about these creatures. One point of warning, they are extremely ferocious and possess superior strength."

"Yes, I've seen that before."

He glanced across the corridor, into the opposite cell, all the time making sure he kept a level aim on the Brog. But the creature did not move. The other cell was dark, and he could not see within, but something was there. He moved closer, turning his helmet lamps to full power. Humans! A group of them huddled together in the darkness.

He could feel the Brog watching him, but still, it had not left its cell. *That was a good sign.*

He stepped into the cell with the humans. The room was filthy with floors covered in vomit and excrement. The visual display in his helmet showed the temperature to be 105 degrees, humidity at 80 %. He was glad to be in his suit.

They moved away from him quietly, pressing themselves up against the wall. A quick scan of faces - Aviore was not one of them. Ryan's small amount of hope died.

"Captain, there are indications that an internal fire is approaching the main power conduit. The magneto containment still contains antimatter. It is in jeopardy. I suggest you rush."

"Gem, run a scan, look for any other humans on this ship, exclude this group. I need to know if Aviore could be here."

He decided to start with English and flipped on his outside speaker. "I have come to rescue you. There is not much time, so gather up your sick and come with me."

Some seemed to understand him, as they started to get up. One of the men spoke to him in English. "Are you from Earth?"

"No time. Move now, or we will all be dead." Ryan stepped out, and they followed. The Brog was gone. It had moved to the end of the corridor. "Stay close to the wall." A surge of intense vibration shook the deck.

"My scans reveal no other humans aboard," reported Gem, "and deck four just lost all atmospheric pressure. Deck two is in danger of immediate decompression."

"We'll need an alternative route. There should be an airlock just down this corridor."

"Affirmative. I will detach and reseal to that lock. Estimated time is five minutes."

"Good, get moving and run the flex-tube to the cargo hold airlock. I'll have company."

Ryan checked the other cells and found the remaining empty. The slaver probably unloaded most of its cargo on its last stop. He made his way back quickly. Some of the Showmish had moved out to see what was happening, but most remained where they were, too sick to move. He approached them cautiously.

"Gem, set up Showmish translation through my external speaker."

"Done."

"You must collect your sick and follow me if you want to live."

The Showmish language echoed through the air with a lyrical string of tones. The aliens took a moment to acknowledge him. With a nod, they began to prepare to follow him, the healthy hoisting the sick to their feet. The two groups were ready. They looked to him expectantly, waiting for his next command.

Ryan started down the corridor beckoning them to follow. They followed behind as quickly as possible. "Gem, what's your status?"

"The ship has been relocated. I have just established a seal. You must open the airlock from inside."

They arrived shortly after. Ryan searched the wall for the control panel and activated it. The panel lights flickered, then died.

"Damn it!" He banged it with the butt of his rifle. It lit up. He triggered the sequence and hoped the lock still had enough power to operate. It was common practice for each lock to have its own backup circuits, but this one was obviously on its last legs. The outside hatch opened slowly. A minor pressure change shook the flex-tube, but the seal held.

"Gem, we look OK. I'm opening the inside hatch." The inside airlock door clicked and began to slide. The power drain dimmed the panel's lights.

"A large heat signature is emanating from within the main power conduit. You have very limited time, Captain."

"I know, I know."

The door was open enough. He signaled to the group to start through. They were caught off guard by the absence of gravity, but they somehow managed to keep moving through to the *Dancing Queen*'s cargo hold, mostly by sheer momentum.

"Gem, I have to go back. The Brog may be able to understand me."

"You may not make it!" warned Gem.

"Just close the lock and wait."

Ryan ran, heart pounding, breathing fast. He passed the Brog cell and slid to a stop. Another Brog, smaller than the first, lay motionless in the middle of the cell. He stepped in, reached down and touched it. Was it alive or dead? Watching it briefly, he noticed an almost imperceptible movement. It was breathing, but very shallowly. It must be close to death. He tried to move it, but it was too heavy. A growl from behind him caught his attention just in time to see a waist-thick tentacle swinging down at his head. His reflexes saved him. The months of combat drilling took over. He rolled and he came up with his rifle leveled at the midsection of the Brog.

But he did not shoot.

Surprisingly, it reached down and purred at the other Brog, running its tentacles through its fur.

It must be its mate!

A shiny glint of metal flickered in another of its tentacles. It was the control panel of the escape pod.

This is no damned animal, this is an intelligent creature!

He lowered his rifle and walked around the beast to the doorway, hugging close to the wall. He could feel it watching him under all that hair, but made no further effort to attack him. It just sat there and mewed. He stood at the entrance and beckoned at it to follow. No reaction. He waved again and still, it continued to ignore him. Finally, fed up, he re-entered the room, approached the smaller Brog, bent down and ever so slowly, tried to pick it up.

It growled, and he jumped back. He had seen these things in action before and was not about to get killed by one.

Surprisingly, it seemed to have understood. In one deft movement, it wrapped its tentacles around the smaller Brog and hoisted it over its shoulder as if it were a mere matchstick. Another tremor vibrated through the ship.

"An explosion has breached the hull on your level. Fortunately, your corridor's emergency hatches held. However, the primary power conduits are collapsing," reported Gem.

"On my way." He rushed out into the hallway. To his relief, the Brog and its precious cargo followed him. The way to the airlock was still open. He ran as fast as his legs would take him. The Brog stayed on his heels effortlessly, unhindered by its tremendous burden.

"Gem, open sesame."

The grav plates gave out with a sickening lurch just before they reached the lock. Ryan's momentum kept him moving toward the airlock. With a few small adjustments off the side of the hall, he flew right through, without breaking his neck in the process. The Brog was close behind, managing the null gravity without concern, adjusting his course with small nudges from his many powerful tentacles, which spanned the width of the corridor, it barely fit through the tube.

Ryan arrived at the *Queen's* brightly-lit cargo bay, half expecting to be slammed face first into the floor, ready to roll. That didn't happen. Gem had lowered the grav plates to a minimum. The Brogs sailed through a second later. The bay was a confusion of twisting, turning bodies.

"Gem, gradually increase the gravity to normal."

Ryan closed the locks and activated the sterilization jets. They soaked the inside of the life tube along its length. He brought the pressure down to slightly above full vacuum within the airlock and broke the seal of the life tube. Sterilizing droplets blew out into space, and the tube contracted in. Satisfied, he closed the outside hatch. His feet, now firmly placed on the floor, began to feel the weight of his body return. A quick glance back showed that the slaves were sorting themselves out, reorienting to what is considered 'up' and 'down' - a meaningless concept where gravity does not exist – although its effect was increasing.

"Gem, release the grav lines and move out to a safe range."

He headed to the cargo bay's interior airlock. The decontamination sequence started automatically when he entered. In a second he was through. Within a minute he was in the pilot's chair.

"Gem, display sensor status on tactical."

"Tracing sensors indicate no other vessel within scanning range."

"Good. Calculate a course to Xeronia. We have to get these people help, some of them are very sick. We'll move out on standard random evasive, I don't want anyone second-guessing our destination."

"And I need simultaneous Showmish, Earth-English, and Brog translation, Gem."

"I do not know Brog, but I will make an attempt."

"Good enough." He flipped on the ship's intercom system. "Everyone please remain calm. For those who understand, we are heading for a safe place and will be accelerating. Please stay seated on the floor and avoid moving around."

"Gem, I think it would be worthwhile to retrieve their computer core. Do you think it's still intact?"

"The bulkhead behind the main bridge is where the design specifications indicate its original position. However, most of that bulkhead has been destroyed."

"Oh. Yeah. Remind me to check where the core is before I attack our next slaver, OK?"

"I've been scanning the condition of the ship. It is deteriorating rapidly. The main auxiliary power circuits are nearly drained. An antimatter breach is imminent."

"I'm sure the residual magnetic signature will hold up a little while longer, Gem."

"Nevertheless, I would suggest sending the robot for retrieval. Core extraction is not within a human's capability."

"Fine."

Ryan brought the *Dancing Queen* around and positioned it a few hundred meters from where the slavership's bridge used to be, which was now an exposed jagged, gaping hole.

"Well, is it still there?"

"Yes," replied Gem. "It is intact."

Ryan ran down to the machine shop and yanked out a box about the size of a small storage chest.

"Wake up, Ziggy."

The unit sprang to life. The legs, arms, and antenna extended out. It twitched and turned as it went through a self-diagnosis check then rose up on three long legs. Ziggy was now looking down on its human master. The robot was gangly, with three long arms and an even longer set of legs. With a saucer-shaped head and a short, cylindrical body, it looked somewhat like a spider.

Ryan smiled. *Quite a creation.*

"Time to go to work, old boy."

The robot's single red eye blinked back at him.

"I need you to retrieve something from the other ship - the memory core. You can exit via the pilot's airlock. Gem, download the information to Ziggy."

Ryan headed back to the cockpit, Ziggy at his heels, hydraulics and motors humming. The robot exited through the airlock and was out in space a moment later, his small burner unit navigating him towards the ship.

Ryan watched the robot in the monitors until it disappeared into the gaping hole.

A few minutes passed, and Gem provided an update. "Ziggy reports he has located the core, Captain."

"Good, tell him to move fast."

The memory cores were standard pieces of equipment on Xi-Empire ships. They function as a primary storage pool for all the computer systems on the ship, holding literally every important piece of data. This included navigation maps, system software, and the ship's personnel logs.

A Bellicose Dance

They were designed to be as indestructible as possible and easily jettisoned in the event of a disaster. Extracting these units was tedious, as they were usually tied into a number of self-destructive circuits. It was simply impossible for a Ryan to pull out the unit successfully, but not so for a robot like Ziggy.

"E.T.A is 45 seconds," reported Gem.

"Very good," Ryan replied as he checked the antimatter dispersal controls, prepping for the jump to acroluc. "We'll have to fabricate an interface to access the core," he thought out loud to Gem.

"Ziggy has returned."

Indicator lights on the airlock showed pressurization in progress. A few seconds later Ziggy stepped out, a thick layer of frost covering his metallic body.

"Thank you, Ziggy," nodded Ryan.

"You're welcome," came the reply, through Gem.

"See if you can build an interface for that thing."

The airlock door hissed shut as Ziggy headed back down to the machine shop.

Ryan brought the *Dancing Queen* around the derelict one more time with tracing scanners on full, searching for any missed survivors. The tracings exposed two Xilozaks within the port side of the ship. Ryan aimed the cannon and fired. The front port section of the ship disappeared, exposing many levels of mangled decks now open to the vacuum of space. A chain reaction of explosions chased down the centreline of the ship from stern to bow. The antimatter containment finally failed. The remainder of the stern disintegrated in one last violent blast, rolling the wreck over end-for-end, leaving parts of itself in its wake. Whatever atmosphere was left now billowed out in flaming clouds of red, orange and purple.

His first kill but it wouldn't be his last.

He brought the *Dancing Queen* on course and fired the burners, leaving the wreck far behind. It would drift on indefinitely, locked within its death roll, forever lost in the cold dark endless night of space. Space, so incalculably vast, rarely surrenders her dead.

Ryan watched as it disappeared in the rear monitors. It would make such a nice warning to the slavers out there. Next time, he'll let them broadcast a general SOS.

The ship powered up her antimatter dispersal circuits as it began to accelerate. The anti-gravs whined their familiar protests as they fought to maintain the constant gravitational field within the ship. The jump to acroluc was quick, and subsequent jumps even faster: 10x, 25x, 100x the speed of light. Ryan curbed the acceleration and leveled off. The *Dancing Queen* was capable of much higher speeds, but operating forward tracings could not provide a suitable warning of impending collisions. The onboard navigation computers, subcomponents of Gem watched far ahead, analyzing tight band tracing emissions. They constantly made slight adjustments to keep the ship from colliding with a star or some other celestial body as the ship flew on its predestined course.

In the cockpit, Ryan watched the stars blink in and out of existence as blurry streaks of light. He felt mesmerized by the kaleidoscope of colors. It was a sight he would never get used to. Once satisfied everything was in order, he headed back to the cargo hold, medical supplies in hand. When he walked in, all heads turned his way. He could feel their questioning eyes.

"Gem, ready translation through the intercom. How'd the Brog translation work?"

"Unknown. Need more feedback."

"Regardless, I don't think they are the best at talking."

He addressed the small crowd. They watched him intently. They didn't know who he was, or what his intentions were, exactly.

"Friends, you are no longer slaves. We share an enemy, which is the Xi-Empire. We are headed toward a Xeronian colony, where you will be fed and cared for. The people of this planet are peaceful and kind. They are not like you or me, but I ask you to treat them as your friends."

"In the meantime, I will tend to your needs as best I can. I need to check each of you; the sick will be given priority. I ask that you follow my orders and hold your questions until I have seen to everyone."

Difficult and tiring hours followed. Each of the slaves needed to be sterilized and medically scanned. Most were in poor condition, weak, malnourished, and suffering from a number of infections and parasites. But no matter how bad they were, they all had a strange look on their faces.

Disbelief? Shock? Relief? It was the look of freedom. He probably looked the same way that day he arrived at the Xeronian colony.

Ziggy set up a portable shower in the hold. It helped to wash off the filth off before he examined them. The robot was also the attending tailor and barber. The robot tried his best to meet everyone's wishes, although it had some difficulty fabricating the Showmish clothing.

Ryan was not a doctor, although his studies had covered the physiology of many races. If one of the slaves were in serious enough condition, he would have to bring him/her to the medical bay. So far, it wasn't warranted.

He felt them watching him, relentlessly. Every time he turned, he caught them staring. It was annoying as hell, but at least they followed his orders.

There were 11 humans altogether. Six females, five males. Most of their wounds were infected. It was a wonder any of them were still alive. One woman, a victim of the charged whip, had deep cuts running down her back, onto her arms and hands. They were probably inflicted when she tried to protect herself. She was very young, early 20's. She had a kind face with high cheekbones and a small mouth. Her hair was a rich brown that matched her deep, dark brown eyes. When he looked into them, he felt like he was looking into her soul. He turned away quickly, not wanting to feel her pain.

He was almost done her dressing, just her arm and hand remained.

"Who are you?" she said softly.

"What did you say?" Ryan replied, caught completely off-guard.

"Who are you?"

"I didn't know you knew English," he smiled back at her. "My name is Ryan. I am from Earth - are you?"

"And this is your ship?" A man stepped forward to ask. He was the same one who spoke to him in the slave cell - a strong looking man, average height, blond hair, probably early 30's. His face showed the lines of stress, making him look older than he should.

"I didn't know our military had starships."

"Yes, this is my ship. I call her the *Dancing Queen*. No, I am not with the military."

"You are a long way from home," the brunette said quietly.

He turned his attention back to the woman. "Pardon?"

"My name is Alexandria."

"Glad to meet you."

"We have all been captured by these damned aliens," interrupted the man. "There were more of us, but this is all that is left. Only four of us can speak English. The rest are crazy or speak something some gawdawful gibberish."

"You two – and the others?" asked Ryan.

A red-headed man stepped forward. He was lean, with a face that was weathered from years of pain. His eyes were sunk deep into their sockets. By his features, he looked like the type that was quick to laugh, but that had been long ago.

"My name is McClary. The mouthpiece over there – he pointed to the blond man – his name is Jim Smith. He's a nervous type, so don't mind him... You said your name is Ryan. A downright Irish name if I may say."

"Well, American actually."

"You said you pilot this ship, lad?"

"Yes."

"Then you can take us back home!" Alexandria's eyes were wide and she could not hide the pleading in her voice.

"No, I'm sorry. I can't. I have a promise to fulfill, a debt to pay. Besides, I don't know where Earth is, at least not yet."

Alexandria's brown eyes began to fill with tears.

"I'm sorry," he repeated, fighting to clear his throat.

She turned away resentfully.

Could he blame her?

A hissing sound behind him caught his attention. A lone Showmish spoke. The translation came through the intercom.

"We are in your debt, Earthman, we of Shawma. I am called Wharsoff."

"Wharsoff of Shawma, your debt is already paid."

"Such a debt can only be repaid in blood."

Ryan assessed him. A slight creature, but capable. He remembered them from the mines. Their strength was surprising.

"You owe me nothing."

"You have no escorts. You destroyed that slavership all alone, did you?"

"I'm just starting."

The Showmish hissed with amusement. "You have a sense of humor. That is required if you intend to fight the Xi-Empire on your own."

"I do not intend to fight the Xi-Empire. I intend to destroy it. Completely."

The Brog growled spasmodically. Its body shook in concert.

The damn thing was laughing. How the hell was it understanding Showmish?

As its performance died, it spit out a guttural form of Trinarieit. "Your goals are too grand, Earthman!"

"So you can speak, Brog," replied Ryan. "And I thought you were incapable."

"I listen. You are only one, one against millions."

"Look buddy, I don't want to be stuck in the middle of a war!" Jim intervened, his voice bitter, desperate. "I just want to go home."

Ryan glanced back, irritated. Desperate human faces were awaiting his reply.

"You don't have a choice," Ryan stated flatly. "And neither do I. That's just the way it is."

He tightened the last bandage with a jerk and stood up.

"This war started a long time ago, way before us. Whether any of you like it or not, you're already involved. You, Brog, you should know I don't intend to fight this war on my own, but I will."

"So are you looking for recruits, Earthman?" hissed Wharsoff.

"I won't refuse the help."

"Then I will join you, and we will die together," announced Wharsoff.

Ryan laughed. "We'll bring a lot of them with us."

"All wars lead to death," stated the Brog. "I am Gor, father of the Tatunckt, High Chieftain of the northern tribe of Grak. I will join your crusade - for a price."

"Which is?"

"My mate is sick. She will die. Help her."

"I've done everything I can for now. The Xeronians, my friends, might be able to help. If anyone can, they can. But you must trust me on this."

Gor shifted his tremendous bulk from one hidden foot to another, obviously contemplating. "Trust I will."

"Good."

He turned to the Showmish. "Wharsoff, this is not your native atmosphere. Is it endangering your people?"

"No. Malnutrition is our enemy. This atmosphere will suffice."

Ryan pointed to Ziggy. "He will see to your food. If you require more, just ask." The spindly metallic servant bowed ever so slightly.

McClary stepped beside him and reached out his hand. "You did save my life, even if you will not give it back to me." A wide grin flashed across his face.

"How's he doing?" Ryan was referring to the man McClary and Jim had carried to the ship. The man was in the worst condition of them all.

"Better."

A quick check with his portable scanner showed he was stable. He needed rest and time to heal.

"What happened to him?"

"They beat him. Took four of them. He just wouldn't stay down, damn fool. All he had to do was stay down."

Ryan eyed the Scott closely; the man was visibly shaking. "Why don't you sit down? I'm pretty sure he'll make it. You've all made it. You're safe – I'll see to that."

A few more eyes moved in his direction, no longer averted.

He did, after all, save their lives. What was their damn problem anyway?

"I've work to do. Ziggy will take care of you while I'm away. I'll ask you to remain in this part of the ship during our return flight."

"What is this place like that we're headed to, this colony?" asked McClary.

"Trust me, it's heaven in comparison to where you were."

* * *

The slaver's logs were extensive. Ryan scoured through every last entry, every file. Something was there that would be useful, and he was sure of it. An entry jumped out at him on the final approach to the Xeronian colony. It was in the Captain's personal logs: an excerpt about a slaver captain - an old friend who paid a large sum of credits to the empirical Admiral for the daughter of a Signite Governor. The slavership was called the *Xabunzt II*. He read it over three times. The information was old, but it was a starting point.

Gem diverted his attention with a navigation update.

The Xeronian's planet loomed ahead, red and angry. The Par resonated weakly even at this distance. In a moment they knew he had returned.

"This is the *Dancing Queen*, E.T.A - two minutes," Ryan relayed. A welcome was returned, both cordial and dry.

He dumped over a block of information onto the Par reserved for his log entries. It provided the Xeronians with a complete update of his travels – and the ex-slaves he had on board.

He flew the *Dancing Queen* in low, down into the cover of angry winds, and between the mountains. She slid into the bay gracefully. All around, Xeronians scurried about, carefully shuttling about a maze of transparent structures.

Tsaurau called to him. "We are not ready yet. We need to follow stringent sterilization procedures."

"Of course, we'll have to wait, but..."

"This Brog you have brought us is near death."

"Yes. And I don't want to be around her mate if she does pass away."

"We will exercise precautions. I will ensure we have the medical teams ready. It will not be long."

"I understand. Tsaurau, I've found something else in the logs. It's an outside chance. I don't know how old this information is, but I might be able to find her."

"Her? You are referring to Aviore?"

"Yes."

"There is something else, Ryan. I suspect it will interfere with your plans. Our surveillance probes have picked up some disturbing news. The council has requested your presence."

"Alright," he replied somberly. "After I see to our passengers then."
Whatever this was, it wasn't good.

He went down to the cargo hold. This time he was greeted with a wall of silence. They watched, and waited, studying him carefully. He could read the humans: pale, taut, fidgety. They were nervous, awaiting the possibility of a continuing nightmare. Was he a slaver or wasn't he? As for the aliens, their thoughts were probably the same. He just couldn't read them.

"McClary," he called.

The Scott approached. His color was not quite there, a visible shakiness in his gait.

"You may have guessed we've landed, but we'll need to wait. We present a biological hazard to our Xeronian friends. Safety measures need to be taken."

"Are you on the level with us?"

The Brog shifted its stance, ready to pounce. Three meters away but close enough to rip him in half in the blink of an eye.

"Of course. Everything is OK. I'll prove it soon enough. Just remain calm." He turned to address everyone. "I will repeat, you are safe. I'll wait here with you."

Most seemed transfixed on the cargo doors. A few swung their gaze back and forth, assessing him silently, looking for any hint of deceit. Ryan waited calmly, bouncing navigational charts through his mind, planning.

News came over the Par. "They are ready." He announced, opening the cargo bay door. The ramp lowered to the floor quietly. No Xi-troopers marched in to meet them. Outside details were blurred behinds a maze of imperfect transparency.

"Our Xeronian friends have erected a containment system. You need to stay within it and do what they ask you. Right now you could be carrying some kind of pathogen that could kill them or, possibly, the other way around. Just listen to them, and we will all be out of quarantine shortly."

Pale but tentatively trusting faces nodded.

He turned to the Brog. "Gor, if your mate can be saved, the Xeronians can do it if you can trust them."

"Trust you earn when I see I am truly free."

"Then go," motioned Ryan. "Be the first."

The Brog marched down, his mate tucked close to his side. Behind him, others followed, all cautiously, many carrying the sick and injured with them.

As they moved down the short tunnel, they could see Xeronian faces peered through the containment tunnel.

"They're ugly as sin," remarked McClary.

Ryan laughed and patted the Scott on the back. "I see you say what you think, McClary."

They had enveloped the ship's exit with a transparent tunnel leading to a circular area in the center of the bay. Multiple decontamination booths stood ready. A surgical team, fully equipped with envirosuits awaited at the main receiving area.

At first sight of the ferocious-looking Brog, the Xeronians backed away. Ryan quickly moved between them, simultaneously waving over the medical lead.

"Gor, this is the chief surgeon." He stated in Showmish. "His team will do everything they can for your mate. Please follow his direction."

He nodded to another Xeronian. "Can you help the Showmish?"

"We have constructed an area with a more adequate atmosphere. We will attend to their needs there."

"Good."

"I need to see Tsaurau." A familiar crew of faces outside the transparent walls nodded to him a minute later. A fog filled the bay no more than a meter high; a product of the cooling vents discharging from the *Dancing Queen*. Xeronians scurried around, often invisible under the blanket of white haze. They had already scurried into the ship to perform a myriad of tests and follow-up maintenance activities.

Tsaurau stood waiting. "Good to see you, my friend," he said with a pert nod. "You have already started to make a difference."

"Less than a scratch. I'll call it luck. You'll note in my report I managed to pull the slaver's memory core. I'll leave it with you to further analyze before I go. I'd appreciate your insights on some possible course vectors."

"When are you planning to leave?"

"I guess it depends on what you have to tell me. I..."

They were both interrupted by McClary yelling at him through the environmental seal, an anxious look on the Scott's face. "Are we going to see you again, Captain?"

"Yes," Ryan yelled back, "If you're lucky," he chuckled. McClary gave a wide smile and a thumbs-up sign.

"The council wishes to discuss your trip."

"Already? I've been away less than a week."

"Remember Ryan, two days to you is relative, it has been three weeks for us."

Right, relativity, always a strange concept to grasp.

He gave the *Dancing Queen* one last look before stepping out. A weak plume of steam was still billowing out from her rear burners as they cooled. Swarms of Xeronian technicians were running in and out of her through the auxiliary airlock. He heard Gem address them sarcastically over the Par as his A.I. friend directed them on a number of different tasks.

He did not like leaving her.

"If you prefer, you may rest for a few hours before meeting with them."

"No, let's get this over with."

"We will need two to three hours for our technicians to check over your ship."

"That's alright, I need more time to dig through the slaver's core. I found something that can lead to Aviore."

Tsaurau decided to fill him in on some of the details. "We have had some distressing news from the Signus system."

"Signus? That is where Aviore was from."

"I assume you are ready for combat?"

"Yes. Why?"

Tsaurau remained evasive, "You'll see."

The council had already convened anticipating his arrival. Tseman welcomed them warmly. "Ryan, you have had your presence requested because of a dire matter. The information we have received through our remote probes indicate a massive organization of slave traders headed toward the Signus system. As you already know, Signus has recently fallen to the Xi-Empire. We expect this fleet will perform a collection run of close to five hundred thousand Signite citizens. We estimate their arrival at the Signite system to be imminent. As you can surmise, we require an immediate decision on your part."

"What is it that you want me to do?"

"Intercept this fleet and destroy it."

"At Signus? The full force of their attacking fleet is there. I won't have a chance against that many."

"We know they have migrated their forces to attack the multiple Signite colonies. Only a few residual guard vessels remain at Signus."

"Exactly how many of them are there?"

"The exact count is unknown."

"As long as I have a fighting chance, I guess."

"We have discovered one other, possibly significant, fact. Our monitoring of their communications has revealed this slave fleet is led by a Xilozak named Zorlog."

Ryan felt something stir within him. *Zorlog. He knew that name too well.* He didn't realize he was rubbing his scar.

Tseman had already sensed something from him. "So you know of this individual?" she asked.

"Yes, I know of him."

"Will you intercept these ships?"

"But I've just found a lead on where to find Aviore... the woman in my visions. I'm sure the trail will grow cold if I'm too late."

"I do understand what we ask of you," Tseman said gently. "She is but one life. Thousands more will be enslaved or killed if this fleet is not stopped."

"I know." Ryan took a long agonizing minute. "I'll intercept the fleet."

* * *

9. Into the Breach

The *Dancing Queen* was ready. All systems checked over, all tests completed. A small group had stayed to see Ryan off, among them McClary and Alexandria. They looked a little better than the last time he had seen them.

"Will we see you again?" asked Alexandria.

Fear was in her eyes, an enduring, entrenched fear.

Would she ever see her home again?

He touched her cheek tenderly. "You're safe in this place. Probably safer here than anywhere else in the known galaxy, and you're not a slave anymore."

She smiled back, eyes wet with tears.

McClary stuck out his hand. "May I shake the hand of a truly brave lad," he stated with an earnest smile on his face.

Ryan took his hand, smiling at the Scott, who managed a firm grip despite his condition.

"Good luck to you. You are doing good out there."

"McClary, maybe when you're feeling better you'll consider helping me out."

"I'm as fit as a fiddle now, my boy. Consider me volunteered. I'll help you bring down these devils." He stood straight as a rail and saluted, but only briefly as a gut-wrenching cough ripped through his body.

Ryan glanced over to Tsaurau, who motioned, via the Par, to a nearby doctor.

"First things first, McClary. A sick man makes a poor soldier. But don't worry, I'll be back to take you up on that offer. You can count on it."

* * *

The *Dancing Queen* was on her way within minutes, course inlaid for Signus. Expected arrival at the system was about two weeks, approximately the same time the Xi-Empire fleet was scheduled to arrive. It would be close. Ryan was pushing the remnants of his good luck, and the ship, to the limit. Traveling through Xi-Empire controlled space required more than a cautious approach, but there simply wasn't time. The possibility of being discovered was high.

He knew, in retrospect, that was the least of his worries. What awaited him on arrival monopolized his apprehension. There would be more than slaverships to contend with. At least one military destroyer-class starship would be stationed there with unmistakable intentions - to ensure any and all threats were decimated in the usual thorough Xi-Empire fashion.

Could he do this? Would his ship hold together – hell would he hold together? He had to take the time to review a few key battle strategies from Taldig's lessons. Also, the logs from the old warship were barely dented. They were a maze of disjointed information, a collection of vector images and alien symbols, linked with Xeronian translations accompanying captions and footnotes.

After a few intense hours of research, he found his mind wandering, possibly due to anxiety or mental fatigue. Whatever the cause, his thoughts always seemed to follow down that same, twisted, pain ridden-path of never finding Aviore, or worse, finding her too late. His mind tortured itself with that awful game of self-directed anguish. Like a nightmare out of control, he conjured images so horrible it made him shudder. He could play out scenarios in infinite detail. It plagued him like an ulcer, eating away at him with no remorse.

Enough. Was he going crazy?

He leaned back in his chair and rubbed his temples. It would be so easy to change course, head toward Xilo and locate *that* ship. But at what cost? This was not a single slaver raid. This was an empirically funded mass abduction. There was not just hundreds or even thousands, but hundreds of thousands of lives at stake. To betray the innocent would be the ultimate sin.

Could he pay this price? It seemed unfathomable, and therefore, unreal. Could he live with himself after?

The question left a cold knot in his stomach that wrenched at his gut in sickening tugs.

No. No, he couldn't. That he knew. He had his duty.

Indifferent to its Captain's doubts, the *Dancing Queen* thundered on. Gem monitored her course and Ziggy kept active completing odd jobs. The robot would be an essential crew member during battle, along with the thousands of nano-bots that circulated throughout the ship – all creatures of mechanization living out their lives in focused, dutiful execution, making repairs as needed.

The monitor blipped at him. The requested archive file appeared onscreen.

"Gem, why is this archive of the Captain's log so fragmented?"

"A significant portion of data was damaged. I have been working on reorganizing the affected files. I have been successful in reconstructing a number of related data logs."

"Did you find out anything of interest?"

"Yes," Gem replied curtly. "The archives in question represent the personal log of Captain Grammul Dente-Ala-Pier. Entry log date 577 78:35:00 A.D. Duration: 22.5 seconds."

"Hmm. Sounds almost human. This A.D, does it stand for Anno Domini?"

"No, the acronym refers to a historically significant event that had occurred during the years of the Ancient Ones. I've not discovered any further definition."

"So you have no idea?"

"Unknown, I have insufficient information. I will not even attempt a guess."

Ryan chuckled, "You? Make a guess?"

"Yes, a statistically probable conclusion. I can guess, just like you."

"But just not this, right? Anyway, pull the log up, I'd like to review it."

An image appeared, distorted and continually barraged by white noise like a bad analog TV signal during a thunderstorm. Within the frame stood a man, graying and distinguished looking, wearing a red uniform with a tunic neck. On his left breast were a number of medals, the distinction of a high-ranking officer with years of experience. Although the video revealed he was talking, the corresponding audio was scratchy and distorted, playing out in a choppy delayed fashion. The man's voice presented a thickly accented foreign language. The playback lasted a full 22.5 seconds in duration before turning to white fuzz.

"Gem, this is... he's human. I didn't know Flukkens were human. Where did you say this log came from?"

"This recording came from the vessel 'D'all Zermifacta-9502877' or simply translated *The War Spritzer - 91009D* main library of the crew's personnel logs, and you are mistaken. This life-form is not Flukken. His race is called... I am scanning available data. Please wait a moment." The pause stretched over minutes. Ryan drummed his fingers anxiously on the console. Finally, Gem came back from the recesses of her fractal world. "I am not able to find the official name of the Captain's race, in any context, however, I am convinced they are referred to by the Xeronians as the Ancient Ones."

"Are you sure?"

"I am."

"The Xeronians must have known this, why didn't they tell me?"

"I have not had sufficient time and opportunity to review all the available libraries in detail. I will state that of all the information I have researched, there are no physiological references provided describing the Ancient Ones. The information is unusually sparse in context."

"So they don't know, you mean? If they did, why wouldn't they have told me?"

"I'm sorry, Captain, the facts are elusive."

"Are you continuing to reconstruct the damaged memory on this log entry?"

"Yes, it is an ongoing task. I am about 40% complete."

"Can you try to translate whatever he is saying and sharpen up the image?"

"That may be possible, but I will provide no guarantees."

"I'm satisfied with that."

"I can download all relevant archives to you through your vaskpar."

Ryan scanned the total size of the logs before agreeing.

"Umm, OK Gem, but I can see this is going to take some time."

* * *

Days passed into weeks. The ship passed by a number of vessels in the outer range of the scanners, but without any concern of engagement.

"We are now five hours from Signus," Gem announced.

Ryan was jogging on his flex-motion machine but quickly stepped off, wiping the sweat dripping down his forehead. "Alright, bring all tracing scanners up to maximum range and ready the weapons systems. I'll be in the pilot's chair after my shower."

The view from the pilot's chair revealed little but the blurred image of stars. Nothing showed on the scanners. The ship's navigations displays gave little clue of any major concerns.

Ryan doggedly returned to studying the battle logs. The dry research soon took its toll, and he fell asleep at the console. He awoke 30 minutes away from Signus barraged by persistent and piercing sirens. His drowsiness vanished as intense details flooded into his mind. The tracing sensors projected a holograph of the system above the cockpit's instrumentation panels, superimposed over the brightly lit background of stars, which cut through the open quartz viewports with resolved clarity. The situation became clear quickly.

There were Xi-Empire destroyers and slaverships in orbit around the planet. The fleet had arrived early.

Ryan modified the course to bring the *Dancing Queen* behind the outermost planet of the Signus system. The sudden deceleration was intense, barely halting them in time. But they made it, and were drifting along, safely obscured behind the planet – their arrival hadn't been noticed.

He ran the tracing scans, and his heart sank.

There were more ships than he anticipated: two destroyers, eight slaverships, all heavily armed. Three of the slaverships were in high orbit, which probably indicated they were already full of slaves. Shuttles were moving to and from the successive ship in line. He had expected a full stream of simultaneous shuttles between all the slavers but something, obviously, was hindering their progress. Possibly the task of rounding up their victims had proven more difficult than they had expected.

"Gem, I am not sure about this. Timing is critical and we will have hit all of them simultaneously. And our missiles cannot be dispatched this far out."

He pulled up multiple tactical views. The three slaverships needed to be intercepted at the same time the destroyers were disabled or they'd scatter in all directions.

There had to be some way to pull this off.

Since the Signites were giving them some grief, they probably have many troops on the surface, and most likely running sparse crews on those destroyers. That could work to his advantage, but he had to get in closer without being detected.

He pulled up a full inner system display. Signus was one of five planets within a single sun system. The system had its share of moons, asteroids, and comets - enough to provide some level of camouflage. There were ghost images on the edge of the tracing image, fuzzy shapes, probably space debris or tracing noise, but nothing that would warrant a closer inspection.

He scoured the holographic map, looking for something - anything that could work to his benefit.

If he could find something large enough to hide the Dancing Queen, close enough in range to launch an attack...

The solution presented itself quickly: a comet on a flyby no more than a stone's throw away from Signus.

"OK, Gem, I think we can make this work. The ice tail should distort the *Dancing Queen's* signature just enough. From there I should be able to launch missiles to hit the destroyers, and engage in direct fire to disable those three slavers."

"We could initiate an acroluc jump directly into the tail. But this would be a challenging manoeuver," offered Gem.

"Show me."

Gem replayed the plan through the vaskpar. The *Dancing Queen* would slingshot around the sun but stay out of tracing range of the destroyers, then make a jump to acroluc and decelerate quickly enough to drop precisely within the tail without colliding into the comet. Undoubtedly, their tracing sensors were calibrated to catch any objects moving in on an approaching vector, so they just might miss this. Gem had already isolated the frequency of their tracing search pulse. If they timed it just after the sweep, there would be a large enough window to pull it off.

"The probability of successfully completing this maneuver is statistically low," Gem stated.

"Do you have any better ideas?"

"Not at this time."

"Then we go with the plan," stated Ryan. "Besides, you can do it. You're the most advanced... ah... control system the Xeronians ever created."

"ConPar is the Xeronian term."

"Alright then, I won't call you a computer, I'll call you a conPar, that make you happy?"

"My happiness is not relevant to this discussion."

"Right. Well, we move at T-minus 60, so start the countdown." He communicated with Ziggy through the vaskpar. "Ziggy, prep the long-range missiles. Four of them."

"15..14.. Are you sure you want to do this?" inquired Gem.

"I thought you came from a warship," Ryan returned sarcastically.

"Very well. Be prepared for acceleration."

Ryan pulled the restraints tighter and patted the console. "You can do this, baby."

"3..2..1."

The ship lurched as the gluon burners flared to maximum. The gravitonic flux inverted them within the antimatter blanket and they jumped to acroluc. He fought the urge to grab the controls.

"Please, do not override my control, Captain," warned Gem.

"Yeah, I know, just get me there in one piece, Gem."

The *Dancing Queen* completed the loop around the sun, leveraging the star's massive gravitation field to help swing it around.

"Approaching destination vector now. Deceleration in 2..3..1."

The anti-gravs whined as they tried to compensate the inertial forces within the ship. They were not completely successful, as Ryan was compressed so tightly against his restraints that he almost blacked out. It was all over in a matter of seconds.

He gratefully gulped in some air and checked the ship's systems. The *Dancing Queen* had matched the speed of the comet perfectly and was positioned well within the cover of its tail. Ryan could see the icy dust floating over the ship's hull through the quartz viewport.

"Dropping to low energy emissions," reported Gem. Multiple ship systems shut down or migrated to low energy levels throughout.

"Good job, Gem. Wasn't that hard was it?"

"We have accomplished this contrary to statistical evaluation. We should have crashed."

"Have some faith in yourself. Let's check on our enemy."

Using a low power trace in order to avoid detection, he mustered up a visual tactical of the situation. Gem had to process the image a number of times to remove the distortion caused from the ice particles.

The three full slaverships were beginning to maneuver into trajectory alignment for departure, but the destroyers hadn't moved from orbit. There was no indication they had a clue about their arrival.

He would have to move quickly now as the slavers were getting ready to depart. At this range, the missiles would easily slip through the destroyer's short-range tracing arrays. By the time they completed a confirmation sweep they would already be within lethal range of their targets. Only blind luck would save them.

"Gem, do you believe in luck?"

"I am familiar with the concept of statistical significance being altered."

"So, yes? Really? You surprise me sometimes. Do you realize that? Anyway, cross your fingers – or what have you."

Ryan took a deep breath and deployed the missiles, each destined for a destroyer. He waited only a second before pulling the *Dancing Queen* from its lair, high acceleration, palms sweaty, heart pounding in his temples.

As expected, the destroyers didn't have time to react. The missiles bore through their antimatter shielding effortlessly, warping their protective shields just enough to allow them to reach the outer hulls and explode. Two bursts, intense as the sun, lit the heavens. The blast radius expanded to engulf a number of the nearby slaverships, savagely tearing them apart.

The *Dancing Queen* was on course to engage with the slaverships. They were already attempting to scatter in disorganized haste but fell prey to his intense, precise cannon bursts. Main drives shredded into misshapen fragments, alive with hues of color, as briefly surviving infernos faded to darkness.

A second volley and then a third. All three of the laden ships floated on, severely crippled and helpless. Behind the Dancing Queen, the remaining slaverships were going on the offensive.

Ryan flipped the ship and maximized the rear burners. The *Dancing Queen* shot toward Signus, as the collection of slavers were rushing out to aid their fallen sister ships.

Ryan started a barrage of cannon bursts. A wall of deadly plasma burned into the oncoming ships. A particularly able Captain managed to avoid the onslaught, quickly pulling his ship out of range and then maneuvering to fall in behind the *Queen*. The slaver began its own suppressive firing. Ryan reacted, dropping down into the Signus atmosphere. His pursuer followed, and two others joined in the chase.

A Bellicose Dance

The *Dancing Queen's* streamlined design allowed her to maneuver through the atmosphere with grace, combating friction easily in comparison to the large, clumsy slavers. As Ryan guided her down, targeting statistics fed directly into his mind. He made a slight adjustment to his course, and the tail cannon found its first target, blasting a lethal blow into the pursuer's midsection. The slavership fell to the surface, leaving a trail of thick, black smoke behind. The others, coming in from oblique angles, spread a volley of bursts at the *Queen*. Ryan pulled the ship through and up the tower of black smoke, briefly following the pillar, climbing above the pursuing ships under cover. The maneuver left him at a distinct advantage. The other ships did not take long to realize his position, but their main cannon were momentarily diverted as they struggled to follow. He turned and dived, splaying out his own volley of blasts directly into both. One exploded into fragments, another careened off, critically damaged, and fell rapidly. It hit the surface with such savage force that it disintegrated into a ball of fire.

Ryan refocused his attention on tactical feeds. Mental images swarmed through his vaskpar. Three slavers left – one still actively filling its holds with slaves. Strangely, none had jumped to acroluc.

Arrogant enough to wait for the outcome of the battle. Typical. A fatal mistake.

He pulled the *Dancing Queen* up and out of the atmosphere and back into frictionless space catching up with his new targets easily. Their underpowered drives and overextended mass restricted their acceleration.

He was sure they were regretting their overconfidence as they scattered in obvious haste to avoid their unknown assailant.

Ryan dispatched a missile. Unhindered by biological passengers, it accelerated past the retreating slaverships and detonated well ahead of them. The ships veered away, avoiding the destructive blast. They would have to recalculate new vectors, and this provided a brief delay in their jump to acroluc.

"Captain, we now have definite resolution of a Xi-Empire cruiser approaching on an interception course."

"A cruiser? How the hell did we miss that?"

"The initial tracings did pick up it. However, the image was poor and we chose to ignore it."

"E.T.A and course?"

"3.5 minutes, and for all intents and purposes, dead ahead."

"So that is where they are headed," Ryan muttered to himself. "Running to mamma. But they won't make it." He targeted the first with the forward cannon. The alignment systems took over, locked, and fired. The ship faltered - direct hit in the central power conduits. With its main drive useless it coasted in the vacuum, defeated and crippled. Something exploded from the stern, and the ship started spinning.

The *Dancing Queen* shot by leaving it behind.

Two ships left.

The slaverships' antimatter shielding were each glowing bright blue. They were preparing to jump. But the *Dancing Queen* was almost on top of them now, and well within range. He fired again, this time with both long and short-range cannon simultaneously. The blasts of the two cannon worked in tandem. The short-range pounded the slavers' shielding, effectively overloading their systems, disintegrating their capacitors and wreaking general havoc internally. The blasts from the long-range cannon ripped into their hulls with measured precision, cutting through their engineering decks.

They were finished. Now Ryan had a bigger problem to worry about: the Xi-Empire cruiser closing in.

"Ziggy, ready five missiles. I want them deployed dormant."

"One minute until interception," announced Gem.

Ryan set them for remote activation and pulled the *Dancing Queen* 90 degrees from their present course, quickly firing the deadly payload out into space. "Gem, lock on those missile signals and stand ready to activate."

The magnificent cruiser appeared like a ghost, dropping out of acroluc in a silent scream of power. The two ships were just kilometers from one another. Unmercifully, Gem activated the four missiles that were in range. As they shot toward the cruiser's hull the giant vessel's shielding sublimed the weapons before they could detonate. Immediately the warship brought its cannon array to bear upon the *Dancing Queen*. Ryan yanked her around, just avoiding a decimating barrage of disruptor blasts. A stray shot made partial contact with his hull shielding. The port wing was briefly enveloped in a blue-violet haze. The shields held, however, and the damage from the menacing salvo was limited to turning part of the *Dancing Queen's* white hull to a dull black. Ryan reviewed the stats: the capacitors had nearly peaked containment with that single shot.

"Damn it, that was close! I need some info on this thing."

It came up immediately, a background vaskpar voice began a familiar murmuring directly into his mind. He brought the *Dancing Queen* around again barely avoiding another volley.

"It has a weakness, where is it?"

"Information is limited. This is a modified version of a cruiser-class warship. Scans indicate known targeting areas have been upgraded."

"Then find one that hasn't."

"There is one possibility - the rear burner plates near the cooling channels."

"Possible? Aren't you sure?"

"Insufficient information - it is a guess."

"Gem, those burners can handle intense, concentrated blasts. The shots will disperse. It'll be like firing into the sun."

"A missile will penetrate successfully."

"Yes, if it doesn't get vaporized first."

Ryan had the *Dancing Queen* moving perpendicular to his previous course, jumping away at maximum burner acceleration. The gigantic cruiser, with its imposing mass, was still attempting to intercept, but it was much slower. Its weapons systems, however, were not as restricted. In a few more seconds it would be in position, yet again, to pound them into dust.

"Ziggy, ready another five missiles."

"That will deplete our current stores. Just to remind you - there is still one inactivate missile remaining."

"That's right. Of course, that's it! Gem, be ready to lock on and wake that missile. We'll let that big bastard chase us right by our little surprise. When it gets into range, nail it in the ass. They won't see it coming."

The distance between the two ships began to close. The Xi-Empire cruiser's cannon were firing heatedly. Walls of white and blue lit up the dark vacuum of space around the *Dancing Queen*. Ryan pulled the ship into a full 180 degree reversal. The forward burner reaction plates lit up the cockpit with intense brilliance even though the quartz filters compensated to keep the radiation to a minimum.

The cruiser readjusted its course quickly, maintaining pursuit.

Another direct volley into the *Dancing Queen's* shields could be fatal. The ship's shielding was not built to channel that much energy.

"The enemy is within optimum target range. Activating missile," reported Gem.

Ryan flipped the ship end for end and pulled the nose a further 60 degrees, bringing the main burners to maximum thrust. She jumped ahead as the cruiser attempted to correct its course. The monitors told the story. As the missile hit and explosions rippled through the rear of the cruiser, blowing out seals and its interior contents into the blackness of space, including some crew. Parts of the outer hull glowed to white hot as a chain reaction fired through the drive systems, demolishing bulkheads and contorting the massive ship's back as tremendous forces pushed and pulled at the spectacular vessel. In a brief second the cruiser's main drive was obliterated along with a large portion of its stern.

"She's not going anywhere now," chuckled Ryan. He checked his tactical. The slavers were still floating aimlessly in space.

The cruiser sat helpless before him, its main drives obliterated, all power systems down, fires billowing throughout its corridors. A couple well-placed cannon shots would end it permanently.

"Captain, I do believe the prisoners within the slaverships are in duress," reported Gem.

Ryan moved his finger off the trigger. *More important work to do now.*

He maneuvered the scarred *Dancing Queen* to intercept the closest crippled slavership.

"Gem, open a channel with that slaver."

"They could attempt a hostage negotiation."

"Maybe, let's see."

To Ryan's surprise, they responded. What should he say? Keep it short and precise. He thumbed the communications relay.

"Slaver crew, cooperate and you will live." He dropped the link.

"That's it?" asked Gem.

"What do you want, a speech?" retorted Ryan. "Can you do a structural integrity analysis from the tracings?"

The report flooded in over his vaskpar, design details of the slaver, from bow to stern, all supplied via the Xeronian intelligence libraries. Key attachment locations were revealed.

Ryan deployed the grav lines. "Gem, how powerful do you think these grav lines are?"

"Do you wish torque and shearing strength ratings or an electro-gravimetric statistics?"

"No, just tell me they'll hold if I bring this ship down onto the planet's surface."

"The load will surely exceed maximum tolerances."

"That's what I thought, but I've decided that they'll hold."

"How do you know this?" Gem asked curiously.

"I have a gut feeling."

"I hope your gut is more accurate than my calculations," replied Gem dubiously.

"It's the only way I can think of to get our fellow Signite prisoners back to safety unless you have another idea?"

"You could board the ship, locate and pilot the shuttle."

"Not enough time."

"You will be exceeding calculated limits marginally. Deploy extra grav lines and that should alleviate the concern of failure."

Ryan deployed additional lines, each finding a firm locking position on the hull. With the slavership in tow, they headed toward the planet. The extra burden seeming negligible to the *Dancing Queen* but that would soon change with the added pull of gravity.

The planet's sun, a yellow dwarf, glared white-hot in space, bathing the day-side of the planet in life-giving warmth. The view from above revealed vast oceans with masses of connected continents, reflecting back a whole spectrum of greens and browns.

"Amazing. Looks a lot like Earth from up here, all you need to do is rearrange the continents a little," stated Ryan out loud. He knew he couldn't enjoy the scenery long. They were descending into the atmosphere at a faster than recommended speed. The dead weight of slavership was pulling tenaciously on the *Dancing Queen* now. She battled to compensate as Ryan struggled to balance the ship's thrust against overstressing the grav lines. Knowing it was going to be close, he guided the ship in over an ocean in hopes the water would cushion the impact of the descent.

They sank down into the atmosphere, Ryan desperately attempting to slow their descent speed enough to bring it to a full stop before making contact with the surface. The slaver hit, plunging down into the depths, pulling the *Dancing Queen* down with it. Ryan adjusted frantically, managing to stop the descent just meters above the surface of the water. He held the *Dancing Queen* there, momentarily in a hover, and let out a breath he hadn't realized he was holding. He wiped the palms of his shaking hands.

"Well, there you go, Gem. Instinct over mathematics. Checkmate."

He proceeded to pull the larger craft up and out of the water and headed toward the nearest land. The slaver had taken on water and had gained substantial weight, but with Ryan's gentle coaxing, the *Dancing Queen* managed to skim its burden along the water's surface, leaving an intermittent wake behind. Within a minute they reached land and managed to drag the vessel up onto the beach.

He detached the grav lines, quickly checking the monitors. The slavership imparted an unusual contrast, a black towering pillar of technology, strewn upon the pearl-white sands of a natural shoreline. Torrents of water poured out of it from the breached areas of its hull.

"Let's hope we have survivors in there. No time to wait and see. That's only one ship and there's more to go," he stated with satisfaction, then quickly guided the *Queen* up to retrieve the next. He followed the same procedure. The grav lines held each time.

Four ships, four trips, each successful. Four carcasses of slaverships now rested on the beach, each full of Signite abductees.

He could attempt to board the ships, take out any remaining crew, and free the slaves. Or possibly, a better plan was to locate and destroy the newly formed Xi-Empire military bases and help the Signites reclaim their planet. Let them do the dirty work of reclaiming their people. As this planet was a recent conquest, the Empire hadn't had time to build their usual vast fortified defenses.

It was doable.

He bounced his idea off Gem.

"Yes, the Signites should be able to regain control, at least on the surface - assuming there are any resistance left."

"Anybody ever tell you that you are incredibly positive?"

They proceeded to scan the area, hunt down the bases, and then systematically blast them into open craters. A few of Signite resistance fighters waved at him as he passed. To them, the graceful white ship was an angel of retribution.

The exercise took hours to complete. Once complete Ryan returned to the beach. A stream of people were making their way out of the many air locks within the ship using makeshift ropes of clothing and materials to traverse the distance to the ground. Those that were lucky enough to reach the safety of solid footing found they were easy prey for a group of surviving Xi-Empire troopers. The unmerciful troops had littered the white beach with the blood of Signite men and women. Luckily, some of the resistance had arrived at the scene and were pushing the rogue aliens into a tight circle. The troops had dug in under a cover of rock and driftwood and remained steadfast between the escaping slaves and the encroaching rebels.

Ryan wasted no time putting the *Dancing Queen's* cannon to work with a number of precise, low-intensity bursts. The alien invaders disappeared in a shower of sand, fire, and blood. He watched from above as the rebels stormed onto the beach in hordes, waving their weapons and blasting at anything left moving.

He came up close to each of the wrecks and checked their hulls, searching for any identification, any familiar symbols. None showed the vaguely familiar markings of the *Xabuntz II*.

Yeah, it was a long shot. Was that dream real or was it a collection of haphazard, manufactured images with no relevance to reality? He had nothing else. The contents of that Xeronian vile had given him something - an experience he would never forget. And it gave him knowledge that there were things about this universe he could never understand. That fed his hope.

He scanned the beach area one more time. The rebels were already setting up camp and were busily shepherding others from the massive hulks of the slavers.

They clearly didn't need him.

Pulling the *Dancing Queen* into a vertical climb, he left the picturesque planet behind. As he passed beyond the third planet, the tactical scans revealed the cruiser, still drifting, still totally crippled. It was only then that he remembered Tseman's words: Zorlog was on that ship.

Maybe if it had been any other Xilozak, any other Captain of the Xi-Empire, he would have just pointed the *Queen* to Xilo and moved on.

But it wasn't.

Thoughts were churning within his mind. He rubbed the scar on his forehead, remembering the last glint of metal, the vicious strike. *He should move in right now and destroy her. No, that would be too easy. Perhaps the embarrassment of failure would do him more damage.*

Let him suffer one more hit.

* * *

A very angry, very irritable Karvok stood on the deck of the cruiser, yelling out a stream of orders, words muddied with strings of demeaning curses. The ship was slowly recovering. The fires were finally under control, and all decks had been successfully sealed, oxygen and methane levels were down to dangerously low levels - they would have to convert some of the water supply over as soon as possible.

The secondary drives were repairable. In time, they would be operational again. Just as well. The alien ship had left Signus and by its trajectory, was going to pass close by. He still could not believe the arrogant luck of that alien pilot. It had managed to do a considerable amount of damage to the Xi-Empire's most powerful warship - something unprecedented.

Worse yet it was he, Zorlog, that had made the mistake. He should have destroyed that alien ship instead of trying to capture it. He cursed again as another explosion ripped through the engineering section. How did *it* slip that dormant missile by? How did *it* know where to hit? It was one of the only weaknesses this ship had left. Obviously, *it* knew something about Xi-Empire design.

With detached eyes, he studied the chaotic picture around, looking for key crew, the ones that held their cool under the pressure. Many of the arrogant ones, the confident and cocky, were staggering about numbly, thoroughly shaken to their disgustingly impudent cores. These he would replace. There was no room for incompetence and no patience imparted from their commander. He watched them falter about briefly, thinking how he would have even found it amusing if it was not for the fact that he was in command.

"Zuvok, we are being hailed."

Zorlog glared at his Avok, irritated by the interruption in thought. "What?"

"The alien ship is hailing us."

He paused a moment. On an Xi-Empire channel? Strange. Could it be a Txtian trick, a possibly twisted scheme of the Emperor himself? "Answer the hail. Put on the visual."

"Link established. We have audio only."

"Then we can assume the pilot has ears and a mouth. That's a start. Link it over the intercom." A second later, a voice rang over the bridge. It was a basic form of Trinarieit, accented strangely. Zorlog had heard this same tone before, but where?

"Who's in command?" the voice asked.

"It is I, the Empirical Karvok Zorlog, of the Xi-Empire fleet. You have just declared war on the Xi-Empire by your actions. That is a very foolish thing to do. Exactly *what* am I talking to?"

A pause.

"You are talking to your past, Zorlog and you will feel my wrath, you waste of skin."

Zorlog lip's curled back in tight irritation, exposing his fangs. Trinarieit curses always translated too loosely. "I ask again, what are you?"

"Lost him, my Zuvok. It dropped the link."

Zorlog crashed his arm down on the nearest console, growling in hateful disdain. "Ready the cannon arrays. Activate all missiles."

The Tracing Avok yelled out, "Enemy vessel modified course - on a direct intercept trajectory, Zuvok!"

"Ready stations!" yelled Zorlog, although his urging was not at all required. The crew attended their posts in a panicky haste. A thousand troops watched the small image of the approaching vessel, a select few waiting anxiously within their gunner's spheres. The engineering crews, already exhausted from the effort of rebuilding damaged ship's systems, fought on wearily, attempting to keep the many conduits open to the ship's main capacitors. Turrets powered up and down in a traveling dance along the *Bzak's* outer hull, the gunners watched with desperation as their consoles flickered off, on and off again.

"Status!" ordered Zorlog

"The vessel is coming in on a collision course, my Zuvok. At the speed it's going, it'll cut us in half!" The Avok was nearly euphoric.

Zorlog remained calm. "No, it has another purpose in mind. Bring all weapons to bear and fire at will, immediately."

"Third bank deployed. Missiles attaining target... Alien ship firing. First bank, second, third, all missiles destroyed. Deploying fourth bank..."

The cruiser's formidable cannon turrets, the first of all of its systems brought back online, aimed squarely on the small white dot, which was only slightly camouflaged in the background of stars. They remained silent, however, as the alien aggressor was not yet in range.

Without warning, the bridge's power systems failed in unison, leaving Zorlog in darkness once again. The blackout was only momentary. Systems struggled back to life in a defiant resurgence. It was enough, however, to increase the tension tenfold.

"Zuvok! The ship is jumping to acroluc!"

"As I suspected. Fire everything!" yelled Zorlog, barely able to mouth the words before the very walls around him started vibrating. The whole ship began contorting as if a gigantic pair of hands had grabbed hold of each end and started twisting back and forth mercilessly. Micro-thin fissures snaked along outer and inner hulls. Internal bulkhead plating popped loose, some sections literally exploding across corridors. The groaning and creaking from the superstructure turned into high-pitched screeching, a thousand tuning forks ringing in unison, all with different frequencies. The vibration became so intense the decking seemed to turn to liquid, and the crew were tossed about like rag dolls. The power systems, not built to withstand such conditions, fused together and shorted out conduits. Blue arcs raced along the ship's hull. Immense surges of pure energy let loose, literally frying unlucky troopers to charcoal. Throughout the ship multiple power relays shut down as gravity plates fluctuated and failed, throwing the others against bulkheads and snapping limbs in the process.

Just as suddenly as it had started, the havoc subsided, surrendering to a high-pitched shrieking of escaping atmosphere that echoed down the ship's corridors. Thousands of new leaks had formed throughout, and the ship was hemorrhaging atmosphere.

Zorlog removed his hands from his ears, stood up from the deck where he had been thrown. His arm throbbed where he had landed upon it.

Probably a fracture, but could be broken.

He watched as the bridge systems struggled to come up. Redundant backups were supposed to protect these systems, even in the case of multiple power failures but the engineers had never imagined such abuse.

"Seal every hatch in every corridor. Now!" Zorlog growled.

"What was that?" asked an excited young Avok, his face full of nervous fear, fangs indecently dripping saliva.

"Didn't you learn anything in militia training? That was the wake of a gravitonic distortion field. It is what happens when a starship launches into acroluc and passes too close to another."

Zorlog blew out his breath in exasperation. This interference effect sets up a harmonic imbalance in the superstructure of the resting vessel. The bigger the vessel, the worse it is, and the effect is amplified through its gravitational plating. They were lucky the cruiser held together at all.

"My Zuvok, all the power networks are now offline. All ship's systems are compromised."

Zorlog laughed his icy laugh. "But we are still alive! I've seen ships rip apart like rotten razum from this. Not even a cruiser is safe from gravitonic distortion. The only protection is to blast the enemy before he gets too close." Zorlog's laughing suddenly stopped. "Of which you obviously did not do...

Stop standing around! We're losing atmosphere!"

He slammed the ship-wide intercom. "This is a conservation alert. If we don't get this leaking situation under control within the next few radii, this ship will be returning to Xilo with only corpses aboard!"

That should get their attention, he thought with grim satisfaction. Who was this alien adversary? This creature had engaged two empirical destroyers, a cruiser, and a group of heavily weaponized slavers. It knew no fear.

A sudden sour realization sunk in. Due to this his reputation is now irreparably damaged. He did not look forward to returning to Xilo. Everything was going so well before. Why do things always seem to twist the wrong way at the most inopportune moment? Perhaps there are a few Txtians left aboard he could kill. That would cheer him up.

He suddenly laughed. The officer near him looked up, puzzled and wary.

"Get me the crew roster."

As always, he will adapt. Things change. Plans change. The goal remains the same. He will just have to accelerate the schedule.

An old, familiar hate burned deep down within his gut.

* * *

The *Dancing Queen* was almost 10 weeks away from the Xi-Empire capital planet of Xilo. She was traveling at maximum cruising speed with her forward tracing scanners sweeping a tight beam. Few ships, if any, could match the velocity of her, and of those, none were of Xi-Empire origin.

Ryan stayed busy reviewing the ship's systems. The engagement with the cruiser was taxing on her systems and everything needed to be inspected thoroughly. On the initial overall pass, everything seemed fine, but he felt, no he *knew*, something was amiss.

"Captain," Gem interrupted.

"Yes, Gem."

"I have completed all drive system diagnostics. Nothing is operating outside established parameters."

"Well, maybe the parameters are wrong."

"I do not understand your concern."

"It's called human instinct. Something is wrong. I just know it."

"I will endeavor to review all parameters and review all test data again."

"Good idea." Ryan began to climb into the port-wing maintenance tube. He felt himself become lighter as he left the effects of the gravity cone generated from the grav plates.

"Captain."

"Yes, Gem," he replied with an edge of frustration in his voice.

"There are a number of tests that I cannot complete as I do not have the required detection and monitoring devices."

"What type of tests?"

"The navigational interface units on second and third channels."

"OK, and?"

"Power transfer feeds to main drive."

Ryan sat there for a minute, thinking. "Gem, would that include the capacitor feed systems to the main drive burner plate?"

"Yes."

"That's it! Listen, don't you hear it? It's a high-pitched whistle, like a bad CRT tube."

"A CRT tube? I do not know..."

"A high-pitched whistle. Can you hear it or not?"

"Dropping audio sensitivity filtration. Yes, I have now detected the sound in question."

Ryan quickly wriggled out of the tube and ran over to the drive balance indicators. "We're at an imbalance of 0.02%, Gem!"

"That is not within acceptable parameters. I would suggest an adjustment in the array immediately."

"Already on it. Well, well, looky here. Got it. Looks like we have a bad resistance on this pathway. I am switching over to an alternate route."

The high-pitched whistle disappeared. "That's it. What's the damage Gem?"

"I estimate it has added approximately three days to our arrival time. I would like to point out that I would have spotted our navigational drift within the next hour. We would have certainly isolated the problem by then."

"I know, but nobody's perfect, not even your computers – I mean conPars."

"Captain, I have as much in common with a computer as you have with an amoeba."

Ryan chuckled, enjoying Gem's irritability.

"I suggest that we construct a monitoring interface into these circuits. I must be able to measure this activity more effectively."

"I wholly concur. Have Ziggy fabricate the interfaces for you. Such a complicated task is beyond a mere biological being as myself."

Ryan was now satisfied to wrap up the diagnostic scans. They had done well - and they were still alive. It reminded him of a previous discussion. He wondered if Gem felt any fear during the battles.

"You know, Gem. We did OK, all in all. It looks like we've weathered our first battle with flying colors. You handled yourself well."

"We did achieve our goal. Something not always accomplished in similar situations."

"How did you feel during the battle?"

"Feel? Why do you ask such a question?"

"I must understand your state of mind, determine your stability."

"I am very stable, thank you."

"I must have confidence I can count on you when things get difficult. So again, how did you feel?"

"I felt... afraid, excited, apprehensive, anger... However such emotions do not interfere with my function."

"No, in fact, they sharpen your abilities. It is good you embrace your emotions and use them to drive you.

"I am... working through this process."

"Good. By-the-way, have you managed to get anywhere with the memory reconstruction?"

"No, I am continuing to work on this."

"Please continue – there may be something very important in there."

Ryan situated himself in front of the wall-sized display in the navigations center, leaning back into a much too comfortable chair. He began the difficult task of establishing a tight-beam communications channel to Xeronia. It was a difficult task, virtually impossible, had it not been for the Xeronian surveillance relays positioned in certain key regions of space. Although their coordinates had been stored within Gem's vast memory, securing a connection at such high velocity was tricky at best. Regardless, within the hour a channel was secured. Ryan switched it over to full visual. He preferred to see who he was talking to, although he had no doubt that Tsaurau preferred a mind-to-mind link.

Tsaurau's face appeared on the monitor, the image flickering, shifting in and out of phase. It was the best one could ask for, given the situation.

"Tsaurau, how are your new guests?"

"They are doing well. I am glad to hear the news on Signus. Did you have any major difficulties?"

"Yes, I was almost blasted into oblivion. These shields are not equipped to handle a full-on barrage of a Xi-Cruiser. I don't expect I will be as lucky next time. I need a better solution."

"We do have alternative designs for the shielding, such as employing some of the design aspects implemented on the shield we used to protect Xeronia, but its energy requirements are restrictive. Such technology requires the enormous reserves to operate. I am not sure we can scale this down.

"Get your people working on it. I'll take a look at that angle from here."

"What is your current mission?"

"You know where I am going. I have to find her."

"You are traveling through very dangerous space."

"Unavoidable."

"Only love would lead one into the very center of death. Patrols are numerous as you approach the capital. I must warn you, you will not remain undetected for long. You may not make it back to us."

"Don't give up on me yet. I've some distance to travel and time to prepare. This shield problem should keep me busy. I will communicate with you when I'm able."

Tsaurau acknowledged Ryan's response with a nod. He knew the Earthman too well. Nothing he could say would convince him to turn away. "Be careful my friend, and good luck."

"I may need some. *Dancing Queen* out."

* * *

Ryan spent the following weeks working furiously. The mental work was challenging, but satisfying, as it drew him away from his own troubling thoughts. In comparison to the past, things that he'd never been able to understand before were now just simple ideas, trivial facts. His confidence was always short-lived, however, as it was often dashed into unpretentious confusion once he delved into the Xeronian advanced concepts and mathematics, especially those employed in shield engineering. He pushed on, determined as ever, and by the end of the first two weeks the fruits of his labor paid off. He had developed a new model. Granted, there were still questions and unresolved details, but the model would and could work. He transmitted his proposed designs to the Xeronians. They replied back quickly, putting forth a mountain of questions and additional ideas. Their combined efforts resulted in success. By the end of the seventh week, the model was a working prototype that could be integrated into the ship.

Ryan had little time to get it operational. He worked with Ziggy around the clock, printing and machining the parts, growing the circuitry. The power issue remained the one main stumbling block - and the biggest compromise. Two extra capacitors were constructed and installed, and the energy collection system was reinforced. The most significant task involved the installation of additional conduit throughout the length of the ship. The new shield's energy requirements were enormous. Charging the capacitor array took time, and once the energy reached the required operating level the shield's duration, once activated, was very short, lasting only minutes. But that was all he should need. The system was designed to be activated only when the ship was under heavy fire. Each blast by the enemy would be absorbed by the shielding and then channeled back into the capacitors, which in turn powered the enhanced shielding. The risk of an overload still existed, but that's where his piloting skills compensated. The bottom-line trick was the timing of the enhanced shield deployment. If activated too quickly, energy reserves could decrease to dangerously low levels, starving the primary shielding and literally leaving the ship exposed, which in the end, was self-defeating.

The most tedious of all tasks was the replacement of the shield projection devices along the hull. Ryan had never been out in space before, least of all running at acroluc, which was considerably more dangerous.

He took his time pulling the suit on. As he locked the helmet on, he let out a slow breath. Everything seemed louder: heart pumping in his ears, breathing resonated as if he was in a spacious cavern.

Calm down. No mistakes now. No mistakes out there.

He held out his hand. It took a moment for his shaking gloved fingers to steady.

The airlock doors closed and evacuated to vacuum quickly. The outer door opened to reveal a spectacular view. The stars were a myriad of swirling colors, sharp, piercing lights and solid lines of blurred brightness, all in a canvas of utter silence.

He locked the toolbox to his suit. An extra toolbox was also in the airlock, but it would remain there, unless of course, he needed something special. Hopefully, if everything goes right, he had everything he needed. He disabled the anti-grav plates and waited for the slight nausea to pass as he adjusted to the weightlessness.

"OK, Gem, looks like I'm ready," he relayed, a bit too shakily.

"Have you deployed the outside handholds?"

"Yes, they all are deployed. Captain, are you prepared?"

"Why, do I sound nervous?"

"Yes, you do. I believe this would be considered in human standards, ironic. You are a starship captain after all."

"Good choice of words, Gem," replied Ryan, barely hearing her. He attached the lifeline to the outside anchoring point and with a deep breath, pulled himself out of the safety of his ship – only to look down at the stars below his feet. His stomach flipped end over end. Below him, above him, nothing – an expanse of space - the black vastness of the universe. There was no up, no down, and everything seemed endlessly far away.

But everything was moving, swirling, churning, even at acroluc the movement was apparent. It was mesmerizing. His grip on the handhold seemed the only thing between him and insanity. He wondered if he let go, would he fall forever? Would he crash into a planet, come too close to a distant star?

Like a momentary case of vertigo, he was overwhelmed with an urge to let go, but then there was the lifeline, he'd not forgotten about the lifeline.

Calm down. Enjoy the view. You're OK.

The helmet stats looked good, although the vitals monitor showed he was breathing a little too quickly. He had to slow down, be careful not to hyperventilate. He looked down the length of the ship. It seemed to go on forever.

"Tell me, Gem. Do you ever get nervous?"

"I do not believe that is an emotion that I am overly familiar with."

Ryan edged his way along the ship's hull, grasping each handhold successively. "Of course not, that comes with self-doubt which I know you are a bit short of, but you could use some self-reflection."

"Possibly... I do not always feel I will be successful at everything I attempt."

A long pause followed.

"If you can keep talking, it helps me to stay calm."

"Oh, very well. To explain further, I have the ability to realize when the odds are not in my favor and can determine with high probability when I am in danger. I must say that I do not wish to be exterminated, of course."

"Right. Perhaps we modify the conversation slightly?" asked Ryan. "I'm nervous enough out here."

"Yes, that is perfectly understandable. One slip and it may lead to you moving uncontrollably away from the ship. I have been monitoring your thoughts. You are constantly revisiting images of quite dire circumstances. I can assert, however, that you are wrong in your prediction that you would float on forever in the case where you did stray too far away from the ship. Of course, I would react as quickly as possible, correct this situation. As a matter-of-fact, I would even shut down the shielding to ensure you would not be vaporized at its horizon, at the advanced risk to the ship and myself. The truth is, in your present atomically excited state your chances of survival would be extremely slim. At such velocity, you would literally decompose as external gravity wells you pass by tug at your body. Most certainly, a dust particle passing too close would simply rip you apart."

"Enough already, Gem! Change the topic why don't you?"

"I am just attempting to point out, as you are looking for reassurances, you can be guaranteed that I will do my best to retrieve you in such an event. I would immediately deploy Ziggy. Of course, there are timing factors involved, and if you were to somehow stray behind the main gluon disrupters..."

"Just stop. No more talk, OK!" yelled Ryan.

"Very well," replied Gem in a hurt voice.

"Alright, I've reached the first shield deployment projector."

He pushed the arm control and the rear tool rack swung around on projecting arms to rest on his right side.

"Disabling the projector node," announced Gem. "The others are compensating favorably. Ready for unit replacement."

He pulled the tools from the rack and went to work on the first node. It came off with some effort. He replaced it with the new updated unit.

"Here goes. Gem, run the diagnostics."

"Testing. Tests are complete. The new projector node functions correctly."

"Good. Activate it."

"Shield energizing rebalanced."

"Onto to the next one. Only 233 left to go."

The work continued for over half a day. Ryan found himself becoming adequately comfortable out in space, though not necessarily confident. Regardless, he was incredibly relieved upon re-entering the airlock, enjoying the returned freedom through escaping the confines of his suit.

He was soaked to the skin with sweat, and he felt weary to the bone. Regardless, he had little time left, and he knew what time he had would not be enough to complete a full testing cycle of the new shields. He managed to arrange a link to the Xeronian colony and reported in to Tsaurau.

"Everything is in place and working. It'll take a couple of days to charge the secondary capacitors."

"You will have reached your destination by then. Do you not plan to test the new shielding before you encounter an enemy ship?"

"Exactly. I'll test it in battle. Gem's run a number of internal simulations already. It'll work."

The alien's reaction was constrained, his face reflecting placid uniformity. Ryan could tell the Xeronian was studying him, trying to sort out of his behavior.

"Also, I almost forgot to tell you. I have learned some information about the Ancient Ones. Gem has managed to reconstruct some of the damaged core memory, and I've found out something that no one cared to mention to me. The Ancient Ones were humanoid."

"Yes."

"Why didn't you tell me?"

"We have our reasons."

Ryan hated it when Tsaurau did this, keeping him in the dark until the 'proper' time came. "Alright, I've heard this all before. I warn you I'll be looking forward to you filling me in when I get back on these so-called reasons. And another thing, why was there no mention of this in any of your libraries?"

"That information was deleted intentionally. It is too dangerous to keep. I must ask you now to delete all details that you have uncovered."

"Why?"

"I must caution you, it is for your own good to ensure this information does not fall into the wrong hands."

Ryan found himself irritated by the mystery Tsaurau seemed so bent on not sharing. "Your advice is duly noted. Now, since I am less than two days away from Xilo, there will be no more communications from now on. Take care of yourself."

"*Dancing Queen* out."

* * *

Tsaurau reflected in silence. Would he ever see Ryan again? The Earthman was well within Xi-Empire controlled space now. If discovered by a patrol it could prove fatal. Such a strange creature, this human, to risk everything on the slimmest chance of finding this female, of which he had only the briefest of relations with. Perhaps it was his biological drive, a need to procreate, to bring forth generations as a counterbalance of mortality, or possibly this was an obsession brought upon by internal chemical reactions, of which he refers to as love.

He recalled in vivid detail Ryan's experiences after he had consumed the contents of the vile. The human's feelings had been so intense. It conveyed, in that brief moment, what it was like to be human. Such raw emotions, anger, happiness, fear, love and hate, all so overwhelming. He scoured his memory for the Earth-term Ryan had once mentioned: passion. Passion drove men to greatness or ground them to dust, but its poison was never avoidable.

Perhaps that is why Ryan was the chosen one. There were other, much more suitable races, that could have fulfilled the role of a soldier. Indeed, a human was nearly as frail as a Xeronian. He could only hope they had taught him enough to remain alive.

"Take care, my friend," he said out loud, voicing into nothingness.

* * *

Even at this distance, Ryan was already picking up numerous ships on the tracing scans. Ironically, the closer he moved in, the odds of being attacked were actually decreasing. He found that he was all but ignored. Other vessels stayed to their courses, and no attempts were made to hail him. No one expected a lone enemy ship to be on approach to the Xi-Empire capital planet. No one would be foolish enough. His arrival generated nothing but disinterest, if not a passing curiosity that was mistaken as a Torzon private yacht. Regardless, the approach of an unidentified vessel was a matter for Xi-Empire security patrols.

Ryan came out of acroluc and pulled the *Dancing Queen* within the spartan safety of an impact creator bored deep within a large asteroid. He deployed the grav lines to bring the ship flush to its surface and then proceeded to power down. To other ships, he would be all but invisible, unless they drew too close.

He was a fox awaiting a rabbit. He would lie in waiting for another Xi-Empire ship to pass by, close enough to engage in a limited communication. Since he was in the shipping lanes of Xilo proper, it did not take long.

"We have a candidate vessel. By the analysis, looks like a merchant trader. Gem, you ready?"

"Yes. I have managed to create an image of Captain Gick from the *Joahack's* logs. There will be a slight delay in retransmission."

"That's OK, it'll hold up the illusion that we are far away. Keep the link on wide dispersal and as weak as possible and hail the merchant."

The Captain of the ship was Txtian. He was a shrewd and ruthless trader known as Katar. He was surprised to be hailed so close to Xilo. The image on his viewscreen was that of a Xilozak named Gick, Tarvok of a slaver called the *Joahack*. One look and he could tell this one was of limited intelligence, as most Xilozaks are. He despised them all.

"What do you want, Tarvok?" he said hastily. He wished for this discussion to be brief.

"I am trying to locate a slaver called the *Xabuntz II*."

"You've forgotten your protocols, Tarvok? I am Torzon and shall be addressed as such."

"Very well, Torzon. Do you know of this vessel?"

"I am not Xilo Port Authority. Ask them. Do not bother me with your mundane inquiries, slaver."

"We are transmitting from the Platzick quadrant. We were supposed to rendezvous with the Xabuntz II three sadii ago. I cannot reach the Xilo Port Authority to ask them if they have located this ship."

"Seems quite strange, that you can reach my ship but not the Port Authority. We are barely a parsec away from Xilo, most certainly you can reach them directly. What are your coordinates?"

"As I stated, we are within the Platzick quadrant. It is truly amazing that we have managed to reach so far. Probably due to some natural phenomenon amplifying the signal."

"Yes, possibly," the Txtian replied with a slight skepticism. He considered the story for a few seconds and decided it was plausible. Damn Xilozaks couldn't navigate through a star system without help.

"Very well, I will relay a message to the Xilo Port Authority if you wish," offered Katar, wishing to cut the correspondence short.

Gotcha you sonofabitch. Ryan smiled.

"Yes, my Torzon, and quickly, I must insist." He had to be careful not to seem too nice. Xilozaks were by nature, miserable creatures. He suspended the link, not wanting to view the Txtian's repulsive features any longer.

"Communications, hail Xilo Port Authority, ask them about the last known location and course of the *Xabuntz II*, and that Tarvok Gick of the *Joahack* is requesting it."

A moment passed. The Avok reported back in. "The *Xabuntz II* left Xilo port a little over one zanii ago, last reported in the Ceros quadrant on a slave raid to Shawma. Additional info coming in: The *Joahack* is overdue at E-0017. End-of-message, my Torzon."

"Put the fool back on," ordered Katar dryly.

"Gick, the *Xabuntz II* is on a raid mission to Shawma, Ceros quadrant. You do realize you are overdue at E-0017?"

"Really. Tell them I've changed my plans. Thank you, Torzon."

"Gick, I will not..."

"Link dropped, my Torzon. Shall I attempt reconnection?"

Katar pondered momentarily. Something seemed suspicious, not quite right. "Did you get a fix on the source of that transmission, Avok?"

"Too dispersed, seemed like it was coming from our quadrant, but that signature doesn't make sense. Could be Platzick though. I've heard of this phenomenon before."

"Fine. The *gehrzick* doesn't even know his own schedule. Log this correspondence, include all transmissions. We'll pass it to Xilo Port Authority on our return. They can deal with him."

The Txtian ship continued on its journey. It was not scheduled to return to Xilo for another four zanii.

Ryan gave a big sigh of relief. He was lucky. He had made no mistakes and managed, somehow, to glean useful information. Time was of the essence now. He had to find that ship. Even when or if he found it, she may no longer be on board.

He waited for a lull in the traffic and powered up the ship's drives. Gem calculated the course. It came up on the tactical. The Shawma system was at least three weeks away at maximum. He broke from the asteroid, aligned the *Dancing Queen*, and jumped.

* * *

Was he dreaming?

Inside the ship, everything was where it should be. He leaned back in his seat and flipped open the cockpit shields. They seemed to move too slowly, curving around and past him like a ray of light through rippling water. He felt the heat of a thousand suns on his face as the heavens glowed through the transparent quartz. The universe was so full, billions of galaxies containing billions of stars, too numerous to fathom. Out here, they seemed painted against a backdrop of black velvet, many swirling rich in color: the anger of red, the calmness of violet, the sharpness of blue, the softness of yellow, and the piercing purity of ebony white. Every star beckoned him, like the mythical sirens of ancient oceans, they called to him.

He was dreaming.

Reality slipped over him like a cold glove, quenching his hopes with a crushing strength. He sat up on the edge of his bed, holding his head in his hands, only one thought on his mind.

Aviore!

From memory, he could picture her as clearly as it had been yesterday.

But there are so many stars between them.

He clenched his fists and fought off a rising feeling of hopelessness.

No, he would find her. He had to believe.

He sought out his clothes and dressed clumsily, then stumbled to the cockpit, still half-asleep. From his chair, he thumbed the switch to open the cockpit shields. They pulled back, folding over themselves, eventually sliding down into the ship's hull.

The stars were there, just as in his dream, in all their glory, but this time they were just cold and distant dots in the darkness.

He checked his course, glanced over the multiple monitors, and reviewed internal stats. They were on course. The ship was running well as it raced through the immense span between stars, expending its energy precisely, pushing on without compromise. It had achieved a harmonious balance amongst the forces of the universe.

But would he arrive in time?

He knew the odds. A betting man with any sense would have folded by now. But he had no alternative, no choice but to follow the slimmest of leads. He was on an impossible task, in a starship that could cross the paradox of time and space in a blink of an eye. In a way, it all paled in comparison to the power that drove him on. It made the suns that boiled around him appear flat, featureless, and made time itself hold in anticipation. Somehow, he could still feel her touch. She persisted within his mind, softly, lovingly.

I will find you, Aviore. I will find you.

* * *

10. Rescue

The days passed by quickly. Apprehension ate at him the whole time, creeping through his body, burning into his gut. He had slept no more than a few hours each night. The thoughts raced through his mind incessantly: Would he be too late? Was she still alive? Was she even still there?

He had tried to keep himself busy by reviewing the *War Spritzer's* logs and conducting various tests on the new shielding. Other times he paced the decks or worked out in the lower gallery. Eventually, he would fade into exhaustion, lulled by the low, reassuring rumble of the main drive echoing throughout the ship, and would find sleep. And then the dreams would come.

Planet Shawma was a welcomed sight, but he did not rush in, recklessly announcing his arrival. He chose to bide his time, move cautiously, bringing the *Dancing Queen* into a far orbit and hide within the remains of its long, wrecked moon, which was now just a string of broken rocks.

Initial tracing scans showed a main relay satellite sitting in geosynchronous orbit around the equator, of familiar Xi-Empire signature. That would need to be disabled before moving in. No other ships were in orbit. If there were any, they had to be on the surface.

He did a tracing sweep of the planet, systematically and carefully. He was not going to miss anything this time.

In many ways, Shawma was surprisingly similar to the Kalmaka. Its surface, rich in vegetation, an atmosphere thick in methane, oxygen, sulfur, and nitrogen roiling in a constant state of forming or evaporating storm fronts. Bodies of water lay throughout, fed by a vast network of rivers and canals. The density of atmosphere interfered with the scans, distorting the tracing image feeds so badly multiple scans were required. It took some time for Gem to analyze them before they could be interpreted with some reliability.

Ryan reviewed the images in a three-dimensional holograph from the cockpit. The planet rotated above the navigational console very slowly. Coded key areas revealed themselves as bright blue marks - the probable location of Xi-Empire base camps, and in red - the possible location of the slaverships.

Five vessels had landed at various locations throughout the planet in a haphazard fashion, with no regard to base camp locations. This held no surprise, as these were independent slavers slipping in to collect their, more accurately stated, unsanctioned cargo.

Page 267

But which one was the Xabuntz II?

He would have to move in close to each to know for sure.

"The atmosphere can be used to our advantage," offered Gem. "The shields can be modified to enhance our tracing imprint, essentially, make the ship look like a gaseous formation, which seems very abundant on this planet."

"So the trick is to act like a gas cloud, move slow."

"Yes."

"Then tweak the shields."

Ryan pulled the *Dancing Queen* from its hiding spot and promptly destroyed the relay satellite with one well-placed shot. The descent was quick and well away from the ships and the bases. He came in low, cutting over treetops, taking advantage of the dense atmosphere. The odd time a tall twisting branch would reach up and scrape along the belly of the ship.

"Our image should reflect back as a gaseous anomaly," commented Gem.

"Well, we'll know soon enough. Coming up on our first ship. Ready the tracing scanners, I need a full report."

Flying slowly, and shifting directions lazily in the process, he eased closer to the ship but stayed far enough away not to be noticed. With the first ship complete, he adjusted course to the next, taking time to avoid moving too quickly on their exit, and hiding within the dense rain clouds in transit.

Tracing sensors revealed an unexpected surprise: signatures of humans in every ship. To make matters worse, it was impossible to determine which was *Xabuntz II* due to the opaque, yellowish air, which made a definitive visual inspection near impossible. He would have to land and visually inspect each ship on foot.

"Well, Gem, which one first?"

"Logic would dictate the nearest vessel."

"That's your best guess?"

Silence.

"Well, it's not like I have a better idea anyway."

He brought the *Dancing Queen* down a couple kilometers away from the slavership in order to avoid blasting open a clearing. The ship created a landing area through brute force, bearing down upon the foliage until branches snapped, stopping only once ship's legs finally came to rest upon the forest's thick loam.

Ryan wasted no time preparing for the trip, putting on his armored suit and checking his weapons with involuntarily precision. His mind reeled with the local tactical status reports from Gem. He grabbed his blade on the way out. Or would prove a useful tool for cutting through the overgrowth.

A Shawma aqueduct line, probably constructed before the Xi-Empire's occupation, ran tangent to the landing site. Its shores were no more than 100 meters from his ship - a perfect guide to the slaver as it would help him maintain his bearing in the dense fog.

Ziggy intercepted him at the airlock and handed him a small black box. "What's this?"

"A universal interface," replied Gem. "Clip it to your belt. When you get into the slavership, fasten it to the closest interface panel accessible to the main control core. I will use it to infiltrate the core's security systems and keep the bridge crew in the dark while you secure the ship. It is the least I can do."

"Can it work standalone, in case you cannot establish a link?"

"Yes. All programs have been downloaded to it. However, I do intend to establish a connection."

"How many more can you make of these?"

"Ziggy has already manufactured two. We will manufacture units for each vessel incursion."

"Then give me both. You may need to access a security clearance panel."

Giving Ziggy a nod, he moved out quickly, leaving the *Dancing Queen* secured under Gem's control.

The forest floor reminded Ryan of Kalmaka. His feet sunk deep into the thick vegetation and muck, making the walk slow and arduous. The air was dense, too thick for the unaided eye to see. He had to constantly adjust the visual acuity on his helmet to compensate. Often he would have to cut a wide swath with his sword just to forge a path. He was quickly covered in sweat, as his suit fought to rid itself of the extra heat.

The aqueduct appeared before him, a concrete-banked river more than 50 meters wide. Its waters surged by angrily, carrying with it debris ranging from small logs to whole trees. Upstream, the surging waters were tossing along a massive derelict - a long dead tree, pulled out by its roots, with thick limbs scraping along the concrete bank.

Vibrations carried through his feet as the immense carcass washed past. Ryan stepped back quickly in order to avoid a stray branch that reached out for him menacingly.

The green water raced by with an unyielding power, a fabricated river barely contained. Something upstream had to be dreadfully wrong. Perhaps a dam had given away? The original engineers were no longer present to do the repairs. How long had the Showmish been conquered?

Ryan eyed the river warily, tossing a large stone into the raging murky surface. He must be careful not to slip - to fall into such water spelt death. He started up the shoreline toward the camp, covering the clear ground with a quick jog. The slavership sat fat and rudely, under the canopy and adjacent the river. Its scarred twin towers loomed far above him as blurry silhouettes in the thick yellow fog.

Confident he was still far enough away from the immense vessel to be relatively safe, he searched out a tall tree to provide a vantage point to inspect the whole area. The climb left him breathless and his mouth dry.

He should have filled the suit's water jackets, damn it!

Pulling a large dripping leaf away, he scanned the area. He could make out a view that alternated under lazy, shifting clouds that refracted dense and light patches. From this vantage, the ship was only partially visible. His helmet's magnification did its best to cut through the haze, but it was fruitless. There were no markings on this ship's hull, at least none that he could find.

Movement from below caught his eye. They were Showmish, walking in a long line, moving slowly. Slavers, dozens of them, accompanied the hostages. Whips sang in the moist air, followed by hoarse growls and Xilozak curses. Ryan gritted his teeth, fighting down a familiar rage.

He checked the ship again. His visor magnification cut through the haze enough to expose a large assembly of Showmish collected at the base of one of the many ship's cargo bay ramps. The newly captured slaves trudged slowly up and into the ship. He estimated the numbers to be in the thousands.

But how could he help them? He had to find her and time was running out.

"Gem, it's the wrong ship. I'm pulling back."

It seemed to take forever to get back to the *Queen*. He was beginning to feel panic. Any one of these slaverships could take off at any time.

He had to move faster. He had to find her.

Gem reacted instinctively, putting the ship in motion before he had reached the top of the ramp. They moved onto the next ship. This one, as with the one before, did not bear the markings.

They moved again, dropping the *Dancing Queen* in a small clearing. He headed out quickly, avoiding his usual perimeter checks. He didn't notice the slaver guard approaching until he was practically on top of him. A lone Txtian on patrol had decided to stray from his usual path and take a stroll through the forest. Had his reaction been slightly quicker, Ryan would surely have been dead. But the Earthman's response was a conditioned reflex, ground into him by an unmerciful schedule of training. His rifle blasted in his hands, although he didn't recall taking aim, and the shot struck home, cutting the alien neatly in two.

"That was close, Captain," Gem commented.

He was becoming careless, and that wouldn't do. He was too close, too close to finding *her*. Not waiting for another guard to appear, he started running back to the ship. This planet was reminding him too much of Kalmaka. Years of suffering swarmed through his mind.

"Gem, it's not the right ship, either."

Ryan arrived at the *Queen*, out of breath. He scrambled up the ramp as she rose from the surface and started skimming over the treetops, heading toward the next ship. They made a temporary diversion off course to give a wide berth to a Xi-Empire camp.

"OK, we're as close as we can get. Look for a good landing spot and put her down."

Ryan dashed for the airlock, only to wait impatiently for the ship to land. Before the ramp touched the soil, he was in the forest, making a beeline for the slaver. The run was short, but he arrived out of breath and sweating from the intense sprint.

This was starting to wear on him.

His suit constantly worked overtime attempting to moderate the internal temperature. Ryan felt like tearing it off and running free, to feel the air upon his skin, but that would be foolish. He hadn't had time to study the atmosphere or the local flora. A brush against the wrong plant could easily poison or kill him.

Damn it. He didn't have a suit for her. Better to not get ahead of yourself. She might not be here either.

The slaver was parked in an expansive clearing. Its back raised high above the treetops like an ancient prehistoric predator. Its dark massive shape appeared and disappeared behind drifting clouds of murky fog.

The clearing worried Ryan. The varying fog cover made an approach foolhardy. Adjusting his visor, he scanned the ship for identification. Again, nothing evident on the hull. Maybe it wasn't common practice to mark a slaver's hull. But this was the ship - it had to be. He moved around the perimeter, staying in the underbrush, careful not to disturb the vegetation around him. Then he saw it, standing out clearly in bold white Xilozak letters on a scarred and blackened hull.

He read it twice, fighting disbelief, the letters were clear: *Xabuntz II*.

He fell to his knees, tears welling in his eyes.

"Captain, are you alright?"

"Give me a minute. I'm OK."

His senses sharpened up. "I ah... It's our ship. The one we were looking for."

"Very good. As you expected, Captain."

"Yes, as I expected."

"I've picked up a sketchy tracing image. I suspect it's a ground vehicle moving towards the ship."

"What direction?"

"262 degrees from your perspective."

"What's the E.T.A?"

"Approximately three minutes, given current speed."

Ryan scanned the area and spotted an opening at the edge of the clearing - a makeshift road. The rover would be coming from there. He headed for it as quickly as he could without compromising his cover, emerging from the underbrush in time to spot vehicle lights dancing down the road. He stood at the apex of a sharp turn, where the road wound its way out of the forest and into the clearing.

He should be all but invisible from this spot, hidden by thick underbrush within the pasty fog. The image of the rover was becoming sharper, although still blurred behind the mass of yellow gaseous air and hidden behind the glare of the lights. The rover was heading toward him at a fairly good clip. Passengers on the top deck were doing their best to accommodate for the bumpy ride.

He stepped back into the underbrush and waited. Droplets of condensation crawled down his visor, leaving wet streaks behind, like the trails left by snails over a piece of glass.

The throb of a powerful engine carried through the air in a rude announcement. The rover passed by, a wall of shiny metal and monstrous tires. It slowed for the oncoming curve. Ryan sprang, grabbing at a rear handrail, and missed. He ran, grabbed again, this time taking a firm hold. In one massive effort, he pulled himself up the rail. The rover had already negotiated the curve and was accelerating. The ground below passed by in a blur.

Above him, shadows of movement. Showmish faces looked down at him, but only briefly. Ever so subtly they crowded together, tightly, blocking the guard's view. Ryan had less than a minute to get down below the rover, behind the cover of the gigantic wheels. Alternating, one hand at a time, he lowered himself, attempting to keep his legs from dragging on the moving ground. Reaching under the belly of the immense vehicle, his fingers found a solid hold. With a deep intake of breath he swung down, flipping over, his back facing below, free arm dangling. The strain on his other arm burned like fire. His lungs felt ready to burst. Muscles shaking, he had only moments to search out another grip with his free hand. He felt a length of pipe and grabbed. His heels dragged along the road's rough surface, bouncing painfully, feeling every protrusion. With intense determination he freed his strained hand, searching again for another hold, inching his way between the wheels. He was relieved to find a line looped down below the undercarriage. He threw up his leg, catching it, then he threw up the other leg. Finally, he was off the ground.

A Bellicose Dance

Every muscle in his body was burning, fighting to stay rigid.

Minutes passed by painfully, each bounce threatening to throw him off.

But it wasn't long before the machine finally ground to a halt, its engine dying to silence. Guards from the ship ambled toward the rover, red stained whips dragging on the ground.

Ryan could only catch a portion of the picture through a crack between the tires, but he could hear it all too clearly. Familiar sounds, the snapping of electrified whips, the shrill, desperate cries of pain. Ryan pulled himself closer to the rover's belly, ignoring his quivering muscles. He had little time, as his arms were taxed to the limits of exertion. He closed his eyes and waited, fending off mental playbacks of times not so long ago. Across from him, legs moved with no attached faces, many shuffling, others limping, an endless stream of Showmish.

Every second felt like a minute. Every minute an hour. How much longer?

The rover roared to life. Its gigantic wheels spun as the driver jammed the multiple differentials into gear. It rolled in a slow circle around the ship, away from the busy cargo loading areas and to the side of the ship that was quiet, with no guards. Making a quick decision, he freed his legs and let go. Falling to the hard ground with a painful thud, he lay still, watching the metal frame of the rover dissolve into the yellow fog as the vehicle drove on.

His arms felt like rubber. For a moment, he just rested and listened. There were no sounds, no movement around him. He was lying in a shallow trench created by a rover's enormous tires.

There was nothing but the stillness of the slowly drifting fog.

He slowly rolled toward the ship, falling into one rut and then another, eventually coming to a stop at the base of one of the ship's colossal legs. Rising up to a crouch, he scanned the surroundings. A maintenance hatch was open above with a ladder extending down, no more than a yard away - an opportunity too good to be missed. He went up it like a cat, his tensed muscles loosening with each movement. A guard, unlucky enough to start down the ladder at the same time Ryan was going up, fell victim to a lethal jab of his disruptor sword. Ryan threw his body down, continuing up the ladder using every other rung. In a second he was in the airlock, its hatch closed and secured behind him.

He moved through the ship quickly and came upon two more Xilozaks. They wore uniforms indicating they were part of the crew - not common slaver guards. Their rank did not save them from Ryan's blaster, which had no prejudice. He pulled them into a nearby room and closed the door behind him. A Xilozak lay sleeping, unaware of his entrance. Ryan employed his sword, piercing the alien through both his hearts.

He looked for a core panel and found one on a retractable pedestal that rose off the floor, probably the Xilozak's study center. Unclipping the small box from his belt, he laid it on top the glass-smooth panel and pressed the single recessed button on the unit. Small spider legs appeared from underneath and it crawled across the panel to the upper left corner. With a puckered kiss it sucked itself onto the panel and again sat motionless.

"I've activated the unit - anything?"

"Yes, link established. It may take a few minutes to bypass the security blocks."

"Not a problem. Standby for a tracing relay."

Ryan unclipped another small box from his belt. He gave the portable tracing unit a slow wave in a long arc above him, intending a full scan of the upper decks.

"Gem, you get that? Can you locate the humans?"

"Yes, four on deck three and one on deck two."

"That's it?"

"Yes. I have not been able to locate any others. There are 14 crew on your level. A party of four is approaching your position now."

"Thanks."

He readied his rifle. The four passed by. He could hear them joking and laughing vigorously. Ryan stepped into the corridor behind them and blasted all four. The laughing stopped abruptly.

"So far, so good, 10 more to go. Where are they?"

"Within the cafeteria," replied Gem.

A mental image appeared in his mind, the schematics of the ship. *Now that's handy.*

Using the new information he traveled through the maze of corridors directly to the kitchen, killing the unsuspecting cook in the process. He peered into the cafeteria. Six Txtians and three Xilozaks seated around various tables, some engaged in conversations, others actively gorging themselves. All of them were armed.

He knew he couldn't kill them all before at least one managed to retaliate. The cafeteria's ceiling provided him with another idea. It was a maze of pipes and conduits.

"Gem, can you verify that the secondary coolant lines go through there."

"Yes, the secondary circuit should be represented by a large yellow colored line."

"Umm, they're all yellow - just different hues of yellow."

"Look for a large diameter line, it's a very dark yellow."

"I see it." Pushing the door slightly ajar, he perched his rifle through the crack taking careful aim at his target. He squeezed off a blast and yanked the door shut. Within the cafeteria the ruptured line spewed out superheated gas, filling the room within seconds. They didn't have a chance. Ryan's battle helmet status display showed the air intake had automatically switched to internal storage. Gas was seeping in through an adjoining door.

"Gem, I need to get all the hatches closed and locked, and I need that leak alarm taken care of."

"I expect to have control of all ship's systems within 5 seconds. I have access to internal tracings."

"How many crew left on the ship?"

"There are 12 at present. Two on level five below you, two on level three, one on level two, and seven on the bridge."

"Notify me if any of them move. I'm going up to level three."

He crawled up the maintenance tube and found two Xilozaks playing some kind of game in front of the corridor where the humans were kept. He crept up as silently as possible. One of them hammered his fist on the small table and yelled at his partner that he was cheating. They both stood up ready to fight each other. Ryan interrupted, his blaster leveled at them.

"You both lose," he said icily.

They scrambled clumsily for their weapons, but neither succeeded. Ryan stepped over their bodies and opened the door. The room was dimly lit and littered with excrement. His suit was still on internal supply, but he could only imagine the foul odors. Huddled in the corner were four humans. They watched him intently. One woman and three men, but she wasn't there. Ryan backed out, leaving the hatch ajar.

"Going up to level two."

He crawled up another maintenance shaft and arrived on the second level. The corridors were dark as lighting was off on most of this level.

"Gem, can you help me locate the last human?"

"I can give you an approximation of two corridors to your left."

He moved quietly down the narrow corridor, holstering his blaster and pulling his sword in the process. A loud blaster shot would tip the others to his presence. If the bridge crew caught on, they'd realize Gem's interference and cage him like a rat. He heard a woman scream, and he picked up his pace, searching for the source. He was deep within the slave storage areas now. The rooms were dingy and dark. Another scream followed by a Xilozak laugh.

Ryan found the source. The door was open and he moved in.

The Xilozak was there, prone over a woman on a metal slab. He had one grasping claw wrapped around the woman's arms. Outmatched in his strength, she could only struggle weakly, desperately.

The Xilozak turned and saw him.

Ryan would have carved him up on this spot, but he was too entangled with the woman. He slid the sword over his shoulder and into its scabbard.

The Xilozak grinned at him through the darkness, its white teeth reflecting in the meager light. He reached for his belt. A communicator!

Ryan grabbed him by the head and smashed him up against the wall. Unfazed, the Xilozak seized him by the arm. Ryan countered, turned and catapulted the alien onto the floor. It hit with a bone-crunching thud, but still managed to raise up in a blur, grabbing for him again. Ryan reacted instinctively, bending back and kicking the tough alien viciously in the midsection, ensuring to leverage all his weight. The alien flew out of the room and hit the opposite wall. Ryan pulled his sword and lunged. The blade buried itself into the Xilozak and simultaneously through the communicator and into the opposite wall. Ryan in blind fury grabbed the Xilozak by the neck with his right hand and squeezed. Arm muscles rippled as his grip tightened. The Xilozak neck snapped with a final audible crack, and the alien went limp.

Ryan withdrew the sword, now drenched in green blood, and disabled the molecular vibration.

A soft shuffle behind him. He swung around, ready for another attacker.

The woman had pulled herself upright, a mere shadow. He moved closer and she pushed away, eyes wide, body covered in filth and blood, tattered rags for clothes. A hard, cold look covered her face.

Aviore? He flipped the helmet control to full opaque.

She looked past him, eyes wide, body shaking uncontrollably. He reached for her, but she moved away. "No, it's really me, you're safe now. Nobody's going to hurt you again. It's Ryan. I've come back for you - like I promised."

"Can't be, you're dead. You're not real." Her words were distant, gaze averted, dismissing him as an illusion.

"She's in shock, Captain. Please note another Xilozak is coming down to your level."

"Aviore! Aviore! Listen to me. I'm here - alive. No, you're not dreaming. You have to come with me. Do you understand?

He didn't think she'd answer.

"Ryan?"

"Yes. It's Ryan. I'm here - for real."

Her brown eyes turned to him, softened.

"Is it you?"

A single tear flowed down her cheek. Ryan reached over and wiped it away. "We have to go now." He picked her up, carried her out into the corridor and quickly stopped. Footsteps were echoing down the corridor - too close. He set her down gently. "Stay here."

She grabbed his leg, tightly. "No, don't go, not again." Her voice was filled with sadness, desperation. He pulled her clutching hand free and yanked out his sidearm blaster. "You know how to use this, yes?"

She nodded, and he placed it in her scarred hands. Without another word, he turned and ran down the corridor.

The Xilozak had changed direction and was now walking down an adjoining corridor. A sound caught his attention. He turned in time to see the glint of steel as the sword buried itself into his chest. Ryan left the alien where he fell, then quickly moved up another level, to the bridge. He readied his rifle, stepped in and fired, relying totally upon his reflexes for aim. One of the crew managed to get a blast off and missed - but Ryan didn't. He made a final sweep over the bridge, selectively finishing off any alien left alive.

Every airlock door shut simultaneously.

"Gem?"

"I've accessed the core. All locks are sealed, all hatches closed."

"Bay doors?"

"They are closing, but slowly."

"I've secured the bridge. What about the crew?"

"Two crew are now coming up the turbo shaft."

"Oh, really?"

Ryan walked over to the door of the shaft, stepping slightly aside with his blaster leveled. As soon as the doors slid open, he fired. The unsuspecting crew couldn't even discharge their poised weapons.

"Anymore, Gem?"

"No. The ship is sealed, with no other crew."

"You have found Aviore. She does not look well."

"Prep the surgeon, Gem. Medical emergency. I'm bringing her in."

* * *

Ryan found Aviore lying on the corridor floor, the blaster still held tight in her hand. Her face pale, her breathing light and raspy.

She watched him with a desperate stare.

"It's me. I'm going to bring you somewhere safe."

As gently as possible, he wrapped his arms around her. He could feel her shaking. She was going into shock. Her eyes rolled up. The blaster fell to the floor.

He was scared. "Gem, I have to get her out of here. How many troopers left outside the ship?"

"Two that can be determined, possibly more. They are currently circling the perimeter."

"I need some help. Where are the weapons stores?"

"Fourth level storeroom off the main corridor."

Kicking two dead Xilozaks out of the way, he stepped into the turbo shaft, arms full with his precious burden. With a free finger, he pressed the control console. They shot downwards at a dizzying speed. The turbo shuttle stopped at the fourth level. Its doors opened to an empty corridor.

A short walk and he reached the armory. The room's walls were lined with arms of all types, the Xi-Empire's weapons of murder and torture. He shifted Aviore over his shoulder and hoisted up a couple rifles with his free hand, then headed to the lower slave holding tanks.

The Showmish were crammed into their cells so tight he wondered how they could breathe. He felt their reptilian eyes staring at him as he passed. Walking these corridors brought back memories. The foul smells, the darkness, the fear. He swore he could feel the bite of the whip on his back, the blood in his mouth. He turned quickly, to find no one. His imagination playing a fool's game.

He found the master switch and flipped it with his elbow. Every door slid open simultaneously. The Showmish flooded out from all directions, relieved to be free. They all seemed unusually calm.

Ryan stood amongst them, holding Aviore, waiting.

"Gem, I need a Showmish translation through my external speakers."

"Everyone," he announced. "I have taken control of this ship. All the Xi-Empire troopers are dead and the airlocks secured. There are troopers still remaining outside - at the very least two, but probably more."

A few of the Showmish moved into the outer corridors, checking for signs. Did they believe him? He tossed the extra rifles onto the floor.

"I need help. I have to get back to my ship. I want to set a trap for them."

A few reached down to grab the weapons.

He continued on. "They do not know what has happened. As soon as I open the main lock, they will rush in. If they notice all of you out of your cells, they will come in shooting. This must be a complete surprise or someone will die. Do I have any volunteers to help me?"

Two very large, tough-looking Showmish stepped forward. "We will help." announced the larger of the two. "Who, and what, are you?"

Ryan realized they couldn't see him through his helmet. It had automatically reset itself to combat parameters. He switched it over to full opaque.

"I'm a human. I was a slave once, as well. You need to trust me. There is no time. Are you the appointed leaders?"

They looked around at the group behind him, hissing menacingly. The others nodded acknowledgment. "Yes, we are the appointed."

"Send your people up to the fourth level. Just off the main corridor, there is a weapons storeroom. There should be enough to outfit the lot of you. I hope you know how to use these things."

The leader looked at him, a strange expression on his face, with its forehead crinkled over its eyes. On a human, one would call it a frown, but on a Showmish, it was pure guesswork.

"We are not savages, human. We may live close to nature, but we have also developed advanced technologies that are well ahead of this Xi-Empire scourge."

"Of course."

"But that was before they came," said another. "They took all. Destroyed what they could not take. We lost everything during that time, our technology, our homes, our families."

"They must be destroyed," the leader hissed, his teeth bared as his lips curled back. He reminded Ryan too much of a crocodile ready to pounce.

A group of Showmish started up the corridor. "We will take care of the remaining Xi-scourge, Human. You can go to your ship, spare no more thought on this."

"There are more. Four other slaverships," Ryan announced.

"Do you know their positions?"

"Yes."

"We wish to converse with you more about this. Take care of your sick first."

Ryan suddenly remembered the four other humans. He had been so worried about Aviore he had forgotten about them. He would have to get them himself. A Showmish might frighten them even more - unless they were all Signites. Regardless, Aviore was in a bad state. They would have to wait.

"Four other humans have been captured, if you can, bring them to my ship."

"Wait, Human!"

An older looking Showmish female stepped forward. She was stout, no higher than a meter and a half, and slightly bent over. She held out her stubby arms.

"Give her to me. She is not well. She will not survive the trip. You get your fellow humans. I will keep her safe until you return."

Ryan looked down into those strange reptilian eyes. They were not at all like the eyes of a Xilozak. They were soft and warm, like the eyes of a grandmother who missed her grandchildren dreadfully.

How strange to apply such a human trait to an alien. She means to help. Could he trust her?

"Please. I know a little of the human *kera*. Her breaths are shallow. This cannot continue - her heart will arrest. I can help. I must help."

Ryan felt for Aviore's heartbeat. It was weak, weaker than before.

Maybe she could help.

"Set her down. I will take care of her. I will not move her from this place. Go, get your people. She will be safe with me."

Ryan yielded, lying her down as tenderly as possible. "Thank you. I'll only be a minute."

He ran down the corridor, scarcely avoiding a collision with a weapon-toting Showmish. The maze of corridors seemed to wind on forever. Finally, he found the humans' cell. Surprisingly the four had remained waiting. He half-expected them to have attempted escape.

When they saw him, they rose, excited looks upon their faces. One of them babbled Signite at him loudly.

"Follow me," he ordered in Trinarieit, ignoring the obvious inquiry. They understood him well enough to obey. By the time they had made it back down to the fourth level, all the Showmish had disappeared. The only one left was the old female, who was sitting on the floor, awaiting his return. She was holding Aviore like a newborn and hissing to her softly. She spoke to him, this time in Trinarieit. "This one, she carries the mark of prominence. I have put her into *hutah*. She is resting in harmony now. But there are many injuries. A great healing is required. Do you need help?"

"I have medical capabilities on my ship." He took a quick glance around, apprehensive of danger. A breeze blew down the corridor, ruffling Aviore's hair.

"Carry no concern. We have already taken care of the scourge," she stated. "The danger has passed."

Ryan did not need more urging. Taking Aviore in his arms, he turned to start out.

"Gem, are there any more rovers heading back?"

"One rover is now returning, although very slowly. I believe they are having mechanical problems."

"Bring the ship to us then, quickly."

"In-progress, Captain."

He stopped and turned to the old female. "Tell your people another rover is on its way here."

"That fact is already known, Human of Earth. We will not forget this."

"You're welcome," he quickly turned and headed down the corridor to the outside.

"My name is HishTar, and I will see you again," she called after him. It was not until Ryan had made his way down the airlock ramp did he realize what the old female had said. He had not told her that he was from Earth, just that he was human.

No time to wonder about trivial things now.

As they walked out to the clearing a tell-tale rumble echoed above as the *Dancing Queen* appeared overhead, its dark image fading in and out of the fog. The landing legs jutted out with a hydraulic whine as the ship settled onto the open field.

"Gem, we'll follow the same procedure as last time."

"Acknowledged."

He turned to address the four Signites in Trinarieit while maintaining a brisk walk toward the ship. "This woman needs medical attention, just follow me up the cargo bay ramp and stay in the first bay until I come to get you. I will talk to all of you as soon as I can."

They seemed to understand as they did as he instructed. Once they entered the cargo hold, they proceeded to sit down on the floor and rest. Ryan took Aviore directly through to the internal airlock and triggered the sterilization spray. It washed over them both. Aviore opened her eyes. She smiled weakly. He smiled back. Once in the ship, he laid her down on the floor and took off his helmet.

"I have an automated medical bay to treat you. How do you feel?"

She had lost a lot of blood. Her face was very pale. "I am not well," she whispered. "The old one, she helped me." She held up a swollen hand to touch his face. He picked her up and headed for the medical bay.

Ziggy was waiting for them. The medical bay was a circular room, with the operating bed situated in its very center. The room was lit brightly with polished walls of stainless steel.

Like a sentinel spider, the automated surgeon hung from the ceiling above the bed. A varied collection of arms and medical instruments jutted out from its spherical body in all directions.

Its brain was independent of all other ship systems, a feature designed as a safety precaution, although it could interface into Gem's network, it acted autonomously. Gem could act as a consultant to the surgeon if it ever had difficulty making a decision, but that was a statistically low probability, considering all the medical knowledge that the Xeronian's had imported into its core memory.

Swarms of telescopic lenses were nestled throughout the room, which aided the surgeon while it worked. The surrounding walls revealed a matrix of lines which subtly revealed the presence of drawers that reached up and through the ceiling. The surgeon could reach into any one of these drawers to retrieve required medical supplies or surgeon's tools.

Ryan laid her on the medical bed and Ziggy helped him strip her down. What remained of her clothing were a few filthy rags which he discarded into the waste. They sponged her body clean with a sterilization fluid. The grime hid a massive collection of cuts, sores, and infections. A contorted swelling on her left ankle worried him. Ryan signaled the surgeon to start the scans while he finished off. The results came up on the monitor at the head of the bed. It read like a grocery list.

Rescue

Prognosis: CRITICAL: Immediate surgery required.

The word CRITICAL blinked red on the monitor like a loudspeaker blaring in a closet. Things were far worse than he could have imagined. The surgeon dropped over her, anchoring its legs onto the side of the bed, and proceeded to make its first incision.

"Captain, once we have the internal hemorrhaging under control she will be stabilized," Gem offered reassuringly.
Ryan noted it in the back of his mind, but it did not make him feel any better. "Have you scanned all the viral composites?"

"Yes. None are alien to me. All the infections will be treated successfully. Immunity agents and nanites are currently being injected into her bloodstream as we speak."

"Parasites?"

"They are also being flushed out. We have nanites developed to destroy the parasites identified within her."

Her face, no longer covered with the grime, revealed swelling and bruising to her cheeks. "What about her jaw?"

"We will have to cut and reset the bone. The healing process will be accelerated once the corrections have been made. The damage to the spine will also be repaired through a similar treatment."

Ryan was frustrated and angry. He had taken so long to find her. He clenched his fists tightly, containing the rage building inside him. What had they done to her?

The surgeon moved swiftly, pausing only briefly to make adjustments to Aviore's prone body. Ryan watched it work, oblivious to everything around him.

"Captain."

"Captain."

"Ryan."

He broke from his trance. "Yes, Gem."

"She would not have lasted another night on that slavership - you did find her in time."

The surgeon began to fuse the epidermal incisions. It would not be long before it was finished. One more check on the monitors. They beeped in synchronous intervals with their displays.

Ryan finally processed the words Gem had said. "Thanks, Gem."

He took hold of her hand. It took all he had to fight off the tears welling up. The emotion ripped at his insides: guilt that he had not found her sooner, the fear, now lapsing that something could still go wrong, relief, and joy - the most unusual emotion of all. For all that she must have gone through, he could still marvel at her. She had this beautiful look of peace about her, even now, as she lay there. In the airlock, when she'd awakened. She had known this wasn't a dream. The old Showmish had pulled her out from the shock.

The surgeon was finished. The first phase of operations were successful with no complications. The internal bleeding had stopped, and all critical wounds repaired. The spider-like robot silently raised itself back to the ceiling.

Now, it was time to wait.

Ryan went into one of the drawers and pulled out a thick blanket. "We will hold off with any further surgery until she regains her strength," he stated flatly. "I want her on a full I.V supplement. He covered her with the blanket and looked over at his robot friend. "Keep an eye on her, Ziggy. If there is a problem, let me know immediately. Take care of her."

Ziggy nodded silently.

"I'll be back," he told her gently and kissed her on the forehead. "I've got a war to start."

* * *

11. Recruits

They moved in quickly, quietly. The Showmish slithered along on all fours, dashing through the undergrowth. The rover clambered through the muddy trail, wheels spinning as they fought for traction. Ryan waved to the party on the opposite side of the hill. The guards walking alongside were the first to be taken out. One at a time they were pulled into the bushes and killed. By the time rover emerged into the clearing it no longer had an escort. But the driver hadn't noticed. He gunned the engine and covered the distance to the ship quickly.

They waited for the laden vehicle to roll to a stop. Ryan could feel the tension increase in the group around him. They hated the Xi-Empire. Too many times they had seen their women and children taken prisoners, to become slaves on some unknown world.

The driver called out for a guard. No one came. A moment later a Txtian swung open the hatch and started marching toward the ship, cussing in his native tongue.

Ryan gave the signal.

A very brief but intense exchange of blaster fire followed. It was over before it started. The overzealous Showmish made quick, savage work of their enemies. Then they formed a line to help the captives down from the rover.

This was the last of the *Xabuntz II's* deployed rovers. The next step was a little more complicated - to take over the other ships. But night was approaching, and the Shawma sun bathed the yellowish-orange sky with bluish-green as it slowly settled on the horizon. They all knew they had a lot of work to do before the next dawn.

Ryan motioned to the group leaders to meet. There were about a dozen of them now. The Showmish had quickly organized themselves into small, effective groups. The aliens were very efficient at creating and working within teams.

The leaders formed a circle. Ryan addressed them in Trinarieit. "That's the last of this ship's crew, but we have four more ships to go. Does anyone have an idea how long we have before they are ready to leave?"

"They like to stay planetside for many cycles. They attack our homes during the day, take their prisoners, and drink their intoxicants during the night." It was an older Showmish who spoke, his words were hissed out sharply, a Showmish expression of distaste of the topic.

"This time has become less brother. No more than one more day," hissed another. "I have sent word. It has come back. When the sun had reached its *quiche* the first one lifts off."

They nodded - an almost human quirk.

"Then we'll move on them now, on both sides of the planet," announced Ryan.

"It is a shame, my brother," hissed another.

"What do you mean?"

"This fog which provides your camouflage lifts under the cycle of darkness. One cannot sneak up on a vessel when its tracing scanners are active. It is suicide."

"Then we move on the ships on the day side of the planet now, and we wait until tomorrow for the others."

"Human, if a ship leaves before we seize it, then you must destroy it. It must be done."

"And what of the captives? You want me to kill them too?"

"It is better that way," added a newcomer, an especially old looking Showmish. The small crowd parted for him as he hobbled into their circle. His head nodded constantly, unable to hold up his heavy jaws. His skin was speckled with spots of gray.

"It is better that way. The sisters have spread the word, and the word has traveled well. No more."

The Showmish surrounding him raised their weapons in a cheer.

"Listen, I am not destroying a ship full of slaves. I'll disable it, but I am not going to kill innocents."

"Very well, Human, attempt what you must, but you cannot save us all. We are strong. Let us focus on the task at hand. We ride the line of darkness and strike!"

Another cheer.

Ryan rather enjoyed this cantankerous old Showmish.

Another group leader spoke up. "There are those of us who can pilot these slaverships. We shall use these vessels we capture to move our brothers to the next site."

"I can load a party into my ship as well," offered Ryan. "Remember, we will have to stay low, just over the treetops, and the shielding for each vessel should be modified for maximum deployment. Their tracing scanners will pick up a signature, but they'll think they are just gas clouds."

"It is an old trick we used during the Great War," offered the older Showmish. "These slavers are ignorant compared to the Xi-Military. They are the lowest of the filth of their system. They have no honor, carry no discipline."

"To their demise," stated Ryan. "And I have a few presents for them," he announced, producing a half dozen black boxes. "These boxes will assume complete control of their ship's systems."

The Showmish took the offerings appreciatively. "How are they used?"

"Attach them to any core access panel and press this button. They start their dirty work immediately. But I must warn you it may take time before they have full control."

"How much time?"

"Possibly as long as an hour depending on system encryption – that's about how long the sun takes to move to about there," he explained moving his arm in an arc.

"So be sure to attach them somewhere inconspicuous."

"Very good, Human, this will be of great help."

"Then let's move. Secure the rovers and tend to your injured. Whoever is coming with me, get organized. I'm leaving before that sun disappears. Have you selected the leaders for the other raids?"

Three Showmish stepped forward, one carried an air of command about him – he was once, possibly, a military officer.

"Good. Remember our strategy. Infiltrate first, quietly and quickly. Get in and plant the boxes. If they suspect something, they'll lock every hatch in the ship and leave you sitting there as they fly away safely to Xilo."

"We will do our part. We have an advantage. They do not fear slaves. They are too arrogant. They do not expect us to be armed. We will succeed, Human, and we thank you, for all you have done."

"Don't bother thanking me yet. There's one more thing. If any member of either ship's crew gets a transmitter link, we'll have a visit from the Xi-Empire Military fleet. You won't have anything to thank me for then."

He turned to address as many of them as he could. "Tomorrow afternoon, on the ah...*quiche,* bring all the ships to this clearing and any volunteers that you can spare. I intend to wage war against the Xi-Empire, and I'll need all the help I can get. Some say that what I mean to do is suicide - and it may well be. Either way, I'm looking for volunteers."

They understood him. What he had said had sparked a number of conversations throughout the camp. Ryan watched with interest. He didn't bother translating, he could almost guess what they were saying. Before long, quiet came over the whole camp. They had somehow come to a unanimous decision.

That was something you would never see on Earth.

The old Showmish stepped forward. "All of us would gladly join with you Human, but there are some of us that have families to care for, others are too young, or too old. We will crew these slaverships and provide as many Showmish fighters as we can spare, before the end of the cycle."

He bowed his head humbly. "We wish we could do better but we are scattered throughout the planet and throughout the galaxy thanks to the Xi-Empire. There are many Xi-bases here on Shawma that we must liberate. Our people are suffering."

"Don't apologize, your offer is more than satisfactory. I thank you. I destroyed the main relay satellite to Xilo when I arrived. That should slow down their ability to establish a link and give you the time you need to reach the bridge. If we move quickly and succeed, Xilo may never know."

Ryan looked up at the darkening sky. "Prepare your fighters. Time to go."

* * *

He checked in on Aviore. She was sleeping soundly. The monitors indicated she was stable and recovering well. He kissed her on the forehead.

"Gem, did Ziggy get the medical tests on our guests finished?"

"Yes. They are all in suitable health. No alien virus, bacteria or parasites have survived sterilization."

"Good, I need to move them to the main living area. We're not done here."

Ryan stepped through the cargo bay airlock to find the Signites fast asleep. Ziggy had made them comfortable in their makeshift quarters. They were content, with full stomachs, clean bodies, and new clothing. Ziggy had manufactured some air mattresses and bedding for them. He shook the closest Signite awake. The woman looked up and smiled.

"Hello," she said. Her accent was thick. Her words seemed to die off in a rounded twist. "So this is what you look like. You are very similar to us, but that is what I expected... I must thank you. You saved our lives. We can never, ever repay you."

"You're welcome." he smiled back. "This is not just a social visit. I need all of you to move out of the cargo bay. We are going to have some Showmish guests using this area."

"I'll wake the others," she offered.

The four grabbed their cots and bedding and followed Ryan. He led them through the airlock and into the main living area - to the lower deck in front of the main system research console and filled them in on the past events. One of the men offered his help in the upcoming raids.

Ryan half-chuckled his response, "You're in fine shape to help. All of you need rest and you need to heal. If you need anything else, just ask your questions to the ship's computer. Her name is Gem. Just talk out loud."

"Hello, Gem," said the woman.

"Hello, female Signite. How shall I address you?"

She looked at Ryan, slightly confused.

"You do have a name, don't you?" asked Ryan.

"Of course, my name is Steffereni, Gem."

"How is the other Signite woman?" she asked, genuinely concerned.

"She has been stabilized. Her condition is improving. Do you know her? I mean. I'm sorry, I just thought..."

"Yes, I do. We met a long time ago. Her name is Aviore Tem Enova. The late Governor Tem Enova's daughter," stated Steffereni. "She is very important to us."

"The Governor? "

"Yes, the elected leader of our government, now dissolved. He was a casualty of this war. Until you carried her past us, we did not even know she was on the ship. We assumed they would have thrown us all together. They are a ruthless, cruel race."

"They will pay," said Ryan. "Gem, - night simulation. Please, try to get some rest, all of you. If I do need your help, I'll need you rested up."

Ryan headed back to the cargo bay. The Showmish warriors were waiting to file in, a lethal regiment of 50 armed Showmish warriors.

They were off in short order, heading towards their next target slaver. Ryan landed the *Dancing Queen* approximately five kilometers from their target. The Showmish deployed quickly. He went to join them, but their leader stopped him.

"Human, you have done your share. Let us take the risks now. If we do not succeed and the ship takes flight for Xilo, we will need you to destroy it."

"I've told you before I have no desire to kill innocent captives."
The Showmish alien face showed an unfamiliar expression. "You do not understand, Human. We would rather die than become slaves. What we have needed has been provided, with your help. Our weapons have been reduced to meager projectile launchers. It is no match for these." He held up the Xi-Empire laser rifle. "Our population has been reduced to mere thousands. Many of us have given up all hope. You have renewed our spirit to fight. Never fear, Human, we will succeed in our mission. We have no choice."

Ryan watched him disappear into the thick vegetation then closed the hatch.

They have no shortage of courage.

"Gem, I would like to learn Showmish, can you set up a subliminal program."

"Very well, Captain."

A familiar wave of background murmurs started in the back of Ryan's mind. He reached deep into his thoughts, deciphering the gibberish into concrete memories – fabricated memories. Satisfied, he turned his attention back to his monitoring systems.

The Showmish had already approached the slavership. Their images faded in and out of the tactical display as he watched. The tracing scanners did their best considering the heavy interference.

"Gem, what do you have on the Showmish?"

"The Xeronians have a vast collection of information on the Showmish. First contact with the Xeronians was over two hundred years ago. A number of trade missions were accomplished between the two races before the Xi-Empire intervention."

"Bring it up on the main monitor. I'd like to review all the contents of that library."

"Wouldn't you prefer to review the information through your vaskpar Captain?"

"Gem, you don't give up, do you? Us humans are physical creatures. We like to see, to touch, to smell, to feel. I would much rather view it on the monitor, and absorb it at my own control. I do not like to use the vaskpar as my only source."

"I understand. You are strange creatures, you humans. You continue to surprise me with your imperfections."

"You know, Gem, you're sounding more human every day. You've even developed a dry sense of humor."

Ryan caught himself, something about what Gem had just said was nagging at him and he just realized what it was. "Who is your creator, Gem?"

"You are."

"Not me personally, Gem. The Xeronians constructed your neural gel matrix. I only helped in the process."

"Allow me to clarify," Gem interrupted. "Humans are my creator."

"What are you saying?"

A long pause followed, and finally a reply. "The ones referred to as the Ancients were human."

"I see," Ryan said aloud. He pressed a few virtual commands on the console. The black-glass wall took on the form of a huge display monitor. The whole room was bathed in a shimmering, blue light. One of the Signites behind him stirred but went back to sleep.

"So, logically, you are my creator," continued Gem.

Ryan decided to drop it as there was more important work to do.

"Gem, pull up the library directory, split the screen and pull up a status of that slavership, split again with a long-range tactical into space. I don't want any surprises dropping in on us. Oh yes, break up that tracing scan, scan for life signs on the ship on a, say... two minute interval. Keep count of the life-forms and tell me when the Xilozak and Txtian count starts to go down."

"Very well, Captain."

The display split into multiple sections, immediately providing Ryan with an up-to-date tactical.

He glanced at the Signites behind him. They were still fast asleep on their cots. Ryan made a mental note to stay quiet, then glanced back to the library index display and pulled up the Showmish links. "OK, Gem," he relayed over the vaskpar, "let's start at the beginning. Review of their physical makeup."

Ryan was deep into understanding Showmish physiology when Gem interrupted to inform him some Txtian life-forms had disappeared from his tracings.

"Looks like they've started." He glanced at his wrist chronometer - part of the equipment Ryan had his engineering friends manufacture while on Xeronia. This one, however, had a few more functions included: radioactivity sensor, internal body function monitors, even an old-style magnetometer.

"You'll see more of that yet," he informed Gem.

And they did, until every last Txtian and Xilozak life-form within tracing range disappeared. A few hours later, a lone Showmish approached the ship relaying the good news. Ryan met him at the base of the ramp. The messenger was a young warrior. His claws were covered in green and yellow blood. He was still excited from battle, wheezing loudly from his mouth. He reported that the raid was successful and that a number of freed human slaves were being escorted back to the *Dancing Queen*.

Ryan thanked him for the update and watched as the alien faded noiselessly into the trees. Stars were coming up, peeking through the dissipating fog. Again, their camouflage was lifting.

Ryan went back to reviewing the library.

"Gem, it says here that these creatures are slightly telepathic. Is that correct?"

"Yes. The archived information was checked for all conceivable errors."

"So is that how she knew?" he mumbled out loud to himself. "Gem, why didn't you tell me about their telepathic abilities?"

"I did not know that you thought that to be important. How can I measure that piece of data in relation to so many others? They also have the ability to diffuse certain minerals directly into their blood by osmosis through their skin. That is a fact that you did not know as well."

"That's not so important, it's whether or not it affects me."

"That does affect you. They must have a high degree of zinc in their environment, possibly suspended in the air to be comfortable. That, in turn, could be detrimental to your health over a long period."

"No, that's not the point either. Just forget it."

He should learn not to argue with a computer.

* * *

The party of humans arrived, 10 in all, with one Showmish escort. Ryan went out to meet the newcomers. Their escort, strangely enough, was the same old female he had met before. There were three women and seven men in the group. They all looked very confused and very much afraid.

"Hello everyone," he said in Trinarieit. They looked at him incoherently. Gem translated to Signite. No response.

"Hello," Ryan said in English.

One of the women almost fainted. A man stepped forward. He had a thick scraggy beard that hid his filthy face.

"You speak English? You are from Earth?"

"Do all of you understand me?"

They nodded back. A number of them started to talk all at once. Ryan held up his hands.

"How long have you been in captivity?"

"Two, maybe three weeks," shrugged the bearded one. "What the hell are these things? They killed my buddy. They almost killed me - more than once! And are these things your friends?" he pointed at the Showmish.

"Yes. They certainly are our friends. Are any of you sick?"

"No, just cuts and bruises mainly," said another.

"Good. You will have to go through a sterilization process. For now, just make yourselves comfortable in the cargo bay."

He waved them inside. They hesitated.

"It's OK. You will be safe in here."

The party trudged in quietly.

"I'll join you in a moment." He turned his attention to the Showmish. "Thank you again. I'm sorry, you said your name was Hishkar?"

"No, HishTar." She bowed her head respectfully.

Ryan mimicked the movement.

"You are the one," she said as-a-matter-of-fact. "So it is a human that will hold the peoples together, unite them against the oppressor."

"You talk prophetically, like another old woman I know."

She hissed to herself for a moment, as if in realization. "I am too humble to accept such praise. I am merely one with a gift of sight."

"You read minds?"

"I am of the Sisters-of-Soom. We exercise our minds to reach out to others. I am here to reach out to you."

"What do you mean?"

"I am here to teach you. You will see. First, we must return to the plain. They are waiting. We are to have a celebration of your arrival."

"But there is still another ship left, it must be..."

"Not so," she shook her head. "All ships have been seized. I know this.

"How can you know?"

"We are all connected through the weave of life. The weave is thick and strong on our home. My sisters have informed me the warriors have taken all. They will be there when we arrive."

"Confirmed," reported Gem. "The vessels in question are lifting-off and traveling toward said destination."

He looked into those strange reptilian eyes and was almost lost in their hypnotic effect. "I'm impressed. Please, come in and make yourself comfortable, HishTar."

He helped her up the ramp. We'll be lifting off in a few minutes. I'll have to leave you in the cargo bay – sterilization protocol – you understand?"

"Of course. You need not concern yourself with my needs. Go, fly your ship."

He glanced at the humans as the ramp closed.

"I'll be back soon. My robot will bring food."

"Gem, what do Showmish eat?"

"They are vegetarians, our food stores should be compatible."

"Arrange something for her, as well, Gem."

"HishTar, I'll be back soon."

She nodded. The frail-looking Showmish had lowered herself to the floor and was seemingly meditating, somehow content.

Ryan went back to the cockpit but not before stopping to check on Aviore once again. Ziggy was standing over her, monitoring patiently.

"How is she doing?"

"All medical data shows that she is recovering quite nicely. Her systems are functioning within adequate parameters considering the scope of the damaged components."

"She's not a machine," Ryan stated with annoyance. He ran his hand over her cheek. She was warm. Her temperature was high, a slight fever, but her color had come back, and her breathing was strong.

"Ziggy, Gem probably asked already - I need you to do guest duty again. More captured slaves. Same as before, OK?"

Ziggy nodded but didn't move.

"Don't worry, I'm sure she'll be OK. She's out of the tough spot now. Go ahead now."

Ziggy hobbled off.

Ryan gave Aviore's hand a squeeze. She twitched a little but remained in a deep sedated sleep. He headed for the cockpit.

* * *

The sky was a bright yellow when the *Dancing Queen* landed in the meadow. The morning had long since passed. The recently captured slaverships were also present. Thousands of Showmish were moving around the clearing, busily loading and unloading the ships with a variety of materials.

Ryan donned his envirosuit and opened the cargo hatch door. All the humans were busily eating and Ziggy was shaving a bearded man. It was a sight to behold. Ryan laughed.

"Make sure you get behind his ears," he chuckled. Ziggy's small light indicators blipped a confused message at him.

"Forget it, Ziggy. Just a joke."

He addressed the Earth-group again. "I'll return in a while. By the way, my robot's name is Ziggy and he understands English."

HishTar was already at the hatch. He joined her.

"You will not need that suit, I assure you."

He hesitated a moment, then twisted off his helmet and tossed it onto the cargo bay floor.

As the ramp lowered the fresh yellow jungle air swept in. It smelled sweet and rich like fresh cut grass, and flame. Fires were burning in the camp.

"We will be having a celebration tonight in your honor. It will be a joyous event. The coming of the warrior."

"Isn't that a bit premature?" He was feeling more than a bit fed up at all of this hocus-pocus crap. *First the Xeronians and now the Showmish.*

"You cannot discount the smallest flame, as it can turn into a raging fire."

"Yeah, sure," he said under his breath, inspecting the clearing. It was absolutely crawling with Showmish. *Where had they all come from?*

The five slaverships around the edge of the clearing formed a circle. Ryan had landed the *Dancing Queen* near its center.

"You shouldn't have such a population so concentrated. They should be dispersed. If a Xi-ship comes..."

"Nonsense. We have survived a long time under the great oppression, and we will continue to survive, and we shall see our day of freedom!"

"Are there any more humans?"

"Yes, they are being fed and cared for. I will have them all escorted to your ship now if you wish."

"How many of them are there?"

"There are 22."

"Oh, quite a few then. Please have them escorted to my ship. Ziggy will take of them unless there are some individuals that are very sick or hurt."

"None of the humans are deathly ill. A few have sustained injury. We have already attended to them."

"Thank you, HishTar, and please convey my thanks to the others. It has been a successful operation. I would appreciate it if I could meet your leaders and the prospective captains of these ships."

"That is where we are headed," she announced.

"Of course," said Ryan, not surprised in the least.

They approached a large group. The surrounding Showmish were busily constructing strange wood erections. Each reached all the way across the clearing.

HishTar introduced the captains one at a time.

"Captain Shobotsh, of our newly ordained ship *Sbash Nateer*."

They exchanged respectful bows.

He leaned over to HishTar, was about to ask what Sbash meant, but she answered his question before he could ask it. "Sbash means Freedom. Nateer means... one. I will translate our numerology, as well."

They continued with the introductions.

"Captain Roshesh, of the ship *Sbash Two*. Captain Hushob, of the ship *Sbash Three*. Captain Whushob, of the ship *Sbash Four*. Captain YushTar, of the ship *Sbash Five*."

He had to give them credit for originality. At least he wouldn't forget the names, though he would probably mix them up.

"Have any of you captained a ship before?"

They all nodded in affirmation.

"All of you have?" returned a surprised Ryan. "That's great! Do your crews have the necessary skills – you know, navigation, engineering, tactical, medical?"

The all nodded again.

"Really?"

"Do you realize what the stakes are in this war I am about to wage?"

Captain Roshesh spoke softly. "We are all aware of the probabilities of meeting death in this war, Captain. We are ready. We are at your disposal to fight at any time."

Captain followed, "We are reviewing each vessel's condition at this time. Some have sustained rather serious damage. All repairs must be complete, and all systems checked thoroughly before we lift off. We expect this will take a full day before we are ready."

"That sounds exceptional. I'm impressed that you have the knowledge to accomplish this."

Each captain bowed.

"As for my plans, I am heading to the Signite system first. I expect we may run into other Xi-Empire ships on the way there. I intend to hijack these ships and add them to our fleet. We will free, and hopefully, enlist any slaves we find on board. We will aid the Signite resistance in getting control of their home again."

They went over a number of different strategies that Ryan wanted the captains to know intrinsically. It took most of the day, and part of the night. The captains proved to be very knowledgeable in their field and had interesting perspectives on engagement strategies.

That night the air cleared, revealing the stars at their ultimate beauty. A vast golden nebula streamed across the northern part of the sky. If one looked close enough, one could see reds and blues interwoven within. Ryan couldn't help but admire the sight.

"The night skies of Shawma are truly beautiful."

HishTar had come to join him. "The magnificence of the Gushwan constellation there," she pointed to a formation of stars to the east. "The Great Warrior of Gushwan, can you see him?"

It took a second for Ryan to make it out. "Yeah, I can. Compelling isn't it, how we can draw so much from randomness."

"Not all is random, Ryan, you must realize that by now? Come," she took his hand in hers, a soft, warm, leathery touch, "my sisters have arrived."

Some of the other Showmish had started dancing. It was as if electricity was charging the very air. The arrival of the Sisters-of-Soom was a big deal.

Lines formed into concentric circles around the primary fire pit. HishTar led Ryan through to the innermost circle, reserved for the sisters. He sat down on a log, passing a nervous glance around. There were familiar faces, the captains, the leaders of the raiding parties, seemingly all the Showmish of demonstrated power.

The fire was fed with more fuel, allowing it to grow higher in the night sky, crackling and spitting sparks as it roared. All around him, the Showmish began to hiss and chant musical tones. Drums started, and the dances began.

HishTar looked over to him. "Have you decided?"

The question caught Ryan off-guard. "On what exactly?"

"Who you serve. Who you are. Who you will be."

"I don't understand."

"This." She tapped a clawed finger upon his chest. "Is filled with anger, with hate. It will tear you apart. It will make you weak when you must be the strongest of all of us. Will you let it?"

"I don't know."

"You must listen to the authentic you, the core you, to survive what is to come."

"Sure," Ryan replied, more confused than inspired.

HishTar clapped her claws together, and the music raised in volume. Sparks flew up into the night sky as the fire roared.

"Your bravery has earned you a special gift from the heart of Shawma. You are to learn the secret of the eye of the mind. There will be a time where this will be the only way to save that which is yours."

"What?"

She cut him off with a raised palm. "First, you must calm yourself. Close your eyes and listen. Hear what is in the wind."

Great, more hocus-pocus.

He closed his eyes as requested. The fire was hot on his face and the drums sounded a steady rhythm that seemed to permeate through his body.

The Sisters-of-Soom sang into the wind.

A soft rhythm of whispers grew louder, it was a haunting sound. He could feel the hair on the back of his neck stand up. Unusual smells were drifting in the wind, pungent and bitter with a taste of vanilla. He was getting a little light-headed, a little dizzy, but didn't seem to care. He followed the music, so beautiful, flowing on different levels. He could feel HishTar beside him, a comforting warmth.

"Come," she said, with a slight touch. "Let me show you."

He floated around the fire, touching each sister, feeling their thoughts, merging, becoming one. He could feel the others, out beyond the fire, thousands of minds projecting their fear, their joy, their pain. He pulled back, panicking. It was too much. HishTar was there. "Focus. Control what you receive. Someone out there needs you. Go to her."

There was no distance, no travel time. He was just there. He felt the cold blue of machines, at the same time, felt the blood coarse through his body, and the beating of his own heart. He looked outward through eyes so alien and saw out further than he could imagine, into the very depths of space.

He turned inward, touched the knowledge, skimming over it. It was overwhelming. A small orange signature worked amongst hot red ones. He felt... fondness?

He pulled out of the metallic memory and touched her. A dream, so dark. A feeling of helplessness and unbridled fear unquenchable. Dark shapes crept amongst terrible images of violence and pain. The hopelessness. He was frozen, unable to move, a powerless victim. He had to fight it back, to destroy it. He searched for warm memories, let them flood over the bad, suppressing the darkness. He scoured through the memories, a researcher desperate for the proper material, tossing through libraries of memories, touching them only momentarily to be recalled, relived. Old memories came, like waves in the ocean. But they were jumbled, poisoned by the recent thoughts. He shared his own, remembered the Shawma sunset, day turned to night, and the sky lit with the colorful nebula and stars dancing above, and he impressed the image and the feelings of the peace. He could feel the warmth grow, the pain, the fear, subside as memories faded to only lingering hints. What was left was a quiet, comforting, peace.

A cold rush and he was back. The bonfire was crackling, the drums reverberating. The Sisters-of-Soom were looking at him, eyes judging yet soft. They did not say a word.

The music was still there, as an echo coursing through his veins. He heard a whisper in the night wind... "You do have the gift."

He looked into the fire and watched it burn, and said nothing. There was nothing to say.

The circle opened. Two figures walked forward slowly, a spindly mechanical man supporting a woman layered in bandages. Her face, though scarred, beautiful by the light of the flame.

Aviore.

He went to stand, but too quickly. A brief bout of dizziness surged over him. Reaching out, some steadied him, and he moved more slowly.

She was there, in front of him, as big as life itself. Her gentle eyes watched his every move. A warm smile danced on her face in the firelight. With one look, he knew why he had fallen in love. He was at a loss for words.

"Hello, Ryan."

"You shouldn't be out here, you could..."

"No, Ryan," she cut him off. "I want to be here, with you. I need to." She stepped forward and stumbled a little. Ziggy was there. Ryan had a hold of her just as quickly. He held her in his arms and looked into those captivating eyes.

"I knew you would come for me," she said to him softly. "Somehow, I knew you would find me."

They kissed, passionately, devoid of anything around them.

She was trembling, standing was taxing her strength.

"Here, sit." Ryan kept his arm around her. She leaned against him.

"These are my new friends and allies."

"Let me see." She spoke an eloquent Showmish, matching every subtle nuance expertly.

HishTar replied back, a very pleased look on her old face.

Ryan watched her with utter fascination.

"What, did you forget so quickly?" she teased, "I am an expert, after all."

"That you are." He said, unable to hide his admiration.

She drew closer. Her hair tickled his nose, but he didn't mind.

The night passed too quickly. They talked of many things but avoided the topic of war, the Xi-Empire, the torture of slavery. Aviore's knowledge of the Showmish culture was impressive. She had clearly devoted long hours to the study of these people. Ryan often found himself sitting out of the conversation, just enjoying the night. Ziggy sat perched near the fire, his metallic body glinting reflected firelight. He seemed to be enjoying this – in many ways he was sentient, and tonight he was simply - living. Ryan made a decision not to deactivate him again. It just didn't seem right.

The night passed into a spectacular sunrise. With it came the mist of yellow, growing denser as it reacted with the sunlight.

Aviore was exhausted, and he could tell she was in pain.

"It is time we retire," he announced. He bowed slightly to HishTar. "Thank you. I don't understand these things very well, but I will attempt to practice what you have shown me."

"The time will come, Commander, when you will need it. I assure you."

"You mean, Captain," corrected Ryan. He picked Aviore up in his arms and carried her off to the ship. Ziggy ambled behind.

"Ryan, what happened to you? You are... much bigger than I remember."

Ryan chuckled. "That's what hard physical labor and steroids do to you, I guess. Don't worry, I've been checked out by some very good physicians, and I'm fine." He strived to change the subject, knowing full well certain things may not be complete truths.

"We have so much catching up to do. I'm just glad to have you here."

"So am I," she said warmly.

The *Dancing Queen* loomed above them. Her eyes turned back to him, amazement on her face.

"I know. Like I said, we have a lot to talk about. This is my ship - the *Dancing Queen*."

"It is beautiful! Truly. I've never seen a starship so graceful in design."

Ryan laughed, finding he could not help himself.

The ramp lowered as they approached.

It was time to meet the newest of his guests.

"I have to warn you, in case you don't already know. We have company. In all 22 humans, most from Signus and a few from Earth. A few have asked about you."

They stepped into a crowded cargo bay. Eyes turned their way from all directions. He nodded to them as they passed through quietly.

Many were sleeping, others were talking amongst themselves, some were even playing games with small trinkets they must have brought with them. The Signites nodded to Aviore, many recognizing her features through the bandages.

Too many people. He was not used to so much company, and he wasn't sure he liked it.

"First things first. Ziggy, it's mealtime."

"And you," he looked into her soft brown eyes, "I need to run some more tests."

He carried her into the medical room and sat her down gently. They kissed again, very passionately. He broke off regretfully.

The surgeon lowered and commenced the scans. He watched patiently, noticing positive changes. A stern low voice emanated from, well everywhere. The voice of the surgeon. Somehow, it carried with it a calming confidence.

"We will focus on your primary sources of pain. We are going to have to reset your jaw, as well as repair your broken teeth. One of the discs in your neck requires attention. These will be rebuilt by our nanites. Your blood has been analyzed, and we have noticed your hemoglobin is almost back to normal, but you still have traces of a viral infection, so we will need to temporarily enrich your immune system."

Ryan scanned the status display on the main console. "Aviore, given this status you should not be up yet. I don't know how you are standing."

"I don't know what woke me up, but I needed to see you. Besides, relatively speaking, this is the best I've felt in years. And I wasn't alone when I woke. I met your friend, Gem."

"You've met her already?"

"Yes. She introduced herself. I have to admit for a second I was... well jealous, maybe heartbroken, until she explained herself." She smiled, hiding a brief wave of sadness. "Gem told me where to find you, and Ziggy came to help. I wanted to surprise you."

"Well you did," Ryan said with a chuckle.

The surgeon dropped down its snakelike arms. "I must inspect your oral cavity, please open."

"There is considerable damage to repair."

"It hurts," she said, or more accurately attempted to say, given her mouth was still pried open. Metallic fingers released, giving her back full motion.

Ryan ran his fingers along her face. "Do you feel up to some more surgery?"

"To tell you the truth, no."

"Well, we really can't wait. I know you're tough. We need to address this now."

She nodded quietly, accepting her prognosis.

"Your hands, let me see them."

She laid them over his. Some of the fingernails had grown back, others hadn't.

"I was tortured. They wanted me to tell my father to give up, but I wouldn't."

Ryan inspected her fingers quietly. "We can take grafts from your other cuticles and grow new ones. It'll take a few months, but they'll be as good as new." He smiled at her.

She looked at him quietly, bravely holding back a sob. "Then go ahead Doc, cut me."

"We need to brace you first."

He locked her down on the bed, including the head brace as per direction by the surgeon. She had to remain absolutely still.

The first set of operations took almost an hour, the most critical occurred without any visible action, deep within her tissues. Nanites worked diligently under the surgeon's direction to rebuild the damaged disc in her neck.

Ryan watched from the main surgery console, via the multiple imaging feeds which the surgeon used, some exploding out magnifications at the cellular level. Once complete, the surgeon focused on the dental work, leaving Aviore with two artificial teeth and two new crowns.

"How are you doing?" he asked her.

"Oway," she said, her mouth still wedged open.

He disconnected the holds. Her eyes were red. She was holding back tears. She was obviously in pain.

"Hurt?"

She nodded.

"The surgeon wanted to use local anesthetics only. Given the type of surgery, I know your jaw must be aching. We're going to have to re-break and reset it."

Her eyes went wide.

"Don't worry, you'll be on pain suppressors and you won't feel a thing. But you will definitely be sore tomorrow."

"I'm already sore, and you haven't even started. Are you sure you have to do this now?"

"Yes. The reason you're sore right now is because your jaw hasn't healed right. You can't leave it the way it is. I'm afraid that this is going to be a tedious surgery. The auto-surgeon will have to go in behind by the ear and remove scar tissue as well to ensure..."

"Don't tell me about it, just do it. When I wake up tomorrow, I want to be all done. Then it'll be up to me. I'll do the healing myself."

Ryan chuckled. "You got a deal."

Hours later, Ryan carried Aviore to his bedroom and laid her down as gently as he could. He put an armband monitor on her and covered her up, being careful of her bandaged hands. He had decided to do everything like she asked. Now it was all up to her.

He hooked up an IV and left her to sleep.

* * *

The new human guests were surprised when he appeared. All of them looked relatively good, considering.

Ziggy had been busy.

They convened in the cargo area, the only spot large enough to house everyone. He addressed the crowd in Trinarieit, with Gem translating to Earth-English.

"We are about to leave Shawma and travel to the Signus. Those of you that wish may return to your home, but I must warn you, there is not much left, and living conditions for the resistance is hard. Those from Earth will have to stay with me for the time being."

The small crowd shuffled uneasily, an Earth-woman hid her face in her hands.

He couldn't get them home. He couldn't afford the time.

He pulled his eyes away from his fellow Earthlings. "You do have an option. I am looking for volunteers to join me, and fight the Xi-Empire. I need to build a fighting force. I know this sounds impossible, but we've had some success already, arranged some allies with the liberated Shawma."

"For how long?" uttered a Signite man. Others nodded.

"I don't know - as long as it takes. To be clear, I'm not forcing you to join me. What I am asking for is dangerous, and you will be putting your life on the line. I will not fight beside anyone who is not willing, but please think about it."

"I just want to see my family again," one man stated, quietly.

"I understand, believe me. I know what you have been through." He pulled up his pant leg, exposed ugly scars of scorched skin. "The brands burn into you, but they heal." He put his hand to his head. "But not in here. You want to find peace? Help me destroy them. Think of all those that you've watched die. I know, sometimes, you wanted to be the one – but you survived, didn't you? Now you know why."

A sarcastic laugh bit into the thoughts of the crowd. "Who are you kidding? They ripped us to shreds - and they didn't even use their whole fleet! Look at their technology, their weapons, their ships. And we thought we could hold them back."

This started an uproar of voices.

A Signite woman spoke up, she was favoring her arm, and her one eye seemed damaged. "When they force you to have children, only to rip them out of your arms and sell them to the highest bidder. Are you still going to tell me how it's right to give up?"

The group quieted to a solemn silence.

"What are we going to fight them with? A couple broken down slaverships! Maybe we can stock up on some extra large stones," stated a Signite sarcastically. He carried the features of an ex-military man. He was angry, face flushed red. "And how many other races have they enslaved? Do you know, Earthman? You don't, do you? You know how many times others have tried what you are talking about? You think you can fly that one insignificant ship of yours against their entire fleet? You're as good as dead, along with anyone else that's stupid enough to follow you."

The others were watching him, some nodding in agreement.

He was already losing them, and it was beginning to irritate him.

"How much is your life worth to you, Signite? Would you rather live as a slave or die free? So you tried before, and you lost. I'm giving you the opportunity to try again. How long has it been since you were captured?"

"Three to five weeks I think. I've been locked up in that slaver cell. It's hard to say to the day."

Ryan spat on the deck, openly pissed. "So you don't have a damn clue. You've never seen them break someone, have you?"

With that, he stepped forward and grabbed the Signite by the collar. "You don't know what I mean, when you're past exhaustion, when all you know is, if you don't take that next step they'll slice you in half, like they did to the one beside you. You're broke when you fall down, and you don't get back up because you don't care, because you've already died!"

"Captain. Calm down."

It was Gem.

Ryan looked around, saw their faces. Fear, all too familiar. They were afraid of him, or maybe they were afraid of what he was saying. Afraid of what their future holds.

The Signite man he had hold of was trembling. He let him go.

"Sorry. I, ah..."

"It is perfectly alright, Captain," said an older Signite in the crowd. "I've seen it. I was captured about five months ago. I've seen all the things you talk of. I've lived them."

"Then join me."

"Captain, all I want to do is get away from this - to get back home, to my family, to my home."

"And where's your home?" Ryan asked.

"Alterra. Just outside of it, actually. It is a beautiful city."

A woman beside him grabbed his arm. "Alterra is gone, completely destroyed, it's just a crater." The color faded from the man's face.

The woman turned to address all of them. "He's right, you know he is. Signus is gone, the world that we knew is only a memory. They are attacking our colonies, and soon there will be nothing left of us. We have nowhere to run. We have nowhere to hide. This man is offering us a chance to fight back, to try again, but most likely die, die for the things that Signus once stood for. Since when do any of you feel like we even have a choice?"

Eyes turned to him as if he had something incredible to say, like he was some damned hero that could destroy the Xi-Empire all by himself. He despised that look in their eyes.

"You need to decide for yourself. If you don't want to fight, I'll try to find you a safe place. But there are no guarantees."

"What about us, what's going to happen to us?" asked one crow-nosed man, with rich black hair. He spoke in Earth-Spanish. Gem had translated for Ryan's benefit.

"Those of you from Earth – I know you want to go home, I know. Don't fool yourself. You're not safe there either. They know about Earth now. Once the Signite colonies are out of the way, I'm sure our home is next. Only this won't be like Signus. Our technology is pitiful in comparison. It'll be a damn slaughter."

"You asked me what is going to happen, you're not going to like the answer. You're either going to hide out or fight with me, but there will be no returning home."

"We don't know anything about space stuff," another woman said, already in tears. "I'm just a housewife. I want to get back home to my family. I have a daughter, she's only two. She can't sleep unless I read to her each night."

Another woman wrapped her arms around the sobbing woman, providing as much comfort as she could.

"You are here now so you can protect your daughter, save her from a life of slavery. That's the future that lies with Earth, and everyone on it, unless we stop them. I'll train you as best as I can. Maybe we can slow them down for a time."

"But we've got to get word back."

Ryan laughed. "You think the governments in control would allow this to get out? If I brought you home and you started telling others – they'd lock you up in a tiny cell and throw away the key. He looked over at the woman who was still crying softly. "Be strong, for them. Maybe you've been called upon to be here for a reason."

He turned abruptly, putting his back to them as he left. He was sick of holding their hands.

"Make your decision." He yelled back.

The airlock door closed, shutting out the noise.

* * *

Three days passed.

Ryan had spent most of that time with the Showmish discussing battle strategies and boarding procedures. All known information of the enemy was collected and shared, including the specifications of every class of Xi-Empire starship. The slaverships' logs were extracted and dissected for every useful tidbit of information. It was a mammoth task. The Showmish were overworked and tired, but they were remarkably resilient.

The last meeting was held in the makeshift boardroom in the *Sbash Four*. It included Ryan, the five Captains, and the assigned leaders of each regiment of Showmish warriors.

Ryan spoke for the majority of it while the Showmish listened attentively, not missing a word. Sometimes a question would be posed which would lead to a discussion. Ryan struggled to keep on track and keep the focus on the important issues, the most prominent being the difficult task of increasing the strength of their meager fleet.

"We'll keep hitting them where they're most weak - single ships, traders, slavers, whatever we find without escorts. When and if we encounter military vessels everyone else scatters. I'll take care of them. We avoid anything big such as cruiser-class interceptors, at all costs. They have enough firepower to annihilate the lot of us."

"We can board and take over any ship, but we must have sufficient firepower to protect us while we are doing it," grunted Captain Roshesh.

"As soon as they see us, they'll transmit a distress. We'll have Xi-militia all over us before we can blink."

"No, no," Ryan said, frustrated. "The galaxy is a big place, and we'll be choosing when and where to hit. We'll know if there's a patrol in the vicinity. The trick is timing, to know when to hit, when to move, and when to keep our forces dispersed and hidden. We hit and run, hit and run. This is what we call guerrilla warfare where I come from."

"The Empire will soon notice. They'll send a fleet out to destroy us."

"They can't destroy what they can't find. We have access to superior technology. If we can integrate it into our ships, our shielding and weapons, we'll have the upper hand. All we need is time, know-how, and the raw materials. We can't build a fleet, so we'll steal it piece by piece. All we need is willing and able fighters and pilots. That's why we're headed for Signus. I think they will still have a worthwhile resistance. The Empire was too overconfident with them. They're in for a surprise."

"How do you know about the Signite strengths, and from what source?" asked Captain Shobotsh.

Ryan chuckled, "From an old friend named Taldig. Tell me something - what is a basic strategy employed when you know you are going to meet a superior force and will most certainly lose?"

"You retreat," joked one of the leaders. The room filled with Showmish laughter. Ryan waited for it to die down.

"He's right. You don't run, and you don't engage either, at least not with your full arsenal. You leave a skeleton force of volunteers behind. You disperse and build your forces somewhere safe."

"Surely, the ones left behind know they will be destroyed," commented Captain Hushob.

"Yes," Ryan agreed, "yes they do."

The room filled with silence for the first time in many hours. Ryan stood up, effectively signaling the end of their meeting. "You are going to have to elect a single representative for your people - someone with a strong military background and leadership qualities. I'll be waiting for your decision back on my ship." He turned to leave.

"We have decided already," announced Captain YushTar. "It will be you. You will be our leader."

Ryan turned back to face them. "No way. I'm not a leader. I'm not even Showmish. You'll have to choose amongst yourselves. I will not lead your people to their death."

"But, sister HishTar said otherwise," disputed Captain YushTar. "I have never known my great grandmother to be wrong. You have full authority amongst us. This matter is settled."

"No. No, it's not," refused Ryan. "I have my own kind to worry about."

"You represent us all, Commander," said Captain Shobotsh. "There are many other races under the oppression of the Xi-Empire. It will take a strong leader to bring them together and make this succeed. That leader is you. You cannot refuse."

Ryan checked every face in the group. There was one look he was sure about when it came to Showmish expressions. They were steadfast in their decision.

The idea raced across his mind. Leader. He didn't know the first thing about leading. He didn't want that responsibility. What if he doesn't have what it takes and they all end up dead? Or worse - he survives to live with that failure.

Taldig had told him something about leadership. He recalled vividly: "Those that lead, bear the weight of their own self-doubt. It is their greatest enemy and their greatest ally. Doubt stays impulse and avoids mistakes. If a leader must, he can use arrogance to provide missing self-confidence, but only instinct can compensate for missing information. And you, Ryan, have that instinct, more than any of us here. You survived inescapable odds. That is what a leader needs to keep his people alive."

Ryan studied the grimy floor, followed hairline cracks that spread up the bulkhead walls. This ship, like most of them, was falling apart. It took courage just to fly in one of these vessels, much less go to war in one. The Showmish were no fools, they knew this, and yet they had still chosen him. Maybe he had something, something extraordinary, or maybe he just had a plentiful dose of good luck.

Hell, maybe he was their good luck charm! If they believed it strong enough, it could keep them alive. And that carried a lot of weight.

He nodded to the group. "If that's the way you want it. I'll do my best to live up to your expectations, but sure as hell don't expect perfection."

The Showmish stood in unison, and each bowed ever so slightly – similar, but exact in meaning, to salute.

Ryan returned the gesture in full respect.

"Then Commander it is."

* * *

They approached Signus from six different angles, jumping out of acroluc just behind the cover of the multiple moons and some of the larger asteroids. Their cover was at best, temporary. Coordinated multiple tracing scans passing over their hiding places would have easily exposed the majority of them.

Signus, this time, was well guarded. There were six destroyers and three slavers in orbit. The cruiser that Ryan had crippled was long gone. Ryan double-checked the tracing image for ghost signatures, just in case. This time both he and Gem agreed they were clear.

They moved in quickly, the *Dancing Queen* in the lead. The destroyers caught the bait. Word of his ship must have spread and he was sure that it would be considered a valuable trophy. Five left orbit and went into pursuit. Ryan gave them time to close in, and veered out, away from the system.

He kept an eye on the tactical. Their five slaverships were converging on the last destroyer, after that they would hit the other slavers. Showmish boarding parties were standing ready for infiltration. The destroyer had not as yet initiated fire on them – they've not figured out they were under Showmish control.

A range proximity warning pulled his attention back. The five destroyers were coming in hot and fast, but he had anticipated this and had studied the area. He knew just where to go. The *Dancing Queen* was on a tight trajectory between two stars that were less than three million kilometers apart. Skiting a gravity well so close at acroluc was insanely precarious. The gravity wells were already making their presence known, tugging at the ship in opposing directions. Two destroyers were following the same trajectory, while the others broke off pursuit.

Ryan slowed as much as he dared, wanting them to draw near. He dispatched two missiles hoping they would do some damage. One did, brushing alongside the destroyer's hull, exploding on impact. In normal space, the ship would have suffered only minor damage. But here, the stresses were overbearing. The ship ripped apart, still in acroluc.

Distortion waves started, ripples first, relatively small, bursting circlets of purple and blue light, churning, jumping. More and more appeared, numbers immeasurable. The waves traveled along the intertwined lines of gravity, as an unstoppable force of chaos. The other destroyer, now in mortal danger, immediately dropped out of acroluc to avoid the encroaching turmoil, only to find the attraction of the star too strong. This ship, like the other, twisted and contorted, and eventually disintegrated to pieces as it fell into the deadly gravity well.

Tendrils of destruction reached for the *Dancing Queen*. Lost in a wall of white noise the vaskpar flooded with jumbled chaos, interference dropped his link with the ship.

Switch to manual. Keep focused.

A precious millisecond had passed, and the storm was still coming.

"Gem, could use your help here."

No use. The vaskpar link was dead.

He had less than a second.

Shields to maximum.

The threat was upon them. The *Dancing Queen* lunged as her burners were pushed far beyond their designed limits. The anti-gravs, unable to compensate, overloaded successively, each failing over to its redundant twin backup as the ship went through a dance which no human could have ever orchestrated.

Death fell away, and they were free.

He opened his eyes and verified what he already knew. Three blips on the tactical, now converging toward him. He pivoted the ship around the nearest star, banking the burners on full, watching the blips scramble to divert, moving at hard angles.

The vaskpar link recovered. He waited briefly for Gem to vector the trajectory toward a certain small white dot on the tactical, the *Dancing Queen* was climbing out of the gravity well steadily, leaving the destroyers far behind, fighting an unforgiving force of nature. He had a brief moment to relax. He cut the burners back, allowing the cooling systems to catch up. The course brought the ship directly toward the star. Ryan's plan was sketchy, questionable even, but he was outnumbered.

"E.T.A. T-minus 33 seconds," reported Gem.

"..5..4..3..2..1."

The *Dancing Queen* jumped out of acroluc, bearing in close around the star. The destroyers were catching up in a hurry and he was waiting for them.

Come to Papa, you bastards.

The tracing scan stats came in. Ryan reviewed them, watching the tactical warily. The tell-tale dark spots were there.

"Modify three missiles for implosion, Ziggy."

He flipped the *Dancing Queen* end for end as she plunged toward the star. Self-protection systems engaged. Her cannon withdrew as shielding enclosed over them, and she began to rotate to evenly disperse the radiation they were taking on. Already her wing tips were glowing white hot.

From the cockpit Ryan watched as the shielding crept closed, blocking off the encroaching picturesque view of hell. He didn't mind.

One of the destroyers had been pushing to the maximum and had left the others behind. It was almost in range. The destroyer's cannon had already started blasting away, but their energy dispersed harmlessly.

This Captain was a bit too eager for his prize. Then again, he was counting on that.

And they sunk down even closer.

"Hull temperature approaching critical limits," reported Gem.

"Just hold together baby," urged Ryan.

The destroyer had just started to rotate.

They must be baking in there. The thought made him laugh.

"You starting to feel the rage of God, Captain?" he yelled.

"Deploy the missiles."

Again, he was counting on the *Dancing Queen's* superior drive. He started to climb, pushing the burners to maximum. The cooling systems were overloading. Ryan diverted all available life-support water to the cooling matrix and vented the super-heated steam.

A finger of flame erupted from the star. An incredibly powerful explosion triggered by three relatively indiscernible ones. The destroyer was slow to react. Its overheated crew did not appreciate their Captain's sense of urgency and its drives lacked the raw power needed to push them clear. The gaseous stream engulfed the fleeing vessel and vaporized it in milliseconds.

The *Dancing Queen's* course compensated for the predicted path of destruction, riding the edge of the gigantic firestorm, now on course for the nearest planet, a gaseous giant fueled by the sun's continuous onslaught.

Ryan checked the tactical. The other destroyers had opted for safety, curving around the star at a higher orbit. They had come around successfully on a vector to overtake. The *Dancing Queen*, still climbing up the gravity well, was at a disadvantage.

Gem laid out projections. It would be close.

"Enemy vessels within weapons range, Captain," reported Gem.

"Take over evasive, Gem."

The *Dancing Queen* lurched as it avoided a missile. The turrets, now on auto-fire, destroyed it as it came around for a second pass. The destroyer's cannons, however, found their target. Ryan activated the secondary shielding and brought up the overload response systems monitors. A ceaseless barrage of plasma lit up the exterior of the *Dancing Queen*, without leaving a mark. He watched as the capacitor feeds rose, channeling newfound energy. The updates were working flawlessly. No doubt the destroyer Captains were wondering why their cannon had no effect.

A Bellicose Dance

Next engagement with a cruiser, he'd be ready.

The planet coming up on the tactical reminded Ryan of Jupiter, with alternating multi-color bands of atmospheric storms. His plan was simple, bring his followers with him as he dove down into the hostile atmosphere, then take them out. As usual, reality did not follow to plan. Only one destroyer kept on his tail as the other broke off to maintain high orbit.

Ryan fought to keep the ship on course. The atmospheric winds moved at cyclonic speeds and kicked the ship around like a toy. Internally, the ride wasn't much better. He wondered how long they could take this abuse.

"Tracing scanners operating at 30% efficiency. Too much interference."

"Captain, I have been requested to relay to you that our passengers are concerned."

"Tell them to remain calm. We are engaging the enemy."

He had repositioned the group into the main living section and Ziggy had fabricated chairs with full restraint harnesses.

He flipped the intercom. "Aviore, are you OK?"

A soft voice came over, carrying a nervous edge. "Yes, I'm ready in the upper turret. Do you ont me to depoy?" She was hard to understand, as her jaw was braced shut.

"What the hell are you doing up there! Damn it!"

"Depoy?" she replied, all but ignoring his outburst.

"No. Don't deploy, wait until I'm out of this sonofabitching atmosphere!"

How the hell did she learn about the turrets anyway?

"Gem?"

"She asked me, Captain. I saw no reason not to inform her."

Ryan grunted a distasteful curse and focused his attention on the tactical holograph. He looked for the eye of the storm - a small dark area in the center of the gargantuan hurricane that all but engulfed the northern hemisphere of the planet. He caught glimpses of the destroyer now and then and noticed it had slowed pursuit.

They must have lost track of him.

Ryan pulled the ship into the eye and began to descend downward.

Minutes passed.

The destroyer started to traverse the storm in a standard grid search pattern and soon started crossing the eye.

Ryan was ready. The *Dancing Queen* shot upwards, all cannon blazing. They were too close for their shields to hold long. The blasts penetrated and hit the hull with devastating results. The ship literally split apart - and began to fall. Ryan pulled the *Dancing Queen* into a spin like a drill, its cannon on wide dispersal. It flew right through the descending, burning wreckage. The roiling horizon fell away, giving way to vacuum and starlight.

"We're out!" he announced. "Aviore, you can deploy!"

Aviore, sitting in the gunnery chair, pressed the virtual control on the command console. The turret dome ascended up through the hull, and out into the stars. She rotated the turret and watched as the planet fell away. The turret was a dome of clear ceramic-quartz. It provided a clear line of sight to anything within her 180 degree plane.

She took a deep breath, primed the cannon, and smiled.

* * *

Ryan checked his tactical. The last destroyer was approaching starboard, and fast. He adjusted the incline and locked onto it with the main cannon and began firing. The blasts dispersed over the destroyer's shielding.

Just a little closer.

But the destroyer was breaking off.

"Now, Aviore, Now!" he whispered.

Turret cannon started firing from amidships. Aviore had the superior angle from on top. The cannon found their mark, penetrating the destroyer's stern. The ship's primary burner faltered and then she began to lose acceleration. Another secondary burner flamed out. The warship began a slow rotation from the uneven thrust.

He thumbed the intercom. "Nice shooting, Aviore. Didn't expect that."

Ryan maneuvered the *Dancing Queen* around, aligning the main cannon to the now crippled ship. Although the destroyer was crippled and unable to align its main cannon, it was still able to let loose a barrage from its secondary turrets. The plasma dissipated over the *Queen's* shields without issue. Ryan all but ignored their futile attempts.

"Gem, I'm going to need you to do some tricky shooting for me. You up to it?"

"Always ready for a good test of my marksmanship, Captain."

"You know where, right?"

"Yes, I will be firing on the ship's next rotation."

The cannon blasted. A large explosion followed as most of the ship's atmosphere decompressed out of its belly in one tremendous blast.

"Bad design flaw," he chuckled. "Looks like we have ourselves a Xi-destroyer."

He hailed the Showmish.

Captain Roshesh answered. "Commander. All operations were a success. Three slaverships have been boarded and reclaimed. How did you fare?"

"Good work. I have a destroyer that needs to be boarded, and quickly. Hopefully, you can bring its secondary burners online before it tumbles into this planet's atmosphere. Can you do it?"

"Dispatching ships immediately."

"I'll wait for them."

He thumbed the intercom again. "You can retract back in, that's it for excitement today, Aviore."

"OK. I'll be gad when I get dis race off my jaw."

"Sorry girl, liquid food for a month," he replied with a half-smile. "And you need to rest."

"Gem, run a full systems check. This was a rough ride."

* * *

A ragtag fleet moved onto Signus. Any rebuilt Xi-Empire bases were blasted back into dust. This time they made sure no stone was left unturned. The newly captured and half-crippled destroyer was towed into orbit, and the Showmish contended with any surviving crew under Ryan's direction. Initial assessment of the damage was positive. The ship could be repaired – and the secondary burners were intact enough to manage a landing.

A few of the Showmish captains were intrigued by Ryan's ability to cripple the Xi-destroyer. But he couldn't take all the credit. The design flaw had been found by a Xeronian technician long ago. The Xi-Empire had undoubtedly never learned of the inherent weakness as they had never modified the design.

One well-placed shot into a certain section of the ship would lead to a series of internal explosions, which would cascade and effectively decompress a large portion of the ship, which included the main bridge area. They would ensure this particular weakness was addressed when they restored the vessel.

Almost all the ships were in need of repairs in one way or another. They needed raw materials, time, and if they could find it, more help.

They would find it planet-side.

Ryan coordinated the landing effort, having the first ship set down near the slaverships that he had dragged onto the beach, their hulks were still present although there was no sign of the Signite resistance. He monitored the activity from orbit, watching the events unfold as he had expected.

At the Xi-bases, unsuspecting Txtians and Xilozaks raced toward the Showmish-claimed ships thinking it a rescue attempt. Showmish militia surprised them, but to their credit, held back on their opportunity to fully massacre the lot. The killing was to be controlled and precise, as Ryan had given explicit orders that as many prisoners were to be taken as possible. With primary targets secured, the remaining ships started streaming down to the surface. Some remained in orbit, with long-range tracing scans set to maximum.

Ryan brought the *Dancing Queen* down to rest on the beach adjacent to the others then checked on Aviore.

She watched as he pulled on his envirosuit and strapped on his blaster.

"What are you doing?" she asked, trying hard to shape her words carefully.

"I'm going to talk to our fleet captains and interrogate some prisoners."

"I don wunt you to."

He glanced over at her, frowning slightly, "Don't worry, I'll be fine." He could tell she was sore, the metal brace around her jaw was uncomfortable at best, and she definitely needed more rest.

"It's safe enough, and you need more rest."

"I want to go wit you."

"No. You are still too sick. Look at you, you're a mess. Your hands are all bandaged, you're wrapped like a mummy. Your jaw is wired together. You are recovering from some substantial internal injuries. You shouldn't even be walking!"

She knew he was telling the truth. She was tired, and maybe it was foolish to get in that turret, but she had to help. She gave him a hug, and couldn't resist kissing him despite the brace.

"Hey, you're the one who finished off that destroyer. That was a hell've shot by-the-way."

She tried to suppress a smile – as it hurt.

"Come on." He gently helped her onto the bed. "I won't be long, and you need to get your strength back."

She complied, a bit frustrated but utterly exhausted just the same.

* * *

Ryan met with his passengers and they were full of questions.

"Just what the hell's been going on up there? We've been bounced around like basketballs in here."

"I think I've fractured my wrist," announced one of the women.

"I'll get Ziggy to look at that for you. We've been in a few... ah... conflicts. We have now landed on Signus. Everyone is welcome to exit the ship and enjoy the fresh air. Please, come with me." He glanced back to the robot. "Don't just stand there, you're on medical."

They arrived at the top of the ramp to see the resistance forces securing the beachfront. Some of the Signites ran past him, onto to the beach, only to fall on their knees and kiss the ground.

"Should we go too?" asked one of the Earth women. Her accent was thick, possibly Australian.

"Sure, I would. Just stay on the beach though. Signus is – well was - a beautiful planet. It would be good for all of you to get some fresh air."

He left them to make up their own minds. The walk on the sand was enjoyable. The sun was bright and hot on his face. The wind was soft and persuasive. The destroyer towered high above, casting a long shadow down the shoreline. The other ships, along with the hulks of the other dead slavers, were lined up like the beached carcasses of gigantic whales.

The abandoned slavers he had brought down had sunk into the sand considerably, due to their weight. One was at least a third buried into the sand. A storm must have come up. Mother nature tends to swallow up everything given enough time. Even the pyramids of Earth are wearing down. With enough wind, enough rain, enough salt, enough sun, nothing lasts forever.

He noticed one ship had a few new patches on its hull. Someone had been attempting to rebuild it, probably scavenging parts from the other.

Under a hastily built shelter, the Showmish captains had formed a small circle, waiting for him.

"Good afternoon, Captains of the resistance."

"We had to annihilate some of the enemy vessels, I regret," announced Captain Hushob.

"We've a start given what I see on this beach." He ran inspecting gaze over the destroyer. A large dark gash ran along its hull, exposing some inner framework. "You think you can you make it spaceworthy again?"

"Yes," answered Captain Shobotsh. "But it will take some time."

Ryan glanced down at his chronometer. "Unfortunately, I don't expect we will have an abundance of that, Captain.

We need to get every workable ship repaired and back into space as soon as possible. Captain Roshesh, I want your technicians to look over those three, especially the one that has work done on it. Someone obviously thought it was worth resurrecting. Captain Hushob, you've secured the area, I presume?"

"Fully Commander. We have a Signite visitor, as well. He claims he is a member of the resistance and wishes to meet with you."

"Bring him up. Let's have a talk."

The Signite was escorted over to the front of the group - a small man, with very pale skin, and a long face. His chin pointed outward at a sharp angle. He approached Ryan with a quick gait, his chest boasting of self-importance. Not the look of a hardened veteran reflected Ryan.

"You are the one from before, the one who brought down those ships and rescued the slaves aboard?" he said in Trinarieit, pointing towards the derelicts.

"Yes."

"I would like to thank you personally for that rescue. It has been said that you crippled a cruiser with only one ship!"

"Yes, I did that as well."

The Showmish looked at him with curiosity. This was a piece of information they had not known.

"Look, I don't have time for thanks and praise. I want to talk to your surviving head-of-military."

"That's me," the Signite replied quickly.

Ryan evaluated him. The little man looked away, uncomfortable under his gaze.

"I need as many troops and ships as you can spare."

"For what purpose?"

"To destroy the Xi-Empire," replied Ryan flatly.

The Signite almost laughed outright, his face twisted with a sarcastic jeer. "How do you intend to do that?" he asked, the critical smirk ugly upon his face.

Ryan had already decided he did not like this Signite. There was something about him, something that was wrong.

"You're wasting my time."

Gem's voice sounded through the vaskpar. "Relay coming in from deep tracing sentry. There is a fleet of vessels approaching, 35 in all. They do not carry the signatures of Xi-Empire vessels."

"It appears we have visitors approaching," announced Ryan. "We'll need to launch what we can. Let's move."

The party broke up without a word, all the officers disbursing to their ships. Ryan glanced over to the Signite who was starting to make his way back into the woods.

"Grab him!"

One of the Showmish troopers intercepted the man, making his point clear with his blaster. The Signite's features drained of all color.

Captain Hushob gave Ryan a typical Showmish perplexed look, eyes squinted, lips pouted.

"Captain, why don't you bring him with you, actually, put him in lockup."

Hushob nodded acknowledgment and waved to a trooper to escort the Signite back to the captured slaver.

Ryan waved to his people to get back on the ship. The Signites had already disappeared into the forest. Only a few remained, waiting to talk to him before he left. One intercepted him as he hurried toward the *Dancing Queen*.

"Captain, we want to meet up with you again."

"Fine, just clear out of this area quickly."

The man seemed to want to say something else.

Ryan stopped. "I've a fleet of ships headed this way. What do you want?"

"Just to say thanks, and that we, he pointed to the others, we all want to join your forces. We just need to check on our families."

"Fair enough. So what are you standing around for? Get going!"

The Signite gave a half bow and ran off.

Ryan started jogging, signaling the humans to follow.

"What's happening?"

"We have unknowns coming in. Let's go!"

They took the hint and filed into the ship without hesitation.

"Gem, fire her up."

As the *Dancing Queen* lifted off, Ryan checked the tracing scans on tactical. The fleet was taking its time on approach.

"You're right, Gem. These aren't Xi-Empire ships."

Captain YushTar on deep sentry patrol came up on the communications monitor. "Commander, these vessels are not Xi-Empire. I believe they could be Signite. What are your orders?"

"I would not automatically assume they are hostile, either. I suggest we hail them."

"I agree."

"Monitor my channel."

Ryan modified the frequency to Signite known bands. He hailed the oncoming fleet. It took a few attempts to obtain a reply. The hail was acknowledged on the upper frequency range.

Gem's voice perked up through the vaskpar. "A video translation can be transmitted within this bandwidth, attempting translation."

A picture of a human appeared on the screen. The image of the man who was transmitting the signal bore the customary uniform of a high ranking officer.

"This is Commander Ryan James of the Xi-Empire resistance."

"Hello, Commander, we have been monitoring your activities. I am the Commander Lortay, the commander of... what remains of the Signite fleet. We have an old saying amongst our military, an enemy of my enemy..."

"Is my friend," interjected Ryan in fluent Signite. "Yes, I am familiar with this wisdom."

"Forgive me for being blunt, Commander, but would you consider an alliance?"

Ryan laughed. "Aye, friends are hard to come by. I do accept even though you outnumber my forces ten to one."

"I would like to meet you, face-to-face, if we could arrange it."

"Perhaps on your home planet? I have just the spot picked out."

"Absolutely. I'll be instructing my fleet to take up certain positions, as we cannot be too careful. Expect three ships at your designated landing site."

"Commander, assuming you have been monitoring our activities, you should have no reservations in believing we are friends of Signus. As a matter of fact, my future wife is Signite."

"Indeed. Perhaps I know of her?"

"Perhaps. Her name is Aviore Tem Enova."

"By any chance, would you know if she is the former Governor's daughter?"

"I do believe she is the same."

"Then she is still alive! I look forward to meeting you, Commander Ryan James - and definitely the Governor's daughter, as well."

The monitor went blank.

He opened a channel to his fleet. "Cancel the scramble. Friends are arriving. Leave two ships in orbit, send two other vessels to these coordinates – you may find additional parts, possibly ships along these paths." He passed them the location information from his previous battle. "And Captain Yushtar, we need to keep moving on the repairs as time is limited."

Once again the ships landed. Once again teams scrambled to multiple areas to resume repairs. Captain YushTar put a small group to work on constructing a proper command center with a suspended floor and tented roof.

"Captain, the Signite fleet will arrive within the hour, will it be finished by then?" asked Ryan.

"It will be complete," replied the Showmish, not one to waste words.

He checked on Aviore one more time. He would not wake her. It could wait.

* * *

The temporary building was complete, and furnished with tables and chairs. The main tables were positioned in a semi-circle fashion which allowed for efficient inquisitions of prisoners.

The leaders assembled slowly, and quietly, acknowledging one another with nods, most weary from strenuous hours of work. They each wore what would loosely pass as uniforms, mostly tattered and torn, and stained. These rags bothered them little, for image meant little to them. If one looked close enough, it would not be difficult to witness their scars of enslavement.

Ryan sat amongst the captains, at the apex of the semi-circle, finding a surprising closeness with his company.

The prisoners were brought up one by one for interrogation in a continuous procession. For the most part, Ryan stayed quiet, subconsciously noting what was being said, but not getting too involved. His interest was captured when the Txtian Captain of the destroyer was escorted up. He looked a little worse for wear. Yellow blood dripped off his left mandible, his garments were tattered and burnt. Despite his appearance, he still maintained his dignity, walking with an unexpected confident stride. He towered above the Showmish, looking down at them with disdain.

"You will all die at the hand of the Emperor for this!" he screeched in native Txtian. His voice shrilled like a whistle and clicked intermittently.

Ryan signaled to the Showmish guard, who promptly stepped over and gave the arrogant captain a blow to the abdomen. The Txtian doubled over. When he straightened up, he spat out a stream of yellow blood onto the platform.

Ryan leaned ahead in his chair. "You will address us in Trinarieit, Txtian."

He focused his glare on Ryan. "What is your plan now, Signite? We have already conquered your planet. We will return to take it again. You are all just as dead, now as later."

The Txtian followed his statement with a clicking laugh, spitting out even more yellow blood, which ran down his chin obscenely.

Ryan spread his arms, gesturing a mock welcome. "How wise you are, I see. You believe I am from Signus. How quickly one can make assumptions. This is not my planet. And you have never had the privilege of facing me."

For a moment the Txtian was speechless. "So you are the captain of the white ship, I presume?"

"I am asking the questions here. We'll begin with a simple one: You're still alive when you should be dead. The bridge decompressed along with most of the other levels. Why did you survive? Perhaps you were attempting to abandon your post? Deplorable behavior for a high ranking officer - such a disgrace."

The sarcastic words seemed to have struck a nerve in the proud Txtian Captain. The alien had no rebuke, no words to make right the obvious. He shifted about, chest no longer swollen with pride, shoulders now slightly hunched. "I was following standard military procedure."

"You are a coward!" The effect of the translated word in Txtian seemed to drive his point home. The Txtian glowered back. His bulbous red eyes seemed to contort, turn oval in shape. His mandibles pulled wide, and the slight dark fur of its face stood on end.

"You will all die slowly and painfully for this outrage. You will not insult a Torzon. In 10 zadii our fleet will arrive from Gedricka and crush you!"

Ryan sat back in his chair. The Txtian realized what he had said, and he hung his head, disgusted with himself. For a moment Ryan let the silence stand, and enjoyed the cool ocean breeze.

"Such cooperation should be commended, but I have neither the time nor the inclination. I'm sure you have many more secrets within that tiny brain of yours. We have some very proficient interrogators. I pity you will not survive. But that, I guess, is of trivial concern. The truth is Xilo is doomed. You have been successful for too long and you've grown arrogant. Humility is a painful lesson to learn, and we will teach it to all of you."

With that, he waved the alien away.

The guards pushed the Txtian off the platform, then employed the whips viciously over his back as he stumbled toward the hold. Ryan ignored the savagery, jaded to its sight. He passed a slow appraising glance to the Showmish on both his sides. Something eager danced in their eyes. It was the look of a wild animal preparing to strike.

This information would prove helpful. Maybe they would find out more.

They were very lucky to have captured a proud one. He doubted they would be so fortunate next time.

Captain Roshesh commented, "Gedricka is not far away. I would guess that it is to be their new military base for this quadrant. "

"And now we know how long we have," added Captain Hushob.

"Yes. Not long at all," added Ryan quietly.

"Let us continue."

* * *

The Signite Commander arrived in the late afternoon when the sun was hanging low on the horizon, glinting off the restless waves of the ocean. White trailing streaks crawled across the sky above them. Three ships, each only slightly smaller than a Xi-destroyer, roared by to settle on the beach, billowing out clouds of white sand. They had positioned themselves cautiously, farther down the shoreline.

Ryan could see their silhouettes exiting from his vantage point on the platform. Even from a distance, he could make out their leader, who walked with an unmistakable confidence. Unlike the others that escorted him, his gaze remained focused on his destination. The dying sunlight reflected off insignia hanging thick upon his chest. As the party drew closer, he could see the officers were dressed in full uniform. Everything about them was spit and polish.

The visitors came to a stop a few yards from the open platform. They fanned out slightly, weapons lowered, but ready. The pasty look upon their faces revealed their nervousness. Ryan walked out to meet them. The Commander stepped forward, eyes scrutinizing him thoroughly. He spoke in Trinarieit. "Tell me, what do you fear most - death or slavery?"

"Slavery," responded Ryan, perplexed at the first exchange of words.

"If you had said death, I may have shot you myself."

"I'm sure you would have tried."

"You are the pilot of the white ship?"

"I am."

"It is good to meet the one who single-handedly destroyed a slaver expedition and crippled a Xi-Empire cruiser. An admirable feat, even if it had been accomplished by a fleet of ships."

Ryan smiled. "I see you are well informed, but I am at a disadvantage. Many think the Signite resistance is decimated, yet you stand here in front of me."

"Aye, not all is as it seems. Commander Aben Lortay of the Supreme Signite fleet - at your service." He gave a stiff Signite salute, fist tight, touching the shoulder.

Ryan returned the salute as precisely as possible, simultaneously doing his own inspection of the man now standing in front of him. The Signite Commander was probably in his late thirties. His black hair streaked with gray. His face was square, jaw strong and pronounced. His eyes were also gray and seemed to carry a glint of arrogance. Most notable characteristic about him was his air of superiority. It infected those around him. Ryan scanned over the medals he bore on his chest.

Thousands of light-years away and the military types still wear medals. Some things never change, no matter what.

"Good to meet you, Commander. These are my Showmish allies."

The Signite walked down the line, bowing to each Showmish captain. One captain recognized the Signite from a meeting, from years before. The tension dropped immediately. The Signite introduced his key officers one by one. Ryan waited, a bit impatiently. Once the formalities were over, he wasted no further time.

"I'm sorry, Commander. I regret we do not have much time for pleasantries. I have a number of plans I wish to set in motion. You are welcome to be part of them."

The Signite Commander looked him up and down. "If I am to become part of this alliance, I assume it will be under your command?" He was staring him straight in the eye, awaiting a response.

Ryan provided none, remaining steadfast and mute.

"You *are* in command, are you not?"

"We could always arm wrestle for it," Ryan refuted, breaking a smile.

The Commander shrugged, a grin also on his face. "I'm afraid I'm not quite up to speed on that custom."

He didn't get the damn joke. Of course not.

YushTar stepped up, "We follow our Commander only," he hissed. Lortay shifted his gaze over the grizzled Showmish captains.

"I see. Tell me, Commander James, what are your qualifications for this position? Have you ever served in a military role?"

Ryan smiled, then swung his leg onto the table. He pulled up his pant leg. "You see Commander, these are my medals."

The Signite uniforms shifted uncomfortably, few had experienced the pleasure of slavery firsthand.

"I know the enemy. You don't. You already lost, your planet, your colonies, your war - the way you make war, it's all lost. Your medals are irrelevant here."

"We can join forces."

"We could, but I will not follow you, and neither will they." He cast his hand across the room.

"This war is no longer yours, it is ours."

The Signite Commander nodded his head slightly. "I see. You understand my choices are limited, Commander James. This fleet circling above you is all that is left. Our colonies have fallen. Any stand I take is our last. What have you to offer us that is so different?"

"It is the same for you, me, and everyone here. I offer an honorable death. Hope offers little solace, revenge possibly, some. We do not fight for ourselves here. We fight for our children."

The Showmish put their fists to their chests, a show of solidarity in many ways, for Ryan's words rang true.

"Very well, Commander. I am, and the complete 3rd Signite Protectionary fleet, are at your disposal."

"Good," Ryan said curtly. "Then it's time for us to strike."

"Open up this area here, grab those torches, and give me a stick or something." Someone handed him a branch and he started drawing out the quadrant on the sand that had already drifted onto the deck, talking as he worked. "Before, our tactics were simple. Hit and run. Attack, grab what we can, and move out. This is because we are working at a definite disadvantage: the lack of resources, the lack of ships."

The group around him nodded in agreement. "For the next few months, the accrual of ships will continue to be our sole purpose. Board anything and everything. Doesn't matter how small, as long as it can fly. The rules of engagement are simple. If you cannot board it, destroy it, and tow the parts home. In the event that your ship is captured, you will initiate a self-destruct. We all know how to set up a deadman counter. The Empire cannot obtain any information about our existence."

"We will disperse throughout these quadrants." He ran a circle across the sectioned areas. "But no more than three ships together at any one time. I do not want to draw their attention. When the main fleets shift occupation of an area, we adjust accordingly. Cellular communications only for each group. We'll use codes for verification and emergencies and implement a shared encryption system to avoid infiltration. Most important of all: from this point on, everybody operates on a need to know basis."

He stood back from the huddled group. "I need you to understand this is not military-style conflict. Not as yet, anyway. We are too insignificant, too weak..."

He nodded over to the Signite Commander. "Commander Lortay, this will be an adjustment for your style of warfare. I will mix your fleet vessels in with the others. You'll need to coach your captains on this type of warfare. If you encounter superior numbers, you turn-tail and run."

He passed his gaze over the group. "I'll assign each of you the areas in which you will be responsible. We follow the program. No mistakes. No heroics... Any questions?"

YushTar presented one. "The ships we capture, they will be damaged. We can only repair what we are able."

"We'll coordinate a relay to transport damaged ships to appropriated spaceports where they can be repaired. It will be up to each of you to move the ships to a safe area and sit on them until the relay shows up."

"There are many variables, many holes in this plan," stated Lortay flatly.

"Yes, and we'll fill those holes with our blood. This is a start, the beginning of an overall strategy, that's all. When we see a new opportunity come up, we'll seize it."

"You can be sure there is one particular opportunity: others will want to join us," offered Roshesh.

"I am counting on that. New cells, we need them, and skilled workers, especially those that know the trades, the ones that can repair ships, the ones that can fly'em, and everyone in-between. But remember we operate under the need to know basis. I expect informants. Sooner or later they're bound to infiltrate our ranks and we will lose cells in the process."

"When should we start attacking outright?" asked YushTar.

Ryan nodded his head. "I know what you want. If you ask me if I have a great master plan, I will say no. But I won't be doing this alone. I'll expect leadership from every last one of you. These are basic principles I've proposed. We have to work as independent cells. We have a limited amount of time to build a suitable force. It will not take long before they catch on and start running militia escorts. If we're going to win this war, we'll need ships, and there is no better way to obtain them than by stealing them, as fast and as frequently as possible."

"I see the next step will be to establish a secure communications net. With the proper positioning of ships and bases, we'll have the intelligence to know what the enemy is up to. That should help. We'll learn everything we can, no matter how trivial it seems, and compile it centrally. We will find their weaknesses."

The conversation died to silence. They all knew what to do, what had to be done.

"Alright, then, this meeting is adjourned."

Hushob approached Ryan, insistent upon discussing the ship rebuilding issues, but Commander Lortay interrupted them both, clearing his throat loudly.

"I'm sorry, Commander," Ryan apologized. "Just trying to wrap up a few details. I would like to talk to you in a few minutes. Come to think of it, we have a certain individual that would like to meet you. Claims to be the leader of some local resistance. I have my doubts."

Hushob waved to a Showmish guard. In a few minutes, the Signite was escorted out. Lortay's face turned pale, lips drawn thin. "Commander, this is not a leader of a local resistance. He is a known informant of the Xi-Empire."

The announcement didn't actually surprise Ryan, but it did seem, somehow, humorous. Oddly enough, he laughed.

Guess no one else saw the humor, or was he getting twisted?

He turned his attention to the unlucky Signite. "Well, well, looks like my instincts were right about you."

The man was nervous, constantly wetting his lips, shifting his weight from one foot to the other. "I don't know what you're talking about. You can't be serious. Commander Lortay is mistaken. I never even met him."

Ryan paced in front him. "Oh, but he's not in command here - I am. That does not make things better for you, I'm afraid. It makes things far worse. You know, I have a hard time tolerating your kind. I was a slave for a long time. I worked in the mines you see – probably the most difficult place to survive. Showmish, Human, Brog, Kalmakan, all trying to stay alive, the average lasting less than a year. But then there were the moles, selling out for that extra morsel of food, that brief added privilege. In the end, however, they all died too, and they did not die well. Your kind is too short-sighted. You can't see ahead far enough to maintain your own self-respect."

He reached out and grabbed the Signite by the collar. "Listen to me, little man. You are about to make the hardest decision in your life, so listen very carefully. You'll tell us everything you know, and that means everything, or you will die more painfully than you ever imagined."

He tossed him backward. The Signite flew off the platform and landed on his back in the sand.

The anger surged through him - a dark ravenous force. He felt like he could rip this man apart with his bare hands. It took everything he had to turn away.

Breathe.

The rage died down and he regained control. They were awaiting his decision. He turned one last time to look the informant straight in the eye. The Signite squirmed under his gaze. He reached down and pulled out his blaster, and aimed it between the Signite's eyes.

"You must make your decision now."

The muzzle did not waver.

"I'll tell you! I'll tell you everything! I was just trying to stay alive. It's not my fault. They said they would kill me."

"Of course they did." Ryan scoffed and holstered his blaster. "You're a damned fool."

"Lortay, he's yours. Get him out of my sight."

Lortay motioned to a couple of his troopers, they grabbed the Signite and escorted him back to their ship. Ryan stood there quietly, hands on his hips, staring down at the sand. He could feel something shaking inside him.

"There are traitors among all our people," Hushob said. "It is... expected."

"Yeah, I know. I'll communicate my plans to all of you once I have them figured out. Lortay, I feel like a stiff drink, would you like to join me?"

"Certainly, in my ship?"

"No, in mine."

The two went into the *Dancing Queen*. Ryan located a certain bottle of Xeronian brandy from the galley and joined Lortay in the lower level.

"Commander, I know a little about militia strategy. Just how many ships do you *really* have?"

Lortay took a sip of the drink. "Remarkable stuff, kind of smooth. I'll have to introduce you to some of my personal stores. And it is possible that we may have almost one hundred ships, fully operational and outfitted."

"You have a manufacturing facility?"

"Yes. We have been working furiously for the past year now. We've had some close calls, though."

"Your technology is not as advanced as the Xi-Empire's. In combat, they'll rip your fleet to shreds."

"I am very aware of this, but we have no recourse."

"I have friends. They'll help. I suspect we can re-outfit your ships relatively fast."

"How much will this cost?"

"Don't be so suspicious. We're on the same side, remember."

Lortay's eyes landed on him squarely. "So we are... I don't believe I ever recalled meeting you, Commander, In all my years of service."

Ryan chuckled. "Of course you haven't. I'm from Earth."

Lortay leaned back, nothing short of wonderment in his eyes. "From Earth! I would have never dreamed. Of course, I couldn't place that accent. My apologies, Commander, I was only being cautious."

"I know."

Lortay relaxed. "Currently, we have a little over two hundred ships ready to go."

Ryan chuckled. "That's a good start for a rebellion. I think it's time for you to meet some friends of mine. We have little time left before more Xi-Empire patrols arrive. Dispatch your escort ships. I don't want them to be around when someone finally answers those distress calls that were sent. I want you to follow me. With your help, we may just win this war."

"You mentioned Aviore Tem Enova, is she really here?"

"Yes, but she's asleep right now, otherwise, I would introduce you."

"Oh. The last news I heard she had been captured by those animals."

"Yes, I'm afraid she was. But she's safe now."

"Then perhaps another time, then. All of Signus is indebted to you." He stood up, ready to leave. He could not sit for very long. "I will issue the orders to put your plan in motion and await for your departure."

"Good, and will you do me a favor? Have that destroyer put in tow and brought back to your base. It's too valuable to leave here."

"I'll see to it myself, Commander."

Ryan held out his hand. "Earth custom - to shake hands,"

The Signite's grip was surprisingly strong.

"Interesting custom. Physical contact, however, is not always advantageous, especially considering the biohazards."

"Consider yourself infected, Commander," replied Ryan with a half-smile. The Signite returned a wide grin and exited promptly. Ryan turned his attention to Gem, setting up communications channels with all the Showmish captains. They planned out the missions swiftly and were soon passing on farewells as the small rebellion disembarked one by one.

Ryan stepped down the ramp to enjoy the evening breeze.

Signus was, after all, a beautiful planet.

He watched as each ship lifted off, throwing up a massive column of sand as the burners engaged. By now the Signite sun was lost beyond the horizon, leaving only the slightest pale reflection. In the fading light, the departing ships provided a spectacular light show. Captain Hushob's ship was the last to remain.

Ryan pulled up communications via the vaskpar, projecting a mental image of his features.

"So you are going to be able to launch that slaver shortly? Are you sure, Captain?"

"Yes, the vessel is indeed sound. We will lift off seven or eight days.

If the Txtian was correct, we may have visitors soon. It will be very close."

"You won't be alone. Lortay and his ship will be leaving with me, the other Signite ships will stay and depart with you. But if you can't get that ship spaceworthy in time, get the hell out. I want to see you again, right?"

"We will meet again, Commander."

"Good luck, Captain."

"Good luck to you as well," he hissed back.

Ryan reluctantly headed back into the ship.

The show was done anyway.

Within the hour Lortay called in to let him know he was ready. Ryan thumbed the intercom to the rest of the ship. Most of the humans had decided to stay with him and he needed to keep them informed.

"Hello, everyone. Ziggy will be escorting all of you through the sterilization lock. Your quarantine period has elapsed. Please make yourselves comfortable. I've arranged a nice view for you as we take off. I imagine you'll enjoy it."

He ran a quick systems check before lifting off.

In a minute they were ready.

The *Dancing Queen* roared as she climbed up and into the night sky, leaving the peaceful ocean waves lapping on the sandy shore. Moments later the Signite ship followed, dispersing clouds of sand that drifted lazily across the beach. Soon the water would erase any evidence that they had ever landed.

* * *

Captain Hushob stared into the skies above. He watched as the ships shrank to tiny dots, intermingling with the stars of the night sky.

Far above him, sparks flew, bouncing against the ship's hull as they fell. Brief flashes of light blanketed the beach like sheet lightning as fusing tools flared. The repair teams were pushing on furiously to replace the damaged outer hull plating. They were working against time itself. Hundreds of meters above, suspended on tethered lines, they were hanging precariously, struggling with heavy tools and unwieldy materials. He watched as a large section of replacement plating slipped and almost fell. Hushob hissed a small Showmish prayer under his breath.

They were good Showmish, all of them. Most had been enslaved and they bore the scars deeply. Now they had a chance, albeit a remote chance, for freedom. They would rather fight and die than continue on surviving as slaves - and they were not alone. Countless Signites had appeared during the day and offered to join their small force. They all seemed to share in the same insane belief. That is the very seed that continued to drive them now, slugging on at the brink of exhaustion.

He thought about the Earthman, their elected Commander. There is something about him. It is more than one thing really. What could he ask of a leader? Make the right decisions. Take the risks when it was time, and above all - win.

No.

He and his brothers expected only one thing from the Earthman – an opportunity to fight, to live free, and to die well. If they had even a remote chance of succeeding, that was already beyond what they could hope for. Ironically, the Earthman had done the impossible already - multiple times it seemed. But it would be arrogant to assume one could actually defeat this enemy.

Far above the lone Showmish captain, two starships turned from Signus and headed for Xeronia, jumping into acroluc, their speed increasing exponentially, the *Dancing Queen* leading the way.

Her captain knew the trip would take some time, but he could use it to make plans, possibly take advantage of the precious moments with a certain Signite woman. Time was precious.

They were beginning a war, and people died in wars.

* * *

12. Confrontation

The return trip to Xilo was painfully long. The cruiser *Bzak* had crept through space with one of its main burners out of commission for almost a full zanii. The crew was miserable and Zorlog did not help matters. They were tired of his constant drills and repetitious persecution. Zorlog blamed all of them personally for the failure at Signus, and they were paying for it every sadii. After the encounter with the alien ship, everybody went on double shifts. Even the officers were run ragged as they tried to measure up to Zorlog's standard. But it was the Txtians that suffered the worst of all. The Karvok's prejudice was all too evident. When the ship came upon Xilo's remote navigation transmitter, the whole crew breathed a sigh of relief.

A collection of long-range port guides had arrived to put the cruiser in tow shortly after they passed the markers. After that, the news could not be contained. The port guides, under military jurisdiction, had reported back directly to the Seven Karvoks of Domination. The unsettling news had trickled down to the ears of the common citizen. It was treated as a joke, to the detriment of the Xi-military, and obviously, Zorlog.

The Seven Karvoks did not find this humorous, nor did their officers. None liked Zorlog, but they all knew his cunning and respected his abilities in a battle. They could only wonder what had happened at the Signus system.

Zorlog's fate hung in the balance. The Emperor was known for his lack of patience. A reprisal was due.

Zorlog was on the bridge when the order came over - he was to report to the Emperor as soon as he arrived. He laughed a dry, cold, seething laugh - a kind of insidious, almost insane response. Indeed, his crew watched him intently as they had weathered too many sadii of his wrath. The Zuvok's laughter was not misplaced, however, only misunderstood.

The Xilozak Avok who announced the news was put on indefinite waste recycling duty. That did little to soothe Zorlog's damaged ego. As each sadii passed, and the *Bzak* drew closer to Xilo, Zorlog could not bear the waiting. He walked the corridors, unable to rest, his mind spinning with details of which he alone knew. They were incredible details, outlining plans that would unfold and bring the Xi-Empire to a grinding halt.

All his grand ambitions seemed diminutive the day the *Bzak* arrived at Tikonda Station, the main docking base orbiting Xilo.

The images from the tracing scans twisted his gut into painful knots.

Confrontation

Ships of all kinds, too innumerable to count, were awaiting the *Bzak's* arrival. Gawkers, all wanting to see what had been done to the most powerful class of warship ever built. Zorlog spit razum on the deck. A filthy habit, but it calmed his nerves, albeit temporarily.

There was a deathly quiet on the bridge. More than one Avok would have liked to have distanced himself from this moment, but their Zuvok had insisted that all Avoks be at their posts during docking maneuvers. No exceptions.

Zorlog barked out orders with an automatic precision, barely paying attention, his mind reeling with rage. The gigantic cruiser finally came to rest within the grapples of Tikonda Station's mooring couplers.

With a brief salute, he relieved the bridge to his Charvok and wasted no time leaving the ship. Not surprisingly, the Karvok aides of the Xi-fleet were present at the end of the relay tube. He brushed past them, ignoring their questions - and their comments. The shuttle was empty, with the exception of its pilot. The trip down was quick and for a few bare moments, peaceful. It gave him time to assemble himself.

A jarring thud announced their arrival. The ramp lowered unceremoniously onto the hardened tarmac of Xilo's main spaceport. Again, there was an armed escort ready to welcome him. They were wise enough, however, to maintain a healthy distance from him, and none dared to request his weapons. After all, he still retained the full authority of Karvok. That title could be revoked only by the Emperor himself.

He found, as before, the streets of Zenux were hot and dusty. They marched into the sprawling city. Its citizens, both Xilozak and Txtian stopped to watch him pass. He could feel their stares, could hear the hushed muttering. It ate at him, like a dull-toothed parasite gnawing on an open, festering wound. A drunken trooper staggered out of one of the local drinking establishments and almost collided with Zorlog. His eyes went wide with recognition, and he muttered a slur that one would expect of a fool.

Zorlog's weapon of choice hummed in the hot breeze, its disrupter settings at maximum. The bar cut clean through the drunken trooper. It was a quick death.

The guards stood in shock, the citizens in horror. Zorlog only glared back defiantly. None met his gaze.

Without a word, he resumed his march. His escorts hurried to catch up.

He had a slight spring in his step now.

It was good to kill, to vent some of his anger. But this was not near enough satisfaction. This was merely a start.

He felt his hearts triple in beat as the towers of the Zenux came into sight - the home of the Emperor.

Gulin stood waiting just before the entrance. With flat harshness, Zorlog barked his orders to his escorts to disperse, and give him a moment to confer. With fleeting hesitation, they complied, not wishing a conflict with their prisoner.

Zorlog approached his old Lavok, a twisted smile upon his face. It was surprising. He actually felt a bit glad to see Gulin.

"Good morning, my Tarvok." Gulin greeted him in his usual official manner.

"Yes. Morning it is? Good, it is not. What have you to report?"

"Full saturation throughout the planet's water supply. I've been told to pass on a message: *the red sun has risen.*"

Zorlog's smile widened exposing his full host of fangs. "Good work, Gulin. Be prepared with the *Gohk II*. The time is at hand!"

Gulin glanced down the crowded street. He felt uncomfortable. There were too many eyes, too many ears around. Zorlog was much too bold.

"We have everyone in place. We are ready on your signal."

"The signal will be clear enough, Gulin." Zorlog brushed past him to the entrance of the towers, but then stopped short.

"Gulin, how would you like to become Charvok on my Xi-cruiser?"

"I would be honored, my Zuvok!"

"Then it shall be. Transfer your Tarvok role and report to the *Kirbetz*."

"Thank you!" replied Gulin, a hint of excitement in his voice.

Zorlog marched on, disappearing into the massive arched entrances of the Towers of Zenux. His escorts scurried up to match his quick pace.

Zorlog made a mental note as the corridors darkened and the path descended, first as a gradual slope, then through winding stairs. The Towers of Zenux ascended into the clouds, but they also descended even farther.

He enjoyed the walk. It gave him time to think. There were no distractions. His escorts had abandoned him far above, as only a chosen few were allowed within the depths of these towers. Very rarely did he meet anyone in the cold, dark corridors, and when he did, they ignored him as much as he did them. Most of the Zigot servants couldn't even speak. It was the price of servitude to be mutilated into silence.

Just before the Hall of the Apocalypse, he stopped and faded back into the shadows. He began systematically pulling off different parts of his clothing: a belt buckle, a button from the cuff, a small plastic cylinder from the heel of his boot. When he was done, he held a small tranquilizer gun, able to be completely hidden within the palm of his hand.

For all of their searching and scanning, they had missed what was right under their muzzles. He laughed throatily.

When he arrived at the entrance, the two massive granite doors swung open into an empty, dimly lit room. Zorlog proceeded in, careful to position himself within the exact center of the Star of Domination. Exercising unusual self-control, he pulled his body rigid, every muscle taut at full attention, and waited patiently. His mind danced, preoccupied, effectively ignoring the pain and discomfort emanating from his distressed muscles. It was with pleasant satisfaction that he discovered he did not have to wait long.

"Zorlog, you incompetent razum!" The Emperor cursed at him loudly from the darkness.

"My Emperor," greeted Zorlog flatly, bowing his coiled body ever so slightly.

"I thought that you were different, Xilozak! I had thought that you would aspire to so much. But you are no different than the others that surround me! You could have become a Karvok of Domination. But now..."

He shook his massive head, still moving in closer. The obtuse lighting alternated over the fearsome mutant as he advanced. The Emperor was almost upon him now. Zorlog could stare directly into those red eyes. His hand kneaded the small tranquilizer gun. His legs ached, pulled tight as springs.

"Tell me how does one small alien craft disable the Empire's mightiest cruiser?"

Zorlog remained silent.

"Speak, Xilozak!"

The Emperor was close, spraying spit onto Zorlog's face with each word.

Zorlog cracked his toothy grin. "Your mighty military has much to learn about designing vessels of war, Emperor. Your crews perform poorly and they lack discipline. Your Txtian filth has tainted their spirits and destroyed their ambition!"

"So now you admit your affiliation to the Purists!" growled the Emperor, hands raising to wrap around his mutinous subject.

Move! Zorlog could hear that little insane voice in the back of his mind. He brought his left arm up savagely, aiming at the Emperor's head. But, as expected, the Emperor's reflexes were much too fast. The Zigot blocked the swing effortlessly, catching its full ferocity in the palm of his oversized hand.

The Zigot laughed as Zorlog put the gun to the Emperor's midsection and fired. The tranquilizer bullet penetrated through the robing easily and buried itself deep into the flesh.

A look of shock came over the Emperor's face as he realized what had happened. He crumbled to the floor, his limbs numb and useless.

A Bellicose Dance

Zorlog kicked him with contempt. "Mighty Emperor! Long on oppression, short on strategy!"

He laughed. The twisted sound of it bounced off the stone walls of the expansive hall, changing pitch eerily. Zorlog enjoyed the strange effect, and soaked it all in. He circled around the prone body of the Emperor, all the time keeping one eye peering into the darkness.

There were no servants racing in to attack and protect.

"What arrogance!" He looked down at his victim with satisfaction. "You did not see fit to bring your servants with you. You can now see how that was a fatal mistake."

"What have you done to me, Xilozak?" rebuked the Emperor as he struggled to move.

"A small injection of gridzilliam. No known cure I fear."

Zorlog shook his head slowly. "A shame it is." As suddenly as it had appeared, his pleased expression dropped away like a curtain. He knelt down, glaring into the eyes of the dying Emperor. "You want to know why, Zigot?"

The Emperor's breaths were quick and shallow now, his eyes already glazed and vision blurred. The poison was moving quickly. A strange emotion surged through his contorted mind. He had never felt it before - fear.

"Yes, you will know why before you die. My sire was a very prominent member of the Purist Council - a *Huzan-Gaurd*. You do remember the *Huzan-Gaurd* Emperor? They concerned you enough that you dispatched your Zigot drones to silence them."

"I was a mere fledgling then, they would not listen to me. I knew how you would react. I warned them both what you would do. But they lacked belief. They simply could not understand that their own Emperor would kill them for a mere belief. Their foolishness became clear as your drones butchered them like common slaves. It is true, they were weak, lost to their ideals, pitifully naïve.

The irony of today, you must understand, is that the drones were sloppy. They missed me. And so I vowed as a youngling to take these towers down and leave your rotting corpse buried under the rubble."

He spit in the Emperor's face. The slime slid down off the ex-leader's mandibles, onto the cold black floor. He laughed. The most powerful being in the known galaxy lying on the floor at his feet, helpless.

"All your dreams of domination!" Zorlog howled, standing quickly, then twirling in a dance. "The Emperor's grand plan to conquer the galaxy."

"Ah," he stopped. The spinning was making him dizzy. "Such a pity you will never see it. See what all your efforts add up to? A helpless, dying, pitiful climax. Pathetic, isn't it?"

He dropped back down to the floor. "I remember how you justified their murders, labeling it an Empirical campaign, an ordained purge!"

"Purge the Traitors!" you cried. "They and all your followers on a quest for purity!"

"You.. will.. die.. Xilozak!" The Emperor labored over every word, knowingly using up his last reserve of strength.

"Yes I will, but where you are wrong, is in the timing, my exalted one." Zorlog reached down and grabbed him by the top of his head, wrenching it askew viciously.

"At this very minute, my Purist forces are freeing our Xilozak brothers and sisters from your oppressive Txtian mind-twist. Nothing will save your kind now."

He noticed something in the Zigot's eyes. He had seen that familiar look - many times before. He laughed outrageously at the realization. He slammed the Emperor's head down on the granite floor. "Many Txtian's have tried their mind-twist on me. Try, try, try. Try as you might, mutant!" He laughed with contempt.

"Oh, but you never knew! I am more than a mere slaver, more than your eager to please Karvok. I am special, you see. I was born with a gift, shall I say, my own natural defense. I saw but never felt what brought my brothers to their knees. But I knew enough, even as a child, to mimic it. They never suspected. Not even the headmistress at my school. And she was such an evil *geretok* of a Txtian." He grinned coldly.

"Because of my gift I knew what I was born to do. So I scoured the worlds looking for a cure to your cursed ability. A slaver has access to so many planets, so many resources. It is truly glorious."

The Emperor was fading now, death was coming.

Zorlog viciously slapped him across the face. "Stay alive, Zigot, I'm not through with my story yet. You must stay alive for the climax! You must know that I found it. And I have introduced it into Xilo's water supply. By now, most of the planet will be immune! You can take that to your grave."

The Emperor closed his eyes. *It was over. Nothing left but to die.*

Zorlog glanced down at his chronometer. "I must leave now, my Emperor," he stated quietly, giving the almost dead, once invincible leader, one final glance. "And we followed your kind," he growled with disgust. "You are pathetic!" With one last savage kick, he turned and moved quickly out of the gloomy hall.

The Emperor muttered a small phrase of native Txtian with his last breath, and died.

* * *

This was the start of the Xi-Empire civil war - the collapse of a thousand zadii of peace. It sent ripples tearing into the very existence of the colossal Empire. Both sides eagerly embraced the fight. Segregation of the races followed and the great cities of Xilo divided. The Txtian's mind-twist no longer affected the Xilozak population, as the drug had become widely available through Purists channels. The secret was out. The old fear was gone. Txtian control deflated into chaos. Old familiar hates between the two races sprung up like a plague. The streets turned into havens for riots and bloodshed.

Surprisingly, there were those that remained cool in the heat of internal strife. They had realized there was too much to be lost by fighting amongst themselves. These idealistic individuals were in positions of power, heads of corporations, institutions, rich merchants, and government leaders. Not without irony, many were Xilozak.

Their denouncing of the Purists and their backing of the Zigot league swayed the public opinion. It helped, somewhat, to slow the Purist movement.

The common citizen resisted change. Xilozaks and Txtians, conditioned through the generations, simply did not see the need. They retreated into their homes and waited.

The Zigots used this to their advantage. They moved quickly, taking advantage of the temporary confusion, knowing this was a momentary quiet, the undercurrents of a building storm.

The Zigot League was practiced in the art of manipulation. Propaganda was a powerful weapon. It was easy to convince the average citizen of the dismal effects of an internal war. The public's eyes and ears were already barraged with troubling realities: the drop in the standard of living, the loss of assets, not to mention the prospect of losing their slaves.

Their campaign was working.

Confusion and fear beleaguered the Purist movement, holding back its momentum. Slowly, ever so slowly, the Zigot League turned the population's opinion in their favor. The Purists were painted as rogues, enemies of the Empire, common criminals working against the well-being of the average citizen. This did little to regain control of the divided military.

But beyond Xilo, like a plague impossible to control, the war was spreading. Every Xi-colony within the known galaxy was affected. Expeditions were canceled, ships recalled, expansion efforts recalled. The Empire withdrew into itself.

Returning Tarkovs made their decisions enroute, declaring their alliances openly. Some suffered the insult of mutiny, while the majority reinforced their standings with their crews.

Txtians had a habit of abusing their power, especially outside of Xilo's influence. This reinforced the Purist cause with vigor. Young, eager Xilozak warriors rallied to the Purists' strongholds.

During the confusion and chaos, Zorlog launched his own campaign, countering the League's with his own. He attracted recruits with poisonous words that rang of many truths, as Xilozaks' memory of the mind-twist was all too recent, swaying previously neutral Xilozaks onto the Purist path.

Their momentum was unstoppable.

The Purists' fleet continued to grow with each arriving defection. Its fleet had absorbed beyond a third of the entire existing Xi-forces, and at its helm was Zorlog, in the cruiser flagship *Kirbetz*. Three of the Seven Zuvoks of Domination now enrolled under his command.

The Zigot League made the mistake of first strike. Zorlog's reaction was swift and merciless. The Purists left the engagement with minimal casualties but the League lost their fleet. Zorlog's reputation, once tarnished, was now restored. But this did little to satisfy his thirst for power. Ports and colonies were attacked, and ships, equipment, and supplies were seized.

Zorlog was hungry for more.

The Zigot League's military prowess was fractured. Action needed to be taken. A new leader was appointed to the precarious position of Emperor. Not surprisingly, it was the brother of the late Emperor. He was enthroned in a quiet ceremony within the depths of the towers of Zenux. The news spread quickly throughout the planets, but it did not ease unrest. The discreet ceremony left many unanswered questions in the minds of the Empire's citizens.

Was this new Emperor so weak as to hide from the Purists? Did this appointed Zigot lack the will and charisma of their previous?

The new Emperor carried with him years of study, the knowledge of the scholarly. That was unheard of in the previous tyrannical types that had preceded him. He led with a firm and confident hand and quickly earned the reputation of lacking any tolerance for incompetence. Within the span of one zanii, the old inherent corruption within the Empire was literally annihilated. The collection of 'additional' non-sponsored taxes and levies was outlawed. Heads rolled, literally, within the towers of Zenux. No one in the position of power was allowed to abuse his privilege under risk of death.

The new Emperor again broke with tradition - he delegated. He designated his loyal and capable followers to their own areas of responsibility, making the day-to-day running of the immense Empire that much more efficient.

The failing Empire began to show signs of stabilization. The citizens had a leader who dared to walk upon the streets of Zenux, who dared to step beyond all pre-established boundaries and establish new order, new procedures, new traditions. His abilities were unparalleled by any and all who preceded him.

Once the Emperor completed the foundational changes of the Empire's new order, he turned his attention to the war, and to his brother's killer. On that sadii, Zorlog's campaign became much more complicated. Victories of the Purists rebellion turned to losses under the gigantic war machine of Xilo.

Zorlog saw all of this and could do nothing but laugh at the knowledge that he alone had seeded this change. He had killed the old Emperor and caused a brother, who should have never known power, to be appointed.

He alone had brought forward his own greatest enemy.

* * *

Ryan enjoyed the trip back to Xeronia.

Aviore was getting better with the passing of each day. He could tell she was in less pain. She seemed happier, more carefree, and less haunted by her past.

He outfitted her with a less constricting brace for her jaw and removed the cumbersome bandages from her fingers. They were healing so well that there was virtually no sign of the reconstructive surgery that had taken place.

She was feeling so good after the first week that she could not sit still. Ryan drafted her help in managing the passengers. Since she had a background in psychology, she was able to help them through the horrors they had suffered. Aviore asked Ryan to join them, but he refused, citing the large amount of work he had to do before they arrived.

She knew him well enough not to push it.

Ryan had handled things in his own way, and he had managed to survive. For the first time in years, he felt strong again. He wasn't going to trade that off by baring his soul in some group session. It was better to leave the past buried - for him, that is.

He wasn't particularly proud of himself for eavesdropping when it came to Aviore's turn to talk. But he *was* busy, otherwise, he would have been right there, in the group, listening like the others. So having Gem patch the audio over wasn't really doing anything wrong.

He had to know what happened to her.

The first few times, she spoke only of cursory details, avoiding anything that would take any strength to work through. As the group opened up, so did she, and the stories became more horrific. She started at the beginning, enroute to Earth. Their ship had been attacked and the survivors enslaved. She told them of the slavership conditions and of the subsequent transfer to a military detention ship.

Strangely, she didn't tell them about him.

She was interrogated and nearly killed in the process. They tortured her over and over. They were looking for information, anything that they could use, anything against Signus. They broke her, Ryan could tell. Her voice turned hollow, distant, like she was carrying some awful truth, some unforgivable guilt.

He was in the cockpit at the time. He wanted to run over to comfort her. But that wouldn't help. He knew that much.

So he stayed there, and he listened.

She stopped and wouldn't tell anyone more. No one forced her. It was an unwritten rule. Although, after a few more sessions, she was able to continue.

After the fall of the Signite resistance, she was finally released. They transferred her to a space station, barely alive at this point. Fellow slaves nursed her back to health. Apparently, the station doctor provided some help as he had some knowledge of Signite physiology. Her wounds healed poorly.

She was assigned to a hydroponics dome as part of the food production labor pool. She was lucky. Given her condition, hard labor may have killed her. She stayed there for the majority of her captivity. They fed her just enough to get by. She would steal food when she could. Her masters were moody, which often led to beatings. She talked about them to the others, how she had felt so powerless, so helpless. She had learned to block out the pain.

She had seen others go through worse.

Things changed dramatically after the arrival of the slavership *Xabuntz II*. Its captain had contracts to fill. He bought up most of the slaves from the spaceport administrator. It was rumored that he gambled, and couldn't refuse the credit.

This was where Ryan pieced together a bit of history. Apparently, Aviore was particularly valuable, given her previous military inquisition. Captain Gick of the *Joahack* had known about Aviore's credit worthiness but had failed to make it to the station on time. Gick had connections. He knew the Zigot League would pay handsomely for a high profile Signite citizen. The League had made it clear that it would pay significant bounties to any Xi-Empire citizen who would produce such slaves. No questions asked.

They were looking for something, Ryan just didn't know what. But that explained the connection in the *Joahack's* log - a bitter entry, a minor reference to a profitable slave from a wary slaver looking for easy profit – all twists of fate.

However, the captain of the *Xabuntz II* was ignorant of anything about her. In fact, the captain had made other plans for Aviore. He had developed a liking for humanoids, for her in particular. He isolated her and kept her for himself.

In the beginning, Aviore did not know why she never saw any other slaves. After the captain's visits, she began to understand. In time, she realized she would never be sold. She was his personal property. Others may have faded away, lost all hope, given up, but she didn't. That was when she told them about him. About how they met, about how she fell in love. She told them she hung on because of him. Because he would, somehow, come for her.

But there was something she hadn't counted on – the effect of time. There was no way to measure it. No way to know how much passed by. Her feedings, which were irregular at best, provided no point of reference. It tore her down, little by little. The knowledge that time was passing away. The strength she once had, was fading to nothing. She didn't have it in her to keep going.

But then it happened, like a fairy tale come true – he came. She thought it was a dream, that she had finally died. It wasn't until she awakened on this ship that she realized it wasn't a dream. He had come and saved her. The very captain of this ship, her hero.

Stuck in the port wing maintenance tube, wrestling with a release valve, he momentarily stopped what he was doing. He swore he could feel her smile.

Her manner seemed to change in the following days. The haunted look, the pain, all seemed to have lifted. The group sharing, talking through the torturous past, seemed to be helping. She carried a playful ease about her, and it drew him in even closer. He brought up the Signite Commander in conversation, and the fact he claimed to know her. Aviore's reaction was of immediate excitement. Turned out he and Aviore had known each other quite well, something about him being a close friend of her family.

Ryan had managed to arrange a com link just before they had closed off to go dark. As he guided Aviore down into the study, her smile lit the room and tears streamed down her face. She spent the next few hours catching up with an old but dear friend. They had talked mostly of Signus, the way things had been, before the Xi-Empire.

It was the end of the sixth week since he had found her. She lay beside him, in their bed. Bandages and braces were part of the past, although she was still very sore, still on the mend.

She pulled him close.

"I love you, Captain Ryan James."

He looked into her with those brown eyes and they stripped him down to his very soul.

"And I love you," a tear flowed down his cheek. "I never truly believed..."

"Shhh..." she put her finger to his mouth.

"Believe it. I am here. I am yours, forever, if you want me."

He laughed, eyes twinkling. "I do."

Confrontation

"Then come here." She pulled him over. "I want you."

They made love.

Near the end, she held him so tight, she could not let him go. Her tears wouldn't stop.

He stayed quiet. He didn't ask her why.

He just held her close.

* * *

One of Ryan's many self-elected duties was the ongoing task of teaching himself everything about the *Dancing Queen,* again and again, until he had it all committed to memory. He drilled himself until he knew every facet of the ship, every subsystem, every control, every circuit. He crawled through every maintenance tube, every access hatch, reviewed every specification.

He had to know everything. The *Dancing Queen* was his ship.

He vaskpar continued to help him. His Signite was almost there. He surprised Aviore one day by asking her, in Signite, what time it was. She replied automatically, realizing only after, just what he said. Unfortunately for Ryan, she haughtily decided to test him. It was not long before she left him scratching his head and wondering what gibberish she had just said. Sure, he could have accessed Gem's libraries but that was too much like cheating.

"I don't like linguistics anyway," he retorted back to her in his own defense.

"If you get stuck, I'll do it for you," she replied teasingly. At that, Ryan picked her off her feet and carried her into the bedroom. They did not get much work done that day.

On the night cycle, when the ship was quiet, and her interior lights dimmed, Ryan would sit in the cockpit, amongst the stars.

He loved the stars.

Aviore would join him and melt into his lap. They would stay there for hours, often in silence, and watch the universe pass by. Familiar constellations began to appear and Ryan knew they were drawing close.

"Not far out now, we are almost there. So this means we've some work to do beforehand."

"What are you getting at, Ryan?" Aviore had learned enough of his ways to be suspicious.

He was determined to show her how to pilot the ship before they reached the Xeronian colony. It was a complicated task, and he knew she would not like it.

"I need you to learn how to pilot her."

"Oh, her, as in your baby here? Why is it this ship is a she, and Gem is a she too? What is it with you males? Oh, and by the way, Gem can land

Page 338

this ship just fine."

"Ah, you still need to know how to pilot this ship."

"Fine then – show me."

Which he did, a number of times. It did not help that her frustration levels climbed every time she failed. She just couldn't remember all the control functions. There were simply too many things to keep track of.

Then he told her about the vaskpar.

It all made sense to her then, how he had learned so much in such a short time. How he had done the seemingly impossible in such a short time. She had heard of similar devices before but found the idea of it somewhat vexing. She was not at ease with having a metallic impostor embedded in her brain. Of course, it didn't help when he suggested she get one.

"I don't want a thing like that in my head. No way."

"You just don't understand it. You can communicate with others, and you have access to all the knowledge..."

"No."

"This will help you do things as well - like pilot this ship. I am going to need you to fly her one day. You know that. We're going to war and anything can happen."

She winced. She would do anything for him. Well, *almost* anything. But he was right about this. She needed help.

"It won't hurt, will it?"

"No."

"They're not going to give me a lobotomy by doing this are they?"

"No. This device sits on top of your cranium and interfaces into your brain. It is not embedded in your brain. You will find that it will help you store and recall information quicker and more accurately. That doesn't sound so bad, does it?"

"No, but I suspect you there is something more to this you aren't telling me."

He laughed.

She liked seeing him laugh. She wrapped her arms around him and kissed him.

They were interrupted by Gem announcing they were in safe communications range of Xeronia. Ryan established a link and exchanged updates.

Long distance reconnaissance probes had picked up something remarkable - a war had started within the Xi-Empire - a civil war. Additional probes were deployed and a Xeronian scout ship was currently being prepped for a mission. Ryan reviewed the new information, excitement building within him.

This was it!

Of course, they needed more information and Xeronia was the intelligence source for their tiny rebel force. What they needed was a communications network that was bullet-proof. He conferred with Tsaurau on this. Xeronian specialists were assigned to the problem immediately.

On final approach to the mountainous red planet, Ryan set up the main monitor so everybody could view the flight. Needless to say, most of their passengers were not impressed with the barren world until they saw the side of the mountain slide away to expose a full starship bay.

On arrival, the crews and passengers of both the *Dancing Queen* and the Signite destroyer needed to go through the required medical quarantine. Everyone was checked thoroughly. The delay cost valuable time, which was yet another problem for the teams to consider.

Ryan's first order of business was to visit his friend with Aviore at his side. Tsaurau attempted his all-too-inhuman smile as he introduced her. He spoke with unprecedented expression and even attempted to exercise some 'human' charm. Ryan enjoyed the spectacle, laughing to himself. Unfortunately, their friendly chatter soon changed to plans of war and Aviore left for a full Xeronian medical work up.

They retired to Ryan's old apartment, requesting the Signite Commander, Tmaurau, and Taldig to join them.

The ad hoc meeting started with a celebratory drink of brandy. Taldig took only a sip before setting his glass down. He preferred vegetable juice. Tmaurau rather enjoyed it and guzzled down his first greedily. Ryan provided his obligatory warning to be careful, as it would sneak up on him.

Once everybody was seated comfortably, Ryan began. "All of you have reviewed my report?"

They nodded. Taldig commented, "I must compliment you, a rather impressive piloting effort on your behalf, Ryan."

"Thank you, Taldig. Your training has more than helped. Gentlemen... if I may call you that?"

They nodded. Translations were always getting in the way anyway.

"I have a problem," he continued. "We are commandeering as many ships as possible in order to provide a healthy force against the Xi-forces. We have a limited number of ships and limited know-how. The people that we free from bondage are not always the ideal military technicians or pilots. The act of assembling this fleet will prove to be a very difficult endeavor and will cost us time and resources. In addition, resources are very scarce, especially the ones needed to provide repairs to our captured ships. These logistical issues need to be solved, otherwise, we are never going to be ready. Here's the rub, this civil war is the key to our success, but it won't last forever. The time to move is now, while our enemy is divided. We have to do the impossible, and quickly."

Ryan looked over to Lortay. "Commander, could you provide some information on your base?"

"Gladly. We have established a military spaceport on a planet in the 63rd-quadrant. I don't know what coordinates you people use, but..."

Tsaurau interrupted. "The recent communications with your computer systems have helped out a great deal, Commander. Please..." He gestured to the fireplace. A holographic image of the constellations appeared above the mantel. The image, finely detailed, displayed hundreds of small colored dots blinking and swirling slowly. "The red dot is us, the blue, your base in the Gamian Quadrant," explained Tsaurau. "You must forgive me, as this is not to true scale."

Lortay recognized the references. "Oh, of course, I see now. This is a tremendous help. Thank you." He continued on, referring to the holographic image intermittently.

"So, in summary, we have at our disposal, approximately two hundred and twenty-five Signite ships. Unfortunately, from our own recent experience, we know they are no match for the Xi-Empire's fleet."

"Your technology is not exceptionally inferior," stated Tmaurau, attempting to convey encouragement.

"Just the same, we will have to upgrade all of their ships," interrupted Ryan.

"You may note that previous patrolling of the Gaminan Quadrant was very heavy, but this has changed since the start of the Xi-Empire internal conflict," commented Taldig.

"I am willing to form a group to help your technicians," offered Tmaurau.

"Indeed, I'm sure things have changed," stated Tsaurau, "But the possibility of exposure is still very prevalent. Father, you do realize that your members must volunteer for such a role? This may be quite dangerous."

"Yes, Tsaurau. My engineers are an eager lot. They desire some excitement. I expect we will need to refuse some requests."

"Thank you," said Lortay. "We welcome all the help we can get."

"Before continuing, may I recommend two other members attend this meeting, Ryan?" asked Taldig.

"Of course, who do you have in mind?" Ryan asked.

"Wharsoff and Gor. We have need of representatives for the Showmish and the Brogs."

"Of course, my oversight. Invite them in, please," agreed Ryan. "The more, the merrier."

Taldig took the floor. "We can operate two central spaceports: the Signite base and here. We'll try to keep a good balance of trained personnel on both ports. Ships will be shuttled to either base for repair after they're captured, depending, of course, on their proximity."

"This will also raise the risk of being discovered," offered Tsaurau. "The council must agree to such a measure."

"And we're going to be spread very thin," commented Ryan, pessimistically. "We'll need to bolster base defenses and have emergency escape vessels parked at each base, just in case."

"There are other issues, as well," added Tsaurau. "For instance, the projected influx of escapees from captured vessels will pose a very real burden on the hosting infrastructure. These victims will need medical attention, food, clothing and a host of other resources."

"In addition," added Taldig, "we must establish an effective sensory network to provide adequate tracings for intelligence gathering on enemy activity."

"Yes, we need to build that network as soon as possible. I also propose each of our ships be outfitted with some sort of tracing scanner jamming device," offered Ryan.

"We do not have such a device," returned Tmaurau.

"Then we need to invent one," replied Ryan flatly.

Just then the doors opened and the two new members arrived. The Brog, named Gor, stepped in first. The group moved to allow him space, then Wharsoff followed.

"Hello, Commander Ryan James," hissed Wharsoff. Gor followed with a grunt.

"It is good to see you are both doing well. Would you like some brandy?"

"No thank you, it does not agree with my palate," replied Wharsoff.

Gor declined with a tentacle wave. Ryan had wondered if the Brog could even drink.

Just as well. More for him, if Tsaurau didn't drink all of it first.

He brought the two aliens up to speed. Surprisingly, it was Gor who spoke up once the true scope of the issues were explained. His guttural snorts and whistles came out in a delayed dance of sounds and gestures.

"We have a functioning base. Our technologies do not match, but we overcome."

"How did you manage to keep a base hidden and operational for so long?" asked Ryan.

"Through the years, after the Great War, we had made an arrangement with the filth. We gave them something and they stopped their constant scrounging."

"An arrangement?"

The Brog growled, his way of laughing. "We grow a type of plant and keep them in supply, and they leave us alone. It is but a weed and grows naturally between the ice layers. But they do not know that."

A drug more than likely thought Ryan to himself. Probably an arrangement made without the Emperor's official signature. "Where is this base - on Grak?"

"No, it is on a moon in our system, beneath the surface. It is hidden very well. The filth found our others but they could not find that one. We have only a small count of ships that are spaceworthy. They are very old and are no match for the filth. We need your help to make the filth feel good fear."

"You will have it," granted Ryan.

Wharsoff spoke up. "I regret to say, we no longer have such facilities or technology left to offer."

Ryan noticed he had his stubby arms crossed - a Showmish demonstration of shame. "Wharsoff, your people have helped out a great deal already. The Showmish are noble warriors."

"The personnel problem remains paramount," interrupted Tsaurau. "A place is required where members of all races can be trained for combat. At the same time, there must be an availability of supporting infrastructure. One of the most important requirements of such a base is its ability to avoid detection by the Xi-Empire for an indefinite period of time, and remain functioning effectively in the event of an interruption of supplies."

"We will need to find something that will work for us."

"This base would have to be independent and self-sustaining, mobile perhaps, and equipped with adequate weaponry for protection," hinted Tmaurau. "Perhaps a compliment of fighting vessels, as well. Would access to over a hundred retired warships interest you?"

"Of course!" Ryan exclaimed. "The ships within the Maskaffa Spider!"

Taldig interjected, "We were instructed not to board the mothership by Tseman. I believe it would be unwise to consider that option at this time."

Ryan heard a persistence in Taldig's voice that was highly unlike him. But the suggestion remained a good one. "What's this mothership?" he inquired.

"It is a very large vessel constructed by the Ancient Ones, comparable in size to 10 Xi-Empire cruisers at the very least."

Ryan was excited at the prospect. "Can we get it operational?"

"It is too dangerous, there are too many unknowns," retorted Taldig again. "Tseman does not provide idle warnings, there is a reason for her request."

"Maybe so, but we must consider all options!" scoffed Tmaurau. "We cannot be afraid of shadows within the hulk of an abandoned vessel. You know as well as I that this vessel presents a perfect solution to the problems we have mentioned."

Ryan remembered the damage to the *War Spritzer* - signs of a powerful and incredibly fast creature.

That must be what the two older Xeronians were concerned about - something incredibly dangerous.

"I recall some evidence of an alien life-form on board the *War Spritzer*. Is that the danger, Taldig?"

"I cannot say with certainty," he replied grudgingly.

Ryan continued on. "Either way, it's been over a thousand years, and this vessel is exactly what we need."

Silently, he put a question to Gem, asking her to dig up every piece of information on the creature. The investigation teams might have found more information since he had left.

"Let us not conjecture," offered Tsaurau. "I propose we bring all of this information to the council and await suggestions. We will ask Tseman what precisely her concern is."

"Fair enough, Tsaurau, please arrange it with the Elders."

The small group broke apart slowly. Ryan and Tsaurau waited for everyone to clear out before he topped up both their glasses, once again.

"You are beginning to like this stuff, old friend."

"We synthesize alcohol differently than humans. It is present naturally in many of our fruit genus."

"Oh, well, OK then. On a more serious note, I feel like we're dragging in the mud. This civil war is a gift that we cannot pass up. We must begin attacking Xi-Empire bases soon."

"Perhaps you are approaching this problem from the wrong direction."

"What are you suggesting?"

"The one who wins in a conflict of brute force is the one who has the most force available at his disposal."

"OK, I'll agree to that. So where does that put us?"

"If this is the case, we must find the superior force that will work against the Xilozaks."

"What are you leading at - biological warfare?"

"Such a weapon could be deployed to affect a large portion of the population in one single coordinated effort. There are, however, the moral arguments of killing non-military citizens."

"Well, Tsaurau, the argument is simple. If the act of destroying the enemy makes you worse than them, then you have become them, haven't you? How can you justify yourself, then?"

"I certainly understand the moral dilemma. I wanted to understand your position."

"Consider me officially on the fence. I wear too many scars."

"Then you feel you can justify such an action?"

Ryan changed the subject, irritated at his friend's line of questioning.

"Tell me, what was Taldig so worried about?"

"I am not sure. Tseman's words should not be considered lightly."

"Do you know what her concern is?"

"I do not know. We must ask Tseman."

They walked out into the brightly lit corridor. Ryan squinted.

"You realize this mothership could be the answer to a number of our problems."

"I do comprehend the nuances of the situation."

"If we go out there and get it, I'll guarantee you one thing."

"What is that, Ryan?" Tsaurau was intrigued.

"The lights will not be set so damned bright."

* * *

They met up with Aviore in the medical center. The doctors had completed their recovery work on her jaw.

"Looks like they've given me the A-OK," she reported perkily. "Apparently you do good work, Doctor Ryan James."

"Thank you, and you make a good patient," he kidded back.

"You have requested a vaskpar implant for her?" Tsaurau inquired more for confirmation than anything else.

"Yes. Can you do it?"

"I assume you have already discussed all implications involving the surgery?"

"Yes and no."

Aviore frowned. "What implications?"

"There are always possibilities that things will not go exactly to plan," Ryan replied, in his own self-defense.

"Like?"

"Things go wrong, could result in anything ranging from insanity to death, but our Xeronian friends are experts in this field. They didn't make a mistake on me."

"Are you sure?" Aviore answered back coyly. "Just tell me, again, why I need this thing."

"Because you're my backup. Unless you're a bloody genius, there's no way you're going to learn everything you need to know before we move out on our next mission."

She took a moment to respond. "Fine. Let's just get it over with."

"I have already conferred with the medical team about your request. They will be able to do the operation tomorrow."

"Tomorrow! How? Have you already constructed her vaskpar?"

"We have constructed many, although they are not exact replicas of your unit. Your version had modifications that introduced additional risks with interfacing. We cannot justify such modifications with others."

"Oh. So, I was the guinea pig? No need to expose anyone else to insanity or mental breakdown."

"The modifications to your unit were necessary due to the time constraints and extended transfer rate saturation."

"Of course. There you go, Aviore. They inserted an experimental unit into my brain and they didn't even bugger it up. Your unit will be plain-jane vanilla. That should make you feel better about the whole thing."

"Well, it does help, but I'll feel better about the whole thing once it's all over."

He pulled her into a hug. "Don't worry. I trust them implicitly."

"I forgot to mention. Your fellow humans have been asking about you. I am sure they would like to see you."

"Oh yes, my fellow Earthlings." Ryan chuckled. "They've all been sterilized I assume, and allowed to move about freely?"

"Yes. They have proven a bit... troublesome. They tend to explore areas where they should exercise more caution."

"Typical," laughed Ryan. "I feel like a walk. How about a field trip?"

Aviore smiled. "Sounds great."

* * *

McClary was the first to spot them when they turned the corner. He announced their arrival in his familiar Scottish tone. "I believe our hero has arrived!" He jumped ahead to become first in line to provide a warm handshake. "Good to see you made it back, lad. I was beginning to fear the worst."

"Well, I am back, and the worst didn't happen." He turned their attention to Aviore. "Meet my future wife, ladies and gentlemen."

They acknowledged her with friendly nods and the odd hello. One of the women gave her a warm hug. "You are a lucky girl. You have the catch of the galaxy."

"So, you've decided to take the big plunge, my boy," exclaimed McClary, his eyes twinkling.

"Don't do it!" laughed Smith, joining in on the fun.

Ryan smiled, he looked over at Aviore. She was biting her lip, and a single tear was rolling down her cheek.

"What did I say?"

"I love you, Ryan James," she said to him softly, "I just didn't know you wished to marry."

"Oh. Um. It's just an Earth custom. I assumed you would be fine with it. Well, what do you think? It's a yes, right?"

"Of course," she sniffled, a bright smile pushed away her tears. "As you can tell, I certainly understand the meaning of this custom of yours. And yes, we have a similar one on Signus. I gather this is your form of a proposal?"

"I ah. Yes, I guess I should have made it more formal?" fumbled Ryan.

She only laughed. "Yes, I will be your wife, Ryan James."

They kissed – a little more passionately than normal.

The small group of humans cheered.

"Well, we were going on a tour," announced Ryan. "If anyone else is interested. Doesn't matter if you've seen it before. I understand more than a few of you have been itching to get out of your sanctioned areas."

The Native American, the one the group they had called Geronimo, approached Ryan and held out his hand.

"I am indebted to you," he said quietly. "I am Kanook." His grip was firm and sure.

"You've recovered well, I see."

"I understand you have requested volunteers. I tell you now, I will join you and fight by your side, and I will not accept any form of refusal."

"You won't get one, am proud to have your help."

"And what about me, lad? I did lay out that there offer, prior. You did bother to think about it, didn't ya?"

"Of course I did. This applies to every last one of you. If you wish to join me, you're welcome. If you don't - that's fine too. But I'm afraid a trip to Earth right now is still out of the question. I'm sorry."

Low murmurs emanated from the small crowd. Faces turned away. Some did not want to share their disappointment.

"What are we waiting for? Let's go on this grand tour!" Aviore stated enthusiastically, at the same time taking Ryan by the arm. The group started off, those with dashed hopes falling into step last. The tour, if anything, took all of their minds off their grim reality, if only for a short time.

* * *

Ryan and Aviore married that evening. The ceremony was short and quiet. Captain Lortay gave the official sermon, standing on the ramp of the *Dancing Queen*. Tsaurau was best man, and McClary gave away the bride. Ziggy was the ring bearer.

A large portion of the colony managed to cram into the starship bay - a strange array of Humans, Signites, Showmish, Brogs, and Xeronians to witness the earthly custom.

Aviore wore a dress that Ziggy had secretly manufactured on the trip back to Xeronia. He had done an incredibly good job considering the limited information Ryan had supplied.

He couldn't take his eyes off her, to him she was absolutely radiant.

At the end of the reading, they sealed their marriage with a long, passionate kiss. The Humans and Signites cheered, the Showmish hissed, the Brogs purred, and the Xeronians flooded the Par with their shared kind thoughts.

When the two turned to face the crowd, Ryan heard a familiar voice in the back of his mind - a voice of a friend.

"Congratulations, Captain Ryan James."

"Thanks, Gem."

The celebration came afterward. It was an ad hoc deal, thrown together in no less than an hour by a collection of volunteers, mostly human, and a few Xeronian.

People of mixed races intermingled and talked, aliens no longer.

Ryan couldn't believe it. It all seemed to be moving so fast. His freedom, a pilot of a starship, and a wife - a beautiful, complicated woman from another star system.

Was this all a dream?

She looked up from her discussion with Wharsoff and smiled.

He felt like he was going to wake up any second and realize that he was laying half-dead, immersed in a cold puddle, mining machines rumbling by.

"Ryan, are you OK?"

She wrapped her arms around him and pulled him down to kiss her.

"You're real, right? This is real?"

"Yes, this is. I know what you're thinking. That you don't deserve to be happy. I've asked myself the same thing so many times. No, we're not moving too fast. We're not. We are living. We are seizing the moments. We have to make up for all the lost time." She stared into his eyes. "I am real and you aren't dreaming."

The party broke up in a few hours. Ryan and Aviore escaped into the *Dancing Queen*, alone.

"Finally, the ship to ourselves."

"You are quite the hermit, aren't you?"

"Let's go on a little trip, just you and I."

He relayed his intentions to the Xeronian docking steward. The bay doors slid open to the dusty winds outside. Ryan fired up the *Dancing Queen* and brought her out slowly. Once safely positioned, he pointed the nose up and shot up into the night sky. The winds and the dust fell away to a silent darkness, interrupted by a million white specs called stars. He hit the controls to retract the ceramic-quartz shielding fully.

The cockpit was bathed in a soft, white light.

He looked over. She sat beside him in the co-pilot's chair, eyes twinkling.

"Still think this is a dream? The first time you took me up here that's when I knew that I wasn't dreaming. I knew I wasn't just imagining this new life while I slowly died in that dingy slaver cell. No dream can make these stars. Your mind can't create this clarity of detail." She smiled warmly, softly. "You see?"

He did. *God, he loved her.*

"Aviore, no matter what happens, I'll love you forever."

She leaned over, her beautiful face radiating the colored starlight, and placed her hand softly on his cheek. "Till death do us part then, Ryan James."

She slid over to nestle in his arms.

"I know this can't last forever. I can't help but feel something bad is coming."

He shivered.

"Shhh... Live now. No one can take this, what is now, away from you. And this can last forever. All you need to do is remember it."

He held her quietly. They gazed at the beauty around them, and for a moment they felt a true peace.

For the moment.

"Captain, you are requested to join Tsaurau in the Chamber of the Elders," interrupted Gem.

"Damn it. It's time for the Xeronian Council meeting. They always seem to have this unique sense of timing. We have to go back down."

"The good things never seem to last long enough, do they?"

"No, they don't. You realize they'll be prepping you for the operation shortly. Tell me you are you ready for this?"

"I will be fine," she replied confidently. "So I guess we have no time at all to consummate our marriage?" She moved suggestively over him. "You think they could wait a few more minutes?"

They kissed passionately.

They arrived in dock slightly later than planned.

* * *

13. The Strengthening

Lortay, McClary, Wharsoff, Gor, and all the members of both Xeronian councils were already present. All heads turned when Ryan came in.

"Sorry, I ah... go ahead, continue."

Tseman's old eyes gave a twinkle of amusement. "Ryan," she said, "you have done well. Events have put into motion a greater destiny that awaits us all." Her mysterious old voice demanded the attention of all of them.

"Elder Tseman," he addressed her respectfully, bowing slightly. "As you must already know, the Xi-Empire has fallen into civil war. This is our chance to move. We need to make plans, cultivate ideas on how to attack when they're weakest."

He waited for her to respond. But she was not one to answer quickly, be it her age, or her own ponderous wisdom that held her back.

"You must ask yourself man-from-Earth: What is your purpose? When does the value of life decline? These questions hang heavy on the soul, far beyond one's death and regrets can slowly tear one apart. There are those that can disassociate from others, stand apart and claim oneself superior. But you are not that way, are you, Ryan James? There will come a time when you must look inward, and ask: Who do you serve? It is the authentic you who must answer, for there is no one else who can."

What could she possibly be talking about? She sounded like the Sisters-of-Soom with this line of questions. He had a hard enough time sorting out Tsaurau sometimes, let along these Elders.

"Not quite following you on all this. What, exactly, is your meaning?"

"It is what you make it, Ryan," she replied. "Time will explain, much more effectively than I can aspire to. Reflect upon my words. You need to consider what you have not already."

She stood up slowly, her brethren followed suit. "We can serve no further purpose here. Do what must be done, ask of my people, ask of our allies, but only do what must be done."

They left, filing out quietly behind the massive semicircular bench. Their bent gray forms faded into the darkness like ghosts.

Such a damned penchant for the theatrical - answering questions with questions. Do only what must be done.

"Tseman," Ryan called after her. "I need an answer I can understand."

But she was gone.

"She has answered your questions," stated Taldig, the only remaining Elder.

"How?"

Taldig only blinked his large, glassy, dark eyes, providing more of an impassive response than an answer.

"Great." He took a deep breath. *This was going nowhere.*

Tsaurau took the floor, effectively seizing command of the meeting. "Work is to be done. Decisions must be made. Issues have been put forward of which we currently have no resolution. I encourage all to open the discussion. Plans must be formulated."

Troyka, the head of engineering, offered some good news. "I am obliged to announce that we have established a model for an acceptable communications network."

"How soon can it be implemented?" asked Ryan.

"It is necessary to upgrade the communications systems of all ships, all nodes, that are to be integrated into the network. And we must deploy a large number of communications relay probes."

"Right," stated Ryan. "We'll need to outfit all our ships, and since our priority is also improving the surveillance on our enemy, to integrate this system into our probes and relays throughout the network."

"That," stated Taldig, "requires reconnaissance vessels that are able to move about undetected by the Xi-Fleet. That includes surveilling Xilo Prime Quadrant. Xilo's security tracing perimeters are unparalleled. Given their heightened alert status, I fear we may not be able to successfully infiltrate their system."

"The ability to remain undetected by Xi-Empire's tracing scanners is not impossible," commented one of the council members.

It was Tsaurau's cue, as he was head of sciences. "Yes, such a feat is not impossible. However to move in very close, and maintain position for an effective duration, is difficult. Such a vessel must undergo the continuous scrutiny of continuous scans. We have looked into the problem. Some consider such an achievement to be virtually impossible. We will not surrender so easily. In the meantime, we have discovered an interim solution."

"What's that?"

"The actual physical design of the ship plays a large role in this problem. A very small ship, with confined living quarters, can be very successful."

Wharsoff stepped ahead. "Perhaps we assign these missions to the race best equipped to deal with limited space, as this is a collaborative effort."

Gor growled. "The Narkusites would readily join our cause, as well as the Domeheads."

The Strengthening

"Yes, you are right my friend," hissed Wharsoff. "Unfortunately, the Narkusites are but a few now. Alas, they are almost extinct - they were one of the first victims of the Xi-Empire. It is said one cannot even find a Narkusite on Ikaire. Their greatest remaining population resides only on Xilo itself, as generational slave descendants."

"Gor, who are the domeheads?" asked Ryan.

"The Nuboks," corrected Wharsoff. "They do not appreciate being referred to as domeheads. It is true they are of small stature, and their heads are somewhat domed shaped..."

"Yes, domeheads," interrupted Gor.

Wharsoff hissed. "They would be ideal for travel in a compact vessel."

"Have we made contact with any of these Nuboks?"

"We had a very good trading relationship with them," announced Wharsoff with pride, tongue forking out in swooping circles. "But that was before the war."

"Good. Wharsoff you are in charge of opening communications with them, and any other known races. I'll want a representative for each one here, on this base, as soon as possible."

"There remains the question – where shall we find the required starships, if we cannot assume them," Taldig announced.

Ryan held his tongue, waiting to see if anyone would mention the ships within the Maskaffa.

"I have had a recent communication from my base," announced Lortay. "We have had 12 more ships brought in, in as many days, by the Showmish Captains. There are promises of many more. Apparently, the civil war has caused an unprecedented retraction of the Xi-Empire fleet patrols. Xi-traders have been left defenseless."

Ryan expected as much, but he did not want the group to be overly optimistic. The tide of civil war could cease as quickly as it had started.

"Yes, as I said before, we have an opportunity. I cannot stress enough, however, that this bit of luck will not last indefinitely. I want the word spread. We must become more aggressive. Seize everything and anything we can get our hands on. Then we move on the fringe planets, take what we can there. That means offensive disabling of Xi-colonies."

He glanced over to Lortay. "Lortay, your communications are not secure. No further transmissions until we upgrade to the Xeronian system. All messages must be sent via messenger until the network is up."

Tmaurau added, "I have already inspected the Signite ship. If its construction is typical of the other Signite vessels, refitting time for adaptive shielding, improved weapons and drive systems will be minimal. Once I have finished at the Signite base, I will travel to the Brog moon. I am not familiar with their technology, and so, I cannot estimate refitting time on their vessels."

Tsaurau was quick to dispute his new offer. "Father, are you sure? Perhaps your younger apprentices can..."

"Nonsense. I shall lead the engineering parties myself. We are at war, my son. If the stress kills me, so be it. I shall die honorably, not as a Xi-Empire slave."

The aggressive words shocked the Xeronian crowd. The Par flooded with a disarray of concern. One awareness resounded ever so strongly, gaining momentum: they were at war as war had arrived.

Ryan pulled away from the Par, as their realization seemed almost painful. He had a hard time understanding them as it was. Their thoughts bleeding into his mind through the Par was disassociating enough. *It was all too alien.*

"Thank you, Tmaurau."

Eyes turned toward him. Eyes full of concern, and of fear. "Wars are won as battles are won. Battles are won through strategy, logistics, weapons, and most importantly, sheer willpower. Every step a person takes to help this movement is a step toward victory. Even with the Xi-Empire overmatching us in numbers, we still have superior technology, because of our Xeronian allies."

"This will be a war of skill, as well as technology," Taldig proclaimed. "The training of the new crews will decide the outcome of the battles. They must be trained to be properly prepared."

"We have a training base set up already, with ample room for more recruits," proposed Lortay. "But we cannot undermine our training program by flooding it with those requiring general combat training. I suggest the Xeronian and Signite tactical experts join forces and design a comprehensive and focused program. Compartmentalize the effort."

"Your logic is sound. Such a venture will be very effective," Taldig agreed.

"Which again leads us back to the problem of people," Ryan said, unconsciously verbalizing his thoughts. Attention turned to him. "We must have starship pilots, technicians, people with advanced knowledge and skills. Hard to find. They do not grow on trees."

"I do not understand the relevance to trees, Ryan," Tsaurau stated. "This comparison is quite confusing. Botanists are definitely a requirement for managing a ship's food management system."

"No. No. Don't be so damned literal. I just expect we won't have enough knowledgeable, educated people."

"Xeronians have much knowledge and skill. I am sure they can teach and we will learn. Then we will become the teachers," added Wharsoff.

"We cannot join you in your war vessels. We are not a violent race. We cannot control the machines of war."

"Do you think you are better than us!" growled Gor.

"Hold!" yelled Ryan, attempting to squelch the Brog's inflammatory thunder. "The Xeronians are my friends. What you see around you are the only known survivors of their entire race. They cannot afford to lose even one of their people. There are many of us. We do not fear our own extinction if we die. Not even you, Gor, can say that your death will mark the end of the Brogs."

"Everyone does their part. The Xeronians are helping. They have offered to train us, to teach us, even provide us the means to protect ourselves and fight back. We are all allies to the core, am I clear?"

Gor grunted an acknowledgment.

"Commander," Wharsoff spoke, addressing him respectfully in his newly assigned title. "The problem may not be as bad as you think. The Narkusites, Brogs, Nuboks, and Signites were all once proud space-faring peoples. This is just a logistical matter of coordination of effort. You will find that freeing those enslaved will provide us the resources we require."

"Thank you for your optimism, Wharsoff. However, to accomplish this, we need to free our brethren. The next question is - do we have enough space in our two bases to train and feed these people?"

"We do not have any idea of the numbers of individuals. Any estimate would be too premature," suggested Tsaurau.

"Fine," stated Ryan. "We'll cross that bridge when we come to it. As of this moment, we start putting our plans into place. Collect your ideas, no matter how small, or unimportant - everything counts. Let's take a break and reconvene shortly."

Tsaurau approached Ryan. "You have been invited to talk with the Eldest. It is unusual for Tseman to see her subjects out of the council chambers."

"Yes, I sort of figured that. You're going to have to show me where she is. I'm afraid her location is not within the Par's records."

Tsaurau responded with a matter-of-factly, "I know."

On the way to Tseman's quarters, Tsaurau seemed unusually brisk, his movements stiff and deliberate.

Something was troubling him.

Ryan quietly waited for him to divulge his problem, as it was a Xeronian custom to respect one's silence.

"Ryan, we have found a small inconsistency in your recent medical examination. We need to verify that this aberration truly exists, or if we are experiencing problems with our equipment."

"What kind of inconsistency?"

"We may have discovered a degenerative condition within the central muscle controlling your circulatory system - I believe you call this organ the heart."

"What's wrong with my heart?"

"I do not wish to worry you. My announcement is unsubstantiated. More tests are required."

"Really, Tsaurau, I find that hard to believe. Your people's medical examinations are thorough, results of every test reviewed meticulously. This much I know - firsthand. So don't be offended if I find your unsubstantiated findings substantial. What's wrong with my heart?"

"We believe certain compounds ingested during your period of slavery may be having latent adverse effects on your internal organs, your heart in particular."

"Can your people do anything about this?"

"Surgery is required. Re-constructive grafts must be cultured. This takes time and the corrective procedures will have a dramatic effect on your body. You must allot for adequate recovery time."

"That's the one thing I cannot afford, my friend, time."

They arrived at the entrance to the Elder Tseman's quarters. Two large, ominous, white and gray-veined granite doors blocked their way. Tsaurau announced their presence over the Par, following Xeronian protocol.

He looked back at his Earthman friend. "Please reconsider. We believe the degradation is accelerating. You may be in very real peril."

Ryan found the choice of words amusing. In peril - now that *was* funny.

"Don't worry so much, Tsaurau. After all, the Xi-Empire might take care of this little problem for me."

The doors opened, swinging inward into Tseman's quarters without a sound. The room was dark in comparison to the standard Xeronian's. The Elder's affinity for bright light must dim with age. They stepped in, Tsaurau taking the lead. Ryan gave the area an inspecting sweep with his eyes. The walls were bare rock, the floor, a black gloss of midnight. There were no ornaments, no multi-dimensional art, no appeasing furniture. Only two fountains positioned in the center of the room. Water shot upwards toward the ceiling and fell back down into small wading pools at the base of each fountain. Something was out of place. It took a few moments to register in Ryan's mind. The noise of lapping water was hushed, somehow suppressed to a whisper.

Seated between the two fountains, on a large, red, velvety pillow, was the familiar outline of Tseman. Her head was tilted back, her face to the ceiling, her eyes closed. She had to be meditating.

They stood there for minutes. Ryan checked her, then Tsaurau, then her. *Couldn't she tell we were here? It would probably be a little too rude to clear his throat or something.*

When she opened her eyes, Ryan almost jumped. She was staring at them, but she didn't seem to see them. It made Ryan's hair on the back of his neck stand up.

Then she was back, back to reality from wherever she had been.

"Join me," she said quietly, beckoning with a wiry limb. "Sit."

The two lowered themselves onto the hard floor, into a cross-legged position.

"I have reached out beyond. I have found what I did not wish to find... You intend to claim the mothership within the Maskaffa."

"Yes," stated Ryan.

She watched him with those eerie penetrating black eyes. Tsaurau nudged him in the ribs.

Apparently, his answer was not required.

She glanced over to Tsaurau. "You cannot claim such a prize without a price." Her old body literally creaked as she shifted her weight on the pillow. "I must repeat a story once told to me when I was a child. It is the truth about the Maskaffa spider. The truth about the Flukken war, beyond the data contained within the libraries."

"There were once a people called the Flukkens, of the planet Tolum. The Flukkens had achieved many great things in their time, but not without sacrifice. Their science, their technology, their vast knowledge, had all been accelerated prematurely. They obtained wisdom without earning it. You see, the Ancient Ones had befriended them, and with mistaken good intent, had decided to help them. They adopted this race, acted as a sponsor for them, and cleared barriers to allow them relations with other races."

"Inevitably, internal conflict arose within their peoples. It spread to their colonies like a disease, escalating to the atrocity of war. All Flukkens were pulled into this dissension, as none could see through their own barbarity. Their lives, filled with such passion of what one could only label as religious ideals, drove them with an unbridled insanity. "

"This war distressed the Ancient Ones. They offered to help in negotiating a peace, to function as arbitrators. A special envoy was sent to Tolum. Part of this small fleet included the vessel we call the mothership."

"Unfortunately, their arrival was misinterpreted as a threat. The Flukkens, overcome with fear and distrust, struck out at them in reflex. The Ancient Ones retreated to the safety of the Maskaffa Spider. But they did not abandon their purpose. One lone ambassador returned to Tolum.

The Flukkens, realizing what they had done, were profusely apologetic. That was the foothold needed to allow their ambassador to begin the negotiations."

She stopped, out of wind, her breathing short and raspy. Ryan went to stand up, to offer help, but she held up her hand, motioning him back down. "I am very old, Ryan James. Time takes its toll, the body loses strength, it cannot be stopped."

She continued on, her breathing labored but stable. "The Flukkens were accomplished biologists, in such a context that all of their other technologies paled in comparison. A Flukken researcher, a very brilliant and confused individual, led his team to develop a new weapon - a new and incredibly dangerous life-form. It exceeded their expectations in its ability to kill, including their ability to control it."

Her dark eyes roamed, mesmerizing, beckoning. Ryan could feel himself being pulled into them, back to a world of death. Visions of pain, confusion, fear - so great it wrenched at him, jerking into one twisted, sickening moment. He looked away.

"Yes, so you see, since they were not able to control this creature, it spread like a plague throughout their planet. Reproducing at an incredible rate, its offspring infiltrated every continent. There was nowhere to retreat. This weapon did not choose sides, did not follow direction, it knew only how to kill and consume, and so it slaughtered ceaselessly, decimating the population, unchecked."

"Truly a tragedy," Ryan acknowledged.

"The greatest tragedy of all was that their civil war had finally ceased. A peace agreement had been successfully brokered by the Ancient Ones. They had already initiated the first phase of operational peace through the disarmament and reduction of war vessels. At the time of the breakout, warships of the Flukken fleet were being taxied into the Maskaffa Spider for decommissioning. The creature managed to find its way into space in very short time, infesting the escaping vessels from Tolum, which unknowingly carried the deadly cargo. Panicked captains issued distress calls, and in turn, their rescue ships became infested. The creatures spread from ship to ship, eventually reaching Ancient Ones' vessels. An emergency force was dispatched to their aid. The Ancient Ones', regiment arrived in time to rescue some of the Flukken population, and some of their crew members, but they were too late for most. It is rumored that there are ships adrift inside the Maskaffa Spider that contain these creatures to this very day."

"Tseman, correct me if I am wrong, but that must be well over a thousand years ago," commented Ryan. "They can't still be alive."

"Time is a strange thing. A thousand years to some is but a blink of an eye to others. Who is to say for sure?"

A chill ran up his spine. This spooky talk made him uncomfortable.

"Why so secretive?"

"Knowledge can be dangerous. From stories come rumors, from rumors, come seekers. Things are often better forgotten."

A long silence followed. The old Xeronian woman shifted her weight slowly, her eyes now dimmed with sadness. "What you must understand, is that millions of lives fell prey to these creatures. The Ancient Ones attempted to save them, but it was in vain. They found Tolum teeming with these monsters, and all native life obliterated. The creatures had resorted to feeding upon themselves. The Ancients, in disgust, incinerated the surface of Tolum, eliminating any threat of further contamination, but in the process making Tolum inhabitable."

Ryan glanced over to Tsaurau. The Xeronians face was typically placid, but he could sense the alien had withdrawn within himself. He had even removed himself from the Par. Ryan understood why. It would not do to share such horrors with others.

He contemplated the grim tale. A whole planet wiped out - like Xeronia, lost with so many lives. It was unfathomable.

"But you said they saved the Flukkens didn't they, and what of their colonies?"

"Yes, some of the population survived, but their hardships were not over for them. Their colonies suffered diseases and catastrophes. Death followed them with an insatiable desire. Their population faded soul after soul. Within a few centuries, a once proud flourishing people were reduced to only memories."

"Everyone?"

"The Flukkens are lost to time."

"What do you remember of these engineered creatures?"

"What about the Ancients? What did they do to combat this life-form? How did they kill it?"

Tseman coughed, her body racked with the strain. "I am sorry. It was so long ago. My memory is compromised. It may be, the creature has a soft underbelly, such as the nature of things. It is also possible, by my recollection, these monstrosities moved so quickly they would seem only a blur to our sight and senses. They procreate by injecting their eggs into its victims, or any other biological matter. In a matter of hours the eggs turn into larva insectum, within days they would grow to a formidable size. They are creatures of consumption. Their metabolism remains elevated until all food sources around them are depleted. In their own way, these creatures are slaves, that is, to their obsession to consume."

"Yes, fitting they would die of starvation," Ryan sounded off more to himself than the others.

Old Xeronian's eyes again came to focus on him. "Perhaps so. That is all I can provide. The old ones from that time have become silent. I am the only one who remembers the truth, and now you know."

"Then I thank you, Tseman."

"Good luck, Commander," she whispered, and quietly pulled herself into a more rigid posture, resuming her trance-like state.

Ryan and Tsaurau got up and bowed respectfully before leaving. Once outside, they resumed conversation.

"Before you say anything, you do realize these retired warships are key to our success, regardless of any possible risk," stated Ryan.

"Yes, I realize this, and yes, we should be able to recommission these ships once again," replied Tsaurau.

"So, we'll exercise necessary precautions and get those ships."

"Yes. We will."

"Then the matter is decided. More importantly, can you tell me of Aviore's status?"

"We must proceed to the medical area. They are ready, but Aviore has insisted that you be there before they begin."

The walk was quick, Ryan's mind distracted as he attempted to suppress his own dark thoughts.

This will go well.

Aviore smiled at them as they arrived. "We've been waiting for you."

"I heard. How are you doing?"

"I'm as ready as I'll ever be. I hope this doesn't hurt too much."

Ryan chuckled, "Considering what you've been through, this will be a pinch."

He held her hand throughout the procedure. Everything went smoothly, which was not surprising, considering the caliber of the medical team.

* * *

A few from Earth decided to join the ranks. A few of these were brave enough to follow Aviore's example and request a vaskpar implant. Those volunteers were given an accelerated program of training. Ryan oversaw the group's development, which included Aviore. Notwithstanding, she was, of course, his favorite student. Unique in many ways, her hunger for knowledge grew as her vaskpar evolved. It was not long before she mastered the *Dancing Queen's* becoming a proficient pilot.

Gem was also quite happy that she had a new friend. She learned tricks from Aviore to contest Ryan's wit. The resulting humor helped keep all of them sane. This was a welcomed side-effect as captured ships began arriving in noticeable numbers. The Showmish captains had joined forces with the Brogs and Nuboks. Wharsoff coordinated the efforts to secure each sector, maintaining an organization of small cellular forces, each with a focused set of goals. Xeronian technology was applied to the communication network, and soon relay points and surveillance nodes were being deployed to every quadrant of the explored galaxy.

Intelligence information flooded in, targets identified, and enemy vessels seized. With each ship, cargo and slaves were liberated, and their crews shipped to prison camps on Signus. More and more recruits flooded in, all wishing to join the growing armada.

Seven races had joined the cause to date: Signites, Showmish, Brogs, Nuboks, Narkusites, Krelps, Xeronians, and of course, Earthlings. The Krelps were the most recent addition. They required an atmosphere of nitrogen dioxide, methane, sulfur dioxide and carbon monoxide at a mixture highly poisonous to humans. Their environment suits allowed them to intermingle with others and effectively hid their appearance. Very few had seen them in their natural state, with the exception of Aviore. She was, after all, one of the few resident linguistics experts. Her work required her to suit up and enter the Krelp vessels. What she saw initially shocked her. The aliens resembled a very large caterpillar, with skin of gold, laced with dancing lines of white and purple that followed the lateral lines of their body from tip to tip. An array of tentacles shot up from under their 'belly', each narrowing down into three joint-less, opposing muscular fingers at their end.

They were an imposing creature, an adult Krelp easily exceeding the total mass of three or four men. Holding up their tremendous body were six legs, similar to an elephant's, exempting the toes. Their language was based on vibrations, much like the audio vibrations through the air, although they were much more sensitive. Once Aviore managed to establish a baseline for communication, she was able to build an equivalent symbolism. From there she and her team attempted to build a Krelp translator, albeit with limited success. The Krelp's language held meaning, ideas, that were simple but untranslatable. Language was based on perception, and the Krelps' view of the universe was radically different from humans'. Regardless, the translator was successful enough to bridge the gap needed, although crude.

Wharsoff was attempting to oversee the massive organizational problems occurring throughout the multiple bases, but the burden was becoming increasingly difficult, if not impossible. His last report to Ryan made it clear something needed to be done.

Ryan called a general assembly with all leaders currently on base. The first order of business was a simple challenge - assign a name to their movement. A number of ideas were submitted, but Ryan appreciated the most simple and direct: The Galactic Alliance. The next priority was defining the exact organization the Galactic Alliance would implement as its overall structure. Ryan had requested the help of many to pull it together. In essence, this structure was to be the glue that would hold the Alliance together, during and after the war - assuming of course, that they succeeded.

There were to be two arms of the Galactic Alliance, the Council, and the Militia. On the Council, each race had an elected Ambassador, three Trade Ministers, and three Judicators of Galactic Law. All positions were to undergo a re-election process every five years, or three cycles in Galactic time. That rule was put in place to control the very real possibility of corruption. On the Militia side, each race provided three generals, who reported directly to the Commander of the Militia, who would in turn report to the Council. It was a structure defined to manage the true power of the growing militia.

Once Ryan finished and tabled the completed proposal, he wrapped up by explicitly outlining his position as Commander of the Alliance as a transitory one. This started a heated debate, which eventually forced Ryan to accept an honorary title within the organization, post-war. He accepted grudgingly, as he did not feel he was worthy of such a title without extensive experience in war. It did not seem to matter to the members of the assembly. The decision was made, and he was the obvious choice. In the end, everyone was satisfied, if not totally, then partially, and so the Galactic Alliance was born. Its birth marked the beginning of hope to a quiet and vigorous rebellion, which was methodically gathering strength.

Luckily, the Empire and Purists forces had ignored the cries for help from the fringe colonies. Neither had the resources free to investigate the allegations of rebellion. Such news was expected, since all crucial military strength had been withdrawn into the core quadrants. The primary worlds of the Xi-Empire did not, however, realize the full extent or success of the rebellion.

Accurate, authoritative information was difficult to collect in a background of chaos. Collecting statistics on lost merchant and slaverships that wandered out into the fringe systems was all but impossible. Indeed, when such news did filter up to command level, it was often dismissed as mere casualties of war. Such news served little advantage to either party.

* * *

The Galactic Alliance Militia's first significant target was an outer planet in the Gamian quadrant called Gedricka. It was a relatively new docking and ship repair facility for the Xi-Empire fleet, which was now under the ownership of the Xilozak Purist organization, and would prove key in helping the Alliance repair and refit captured vessels.

They planned the raid in phases. The first phase encompassed infiltrating the bases to strategically place bombs on the communications network hubs and the tracing relay centers. Second phase was the assumption of control of as many ships as possible without causing a distraction. Third phase was attack and obliterate – that is, obliterate everything that would serve no value to the Alliance.

Ryan led the ground attack on the spaceport personally, contrary to the disapproval of many of his generals. He found they were not near as difficult to circumvent as his wife, as they eventually compromised. Aviore eventually agreed to follow along with the mission in the *Dancing Queen*, maintaining an acceptable safe distance from the base, on standby in case he needed her.

Multiple teams landed on the spaceport under the cover of darkness, using captured ships and fake clearance identification. They dispersed quickly, their targets known intimately. Ryan led his particular team on a mission to disable the backup sensor array near the spaceport. There were five on the team, two Showmish, McClary and Kanook.

They terminated the guards with stealth and positioned the bombs where they would be most effective. He ordered the group to move up into the forward array tower and came face to face with five Xilozak officers. Ryan killed the first with his disrupter sword and shot another with his blaster. Two others were taken down by Kanook, and McClary took care of the last. Ryan progressed through the tower hastily, Kanook and McClary on his heels. The Showmish took up the rear, covering the entrance.

"What's up my boy? Why this tower?" whispered McClary.

"Let's just say I want to know if they're expecting any new arrivals. Our tracing scans are only so good. This base has an extended range."

They hit the primary control room and made quick work of the inhabitants. Ryan signaled them to fan out and took a second to survey the spaceport through the tower's windows. He could see a few remaining guards shuffling through the maze of landed starships, but that was it.

No surprises so far.

He examined the system consoles, and with Gem's help, managed to pull up an arrival list. "Shit," he exclaimed out loud, rushing to adjust the tracing sensors.

Kanook moved in beside him. "Trouble?"

"Hit that switch over there. We need to initiate a long-range scan."

It took a second for the images to appear on the graphics display. "OK, this is now verified. Boys, looks like we're going to have company."

"What's up, Commander?" asked McClary.

"Just a few destroyers and a couple cruisers, coming in at acroluc."

He checked the tracing scanner image one more time, hoping his interpretation was wrong. In one way that was a remote possibility. The Xi-Empire controls were a mishmash of Txtian and Xilozak equipment. How they ever managed to marry their technology together was beyond him.

"I estimate we have about 10 minutes before the first squadron of the Purist fleet arrives. I expect the majority of the fleet will remain in orbit, but we'll definitely have company down here. It's time we adapt our plans to the new situation."

He issued the orders to the other teams: stop and secure. Whatever number of ships they had seized would be what they were taking. Gem relayed the news to the support teams in orbit using a tight band transmission. The Alliance ships retreated, putting the sun between them and the approaching enemy's vectors. They dispersed on different trajectories to avoid creating a strong tracing signature. Aviore, however, had a different strategy. She landed the *Dancing Queen* in a crater on the nearest moon and shut down her systems to avoid detection.

Within the tower, the tracing scanner image was already coming alive with signals. Voices rang over the tower communications station.

Ryan went to acknowledge. McClary grabbed his arm. "Are you crazy?"

"They need to think everything is OK here. Otherwise, they'll come in fully armed and expecting trouble."

Ryan cleared his throat and acknowledged using his best Xilozak. A few painful seconds later, they acknowledged back.

"Let's get the hell out of here – and quickly."

They were just exiting the tower when the Purist fleet arrived.

The ships flew overhead in a thunderous rumble, shaking the buildings around them. For a brief moment, night turned to day as a dozen Xi-Empire destroyers landed simultaneously on the spaceport's hardtop.

Ryan and his team retreated to cover between the nearby buildings. He chanced one more long-range transmission over his vaskpar.

"Aviore, when you get the chance, get out of here."

He clicked the transmitter one more time.

Nothing. Why didn't she acknowledge? No more time.

A quiet settled over the spaceport once again, until the hatches opened and the ramps dropped. They watched as Xilozaks began to file out of the monstrous ships, noisily growling and spitting out comments to one another. A couple started fighting, bashing and kicking one another. What seemed to pass as officers broke them up only to contend with another fight.

"Damn animals," Ryan commented dryly. He pulled out his portable communicator and switched to an encrypted channel open to each of the boarding teams. All but one had secured their target ship.

He made another visual check. Fleet officers were filing out now, garbed with more colorful and ornate uniforms.

"Commander, we are ready," the last team reported in.

"Good. On my mark, fire the burners and power up your cannon. Get ready to blast the shit out of these Xilozaks and every ship that we haven't seized."

He glanced across the spaceport. Only the stragglers were left now with a handful of officers. His team needed to get to the third ship on the left. They proceeded in pairs, using everything at their disposal as cover. Within minutes they were meters from the entrance. To reach it, however, they were going to be fully exposed.

Ryan, Kanook, and McClary positioned themselves to provide the best defensive cover. Ryan gave the signal and the Showmish dashed ahead, running on all fours, low to the ground, utterly silent, then it was McClary's turn.

A group of Xilozak officers were approaching at a sauntering gait.

Kanook and Ryan pulled back, finding cover behind a collection of storage drums. They were so close now, it felt like he could reach out and touch them. A voice cut through the still night air, giving orders to the others. The group stopped. They passed something amongst them, just like humans would share a smoke.

Why the hell did they have to stop here, anyway?

The sounds of scuffling came from the spaceport's main entrance. The officers turned, distracted - another fight had broken out in the distance.

Kanook nudged Ryan to go, but he waved him on. He had to stay. There was something vaguely familiar about that officer.

Kanook moved like a cat, sprinting silently to the ship's hatch. He slid back into darkness. No one noticed.

Good. Just him left.

The quiet night was shattered as one of the captured destroyers initiated its burner warm-up sequence. The low vibration carried through the night air.

Ryan cursed under his breath.

Who the hell ordered that?

He gave the 'GO' signal to the rest. The other ships fired their burners almost simultaneously in a cacophony of roars.

The Xilozaks began walking in his direction, their attention now focused upon the destroyer powering up behind Ryan. As they passed under an overhead light, Ryan saw something that made his blood turn ice cold.

A long, sharpened disrupter bar swung lazily from his belt as he walked, slapping on his thick leg in a deadly rhythm. He had seen only one Xilozak carry such a weapon – Zorlog.

The big Xilozak must have sensed something was wrong, as he started blasting out angry orders to the other officers. Some of them began to sprint toward the captured ships.

Ryan issued the order to prep the cannon.

Again he peered out. The Xilozak Commander was almost upon him now. He could see Zorlog's snake eyes squinting thin with exasperated puzzlement. The others had the same look about them. Ryan quietly stood up from his cover. Behind him, the destroyer's cannon were pivoting to bear down upon the oncoming group. He stood there with his rifle pointed directly at them, waiting.

Zorlog noticed, but he did not reach for his weapon. He merely stopped to assess the situation.

"Zorlog!" Ryan yelled in Trinarieit. "Remember me, you bastard!"

Some of the officers went for their rifles, but Zorlog waved them still. He stepped closer. Ryan reciprocated, moving into a meager beam of light. He kept his rifle poised and ready.

"You are a Signite?" Zorlog growled in Trinarieit.

"Don't recognize me?" He pulled his hair to the side, revealing an ugly scar on his forehead.

Zorlog's teeth glowed yellowed-white in the darkness, and he laughed so heartily he had to pound his chest.

"You! Yes, slave, I remember you. I should have cut off your head, but I hadn't switched on my disrupter. I lost a few credits on a bet that you would die. But, just the same - I made a healthy profit off your sale."

He laughed again, grabbing his gut.

"What do you want, little Earthman?" he said sarcastically.

Ryan only smiled. "I want you dead."

"Zorlog killed by a slave!" He laughed even louder, straining his vocal cords in raspy growls. The others joined him, forming an ugly chorus.

"Did you enjoy your slow ride home from Signus?" Ryan asked quietly. "Must have liked facing your Emperor carrying all that shame."

Zorlog's laughter died to silence. He glared at Ryan, his eyes afire. "That was you?"

"Surprise, surprise."

Ryan was through talking. He pulled the trigger and swept a cacophony of blasts into the group.

Zorlog had somehow sensed what he was going to do. The Xilozak moved in a blur, diving behind a freight unloader, but he wasn't quite fast enough. A blast caught him in the arm.

A shockwave of superheated air threw Ryan to the ground as the ship behind him fired its cannon. The remaining group of Xilozaks vaporized into a mist of blood and fire, and the air was saturated with the smell of ozone.

Someone grabbed him from behind and yelled. "Let's go!" It was Kanook. Ryan wasted no time sprinting to the ship. The ship was beginning to ascend before they closed the hatch. As they reached the bridge, they were met by a young Signite officer named Dorftal, who saluted them on arrival.

"Bridge is yours, Sir!"

"Kanook, remind me to personally kick the ass of the person who initiated the burner warm-up sequence before I gave the signal. That is, if we get out of this alive."

He glanced at the navigational matrix. Eight ships had lifted off.

"Hard to port, 60 degrees, run her parallel with the surface."

"McClary!"

"Detonating now, Sir!"

The scene behind them turned into a field of fire. Ships toppled, and crashed, second and third waves of explosions thundered, lighting up the night sky.

He knew the bombs wouldn't destroy every ship. A few would survive. That wasn't their problem anymore. The Purists fleet would already be locking onto them with their long-range cannons from orbit. They had seconds before they would start pounding them.

"55 degrees, toward the pole, evasive maneuvers," he ordered.

The ship lurched as explosions raked the surface and concussion waves tore through the atmosphere.

A near miss. Judging by the firepower, that came from a cruiser.

"40 seconds before we leave atmosphere," reported Dorftal.

"20.."

Another barrage. The tracing image showed three Purists destroyers were moving in to intercept them.

"Standby for 270 degree roll. We're going to run right down their throats!" yelled Ryan.

"Commander, we're going to collide!" exclaimed Dorftal.

"Hold course, Dorftal!" Ryan warned him firmly.

Kanook spoke up. "All ships holding formation, Sir."

They had ascended beyond the thermosphere, leaving behind only wisps of atmosphere in the cold of space, and they had shed all drag as they accelerated directly toward the destroyers.

"Drill formation!" ordered Ryan, "Fire at will!"

The eight captured Alliance ships pulled into a revolving circle. The maneuver was referred to as a drill formation for the simple reason, if one viewed it head on, it would look like the end of a turning drill. Such an arrangement allowed the ships to become one virtual gigantic cannon, once they synchronized their firing sequence. No Xi-Empire ship could hold together under that kind of intense power – not even a cruiser.

In short order, the blasts penetrated one of the first Xi-destroyer's hull. The ship exploded, sections cleaving off and into the adjacent ship. The second destroyer suffered a string of explosions and starting falling toward the planet. The third attempted to break trajectory, desperately attempting to avoid the relentless blasts, but it too fell prey. Its shields failed quickly, baring an unprotected hull. In seconds it literally disintegrated.

"Ten destroyers closing in from 9 o'clock," reported Kanook. "And we're heading directly toward the main fleet."

The announcement didn't worry Ryan. He rubbed his left arm as it felt stiff and sore. *He must have hurt it somehow on the surface.*

"New heading!" he ordered, "90 degree vector at T-minus 3 seconds. Prep the anti-gravs. Everybody latch down!"

The ship lurched. All eight followed suit precisely. The 10 Xi-destroyers delayed an additional second before they too changed direction. The navigation holographic revealed another group of 20 were breaking from the main fleet, followed by a cruiser.

Ryan glanced over at Dorftal. The young officer was pale, his hands shaking visibly. "Don't worry, we'll get out of this."

"Relay to all captains: Acroluc at T-minus 5..4..3..2..1."

The ship shook as it jumped.

"We've bought some time, but they're still on us," reported Kanook.

"Who's got the rear, Kanook?"

"Captain Wark, Sir."

"Ask him why he hasn't spread some missiles around."

"Captain Wark acknowledges the question, Sir."

Ryan studied the navigation holograph. At this point, they were pretty evenly matched. They couldn't catch him unless he slowed, or they got off a lucky shot, or they pushed their ships beyond limits...

But that would be atypical. No, they would be playing it safe. After all, they had their main fleet behind them. They would maintain pursuit and wait for the reinforcements.

"Ryan!"

It was Aviore relaying over the vaskpar. He checked the tracing image for the *Dancing Queen*.

"McClary, where the bloody hell is she?"

The Scott made some quick adjustments to deepen the scans. They could make out the fuzzy image of the *Dancing Queen*, just out of range. He flipped on the vaskpar communication relay in his helmet.

"Aviore, you're getting too close. Stay out of range."

"Helm, is everything ready?"

"Yes. We are moving into position. Approaching intercept target on T-minus 2 minutes and counting," reported Kanook.

The fleet of the Galactic Alliance loomed into view as the scene played out on the tracing image. The pursuing Xilozak destroyers saw them a second later. They veered away, breaking course. But a trail of multiple faint images shot past the newly captured Alliance ships. One could have mistaken it as mere tracing noise, but Ryan knew better. These were alliance ships, specially designed to deflect tracing scanners.

The Nuboks made their shots count, anticipating the enemies' evasive maneuvers. Some hit their mark with only one shot, effectively crippling their targets. In minutes they had accomplished their purpose. The Xi-Empire captains, desperately adjusting course, were ushered into a number of oncoming Galactic Alliance fleet destroyers, which were ready to pounce.

Cannons flashed deadly plasma in an exchange of white light. The Xilozak captains were panicking now, attempting to scatter in multiple directions, to avoid the intense barrage of cannon fire by an arm of the fleet. One by one, they fell prey to the devastating wall of destruction. All but three remained intact, although severely crippled.

Ryan checked the tracing image for an incoming second wave. *They had time, if they moved fast.*

He ordered the ships boarded. They had less than five minutes to disable any remaining crew and put the vessels in tow. The boarding parties didn't let him down.

The fleet jumped to acroluc and disappeared with a minute to spare.

The incoming Purist ships caught the briefest of a tracing image before the Alliance fleet disappeared altogether. Realizing the futility of pursuit, they refocused their attention to rescuing survivors within the maze of pulverized, burning derelicts.

Zorlog stood on the bridge of his gigantic cruiser, shaking with an unprecedented rage. He swore, under his breath, that he would kill this Earthman, if it was the last thing he ever did.

* * *

14. Everything Has a Cost

The Galactic Alliance pushed along the full perimeter of the Xi-Empire's guarded domain. Base after base, planet after planet, seized and secured. With each conquest, they gained more recruits and acquired more weapons, more ships. The refit docks on Xeronia and the Signite bases were full, with engineers and trades working tirelessly to keep up.

Regardless of their growth Ryan knew the fleet did not, as yet, have the resources to face a full-force Xi-Empire attack, so they kept well away from the hot spots where the civil war was at its fiercest.

The Nuboks had proven to be excellent spies. Their special Xeronian manufactured stealth ships infiltrated all the way to Xilo undetected. Reports came in daily, divulging information on key Xi-Empire activity. Tsaurau led the task force with the thorough discipline of a seasoned general. Little escaped their intelligence net.

Ryan's tactics and strategies were being refined the hard way, during battle. He learned from his mistakes, not finding it easy to endure failure. Time and time again they were outmatched, either in firepower or circumstance. In one desperate move or another, he managed to pull them through, sometimes with heavy losses, sometimes not, but never were they beaten.

He was a machine. He sensed a part of him was fading away, but he couldn't identify what it was, or how to stop it. His perception of time turned fluid, a constant state of semi-wakefulness, jammed with hours immersed within the tactics of war, revising plans, making decisions, and inconsolable hours of insomnia. He was obsessed with an uncontrollable need to soak in every morsel of information. Maybe it was fear that drove him. To be on the very edge of loss of everything they had built.

He would not fail. He would not feel the sting of a whip, or the heat of a brand again. One day soon the civil war would end, and the Xi-Empire would awaken. Then they would face the full force of the enemy that day. Maybe, despite everything they've done, they would be no more.

And so they pushed on. Others accepted Ryan's driving pace on blind faith, trusting him wholeheartedly, rarely questioning him. He delegated as much to his generals as he did upon himself. He had seen them bear the burden of their decisions with the very lives of their troops. Most proved capable, and others - well not everyone can live up to expectations. As

Supreme Commander, he dealt with these problems quickly, without remorse. More than once he demoted a general and promoted a replacement. His decisions were sometimes difficult to make, as his sources of information were often limited to another officer's report or his own gut instinct. That, more often than not, seemed to work the best. Indeed, his three Showmish generals proved extremely capable. Wharsoff, YushTar, and Whushob outpaced the others, attacking and securing a large portion of the fringe area in an amazingly short time.

Their success began to cost them more than they could afford. Thousands upon thousands of freed slaves were arriving in a steady stream at the Galactic Alliance bases of Xeronia, Signus, and Grak. The bases were stressed beyond their maximum capability. Taldig worked desperately to keep all three bases producing soldiers but the task was insurmountable given the other complications. Food stores were practically exhausted, life supported systems taxed past their design limits, and medical supplies were critically low. The cries for help were becoming desperate, especially on the Signite ice colony of Gairf.

Ryan ignored the suffering, knowing full well what was occurring. He continued to push himself, as if some mad insanity had taken over, and expected everyone around him to match his pace. And they did - most of them anyway, aliens and humans alike. None of them would stop.

Aviore had complained to Wharsoff, asking why they didn't push back, but his response explained it best. "They would have plenty of time to rest when they were dead."

Ignoring their nonchalant attitude, she decided to try and intervene. She could tell something was wrong, but she had no idea what to do. So many times she had found him working like a zombie, utterly exhausted, or collapsed in his captain's chair with everyone moving about in hushed tones.

Aviore knew that she too had been absorbed within the rebellion, coordinating a never-ending training and re-training of troops, learning of weapons, navigation, and technologies contrary to her interest of real desire. After all, they were at war, and everyone had to make sacrifices.

That was his favorite damn line. He threw it in her face every time she tried to talk with him. What could she do? He was so bull-headed.

Taldig provided her an idea, and surprisingly, Ryan agreed to her suggestion without argument. And so, they were off to Gairf and some well-earned rest. The trip provided Ryan and Aviore a much needed chance to break from their relentless cycles. It gave them both time to reflect, and reconnect. But they knew this would not last. Their time together was a precious as it was fleeting.

"We're almost there," Ryan announced from the pilot's chair. He initiated multiple system diagnostics on the navigation sub-systems to ensure everything was within calibration.

"I know, and I've been holding off on talking about this..." announced Aviore as she navigated up the stairs.

He turned around to focus his attention on her. "Talking about what, exactly?"

"The pace you've been working at. I'm worried about you." She moved in close, easing down onto his lap.

"I'm OK. This was a good idea. You recharge me." He smiled, intoxicated with her scent, lost to her softness.

"Oh, is that all?" She kissed him, giggling slightly. "Maybe we should re-examine this effect I have on you."

* * *

Gairf base was strategically located on a small planetoid, well hidden, buried deep within the center of a glacier and surrounded by mountains. The Signites had employed a number of tactics to keep it a secret, but the most effective was the choice of the planet itself. It was a cold dark world, with frequent ice storms, blinding winds of snow and ice, which at times, could exceed 400 kmh.

The ride down was rough. Ryan was hands-off, his co-pilot at the controls. Aviore bit down on her lip nervously as the ship descended. It was the first time she had ever attempted a landing in such conditions. The swirling, battering winds knocked the ship about, raising alarms and forcing continuous attitude corrections.

He watched her calmly, probably with more confidence in her than she expressed. He was ready to help, but knowing enough not to interfere - she hated that.

"The winds are too strong," she exclaimed, an edginess tearing into her voice.

"Just watch your tactical, Gem has the approach vector lined up in red – see? Take a moment and try to pull up the visual image through the vaskpar. If you sway off course, just edge it back."

He attempted to provide her some level of comfort with his advice. But that only worked so well.

"I know. I know. I have this."

"5000 meters and T-minus 2 minutes," reported Gem, through their vaskpars.

"Better slow it down a bit."

"I got it!"

Her jaw clenched tight as the *Dancing Queen* shot through the small opening between the mountains heading straight for the base entrance. If not for their equipment, the entrance would have been all but invisible within the wall of snow.

Ryan opened a channel. "*Dancing Queen* on final approach, will reach the main marker in 45 seconds. We're running blind through a nasty bit right now."

A Signite controller responded, his face marred with boredom from too many arrivals. "Confirmed. Please decelerate to 160 before you pass the minimum depth marker and standby for parking maneuvers."

True to his word, the depth marker whizzed by underneath them, a small synchronization beacon buried meters under ice and snow. Warning signals burst over the channel.

The com monitor flashed on. The flat face of the controller had suddenly sprung to life. "You are coming in too fast. Please decelerate immediately!"

Ryan glanced over to Aviore.

"I am, dammit," she said quickly, her voice inflecting irritation. The *Dancing Queen* ground to a near halt, just in time to allow them to coast gently through the dark hole in the ice. Within seconds they were hovering over the main landing bay area. A flagman signaled them to move to the starboard side. With a few gentle nudges, the ship slid into position and settled down onto the bay floor.

Aviore took in a deep breath and let it out slowly, then turned beaming a wide smile of pride.

"Good work, I'll make a pilot out of you yet!" He laughed.

"See, like I said, no problem."

Leaving the comparatively quiet arrival bay, they stepped out to a scene of organized chaos. The base was bulging with people of all shapes, sizes, and races. Unlike the Xeronian base, the main loading bay was laden with heavy scents of multiple life-forms, so much it was almost overpowering. Ryan and Aviore pushed into the mass, dodging through the bodies, at the same time being careful to watch for and step out of the way of massive cargo unloaders as they whizzed by.

General Lortay was in the midst of all the chaos, pushing through the crowd toward them. Ryan gave him a wave. "General!" he yelled in Signite.

The crowd flowed around them, making it difficult to close the distance, but they managed.

"Good to see you two again," he announced loudly, giving a firm handshake to Ryan, and a warm hug to Aviore.

"Let's get to a quieter place, shall we?" They moved out of the busy bay and into a small side office. The noise dampened to a background vibration as the door slid shut.

"This is the cargo bay supervisor's room," Lortay stated, "Should do for a time." He proceeded to pour hot drinks from a resident brewing pot.

"I haven't had a cup of this in years," Aviore proclaimed.

Ryan just appreciated the pure scent. It seemed to cut through the aftertaste of the crowded bay. He drank it down, allowing it to wash his senses. "This tastes somewhat like green tea. What is it?" asked Ryan.

Lortay looked at Aviore for clarification. "I believe I know what you mean," she confirmed. "It's close - comes from a leaf of a certain tree on Signus."

Lortay cleared his throat, indicating he was through with the small talk. "We have a few things to discuss. Have a seat," he offered. They sat down on two cushioned chairs, in front of a white floating desk.

"I can see you're fairly crowded in here, General."

"Yes, as you can see, we're full. There's simply no more room. People are sleeping in the landing bays now. Our systems are breaking down. Air handlers are down in this section, have been for three days."

"I thought you had transports ready?"

"Sure I do, for almost two weeks now, as a matter-of-fact. Problem is, no one wants to leave, they all want to stay and fight!"

Ryan smiled, "Well, that poses a problem I guess." He sat back in his chair and cradled the warm mug of tea.

"That's not all," Lortay continued. "I know your Xeronian friends are full up as well, even those damn hairy Brogs are at capacity, and they keep it a nice warm -10 degrees at their base."

"Then we need to start moving them planet-side, whether they want to or not."

"That's a fine thing to say, but I can't convince them they'd be better off. Signus is a mess. Their infrastructure is decimated. They are rebuilding slowly but people are starving down there. And don't forget our POW camps – we are dealing with a lot of unrest when POW's are eating better than the citizens."

"Send detachments to get them organized. Get the systems straightened around."

"Already being done, but these things take time and resources. Keep in mind that every planet we've reclaimed is in the same sad shape. The Showmish, the Nuboks, everybody! That Xi-scum took everything, and what they couldn't take, they destroyed. When *we* moved back in, we made the further mistake of destroying the Xi-bases. Unfortunately for us, anything that was left that worked was in those bases. Those damn creatures are like pack rats stealing anything of use or value."

"And how are your supplies?"

"As of right now, we are almost depleted. We have a convoy due to arrive anytime now, secured from our last raid – but that's just the point - we cannot handle this many people. Our infrastructure is starting to fail, sewage reclamation systems are backing up, air management systems breaking down, water pumps failing."

"Then we have no choice, Lortay. We have to move them out."

Lortay hid his face in his hands, wiping away his tiredness.

"Commander, we can't. Those people feel safe here. In the event of a retaliatory attack, we can at least protect them here. If we move them planet-side, we simply can't guarantee their safety, besides the fact we are leaving them to fend for themselves. Add to the fact we are working solid shifts refitting our seized warships, and our people are exhausted. This is difficult at best. Mark my words, however, we are still taking the offensive, despite this situation."

"I see that, General."

"To top it off, we just can't seem to get rid of this Xi-scum. There are still parties of them roaming on every liberated planet. When we ship populations planet-side, we have to arm them, and we can't spare the weapons."

"What do you want me to do then?"

"I just received the latest numbers. Right now, I've two fleets on their way back with no way to handle the incoming. The 20 ships are crammed full, with a conservative estimate of at least a thousand heads apiece."

Ryan let out a low whistle. "Type-G slavers are the only ships big enough to handle that many. I noticed you have a couple being refitted in port."

"Neither of them are ready yet. They can fly, but they need more work. You can't have people living in those tanks when you're tearing apart the hull. It's a damned hazard. That'll be just what we need, a thousand dead due to some freak accident."

"The inbound ships - you should know - are full of your kind... Earthmen."

Ryan took a gulp of the tea, considering the news. *The type-G class are official Xi-Empire slavers. This means they've raided Earth. Why didn't he have intelligence on this?*

"That's not everything. We lost one during the attack. I'm sorry."

"You saved who you could," Ryan replied somberly.

We were all victims somehow, alive and dead. He had to deal with the living.

Aviore reached over and touched his leg. He returned a half-smile.

"Looks like we have only one option left to us, General. I'm going to need about five hundred men. All trained combatants, armed to the teeth. About half of them should be technically proficient enough to repair ships' systems."

"That's almost everybody I have that can keep this base running."

Ryan stood up. "If you want me to fix your problem you'll need to spare your personnel. Maybe we can get away with four hundred, then. Have the ships manned and ready within two hours."

"Why? What do you intend to do?"

"Let's just say I believe I can cure this problem of ours once and for all. But I need the troops."

"How long will I have to wait for this cure?"

"I don't know for sure. We'll move as quickly as possible. It will probably take a few weeks. If we're successful, we'll be able to relieve the strain on all three bases."

"Just keep in mind, Commander, we're running out of time here."

Ryan got up and moved to the door, Aviore followed. Lortay called after him. "Commander, I forgot to mention, the incoming fleet should be here soon. You'll get to meet a couple of my new officers."

"Good. I'm looking forward to meeting them." Ryan opened the door and hesitated. "Do they have any experience in high stress, no-win situations?"

Lortay's eyebrows creased into one. "You're making me feel better about this secret mission by the minute. I guess Ranton would be your man."

"Then we'll wait for the convoy to arrive. Have your best officers, including this Ranton, report to me as soon as they set down. I'll be over with Tmaurau."

"Commander, do you know where he is?"

"A guide would help."

"I'll get you one," he offered, pushing a button on his desk console.

Aviore spoke up. "If you don't mind, Ryan, I want to go through the registration roster, to see if anyone I know is here."

"I'll help you out," Lortay offered. "As things are in a bit of a disarray."

"Thanks."

The guide knocked, opening the door to let in a noisy roar. Ryan set down his mug, gave Aviore a gentle kiss, and disappeared into the crowd. The guide's name was Bartaliue. He was a talkative one. Ryan kept him tuned out, for the most part, inspecting the base as they walked.

"Here we are, Tmaurau should be working on this vessel."

They were in the main repair bay. Repair teams were hustling around in a frenzy. In the distance, a massive Xi-destroyer was being dismantled. Missing hull plating exposed the ship's internals. Cable and conduit hung down in tangled stands.

Before him, perched on the very top of a short ladder, was his old friend. He was bending over, half his body immersed in an open cavity of a Nubok reconnaissance ship. It was, compared to the others, tiny.

"Tmaurau!" he called out.

The startled Xeronian bumped his head as he attempted to straighten up. "Ryan!" he exclaimed, rubbing his bulging bald noggin. "Good to see a familiar face."

"How are things?"

"If I were to pick a word, I would say crowded," he replied. "You?"

"Too many details. I'm buried in details."

"You will be glad to know that we are making significant progress. Most of the Signite ships have been outfitted and are out in active service."

"Yes. I have a few of them in my own fleet. They seem to hold up well."

"A few insignificant design problems... they are not of the same caliber as the *Dancing Queen,* but they are more than a match for the Xi-Empire destroyers. I have to congratulate you. Your modifications to the shield design were quite impressive. I have implemented your ideas into other ships and made an improvement to your design as well. A double-phased transducer allows the shield generation field to change modes. It reduces..."

Ryan interrupted him. "Already did it. I don't know why I didn't think of it when I installed it."

"Oh, very good. You are beginning to impress me, man-from-Earth."

Ryan chuckled. "You are the master shipbuilder here. I'm just the student."

"It is the teacher's purpose to make the student excel beyond his own abilities."

"I'll do my best. What are you working on?"

"A small problem. I was just finishing up."

Ryan gave the ship a closer inspection. "The latest Xeronian achievement," he commented.

"Not really," returned Tmaurau. "Old ideas combined in a new way. No, the real achievement is when we can take one of those," he pointed to the destroyer in the distance, "and make it invisible to the tracers."

"I'm sure you will find out how to do that one day. How's the team keeping up with the repairs?"

"The Signite technicians are very proficient but they are in short supply. We have drafted the help of other technicians from those rescued. We are attempting to employ as many individuals as possible, but this work is specialized. We have a backlog of more than twenty ships, varying in repair requirements. More vessels arrive every day. We put them in orbit around this system's outermost planet and taxi them in when they are ready for refit. What we need to do is avoid inflicting so much damage to them in the process of capturing them."

"That may be impossible, my friend, unless we switch to biological weaponry."

"That remains a possibility. The thoughts of delivering a payload that is able to breach the hull, and inject into the interior..."

"Is a tall order even with your knowledge and skills. I assume you'll continue to work on this. Tell me, do you know how the Brog base is doing?"

"I have been there. Their base is quite small, approximately 24 useable bays. I have reviewed their native ship designs and have provided them with my recommendations. Their ships require extensive overhauls. A few Xeronians from my team are there presently, aiding in the reconstruction efforts. The Brogs are competent and their equipment is adequate to perform the work."

Ryan was about to tell Tmaurau about the decision he had made when a small creature walked, or scurried, up to them. It stood barely one meter tall and looked like a mushroom with eight small spindly stems.

"Bend down please, Ryan," asked Tmaurau.

Ryan got to his knees. He could see there were three eyes located underneath the dome-shaped head. They were glowing a bright green. He could not see a mouth. Strangely, he picked up a slight scent of vanilla emanating from the small creature.

So, this is a Nubok.

Gem informed him via the vaskpar, "He is Nargum of Fragoon. According to the registry, he is capable of speaking the Trinarieit language."

"Hello, Nargum," Ryan stated in Trinarieit.

Nargum replied with a surprising base-filled voice. "Hello, Commander. I am honored to meet you."

"This is your ship?"

"I am the Captain. There are two in my crew. Our next assignment will bring us enroute to Xilo. It is a reconnaissance trip requested by the Xeronian master, Tsaurau."

"Yes, I know him," Ryan smiled and glanced up. Tmaurau smiled slightly, matching the Earth custom with an exact finesse.

"Commander, Master Tsaurau has told me that you have put him in charge of a special project - to study the conflicts occurring in the Xi-Empire civil war."

"I need him to give me some insight on the commander of this Purist fleet, whoever he is. From what I've observed, he is very dangerous."

"I know the leader of the Purist fleet," announced the tiny Nubok. "He is assigned the title of Zorlog, of Xilozak descent."

Ryan's mouth went dry. "What? Are you sure about this?"

"Very sure. We have intercepted multiple communications with reference to this stated individual."

Ryan felt irritated and angry. "So I guess he's not dead, then. Figures I missed the sonofabitch. Seems that lizard has a horseshoe up his ass."

The Nubok blinked, but avoided further comment, not recognizing his Earth-English response.

Ryan remembered what he originally wanted to tell Tmaurau. "We're going back to the Maskaffa to retrieve the mothership."

Tmaurau's eyes squinted. Blue veins popped in his temples. The Xeronian did not like the news. "You must be very, very careful my friend. There are many legends about that fleet, and about that very ship. Tseman is never wrong."

"Let's hope she's wrong about this, we don't have a choice. I don't intend to take just the one ship. I want to take them all. Can you retrofit cores if we bring these hulks back?"

"Such precision work needs to be done on Xeronia, but yes, it can be done. I have a few cores fabricated already."

"Good. Contact Xeronia and let them know that we'll need more."

Ryan noticed a familiar face approaching, Bartaliue's shoulders bounced from side to side as he walked. The carefree teenager arrived slightly out of breath. "Commander, General Lortay wants to inform you that the convoy has arrived. The officers are on their way in as we speak."

Ryan said his goodbyes and headed back.

* * *

"Captain Brush, Captain Ranton." They shook hands firmly. "Good to see you made it back in one piece," stated Ryan. "A fine collection of ships you've pulled in."

"Yes, but we lost one," said Brush somberly.

"I understand you've requested my company, Sir," Ranton said.

"I've got a job for you. I expect it could be very dangerous."

"Could be? That's the most promising news I've heard yet," he half-laughed.

Ryan smiled at the quick response. He liked this fellow.

"General Lortay has recommended you. We are going on a mission to retrieve a number of ancient war vessels, and a very special ship – of significant dimensions. I expect that most of these vessels are still functional, which includes this large transport. This particular vessel's systems, according to my data, has everything we need to support our growing population."

"Where the hell did you find such a gold mine!" exclaimed Lortay, excitement in his voice.

"In a place called the Maskaffa Spider – a very secure area with only one way in and out. This location would be ideal to build a base."

"Sounds like this will really make a difference," commented Brush.

"Yes, that's the point. But it won't be easy. I'm sure the ship's systems will require repair, so we'll need a large number of men to get them up and running, considering the size of the vessel."

"So why the fighting men?" asked Lortay, somewhat suspiciously.

"The ship may be infected with an alien life-form. If it is, it will have to be exterminated."

"And you need 400 troopers to do it?" Lortay countered.

"The ship is very large. We need to scour through her quickly," returned Ryan. "I expect we'll need about four to six ships, whatever's needed."

"Once we've secured the mothership there are a number of other vessels surrounding it. We may need to tow some of them. We're leaving in one hour. Ranton, you're my first, make sure the ships are ready to go."

Each of the officers gave him a Signite salute by hitting their left hand with a closed fist. He returned the motion and quickly left, eager to find Aviore. Gem helped him locate her through the maze of rooms and corridors and bodies. She was in the medical center, going through the roster on a portable terminal.

"Need help?" he offered.

She looked at him sadly. "I thought I could find my mother."

He put his arm around her. "Did you try the cross-references, search by description?"

"No. I was just about to go through it, though."

"Better yet, why don't we just ask Gem?"

He relayed the request. Gem was quick to respond. She liked helping out with things like this.

"Downloading the information now," reported Gem. "The data transfer will take a few moments, as the Signite system is archaic. Please relate all information pertaining to your genetic mother, Aviore."

She did, distinguishing as much information as she could remember. A few moments passed by as Gem searched the database.

"I'm sorry. No individual was found matching all the required physical features, skills, name, or personal history."

Aviore looked down sadly.

"We'll find her," encouraged Ryan, "it will just take some time."

She moved into his arms quietly.

"We're going to have to leave," he announced.

She looked up at him. "Where are we going now?"

"To the Maskaffa Spider."

Her eyes widened. "Tsaurau told me about that thing on the mothership! You're not going to board it are you?"

"We are going to do more than board it. We are going to fly it out of there. Besides, that creature is long dead. It has been for a thousand years."

"Don't you go aboard, Ryan... Please. I'll tell your generals. They won't let you go as soon as they find out. You're too valuable to them."

Ryan looked deep into her eyes. There was real fear there. "What are you afraid of, a bunch of stories?"

"I just don't want to lose you. If you go, I go."

"Alright. I won't board until we've secured it, OK?"

The look in her eyes didn't subside.

"I don't want you to die."

"I'm not going to die," he said, openly irritated. He glanced down at his chronometer. "We have to get going."

"Just remember if you go in, then I go in."

* * *

The ships were outfitted and ready within the hour. They left for the Maskaffa Spider on schedule with the *Dancing Queen* in the lead. The trip took a week at the fleet's maximum acceleration – which was much slower than the *Dancing Queen's* capability. It gave Ryan time enough to brief the crew for their mission. He reviewed the investigation file compiled by the Xeronians on the *War Spritzer* with the other captains and officers over a vid-com session.

"As you can see, these bulkhead hatches were literally ripped apart. The statistics are at the end of the report, but it would take roughly 150 GPa to sheer the alloy that the hatches were made of."

"We'll just blast it before it reaches us," said Ranton.

"The speed of this thing is supposed to be incredible. It would appear as a blur to the human eyes. Make no mistake. This thing kills. If we are unlucky enough to find one, it will probably take out half your men before you aim that blaster."

"I get the picture. Everyone will be on their toes." Ranton's tone was more skeptical than earnest.

Ryan decided it was best to ignore it. "As soon as we've reached our destination, I'll be coming over to McClary's ship. That will be the command center and I will coordinate everything from there.

"This thing could be resident in any of these vessels. I want every last one inspected, cleared, and either made operational or connected up with grav lines for a tow back. We'll finalize the plans to get the mothership operational after we inspect it fully. I want all of you to review everything I've downloaded to you, if anyone has any other ideas, make note of them, and we'll take it up at our planning meeting. *Dancing Queen*, out."

* * *

Aviore was up on the elevated walkway. She was looking at him so strangely, it gave him the chills.

"What?"

"I just have this bad feeling."

"Don't worry, we'll handle this right. We're not going in unarmed, remember."

"I know," she resigned, worry still echoing in her voice.

"Oh, and I've got something to show you!" she announced, a little on the happier side.

"What? You've invented a juicy steak," Ryan kidded.

"Don't be silly," she dismissed his humor. "It's in the hydroponics room, but I want you to close your eyes."

"I won't be able to see."

"Here, take my hand."

They walked through the ship. It tested his knowledge of where everything was. He only tripped but once.

"Come on you big lug," Aviore told him affectionately. "You must know this ship pretty good by now if you can walk through it with your eyes closed."

"You told me to close them."

She laughed slightly and turned him to face a certain direction.

"OK, you can open your eyes now."

Ryan did. He didn't see anything unusual at first, just the rich vegetation of edible plants and the thick moss that covered the walls and ceiling. He was already feeling the heat from the bright, hot lighting and high humidity.

"I don't see anything."

"It's right in front of you."

He looked down at the compost vat in front of him. Perched in the middle of a red cherry vine, was a single yellow flower. It resembled a daisy.

"What? This little flower?"

"Yes. Isn't it something," she said cheerfully.

"Yeah, I guess. So what's the big deal?"

Aviore was beginning to form a cross look upon her face. "You think I planted it there? It grew by itself. I found it when I was picking the cherries. It's absolutely incredible."

"It's just a plant. A stray seed, so what."

"When is the last time you've ever seen a flower with pedals like that? I remember my biology. This flower shouldn't be here."

"I agree, but I'm weak on biology. We'd better get it out of here before it interferes with the other plants."

"No way! Leave it alone. Don't you get it? This is an amazing find. That flower is a desert dwelling plant, its root system should have broken down by now."

"How do you know so much about this one plant? What's so special about it?"

"Well, for one thing, it comes from Signus. I know as I used to have one growing at home. If you watered it, you would have killed it."

"This plant? If I remember right, I've seen thousands of them all over the Xeronian parks."

"Yes. I saw them there too. That's precisely the point. This particular plant is a Xeronian version. I've examined it fully. It's exactly the same plant that is on Signus, almost. Everything is identical except a small mutation that has allowed it to adapt to the different soil. Its cellular makeup is almost an exact match."

Ryan was totally disinterested now. He walked over and checked the flowmeters and the circulation monitors. "Well, everything looks OK here."

"Well, don't act so damned... disinterested!" she said, frustrated at him.

"Look, I'm not..." He cut his sentence short.

"Not what?" she demanded.

"I'm not interested," he stated flatly, with a slight smile.

She gritted her teeth at him, seething, not saying a word.

Gem spoke up. "You are not communicating effectively, Captain."

"I noticed. She didn't like my little joke," he replied.

He tried to sound apologetic. "If you find this so important, you study it. It's possible one of the Xeronians visited..."

"No Xeronian mission has visited Signus," refuted Gem, to both of them.

"OK, then a Signite ship visited Xeronia. Or an identical plant evolved on both planets. I don't know. If you find something out, tell me... I've got to check on the anti-gravs, one's acting up a little."

"Fine!" she said firmly, and a little loudly.

Ryan left, glad to get out of the heat, literally. He kept himself busy in the main drive room almost all day. Aviore never even came out to check on him. Gem informed him that she was busy doing a full study of the flower. She was helping her with the analysis.

He knew she was mad at him, but couldn't fathom why. *For the life of him, he'd never figure out the opposite sex.*

They retired early, 10 hours away from the Maskaffa Spider. She lay on her side of the bed, not talking.

"You didn't call me so we could have dinner together," Ryan said, sounding hurt.

"No big deal, it was just salad."

Silence followed.

"Did you find out anything interesting... about the plant?"

"Why are you interested now, you weren't before?"

"Aviore, why don't you tell me what's really bothering you?"

She turned, facing him. "I don't know. I just have this bad feeling."

"What about?"

"I don't know," she said, exasperated. She moved in closer. "Just hold me."

* * *

They arrived at the Maskaffa uneventfully. Ryan could not take his eyes off the awesomely strange spectacle before them.

"The Xeronian archives did not give this justice," he said softly. Aviore nodded in silent agreement. Using the Xeronian libraries for reference, he guided the *Dancing Queen* through the maze, the other ships following closely. Aviore helped navigate, monitoring the tracing scanners.

"You don't want to make a mistake going through here," she said. "It could be fatal."

"Yeah," he glanced over to starboard at a disturbance that was registering on the instruments. He had seen that same imprint before – a miniature black hole. "I noticed."

"I understand the ancients engineered this... thing."

"How?"

"I really don't know," Ryan replied. He thought about the fleet inside, sitting there, abandoned for centuries. "Yeah, it's a regular Pandora's box," he said aloud.

"I believe we are almost through," Aviore reported quietly.

They emerged out of a thick cloud of blue gas. Floating before them was the long-abandoned Flukken fleet. The ships were scattered about, pointing in all directions. In the very center of the collection floated the mothership, sitting dark and ominous.

As the seven ships approached, they were dwarfed by the gigantic vessel's sheer size.

Aviore stared in utter amazement. "I didn't know..."

"That it was so big?" Ryan interjected. "Now you understand why I think this will answer our problems."

General Ranton's face came up on the com monitor. "I must say, Commander, an incredible find."

"Agreed. Start your scans, Captain. We'll convene on McClary's ship and discuss our strategies."

Ryan brought the *Dancing Queen* up to an entrance hatch on McClary's ship and docked, activating the life tube extension from the airlock as soon as they were secure.

"Are you going to be alright?" he asked Aviore.

"Yes, I'll be fine, don't worry about me."

"I think I've heard that before."

He kissed her and was gone.

Aviore decided to do her own tracing scans. She had Gem start with the standard life-form identifiers. She waited for the results nervously, staring at the dead hulk of the ancient ship, watching the tracing readings as they passed along the monolithic vessel.

* * *

"Now that everybody's here," Ryan announced, staring at the three other captains and officers, "It's time to review what we have so far."

"Something that big could take at least a week to do a thorough search," McClary offered.

"Our scans of the ship reveal nothing. No life-forms. No unexplained images. Nothing at all. Are you sure that we need to do this search? This will take up valuable time," Ranton complained.

Ryan felt a little defensive. "I expected that we would not be able to spot anything on normal tracing scans. I'm sure this thing was engineered to be transparent to such scanning methods. We will assume this hostile life-form exists until we confirm it doesn't."

"Very well, then I recommend three armed parties, Commander. One led by McClary, one by me, and the other by Dorftal."

"What about your technical guys, Ranton?"

"As you know, we also have a Xeronian among us..."

"No, I didn't know," Ryan said, irritated that he wasn't told.

"Forgive me," came a voice. It was Tmaurau. He stood in the entrance-way, not quite sure if he was invited in. "It was a quick decision on my part. I felt that news of my presence should remain quiet until we arrived."

"I see," Ryan said, smiling. "Maybe you thought I would disagree? Regardless, we can certainly use your help, my friend."

Ranton continued. "We have estimated that it will take as many days to review the ship's systems as it will to search it, and at least as many days to run prestart tests."

Ryan shook his head. "We can't afford the prestart testing time, and we have all these other ships to stage up as well. We'll need to run multiple shifts."

He thumbed a display control on the semi-circle table. A holographic image of the large ship came up. "I present to you - the mothership. Tmaurau, could you do us the honors?"

Tmaurau nodded, grabbed a holographic pointer and approached the front. The group studied the holographic image with honest amazement. The mothership's triangular fuselage was approximately 40 kilometers long and 10 kilometers at its widest. The front section sloped to a point, lined with portholes, and somewhere, along there, was the bridge. Two thick rectangular wings jutted out mid-way down its length. They were as thick as the full height of the ship and about 25 kilometers, tip to tip. Along the front of these wings ran the matter collection vents, which charged the ship's systems. The wings were as wide as a full quarter of the ship's length. Along the last quarter ran a thinner section of wing. That section was covered in a mass of external conduits and lines that led to an array of burner plates on the top, bottom, sides, and rear. The rear burners were the largest of all. The top of the fuselage ended in a sharp cone just above the main rear burners. A spaceship bay jutted out from on top of the wing section mid-fuselage. It was a little over five kilometers in width, with entrances fore and aft, easily as wide as any of the Signite ships. This is where they would dock.

The mothership's hull was covered with strategically placed laser cannon turrets and missile launching ports. Four main cannon were located at each end of the square wings. This was clearly a ship of war. The Ancients did not arrive at the Flukken system defenseless.

Tmaurau moved the tip of his pointer to the sloping front of the ship, near the top. He began his instruction. "Within this section, you will note there is a main bridge area where all ship's functions are controlled. There is also a redundant battle-bridge ahead of the engineering area, near the stern. Either will be of use to our team."

"We should start with the battle-bridge," Ryan announced. "It's more accessible from our point of entry." The others nodded in agreement.

Tmaurau continued, bringing his pointer to rest on the exposed fuselage along the burner wing area. "Main Engineering is located here. We believe this area is guarded by a number of dispersion fields, some of these may still be engaged, though highly doubtful. Care must be taken as contact with a dispersion field will burn a victim severely. In the event one was to fall through a field, he would come out the other side as ash. The location of these fields should be clearly marked by this sign."

A small red icon appeared above the ship's image. "Remember it," he warned.

"Once we have arrived at both destinations, work can begin to test and bring up the individual ship's systems. Our preliminary investigations have shown that there is a suitable, breathable atmosphere within the ship, even now, but I suggest all initial infiltration be conducted with the use of environmental suits. There is a very real danger of suspended viruses or poisonous gases."

"Everyone will be in combat suits," announced Ryan. "With full vid-relays and body monitors. Everyone's feeds will be relayed to central control."

"The initial parties are to move in and secure those two areas. Then we'll begin a systematic search throughout the ship. Nothing can be missed. Any questions?"

"About this thing - what do we look for?"

"Anything from live creatures to dormant seed pods. Just look for anything suspicious or unusual."

"Where do we dock?" asked McClary.

Tmaurau pointed to the bay area. "Each one of these bays should open once a certain coded signal is transmitted. The bay control systems should have sufficient power remaining to open. We believe we have that signal and the possible range of codes. Each bay is a completely independent section, closed off from the others."

Ryan pointed to the first six bays. "We'll use these six, and begin a coordinated deployment. Once each ship has deployed their teams, they are to secure all locks. Break up the men into groups of 20 or so and secure each level as you move down. Each of you will be in charge of your teams. Keep your approach in-line. Move uniformly. I don't want to have a group isolated from the others in the event of an attack. Remember, assume we have a hostile on board. Take all precautions and be prepared for anything. Any more questions?"

None came.

"All right, let's move."

Ryan and Tmaurau headed to the McClary's ship. On the way, he relayed a message to Aviore. "Everything's set. I want you to break off from the ship and bring the *Queen* out to a surveillance distance."

"Alright Ryan," came the reply. "Just be careful – and remember we board together."

"I'm not boarding the mothership. I'll be coordinating from here."

When they arrived on the bridge, Kanook was there to greet them. "We have all the reconnaissance teams on the tactical display. They'll be ready in a few."

"Good. Keep me informed."

"Your ship has disengaged," reported Kanook.

"Let's get underway, then. All ships move in," he ordered.

The ships drew up slowly to the spaceport bay entrances. On the bridge of Ryan's ship, the main viewscreen was filled with the sight of the immense bay door in front of them.

"Issuing signals," reported the com officer.

Nothing happened. Ryan glanced over to the com officer. "May take a few moments to run through the possible combinations, Sir."

They waited.

"The other ships report their doors are opening, Sir."

Tmaurau spoke up. "The problem may lie within the mothership. I suggest we try another bay."

"Agreed. Helm, reposition us to the next bay, and we'll try again."

The ship moved around to the adjacent bay. To their relief, the door opened, sliding up slowly, revealing darkness inside.

"External illumination and move in."

The internals of the bay was a mass of equipment, scattered in all directions. The docking deck came into view.

"Helm, deploy grav lines."

They pulled into the docking bay and came to a full stop.

"Testing seal now, Commander," said Kanook. "Seal complete."

They moved over to the holographic tactical display in the middle of the bridge. Kanook brought up a display of the immediate area in the mothership, small corridors outlined by thin blue lines.

"Com, patch me into all troop feeds. Tactical, I want full monitoring of everyone's signal. Ranton, McClary, Dorftal, are your groups ready?"

"Ready as we'll ever be, Commander," came McClary's familiar voice. "Open those doors before I change my mind."

Ryan gave the order and the doors opened into the docking corridors. The bridge crew watched them from the primary tactical image feeds. The troops, signified by little red dots, began to move. Vid-feeds relayed from the individual troop channels.

"Airlock secured, compression sequence keyed. Inner hatch ready to open." They went through a status roll call. "Group 1 ready. Group 2 ready. Group 3 ready."

"Open hatch on T-minus 3..2..1."

The red blips moved into the ship's corridors. No attack. Ranton's voice came over. "We are in the corridors. No signs of residual power in the lighting banks. Beginning dispersion into groups."

The three blobs of red dots divided into six and moved through the corridors.

"Pull in the signals from the other ships' search teams," ordered Ryan.

A small army of red dots disbursed across the search area, progressing forward. A few moments later, another report came over. "Level one secured. Beginning next level."

The red dots moved deeper into the ship, the second level, then the third. Three of the groups broke off and headed toward the engineering section. The other half continued moving down. An hour later the two key areas were secured. No sign of a creature. Ryan felt relieved, but that old familiar nagging was bothering him. The feeling of dread was still there.

McClary's voice came on the intercom. "Commander, we've secured engineering. We haven't met up with anything strange, other than some damage in the corridors. My Signite techs are going over the battle bridge controls to see if they can get these old systems powered up. Apparently, they're like nothing they've ever seen."

"We'll see if we can help remotely." He looked over to Tmaurau. "You know more about this than we do." Tmaurau acknowledged with a nod.

"McClary, Tmaurau will guide the engineering teams. Proceed with section by section. Keep your eyes open. I don't have a good feeling about this just yet."

"Right-oh, me lad. If we do find something, I'll bring it to you on a plate."

Ranton was next. "We've come across some notable damage. Radiation hatches torn open. Whatever did this was incredibly strong."

"Acknowledged, Captain. Check the area closely."

"Already done, we're secure. Continuing with the search."

"Good luck."

The hours ticked by slowly. No creature was found, and no remains. As the case with the *War Spritzer*, the crew of the ship were long missing. They occasionally crossed an area where something had done an impressive amount of damage. Alloy bulkheads, 10 centimeters thick, were pushed in like they were made of tin. Doors ripped off hinges, furniture and consoles ripped and shredded like paper. In a way, Ryan was glad that they found this. It kept the men alert and ready.

Shift change went by, and Ryan was still on edge. He paced the bridge floor in anticipation. The men switched without incident. The relieved troops headed back for a much needed rest.

Aviore contacted him, sounding concerned. "How is it going?"

"Good. No problems so far," he replied. *He could not tell her how he felt.*

"With multiple shifts running we'll have the whole ship covered within three to four days."

"Good, I'm glad to hear it." She sounded detached, far off.

"Don't worry Aviore. Nothing has happened yet. Things are looking good."

"Yes, I know. I am doing my own scans of the ship. Unfortunately, it takes hours to complete."

"Good idea," he replied enthusiastically. If anything, it is something to keep her busy, to keep her from worrying.

Another shift passed without an event. Ryan was growing tired. The hours of anticipation were wearing on his nerves.

Tmaurau reported good news. "We have managed to bring the secondary power grid online, Commander. The bridge is ready to initiate lighting and environmental systems. On your order."

"Do it," ordered Ryan.

The lights came on throughout the ship. A small cheer came from the engineers on the bridge of the mothership.

"Excellent work!" Ryan complimented over the communications

channel. He looked over to see Tmaurau's reaction was not the cheery one expected. He had learned all too well the expressions of the almost expressionless.

"We can expect only about three hours performance from the secondary capacitors. They are almost exhausted. We are beginning to work on the matter collection systems, but there is much work to be done."

"I'll permit more men down there if you need them. I don't want those lights to go out, now that we have them on."

"I recommend six more."

"Kanook, round up six engineers that will volunteer for extra shift duty."

He gave a quick nod and was gone.

Tmaurau went to turn back, then hesitated. "Ryan, this creature may very well be dead."

"Tmaurau, I believe you are correct. Should we say to hell with it now - let's cancel this search and get this beast going?"

Tmaurau's veins pumped in his temples, although he said nothing.

"Yeah, I suppose not. Best we finish the job we started."

Tmaurau gave a slight nod. "Once this ship is completely searched, I will dispel my pessimistic beliefs."

The second shift change came and went.

Ryan had been up for 24 hours now. He felt he was wearing down. His left foot kept falling asleep and his arm ached. It was annoying as hell.

The extra help at engineering was paying off. The power capacitors were charging, albeit, only a trickle, but it was enough.

Tmaurau noticed the Commander's weariness. "Ryan, why don't you get some rest? You will not be able to maintain a clear mind with a lack of sleep."

"Yes, good idea, Tmaurau. You get some rest. That's an order," returned Ryan, with a slightly sarcastic tone.

"Sir?" said the bridge officer. "If I may, the Captain's quarter office has a very comfortable reclining chair."

The temptation to sleep seemed too appealing now. "Alright, you talked me into it. Wake me up if anything happens. You know where I'll be." He ambled into the quarter office, which was directly off the bridge, and fell into the comfortable cushioned recliner. He did not forget to check with Gem before he closed his eyes. Aviore was sleeping comfortably in the *Queen*. All was quiet.

He fell asleep within a minute.

* * *

Ryan was awakened by the intercom. It was the excited voice of the acting bridge officer.

"Commander! We've found something. I repeat, we have found a biological."

It jolted him awake like an electric shock. He was on the bridge within seconds.

"Report!"

"Search team 6A reports finding a dead carcass of a creature. Quite large."

"Bring it up on the main view."

The scene before him was shocking. There were five men surrounding the thing. It lay on the floor on its back, its legs stretched up toward the ceiling. Its skin was gray and black. To Ryan the creature's overall appearance reminded him of a beetle or tick, only it had two pairs of arms, and its legs were in groups of three. There were no eyes. The mouth was oversized, lined with teeth, with mandibles that reached around the front.

As it lay prone, the thing's mouth was hung open, revealing an opening big enough, possibly, to swallow a man whole. Upright, the creature would have stood about three meters tall. Ryan did not want to envision one of those things chasing him down.

"You're sure it's dead?" he asked, half-joking.

The leader of team 6A stepped forward in the picture. "Absolutely, Commander. It's been dead for some time. It seems to have mummified."

He glanced at the tactical to find their position. They were in the rear burner section.

"You guys have covered a lot of territory," he commented.

"We are almost done with this section. A few more shifts and this section will be completely searched," replied the leader promisingly.

"I'll send a detachment down to study that thing. Keep your men moving, and stay alert."

"Yes, Sir."

Ryan ordered a science officer to the bridge.

Tmaurau arrived.

"Scary looking sonofabitch, isn't it?"

"Quite deadly I should think. It has all the ideal qualities of an efficient killing machine. Defenses of an impenetrable exoskeleton, powerful legs to ensure mobility..."

"And don't forget the sharp teeth," added Ryan.

"I have located some libraries that had been previously sealed. The danger of this life-form is augmented through its accelerated life cycle. These creatures begin as minuscule insects that devour all available bio-matter. Their post-larval wings allow them to spread out from the original point of contamination and infiltrate difficult to reach areas. Their appetite, although primarily carnivorous, is omnivorous. Their flexibility of diet ensures they can pull in the necessary calories to grow quickly.

Once they develop into an adult, they are lethal predators. They are an example of excellent bio-engineering, a brilliant yet disturbing accomplishment."

The science officer reported on deck, interrupting them with a salute. He was fairly young but carried confidence in his manner.

"I understand we've discovered a corpse of one of these creatures, Commander."

"Yes. You have your work cut out for you now. Examine that thing. Maybe they have an adequate lab area on that ship, not sure. Just make sure this thing doesn't have any little babies or something inside it. From what I understand, they'll be similar to insect larvae. If you suspect they may somehow still be viable, incinerate that corpse. I don't want any other nasty surprises. Avoid direct contact and sterilize everything, understand?"

"Yes, Sir. I'll try to have something for you in a couple hours." He turned sharply.

"And Lieutenant," Ryan called after him. "Figure out this thing's weakness so we know how to kill it – just in case we meet up with a live one."

"Yes, Sir. Will do."

Ryan punched a few commands on the console, a list of shift reports came up on the screen. He studied them for a moment. "Tmaurau, have you inspected the food and hydroponic area reports. Looks like that's where the creature had spent most of its time."

"Yes. The damage is extensive. The supplies were decimated."

"And most everything else by the looks of it. This thing was destructive."

"There are signs that the crew attempted to fight this infiltration," added Tmaurau.

"Yes, I've seen the blast damage evidence," noted Ryan. "Do you think they were able to kill this thing?"

"The evidence will explain," offered Tmaurau.

"Maybe."

Kanook stepped on deck and joined them after completing his inspection. They both nodded a welcome.

"Do you know who was heading up the team that is searching the stern engineering area?" asked Ryan.

"Captain Ranton, Sir. He just went on shift."

The remaining hours went by agonizingly slow. The search was concentrated to the rear of the ship now. Every other part of the ship had been cleared.

Aviore called in. She was starting another type of scan. Ryan informed her of the news.

Her scan would be a waste of time now. If there's another creature on the ship, they would know soon enough.

"Ranton reporting in, Sir," said Kanook.

"Put him on the main screen."

Ranton's tired but determined face showed signs of relief.

"She's done. End to end. We found nothing alive. Looks like your alien was that carcass we found, and it died a while ago. We found the area where the crew made their last stand. It's a hell of a mess. Everything's melted or burnt to a crisp. Looks like that thing found a way in behind them, went through a 15 centimeter thick bulkhead to get to them." Ranton shuddered, "I pity the poor bastards!"

"Did you find any sign of bodies?"

"No, nothing, thing ate them, I suppose."

"Good work Ranton. Your men can relax now. Start the sterilization procedures. I will not consider this ship secured until we hear back from the science team."

Tmaurau spoke up. "We have the majority of the ship's systems up. Everything is working with the exception of the main drive."

"Even after all those years," commented Ryan in wonderment. "These Ancients were something else."

"Yes, they were," agreed Tmaurau.

* * *

He went to the officer's briefing room and contacted Aviore over a communications monitor. He wanted to see her face.

"Hi."

She smiled sweetly back. "Hi. I've heard the good news."

"Yes. That means I'll be boarding her soon. Do you still mind?"

"No. It's OK." Her voice was shaky. "Just be careful, alright?"

"Of course, relax, it will take at least 12 hours before the ship has been fumigated and the atmosphere filtered. I won't be going in until then."

"Hope to see you soon, Commander."

He smiled, threw her a kiss.

When Aviore signed off her smile disappeared in a flash. Her instinct told her something was still wrong. She'd spent her life denying that instinct, especially when she wanted to believe the contrary. Last time that mistake had put her into slavery. It wasn't going to happen again. She was not going to lose Ryan.

"Gem, I want to start a full geo-matrix mineral scan on the mothership."

"I am not equipped to accomplish all the required scans in that range. Modifications are required on the secondary feedback scan circuit."

"Can I make those modifications?"

"Yes. All equipment and supplies are available. I will guide you through the process. I must warn you, the work is tedious."

A Bellicose Dance

"I'm good at tedious work," she said confidently. "Let's get moving!"

* * *

A refreshed Ryan stepped aboard the mothership deck.

He took a deep breath. The air smelled sharp and sweet. A long way from the rancid, stale smell it was a day before. The environmental control systems were working without fault, even after a thousand year rest.

Kanook stepped up beside him.

"Let's inspect this creature. I want to see this thing for myself."

"It's been moved to a medical bay, under quarantine, Commander. The ship's doctor and the science officer are still examining it."

They found the doctor and the science officer huddled over a monitor of an electron microscope. Ryan cleared his throat. The science officer jumped. His nerves were on edge.

"Oh, Sir," was all he could say.

"Well, what do you have?" demanded Ryan.

"We're not... completely... sure yet. It's dead, we have determined that much. There are no eggs, spores, larvae, no chance of procreation. The way it sits now, it's harmless."

"OK, what are you examining now?"

"A sample from the circulatory system. This thing is absolutely amazing."

The doctor interrupted. "We've already studied a graft of muscle tissue from one of its legs. The cellular energy requirements are unusually high. The mitochondria count is remarkable. The diffusion level of ATP within the blood had to be artificially elevated in order to provide such..."

"Hold it, hold it. I don't want an analysis. I want a summary. What is the potential of this creature?" He moved closer to the inspection window. It and the two doctors were effectively quarantined off, sealed behind a plexiglass door.

"First off, the creature's metabolism is completely variable. We expect that it can hibernate for years. It would appear, in these cases, quite dead."

"Until it wakes up," interrupted the young science officer. "But we can assure you this creature is definitely dead."

"Conversely, it has an unusual base for blood. It is capable of maintaining a sustained elevated metabolism for hours before it must rest. Once its metabolism is elevated, it effectively increases its strength and speed by a factor of at least ten."

"Basically," interjected the science officer, "we estimate it to have been able to move at speeds exceeding 325 kmh and have claws with the clutching strength of 700 kg per square cm. It would, to be more descriptive, move in a blur and rip apart a human being like tissue paper."

"It's no wonder they couldn't kill it," added the doctor.

That point bothered Ryan. "Yes, what about that? A direct hit with a hand

Page 393

blaster wouldn't kill it?"

"The shot would have to be extraordinarily well placed if it was projected from shoulder height. It would have to hit here, in this particular joint in the abdomen, to do any damage. Otherwise a hit, even at close proximity, would only dissipate, easily protecting any and all vital organs."

The science officer pointed to the armored back. "If you look closely, you will see small crystals embedded within the exoskeleton, they're hard to see from your angle."

Ryan peered in close, saw the tiny glinting nodes within the exoskeleton. "Yeah, I see them alright."

"This is why a blaster wouldn't affect it. A frontal shot would be useless, and a side shot would be incredibly difficult if it was moving even at half of its capable speed. The most effective way to hurt this thing is a direct shot into its lower abdomen. But you would have to literally shoot at it from underneath. We think that is what killed this thing."

"Someone got a lucky shot off, I guess."

"More accurately, whoever got that close to it," interrupted the younger man, "probably didn't make it."

"Why do you say that?" asked Ryan.

"This thing is literally a furnace. When it's running full steam, it's throwing off enough heat to give you a third-degree burn within a meter of it."

"There would be considerably less heat being thrown out from the underside," argued the older doctor.

"I guess all these concerns are academic now. This is the last of them," stated Ryan. "I want this thing out of here when you're done."

"This is a most unusual life-form. We would be losing valuable scientific..."

"Before you continue," interrupted Ryan. "You don't know this thing's story. So let me sum it up for you. This creature was genetically engineered as a weapon. Its creators lost control of it. It proceeded to propagate and kill every living thing on the planet where it had been conceived. It wiped out a whole race of people. This is an example of knowledge we can afford to lose."

The senior doctor put his slides down, looked over to the younger science officer.

"Understood. We'll finalize our work and eject the carcass out to space," acknowledged the science officer soberly. "Whoever engineered this ship knew what they were doing. There is a jettison tube in the back of this quarantine bay, and it's big enough to suck a small ship out of here. If something poses a problem, press that button over there," he nodded to a covered switch behind Ryan, "and out she goes. You could eject it from in here if you enter the override codes."

"And kill yourself in the process," added Ryan morosely.

"You do what you need to do," replied the science officer.

Ryan nodded solemnly. "Agreed. Give me a full report once you're done, and keep it confidential. I want all record of this thing encrypted."

Kanook and Ryan headed for the main bridge. They took advantage of the turbo-shaft shuttle system that ran the full length of the ship. Some minor repairs had just been completed and it was now in full service.

"Ready?"

Kanook nodded.

He pressed the destination selector. The car launched with a quiet whine, accelerating with enough force to compel Ryan to either grab the handrail or get tossed against the wall. A moment later and they were there. The doors slid open to the ship's immense bridge.

"Now this is the way to travel," Ryan said with a smile.

The place was a hive of activity. All around them technicians were busily working on the bridge equipment while others hauled supplies and tools throughout.

He glanced up to see the stars. It was a breathtaking view.

Ten meters above, transparent ceramic-quartz view panels spanned across the top of the bridge. He stepped out onto the upper bridge deck, which served as a suspended walkway traversing the full length of the bridge, and served a commanding view of the area below and above. In the center of the room, the walkway branched into a circle flowing around a four meter wide clear globe, which functioned as the navigation/tactical holographic display.

He glanced through the metal grating of the walkway to see dozens of consoles, where bridge officers were actively monitoring and controlling the newly awakened ship's systems.

As he walked down the narrow deck to its end, the transparent ceiling dropped down on a sharp angle. At the very end of the deck, Ryan was able to reach out to touch the quartz panel. He expected it to be freezing, yet it was only slightly cool to the touch. The stars shone through it with an unprecedented, sharp brilliance.

"Quite the ship, wouldn't you say, lad?" commented McClary from below.

Ryan looked down at him, a broad smile across his face. "She's a beauty – a real work of art. I thought your shift was done, McClary?"

"That it is, Commander, but you know me. I've heard we were having a wee bit of trouble with the hydroponics area. I was just about to amble over there and take a look. We have a lot of work to do if we are going to fit the thousands we intend into this vessel."

He gave a quick wave-solute and headed out. "I'll be seeing you, Commander."

Ryan walked back to the main command area, which was situated just in front of the navigation globe. Three seats were positioned there, the one in the center designated for the captain. Sitting down, he found it quite comfortable. He noticed pull-down restraints could be locked into place on each side – just in case of a bumpy ride. A large, slanted viewscreen was directly overhead, which provided a view to the majority of the bridge crew. His chair had quite a few controls on its arms, on which he noted a small light was blinking. He guessed it to be communications. He pressed the button and Tmaurau's face came on the viewscreen above.

"Commander, I see you have found your place."

Ryan chuckled. Tmaurau's sense of humor was very dry.

"How are things going down in engineering?"

"We are ready to run a number of tests on the main drives, but the capacitors are extremely depleted. It will take days to charge them to adequate levels."

"I guess once we start moving this crate, it'll charge a little quicker, right?"

"Yes. But we need to establish a minimum charge in order to engage the drive."

"Ah, yes, the infamous catch-22. How about siphoning off power from our ship's reserves?"

"We already anticipated that course of action. It will require some coordination on both ends, but the connections can be established easily."

He glanced over to his second officer. "Kanook, can you work with Tmaurau on this? I want to be mobile ASAP."

Kanook nodded acknowledgment.

"Tmaurau, Kanook is going to give you a hand. Get this crate moving."

A couple technicians had started work on the navigation holographic. Ryan went down and joined them.

No time like the present to get his hands dirty.

About an hour later, a number of Signites came up from engineering hauling heavily insulated coupling cables. Their job was to link up the Signite capacitors to the main power circuit running through the mothership. The only way to do that was to hardwire it directly.

* * *

On board the *Dancing Queen* Aviore was also very busy. The adjustments to the tracing scanners had taken longer than expected. Mistakes had cost her precious time and contributed to an increasing frustration. She felt a sense of urgency, and her tendency of rushing had set her back even further. She had to force herself to calm down, do things carefully, methodically.

Upon completing the enhancement, she triggered the tracing scanners to start. The scan process literally crawled down the ship's length. She sat back in the co-pilot's chair and watched the readout.

Nothing so far. The bridge area and front section of the ship were fine.

The beam moved steadily, passing further down its length. Suddenly there was a slight blip, a small aberration. Aviore's heart jumped. She backed the sensor beam back over. There it was again!

She called Ryan via the vaskpar.

He answered on the mothership's communications channel.

"What's up?"

"I've got a signal on the sensors!"

"What kind of signal?"

"I modified the sensor beam circuit for a certain type of scan."

"You modified the circuit? Why?"

"I needed to enhance the scan... Wait a second. Gem, impose the ship's structural layout onto the sensor coordinates and determine where that reading is originating."

Ryan waited patiently.

"The tracing source can be located within one of the mothership's medical quarantine bays," reported Gem, a second later.

"Well, great work. Looks like you found a way to pinpoint these creatures. Don't worry about that one, it's dead. So you did the modifications yourself?" Ryan was genuinely impressed.

"I did - pretty good of me if I do say so myself."

He laughed. "Do me a favor and scan the other ships. I want to know if there are any more of these things around here."

"What about the mothership?"

"We already checked it out. Do the others and let me know if you find anything."

"But..."

The monitor went blank.

"Uhhhhhhg! Damn it!" she cursed loudly.

She slammed the release key. The scan resumed.

Why didn't he ever listen to her?

She felt a familiar growl in her stomach and marched out of the cockpit, headed for the galley. *Food would settle her down, maybe a sandwich.*

Gem interrupted her as she took her first bite.

"Would you like to see the scan results?" she asked politely.

"Of course," she mumbled, mouth full.

The display came on the main monitor. She dropped her sandwich.

The vaskpar! She tried, but she couldn't concentrate.

Don't panic!

She yelled, "Gem! Get Ryan, hurry!"

She had to stay calm and concentrate.

Ryan saw the incoming communications signal blipping on his chair. He was halfway down the steps to the lower level, so he decided to route it through the monitor below. The walkway was cluttered with old consoles and rubbish that the repair crews were moving out - damage caused by the thing.

Then he heard, no felt her on the vaskpar. "Ryan! It's in the bay. The thing is in the bay!"

Ryan hit the communications, not to answer Aviore, but to reach engineering.

Tmaurau answered. "Hello, Commander."

"It's in one of the bays. Aren't your boys headed down there?"

"It? The creature? Yes. They are, I'll..."

Suddenly Ryan heard the screaming. Then the sound of a train coming, barrelling down the tracks. He glanced up to see a hatch fly through the air. A blur was in the room. An engineer flew into pieces before him. Something told him to dive. He jumped between two consoles. *It* was right behind him. He felt the heat, felt a tug on his leg.

Everything turned to slow motion.

It was above him hammering down at him, but couldn't reach him. He was lying on a jagged piece of metal. He twisted and grabbed a sheared piece of decking.

Kill it.

He shoved upwards and the shrapnel sunk into *its* belly. A thick rancid fume engulfed him, he gasped for air.

It was off him, going crazy, jumping across the room, denting a bulkhead, demolishing a console. *It* spun in circles, a blur of motion, trying to free the jagged piece of metal lodged within *its* belly. The room filled with the sound of hummingbird wings amplified a thousand times. Waves of heat carried through the air, rippling in intensity. Then *it* raced down the corridor.

Ryan looked down at his leg. It had a large gash, seemed to be all the way to the bone, but surprisingly, he couldn't feel it. *Was he in shock?*

Two meters in front of him was the turbo shaft. He had to move before *it* came back. He pulled himself along the floor, his left leg useless.

He slammed the button and pulled himself through.

He was in!

The door started closing. Behind him, a wind howled and searing waves of heat melted consoles together. *Its* screaming almost burst his eardrums.

His blaster!

He yanked the weapon from his holster.

He could see *it* turn, head toward the closing door.

The turbo shuttle started moving, gaining speed.

Then came a loud crash, and a tremendous shaking.

It was in the shaft with him now, but the shuttle was leaving *it* behind, clipping along at a fantastic rate, but he knew this line would end, sooner than he wanted. And *it* was after him alright. *It* didn't like the little present he had given.

He remembered the Ancients' warship, the men in the cargo bay.

He would eject the sonofabitch!

The medical lab would be his only chance. He wouldn't have time to get any further before *it* caught him. He reset the destination. In seconds the shuttle decelerated. He could hear it coming in the distance, like a freight train.

Down the corridor and to the left to the medical lab.

He forced himself onto his feet, fighting back a wave of nausea, and hopped, as much as jumped, with his good leg, leaving behind a trail of blood.

A loud thud echoed behind him. *It* had reached the shuttle and was forcing its way in through it. Ear piercing screams filled the corridors in all directions.

He glanced back but dared not stop.

It was stuck.

Ryan laughed crazily. He was scared to death and moving as fast as he could. His chest was on fire. His heart pounded painfully.

Turn to the left.

The lab!

He dragged his bad leg through and pressed a button to lock the hatch door. As the door closed a shrill screaming pierced through the bulkhead.

Little time left.

He stepped in and to see the doctor and the science officer standing there, dumbfounded.

"What the hell is going on out there?"

"Do you have any envirosuits?"

"Yes. One in the locker."

"Give it to me and seal yourself in that other room, NOW!"

The science officer grabbed the suit. His face was pale. "There's another one coming down the hall isn't there!" He looked at Ryan, saw the large gash in his leg, looked down at the suit and then into the quarantine room. His eyes went wide with realization.

"Bullshit, Commander! Doc, grab him and lock yourselves in there –
and seal it!"

The doctor grabbed him and pulled him back into the small storage
room.

"Let me go."

The shrieking stopped.

"Oh shit," Ryan said. "*It's* heard us."

The doctor slammed the door shut, and they peered out the tiny
window.

The young officer calmly keyed in the override for the evacuation
sequence.

It hit the door with a tremendous crash. The metal bulged under the
strain but didn't give. The medical hatch was reinforced alloy, triple the
strength of the other hatches. It bought the young man precious seconds.
Instead of reaching for his helmet, he coolly finished entering the
sequence as the hatch door's metal twisted and screeched under
unfathomable stress. In one movement the officer snapped a salute to
them and pressed the button.

Remnants of the door flew in all directions. A dark blur screamed past,
crashing through the lab door and into the quarantine room, which was
already decompressing. Equipment and papers followed the shadow,
sucked through the opening, destined to the vacuum of space.

It was gone.

Sirens began to sound throughout. Hatches closed automatically,
emergency doors sealed. A small whistle started in the upper seal of the
door, but it was holding.

Ryan leaned back against the wall, shaking visibly.

It was gone and had taken a brave man with it.

He heard Aviore on the vaskpar. She had been trying to reach him all
this time. He answered back and he could feel her relief.

Then everything turned to black.

* * *

The doctor worked furiously to stop the bleeding. He had less than a
minute before his patient bled out. He tied the leg off with a tourniquet
and yanked the suture kit down from the shelf. With shaking hands, he
stitched the artery together and loosened the tourniquet.

It held.

He pulled the muscles together and wrapped them closed with sutures
and compression bandages.

It was done.

He collapsed against the door, unable to stop shaking.

Ryan fought against the blackness, pushing through to consciousness, ignoring the nausea and pain and the black veil that tried to envelop him. Everything around him seemed distant, surreal. The heaviness and pain in his chest had faded, but his leg was afire.

The doctor was sitting on the floor, knees drawn up, hands burying his head. He was sobbing quietly.

"He was a good man," Ryan whispered.

"He was my son."

* * *

Due to the decompression, it took some time for the emergency teams to reach them and re-establish atmosphere. The doctor had kept a vigil over Ryan, but despite his efforts, the Commander was unconscious, suffering from loss of blood. Kanook picked him up and carried him back to the *Dancing Queen*, where Aviore waited.

After the event, everyone worked to save as many as possible. *It* had killed a total of 138 and seriously injured another 22.

Ryan was bedridden for days while Aviore watched over him with deep concern. His manner was different, withdrawn. Something had changed within him. She was worried – but not about his leg.

He gained his strength back quickly, all the time remaining quiet and withdrawn. Once he was able to stand, he requested Ziggy to fabricate a walking stick for him. Aviore pleaded for him to continue resting, but Ryan would have none of it. He called on his captains to meet.

They waited for him in the corridor of the mothership. They would accompany him to the bay where *It* had hidden for so long - the bay with the door that had failed to open. The engineers had unwittingly opened the wrong door by mistake. They were the first to be killed.

This time, when the door to the bay opened there were no more surprises. Everything had been thoroughly searched and secured.

Kanook triggered the lights.

The sight before them was worse than they could have imagined. Heaped in piles on the floor lay the bones of thousands.

Victims of *It*.

The air stank of rancidity. Ryan covered his mouth with a handkerchief and limped out towards the center of the bay. All around him was death. It reminded him of his past - of the boy suspended in the brush, with his chest blasted away.

McClary stated quietly. "You know, Commander, we could all be among these bones now if you hadn't acted so fast."

Others nodded their agreement.

Ryan didn't need to hear that. He could only feel the pain. He could only see the face of that brave science officer so coolly saluting him. "I need you to leave me alone... all of you."

They filed out silently.

"And close it on your way out," he called after them.

Kanook ensured the door closed, turned to guard the entrance.

Ryan went down on one knee, then the other, and leaned against his walking stick.

"Why?" he yelled.

God wouldn't answer him. He knew that much. Maybe God wasn't out here, in the cold of space.

He knelt in the room of pain and wept.

He would carry this pain with him for a long time.

Kanook waited patiently by the door. Hours passed before the Commander reappeared. His first order was to seal the door.

No one was to disturb the dead.

The damage was repaired. Equipment rebuilt. Systems brought online. Within days the mothership was ready to move. Any other ships that were functional were repaired and put into formation. Others that had potential were docked within the bays or put in tow.

Thanks to Aviore's adapted scanner, they were able to expose another ship with the genetic weapon aboard. Ryan personally destroyed the vessel. The ship was not worth the risk.

He leaned back in the command chair, with McClary on his right, and Kanook on his left.

The fleet was ready to return back through the Maskaffa.

As they passed through they held a funeral service. A military procession moved through the ship, to end at the bay. Ryan said a few words for all the lost souls, and signaled three troops to fire three times.

The service was over but for one final action. The bay was pressurized to double atmosphere, and the doors opened. Their remains floated out to become part of the universe once again.

The convoy moved out of the grasp of the spider, its poison no longer lethal. A collection of almost one hundred ships in total turned and headed back to a cold, desolate planetoid of ice.

* * *

15. Freedom

The mothership hadn't moved for a thousand years. Problems were to be expected. The ship's main drive started behaving erratically soon after they left the Maskaffa.

Ryan ordered the fleet to a full stop. The technicians estimated 24 to 32 hours to complete the repairs. It was a costly delay, but it was also an opportunity. So many details needed to be sorted out. Crew issues were paramount, such as overall organization, assignments of roles and responsibilities, coordinating specific training by post.

This would all get worked out soon enough, Ryan knew. However, there was an even bigger issue, and it worried him. The ship's defensive capabilities were, as yet, unknown and untested. Until they worked the details, they were fully exposed. That was not a good situation to be in during a war.

Ryan pulled the captains, officers and group leaders together and laid out the priorities all too clearly: Get the weapons systems online and supported by a fully-trained crew.

The main cannon, mounted on the tips of each wing, were the first to be assessed. They were gargantuan devices, with diameters no less than 10 meters and lengths spanning the full depth of each wing. Such sheer size implied an unparalleled capability of incredible destruction.

The first of the firing tests were performed at low energy to ensure no power surges would feedback and destroy the complex array of ancient components. Unfortunately, regardless of this extra caution, they did just that. The energies involved, even at a low level, presented so much stress on the aged equipment that a mid-relay station within the main power conduit in the left wing literally disintegrated, rendering two port cannon useless. One of the starboard cannon suffered minor damage after its cooling system malfunctioned, which revealed that the cooling systems for all the cannon needed complete overhauls.

This ship remained adrift, main drive disabled, with only one functioning cannon, crippled and vulnerable.

Ryan remained on the bridge shift after shift, impatiently waiting while the technicians sweated over the repairs. But things soon turned from bad to worse.

The engineering teams had to shut down all the main power conduits. Every critical system went offline, with the exception of environmental control - no navigational control, no shields.

General Lortay boarded bringing with him plans to organize multiple teams to test the remaining weapon's systems - from turret guns to missile launches.

Ryan ordered engineering to patch auxiliary power feeds for the tests. He watched Lortay as he worked, noted his disciplined style of command, the easy way he moved his troops about. He could only wonder if he could inspire others to follow him like that. He dismissed an annoying tinge of jealousy.

How could he be so immature?

The Signite General was anything if not thorough. The work was completed ahead of schedule with some encouraging results - remarkably few of the weapons had failed.

Lortay passed on the news personally, visiting the Commander on the bridge.

"At least we're not completely defenseless," was Ryan's only reply, irritated by the number of problems they were experiencing. He glanced over at tactical - the odd asteroid, chunks of ices.

Still quiet.

He turned to catch Lortay just as he was stepping into the turbo-lift.

"By the way - good job, General."

Lortay nodded back, a trace of a smile on his face.

"Power may be limited, but we'll get the troops going on some drills. We'll use any piece of junk we can afford to eject out into space for target practice."

"Good idea, General."

Across the deck, Kanook glanced up from the tactical. His face reflected the greenish hue emanating from the navigation globe, making him look pale, almost sickly. "I've just initiated a long-range scan. I estimate that could pull at least 10 % out of our reserves."

"Take what you need, Kanook. We need to know what's out there."

"Commander," McClary called from below. "Our lads have just passed on some more good news. Power is restoring, all systems are coming back online."

Ryan smiled down at McClary. "Now that's good news."

The Earthman was seated at one of the few working consoles that had been spared from the creature's rampage through the bridge. The damage the thing had done in its brief attack was considerable.

"And weapons?"

"Both port, and one starboard cannon showing on standby. Engineering says they're ready."

"Are you sure they'll hold this time?" Ryan asked, somewhat

sarcastically.

"The lads think they've nailed down the problems."

"Alright then, relay the order - we retest in 60."

"Testing in 60 seconds!" repeated McClary over the intercom.

Ryan leaned against the upper deck rail, staring down into the navigation globe. A small blue dot was moving slowly, parallel to their course, approximately one hundred and sixty thousand kilometers beyond the ship. It was a comet, tail-less in the dead of space with no star to heat it. It would make a perfect target and a lucky find, considering the emptiness of the area.

The countdown started with an announcement by a gentle female voice. Gem, through Ryan's request, had reprogrammed the bridge computer to use Trinarieit and integrated the gender to catch the attention of the predominately male bridge crew, which he suspected, in time, would also change.

"McClary, lock onto that comet. Use both port cannon and the functioning starboard one."

"5..4..3..2..1."

The three cannons fired simultaneously, with a massive low-thundering wave reverberated throughout the ship. On the tactical, the small blue dot winked out of existence. Ryan reached for the console near the apex of the globe and pressed in a few commands. Tmaurau's face appeared on the viewscreen above them. "That was pretty far away, Tmaurau. Have you calculated the cannon's range at full power?"

"We have. If we can trust these test results, and there is no reason why we should not, a fully charged, simultaneously focused blast would maintain a 75% concentration before dispersal decomposition to a distance of about 10 million kilometers. That estimation is taking into consideration standard space/matter density. It is an impressive statistic."

"I'd say. We'll be able to poke a hole in a Xi-cruiser's hull and still keep well out of their weapon's range. Do as many tests as you can, but ensure the total reserves do not drop below 40%. You'll be competing with everyone else, including Lortay's men on the turrets. Just keep in mind that I want to have power available if we need it. Give me a full report when you're done."

Lortay's image appeared within the holograph, his head floating in a green opaque sea. Yet another technological perk buried within the navigation globe.

"Commander, our first training round has been assessed and our gunners are going to need some more work."

"As expected, get them in shape, General. There is no telling when we will encounter the enemy. I expect every one of them to know their controls intimately. Tell them to sleep in the turrets if they have to. Do we have any disabled turrets?"

"A good number, but nothing we can't fix with the proper tools and know-how."

"How about the missile launch crew?"

"Well, there's a problem there – we have limited ordnance, and I am hesitant to use our reserves – millennia old or not."

"Do what you can. As soon as the drive repair teams get freed up, I'll have one of the teams report to you. I can't give you any more manpower. The others are assigned to overhauling the cannon cooling systems. Tell those engineers I want every turret online in three shifts."

"We're also assessing the missiles. Most of these existing lovelies are dead. Too many years on their berths I imagine. We're still hunting for some live ones."

"Fire off some of the duds to test the launching mechanisms. We'll need to tear a few apart to see if they have any secrets we don't already know. We should be able to resurrect them if we understand how they're put together."

"Very good, Commander," he saluted as his image evaporated.

"They're warming up the burners, Commander," Kanook stated.

"Excellent. I think I owe Tmaurau a holiday after today. He's been leading two main repair jobs over the past six shifts with little to no rest."

Kanook nodded back an acknowledgment, but his eyes didn't shift away from his monitors.

"What is it?"

"It might be nothing, but I'm getting something. Too far away to know exactly what."

"Can you bring it up?"

A fuzzy area of yellow swirled into formation on the north-east corner of the globe. "Could be a cloud of gas, ejected debris, anything."

Ryan watched the faint image for a few moments. "But you don't think so, do you? I have a feeling about this too... What direction?"

"Toward the Corvellian quadrant. Give me some time and I'll nail down the speed. I'm still figuring this thing out." He punched some more requests into the console. "If it's a Xi-fleet, it could be headed for spaceport Goo15-A."

Ryan pondered, "Last report I read, that was still under Purist control. Hell, this could be a Zigot League invasion fleet. Maybe they're mobilizing, taking on the offensive. Our last intel shows that the Purists are in deep, and they've gained some key territory. Keep an eye on that signature. As long as they stay the hell away from here, I won't care."

* * *

Ryan returned to the bridge on the third shift. The engineering teams were on schedule. The weapons systems were scheduled to be completely restored by the end of the shift. The bridge had been brought back to functioning state, and the drive systems were online and ready.

Ryan engaged the intercom. "This is the Commander speaking, I want to recognize the hard work that everyone has put forth to get this ship operational again, and our fleet is mobilized once more. Thanks to you we are on our way."

He closed off the intercom.

Wasn't much of a speech but it was to the point.

"Helm, let's get this fleet moving. Navigation, use a 10 degree trajectory masking."

A ship, moving through space, flew with specific intention – to get from point A to point B. Unfortunately, an enemy vessel could easily extrapolate an observed ship's destination. Ryan had ordered the fleet to move in a three-dimensional zig-zag. They did, after all, present a large signature on a tracing scan. This would, of course, add time to their trip, and expend additional tracing probes each time they changed direction.

* * *

The end of the third shift was the beginning of the 'night' cycle on the mothership. Every night, Ryan and Aviore returned to the *Dancing Queen*, which was now berthed in docking bay six.

They were becoming familiar with each other's behavioral perks, becoming accustomed to each other. Aviore enjoyed a specific type of Signite tea and preferred to read before bed.

Ryan chose to meditate, attempting to achieve what he had experienced on Shawma. It was not easy. He had been successful only a few times. On Earth, some would call it ESP, to others, it would be the work of the devil. To the Showmish it was natural, and to the Xeronians it was an experience that came in a vile. Ryan knew what it was. It was evolution, either forced on by the vaskpar or triggered by a drug. Either way, it didn't matter. He was experiencing unfathomable things. Indistinct, unclear at best, but something truly amazing. But he had no one to guide him, no chemical to boost his powers. When his sessions ended unsuccessfully, sometimes with a splitting headache to show for his efforts, he often wondered whether it was worth it.

Aviore joined him, more out of curiosity than anything else. She was somewhat skeptical of the whole thing, but her attitude soon changed.

Once Ryan was able to achieve the absolute concentration he required, success soon followed. It came in stages: disorientation, followed by the sensation of physical detachment from his body, followed by, well even he couldn't explain it.

He would drift, life flowing around him would appear as a warm glow. The farther out he would move, the more he would see, like fireflies in the night were the souls of the living.

Aviore was always familiar to him, somehow. The first time he touched her, he *felt* her surprise. The sensation was incredibly close. He withdrew quickly. It was more than a strange sensation to share another's mind. Maybe reality, maybe everything was a dream. He took a deep breath, felt his lungs fill with air.

Did his lungs fill with air? Or was his mind playing games with him? Does it matter? HishTar had told him to let go.

What the hell.

Feeling a little braver, he pulled away. The world around him expanded. The lights of the others faded to dots. He was traveling through space, a wingless bird of energy. He passed planets of lush green and orbs of ice. Space and time were meaningless here, lost in the maelstrom of color under the alternating, swirling streams of darkness. He came upon an orange sun. Its heat beat down upon him with the light of a thousand Sols. He turned away, temporarily blinded. His vision speckled with a kaleidoscope of sparks, quieted onto a sphere. A small planet defined itself. A world of lush green continents and blue oceans enveloped by a transparent sphere of opaque white. It was a beautiful planet, but something seemed very wrong.

He moved closer and saw the shadows surrounding it. Ships - vessels of war - thousands of them, swarming around it, firing upon it ceaselessly. Their efforts were in vain. They could not penetrate the protective shield.

He watched as a new ship approached, much larger than the others. It moved in close, launched its poison and retreated. A stream of flame borrowed through the once impermeable guardian. It reached inside, and the stream widened, a cancerous red blotch painted itself onto the lush green and blue surface. It grew with terrifying speed, spreading, consuming. It engulfed the planet, transforming it into a ball of seething flame. Ryan felt sick. Echoes of pain screamed at him, the souls of millions dying.

The machines of war retreated, their evil now released.

Something else was changing. It was the star. He could feel its steady, persistent heat fluctuate. It was tearing itself apart inside, bulging, throwing out tongues of superheated plasma, its surface rippling in angry waves.

The dying sun swept outwards, consuming all in its path. The evil horde could not escape. Ryan dared to look into the face of the vengeful god of light. It was enough to feel it die a thousand deaths in an instant of time. It winked out, leaving him cold and alone.

A voice was calling him. He could feel a shaking. Images fractured into swirls of color, then darkness. The familiar returned. A sweet scent of perfume. His eyes opened to Aviore's concerned face.

"Ryan, you were barely breathing!" Her voice stressed to a new tenor.

He reached up. "It's alright," he said quietly. She calmed down, the lines on her forehead disappeared. "Thank God," she said in a soft whisper. "I thought you were dead."

"I'm OK."

She pulled away from him, suddenly, violently. "I don't like this. I don't like this at all." She circumvented the room quickly, turned and retraced her steps. "All the time you do this, this thing, I worry. You're meddling with something beyond our science, something scary."

Tears came to her eyes. "I didn't - I don't know what to do." She said in a broken voice.

Ryan got up, his legs stiff from sitting cross-legged. He walked over and wrapped his arms around her. "I'm perfectly safe. I was just in a trance. It's a natural physiological state."

She relented, her arms wrapped around him. "Just be careful, OK?"

He chuckled, "You're the one that married the Commander of the Galactic Alliance, remember?"

She frowned at him. "Don't pull that crap with me. I'm your wife now, and I can't help but worry. At least you have somebody that cares."

"Yes, I do."

"And I'm right most of the time, when I worry, I have a damn good reason."

"Yes, you do."

"What did you see, when you were in that trance?"

Ryan remembered the images clearly, as if it just happened. He could still hear their haunting cries.

"What's wrong? What did you see?"

"I saw... I saw the past maybe, I don't know yet."

She caressed his cheek with the gentle touch of an evening breeze. "I don't understand you. You talk in riddles and see things no one else can. You are so different, like no one else I've ever met. Why don't you tell me exactly what you saw? Maybe I can help you sort it out."

He looked into her brown eyes, his mind still lost in those cold and twisted dreams. "You don't want to know," he said softly.

"I do. I do want to know. I want to help you."

"I don't know what it means and I need time to think about it. It's too early for me to talk about it."

She looked at him, perplexed. "Sometimes I wonder if I'll ever really know you. There's a piece of you in there you never show anyone – not even me. Why won't you let me in?"

Ryan looked away, suddenly finding the floor very interesting.

"Or maybe you don't want me in that close."

"That's not true," Ryan retorted futilely.

A long moment of silence followed.

"Fine." She reached for his hand. "Come on, let's go to bed. You can sleep on your little mystery. We'll be reaching the Signite base tomorrow and I need to work off some stress."

She pulled him into the bed.

He would be a fool to resist.

* * *

Before they were even a parsec from Gairf, Kanook was on the intercom. "Commander, we have a situation. We need you up here, now."

Ryan didn't bother with his uniform. Still half asleep, he dragged himself onto the bridge. He noticed Kanook's features lacked their usual serene composure. Something was up.

"Tactical picked them up a few minutes ago. They've turned toward us."

That woke him up. He inspected the holographic images. Their signatures were unmistakable.

"Kanook, your analysis?"

"I estimate approximately one hundred ships, 10 of them cruisers. Xi-Empire signatures. They were headed for the Signite base, but they've altered course to intercept us instead."

"Lovely." Ryan reached for the intercom. "All hands. Condition Red. Assume battle stations."

"Confirming all available ships have left the docking bays," stated Kanook, anticipating his next question.

Ryan nodded. "Com, open a shared channel to our fleet and keep it open."

"Captains, our situation is serious. Lortay, McClary, Dorftal I want you to be point. Assemble three formations. Branch out 60 degrees in a triangular approach."

Man and alien, in a collection of ships of all shapes and sizes, broke away from the mothership in a multitude of directions. Any dead ships in tow were abandoned in haste, to be later retrieved - if they survived.

Ryan studied the holographic images, refining the tracing scan results to pan across different views. The tracings were invaluable, supplying images beyond what the standard electromagnetic spectrum could supply. From this distance, the human eye could see light, but it was over three years old, unusable in any respect. The tracings operated in an enhanced energy state, multi-dimensional, faster-than-light. Data flooded in, updating the holographic display continuously.

It was obvious the enemy force had diverted from their course, aborting their original target. He glanced down through the decking grid at the weapons control officers - three pale-faced humans and one Showmish. They were waiting for his command - they were all waiting on his command.

"Ready the cannon. Once we're in range, target the closest cruiser. One shot per, as our reserves are low, so make it count. Stay cool. Concentrate on the job."

They nodded back silently.

"Deploy shields to 80%."

Gigantic sheets of plating slowly rolled over the transparent ceramic-quartz panels, locking into place and draping the bridge in darkness. The odd internal light panels adjusted to compensate for the distant starlight.

The soft voice rang across the bridge. "Approaching engagement range. Contact at T-minus 5..4..3..2..1."

The cannon fired. A familiar low frequency rumble echoed through the corridors.

"Direct hit." relayed Kanook. "Looks critical."

"We've got their attention now."

"They're still closing in, Sir, undeterred," reported the tracing officer.

"Yeah, I can see that." Ryan glanced down at the weapons officers. "Fire at will, Weapons. Measured approach. Do not miss. Give'm hell."

The cannon started firing a steady rumbling beat, each throbbed and echoed in thunderous waves throughout the ship.

Ryan circumvented the globe, attempting to get his mind wrapped around the three dimensional positioning. The cannon fire was tearing into them, but they easily outnumbered their small fleet by a factor of 10. A number of Alliance captains lacked interstellar battle experience. This was going to be a difficult battle to win.

"Communications, can you split the channels over the overhead monitors?"

"Aye, Sir."

A secondary array dropped down out of the ceiling. Faces of numerous captains pasted themselves onto the displays. In battle conditions the navigation globe remained strictly reserved for tactical, disallowing any communications imagery.

"Captains," Ryan stated in a calm assured tone. "Standby for engagement." The cannon were thundering, and the noise was pounding down through the corridors leading onto the bridge from multiple directions.

"Ensign, please seal the hatches!" relayed Ryan.

The junior officer below scrambled to trigger all systems that controlled the hatches. Soon the noise was muffled to a low-bass pulse of thunder.

"Captains, we've successfully turned them from engaging the Signite base. Now the heat's on us. Remember to keep an eye on your reserves. I know they are low. I estimate we'll be in full engagement range within 15 seconds. I'll be relaying formation instructions as we maneuver. Coordinate with me where possible and ensure you stay out of my rotation space. Good luck."

"Enemy contact range in T-minus 5 seconds," announced the soft voice.

"Helm, full 15 degree roll, Z-minus 150 degrees. Now!"

The huge starship began to roll end-for-end, no longer decelerating. It was time for the gunners to take over now.

Ryan hit the ship's intercom. "Everyone, keep sharp. Aim well. Trust your instincts. Remember your training... and take those bastards out!"

He closed the channel and hesitated.

Was that enough? Some inspiration he provided - that announcement was weak at best. He wasn't a damned leader. What the hell was he doing on the bridge anyway? He should be in the Queen! He belonged there, not here.

"Helm, alter for evasive at will."

The officers glanced up apprehensively. It was their first battle with this ship. No one knew how she would behave, or to what limits she could be pushed.

Ryan could see the doubt and fear on their faces. It was like a disease that ate away at one's very being, crippling your judgment, causing fatal mistakes. A Commander must provide the confidence, subdue the fear before it eats away at his crew's abilities.

Problem was he didn't feel so damn confident, either.

With an angry mask, he glared back at them. "This ship won't let us down, so you do what you have to do, and do it right."

White faces turned back to their work. They were oblivious to the Commander's insecurity. His brief message was all they needed. Their shaky fears were replaced by grim memories. Hate burned strong within their hearts. The Commander wanted them to take these bastards out, and that is what they were going to do.

* * *

Almost every ship was exchanging fire now. Thick streams of searing plasma hung in the space between the two approaching fleets, the remnants of superheated blasts. The Alliance ships launched a salvo of missiles, many detonating prematurely but some reaching their targets. Ryan monitored the exchanges, reviewed the positions, and ceaselessly belted out commands to coordinate with the other captains.

"Helm, 360 degrees roll now!"

The gigantic vessel rolled gracefully, this fact noticed only by a few, including the Commander. He not only watched how the ship responded but assessed how well the crew guided her. He noticed the weapons officers were having difficulty hitting their targets. The ship's ancient targeting systems were inferior to modern designs and required an overhaul.

"Weapons!"

Heads turned, momentarily startled.

"You have to trust your instinct. Don't expect a targeting lock every time. These systems are too old and out of calibration. Trust your instincts. You won't miss."

The officers were nervous and frustrated, but they listened to their Commander. After all, he knew how to stay alive. He knew how to win.

One... two... three misses. The fourth split an approaching cruiser in two – another fatal wound to the enemy fleet.

Ryan gave a quick glance to the wall monitors. Power levels were down to 55%, even though central engineering had the matter collection vents on maximum. Maybe they should dip into the planet's atmosphere? No, that would slow them down too much. Just maybe...

The mothership's fire remained focused on the cruisers, systematically taking them out, outmatching their steady onslaught of cannon fire. The opposing fleets drew close together. Soon the antimatter shielding would be useless. Unlike the modern vessels, the Mothership did not have the improved Xeronian technology and they would be relying on the outer hull armor.

Ryan had a plan. "Helm 60 degrees on X-axis. Navigations, set trajectory directly underneath the planet, acroluc one. Maximum deceleration on the apex. Engage now!"

The huge ship stopped its spinning and shot past the approaching fleet in a bold flash of light. An Xi-cruiser which had been closing in to wreak havoc on the mothership began to flex uncontrollably. It strayed from its trajectory and collided into a group of escorting destroyers. Kanook looked up from the tactical, a slight smile on his face, and an eyebrow raised in wonderment. Ships in space were rarely lined up on such close vectors. It was either a freak of timing or pure genius.

The mothership's brief acroluc jump had brought it directly underneath the planet. They were now using its gravity to help them loop around at a breakneck speed. Simultaneously, the matter collection vents were taking in a great gulp of energy as they scooped up atmosphere. But the maneuver was chancy as the old ship could break apart under the titanic stresses at play. Vibrations carried along her decks, bulkheads contorted ever so slightly. Monitors glowed red as warning indicators peaked beyond maximum levels.

Ryan ignored them. He could feel the heaving vibrations through his hands.

She would hold.

The tactical was alive with crossfire. Lortay, McClary and Dorftal's forces were firing relentlessly, but the cruisers were beginning to slice them apart.

They had no focus, no precision of fire, Ryan thought angrily.

"Commander! Collision imminent with an Alliance ship!"

"Then tell him to move!" yelled Ryan, watching the tactical, his gut twisted sickly.

Move dammit!

3..2..1.

They scraped by one another.

Ryan swore sourly.

"Weapons, focus fire on those cruisers."

The tactical revealed an ugly picture. The Alliance were in disarray, had lost their cohesive punch. Uncoordinated strikes were yielding poorly. Casualties were climbing.

They didn't need his cue. The cannon started pounding.

Multiple destroyers burst into gaseous plumes and shards under a direct hit from the main cannon. Alliance ships once under duress, found themselves free of the enemy's barrage.

A refitted slaver was running parallel at 200 degrees. A familiar face hailed Ryan on the monitor. It was Wharsoff.

"Commander, we are pleased you have arrived."

"Wharsoff! Regroup those orphan squads, will you? We're moving in."

The Showmish Captain did not bother to reply. His ship veered away, others began falling into standard attack configuration as their courses merged.

They were headed straight into the Xi-Empire fleet. The remaining Xi-cruisers were reacting in frantic attempts to move out of range of the incoming cruiser killer, but they were positioned at a disadvantage, effectively outmaneuvered.

Dorftal's ship was too far in the lead, taking the brunt of the fire. It would hold off the destroyers, but not the cruiser's main cannon. From the tactical, it was clear what the cruisers were intending.

Ryan looked over at Kanook, "Range?"

He shook his head. "15 seconds."

"Weapons, divert all fire to the cruiser at 010-454-554." He read off the globe's coordinates for clarification, although it wasn't required. They had their own tactical display and they knew what to do. The true question was: did they have enough time?

"Just a few more seconds," added Kanook.

But it was already too late. The pursuing Xi-cruiser fired. Part of Dorftal's ship disintegrated. Its shielding collapsed, overloaded by cruiser's massive cannon. The wreckage spun uncontrollably, leaving behind a trail of debris and corpses.

The Xi-cruiser didn't get a second shot. The mothership's cannon blasted directly into its midsection. For a brief, yet eternal second, the huge Xi-cruiser seemed to push on undaunted until a string of explosions started down its length, each blast triggering another.

Ryan looked over to Kanook. He needed a report on Dorftal's ship, although he avoided forming the words. Kanook's eyes hadn't left the tactical. His hands flew over the tracing scanner array controls in a blur.

"Some good-sized pieces left, Commander. There's a good chance of environmental containment. I have multiple life sign tracings."

"Com, give me all Dorftal's deployment lines."

Another line of monitors folded out from the ceiling. Links were established to the additional ships, some small one-man vessels, others larger destroyer class. "This is your Commander, assuming squadron lead. Proceed at a 45 degree vector, course 000-440-334. Spike ball formation."

The spike ball was the most unusual of all the formations. The ships formed a sphere, rotating in a full 360 degree defensive position. This was not used often, as a well-placed missile could destroy the whole lot, but in tight quarters it was deadly.

Kanook gave him a surprised look.

Ryan smiled. "Cat and mouse. That other cruiser will turn away to attempt a shot at them. That Xi-bastard can't resist the temptation."

Ryan downloaded the navigation data from his vaskpar directly into the tactical console. The course vector, signified by a bright red line within the globe's holograph, writhed as it adjusted to the changes. The helm officers, in turn, worked furiously to compensate.

"Helm, bring us around," ordered Ryan casually.

The mothership swung, navigation burners blasting to push the gigantic vessel into position. Destroyers were coming up on their port side, firing unmercifully. The mothership's turret gunners bravely fended them off. Side missile launchers roared successively as they busily spewed out their ancient poison. Still, the Xi-Empire ships pushed in closer, their weapons flaring in vengeful arrogance.

The mothership's shielding somehow remained intact under the onslaught. The antimatter grid dissipated the enemy's fire into waves of energy, the energy reclaimed into the main power network through the outer hull receivers. The powers involved were titanic in scope. Clouds of pure energy raced along the hull, destined to reinforce receiver grids. The nebulous edge of one of these energy clouds touched an external power relay. The result was explosive, leaving sections of the outer hull disintegrated, and fires racing back through the corridors, chasing escaping gases. The horrible shrieking sounded through the ship, and deafening sirens sounded, forcing repair teams to jump into action.

Grim-faced gunners continued on, oblivious to the havoc around them, sealed off in their self-contained gunnery chambers. But no ears could avoid the haunting wails that carried through the corridors, not even those on the bridge.

The tactical was alive with the enemy. Ryan decided on a brash maneuver. "90 degree roll on the X. Now!"

The huge ship banked its gigantic wings again, cycling over quickly. Three destroyers, passing too closely, were slammed by the rotating wings with lethal force. The mothership's outer hull collapsed at the collision points, but the antimatter shielding was already feeding upon the alien ships' mass, engulfing the remnants of the vessels. The enemy vessels collapsed in upon themselves, imploding into successively smaller chunks.

Reports flooded onto the bridge. Ryan scanned them over the vaskpar. Relatively speaking, the damage was minimal. He checked the tactical. The destroyers were no more.

"Cruiser moving into position," reported Kanook.

They both inspected the tactical. The cruiser was slowing, positioning itself to fire into the configuration of Signite starships, just as Ryan had predicted. The Xi-Captain, in his eagerness to destroy the Alliance, lethally exposed his ship through veritable foolishness, by broadening its target profile. The mothership's four cannon fired simultaneously, penetrating through the cruiser's shields and tearing a large hole into the vessel's belly.

Over the vaskpar, Ryan ordered Dorftal's squadron to break formation and move in on the remaining destroyers. With only one cruiser left, the Xi-fleet was in chaos, some were retreating, others had decided to attempt another strafing run. The cruiser broke away, attempting to close into the planetoid.

"He's going for the base before we can destroy him," Ryan commented to Kanook. "Navigation, intercept that cruiser."

They had already anticipated him. Course vectors had already changed.

They were improving.

He watched quietly as his bridge crew coordinated their efforts in the daunting task of destroying the enemy, carefully orchestrating a complex dance of maneuvers, releasing a cannon blast, maneuvering, accelerating and firing again. The Xi-cruiser was elusive, somehow repeatedly dodging sure death, utilizing its shields to the fullest. It was clear this was no ordinary Captain at her helm.

Ryan checked the capacitor levels. They were dropping dangerously low. "Hold your fire. Release your targeting locks and standby."

He studied their target on the tactical. The weapon systems targeting programs were failing consistently, attempting to compensate for the randomly moving vessel, which was pushing burners to the maximum.

"Weapons, deploy missiles to force him into position, then activate the cannon. Send off a full salvo. I want this bastard out of the picture."

They followed his advice with precision. The missiles did their function, and the enemy held course long enough to achieve a lock. The next blast of cannon fire ran true. With main burners destroyed, the cruiser veered away from the planet, searching for another escape route from its gargantuan pursuer.

"Cripple it. Do not to destroy it," Ryan ordered.

The sluggish target was easy pickings for the weapons crew, and the cruiser went adrift, both of its main burners down. The mothership came alongside, her gunner turrets blasting at key areas which dared to return fire. Once the exchange had finally ceased, the cruiser, now dark and lifeless, could be boarded.

Ryan ordered McClary's ships to move in. It was a risk, since the enemy could always initiate a self-destruct, as these were vessels of war. The Xi-military fought by code. Failure was worse than survival.

Ordered to board was out of pure instinct. No one could know for sure what state the enemy vessel was in until they reached the bridge and by then it could be too late.

The Alliance ships docked onto the cruiser in multiple positions, each with a calculated path to critical ship resources. No massive explosion followed and the boarding parties met limited resistance from a devastated crew.

A calculated risk. His instincts had not failed him.

Ryan monitored it all from the upper deck. The last remnants of the Xi-fleet were being chased down and either obliterated or seized. Less than a handful of ships remained, and of those, only two had retreated far enough out to consider abandoning the chase. But then again, that would have been his call, not his allies, who continued pursuit not satisfied until every last one of them were destroyed.

Ryan didn't bother recalling them, instead, he ordered the ship back to the remains of Dorftal's ship and began rescue operations.

A very special deployment of the Xi-Empire fleet had been literally crushed by a much smaller force of the Galactic Alliance. The ramifications of this loss had yet to be felt by the Xi-Empire. The fleet had been under orders to regain and secure all Xi-colonies and then subsequently flank Zorlog's attack fleet at G0015-A.

But they never made it.

* * *

Hours later, the mothership went into orbit around the Signite base of Gairf.

The Commander ordered all the ranking officers to join him aboard. He paced the deck, awaiting their arrival. There were a lot of unanswered questions, and as many problems to solve. His turmoil was briefly interrupted by a warm message. It echoed within his mind, soft and gentle.

"Good work, Commander. You've just destroyed a fleet of Xi-Empire's finest. Something that hasn't been done in centuries."

That made him smile, at least, temporarily.

The resident fleet generals, captains and squadron leaders crowded into the oversized planning room. The lot were weary but still tense from the excitement of the recent battle.

Ryan took the position to address them, felt their eyes upon him, sensed their self-induced euphoria of success.

"Gentlemen – I mean - all of you. We've destroyed a considerable sized fleet. But before we start patting ourselves on the back, I've a few words to say. I'm sure all of you realize it's time to move. A Nubok spy ship came in just minutes ago. We've established that this fleet was part of the Zigot league. They will have already passed the information about the Signite base to Xilo. If I know their leader, and I do, since I've studied every scrap of information on him, they'll drop whatever they're doing to give us another visit. I don't want to be here when they do."

A small rumble of voices filled the room. General Lortay spoke up. "I assume the plan is to relocate the base personnel to this ship."

"Yes, we have the capacity. What's the population at the base now?"

"We're at almost fifty thousand. But we'll be pulling from that number to crew all mobilized vessels."

Ryan turned to Tmaurau. "We must section off areas of the ship to accommodate different environments. You'll be in charge of the modifications. Wharsoff, you handle the political end and make sure everybody is comfortable with their designated locations."

"What about the damaged and seized ships?" asked one of the captains.

"Any work must be done enroute. Put them in tow or dock them in our bays. Assess their value. Destroy what we can't use."

"Now, onto other matters. A number of times during this battle I was monitoring the engagements of your ships with the enemy. Although we won, I cannot help but ask myself why. All of us have a long way to go before we're ready to engage the enemy again."

The crowd shuffled uneasily. They did not take lightly the Commander's criticism.

"Your strategy was shit. Reactions delayed. Coordination sloppy. If we hadn't the advantage of this ancient technology working in our favor all of us would have been floating in space or stuck in a slave barge by now!" Ryan was almost yelling at the top of his lungs. The blood in his temples pounded. The rage was building inside, as it had so many times before, and he was losing control.

His eyes scanned the crowd to meet Kanook's. The second officer looked back impassively, devoid of any emotion, totally controlled.

That's the way he should be now. What the hell was wrong with him anyway? He can't let his emotions rule him.

Calm down.

Breathe.

A moment passed. No one said a word.

Ryan resumed. "Now since I have that out of my system. I suggest we start doing something about this problem. Once we get underway, every last one of you is signed up for mandatory training. It's time we all learned how to fight effectively as a unit."

He looked over and found a soot-covered figure with a ripped uniform. "Dorftal! You were too far ahead, separated from the main fleet. You're lucky you made it out alive."

The tired Captain looked to the floor.

"Just the same, by God it's good to see your ugly face again."

The room filled with laughter.

"Consider yourself reassigned to one of the base ships – destroyer class."

"I don't believe I'm fit..."

"Don't bother arguing with me. You'll only get me more pissed off. I need you in command."

He directed his attention back to the group. "Every last one of you heed my words. Out here battles are not fought with your heart. No matter how badly you want to win, it simply doesn't matter what you want. Battles are fought with cunning and foresight, anticipation and strategy." He tapped a finger to his temple. "Manoeuvres and plans have to be executed precisely. If not, mistakes are made, and every mistake cost lives. Your troops depend on you. They won't trust your judgment if you lead them into battle without that vaguest idea of how you will win. When you make a mistake – learn from it. Many of you have already lost against Xi-Empire at least once. How many mistakes did you make then? Figure them out and whatever you do, do not carry that baggage around with you. It's counter-productive. Remember our advantage, we have nothing more to lose. There is no surrender."

He took a breath. The small crowd remained quiet. "If any of you are offended by my speech. Good. It is your duty to lead brave souls into situations where they will have to give 110% just to stay alive. I expect you to give the same amount. The harsh truth of it is, I expect we will be out-numbered and out-gunned whenever we meet up with the Xi-Empire.

A few of the greener officers glanced nervously around the room.

"There are a few of you here who think you are the answer to this war. I guess that's understandable. You have to be arrogant. You have to have an attitude. Just make sure you back it up with results, understand? You don't, and I'll cut you out of the equation permanently."

He could tell, by the look in their eyes, they didn't like what he was saying. He paced back and forth, again suppressing a familiar building rage. Anger was his dancing partner, but he must maintain control. He stopped and faced the group.

"You may not particularly like me, or what I am saying. Maybe I'm exposing some truths you don't like facing. Maybe you don't think my expectations are realistic. Tough. If you don't take the responsibility of command serious enough or you think you're going to get your crew killed, step down now, before it's too late. So let me repeat the question. If you feel you are not up to command, then feel free to step down now – no ramifications, no reprisals."

Silence.

Someone cleared his throat, another coughed, but no one stepped forward.

"Alright then, consider yourselves committed. We have less than 36 hours to get the hell out of here. I want it done in 24."

"Dismissed!"

The officers filed out, grumbling amongst themselves. Every last one of them avoided his gaze.

He wasn't exactly instilling admiration in them right now. Hell, he expected some of them to step up and resign just to spite him. But they didn't. Maybe they believed in what he was saying. His truth was their truth. They had to improve or they would fail.

As he watched the room empty, his pulse slowed to a steady throb. He rubbed his arm. A wave of tiredness crept over him. He sat down, took a deep breath and let it out slowly.

Was he doing the right thing? This was his role, wasn't it - to push everyone beyond their limits? That is the only way they could win. Go beyond the possible and do the impossible.

Their small victory was just that, small. Once the Xi-Empire decided they were a serious threat...

But no one needed to know his fears – no one - not even Aviore.

* * *

A Bellicose Dance

Despite Ryan's angry proclamations, the Alliance teams met the challenge admirably. The move out of Gairf base was accomplished in record time. Everything was loaded, right down to the smallest scrap pieces of usable metal. The officers pushed themselves as much as they pushed their subordinates, fuelled by anger, challenged by the Commander's deadline.

Gairf was not to be left completely abandoned. A small detail remained at the base for reconnaissance and communications. It was manned by a group of volunteers who were ready to scuttle as soon as the enemy appeared.

The convoy filed away with ordered precision. They were destined for Grak, where they would pick up supplies and recruits. They had very little time to train and prepare themselves for the ensuing battles. Their time to strike was now, but they were not ready.

Ryan reviewed the latest intel from the Nubok spies. Xilo undoubtedly knew about them now, but the Xi-Empire wasn't reacting yet. How long would they continue with this internal war of theirs was anyone's guess. In the meantime, the Alliance would take advantage of it. That was a surety. Things would not be to their advantage forever.

He had a message to deliver, to everyone. He had to be precise, eliminate all ambiguity. They were on borrowed time and they needed to accomplish the impossible.

He set up a rotating schedule to deliver his speech to the Galactic Alliance population. His first address was held in the mothership's auditorium. A crowd numbering into the tens of thousands stood before him. This room had seemed, not so long ago, expansive. One's voice would literally echo off the distant walls, but not now. Every square meter was crammed full of curious Alliance citizens, of all races. Many had never seen the Commander, nor understood the part they were expected to play.

He glanced over to Aviore who was at his side. She smiled at him and mouthed a simple phrase. "They are waiting."

He cleared his throat. "Members of the new Galactic Alliance, I welcome you to freedom."

The hall shook with a roar, the cry of elation welling up from the masses. He had to wait, an eternity it seemed, for quiet once again to settle over the crowd. "We have survived the Xi-Empire by escaping from it. They will not allow us to remain free. We all know they will come for us again. I say to you, not this time!"

A roar started from behind and surged forward. The floor shook with a constant drumming.

"We are the weapons of their destruction. We will succeed because we must succeed."

The crowd started stomping on the floor and clapping out a rhythm that someone had initiated. The chant began to build in volume and tempo.

"Death to the Empire! Death to the Empire!"

He held up his hands. "Wait! Hold!"

Quiet slowly settled upon the room. "We can only do this with everyone's help. We need to know your skills. What did you do before you were enslaved? What do you know? Some of you may feel you have nothing to offer. You are wrong. There is a place for everyone in this war... Everyone!"

He scanned the crowd.

So many hopeful faces.

"Some of you may not be able to fight. I understand this. But this war will not be won by only those who take up arms. There are many critical support functions needed. You can join a medical team, cook the food, repair machines. The opportunities are endless. Choose your task. Do your best. That is all I ask of you. Through your help, we will bring freedom. But, freedom without sacrifice is merely an illusion. It will require all of us to take down the Xi-Empire.

The sea of faces stirred, mulling over his words. He could feel their excitement surging, like an electric charge, building, ready to spark.

"I've made a decision in recognition of this moment. Something I hope that all of us, and I do mean *all* of our races, can appreciate in their own way. This vessel which protects us from the cold of space does not have a name, as yet. As she is the flagship of our fleet, that is simply not fitting. So, I now christen this vessel, the *Freedom*. May she provide a home to the homeless, relief to the suffering, and hope to those who have lost all. And she will, with our help, bring death to the Xi-Empire!"

The crowd thundered. The chant returned, reverberated somewhere near the rear, and raised in intensity, flooding over the cheering in a wave, racing through the crowd in a storm.

"Death to the Empire!"

"Death to the Empire!"

"Death to the Empire!"

Ryan waved, deafened by the roar. He stepped down, and in seconds was out of the room with Aviore in tow.

Too many people. It truly scared him.

"You should have stayed, they love you."

He stopped. "I'm not a politician, nor an entertainer. And I'm not a power-hungry fool." He hit the control panel for the turbo-lift. "And I am certainly not an icon for these people."

Aviore bit down on her lip. *But he was an icon, whether he liked it or not, he had become one. They looked to him for hope.*

Ryan canceled the remaining speeches. Recordings would be sent out to the fleet and further presentations coordinated without him.

He had better things to do.

* * *

Wharsoff had performed exceptional work. Living quarters were modified to meet the varying alien requirements. The ship was subdivided into small pockets of ethnic cultures. Each had their own piece of what they once called home. Even Ryan and Aviore, who determinedly remained on the *Dancing Queen*, finally swayed to the pressure and relocated to the human section of the ship. It was by no mistake this section contained a particularly superior apartment reserved for the likes of a Commander. It was spacious, enticing, with many exclusive features, that made their quarters slightly more impressive than most. They enjoyed their new place, yet neither felt truly comfortable there.

Their work soon pulled them apart.

Aviore utilized her linguistics expertise to teach Trinarieit. Few of the crew had the privilege of vaskpar implants. The most basic of barriers – communication – had to be overcome. She worked long hours, many of which she spent instructing future instructors. She would send them off to coordinate more classes, more training. Every child, every adult of every race needed to know Trinarieit. This was the first step in winning a war.

Once the program had developed a proper momentum, she applied her botanist knowledge to help rebuild the hydroponics area. It had to be restored to operational functionality before existing oxygen and food supplies dwindled to nothing. She worked hand in hand with McClary, who had been assigned the responsibility of atmosphere and water supply.

The Scotsman had to maintain a remarkable juggling act. He worked with Dorftal and Lortay to keep the *Freedom* supplied with air and water and simultaneously helped out Aviore in the hydroponics area.

Supply vessels were constantly being dispatched to raid a nearby moon or planet for raw materials, all under the watchful eye of the Commander as such moves always increased the chance of being located by Xi-Empire forces.

Everyone wanted to see the hydroponics systems fully functional. This did little to alleviate the stress on the rebuild teams. McClary helped Aviore as much as possible, but she was the one who truly understood the marriage of biology and technology. Aviore pulled from multiple botany sources and seed banks, sending McClary on special trips to pull samples. Prepping the main hydroponics decks was painstaking and laborious work. By the time the fleet arrived at the Grak base, seedlings were growing, but the work did not stop there. The central hydroponics area was only one of many. The ship was designed in a nodal, compartmentalized fashion. There were hydroponics cells throughout, nevermind the naturalized park areas which needed to recover from a barren deadened state. All of this had to be functioning before the supply convoys could stop.

* * *

Ryan was pulled in so many directions, he wondered if he would retain his sanity. Officer appointments, duty rosters, role definitions, command structures, all the organizational matters of running a fleet of hundreds of thousands of combatants, plagued him every minute of every day, not to mention the everyday rigors of Fleet Commander.

To top it all off, he also had to fit in time for his ongoing officer training program – where he conveyed his recent studies of history in war to all of his generals, captains, 1st and 2nd officers, examining in detail battle strategies and formations that they would employ in the near future.

Throughout it all, he missed his new bride. He had developed a need for her, to keep her close, but she wasn't – she was lost to him. She had been absorbed into the Alliance war machine.

It was not only Aviore that was involved but Gem as well, who had been drafted by the Xeronians to link into the *Freedom's* main systems and help restore the thousands of ship's sub-systems that had yet to be resurrected.

This had evolved into a new type of war.

Ryan, alone on any free cycles he managed, started his own research project, as the *Freedom* was not without her own mysteries. Artifacts and information were being discovered every day. This was critical information that he was not about to let go. He doggedly continued his research, arranging an hour here, skipping a meeting there.

It was important to him as the Ancient Ones posed an answer to all of this - a race more powerful than 10 Xi-Empires. He searched for but found little that would provide answers about this mysterious race.

The Ancient Ones had ensured their privacy by wiping clean any and all information related to themselves within every computer core. Remnants of the purge programs responsible had been found throughout the cores. Insidious as they were, their purpose was clear. The Ancient Ones were a secretive people, and they had no desire to share their knowledge, or their history.

A few clues did appear intermittently as the ship was opened up for use: the odd printed text, small hand-held computer units that had somehow retained their data, multiple objects of unknown purpose, some artwork.

In a small room that would pass as a chapel, on a wall of polished stone behind what resembled an altar, were etchings so intricate they were no thicker than a human hair. One had to look closely to see the paragraphs of an ancient dialect, mathematical patterns and symbols, and star mappings of age celestial bodies. At the very center of this wall, a truly remarkable shape presented itself. Veins of golden luster splayed out like a silken spider's web, drawing the eye inwards towards a tiny small light emanating from a white crystal. It was a star, unmistakably, of a system buried deep in the fathoms of an undetermined galaxy. If anything, the artifact was a beautiful thing to view up close. But to Ryan, this was much more, for he believed it was the very epicenter, the home star system of the Ancient Ones.

Ryan managed to get word to Aviore. Hoping that it was possible she could decipher the glyphs written upon the artifact.

"Hello, husband."

Ryan stood up so quickly he almost banged his head on the altar.

She laughed.

God, he loved that laugh.

"I've missed you."

"Well, apparently you are the Commander, and you just need to give the order," she taunted.

There were bags under her eyes, lines on her face. She was beyond tired.

"And you need to get some rest."

"Have you looked in the mirror lately?"

He turned to check his reflection on the wall's black mirror-finish. "Yeah, I guess you have a point."

"And what have you been doing?"

Soft hands massaged his shoulders as she drew close to him.

He grabbed her and kissed her passionately.

"I could make love to you right now."

"Who's stopping you?"

He didn't need any further coaxing, proceeding to lock the door and pulling her up onto the altar. They took time after to hold one another, each knowing they were quickly running out of time.

"So what is this mysterious thing you beckoned me to investigate? I am sure the original builders of this room did not have this in mind."

"The wall behind us, do you see this?"

She moved in closer to study the inscriptions. "I can make out some similarities here with other languages, plus a number of very unique markings. This is going to take some time, Ryan." Her features reflected the stress of too many long hours.

He felt a pang of guilt. "Hey, don't worry about it then, really. This isn't that important. How is your work coming along?"

"I am getting close. The restoration teams are working non-stop."

"And then you will get some rest?" He placed his hand on her cheek.

"Soon, I promise."

"You know, I was just thinking about our conversations about religion – and their effect on social structures. How about we turn this room into a church? We must have some priests or preachers or whatever you call them on this ship. Open denomination. What do you think?"

She laughed. "Well, I'm sure some of the crew will thank you for it. I need to return..."

"Yeah, I know, but I think we have a lot of scared people aboard – and I don't mean just humans."

"Maybe you're right. You know, I'm impressed."

"Why?"

She moved in close. "Just the way you think. Like a true leader."

"Let's get together tonight. Let's drop these double shifts."

"I won't if you won't," she said teasingly.

"Then it's a deal."

"But it's OK to spend a little more time on this. I think you're on the right track here. It wouldn't hurt."

That was enough to convince Ryan to find a minister who was willing to take on the challenge. It would be hard work as the minister needed to learn the religions of all the races and keep his own prejudices in check. But he was sure he found the right person for the job: Ashanti of Tawma – a Showmish that had a way about him, a talent to set one at ease.

"I want you to meet the needs of our people. We have so many here of a varying degree of beliefs. I'm not asking you to forfeit your own religion, mind you, only open your house to all, and provide a church that teaches and encourages the essence of most religions."

"Commander, you may not understand what you are asking of me. There are many belief systems represented on this ship, a few of which may actually contradict one another."

"I know, personally, that the Showmish are a very understanding and open people. I am just asking you to promote tolerance and understanding, provide some strength to the ones who need it, maybe some guidance on morality. This should not be such a stretch."

"Morality? Values are not the same across races, Commander. For example, there are certain cultures that promote lying as a highly esteemed skill, others killing is a rite of passage."

"Oh. Well, that won't do. Perhaps the best religion is the law that I set aboard, then."

"Perhaps, but I may be able to find some parallelisms here."

"Great!" smiled Ryan. "That's why I've asked you to do this. Study the crew and draw your own conclusions. I just need you to give them what they need."

"And birth an inter-racial religion, Commander? Stray from the individual truths that we have all learned as children?"

"Truths learned or programmed? What the truth is has been twisted into so many different perspectives, it is unrecognizable. All that extra baggage of history and individual prejudice - that is not what religion is about, is it? No, that's just what it has become."

The old Showmish waved his snout. "Truly, this is a compelling problem."

"Yes, very challenging. I'm sure it will be very difficult to teach such concepts, considering the past that each member of this crew has endured. Such a cause would demand a strong leader."

"Ah. Your attempts of persuasion are all too evident, Commander. However, the answer is yes. I will accept this role, for all the children if not for any other reason. Hashimah works in mysterious ways."

"Or God, or as the Brogs say, Awg," added Ryan with a smile. "Welcome aboard to the Intra-racial, multi-denominational Church of the Alliance, Ashanti." They sealed the agreement with a handshake.

Attendance was surprisingly high on the first day the chapel opened its doors. The Church of the Alliance spanned as many religions as possible. Ashanti did his best to integrate everyone. Human, Signite, Showmish, Narkasite, Nubok, Krelp, and even Brog volunteers had stepped forth to help 'administer' the applicable procedures. Its popularity revealed certain truths. Many drew strength from their religious beliefs. Faith had kept them alive through incredibly difficult circumstances. If that is what his crew needed to have the courage to fight this war, then that is what they would receive.

And so, the Freedom was becoming not only a functioning warship and strategic mobile base but a true integration center of multiple races – a unique example of what the future could bring.

* * *

The Galactic Alliance's arrival at Grak resulted in a further strengthening of ships and resources. The Brog presence within the fleet tripled. It took some time for the others to adjust to the change. Brogs were intimidating, even frightening to many, but they were part of the Alliance and because of that, were accepted. Through all of this, they grew in strength together, for they had moved past the fear and distrust of one another and shared a common purpose – a common enemy. For many, the massive starship called the Galactic Alliance fleet became a new and wondrous home, built on diversity and collaboration.

Regardless of this, no one was foolish enough to consider themselves safe, for they all lived under the dark gauntlet of war. There were many battles yet to be fought.

The fleet then turned toward the Xeronian colony. It was here they would conclude their final preparations for war.

As the Galactic Alliance grew in strength, the civil war of Xilo raged on.

Freedom

The balance of power remained on the side of the Zigot League, though barely. The loss of their fleet at Gairf carried with it devastating effects. Zorlog's Purists had established critical footholds in the outer systems and were now initiating a slow and bloody progression toward Xilo.

The news of the defeated fleet was never conveyed. The Emperor had decided it would damage their cause. An official, sanctioned version was leaked out, very different from the truth. The fleet had succumbed to a freak accident and strayed too close to a supernova. All lives lost.

And so, contrary to the Alliance's expectations, no reprisal was attempted. The Signite base remained operational, acting as a key relay for the Galactic Alliance's intelligence network. This, in turn, provided them with much needed time.

The Galactic Alliance fleet's arrival at the Xeronian colony was a welcomed event. The small colony was saturated, its infrastructure overloaded. Close quarters had tested the patience of many and raised the tension of its inhabitants to a critical situation. Even the habitually emotionless Xeronians demonstrated a sigh of relief on their arrival.

Ryan and Aviore took the *Dancing Queen* down to the planet.

Traffic was heavy, as the port was incredibly busy with taxis shuttling to and from the *Freedom*. Tsaurau was there to greet them, his face gray with fatigue.

"We finally made it back, Tsaurau!" Ryan announced to his old friend with a wide smile.

"I was becoming concerned that we would be stuck indefinitely with our new allies."

"No need to worry now. We've room for everyone, bring'em all on board."

"I reviewed your last report about the engagement with the Zigot League fleet. It was a very close battle."

"Yeah, too close," agreed Ryan soberly.

Aviore commanded their attention with a clearing of her throat. "Tsaurau, I am in charge of the hydroponics system, and I need some help developing a proper vegetation base. Could you direct me to whoever is in charge of your hydroponics and park areas?"

"Certainly, I am responsible for the areas you mentioned, although I do not do the maintenance work. I will contact my friend Targoff, he is Chief-of-Agriculture. I am sure he can help you."

"Targoff." Ryan chuckled. "Now he is a character. You either like him or you hate him."

"I hope that you like him," interjected Tsaurau.

"I am sure I will, Tsaurau," Aviore affirmed. "Don't you mind this big bully. If you can just point me in the right direction?"

"I believe he is in the park on the first level, the one we call Gemoodow. If he is not there when you arrive, you can request his location over the Par."

Aviore gave Ryan a peck on the cheek and left, knowing that the two friends preferred to be left alone.

"Bully?" he asked incredulously.

She answered with only a wave goodbye.

"You think I'm a bully, Tsaurau?"

"I do not perceive you to express such behaviors, Ryan."

"Regardless. Tsaurau, we're a mess. The last engagement proved to me that if we met up with the Empire tomorrow, we'd be cut to ribbons."

"You were victorious, were you not?"

"Yes, but before our convoy arrived at Gairf base, we had already lost a quarter of the ships. Our captains need to learn how to think in three dimensions and develop responsive strategies. I've been attempting to lead some training on this, but I don't have the patience."

They turned and walked towards the bay exit. Tsaurau did not reply immediately, preferring to contemplate the situation for a time.

"The Xi-Empire has reigned over a thousand years. They have been fighting wars for most of that time. It does not surprise me that their captains have superior skills."

"Superior or not, I've seen them make foolish mistakes. I'm sure that won't continue. I'm sure the caliber of our enemy will increase as we approach Xilo. We need to be able to out-think them, out-manoeuver them, out-shoot them. Maybe what we need to do is send my captains on a crash course with Taldig. Do you think he would be willing?"

"He would be more than willing. He enjoys teaching. It is very rare that another Xeronian expresses any interest in Taldig's specialized knowledge. Such research is an unpopular study for most of our people. I'm sure he would be honored to take on such a request. He has expressed interest about boarding the ship you now call the *Freedom*. He has a number of his own interests to pursue."

"Oh, and what would that be?"

"He is an avid study of the Ancient Ones, much like you."

"Really? Then I do have some interesting things of note." He quickly described the icon in the chapel to Tsaurau. The Xeronian was impressed.

"Taldig will bring with him some knowledge. It may provide you with new clues."

"Why so much secrecy?"

"I am not privileged to access this knowledge. Taldig is an apprenticing Elder. He has been taught many things. The average Xeronian is not required to carry such burdens."

"You're avoiding the question."

"Are you sure?"

Ryan thought about it for a moment. He had never known Tsaurau to be purposefully deceitful. Maybe he really didn't know.

"OK, Tsaurau, I'll let this little mystery drop for now. That reminds me - I had a strange experience some time ago. It was disturbing..."

"Tell me about this experience."

"Not here. Are my old quarters still in existence?"

"Yes, certainly. But the area has been in use by a number of humans since. However, I do believe your quarters have now been emptied since your arrival."

"Good. Let's go there. I can scrounge up a nice stiff drink before I tell you about it. I believe it is important."

"Very well, Ryan, though I don't believe I personally could consume another glass of brandy."

They found the apartment in disarray, but intact. The previous tenants had already been relocated on board the *Freedom*. Ryan stoked up the artificial fire, adjusting it to throw off just the right amount of heat. He stared into the coals. Red and glowing, with dark edges, they pulsed with life. It brought back mental pictures. Ryan shuddered and abandoned the fire to focus on the task of pouring them both a drink. Tsaurau would need one, despite his earlier resistance.

"I do not wish to..."

"You will." Ryan forced the glass into his hand.

Tsaurau was perceptive enough the sense something was not quite right. "Very well."

"I've been meditating. Something I have learned from the old Showmish women - the Sisters-of-Soom."

"Ah yes, Tseman spoke of them. It is said they are as wise as the Elders."

"I guess. They are good teachers. My ah... abilities are improving. I've seen things I can't explain." Ryan paused. *Should he ask Tsaurau? Would this just bring up bad memories for him? Just what was it he needed to know? Confirmation or translation?*

"Please, continue," urged Tsaurau.

"Sit down old friend. Please."

"Let me explain my experience. I traveled to a world that was much like Earth. I was an observer. It felt like it was... well, I don't think it was in the future or the present."

"Then an image from the past," Tsaurau added, nodding his head slowly.

"Yes. I think so. Felt like it was a long time ago. As I said, I was watching this scene play out. This beautiful world was being attacked by ships that seemed quite familiar in design."

"Xi-Empire ships?"

"They were, and when they attacked, they failed time and again. They could not penetrate the shield that surrounded this planet. Sound familiar?"

Tsaurau's veins in his temples seemed extended, his eyes a little tighter, an Xeronian expression of emotion, mostly akin to sadness. "Yes, I do know of this story."

"I watched as a ship approached, saw it launch a weapon. Unlike its predecessors, this device managed to penetrate through the shield. Its effect was horrendous, literally turning the planet into a sun. Tsaurau, I am sure I witnessed the death of Xeronia. I saw your world die."

"Your words describe the past accurately enough." He looked away, round black eyes squinted into tight ovals. "Forgive me. The talk of such matters disturbs me..."

Ryan took a large gulp of brandy. It burned on the way down. A burn, like the way the electrified whips felt on his back. Like the pulsating coals in the fire...

"Ryan, are you asking me why you had this vision?"

"I don't get the connection. Why bring me back there? What was the purpose? I'm beginning to think it was just my own mind playing tricks on me."

Tsaurau looked up. "Tricks? There are no tricks. You have a gift. That is why you were chosen." He paused for a moment. "Perhaps you are looking too hard for the hidden meaning when it is not hidden at all."

"What do you mean?"

"What details do you remember?"

"Well, there was something else. The Xi-fleet did not get away with their crime. I think, for some reason, your sun went supernova."

"Yes, it is true. It was intentional."

"You have a weapon that can do this? You understand this could be a way to take down the Xi-Empire?"

"You would use this to drive them back, to their home?"

"Yes," said Ryan quietly, "something not so easily done. We will be moving into Xilo-owned space as soon as the crews and ships are ready. The odds are not in our favor. It'll be seven hundred ships against forty thousand."

"The enemy numbers have grown," commented Tsaurau.

"No. Our intelligence has become more accurate," corrected Ryan.

"It will not be numbers that will win this war."

"Then what will?"

"I don't know. But I do know this - a few of our people have offered to join your crew. The past events have deeply disturbed and split our society. There are those who are willing to fight."

"Fight? Xeronians!" Ryan couldn't contain himself. The thoughts of seeing a frail Xeronian in hand to hand combat with a Xilozak was laughable.

Tsaurau's expression was placid and cold. He was not liking Ryan's reaction.

"Forgive me. It just seems like everyone wants to jump on this downbound train. And what, my friend, do you think of this?"

"I support all of my people. I accept their decisions."

"Your volunteers would be gratefully appreciated. They can join the crews, but I can ensure you they will not be assigned a weapon or expected to participate in combat unless they specifically request to do so. If that is acceptable, we can certainly make room for them."

Tsaurau gave a look of satisfaction. "Those terms would be consoling to a Xeronian mother."

"Tell me about this supernova bomb. Do you still know how to build it?"

"To use such a weapon, it is unconscionable. We were wrong to launch it."

"What do you mean? They destroyed your home and you are telling me they didn't deserve to be wiped out themselves?"

"It was not a fitting legacy that Xeronians wished to leave."

"Maybe so. But you know our odds."

"I will construct the weapon myself... but I ask you, Ryan. Who would be strong enough to bear the blood of millions on their hands?"

Ryan looked into the fire. The coals had now faded to black, only cooling embers remained. "If it meant destroying them, then I would."

"A weight that could crush your very soul. But I will guarantee that you will not bear that weight alone, my friend."

* * *

16. Xilo

Zorlog had a commanding view of the planet below through the quartz panels from the bridge of the cruiser *Kirbetz*. The last campaign had been very successful. He now commanded two-thirds of Xi-Empire space, and a very important planet to the League: G00015-A. It was a dull, dirty planet, not much to please the eye, but a military gold mine, and in some ways very similar to Xilo. He chuckled to himself as he thought of his last visit here, many zanii ago, rebel slaves had done considerable damage. Where were they now? They most likely retreated to their ravaged home worlds, like *thrickets* on dung. He will enjoy tracking them down, killing off the defiant ones. It will feel good to tear the limbs off their leader one by one, to kill that pitiful creature slowly.

"My Karvok."

It was Gulin, his most trusted Charvok, and as such, one of the most envied. The spoils of victory ran thick around them. Charvoks would always have a claim on the most valuable, although the biggest prize has yet to be won. Zorlog had a plan, and it was the plan of plans. In the end, it would be the Txtians that would be bowing to him, and the Zigot scourge would be cleansed from Xilo.

"Karvok, the destroyer *Gimoch* is approaching. Tarvok Brock is requesting your response."

"Tell him to come alongside and board. You escort him up here."

"Very good, my Karvok." Gulin moved off the bridge quickly, eager to appease, content in his duties.

Tarvok Brock appeared on the bridge shortly after, carrying with him a small pouch. He handed it to Zorlog with a wide grin.

"We've got them, Karvok, right where we want them."

Zorlog was studying the pouch's contents. Brock's last proclamation made him look up.

"You looked at this information?"

The Tarvok's features changed like a cloud covering the sun.

"Yes... Yes, I did. I had to know..."

"HAD TO KNOW!" Zorlog screamed. He grabbed hold of the hapless Tarvok and threw him across the deck.

"Where are they positioned? What is the armament? How many ships? Tell me, did you have to know so you could leak that information over to the

Zigot scum?"

"No, no, my Karvok. I am a loyal Purist. I'm loyal to you only." Brock glanced about quickly, snake eyes darting over the bridge. His forked tongue writhed out of a dry mouth.

Zorlog was literally shaking with rage. With the disrupter bar clenched tightly in his hand, he moved close to the fallen Xilozak. Brock cowered on the floor, silently, nervously.

All of a sudden, Zorlog laughed. It raked through the silent bridge like a roll of thunder from an approaching storm. And he continued to laugh. It was insane. Soon the whole bridge crew joined in. The room filled with growling howls. Brock's apprehension faded, his fangs sunk back to their relaxed state. The outrageous laughter, so contagious, forced howls from his gut.

Zorlog offered his hand and Brock took it.

Brock did not notice the twitching eyes of his Purist commander, did not see the raised disrupter bar, not until it was too late. It cut through his thick Xilozak arm, slicing through bone with a sharp crunch. Brock screamed in agony.

Zorlog's grip did not relent, not even when Brock's legs gave out from under him. He held up the heavy Xilozak with his one arm, every muscle intense with excitement. He glared into Brock's eyes.

The laughing had stopped, cut short by a blunt metal bar. The crew were frozen, shock pasted upon their faces. Realization fed traces of fear into the room. Disbelief was reinforced by the pungent smell of seared flesh. Zorlog tossed the severed arm onto the deck. It hit with a wet thud.

"You are alive now because I like you, but I will have to kill you if there is a next time."

Brock swayed dizzily, barely conscious.

"Gulin, see this Tarvok out."

Gulin approached, agile legs stepping carefully, quietly. He took hold of Brock, now fading in and out of consciousness, and hoisted him over his shoulder. He headed for the exit, stooped deftly to grab the severed arm.

The sound of the closing hatch carried throughout the room, penetrating the silence with a rude clang. The crew turned to their work, avoiding the eyes of their Karvok. None dared meet his heated gaze. Grunting in satisfaction, Zorlog retired to his quarters.

Gulin carried Brock back to his ship. The heavy Xilozak was an insignificant burden to Gulin's powerful muscles. Just the same, he expended extra effort to ensure he did not jostle the poor Tarvok too much. As he approached the airlock, he noticed Brock had opened his eyes.

"Let me down. I will walk."

Gulin eased him to the floor, carefully avoiding the severed stump. He wrapped his arm under the Tarvok's, steadying his weak legs.

"There are excellent surgeons that can reattach..."

Brock responded a hopeful look buried in pain.

"But you should not have reviewed that report, my Tarvok. He could have killed you."

"Hah!" Brock snorted weakly. "He will never get that chance. His element of surprise has now been forfeited. Listen to me, Gulin. Get away from that fanatic as soon as you can. He'll get you killed - and everyone else who follows him." Brock's voice was a mere whisper, drained by the stress of the walk. He staggered through the airlock. His Charvok met them on the other side and quickly jumped in to help them through. Brock waved off his questions, quietly cradling his severed arm.

Across the corridor, Gulin gave the Tarvok a sharp Xilozak salute. He gave a nod of thanks and called back a scratchy warning. "Remember what I told you."

Gulin stepped back and closed the airlock door. Peering out the closest porthole, he watched as the ship departed.

He stood there for a long time, contemplating his true situation.

* * *

The Purist fleet was twenty thousand ships strong now. Most of them were military warships, the others were refitted slavers, cargo ships, and the odd converted pleasure yacht.

Zorlog stood on deck, his most trusted Zuvoks surrounding him. The time to move was almost here. One last battle, one more key base and they would be ready to begin their move on Xilo. But this would be the most difficult battle yet. The Zigot League was desperate. They had assembled every ship they could spare to this fleet. It was larger than the Purists' but not by much.

Once they take out this force, it will then be a systematic seizure and purge of every Empire controlled planet until they reach Xilo itself. This would be the beginning of the end of the League.

Their move on Meghellan would take every bit of strategy, every trick Zorlog could muster. He laid out the plan to his Tarvoks carefully, ensuring to cover every detail, everyone's roles, and responsibilities. They would have to move with stealth and position themselves outside of scanning range. This would take time, and leave his main force weakened and vulnerable. His most recent intelligence revealed the fleet was to mobilize and depart from Meghellan within a zanii. Leaving him little time to position the arms of his fleet.

He would let the League fleet get some distance from the base before he would attack. Once they destroyed the base, they would have control of the last remaining deep space communications relay to Xilo.

The fleet would no doubt turn back around as soon as they received news of the attack. But a turnaround takes precious time, enough in fact, that they would be ready by their return. He would leave them surprises along the way using a few strategically positioned ships to wreak havoc upon them, just enough to keep them on edge. They would return into a trap. There would be four separate divisions involved, one hidden in the nearby nebulous cloud, another in close orbit of the sun, one adrift in a dense asteroid belt just inside the system, and the last one – simply the bait. The League Karvok would see their destroyed base, catch the small Purist fleet on their tracings and move in to crush them. As they passed the asteroid belt, the first division would launch, then the rest would fall in. If all went to plan, the League fleet would be decimated before they knew what hit them.

Zorlog left the planning room, confident his officers and Tarvoks would be ready. He waited on the bridge impatiently, often glancing at the tactical.

The divisions moved out to position themselves for the battle.

Soon. They would move soon.

* * *

"I'm worried. It's getting worse. He's sitting up nights. He's always rubbing his arm, although he rarely complains, I can tell he's in pain. Always his left side. When I ask him what's wrong and he says nothing, but I know it's bothering him."

Tsaurau nodded. "The organ's condition is degenerating."

"What can you do?"

"We need tissue samples to grow a new organ. He must submit to a medical procedure. It is very doubtful he will. Aviore, you must put this in perspective. He is about to lead a campaign of war."

"I know this is war, damn it! But it is going to kill him!"

She exploded, pounding her fist against the corridor wall, followed it with a savage kick, and then she sank to her knees, burying her face in her hands.

Tsaurau stood dumbfounded. He did not have the facilities to know how to react to such violent reactions. He waited for another display, but none came. He finally approached her and laid his hand on her shoulder.

She looked up, the anger and frustration drained from her. Her face was pale, and she carried the signs of too many sleepless nights. Tsaurau helped her up.

"Tell me there is another way," she pleaded.

"We could build an artificial organ."

"Will it work?"

"Yes, however, you are departing within one hour. That is simply not enough time."

"I will build it," came a new voice - Gem's.

"Are you sure you can do this?" Aviore asked, trying to contain her hope.

"Yes, most definitely. Ziggy will manufacture the unit and I will aid him. I have many designs to draw upon. However, I would appreciate some pre-manufactured components that the Xeronian medical team has inventoried."

Aviore conveyed the news to Tsaurau.

"I will see to it that you get everything you need, Gem," he offered.

"Very well. Consider this done."

"Is this what Ryan means when he states that you are obstinate?" asked Tsaurau.

Aviore smiled tautly. The words provided a strange translation, but she had remembered it from her studies. *Obstinate: stubbornly refusing to change one's opinion or chosen course of action, despite attempts to persuade one to do so.*

"Well, I guess I am. I just want him to survive this war."

* * *

The Galactic Alliance fleet was on the move. A grueling month had passed since their arrival. One hundred and twenty thousand citizens had worked around the clock at their assigned duties. Generals and captains alike studied under Taldig: three-dimensional strategies, historic battles, mistakes of the past.

They said they were ready although Ryan was not as confident.

Their first target was a small desolate planet of G00015-A. The Commander picked that particular target because of a past sighting of fleet movements in that area, and because it was a key spaceport, and a ship manufacturing and repair facility – which they could use to their own benefit.

Ryan particularly enjoyed the fact that it was under the control of the Purists.

The Nubok spy network was proving invaluable. Whatever they saw via their sensors they passed on directly to the *Freedom*. The small ships moved out well ahead of the fleet, acting as scouts, invisible but deadly to the enemy.

Long-range tracings caught the glimpses of a battle on the fringes of the Zegnite quadrant. As the Nubok relays continued their tracings, it soon became evident that it was none other than the main Purist fleet with ships too numerous to count. They had just made quick work of a small League patrol fleet.

"Kanook, how close are we? Can they see us?"

"Possibly, but our image may not be discernable. We see them so well due to our scanning relays placed by our intelligence network."

"Yes, and if they have their own relays, they can also see us."

"Yes, they could."

Ryan watched the tactical. The Purist fleet was barely a stone's throw away. If they were seen, they were as good as dead. His stomach felt like it was tied in knots. He rubbed his left shoulder.

Listen to your instincts. Too close - they were too close.

"Full stop!"

His order carried throughout the convoy. Ships ground to a halt in veritable unison. The *Freedom's* bridge turned quiet as apprehensions soared. Questioning eyes looked were passed to their Commander.

"What now?" asked Kanook.

"We wait."

The Galactic Alliance fleet remained stationary for over a day waiting for the Purists to move deeper into the quadrant. Ryan had ordered the Nubok ships to move in as close as they dared. The navigation officers soon deciphered jumbled tracing data into clear trajectories. The Purists were moving toward a League-controlled base called Meghellan. Ryan knew from previous intelligence reports that the Zigot League ships affiliated with that base were significant - outnumbering the Purist fleet. He also knew Meghellan was the last stronghold before Xilo.

If they managed to take this base, it would be the Purists that would be winning.

A long 27 hours later, Ryan issued the command to resume. There was nothing holding them back from attacking G00015-A now. It would be an easy target as it was literally abandoned. But he felt compelled to change the plan. It was not good enough to just stand by and watch. He slammed down on the ship's intercom. "Patch me a link to all ships."

"Established, Sir."

"All ships, this is your Commander. We are modifying our destination. All personnel to battle stations. Standby for new vectors."

"Kanook, we're going to Meghellan, what's the ETA at maximum acroluc?"

"It is 38 hours, 17 minutes, Commander. You sure you want to do this?"

"The League's numbers are superior. We need to even out the odds if we are to keep this Purist fleet cutting the way ahead for us."

"Navigations, plan an interception course at full acroluc 10. Download vectors to the rest of the fleet. Helm, engage on T-minus 10."

The Galactic Alliance fleet awoke from its brief rest, reoriented and headed on a new course into the Zegnite quadrant. Aboard every ship there was a flurry of activity. Last minute weapons system checks, combat gear checks, emergency repair drills, medical team preparation.

A Bellicose Dance

Technicians hovered protectively over their drive systems, coddling them as a mother does her newborn. Everyone kept as busy as possible, trying not to think of the impending battle.

* * *

"You fence well."

"Not as well as you, old man. You've surprised me more than once."

"Aye, many years of constant drilling at home, bless'r soul. I can say with certainty too many hours I've sweated through this bellicose dance. "

Ryan wiped the drops from his brow with his towel. McClary had barely broken a sweat.

"Bellicose dance?" exclaimed Ryan with a chuckle. "That is one way to put it for this insanity we call war. But instead of true physical contact, with our swords meeting metal on metal, we exchange hot plasma and nuclear incendiaries in the cold vacuum of space. To tell you the truth, I prefer this type of battle. But we don't have a choice now do we?"

"Aye. Conflict is unavoidable even in the sweetest of times. 'Tis many a time I did have a bit've a tizzy with the Missus. She had a way 'bout her. Up one side, down 'nother."

McClary paused a moment, as if he was conjuring up a vision of her in the air in front him.

"She was a good woman, a lovely creature. This hell was not for the likes of her. I guess it is better this way. She had neither the strength nor the desire to live as we have managed. She was a high strung one, she was. Broke down in hysterics in trying times. I tried to calm her, I did, but as usual, she paid me no mind. It was over before I realized what had happened. They cut her down in front of me." He eyed the length of his blade. "It was a weapon similar to this one, you see."

Ryan sat down on a bench, took a slug of carbonated water. *Yes, he did see. Like many times before, he heard the stories of others. He could only wonder how the human spirit survived such anguish.* He said nothing, for there was no reply. There were no words to heal such wounds. Silence was respect.

McClary abandoned his vision, decided to change the topic. "You know, my dear Commander. I do prefer the finer subtle edge of a sword to these blasted things."

"You don't like these disrupter weapons? Do not discount the amount of damage you can inflict upon the enemy. Activate the disrupter, and this weapon will cut through almost anything, all you need is enough power in the swing."

"Atomic vibrations or something like that ya say? Yes, I understand all of that but this sword I have here just lacks the charisma of a finely crafted weapon. Now yours..." He eyed Ryan's blade with its richly decorated hilt.

Page 439

"You seem to have an exception - a fine tool of debauchery."

"Here," Ryan tossed it to him. McClary caught it by the hilt and swung in one fluid motion. "Aye, she cuts through the air with a perfect balance."

"Present from the Xeronians, but they didn't make it. Apparently, there's a long story behind it."

"I'm all ears, Commander."

"OK, I'll tell you what I know. An Xeronian scoutship found a Showmish ship adrift. They boarded it, found survivors, helped them get the ship's systems repaired and back on their way. The Showmish Captain, out of gratitude, presented the Xeronian Captain with this sword. Naturally, they had not a clue what to do with it, but they received it in good faith."

"I've heard those Showmish blades are worth their salt."

"Yes, and so was this Showmish Captain. Apparently, a Xi-patrol discovered the Xeronians shortly after they had separated from the Showmish. The Xeronian vessel took some hits. Critical systems went down. As the Xi-bastards moved in for the kill, the Showmish appeared and intercepted them. Since their weapons systems were not yet functional, they did the only thing they could - they rammed the sonofabitch. Both ships blew to smithereens. The Xeronians survived though, and they tend to remember things – especially this act of bravery. I've heard them tell this story to their children, I think it's a lesson about faith in other races."

"Aye, 'tis a learnin' that has made all this possible, I'd say."

"Yeah, we can thank the Showmish for that."

"So you say, these Xeronians remember all the details?"

"Like elephants, they never forget. Never. Count on it. Don't cheat a Xeronian. Your children's children will be paying for it."

They both laughed heartily. It really hadn't been that funny, but it was all in the timing.

"By the way, been meaning to introduce you to this - there's something else the Xeronians seemed to have mastered, under my tutelage of course. But I'm sure you can be the judge of that yourself. Would you care for a shot of Xeronian brandy? She burns going down, but it does tend to sharpen the mind. God knows we'll need it tomorrow."

"Don't mind if I do, Commander."

* * *

They were drawing closer to Meghellan with every hour. Ryan spotted a Krelp navigation officer attending his post and beckoned him up. The creature's bulk filled the walkway as he approached. His vibration-translator was blinking merrily, signifying it was engaged.

"What's your name, Lieutenant?"

Vibrations carried through the floor as legs pounded with intention. "Bzbob," came the reply. Most of Krelp names were based on vibrations. The translator could only facilitate so well. Ryan motioned him to view the globe, showing the tactical display of the area around Meghellan.

"I understand the Krelps are from this region. Are you familiar with the celestial formations in this quadrant Bzbob?"

"I am... There are white areas," he pointed with a tentacle.

Ryan moved the positioning image until Bzbob nodded.

"White areas?"

Ryan scanned the Par for the translation. *Empty space*, the absence of all matter, tiny imperfections in the distribution of the universe. The absence of all matter, including the quintessential matrix of dark matter. If anything entered such an area, it would be absorbed to "fill in" the hole as it were. To an outside observer, the approaching matter would simply disappear, literally evaporate.

"You mean *empty space?*"

"Yes. One must not approach *empty space*."

"Bzbob, do you know where these white areas are?"

"The Xi-Empire know few. We know more."

"Where are they?"

"The locations are difficult."

Ryan surmised the meaning. The alien could only provide an approximate location.

"Could you plug in the coordinates of every known white area into the tactical?" He motioned to the other two navigation officers to review the regions with Bzbob.

Kanook watched them curiously, "Commander, what do you have in mind?"

"Just taking advantage of every scrap of information we can collect, Kanook. When you have quicksand in a desert, it is good to know where it lies."

"Com, pass on the new data to the Nubok ships, have them modify their tracing resonance to verify these areas and get solid coordinates. When we get close enough and open a channel to every ship's captain. We're going to review a new battle plan."

He turned his attention to the monitors. "I'm intending to take advantage of this civil war, by altering the numbers in favor of the Purists. By taking out a portion of this Zigot League's Fleet, we will ensure the Purists win this conflict. We will ensure they begin the process of cutting their way through to Xilo and we will be following them all the way in.

I know that the Purists are not about to attack Meghellan with the fleet parked in orbit. They will do what I would do. They will wait for the fleet to break from the base and start their patrols. If the League fleet behaves as per our previous intelligence, they'll break into three patrol divisions. We will destroy the 3rd division."

When the Purists hit Meghellan, we will move on the League Patrol 3rd division. We will utilize our knowledge of this area, including these pockets of *empty space* and we will destroy this division.

"And what of the Purists?" asked McClary.

"They will have their hands full with the other two divisions."

"This plan will work, Commander, provided they do not know where these *empty space* regions exist," stated General Lortay.

"Agreed, but I'm sure that even if they do know about some, they won't know the exact location and shape of everyone in this region. I understand that this *empty space* is a dynamic phenomenon, always changing. They will have to alter the resonance on their tracing scanners, which means they'll lose long-range focus. I doubt they'll want to risk that."

"It will work for the first ship at least," volunteered McClary.

"They may be five or size times or size, but I am confident we will cut them down quick enough. There's more to this plan yet. I'm hedging a bet that they'll break off engagement once they figured out that we can hurt them. They'll try to get back to Meghellan. That's when we'll hit them again with part of our fleet that will be positioned for their retreat."

The generals nodded in agreement. The plan was solid enough, even considering the size of the fleet they were about to take on.

"General Lortay, take three squadrons. You're the fox in waiting."

"So we dispatch our Nubok scouts to Meghellan and track this patrol."

* * *

The Galactic Alliance knew of the Zigot League patrol far in advance. As expected, the massive League fleet broke into three divisions. The third division was on its way as expected. Nubok scouts had picked up their tracings and constantly relayed the activity back to the *Freedom*.

The Galactic Alliance fleet accelerated to intercept. They weren't hiding this time. When the patrol responded to intercept the fleet everyone knew they were committed.

It was time.

The Commander had a channel open to every ship. He had one last moment to address them, and he took it. "In a few moments, the true test of our strength will begin. The enemy is not only out there, but also within our minds and within our hearts. Be brave, live free, die free!"

Ryan closed off the com link. His mouth was dry, his teeth tasted like metal. His officers returned to their tasks, silently, each mind contemplating... something. What they thought, he could only guess - fear they would die today or elation they could exact revenge? He could only hope that those who needed his words found strength in them.

The tactical was a cornucopia of colors. Ships constantly repositioned themselves as the Xi-League patrol bore down upon them.

A wisp of a fragrance turned his head. Aviore was there, dressed in full combat gear. Her face was pale.

But she was stunning.

Ryan diverted his attention back to the tactical. Time seemed to crawl.

Then the thunder began. It rolled with the might of a million troops marching in unison. The powerful cannon fired time and time again. Targets winked out of existence. The weapons crew was becoming dangerously adept.

"Engage all shield plating," Ryan ordered. "Full decompression alert for *all* decks."

Thousands of non-combatants scrambled to their assigned quarters sealing their hatches, others working in the more dangerous outer hull, such as the gunners, screwed on the helmets of their suits.

"In range in T-minus 1 minute," reported Kanook.

10..9..8..7..6..5..4..3..2..1.

The fleet was hit by a savage volley. Missiles cleaved their way through shields and into ships hulls. But the state of the battle was already changing. New tactics were being employed. The Galactic Alliance rebels remembered their training. Ships began concentrating their fire on shared targets. Vessels rotated, swarmed and moved off in unison. It was a long distance death dance, with each drilling holes into their enemy. As League ships drew in close, where the wide expanse of space shrunk to mere kilometers, dormant Alliance missiles sat ready for activation.

Another wave of destruction as League ships faltered and crumpled into floating derelicts.

Then they were within the maelstrom. In what seemed like seconds, the majority of the fleet had passed completely through the patrol, dispersing missiles in their wake. Squadrons pulled together into formation and they began their second phase of the battle.

But the League patrol was struggling to regain formation, attempting to adjust to heavy losses.

The Alliance maintained deceleration, then reversed direction. The exchange continued. The *Freedom* rocked as the helm officers poured over their controls. Power reserves were getting dangerously low. Engineers diverted power from all non-critical systems. Gravity plates fluctuated each time a cannon blasted, bringing with it sickening waves of weightlessness on deck. The engineering crews labored to keep the auxiliary fusion generators online under the chaotic conditions. The new shield generators had been installed at Xeronia as a proactive measure to counter the excessive power drain of the tremendous ship during combat. But the work had been completed quickly and design compromises had been made.

Kanook moved around the bridge barking out orders in all directions. Ryan remained at the tactical advising the navigation teams. They diverted direction, feinting retreat, the League patrol, familiar with a fleeing enemy, pursued with a regained confidence. And they were all closing in on an area of *empty space*. Trajectories were adjusted, calculations made, vectors downloaded into helm control. At the last possible moment, the Alliance ships flipped on their axis and jumped off their original trajectories.

The League ships attempted to follow, but their acceleration was greater, precious moments lost. The first of the League ships hit *empty space*, and then promptly vaporized, literally ripped apart molecule by molecule. Two others disappeared before the Zigot League captains were able to react to the new hazard. Many of them managed to maneuver around the deadly area. A few ships collided in their desperate unorganized attempt to veer to safety. The Alliance captains took advantage of their confusion. They moved in again, this time sweeping away ships in a single pass with a merciless barrage of cannon. In seconds what was left of the League patrol was now cut in half.

The Zigot Commanders reorganized into a tighter formation, but a number of rogue captains broke away, attempting their own attacks, and in the process exposed themselves and others to be destroyed.

Ryan watched with grim satisfaction as they struggled to pull together.

He ordered a star dispersal. Concentrated fire would have no effect on a sparsely grouped number of ships. Each point of the star looped around, changing direction, heading back inwards toward the enemy. One by one, each group moved in on evasive attack formation, blasting in at the Zigot fleet, destroying ship after ship. He watched the orchestra of battle, pleased with his captains and crews. They had learned their lessons well, and in an incredibly short period of time.

A Nubok reported in, demanding the Commander's attention. The Purists were attacking Meghellan base, as expected.

The tactical revealed that the League patrol was in considerable trouble now. The Alliance ships were in position to crush them in one furious onslaught. But Ryan called off the attack, much to the surprise of others. His captains complied, although reluctantly.

They watched as the League ships retreated, sharing a quiet moment of amusement. Things were falling into place. Repair teams scrambled, and rescue operations commenced. They had lost 12 ships in all.

That was 12 too many.

Lortay's group hit the retreating patrol a few minutes later. The engagement was quick, yet devastating and precise, tearing the enemy into floating wreckage. It provided the incentive needed for what was left of the fleet to race back to base.

The Purists were experiencing a healthy resistance from the Meghellan base cannon arrays. The surface cannon were incredibly powerful, inflicting heavy damage to the attacking fleet.

The fireworks started in earnest with the arrival of what remained of the League patrol. It gave the impression the Purists had been over-confident in their planning. As a result, they suffered heavy losses taking back control of a base they had once already defeated.

The original strategy of the Purists was the sign of a devious mind. Ryan had studied the Xi-Empire battles too long now not to know who their Commander must be. His amusement escalated to a full-fledged laugh.

Zorlog had paid dearly for this victory.

"Commander, do we attack? Commander?"

Kanook brought him back. His look of perplexed annoyance was clear on his face.

"No, not yet. Far too many of them swarming that base. I'm estimating the count in the tens of thousands."

"Would be suicide, but we would take many of them with us."

Ryan chuckled. "Appreciate your eagerness, but they still have the numbers. No, we have to deploy rescue teams, and coordinate boarding parties to hit any of these League ships we can reclaim. They have a much bigger battle to fight, yet. We can afford to wait."

The Galactic Alliance fleet pulled back from Meghellan, taking what remnants of useful vessels they had seized with them. Their refuge was within a nebulous cloud, the very same that the Purists fleet had utilized to avoid League detection. Ryan was careful to disperse the fleet over a wide area and move slowly.

The waiting resumed.

* * *

Zorlog was puzzled.

The League patrol had returned, at two-thirds their expected strength. Some of their ships had shown signs of a recent battle, something that he'd never expected from a prominent fleet so close to Xilo. That fleet had been attacked, that much was certain. The question was, who had they encountered?

He pulled together a squadron, leaving the majority of the fleet to sack the remains of the base. It was time to investigate.

They followed the course from which the Zigot patrol had returned, moving cautiously, watching for the tell-tale signs of an enemy in waiting. Precious time passed as the tracing officers scoured the area for evidence of engagement. They found it - remnants of ships, destroyed and scattered - the refuse of war.

They made a full sweep of the area. It did not take long before one of them found the area of *empty space*. The Purist ship and its small crew simply disappearing off the sensors as it disintegrated. Immediately, Zorlog ordered the squadron to a full stop. He had seen this phenomenon before. Probes were deployed and tracing scanners modified to ascertain the dimensions of the region. They pulled the constellation archives – this area had been sectioned off to all traffic due to these anomalies. He paced the deck, putting together facts as the reports rolled onto the bridge.

Scant energy trails uncovered, somewhat loosely, the original course of the ships. Parts of the puzzle fell into place. He knew what had happened. A third party had attacked the Zigot fleet, then retreated to use this *empty space* to their strategic advantage. It had worked all too well. How many vessels had perished here? One could only guess.

"My Karvok, we can confirm the fleet broke into three divisions," interrupted Charvok Gulin. "The one division did not return – at least not fully intact."

"Helm, over there, bring us adjacent to that ship."

The cruiser *Kerbetz* eased through the wreckage to stop at the burned out remains of a destroyer's hull.

"What is it you think could do that to a class-3 destroyer, Gulin?"

His Charvok inspected the remains for a moment before replying. "Whatever hit this was far more powerful than our cannon, my Karvok."

"Yes, that is impressive," he laughed. "But we do not know who deserves the credit, do we? Let us leave a surprise for them on Meghellan."

These are not the slave rebels. They could not have attained enough ships. This must be a new race. A new enemy to contend with...

Gulin interrupted his train of thought. They had found some life signs on a wrecked ship. Zorlog ordered the change of course, then personally fired the blast that obliterated the remainder of the ship. He enjoyed the surge of power. His hate for Txtian blood clouded over him, obsessed him. He ordered the squadron back into formation and turned around. This new enemy would have to wait.

The squadron rejoined the almost twenty thousand strong Purist fleet at Meghellan. With Zorlog's cruiser in the lead, the mass of war vessels resumed course - toward the capital planet of the Xi-Empire.

* * *

On board the *Freedom*, Ryan monitored the Purist fleet with interest.

He had seen the small squadron backtrack and was sure Zorlog knew of them now. But that couldn't be helped.

As expected the squadron had turned about and rejoined the Purist fleet. They had a more important agenda to follow, and they were a mere distraction.

The massive fleet soon mobilized, abandoning the carcass of Meghellan, and disappeared into the heart of the quadrant. Ryan ran a trajectory projection. Straight to Xilo. Zorlog's intentions were clear now.

It would not be an easy trip for them. Squadrons of League ships and perimeter stations barred their way. It would be months before they reached Xilo - if they reached it at all.

He turned his attention to back to his visitors. Alliance generals and captains stood with him on the elevated deck, everyone watching the holographic tactical, whispering quietly amongst themselves.

"What do you plan to do now?" asked McClary.

"Like I said - they're our way in. We follow their wake, staying out of tracing range. The Purists will punch a hole in the Xilo defenses for us. We'll even help if we can, by taking out any League ships trying to outflank them. We will either usher them all to Xilo or terminate them."

"So that is why we helped out those scum-sucking Purists?" exclaimed McClary. "It is little wonder that you are the Commander, my boy, as I would not have the metal to make this call."

Ryan surveyed the group, consisting of a large portion of the top brass of the Alliance. He addressed them with a sober tone. "There is a weapon that was created by the Xeronians. It is capable of causing a sun to go supernova. It is, essentially, the perfect bomb. If one of those weapons were to be launched into the Xilo sun, everything around it within at least a ten-billion kilometer radius would be obliterated. A number of Nubok ships are being re-fitted with this weapon as we speak, including my ship, the *Dancing Queen*."

The group shuffled about, taking a moment to soak in the news.

"So, you may have already have guessed our end game. The focus of our efforts will be to centralize all the Xi-Empire's arsenal at Xilo. That means getting every ship they own into that system. The next few weeks will be critical. This fleet will disperse into five main groups. Each one of these divisions will be responsible for obliterating any Xi-Empire presence outside of the Xilo system. If you can't manage to kill them, at least scare them back home.

I estimate, on the outside, we are roughly six weeks from Xilo, but the Purists, I expect, will need more time than that. I expect they will be securing each base and each planet as they traverse this corridor. That's barely enough time for us though, as we need to literally circumvent the quadrant, move in and pull the envelope even tighter."

"Why think you, that all Xi-Empire war vessels move to Xilo?"

The question came from a familiar Brog - General Gor. He towered above all of them. His voice reverberated throughout the open bridge.

"That Purist fleet out there is the why. As they move closer, any and all Zigot patrols will be recalled as reinforcements. That will mean the majority of the Xi-Empire warships will have to abandon their posts and head home."

That will leave bases, slavers and traders exposed. The slavers and traders are trying to ignore the war. No profit in it. They will attempt to avoid the hotspots and keep their cargo moving. That's where our divisions come into play. We will seize or destroy these bastards one at a time. We close in, determine the right moment, then we strike."

A quiet acknowledgment moved throughout the room. It was not until now that they all fully realized the implications of what had been stated. It was a plan – one that could possibly result in the defeat of the Xi-Empire.

"Just so all of you understand. I intend to launch the missile myself from the *Dancing Queen*. The three other Nubok ships that will also be carrying the weapon will act as a safety measure in the event that I fail."

The room filled with talk. They did not like the idea at all.

"Who will command the fleet!" demanded the Brog.

"Yes. What if you are killed? Is anyone of us here prepared to succeed you?" the question was posed by Wharsoff.

Ryan held his hands in the air, and the crowd quieted.

"I will elect my successor before I leave. I do not expect anyone will contest that, correct?"

No one spoke up.

"Good."

Wharsoff stepped through the crowd, slightly stooped and weighted down with combat weapons. "Why do you elect to do this mission alone?"

"This must be done with stealth. This does not require a fleet, nor will I endanger ours. I cannot delegate this task to anyone else." Ryan avoided his eyes, staring into the globe. "Don't try to change my mind. I've already decided. Just keep to the plan. Everyone will be busy enough herding the last of this scum back to Xilo anyway."

He faced them again. "Wharsoff, Lortay, YushTar, and Gor. You will each be in charge of a division. Leave as soon as your troops and equipment are ready. Split up everything as evenly as possible. Kanook, you manage the details. I want a full complement alongside the *Freedom*. We have a population aboard to protect. YushTar, your area will include the Gedricka base. That's a key port for the Purists. Destroy it. Every freighter, every slaver, every warship, everything owned by the Empire must either be boarded or destroyed. I'll have this division remain here for a day or two until the Purists are out of tracing range. Then we'll take

Meghellan."

"What do we do with prisoners?" asked Lortay.

"We cannot take prisoners." Silence hung in the air for a moment as the gravity of Ryan's words took shape.

"How can we close up this quadrant in such a short time?"

"The slavers and traders will be traveling together for protection. They've been doing it since the start of the war. This should help somewhat. Otherwise, we maintain focus and hope lady luck is on our side. We will be depending on our intelligence network. We have only a few Nubok ships. I guarantee we could use thousands more if we had them. But you'll have to do with the resources we have available. A squadron will be charged with the task of monitoring and following the Purist fleet in.

"So, gentlemen, timing is everything. We have an incredibly tight window to establish a full impenetrable perimeter around the Xilo system. We can't afford any delays. Push your ships and your crews hard. Accomplish what you can, but make this deadline."

"Good Luck."

Hours passed as the crew and volunteers shuffled to and from fleet ships. Taxis buzzed between them like so many bees, transferring equipment, weapons, and stores.

The fleet broke into five separate divisions, branching out in various directions. Each was on a difficult mission. Each was on an impossible deadline.

* * *

Aviore watched her husband, admiring the way he commanded the attention of his generals, pulled them into his feverish vision of victory. He had forgotten she was there, by his side, the whole time. He was so absorbed in what he was doing.

She understood him a little more. It made sense why he drove himself so hard. It was part of him. She reached over and quietly took his hand. He turned, surprised.

"Why don't we go for a walk, Ryan."

Kanook nodded back at him, indicated he had things in control.

"Maybe that's a good idea," he sighed. The energy seemed to drain out of him. She smiled at him. "You could use some time to relax."

She led him out into the corridor. Neither felt like talking, Ryan needed the quiet to wind down, and they were both content to just have one another at their side. Aviore appreciated moments like this. It was not often that he had time for her.

They took a shuttle down into the center of the ship, to an area labeled 'Market Square'. The square was not unlike a Xeronian park - a circle of green vegetation surrounded by large streets. A small artificial sun beat down upon the area, providing a pleasant afternoon sensation. Many people, of all different races, had claimed the storefront shops as their apartments. A few entrepreneurial types had even opened up stores, bartering goods, as money was non-existent.

If this ship ever became an active trader, this would be the business core. He could only wonder if the Ancient Ones once bartered here, with other exotic aliens - people now only remembered in parables and legend.

Aviore pointed to the center of the park to a row of light green and crimson dressed small trees. "We just planted those. They'll grow fairly fast under this artificial sun. Very good oxygen producers, and substantial filters at that. Once we have all these areas recharged and the circulation systems working, we expect to have a complete ecosystem in place, that is, once the system stabilizes."

Ryan loved it. Last time he had seen this area it was gray and dead. "This is beautiful, flowers, bushes, trees. Makes me feel homesick."

"A long way from what it was before. This whole central area was bare, everything was dead - eaten by those things." She shuddered a little as they walked. "Even the soil was dead. We had to replenish and enrich every cubic foot of it before it would grow anything."

"Well, it looks like you have a green thumb - I mean – you have the magic touch."

She looked at him quizzically, not quite catching the meaning of either slang term.

"I see you even have sprouts of grass coming up," he added, attempting to skim over the awkwardness.

"Yes, these grasses are very close to Earth's versions, if I recall correctly. What we call grass is slightly different. It grows like a thick vine, taking root every few centimeters and rolling over the ground like a thick green carpet. I expect these varieties to flourish, that is, if the children would stay off of it."

Ryan saw three of them darting from the trees. Their small voices carried sounds of unabashed happiness. It echoed memories of his past, reminded him of the times of long ago, times when he was a boy. A sad realization came to him. "I didn't even notice that we had children on this ship until now."

"You're kidding me. We've found hundreds of them. Human, Showmish, Krelp, Brog, even Nubok."

"It's amazing they've survived."

"They deserve a better life. We have to give it to them."

"Don't be so solemn. Look at'em. They've already made a home here." He smiled at her. "True."

"You know, I'm really not that bothered that they are wrecking the foliage. If I'm doing all this greenery work for any reason at all, I'm doing it for them."

A small man approached them, slightly balding, but looking no more than 30 Earth-years old. Dark eyebrows covered soft gray eyes. He was dressed completely in brown, with dark, thick-heeled boots. He favored his right hand, carrying it tightly against his chest. It was probably an injury sustained during captivity.

"Commander?" he asked, in Earth-English, hands now joined as if he was praying. Dark eyebrows twitched nervously.

"Yes, what can I do for you?"

"You're from Earth, it's been told. Is that right?"

"Yes, I am." Ryan stumbled over his next words. He had become too accustomed to speaking Trinarieit. "Where were you from?"

"Canada... Vancouver, actually. I was a reporter."

"Got too curious for your own good," chuckled Ryan.

"Yes, I guess I did." Thin lips curled up. Gray eyes shone back amusement.

How long had it been since he'd smiled?

"I just want to tell you that the people around here, they all look up to you. We are 100 % behind you. Whatever you want us to do, just ask."

"I appreciate it."

"You're a legend, Commander, a hero. The real McCoy. I never thought I would actually have a chance to meet you."

"Uh... Thanks again. As for that legend stuff, don't you have to be dead to become a legend? I don't require such fame," Ryan chuckled again.

"How long have you been out here, Commander? I mean in space and whatnot."

"I really don't know. I've lost track of time. It's been years."

"Possibly well over one of your decades by now," corrected Aviore, in fluent English.

"You know, being a reporter and all, I would really be interested in getting your story. If I ever get back to Earth, it would be the hottest news catch ever."

"Sorry. I don't have time for biographies. Even if you had such a story, no one would believe you anyway."

"Yes, they would. You've been away a long time. The raids were a little too numerous and the aliens a little too bold to ignore. Hell, when I left, there was a special UN commission assigned to establish a worldwide defense agreement between all our countries."

"I'd have liked to see that, all the countries joining forces in peace."

"I guess it has been a long time," he stated, more to himself than anyone else. Thoughts of home flooded back, faces of his family, friends. Faces came up with names he couldn't remember, and other memories irritated him with hazy features of those with their identity long lost.

He remembered his black Buick though, long since abandoned in the desert. He had spent countless hours sweating out the imperfections of that machine.

Now it's all gone.

An awkward silence followed as the Commander was lost in thought. The former reporter finally cleared his throat, politely managing to grab his attention.

Ryan jerked back into reality. "Sorry."

"No problem. My name is Johnathan Jones," he stuck his hand out as a formal introduction.

Ryan chuckled heartily, "That's a good name. Like an adventurer. He shook his hand. We'll get together sometime, after all of this is over, OK?"

"Great. Maybe, with a little encouragement, I can convince you to let me write your biography."

"Maybe."

Johnathan turned away but hesitated. With a quick spin on his heel, he spit out his question. It had been difficult for him to work up the courage to do it. "Commander, will we ever get back to Earth? Do you even know where it is?"

Ryan was tempted to tell him he could bring him back at any time but held his tongue. No one goes back home. Not now. After maybe, but not now.

"Yes, I know where Earth is, at least I believe the information I have at this point, is accurate. If it's possible, you'll be brought back home, but only after this war is over."

Thick eyebrows slowly lifted from a creased frown. Johnathan had learned to accept things as they were. After the war, if they survived it, they would be brought home.

Such as it is. He had made a good life for himself on the *Freedom*. Who knows, maybe when the time came, he may not even want to leave? He had been eyeing a certain woman from deck seven. Signite she was, but lovely, once one overlooked the burns that covered her body. She had welcomed him into her bed with that warm, loving smile. He had foolishly declined, citing some ridiculous excuse. She had looked away then, so full of hurt, undoubtedly blaming her appearance. He had to make amends. He just needed to know how long he would be out here. He bowed slightly to the Commander and his wife and hurried away, satisfied he knew how the chips would fall, at least for the near future.

The two watched the man in brown retreat down the corridor.

"What a strange little man," Aviore commented softly in native

Signite.

They resumed their stroll.

"Haven't you told your people you know where Earth is?"

Ryan followed her lead, replying in fluent Signite. "Apparently it's not common knowledge. I'm sure they'll find out soon enough, though. I won't be the only one holding that secret. Last roster I checked we had a handful of Earthmen and Earthwomen signed up for astro-navigation, not to mention those lucky enough to receive a vaskpar, like Kanook or McClary. Word will spread. Either way, I can't be bringing anyone home, not yet."

"Ryan, if we ever do win this war, what are we going to do? I mean - after?"

"Whatever you want," he replied, offhandedly.

"No, seriously, where do you want to live? Earth? Signus? Out here? I want to know."

Ryan was baffled. *He'd never considered it. Strange that he'd never really thought of it. After the war...*

"I really don't know," he answered quite honestly.

"Well, think about it. OK?"

"How about making a home here? I'm sure it will make a fine place to raise a family."

"A family! I see. Now you're talking children," she teased.

He laughed. "Keep your pants on, we're not there yet."

"You mean that literally," she replied coyly.

Ryan looked into her eyes. A familiar flame was burning within them.

They retired early that day.

The war could wait.

* * *

The next day they moved on the Purist base Meghellan. Zorlog had left a regiment on the base to operate the large cannon array. Ryan appreciated the gift of target practice for his weapons teams.

They claimed seven destroyers in varying states of disrepair. They towed them into the *Freedom's* bays for retrofitting and repairs. The warships would make a fine addition to the fleet once operational.

Parties were deployed planet-side to obtain food and water stores, as well as anything else that would be useful. Thousands of individuals worked in unison, around the clock in ceaseless shifts. An enormous amount of food, supplies, water, and air was brought back to the *Freedom*.

Aviore oversaw each and every cargo load of vegetation that was imported up. Each plant was carefully selected and then painstakingly transplanted from the surface of the planet, and also from the remains of Meghellan's hydroponics areas. This was the last shipment of raw material she needed. Once again life was teeming in the hydroponics areas of the ship, within every separate generation cell, and within every living area of the ship.

As the cleanup effort wound down, Ryan managed to free himself from the bridge and search out Aviore. When he arrived in the ship's main hydroponics area, he couldn't help but gaze about in awe. The room was large, with a 30 meter high ceiling and 150 meter circular walls. Thousands of types of trees and plants were jammed into the area, choking off practically every clear spot on the floor. A couple pathways led to the main corridors, allowing the staff to move through the maze. A constant breeze from the air circulation systems swayed treetops and rustled leaves in a serene song.

Aviore was working on the central purification system, a gigantic filtration unit that reached up and into the ceiling of the gargantuan chamber. The central unit was a large cylinder with a diameter of at least 50 meters. Its walls were transparent. Ryan walked up close and peered in. Lines of purplish light traveled through a matrix of filters, like a roving charge of electricity, floating over varying colors of mossy substances that filled each porous layer.

He looked up. She was far above him, on a portable external elevator. A section of the filter was pulled out like a drawer of a chest of clothes. She waved to him from above, quickly closing the layer and lowering the lift to meet him.

"What do you think?"

"Absolutely incredible. It's amazing. I've never been here, but I heard it was a tangled mess prior."

"Yes, it was. Took a lot of work to get it back into shape. We had to pull in the big guns to get this working."

Ryan looked at her, puzzled.

"The Xeronian technicians," she said, laughing slightly. "They understood how this filter system worked right away. But I've never seen anything like it before. After the principals behind it were explained to me, I had to kick myself. It was so simple. Just the same, it's very touchy. Swings out of balance easily."

"Why the lift? Why not just turn off the grav plates?"

"The filters need the gravity for consistency, so we improvise."

"It's hot in here."

She glanced up. Ryan followed her gaze. Embedded in the ceiling, much like the one at the market square, was an artificial sun. Its rays reached every corner of the extensive room, feeding each plant with its life-giving rays.

"Took us a while to get that working again too. It uses a lot of power," she commented.

"I imagine it would. Did Tmaurau repair it?" he asked.

"Yes, he had to, no one else could. Apparently, this particular one taps into the main power conduits of the ship, most other systems run off secondary feeder lines. This one was special for some reason, at least, that is what he told me." She looked back down at Ryan, who was still inspecting the ceiling grid work.

"Don't be such a worry-wort."

"Well, it's an old ship."

"And it was built to last a million years," she added. "These Ancients knew what they were doing. From what I've seen, they've surpassed our technology 10 times over. I even saw a few Xeronians scratching their heads when they first started looking at some of these systems."

"I would have paid money to see that. Are we producing enough oxygen yet?"

"I think we're finally stabilizing. With the addition of the trees from the base, I estimate, if anything, we'll be overproducing within five days. I'll need to get over and check the monitoring systems within the next few hours. Gem's helping me figure it all out. She's been a great help. She helped me organize the vegetation for maximum growth potential and about half a dozen other things at the same time."

"Keep her busy, otherwise, she gets bored, and you know what happens when she gets bored."

"Yeah, she gets cranky."

They laughed.

"Cranky! She gets downright miserable!"

Each of them suppressed transmission over the Par, knowing Gem's moody response could carry repercussions. The smile disappeared from Aviore's face quickly. Her voice turned solemn, and eyes dwindled to the floor. "When do we start heading toward Xilo?"

"Within the next few hours, we're almost ready."

She lowered the lift, bringing it down a few inches from Ryan. "Why do you have to make that bomb run yourself, why not let someone else do it instead?"

"Aviore, are you familiar with the term Genocide?"

She nodded, "Yes, of course - the deliberate extermination of a race of people. I know what it means."

"The missile aboard the *Dancing Queen* – you know that's what it's capable of. I was the one elected to do this from the beginning. It's my destiny, no one else's."

"And when you get there and fulfill your role as the grim reaper, do think you're prepared to live with that action?"

"Do I have a choice? I don't see any right now. Besides, if I don't fire the missile, one of the three Nubok captains will. They'll be positioned and waiting."

"Then let them do it." She wrapped her arms around him, squeezing him with all her strength. "Don't leave me, Ryan."

"You gotta understand, I must do this myself and I will not have you along. I'll be in the very heart of Xi-Empire controlled space. I don't want you to take that risk. It's just too dangerous."

"So what! Everything we do is dangerous!" she yelled.

"Look," Ryan said, exasperated. "The plan is tentative, anyway. You never know, things may change in the next few weeks."

Things did.

* * *

17. Legacy

The Purist fleet approached the Xilo system from multiple vectors. They closed in on their enemy with a reckless abandonment, carrying with them trophies of past battles they had collected along the way. They were too eager, too zealous, blinded by their own overconfidence.

The Zigot fleet was ready for them, in numbers that exceeded the Purists most pessimistic estimates. Zorlog ordered the fleet to hold, but his Zuvoks saw blood and they would not stop.

Xilo, defended like no other, was in many accounts, invincible. Generations of paranoid Xi-Empire administrators had seen to that. Zigot League cruisers were positioned around the planet, each well within the cover of the planetary defenses. Any attacking cruisers that ventured too close would meet a quick end by planetary-sourced fire. Inversely, any smaller destroyer-class ships that were capable of out-maneuvering the formidable blasts were easy prey for orbiting cruisers.

Xilo's moons were fortified with multiple defense stations, protecting not only the planet but a vast underground network of starship bays, storing tens of thousands of war vessels.

When the first wave of the Purist fleet attacked, League squadrons swept up from the planet and drilled through their formations, forcing them into the line of planetary defense cannon, which blasted volleys from the surface and systematically destroyed them with veritable ease.

As the remains of the first wave climbed desperately out of the range. Secondary sentries dispatched from Xilo's moons, chasing down the escaping ships, bathing them in deadly streams of plasma, effectively reducing their numbers even further.

Zorlog, sick with the loss, incensed with frustration and rage, recalled his divisions repeatedly. Finally, after realizing their strategy was failing miserably, the Zuvoks heeded his orders, and the Purists retreated. Luckily for them, the Zigot League armada did not pursue. The Emperor was not about to risk his hold on the capital planet.

The fleet reassembled in a safe orbit from Xilo. Zorlog called for his Zuvoks, then proceeded to execute his rogue officers, enraged into a state of madness. The message he put forth carried throughout the fleet in the color of blood - he was in command, no other, and he expected absolute obedience.

His newly promoted Zuvoks began a detailed process of examining the

Xilo's defenses. Probes were deployed to perform reconnaissance, although not all returned successfully. The information retrieved was sufficient to expose the true gravity of the challenge. Vital facts were uncovered. With every new piece of information, a new strategy began to form. Thousands of simulations were run, each branching into thousands of permutations of scenarios. It took time, but a substantial attack plan began to take shape – one that could defeat the impressive defenses.

Many sadii had passed before Zorlog called upon his Zuvoks again, who were by now growing impatient and irritated. They joined him on the bridge of his cruiser and watched with skepticism as the images of a virtual battle unfolded on the tactical holograph display.

Zorlog's new plan was brilliant. Every weakness exploited, nothing missed. The model played out to end with the Purists' victory. As the holograph faded into darkness, the crowd shuffled uneasily. It was not the complex movement of squadrons or the timing of simultaneous maneuvers that bothered them. It was the foundation of the plan itself. The key to victory was disabling the planetary defensive grid. Zorlog's solution called for a squadron of over 50 specially modified ships to penetrate the defenses at full acroluc and target the key offensive bases on Xilo. Such a bold attack required tricky maneuvering and decision making that would defy any standard evasive logic built into a ship's guidance system. As such, actual pilots were needed. Statistics that had been calculated to demonstrate auto-guided vessels' success rates were at best, minimal. Piloted vessels fared better, yet even then, it was doubtful that only a lucky few would manage to infiltrate the defensive grid. It was clear that once beyond the reach of the long-range defenses, and moving at such acceleration, the attacking ship would never decelerate in time to avoid collision with their impending target. Whoever was at the helm of these ships would be on a suicide mission.

Zorlog called for volunteers.

Who would lead such a defiant attack?

None stepped forward.

The quiet, which permeated the room, was flooded with the raging growls of the Purist Commander. He tore into the group, preaching his Purist message, cursing their cowardice, insulting their character. His followers hung their heads. Others made the bold decision to leave the room, abandoning their rank - and their loyalties.

Still, none stepped forward.

Zorlog looked over each officer. His eyes fell on the one loyal officer he had left.

"Gulin!"

His Charvok stepped forward with an audible swallow that echoed in the quieted room like sharp rap on a tin can.

"Gulin, there are none here that are worthy, or brave enough, to lead such a glorious attack. None but you. I ask you now: Will you be the leader that is absent within this room? Will you bring us to victory?"

Gulin's two hearts pounded in his chest. His eyes watered from the stress on his nerves. He had to make a decision. He glanced back at his peers. They were a tough, hard lot. Many years he had tried to gain their respect, to prove he could command. They had all scoffed at him, and their jeers had leadened his spirit. Their faces carried another look before him now, not that hateful aversion. He saw in them an unfamiliar, yet pleasing emotion - fear.

Yet he was not afraid.

He hated the Txtians more than any of them, possibly more than Zorlog himself. He had watched League troopers kill and torture his family, had felt the pain of the mind-twist so often it left a persistent ringing in his ears to this day. He was, and would forever be, a Purist!

His gaze focused back upon his leader, the only Zuvok who had given him a chance. Strangely though, he did not see the face of Zorlog, what he saw was the pained image of Brock, his severed arm held tucked under his vest. Brock's words rang in his ears, sharp, chilling, echoing again and again: "He'll be the death of us all."

"Well?" asked Zorlog impatiently.

The image vanished, metamorphosing into the sharp, threatening figure of Zorlog. The Zuvok's burning gaze inflicted within him only raw amusement. Gulin understood clearly now, and he stood proud because he was a Purist.

"I will lead your mission," he snarled back.

"Very impressive," Zorlog announced, ever so slightly breathing out a sigh of relief. "You are indeed an exceptional Charvok."

Gulin shrugged the compliment off like water. "I am a Purist."

Zorlog's eyes seemed to dance an evil dance as they glared back at his crew. Few had the grit to face him down. He curled his lips into a satisfied grin. His amusement was fleeting, for around it ebbed the eternal flow of insecurity, and for a second, Zorlog's control deteriorated. His eyes twitched, his snarl cracked, darkness flooded into his mind as the thoughts of death exploded in a thousand painful screams.

Only Gulin noticed the change. Saw Zorlog's true self, exposed for only a brief moment. His Karvok's sanity was no longer a question. Deceptively and masterfully Zorlog pulled himself together. His harsh, fiercely determined composure returned readily enough. He barked his orders.

"Charvok Gulin, I hereby pronounce you the station of Zuvok. Collect your squadron pilots. If none volunteer, then you will choose them."

Gulin nodded, appreciating the promotion, however briefly it would last.

"Then it is time to prepare, I call on my Zuvoks to perform this plan. Begin coordinating your vessels, position your ships and prepare your teams. We will initiate our attack once all is prepared."

The gathering broke up. Each Zuvok left for his command, and each division began to prepare for the final attack. It took almost two sadii to modify the smallest of the fleet's ships for the Xilo runs. Zorlog allowed Gulin complete control over the mission and maintained his distance.

Gulin enjoyed his newfound authority, but still supervised the ship modifications personally. They were loaded with the extra missiles necessary to do the intended damage. Each vessel was stripped of all extra weight, including the life support systems, leaving only enough air for a few radii.

When the time came to draft the volunteers, more than the required stepped forward to be at his side. Gulin was surprised at this.

Why so many? Do they all wish to die so readily for the Purist cause?

As he walked the line, he came to the decision that his understanding why was not important. He felt relieved that he did not have to choose reluctant volunteers. He reviewed each trooper critically. They all carried the same look of determination. It made him proud to stand there with them all, each a Xilozak brother.

The ship's colors were painted red and yellow, the hues of fire, and the name of each pilot was distinctively painted along the fuselage in bright gold letters.

As the day of launch arrived, Avoks and Zuvoks alike filled the bay as the line of pilots marched out. They were all holding a crisp salute as a sign of silent respect. Gulin kept the line tight, and they returned the salute with sharp precision. They maintained that line of precision as each ship taxied out of the bay, the pilots demonstrating their best skills. Gulin's chest was full of pride as he brought the last ship out into formation.

Zorlog stood on the bridge of the mighty cruiser *Kirbetz* He scanned the bridge, acknowledging the intense, excited features of his Avoks, and gave a short, curt nod to each of the Zuvok's projected image.

They were all ready, waiting for his signal.

He grabbed his disrupter bar and activated it. Blue currents of electricity danced off onto the floor and bulkheads in blue sinewy webs. He raised it high and swung it down in a chopping motion, accompanying a growl thick with emotion, "ATTACK!"

* * *

The Galactic Alliance, which included the *Freedom* and a growing division of fleet ships, had followed the Purists fleet's steady devastation as they fought through to the heart of the Xilo system. They stayed behind enough as to not raise suspicion, out of range of the Purists' deep tracing scans. More than once they had passed by a destroyed Xi-base or through the regions of drifting remnants of warships. More than once they had met up with a fleeing Zigot vessel or a small Purist patrol, and each time, with the help of the Nubok scouts, they tracked and incinerated them before they could communicate back.

The Commander insisted all the crew remain at full alert and ensured they all stayed sharp during the long quiet times of drudgery through constant drills and exercises. The crew did not complain as it helped counter the mounting tension. The war was now centered at the Xilo system and the Alliance divisions were closing the envelope on any Xi-Empire remnants.

Ryan was inspecting training certifications for new trainee's when the notification came down of the impending Purists attack. He was on the bridge in minutes. The Nubok relays revealed the undeniable truth. Zorlog's forces were moving into position.

Xilo was now completely surrounded by thousands of warships. Each specifically positioned for a planned attack objective. Xilo defense ships were scurrying to adjust. But they were waiting for something. The fireworks had not started yet.

Ryan was not going to wait, as they had to move to final preparedness. He gave the order. They all knew what to do. All hands to battle stations. All ships systems switched over to energy conservation mode. Fusion generator fuel supplies were carefully adjusted.

McClary, Captain of a divisional command ship, signaled the first 'ready' over the com channel. The others followed through just as quickly.

Ryan quietly watched the Xi-Empire battle progress on the tactical. Aviore arrived shortly, laying a gentle hand upon his shoulder.

"Kanook, you have the bridge." The Indian nodded acknowledgment, uttering not a word, eyes focused on the tactical.

The door to the officer's briefing room slid shut with a deafening silence. Aviore moved into his arms. They held each other for a long time.

"Seems like we've been here before," he said. "A long time ago, in a slavership. Only this time it's my turn to go."

There were tears in her eyes when he looked down into them.

"Don't," she asked him softly, "please, give this to someone else."

The scar on his forehead throbbed, as it often did when he was worried or nervous. It brought back the memories and the pain. He remembered the death of Xeronia and the promise he made to Tsaurau's child.

"I'm sorry, Aviore. I have no choice." He kissed her passionately, pulled her close. Her arms wrapped around him tightly, body trembling.

Then he pulled away. In a moment he was moving toward the shuttle entrance, away from her. He turned for one last look as he passed through the open doors. She was standing there, in the soft light. Her hair was long and glistening, her cheeks wet from tears. He held his hand on the edge of the door, to stop it from closing.

"I love you," he said.

He dropped his hand and the door closed with a hiss. Once again, he closed his eyes and committed her image to memory.

As the turbo-lift rushed down through the core of the ship, he noticed the weight on his chest did not cease with the surge of acceleration. His heart beat an erratic rhythm with the little shuttle as it flew along. The pain helped clear his mind. He closed his eyes, mentally pulling his body back under command. His heart rate slowed and its rhythm resumed a normal beat. The anguish inside him subsided.

But then, a cold fire began to burn through his veins, starting from his closed fists, migrating up into his chest and back through to his extremities. The strength surged as molten iron, encompassing his body and his memories to feed on the fire of hate.

Today Zorlog was going to die.

He gave little more than passing attention to the group of trainees saluting him as he marched out to his ship. At the top of the ramp, he returned the salute with mechanical indifference, then stepped into the *Dancing Queen*. She was waiting for him, her systems linked with his mind in a flood of intimate connections. He eased back into the pilot's seat and closed his eyes. He could feel the ship close up around him. He acquired a second heartbeat, felt the humid air of the bay outside, sensed the warmth of the burners softly glowing.

In an instant, he reviewed the ship's systems as he began taxiing the *Queen* out of the docking area.

"Gem, is the missile ready?"

"Standing ready in the launch tube. All its systems have been checked."

The *Dancing Queen* departed from the bay and left the *Freedom* behind. McClary's division fell into his wake as he pointed the ship on course and accelerated towards Xilo. They would not be alone when they arrived. The other five divisions of the Galactic Alliance were converging. They were hours away from reaching the capital planet. It should be enough time for the victor to claim his prize, be it either Purist or Zigot.

Ryan continued to monitor the battle on his tactical by tapping into the *Freedom*'s relay. With Xilo in sight, he saw a small squadron detach and position themselves out of range from the skirmish. Ryan was intrigued, ran through a mental investigation of what their purpose was. When realization settled in, he knew Zorlog was going to win.

A message was passed back from YushTar's and Gor's fleet: They were in position and ready. Ryan ordered them to maintain their distance and wait. They could not get too close, but when they did strike, they all had to coordinate as one. He could only hope they wouldn't arrive too late.

* * *

Every division was engaging, firing an unending staccato of plasma against the main defenses. He watched his plan unfurl with detailed precision, and laughed when a destroyer took out a primary Xilo communications relay.

The League responded by dispatching squadrons of fighters from the moon bases, swarming in to dissuade the Purist attackers, but Zorlog had multiple divisions at play and had predicted this countermove. As the fighters closed in to intercept, divisions swept in from the rear, drawing the battle back to the surface of Xilo's moons, and back into the vast underground networks.

A smile curled on Zorlog's lips exposing his fangs.

"Advance the destroyers," he ordered.

Hundreds of heavy destroyers moved in under the blanket of fire, their shields pummeled incessantly from below. Knowing they could not take this punishment for long, they quickly unloaded their missiles, depleting their ordinance in minutes.

Thousands of salvos of missiles released to the surface. Surface defense arrays fired incessantly, knocking them out in clusters leaving a haze of explosions across the skies. Seemingly defying all possibilities one missile slipped through the counter-fire, taking out a surface cannon turret.

A hole appeared in the defenses. Destroyers shifted in, concentrating their fire. Xilo's surface shielding glowed red and orange but managed to hold, until it didn't. The resulting explosion toppled an adjacent surface cannon turret which further cascaded across the surface in the form of blue lightning, forcing the planet-wide shielding to momentarily readjust. In that moment, additional surface fire penetrated, again blasting large holes at the surface, and disabling additional defense nodes.

"Pull back all ships. Connect me to Zukov Gulin!" he growled excitedly.

"My Karvok," announced Gulin.

"It is time, Zukov Gulin. You have your entry point. It is up to you to liberate Xilo now."

"To the Purists, Karvok!"

Gulin closed the channel and entered the sequence for navigation targetting, then opened a link to the other pilots. "It is our turn to sacrifice my brothers, may the Purists reign once again. On my signal."

He took one extended moment to stare down on his beloved home planet. Scarred as it was, it was his home. He laid his finger on the control, and went hurtling toward the planet.

From above, the launch of the Gulin's division was invisible, but milliseconds later the planet's surface lit up in purplish, white lightning. The main shield array collapsed under multiple titanic explosions.

"All ships, move in!" yelled Zorlog, so excited his voiced cracked.

"Zuvok," reported his tracing officer. "We have multiple enemy attack vectors."

"Put on the tactical" Zorlog ordered, too excited to give it immediate attention. The destroyers moved, lancing deadly plasma beams into the defending League cruisers, tearing them apart piece by piece. Other smaller ships descended down into the murky skies, systematically bombing the massive surface defense cannon.

Out of the corner of his eye, Zorlog noticed something in the navigation display. The image revealed itself as a cloud of images moving in from all directions.

"Who are they!" growled Zorlog.

"They are our ships, my Karvok!"

Another tracing officer interrupted, his low growl climbing to a shrill cough. "Karvok, the second division is out of formation. It appears they are moving to surround us. Third division ships are also realigning."

Zorlog glanced over to the tactical in disbelief, confirming the maneuvers for himself. The image of Zuvok Zerg appeared on the communications monitor. "Zorlog, I no longer recognize your control over this fleet. I am assuming command!"

"We do not have time for this, you fool. Xilo awaits us!"

"Yes, Xilo is in my grasp. It is only a matter of time for the Purists, but it is time you no longer have. I will not see you become the next Emperor! You are insane."

"Helm! Evasive!"

"Zerg's ship is firing!"

Zorlog marched down the deck and kicked his helmsman from his seat, breathing hotly in seething lunges. The second division was already inflicting considerable damage to the *Kirbetz* and most of the remaining loyal ships of his first division, but some of the first division moved away, opting to stay neutral in the clash, creating a hole.

But instead, Zorlog brought the gigantic cruiser around, pointing it on a course directly in line with Zerg's ship. He racked the cruiser's burners to maximum, and let loose a penetrating wave of fire.

Zerg's ship managed to manoeuver out of the way just in time, but not before sustaining multiple damaging strikes. The *Kirbetz* leapt to acroluc, leaving behind Zerg's cruiser to heave and ripple within the resulting gravity waves, twisting and crumpling in turmoil as its multiple systems

A Bellicose Dance

failed, allowing the massive vessel to sink down into Xilo's darkened, war-torn skies.

Zorlog's cold laughter flooded the communications channels as his ship shot away. His loyal followers clung to the *Kirbetz's* wake, following as closely as they dared, no more than 50 ships in all.

Behind them, they left a devastated Xilo, and an elusive, unobtainable victory.

* * *

The *Dancing Queen* was in position and the Galactic Alliance fleet was well out of range of the impending supernova.

Ryan had not directly witnessed the mutiny occurring within Zorlog's war machine. His attention was focused upon a true and final strike at the Xilo's tremendous war machine.

Three strategically located Nubok captains signaled their readiness. Ryan need only to squeeze the release and the missile would be on its way into the immense Xilo sun. It would spell the end of the most feared galactic military presence in the galaxy.

"Confirming all ships in the clear, Sir."

It was McClary's voice, a man taken from his home planet. Like so many other victims, he had seen his loved ones butchered and tortured, had been sentenced to a life of fear and pain. The Xilozak and Txtians were creatures guilty of so many indescribable, horrific crimes.

Ryan watched Xilo's gigantic sun slowly turn in front of him like a mesmerizing powerful god. A second, smaller sun orbited around it, spinning vigorously to keep from being swallowed up. He opened the shields to full extension and let the light of the heavens lay bare into the cockpit. Unlike other times, the stars seemed flat, their beauty dulled, cold, judging.

Who do you serve?

That was the question Tseman asked him long ago. It was strange he remembered that. It seemed to mean nothing until now.

Who do you serve?

Why did that question plague him so? All he had to do was press this button and end all of this pain and suffering. He had the power to wipe them all out.

Who did he serve? The Galactic Alliance - a rag-tag group of rebels? Or more importantly, the victims of this evil empire, like the Xeronians – a gentle race he literally owed his life to.

He tightened his grip on the firing button, but something held him back. The question would not let him go.

Who do you serve?

Aviore. He served her most of all. But what of God? How would God condone this? Where was he? Not out here. Not in the slave camps. What

Page 465

would the sentence be upon his soul for committing genocide?

Selfish to think of himself, now.

But genocide. The killer of millions – no in this case, of billions.

That is a stain that would blemish the Galactic Alliance as long as it existed. And how long would it hold together with such a start?

"Commander, are you alright?"

It was Gem.

"I ah... I'm having some trouble. Need to make a decision now. Answer me a question, Gem."

"Yes, of course."

"You know you have free will. The Xeronians told you so after we rebuilt you. You didn't have to stay and support me, nor integrate yourself into a ship of war, into the *Dancing Queen*. So why? What is your purpose?"

"When I... became. You were there. I desired to know. Who I am. Who you are. I wish to be... loved."

Ryan almost laughed. "Loved?"

"Yes. By my friends, by you Ryan."

"But you're..."

"Alive. I am another form of life, like the others, your friends, Showmish, Xeronian, Humans."

"Yes, you are, of course. I am sorry, did not mean to offend."

"Have I helped you with your decision?"

"No, not really."

"Is there an answer to this question?"

"What do you mean?"

"I am aware of your question, of course. But there are some questions that cannot be answered. They can only be evaluated for meaning. Lessons are learned through the act of attempting to solve the problem, but the solution to the original problem will always elude you. The important fact is that you are not erroneous in your attempts to pursue the solution."

Ryan thought about the strange reply for a while. His com notification was beeping persistently.

They were waiting. They were all waiting.

He made his decision. It may not be the right decision, but it was sound, nonetheless. "Gem, these missiles require mass to be effective, correct? The more mass, the more destructive?"

"Yes. They need a considerable amount of mass to reach a critical reactive process in order to produce a sufficient explosion."

"Let's just say we drop one of these into the small sun, instead. What would it do to Xilo?"

"Such an impact would vary. Although the inferior sun's mass is well below the Chandrasekhar limit, the device would indeed cause it to supernova. The resulting coronal mass ejections would certainly destroy Xilo if it was at perigee, although the current position is far from that. At its current position, the predominant amount of this energy should be absorbed by the primary sun. This would certainly destabilize the chromosphere of the primary sun, and most notably destabilize output radiation, result in heavy CME activity for an estimated duration of 1,213 years, although the primary sun's mass should ensure it will remain predominantly stable."

"Quite a few 'shoulds' in your answer."

"I cannot be precise. Far too many variables. I assume you have changed your plans?"

"Yes. I am in need of an alternative."

"The missile should be detonated when the smaller sun is strategically positioned partially behind the main sun, as it is now. As I stated, most of this explosion would be absorbed by the primary sun, but the remainder of the energy would escape."

"And Xilo?"

"As I have stated there are too many variables to state with certainty. The planet could experience severe devastation, or remain unscathed. The latter is of reduced possibility."

"But this should definitively destroy the surrounding Xi-Empire fleet. We must remove that threat."

"The powers considered here are vast. This event will most assuredly destroy any vessels orbiting Xilo, specifically on the exposed side."

"Agreed."

"But destroying Xilo, killing billions, that should not occur."

"I cannot simulate this without considerable time and the creation of a number of proven models."

"Then we base our decision on what we know, now."

"Recall the Nubok ships. Instruct them to retreat to a safe position."

"I informed them. The captains do not sound very enthusiastic."

"Are they refusing?"

"No."

"Good. Actually, send them coordinates where we'll convene after we launch the weapon. I want the Nuboks to transfer the other star-killers into our hold. Tell them to ready for transfer."

"They want to know if you intend to launch the weapon."

"Of course, but they need to get the hell out of here."

"They will comply, but they wish to inform you that they have no intention of leaving without you."

"We will be fine, as a matter-of-fact, better than fine. Much more preferable that it's just you and I to worry about."

"Prepare the weapon for launch. You know the new target. Can you make the appropriate calculations?"

"Yes, although the gravitational and magnetic fields do pose a challenge."

"Then guess."

* * *

An insignificant speck of matter in the form of a missile approached the small sun. Its onboard program checked and double-checked its coordinates as it approached. As it first entered into the corona, 10 levels of shielding enveloped the minute device, but that could not protect it fully from the fiery energy ahead. The shields collapsed one at a time, each providing precious seconds for the weapon to inject itself into the chromosphere that much farther. Just as the last shield began to reach its failure point, the missile detonated, triggering a chain reaction that was critically devastating. The sun's corona expanded and transformed into a hot, bright white, which then inverted, momentarily emanating sharp hues of red, blue and violet light.

The core of the sun destabilized, churning as the gravitonic waves rippled across its surface. And then it erupted. Concentric rings of matter, on different angular planes, flared away from the dying furnace. The fiery wavefront crossed millions of kilometers within seconds, losing energy only due to the incessant pull of the hungry gravity well of the primary sun. The wobbling remains of Txtia was hit with the full force of the wave, and the remnant planet atomized in an instant. The menacing wavefront flashed on, passing through the inner rings of asteroid belts and toward the system's outer orbiting planets, dispersing energy as it traveled.

It hit Xilo with one hundredth the power it had when it struck Txtia. The bulk of the mighty Xi-Empire fleet, both Purist and Zigot, thousands upon thousands of vessels were instantly reduced to molten liquid, the enormous Tikonda station included.

Initially protected by the planet, a portion of the mighty fleet survived but only for a few more moments. The concussion wave wrapped around the planet like the hand of death, pulled in by gravity, ripping at the remaining helpless warships, throwing them outward into the darkness, bent and twisted, now unrecognizable in shape, their crews hammered into jelly from titanic forces.

A portion of Xilo's atmosphere ionized as the pulse of incredible energy burned through it, reaching the planet's surface and pounding the land mass into seething seas of lava. The great sprawling cities of the Xi-Empire vanished, driven downward into the crust. Waves of molten metal from the decimated fleet pasted the area like a burning blanket.

A Bellicose Dance

The planet wobbled ever so slightly.

Xilo's moons were next. The smaller moon, Kzak took the full brunt of the energy wave, its underground bases easily permeated and flushed with a penetrating blast, traveling through the expansive network to flare out the moon's dark side. It left no survivors. Arkov, the larger moon, was positioned slightly behind Xilo's shadow, and in turn missed the massive barrage of energy, although it's exposed surface was wiped clean of any sign of Xi-Empire defense systems.

And the wave passed.

Billions had died, instantly, unexpectedly.

Xilo's atmosphere surged back onto the barren, blackened surface, alighting a continuous roiling front of fire. Torrents of storms churned to life, feeding upon intense temperatures and unbridled kinetic energy. Red skies darkened to opaque blackness and lightning danced in spidery bursts from pole to pole.

Seas initially boiling in the heat, surrendered vast amounts of water into darkened, angry cyclonic storms, which raged rivers of scouring rain down upon the blackened, scarred lands.

But Xilo survived.

On the night side of the planet, the sprawling mega-cities yielded to darkness as power distribution systems failed, their citizens struggled against monstrous winds as they sought out safe haven. Skies above glowed in unnatural hues of red and orange and flames danced in the winds, bringing with it the stench of sulfur and fire.

To the survivors - the end had come.

Within the depths of the capital city of Zenux, far underground, the Emperor surveyed the planet with the last few surviving scanners. The destruction Xilo experienced was unthinkable, horrific, and somehow, slightly familiar. He had seen this before, a weapon so powerful it could destroy a sun. He racked his memory, but could not recall where he had acquired this knowledge.

Who or what could have done this? No, it was not the Purists. Zorlog was not mad enough to devastate Xilo to this extent. Something or someone else had done this. He turned the tracing scans outward, searching, and soon found what he was looking for: ships, numbering in the thousands, now approaching in attack formation.

* * *

Far beyond the boundaries of the Xilo system, a string of battle-scarred ships stopped fleeing. They had barely escaped the wall of energy that had scoured over their own home planet, managing to stay ahead of it until it had finally dissipated. They had blasted by the Galactic Alliance fleet undetected, dwarfed by the radiating wavefront that had been produced by the exploding sun.

From a distance, they had witnessed the demise of the Xi-Empire. Their home planet, once clouded with Xilozak and Txtian ships engaged in civil war, was laid barren, wiped clean of any standing force.

A new enemy was now encroaching, and their intention was clear.

The small group of fleeing Xi-Empire ships had little chance against such numbers, and so they watched and waited.

* * *

On Xilo, the last of the Zuvoks scrambled to regroup the remains of a once powerful fleet, in desperate haste. No longer were they concerned about their internal differences. The last of the warships pulled together to form a protective force. These were ships that had been in dock for repairs and refitting on the dark side of Xilo, and a sparse few that survived the onslaught within the underground bases of Arkov, the larger moon. They assembled with brave determination, many vessels barely space-worthy. It was a valiant, bold act.

The Galactic Alliance fleet met the grim survivors with zealous satisfaction. The remnants of the Xi-Empire were blasted into oblivion without hesitation, without concern, and with unparalleled ease.

Ryan brought the fleet into orbit of the scarred planet and ordered the communications officers to send a simple and direct message: Surrender.

The moment had come, despite the incredulous odds.

Throughout the *Freedom's* bridge officers grinned and laughed, letting go the tension and fear of a battle now past. Realization was beginning to sink in. The Xi-Empire had been defeated.

In a short time, the Emperor personally transmitted a message from the surface, in the form of multiple languages.

"We surrender."

* * *

The Zigot Emperor was shuttled up from the surface, leaving behind a chaotic effort of survival and suffering.

Ryan and his most valued generals were seated along a semi-circle table, official representatives of the Galactic Alliance. They shifted uncomfortably as they waited, each reflecting upon their own thoughts.

No one truly believed this day had arrived.

As the Emperor stepped into the room, tension rose exponentially. Not all were prepared for the sight of the tall, fierce-looking Zigot. Stooping to enter, its mere size was menacing. It carried itself across the floor with a flowing grace, attesting to a creature of position and power. It silently glared down upon its conquerors. Its black insect-face a mask.

Ryan stared back. It was the first time that anyone other than a Xilozak or Txtian had ever seen the hybrid race of the Zigot – and lived.

The Emperor spoke, in a low growling voice, countering the expected high-pitched Txtian chatter. "I am Zigot BigarTah - Emperor of the Xi-Empire, leader of the Xilozak and Txtian peoples."

His language was a combination of Xilozak and Txtian, full of clicks and growls. The translator delayed slightly, needing time to decipher it.

Ryan waited patiently. He had understood all of it, but the others may have not. The Zigot's words were repeated in Trinarieit, carefully pronounced by an attending Showmish translator.

"You will speak Trinarieit," Ryan replied icily, careful to sound each click and growl precisely.

The alien nodded.

Ryan played his next move carefully, a calculated, but required bluff. "I have three ships orbiting your sun. They are not detectable by your tracing scanners. Any breach of agreement or further hostile action will not be tolerated. Any sign of such and we will withdraw and leave your planet and its citizens to a complete and fitful destruction. Do you understand the meaning of these words?"

The Zigot Emperor nodded, replying back in Trinarieit. "It is understood. We will not respond with aggression."

"Good. Sit down."

The Emperor stood rigidly for a moment but then decided against making a scene. It would serve no purpose now.

"Conditions of your surrender are as follows: All terms under this agreement must be adhered to in full compliance, or the citizens of Xilo will be subjected to retaliatory action by the Galactic Alliance."

"No Txtian or Xilozak will be permitted to reside on any other planet. Your people are restricted to live out their lives on Xilo. The Galactic Alliance will return what remains of your population to this planet in good faith. In turn, the citizens of Xilo will not be allowed to enslave any other peoples. All slaves will be transferred into Galactic Alliance custody immediately. There are no exclusions. There will be no negotiation."

The Emperor did not shift its eyes, did not flinch.

"All interstellar travel by Txtian or Xilozak is hereby prohibited. All remaining vessels will be surrendered to us. All ship manufacturing facilities will be immediately evacuated, their operations ceased, and control rescinded to the Galactic Alliance."

"All celestial navigational data, star charts, and associated knowledge of planets and civilizations, in all media forms, will be surrendered to the Galactic Alliance immediately."

"All slave asset documentation, distribution, and ownership ledgers pertaining to the peoples of the Galactic Alliance will be surrendered to the Galactic Alliance immediately."

"You are now under the protection of the Galactic Alliance. No other forms of defensive measures will be tolerated. All weapons and defense systems are to be surrendered to the Galactic Alliance. Any and all weapons manufacturing facilities will immediately cease operations and be evacuated, as they will be either dismantled or destroyed at our discretion. All weapons in the possession of your people will be surrendered."

"Do you understand these requirements?"

"Our people will not be safe if they cannot defend themselves," rebuked the Zigot.

"Your population will be governed under the laws of the Galactic Alliance and will be granted citizenship pending applicant evaluation. Your population will also be held under the protection of the Galactic Alliance during this application time. Every citizen of Xilo is subject to a War Crimes Tribunal review. Penalties may include incarceration or death, depending on the nature of the crime."

"So you strip us of all protection, then subject us to your manufactured laws, then issue orders to murder us."

"That is not our intention."

"Just as it was not your intention to kill billions of our population?"

"Do not expect compassion from us, Zigot. But we will attempt to treat you with fairness, although I will state - you are not deserving."

"Regardless, the remainder of the terms are as follows: All assets that your forces have confiscated from other peoples will be returned to their rightful home. Any property the Galactic Alliance deems of interest will be surrendered."

Ryan sat back on his chair. "Do you understand everything I have outlined?"

"Yes, I understand," replied the Emperor.

"There is an individual I am very interested in. He is a Xilozak called Zorlog, do you know his whereabouts?"

The Emperor stirred in his seat. "Zorlog is an enemy to the people. He was engaged in battle prior to the destruction. His ship is referred to as the *Kirbetz*."

Ryan nodded to the closest guard, who left the room.

"Are your terms complete?"

"They are subject to addendum, but for now, they are complete."

"I assume you represent the leadership of the Galactic Alliance?"

"I am the leader of the Galactic Alliance Militia only. I represent the Galactic Alliance in matters of war until a true ambassadorial appointment is established by the Galactic Alliance Federation, of which, eventually, Xilo will be absolved into."

"I formally request ambassadorial status for the citizens of Xilo."

Ryan replied, "As the current Emperor, I assume you are the undisputed leader of your people?"

"Yes, although we have experienced... civil problems. This has weakened us and made possible your triumph."

"As leader, you will have a difficult role. You live in a world that has undergone an ecological disaster. It is doubtful you will be able to feed your citizens or house them for that matter. You are reliant upon a constant stream of incoming supplies. Your industries are suited only for war, and are lacking in areas of rebuilding infrastructure. You have little you can trade, and all trade activities are subject to inspection and possible termination by us."

"Xilo and its remaining population are in trouble. However, we may allow a specific service to be retained."

Ryan made him wait until he asked.

"What is this resource you refer to?"

"Your shipbuilding industry may be tolerated, but then again, how much of that work previously relied on slave labor? We are an alliance of worlds surviving through trade, governed by self-imposed rules. The richest of worlds will be the most industrious and diversified. How will your people fit into this system? How do you see Xilo having a future?"

"Then we are already at a disadvantage, as I foresee your citizens will not voluntarily deal with us. Our only hope will be another war. Only then will we will free ourselves of your treachery. Time is our ally."

"Treachery?" Ryan could feel the anger build within him. "You are incorrect. Time is not your friend. Given your situation, it is time that will kill off your civilization. You cannot survive on a planet that cannot sustain you. Ironically, you may survive through the generosity of the Galactic Alliance, but we will help you only at our desire. Perhaps your weapons manufacturing capabilities can be modified to provide services more fitting a peaceful existence."

"You are offering aid to us? Those who have conquered you, enslaved your people?"

Ryan passed a gaze down the table, both sides. The eyes of his generals held the truth of their anger, a bottled up rage not easily managed. They shifted in their chairs, none satisfied with the direction of the discussion, nor Ryan's presentation of terms.

He eased back in his chair.

This was to be expected.

"Emperor, I was not completely accurate in my previous statements. I will correct this by stating that in a way, it is true that time is your ally in one respect. Time will serve to heal the memory of the past, and allow the ones you once subjugated to find peace. Understanding will eventually supersede hate. It is a simple truth that your people must learn to live with us in peace, or they will all die in war."

The Zigot leader tilted back on his chair. His massive insectoid head turned slowly. Large, unblinking, prism eyes scanned over each of the panel. His mandibles ground against one another, emanating a low grating sound too similar to the crunch of bone. Ryan was relieved when it stopped.

He announced his decision. "Then we will live in peace. Despite my predecessors' examples, I believe it is the way that we should live, in order to truly prosper, we must focus our energies on strengthening our knowledge, skills, technologies. But in order for us to flourish, we must be allowed to compete in this economy of worlds."

"These are the fundamental rights of Alliance planets. Xilo will only be provided that right upon its acceptance into the Alliance, and not before."

The great Emperor bowed his head. "Then we will truly perish."

Ryan did not respond, and neither did anyone else. The words hung in the air for an extended moment.

"Very well, then I would suggest you notarize the agreement as this is a pre-requisite for joining the Alliance," Ryan announced.

A few of his generals stood up, shaking in rage, but holding their tongues. Some responded by leaving the room.

Ryan waited for the room to settle, knowing this was difficult for all of them.

The Emperor did not miss the subtleties at work, and was wise enough to recognize an uncontestable opportunity. He proceeded with the signing of the necessary documents, complying without a word. Once finished, he focused his attention back to Ryan.

"Are you from Signus or Earth?" asked the Emperor.

"Earth."

"Yes, the Grentels were very similar to you."

"Grentels?"

The Emperor scanned the group once more. "You have no knowledge of these people?"

"No. Perhaps you can share some of your history for our benefit?"

The Emperor shifted in his chair, uncomfortable with the line of questioning.

"Are you so afraid of us you cannot pass on events that occurred so long ago?" goaded Ryan.

"Fear? An Emperor does not fear. This is mere knowledge handed down through the generations. It is no longer relevant."

"Consider us curious, then."

"Very well," he sighed, as if readying himself to share to his subordinates. "It was in the days of my Txtian ancestors when the Grentels came. They offered us peace, but we knew only war, and so we killed them. We studied the technology that we seized from them for many zadii. On Txtia it was a time of great turbulence. The planet was beginning its great shift as those have learning had predicted. Through uncovering the Grentels' secrets, the Txtians managed to survive. They used this knowledge to leave the planet and journey to Xilo. It was a difficult time for many Txtians, to leave all they knew. Txtia was near its end, and time was the enemy. Only once the great migration was complete were Txtians able to afford the time to continue to study the sciences employed. It took generations for our people to truly comprehend the mysteries of interstellar travel."

"So you admit these Grentels enabled you to travel the galaxy before you were ready."

The Emperor only glared back.

"These Grentels, are you saying this is the name they called themselves?"

"No, I am unaware, nor do I care of how they referred to themselves. Information is limited. They are from the second planet of 10, from a far star. That is all I have."

The Zigot shook, a shrill shriek razed from its body, followed by a turbulent growl.

A startled guard raised his blaster and leveled it on the Zigot.

Ryan signaled the guard to lower his weapon. "Laughter brothers, the Zigot laughs."

"And what is so humorous, Zigot?"

"Somehow, my brother knew. His last words were recorded. As he lay dying in a poisoned body, he warned us that the Grentels were coming. And I thought it was hallucinations from his poisoned delusional mind."

Again he laughed. The shrill sound pierced Ryan's ears.

"It is an old children's story. The Grentels would come back one day in reprisal, and in their anger, they would destroy half our people with fire from the sky. It is only on that day that we will begin to understand peace."

"I guess your story came true."

"It is true only if you are a Grentel. But you are from Earth, and this story is a mere myth."

The former Emperor rose, towering over all of them. Without another word, the menacing monster turned and started out of the room, pausing only to stoop through the entrance. He glanced back. "I wish you peace, leader from Earth. I have grown tired of death."

"So have I," Ryan said under his breath.

* * *

The panel of generals and captains looked at one another in silence. They had just witnessed the end of the Xi-Empire regime.

Ryan leaned over to his ensign. "Fetch the generals that had left. There is a discussion at hand."

Anger was seething under the surface, it was clear, but Ryan would not initiate the talk until all his generals were present. Within minutes the group was again whole.

"Some of you did not like my terms," stated Ryan.

"They deserve to die. All of them," stated Lortay, his anger kept on the edge.

"Well, General Lortay, tell me, is that what our Galactic Alliance ideals are based upon? Is the first order of business of our Alliance the act of genocide and the total obliteration of another race?"

Silence reigned for a moment.

"No," the Showmish conceded. "But none here were afforded such an option."

"True. It is also true we cannot have it both ways. Either kill them or help them to survive. It is our choice. If all of you agree unanimously with Lortay's position, then I will agree to bomb Xilo from orbit – and we *will* exercise total destruction. Only we know of this agreement before us. We can easily break its terms. But I will remind you, the war is over, and they have been defeated. This is now a matter of how the Alliance deals with its prisoners of war. So, all you have to do is give me a show of hands."

"Their prisoners were enslaved and eventually killed," countered Wharsoff.

Ryan ignored the outburst, intent upon making a point. "Choose your legacy, Generals. Raise your hand if you wish to kill them all, or choose to stand by this agreement!" He waved the document in the air.

Two hands went up, then a third, and a fourth.

Ryan walked around to seat himself in the Emperor's chair.

"Perhaps only a majority is required then? Nine of us sit here. It will take only five votes to reign down death upon the last few billions. Of course, we'll need to continue to bloody our hands as we find remnants of their forces in other systems – and we will. Again, history will define us the conquerors and we certainly have that right. You can tell your stories to your children how you killed off a whole civilization, and you considered it moral and acceptable to erase all evidence of them, adults to children."

So what have you? Give me another vote."

One, two, three raised their hands, another put up and tentatively retracted.

"Then we do not have enough votes to eradicate the remnants of the enemy. Perhaps the function of the military has been superseded by the reality of policing Galactic Alliance citizens. Let us accept it is what it is."

"But now we have more important work to do. Pull together a number of squadrons. We need to get to the surface and start liberating our people. All of you can take care of the details. I'm returning to the *Freedom*. I intend to bring her into Xilo orbit. McClary, make sure you secure the whole area before I return – that includes inspecting those moons. Wharsoff, you're in charge of slave retrieval, be careful down there, and control your troops - no non-sanctioned killing. Lortay, you're on disaster assessment and relief. This destruction was more than I ever intended to inflict. We need to figure out how to get Xilo functioning enough to sustain its population."

Ryan tossed the agreement on the table in front of them.

Wharsoff stood up and bowed. "Thank you, Earthman. I never thought that I would see this day."

Ryan gave him a smile. "Do me a favor and stop crediting me for this. This required everyone's help."

Within minutes he was in the *Dancing Queen* and on his way back to the *Freedom*, and to his Aviore.

* * *

18. Inception

As the *Dancing Queen* came within tracing range of its destination, Ryan noticed something was wrong. There was nothing out there but the desolate vacuum of space.

"Gem, you're sure of these coordinates? You haven't made an error somehow?"

He had visions of being lost without any navigational references, unable to calculate his bearings, drifting until he died.

Gem picked up on his thoughts. Ryan swore he heard her laughing.

"It's not funny. I rely on you, and all this other technology. If you fail, I'm dead."

"That is true, but I also rely upon you for interaction. We have a symbiont relationship."

"Regardless, I think you could fare quite well without me, out here."

Gem did not respond back, realizing the conversation was pointless. "We are at the correct coordinates. This was the exact position where we departed from the *Freedom*. I have located some persistent energy signatures."

"Why did she move? Can you hail her? Start long-range tracing scans, 360 degrees, 1 degree increments all planes. Shit!"

"Initiating full sweep, will take approximately three hours, twenty-five minutes."

Where the hell are they? They would've had to jump to acroluc for an extended time to pass beyond the standard tracing range. Maybe they had an emergency? The best rule was to sit tight. They should return, or at least send a drone back.

Ryan made himself breakfast. He was jittery and the meal did not make him feel any better. His arm was stiff and sore. After eating he decided to meditate. He settled down into a self-induced trance but was unable to concentrate completely. He ached with the desire to know where Aviore was and it plagued his mind. Time and again he attempted to achieve total concentration.

Eventually, it happened.

A darkness swept over him, chilling him to the very core of his being. It was suffocating. He searched around desperately. A small piercing light flickered beyond. He rushed toward it. Warmth returned. He moved closer to the light. It was familiar. It was Aviore. Something was wrong. He could feel it within her. Fear. She was running from something, she kept calling his name. But the cold burned into him, and he could not move closer.

He opened his eyes and found his body draped in sweat. The lights seemed bright and intense.

No this was not a dream. Not this time. Aviore was in trouble.

He ran to the cockpit.

She was out there, somewhere. He would find her.

He slid into the seat, forced himself into a quiet, meditative state again, pushing out the jittery fear.

Focus. Let it come.

Where? Follow the warmth.

His hands moved autonomously to set course. The *Dancing Queen* surged to acroluc. Light-years flashed by, passing by millions of suns, planets, galaxies. Despite the energies at work, the immense power of travel, it felt like he was still far away from an unreachable point.

Time felt like it was standing still. It crept along, second by second, each minute lasting an eternity.

Was he even going in the right direction? Should he turn back, contact the other Alliance ships and start a proper search?

He opened his eyes, focused his attention on the tracing scans, manipulating re-scans to maximize the distance, watching for any hint. The chronometer indicated hours had clicked by. He considered breaking from his course, but could not convince himself to do it.

Trust the feeling.

He could attempt a link back to Xilo, but that could compromise his position if there was an enemy involved. Instead, he adjusted the tracing scanners. Something came up: a faint reading on the outer edge of the tracing image. He manipulated the scans to achieve a tighter beam, his heart pounding in his temples as the anticipation burned in his gut. Deep breaths helped settle his nerves, but a new burning pain began, coupled with a heaviness in his chest, like a burning weight.

Calm down, damn it. Let this go.

He diverted his thoughts, drained the tension from his body, recalling his training with the Sisters-of-Soom. Stress gave way to calm, and the pain subsided.

Images were defining themselves more clearly on the tracing scans. Multiple ships - familiar tracing resonances. It was the *Freedom*. But there were other vessels swarming about her, and the scans confirmed they were Xi-Empire signatures. As he feared, she was under attack.

He deployed all cannon and engaged auto-targeting, simultaneously rolling the ship over end-for-end for maximum deceleration. The *Dancing Queen* blasted down below acroluc, and they dropped into normal space just off the port side of the *Freedom*.

The tactical told the whole story. There were almost 50 enemy ships, and only one of the *Freedom's* escort destroyers remained intact. The destroyer was fighting desperately, engaged with multiple attackers. The *Freedom* herself seemed adrift, her main burners offline. Large gaping holes were strewn along her hull.

There were hundreds of thousands of people in there!

The enemy saw him now. They were already maneuvering to attack. *Let them.*

He opened a com link to Xilo, hoping to reach them before he engaged. He doubted he had time to solidify the link if he could even establish one. Four ships had already aligned on his course and were moving to intercept.

Missiles started for him. Ryan broke trajectory and abandoned the effort. He pulled the *Queen* through evasive maneuvers as the cannon took out the missiles.

He checked the tactical again. The last destroyer took a crippling hit.

Far too many ships. How could he do this? He had to. He had no choice.

The rear cannon auto-targeted and found a victim.

One down, many more to go.

He swung the *Queen* into a tight 180 and laid out a suppressing blast. One enemy vessel took a direct hit, another passed through the barrage unscathed. He brought the *Queen* to bear on the escaping ship and simultaneously pulled into focus three more destroyers as well. They scuttled apart, but not quickly enough. The *Queen's* long-range cannon bursts took them broadside under an incessant staccato. In seconds the plasma burned through their shielding, through their hulls, and into their interior. The destroyers went offline, explosions raking along their lengths.

Four more down. How many to go?

Time and time again, he outmaneuvered around his attackers, their constant barrage had now blackened the *Dancing Queen* with scars of battle. The raw energy of near misses were consistently squelched by the ship's extended shielding. His attackers were beginning to get annoyed at their consistent failure. They broke into squadrons, abandoning the *Freedom* in groups, intent to wipe him out by sheer force.

Now with multiple squadrons on his tail, he maxed-out the lower burners, attempting to pull his caustic pursuers away. The *Queen* jumped forward, just as his followers moved into lethal range.

He checked the ship vitals. Energy capacitor temperatures were climbing into critical range, and the anti-gravs were dangerously close to failing over to their backups.

"Gem, engage the auxiliary anti-gravs, hopefully, it will draw off the capacitors' excess."

The enemy was coming at him from all angles, the black space alight with white, angry plasma. They swarmed in, flying at him in a confusion of trajectories. Ryan saw an opportunity and took it. Some pursuers matched his vectors. He pulled into the path of an oncoming destroyer, sweeping by so close he swore the two ships rubbed hulls. Explosions behind showered debris in all directions.

Two more down.

He passed in close to the *Freedom*. He could see the blurred images of determined turret gunners through their opaque shielding. So he moved in closer, drawing in his pursuing Xi-Empire ships. The turret gunners pasted the unsuspecting ships with multiple concentrated blasts, crippling some, damaging others.

Following along the *Freedom's* hull, he met up with a half a dozen enemy ships that remained clamped on, like so many parasites. He pulled the *Queen* around and fired the cannon with surgical precision, effectively immobilizing but leaving them intact so as not to further breach the *Freedom's* interior atmosphere. The stranded crew would now have to contend with the thousands of armed and angry ex-slaves. They had no escape.

He pulled away and continued down the full length of the *Freedom*, hugging the hull in hopes to confuse the enemy's tracing image and buy an advantage. The tremendous ship's width narrowed as he came up on her nose. Suddenly, Gem seized control, raising the front burners to maximum. A massive cruiser loomed up before the *Queen*, skimming just past the *Freedom's* nose.

Ryan yanked the *Queen* to the side, diverting from impending collision, but the maneuver cost him a precious second. The cruiser's lower turrets had him in her sights now. They bombarded a wall of plasma at close distance, pounding the *Queen* in her belly.

A capacitor blew, filling the engineering bay with lethal radioactive fragments. Containment controls automatically triggered and circulation systems auto-sealed. Gem coordinated her army of bots to chase down the repair. The capacitor cooling system had overloaded, and the temperature inside the *Queen* was already beginning to climb. Both primary and secondary capacitors were peaked beyond their designed maximum, and they couldn't take much more.

Ryan shut the shields down, simultaneously orchestrating a rollover to avoid another approaching barrage of cannon fire. Lethal white and blue light rained past, barely missing him. A destroyer came up on the port side. Ryan fired back. He didn't miss.

"Ziggy, we need to drop their numbers faster. Load a star-killer."

The cruiser had diverted her attention to the mothership and was busily pounding her without mercy. He flew in close, distracting the cruiser's attention, drawing the immense warship into a game of chase.

It took the bait, abandoning its attack on the Freedom, intent upon a small, seemingly insignificant white ship.

"Give me shields again, Gem."

"We are having difficulty stabilizing the feeds. Instantiating the shields may introduce a non-terminating, recursive drain."

"We may not make it this time, my friend. Instantiate the shields."

Ryan pushed the burners, leaping far ahead of the deadly monstrous killer, but it was not enough to dissuade the deadly pursuer. He allowed it to close in on them with each ticking second, sweat dripping off his temples, waiting for a sign from his automated friend.

The signal came into his mind, as a short acknowledgment: *shields enabled, missile loaded.*

Wasting no time, he launched the potent weapon. The predator was almost upon him now. From such a close range, its defenses were useless. The weapon penetrated the cruiser's shields and sunk itself deep midships. A moment later, something dreadful occurred within the ship. The entire top section of the cruiser literally disappeared, crumpling into itself. Outer hull sections peeled off and burst outwards, propelled by some invisible titanic force. An immense section collided with the *Queen*, only to skip across her shields, propelled by invisible titanic forces. In seconds the cruiser lit to bright, white light, then blinked into a maelstrom of twisting energy, ripping and rotating into a reddish sphere that swallowed, then burst into blue-violet rings of energy.

Gravity alarms fired off in deafening screams within the *Queen's* cabin, as smoke billowed up from the lower levels and started to fill the cockpit.

The port anti-grav controller had burst into flame, rippling out a gravity wave that wrenched through the ship. Ryan fought down a momentary bout of nausea as the starboard anti-grav compensated. He scanned the diagnostics over the vaskpar.

"Gem, have Ziggy attend to that fire and replace the control unit."

The *Queen* rocked again in the wake of multiple, external gravity waves emanating from the reddish sphere, which by now was slowly dispersing. He fought the controls, attempting to maintain course attitude, and at the same time run another string of lethal blasts into a group of oncoming destroyers.

Alarms quieted as the star-killer's legacy waned in the distance. Nothing remained of the gigantic cruiser.

Another rash of lethal blasts passed the ship on the starboard side.

A Bellicose Dance

The Xi-destroyers were closing in, obviously angered by the loss of their cruiser. Three more destroyers were now in mortal proximity. He launched a pair of standard missiles and retreated, jostling the *Dancing Queen* through a drill of maneuvers in order to avoid oncoming fire. The ships broke off their attack when they realized they had acquired their own deadly tails. Their attempts to destroy the missiles proved futile. They pulled away from pursuing the *Dancing Queen*, accelerating desperately, but the Xeronian engineered weapons caught up with them easily, bursting them open in a concussion of massive explosions, their internal atmosphere burning away into vacuum.

The tactical showed multiple destroyers converging. Ryan put the *Queen* into a full reverse. The front burners bathed the cockpit in intense white.

Another wave of nausea came on.

"Port anti-grav reinstated into service."

"Could've warned me," Ryan complained.

"I am warning you. Energy levels are building. The feeds remain unbalanced."

"I've bogies crawling all over. Let's deal with one problem at a time. Tell Ziggy to launch another missile, maximum payload. Keep it dark. I want it to detonate where their course vectors meet." He painted the picture in his minds' eye. It was enough for Gem to make the necessary calculations.

"Deploying with minimal signature in 3..2..1."

They started taking on intense cannon fire.

"He watched the shield dispersal energies as they flipped from positive-to-negative crazily. A little closer, a little stronger, and they'd be hitting past critical limits.

Another volley. Alarms sounded as the capacitors peaked extending the shields, only to roll out a cascading ripple – creating a temporary opening in the shields.

A blast penetrated and hit the hull.

Breach.

He winced, literally feeling the pain.

"Rear cannon main power conduit interrupted, re-routing," reported Gem.

Ryan yanked at the controls, pulling the ship straight toward an oncoming destroyer. The *Queen's* cannon blasted away in a continuous stream, drilling into the enemy, leaving behind a cloud of yellowish iridescence. He checked the tactical. Multiple signatures were about to reach convergence.

At least the Freedom was far enough away now.

"Gem..."

"Standby."

The weapon detonated in a wave of atomic destruction. But Ryan wasn't sticking around to witness the fireworks. Instead, the *Dancing Queen* jumped to acroluc, leaving a spiraling, engulfing storm in its wake as multiple destroyers were engulfed in a wave of destruction.

Proximity warnings sounded as the *Queen* brushed past yet another destroyer. Ryan cycled the anti-gravs with only a thought. The destroyer lurched and twisted in an all-too-familiar pattern. As they moved away, the writing metal mass burst apart, spewing out its crew into the black of space. The *Queen* herself contorted slightly, although the anti-gravs auto calibrated to avoid amplification. Ryan rode out the wave, monitoring the ship's stats cautiously. When it subsided, he restored the anti-grav feeds to normal, allow the gravity plates to take hold and pull back into standard gravity.

His heart lurched inside his chest. Pain returned in torrents. With one arm numb, he switched control over totally to his vaskpar, guiding the ship back to the *Freedom*, to drop under its belly.

The anti-gravs protested yet again with a deafening whine as the ship's mass slowed to a near complete stop. He eased the *Queen* up into the recesses of the burner conduits and waited, watching the tactical. He had not seen the explosion generated from the missile, but evidence of its effect lay strewn throughout the space where he had once been. There were only a few of the enemy left now. If he could pull this off, he would have the advantage of surprise. They may think he's been destroyed.

He rubbed his chest with his good hand, concentrated on slowing down his now racing pulse.

Just like the Queen's pulsating capacitor feeds, on the brink of chaos. It was getting bad. Worse than ever before. Maybe he should have listened to Aviore. But there wasn't any time before. Now he was going to die, out here, alone.

But it would be good to rest.

No.

Aviore was still in trouble. He couldn't.

Ziggy walked into the cockpit, his jerky movement graced in a dreamlike haze. The robot injected something into his arm. A burning raced through his body, into every joint, every facet, flowing through every blood vessel, into every cell. Instantly the world around him shattered like glass and came back into sharp focus.

"Thanks, old friend. You may have just saved my life."

"This solution is only temporary," replied Gem. "You need a medical procedure."

"Give me another dose."

"That could do irreparable damage."

"I have to go in. I have to find her. I can't reach her on the Par. Something is wrong."

A long hesitation. "I understand, Captain."

Ziggy administered the second shot.

"The remaining ships have now attached to the hull and are actively boarding. Two remain on patrol. I do believe, as you surmised, that they think we are deceased."

Ryan reviewed the tactical. One of the patrol ships was going to pass almost directly underneath him.

"All the better for us."

"Can you rebalance the capacitors?"

"We are currently printing some replacement components."

"Then we re-engage and cross our fingers."

He waited for the ship to appear, then brought the *Queen* down just meters away from its hull, firing the belly turret into the stern drive area. The destroyer started to explode underneath him. The *Queen* made it out, narrowly missing being crushed between the two ships.

The other patrol was sweeping in, laying down a string of fire. Ryan pointed the *Queen* in the direction of an intercepting ship and maxed the burners. For a brief, almost imperceptible movement, he had the positional advantage and took it. Long-range cannon did their work, carving out sections of the oncoming destroyer's hull. But the ship held course, refusing to veer away. Ryan deployed a missile at close range. It flashed away, penetrated through the enemy ship's hull and shot out the stern, exploding harmlessly out in space. He cussed openly, pulling the *Queen* into an opposite vector. The other ship shot by, powerless and mortally crippled.

The boarding ships were next on his list. One managed to get free but wasn't able to align its cannon in time. The *Queen's* impulse cannon split it cleanly in half.

He brought the tactical tracing out to mid-range and performed as a full sweep. Only two ships remained, and the one was racing up on his stern. He swung the *Queen* down under the cover of the *Freedom's* wing just in time to avoid a ruinous barrage.

His pursuer was rushing in, using the *Freedom* as cover. The ship appeared in an angry flash. He whipped the *Queen* around to avoid another volley of fire and headed along the wing, destroyer in pursuit.

The Par was down, so he attempted a com link to the bridge as this was the only communications left.

Kanook's bloody face appeared, behind him, a bridge draped in thick, black smoke.

"Commander, good to see you. I see you have a tail."

"Portside cannon is still active, if you'd like to…"

"Standby, Kanook. Try not to burn off my ass."

The *Queen* passed into the dispersal range of the gigantic port cannon. Ryan gave it a split second before jumping the burners to maximum. Behind him, a blast of blinding intensity simply vaporized the destroyer class ship.

Only one left, now.

The last functioning Xi-destroyer was tethered to the *Freedom*. He moved in cautiously, systematically firing the cannon, careful to avoid hitting the *Freedom*. His last staccato proved effective, slicing through its shields and bursting open its hull. He left the fatally crippled ship and headed for the docking bays.

"Kanook, still there?"

"We still have you, Commander."

"Where's Aviore?"

He positioned the *Queen* in front of a docking bay, but the doors refused to open.

"Standby, Commander. Disengaging dock locks."

"Nevermind that, do you have a location for Aviore?"

"Sorry, Commander, we don't know where she is."

The massive bay doors crawled open. He guided the ship in, noting the bay was filled with thick black smoke.

"We've a number of serious fires..."

"I'll find her. Just save this ship."

Ryan ran a tracing image to get him as close to the airlock as possible. As the *Queen* settled on the floor, he threw on his combat suit but skipped the helmet. He was on the *Freedom*'s deck plating in a minute, impulse rifle in hand and disrupter sword slung on his back.

He sprinted across the open space, relieved there was no one waiting in ambush to cut him down. At the main corridor, he came face to face with five Xilozaks. One reacted with deadly efficiency, swinging a massive disrupter at his head. Ryan ducked, blasting the whole group with a wide dispersal shot at gut level. They went down, coughing up blood and cursing. The sword yielding Xilozak staggered back up only to receive a savage smash to the head by the butt end of Ryan's rifle.

He pressed himself against the wall as two more Xilozaks appeared down the far end of the corridor, but they saw him. A shot grazed him in the arm. They had him pinned. He retreated back to the next corridor, then jumped down a service pole to the adjacent level and doubled back.

He came upon a Xilozak pulling a woman down the corridor by her leg. The big alien reacted in time to see the edge of Ryan's sword. The woman struggled back to her feet, then turned and ran down the corridor into the smoke.

A Bellicose Dance

A noise down the hall made him instinctively dive into the nearest room, narrowly avoiding a volley of blaster fire that blew the door assembly apart behind him. He ran through into the next room then blasted a hole in the wall, allowing him access into the next corridor. He pressed himself against the wall and waited. His pursuers jumped through the charred hole, expecting him to be retreating down the corridor. They didn't have time to show their surprise. His sword dripped of blood and vibrated heatedly in his hands. He swung it back into its scabbard, it sunk down with a satisfying hiss as a low energy field cleaned the blade of all foreign matter.

Where? He had to find her.

Lower. Have to get lower.

He slipped down a maintenance tube, sliding four levels and landing softly. There was no power on this level. He heard a scream, a shot from a blaster. The flash lit up the corridors enough to make out an image. Ryan swung his rifle onto his back by the strap and carried his sword with both hands. A blaster would attract fire in the darkness.

He heard the footsteps of two approaching Xilozaks. Soundlessly he hugged the wall as they passed, then stepped out and swung. The disrupter sliced through them with ease. He sprinted further into the darkness.

An explosion sounded behind him. The decking pitched beneath his feet and he was thrown further down the corridor. He hit hard, his head crunching against the corridor wall. Darkness passed over him.

He came to a minute later. Emergency lights had come on. Dots of white emanated from the ceiling, barely piercing through drifting black smoke. He went to push himself up, but a sharp pain rushed through his left arm.

His forearm was broke. No, he can't let this stop him.

He pushed up with his knees and glanced up and down the corridor.

Nothing.

Favoring his left forearm, he slung the rifle over to the left shoulder and limped down the corridor. He turned at the next intersection and peered down its length, staying low under the churning darkness of smoke. No more than 10 meters away a woman lay in the middle of the corridor on her side, her legs limp, shirt stained red. She saw him and raised her hand.

"Aviore!" He started towards her in a hobbled run.

"Ryan! Wai..."

A dark shape stepped out into the dim light. A sharp red beam leapt from its arm. Ryan felt a burning sensation go through his side and he went down on his bad arm.

The pain burned into him.

Fight it damn you!

Years of memories flooding him. The whips. The beatings.

Turn it off.

He looked up through the billowing smoke at a familiar evil face - the toothy grin of Zorlog.

"Aviore!"

She struggled to turn, as tears dropped to the floor. She couldn't move. She didn't have the strength.

"Broken spine I think," Zorlog commented. "Had to blast her to slow her down." He walked over and kicked her broadside. She screamed in agony.

"Leave her alone you bastard!"

He inched up his sword, freeing it from underneath him.

A voice came from the back of his mind – it was Gem.

"Stay down, make him think you are weak, draw him closer."

Zorlog laughed. "Think we've been before, slave, remember? So weak you are. How did you get here, now? What is it they call you – Commander?"

He ambled in closer, glaring down at him, his muscled legs flexing in boots stained in blood. "Tell me, what is a Commander?" He howled at his own joke holstering his hand blaster to grab his favorite disrupter bar.

"Yes, slave, you remember this don't you?"

He flipped the switch with an audible click. The bar began to hum. He scraped it along the wall, bright blue sparks danced out in jagged paths, leaping to ground in a mist of ozone.

"Well, maybe not. You see, I did not have this on back then. If it had been, let's just say you wouldn't be here with me now." He howled again. It echoed eerily down the corridor, fading into the dark smoke, which seemed to be growing thicker.

Another step nearer. Two steps away.

Aviore moaned in pain, distracting him for a second.

"Yes, too bad I had to break her. Some Xilozaks develop a taste for certain females. Tends to raise their value some. But not that one. That one is broken, just like you are now. Not worth a single credit."

He stopped swinging the bar. "But to me, I think your skull would make a fine addition to my collection."

He raised his arm and swung. Ryan rolled over, sword in hand. The bar missed, burying itself deep into the floor plating. It gave Ryan time to swing, but the sword only managed to cut a deep gouge in Zorlog's forehead. Zorlog moved back like a cat, then laughed. He flicked his forked tongue out and licked the blood, now oozing down his cheek.

"Ah, the taste of blood. It is so sweet." He reached up and felt the gouge on his forehead.

"Now we're even."

He lunged. Ryan was up and ready, responding with a block. The bar glanced harmlessly to his left. Ryan kicked full force with his right leg, and Zorlog crashed up against the opposite corridor wall.

"You've grown stronger, slave."

"Too many years in the mines," Ryan growled back. He swung again. Zorlog caught it with the bar, throwing a shower of blue sparks. He did a half turn and pushed Ryan up against the wall.

Ryan could smell his rancid breath. He looked into Zorlog's yellow reptilian eyes. They were cold, glaring, and insane.

"You're going to die, slave."

"Then you're coming with me, lizard."

Ryan caught his leg behind Zorlog's and pushed. The big alien fell solidly on his back. He swung down, and Zorlog caught it again with his bar. He kicked Ryan's feet out from under him making it his turn to hit the deck. Zorlog was up in a blur of motion, with his bar bearing down upon Ryan's head in a wild swing. Ryan rolled over and up onto his feet in a single motion. Again, Zorlog missed, and he screamed a blood-curdling yell of frustration.

Ryan could feel the strength ebbing from him now. The effects of the drugs were beginning to wear off and he was losing a lot of blood from the blaster wound. He caught a glance at Aviore. Her eyes were wide with terror, her face pale, her body motionless.

With a growl, Zorlog worked his bar loose from the decking.

"I grow tired of this game, Earth thing."

He rushed in and swung. Ryan ducked and jabbed upwards, driving his sword through Zorlog's bar-yielding forearm. He shoved with all his strength, smashing the alien into the wall with such intensity that the sword buried itself into the thick plating of the bulkhead. Ryan grabbed its hilt and switched off the disrupter switch, effectively freezing the sword within the wall and pinning Zorlog's left arm. But the alien pulled a long-bladed boot knife with his free hand. Ryan powered his shoulder into the big alien, knocking the wind from him in time to slow his strike, and catch the knife in a half-turn with his good hand.

They stood there, arms locked, each straining to gain the advantage. It was a battle of will and strength. Ryan twisted, bringing the knife between them. He could feel the muscles in his arm trembling under the strain, but he would not give, he could not. He could feel the iron of the Xilozak's muscle, like an impenetrable wall of concrete.

He had to win.

He forced himself to remember the whippings, the executions, the face of the boy hanging on the fence, and Bosn, his old friend Bosn. He remembered him like it was just yesterday. A new surge of energy fuelled his exhausted muscles for one last twist and shove.

Inception

The knife, in between them, crept up under the Xilozak's chin. He watched as Zorlog's eyes turned wide and desperate, darting from side-to-side. The knife edged its way into his flesh, letting loose a stream of green blood. Zorlog twisted and pushed, eyes wide with realization and fear.

He started laughing crazily. Despite the Xilozak's frantic efforts, Ryan continued, fueled by the hate and revenge. He heaved, this time raising the heavy alien's feet clear off the floor.

"Goodbye, you worthless piece of shit!"

The alien's grip finally started to fade. Ryan held him there and watched as the life slowly drained out of him, staring into those dancing snake eyes until they turned glassy and lifeless.

Zorlog was dead.

Realization hit him like an electric shock. He stepped back feeling shaky, the corpse slid partially down the wall and hung, suspended by the sword embedded in its arm, like some grotesque trophy.

He turned and staggered over to his wife. She was pale. He lowered down on the floor to caress her.

"I want to go home," she whispered, tears flowing down her cheek.

"I'll get you there. You're going to be OK. I've got to find a brace for you." He searched the nearest room, found something that would work and tied her to it. She passed out from the pain.

His strength was gone from him now. His left arm was useless, his right felt spongy and weak. His wound was bleeding badly, and his chest afire. But he had to bring her to the *Queen*, to safety.

He called for Gem.

He moved as fast as he could, half dragging, half carrying her, his body fighting to let go, but he wouldn't let it. More than once he reversed his tracks to avoid a Xilozak-occupied corridor.

Somewhere along the way, Ziggy met up with him, charred and hot from navigating through a recent fire. The robot swung its arms under Aviore. As the weight lifted from Ryan's arms, his strength faded, and he sunk down onto the floor. In a background voice Gem sounded off stating the fleet was on its way. His chest was afire, and his body was drained. He watched as Ziggy's shadow disappeared down the corridor.

He'd get her to safety. She'd be OK.

He just needed a short rest – to lie down.

Ziggy wasted no time with his precious cargo. The auto-surgeon was prepped and ready to receive her. He was not just a creature of logic, he was more than that, Gem had seen to it with her initial programming of him. He watched as the auto-surgeon began its intricate work, lost in unfamiliar emotions careening within his artificial mind.

He turned with some reluctance but knew he had to get back to Ryan.

He found him where he had left him, slumped over and nearing death. He had the medicine Gem had instructed him to administer. A few moments later the man shifted, returning to partial consciousness.

"Is the surgeon working on her?"

Ziggy nodded, pulling the big man up to his feet with minimal effort.

Ryan leaned up against him, weak and disoriented.

"Get me to the ship, buddy. We need to go home. Bring us home. She wanted us to go home."

He slumped back, unconscious, but Ziggy had already anticipated that. He hoisted the man in his arms and began the trek back.

He would bring him home.

To Ryan the darkness was no longer cold, but warm, inviting. Peaceful. It was so very peaceful.

* * *

Kanook coordinated his troops throughout the kilometers of corridors. They had successfully exterminated most of the Xilozaks with only a few left marauding throughout. Because of this, he assembled multiple extermination teams to sweep the massive vessel from stern to aft. He had given only one order: no prisoners were to be taken.

He personally led the team that included the Commander's quarters. His first responsibility was the ship, his second, the life of Aviore. But when he arrived, there was no sign of her. He had to find her. He would not fail his friend, nor himself. He ordered his men onward down the corridors. They secured section after section, finding many wounded, many dead, but still no sign of the Signite woman.

One of Kanook's lieutenants hailed him on the intercom.

"Captain, I'm one level up. I have something here I think you should see."

Kanook sprinted through the corridors, impulse rifle in hand. When he arrived at the lieutenant's location, a small group had filled the corridor, gawking at the spectacle.

Kanook's heart went to his throat. *Don't let it be Aviore.*

He pushed his way through the small crowd and saw it for himself. It was a Xilozak. Dead, hanging by a sword impregnated through its thick arm, pushed clear through into the solid alloy plating of the bulkhead wall. *It took tremendous strength to do that.*

The lieutenant was standing near the body. "We found it here. No sign of who killed this one, but over here we have a number of bloodstains. We think there were two other people involved."

Kanook glanced over to the Sargent. "Get these men moving! Looks like we have a trail, follow it. I want this ship secured!"

The crowd dissipated.

He walked over to inspect the blood, a dark crimson pool spread over a portion of the corridor.

"Can you run samples down to the lab?"

"Already did, we should hear back soon, but they have a number of medical situations that take higher priority."

Kanook nodded. He knew this man and liked him. He was intelligent and quick. He trusted his opinion. "What do you think happened here?"

"We believe this Xilozak was responsible for a number of attacks leading up to this point. You may notice he has some mark on his forehead, and if you look past all the blood, it has some sort of crest on its clothing. I think this one was particularly high-ranking. I'm pretty sure of this because of this weapon."

He pulled out a sterile cloth and bent down to pick up a large bar on the floor and hoisted it to eye-level for inspection. It was clearly heavy, and its one edge was sharpened, although bluntly. The end of the weapon was bulbous, covered with ornate carvings and embedded with crystals.

"Imagine being hit by this thing. You won't be getting up after that."

Kanook nodded agreement.

"So this Xilozak attacked the first person, a human, and left the victim in the corridor, over there." He pointed. "See the footprints in blood? It then stepped over the body and, I think, encountered someone else coming down the corridor. Looks like he must have shot him, right where you are standing. As you can see, there's smeared blood at your feet there, so this thing hurt him alright. But it obviously didn't take him down for long. Whoever he was, we know he was human and damn strong – so that's why I think it's a male. He took this thing on and somehow won. Gauging the look of that Xilozak that was no easy task.

They moved closer to the dead alien.

"Take a look down the corridor floor, you can see the evidence that he dragged the other victim away. I would imagine that both of them, by that time, required immediate medical attention. If they have not received it by now, well, we'll probably find their bodies."

Kanook stepped in close and grabbed at the sword. He flipped the disrupter switch on and pulled. It took all of his strength as it didn't come out easily. The Xilozak's body slumped onto the floor.

Kanook held up the handle to the lieutenant's view. "Do you recognize this?"

The officer gave shook his head. "Never seen it before."

"It's the Commander's. I'm sure of it."

He kicked the Xilozak's body over to see its face.

"And I think I've seen this one before, though they all seem to look alike. It was on the base we attacked. This was the one in charge. The Commander called him Zorlog, I think."

An excited voice came on the intercom.

"Captain! We have long-range tracing up. We've isolated a signature. It's the *Dancing Queen*. Should I hail it?"

"Yes, plug me through, direct!" ordered Kanook. He waited for the relay to give its tell-tale confirming beep.

"Commander, this is Kanook."

"Commander, do you hear me?"

No response.

Kanook glanced over to his lieutenant. "Something's wrong."

"Commander, this is the *Freedom*. What is your destination?"

"Commander, this is Kanook."

Suddenly the link was dropped, replaced with slight static. The com officer came back on. "She's out of range, Sir. Moving at an unbelievable clip. We'd never catch her."

"Can you extrapolate her course?"

"The tactical system's still offline. We need that operational to figure out the vectors. We might be able to sort it out later, but wait a minute... "

"We've got another signal coming in on the port side at about 60 degrees relative. It's long-range, but they are coming in on an intercept. I think... yes it is. It's our fleet!"

"Hail them. Fill them in on the details. Have them send a ship after the *Dancing Queen* and keep me posted."

Kanook waved his men on down the next corridor. They had work to do. He highly doubted they would find Aviore now. The Commander had come back for her. Somehow, he had known how to find them.

It was lucky he had. He would not have believed it if he hadn't seen it with his own eyes. One ship against almost 50. The odds were impossible, but that didn't seem to matter. The Commander had taken out every last one of them. Kanook only hoped they had the tracing logs, even if they were only partially intact, in order to expose the tactics the Commander had used. It would be invaluable for training the rookie pilots - and humbling for the rest of them.

He could only hope they were OK.

Where was the *Dancing Queen* going?

* * *

The cleanup took days. The main drive was online within a week. The *Freedom* limped back to Xeronia for a full overhaul, this time with a fully armed escort.

At the colony, Tsaurau was there to answer the first hail but was saddened when he heard the news about Ryan and Aviore. He found it hard to join in the celebrations that roared through the colony the following days, keeping himself busy by watching for a report to come in that they had finally found the *Dancing Queen*. But days soon turned to weeks with no news. The search party returned empty-handed. The *Dancing Queen* was lost.

It was Tsaurau's wife that finally lifted his spirits. She suggested to him that maybe he should go and find Ryan himself. Why hadn't he thought of it? It had been so long since they had been able to move freely through the galaxy without the threat of the Xi-Empire. Indeed, freedom was a remarkable thing.

It did not take long to get a ship and crew organized. He had ample volunteers for the mission.

Some of his friends, more than once, asked him if he knew where they were. He didn't know for sure, but he knew just where to start looking.

* * *

"Aviore!"

He awoke with electricity surging through him, ready to fight. Recollections from the *Freedom* were vivid and unforgiving.

"She is doing very well, Commander," answered Gem.

"How long have I been under?"

"Exactly 43 hours, 7 minutes, 28 seconds. Your vitals are strong, but you still need rest."

"How much longer?"

"Go to sleep. Everything and everyone is alright."

His eyes were barely open, just slits, but the light seemed intense. Sleep seemed a great idea.

Sounds. Warm and regular. A pulsing in his ears. She was breathing softly beside him, asleep.

"Gem?"

"It is good to talk with you once again, my friend."

"What's our status?"

"We are enroute to where you asked. The *Dancing Queen's* current course will bring us into the Sol system within the next 72 hours."

"Earth?"

"You wanted to go home. This was my best guess."

"I understand that – but 72 hrs, how's that possible?"

"Ziggy and I have been implementing a number of improvements with the capacitors, anti-grav feeds and main drive. Given the maintenance we needed to perform, it only made sense to upgrade. We've effectively multiplied the velocity capability of the *Dancing Queen* by approximately 10 times."

"Amazing... but how?"

"Improvements, are you sure you desire all the details?"

Ryan thought for a moment. "No, perhaps later, how is Aviore?"

"She is recovering quite well. All her organs have been repaired. The damage was significant. Because of this, her recovery will take longer than yours. And yes, before you ask, she will be able to walk again, but this will require therapy."

Ryan let out a breath. "Thank you."

"I have implanted within you an artificial heart. Your original organ was diseased. I am authorized to inform you that a natural replacement can be regenerated by a Xeronian medical team if you wish to remove this unit. I have stored the removed organ for required tissue samples."

"My heart? You replaced my heart?"

"Yes. You experienced a massive myocardial infarction. Before the incident, I had instructed Ziggy to manufacture a replacement device."

"And the Xilozaks?"

"The Galactic Alliance fleet was inbound to the *Freedom* as we departed. The enemy, I am certain, has been defeated."

"It's over?"

"Yes, the war is over."

He felt tension shrink away with the last few remnants of his discarded breath.

It is over. All of it. It wasn't a dream. The Empire is defeated. Zorlog is dead.

He turned toward Aviore, who was now lying adjacent to him. The light did not seem so bright now, and he was able to focus on her features. His eyes followed her graceful curves. She seemed at peace.

"Aviore." He did not talk. He spoke directly into her mind.

Her eyes opened, brown, sparkling, and a smile stretched wide over her face, yet still, it did not fully reach into those eyes. There was a sadness there. Maybe one day she could find peace within herself, and those eyes would truly smile.

She reached for him, closed her hand around his. Her warmth pulsated within his palm. He tried to shift his body, but his efforts were only slightly effective. He could feel the top of a sharp mountain of pain, previously subdued by suppressants. His arms throbbed, his body leaden, robbed of all energy, muscles seemingly spongy. He stopped struggling.

"Don't, Ryan," she said softly. "Stay relaxed. You need to heal. We both need to heal."

She was right. Neither of them were going anywhere soon. His eyes left hers to inspect their surroundings. They were both nestled into the auto-surgeon's barren, tiny, stainless-steel room, on their backs, in graviton suspension. He could see that her lower abdomen was wrapped under a mass of mechanical devices, all probably designed to aid in the healing of her spinal cord.

Luckily, he was not so burdened with only large square pads of bio-gel stuck to his chest and lower abdomen, and his left arm held rigid in a transparent cast.

"How long do you think we'll need to be cramped up in this little room?" He asked her, dreading the thought.

"Long enough."

"Long enough?" He laughed. "For what?"

"Long enough to decide where we are going to raise our child."

He turned to her, and her eyes smiled.

The End
* * *

Acknowledgments

Firstly, and most importantly, thank you for reading 'A Bellicose Dance'. If you are a fan, and I truly hope you are, please feel free to provide your feedback about this title on your favorite social site, on Amazon, or on my website.

Cover art was provided through **vikncharlie** at www.fiverr.com.

A special thanks to my family (and especially my wife), for their ongoing support during this time consuming endeavor.

Feel free to visit my website at www.patrickmjlozon.com for blog updates and information on upcoming novels.

Other Titles Available

Of Days Gone By, 2018
ISBN: 978-1-7753222-0-7 (ebook), 978-1-7753222-1-4 (print)